Donna,
Wishing you tomorrows!
God Bless,
Debbie Alfuio
4-12-14

Waiting for Tomorrow

by
Debbie Alferio

authorHOUSE®

AuthorHouse™
1663 Liberty Drive, Suite 200
Bloomington, IN 47403
www.authorhouse.com
Phone: 1-800-839-8640

© *2008 Debbie Alferio. All rights reserved.*

No part of this book may be reproduced, stored in a retrieval system, or transmitted by any means without the written permission of the author.

First published by AuthorHouse 5/7/2008

ISBN: 978-1-4343-8754-7 (sc)

Printed in the United States of America
Bloomington, Indiana

This book is printed on acid-free paper.

This book is dedicated to my Heavenly Father with love and thanks for the wonderful gift He has given me.

To Dave, my 'Forever Love.' Thanks for believing in me. It means more than you know.

To my friends, family and loyal 'fans'—you're the reason I keep writing.

With special thanks to Arlene Towne, my editor, mentor, and friend. Without your love, hard work, and dedication, this book would never have been possible. I am eternally grateful.

Chapter 1

April 13, 1988. The honeymoon was over, and real life was about to begin.

I turned the dial on the timer and set it on the counter, found a magazine, and took my place on the couch in impatient waiting. My fingers fumbled to turn the page, and my mind refused to concentrate on the words printed there. Ten minutes. It wasn't long in reality, but I knew it would be the longest, most nerve-wracking time in my existence thus far. Deciding to give up on my attempt at reading, I tossed the magazine on the coffee table and settled back into the softness of the cushions as I let my thoughts take control.

Earlier that day, I had sat in the secretary's office of Lincoln Elementary School enjoying what started out as a casual conversation with my friend, Carrie Jackson. I let my mind replay the scene that had brought me to where I was right then.

"Hi, Dana," Carrie greeted as I fell into the chair opposite her desk. The smile slowly faded from her face. "What's wrong, sweetie? You look like death warmed over!"

"I feel like it, too," I agreed half-heartedly. "I don't know what the problem is, Carrie. For the last two weeks, I've felt drained. Mitch seems to think I'm coming down with something because I've been queasy here and there, too; and night before last, I almost threw up after dinner. I figured that was probably just something I ate that didn't agree with me."

She stood up and moved to a table beneath the window, picked up a pot of coffee, and poured us both a cup. Handing one to me, she sat back down and took a bite of the ham and cheese sandwich lying on her desk. "Have you been getting enough sleep?" She arched her eyebrows in a teasing fashion and gave me a mischievous smile. "I know you and Mitch are newlyweds, but you *have* to rest sometime!"

"Ha, ha, very funny," I retorted sarcastically. "Actually, I've been going to bed earlier than I normally do; once my head hits the pillow, I'm not hearing a thing until morning." I took a sip of the coffee, its rich, smooth taste tantalizing my taste buds. "I'm just thinking it's all the hype from the wedding catching up with me."

"That could be," Carrie agreed.

"Mitch said if I'm not getting sick that it must be PMS because I've been 'overly emotional' lately. He says that I either snap at him or cry over everything, and he can't seem to make a right move around me.

The more I think about it, the more I'm beginning to think he could be right. I do seem to be having trouble controlling my feelings for some reason. Besides that, my breasts have been tender, and I'm either gaining weight or retaining water. None of my clothes fit me anymore. I tried on three pairs of pants this morning before I found one I could actually get buttoned!" I took another drink, this time inhaling deeply to savor the aroma. "Since I'm a week late starting, I think that may be adding to all the symptoms, too."

Carrie suddenly looked stunned. "You're late?" she asked almost as if she were pondering another thought at the same time.

I shrugged off her concern. "Yeah, but no big deal. I've been late before when I've been stressed and stuff." I paused for a moment and tilted my head slightly upward in thought. "Come to think of it, I haven't had a period since about two weeks before we got married. Oh, well, guess it's time for one, then, huh?"

Carrie leaned forward. "Or, time to take a pregnancy test."

I almost fell out of my chair. "A *what*?" I began to laugh. "Carrie, what on earth would make you say something like that? I'm *not* pregnant."

"Are you sure?"

"Of course I'm sure! Mitch is careful about using protection. He never forgets." I finished my coffee and tossed the cup into the wastebasket next to the desk. "Well, except for our wedding night; but it was our first time, so I'm not worried about that."

Carrie sighed deeply and looked straight into my eyes. "Dana, I hate to be the one to tell you this, but everything you told me sounds like symptoms of pregnancy: the tiredness, the weight gain, the breast tenderness—even the overly emotional part of it. Not to mention that you haven't had a period for ten weeks!" She softened the tone of her voice and folded her hands on the desk. "If you were ovulating on your wedding night and the two of you didn't use any birth control, it's possible that you could have gotten pregnant. You really need to find out."

I stared at her in disbelief. "You can't be serious. It was our first time. It just doesn't happen."

Carrie took another sip of her coffee and smiled at me. "Well, honey, I'm here to tell you it *can* happen. Just look at my son Josh. He's the result of the first time Tom and I were together."

"No way...."

She simply nodded.

I sank back into the chair and exhaled loudly. "Oh, this is just terrific. What am I going to do?"

Carrie sat back once more and glanced at the clock on the wall next to the door. "Well, for now you're going to go back to class. Then on the way home, you are going to stop and buy a home-pregnancy test. When you get here Monday, you'd better have results for me; or I'm going out at lunch and buying you one myself!"

Barely able to make it through the rest of my workday, I dismissed my class full of five-year-olds and left promptly at three without taking the time to say my usual goodbyes. On the way I made a stop at Miller's Drug Store, purchased a do-it-yourself pregnancy test, and hurried home.

Inside the apartment, shoes went one way, coat and purse another as I anxiously ripped open the test packet to read the directions. "Remove the testing wand from the sterile package, enclosed, and hold in urine stream for ten seconds. Place on flat surface and wait ten minutes for most accurate results. If the tip turns blue, the test is positive for pregnancy. If the tip remains white, the test is negative." Sounded easy enough. I headed off to the bathroom and prayed it would remain white.

The timer sounded and stirred me from my daydream. Jumping up from the couch, I scurried off to the bathroom to check my results. As I entered the doorway, I stopped suddenly as a wave of fear swept over me. I didn't want to look. What if Carrie had been right? What if I was pregnant? I shook my head to keep the demon of that thought from entering in. I couldn't be pregnant, not after just one unprotected encounter. The chances of that were so low that it was next to impossible. It happened to her, but what were the odds of it happening to me as well? I bravely picked up the wand and looked at it. Obviously, the odds were better than I thought. It was blue. I was pregnant.

I grabbed the instructions off the vanity and perused them again. *"Hold wand in stream, blue pregnant, white not pregnant."* Pretty simple. It wasn't a mistake. I was going to be a mother.

"No, this just can't be. There's no way, just no way!" I collapsed onto the toilet lid and stared blankly at the wand I held in my trembling hand. My mind went back to February 18, our wedding night. Both being virgins, we were so engrossed in accomplishing our 'rite of passage' into the world of holy matrimony, we let our unbridled passion take us beyond reasonable thinking. Well, *one* of us had anyway. I remembered the nervous way I had approached that act, even going as far as to ask Mitch if we could wait. My husband, on the other hand, was eager to "boldly go where no man had gone before," and he did just that. Sure, by the time it was over, the nerves were gone; and Mitch was quite the happy camper. That was until he rolled over to face the nightstand. Awakening me, he showed me the one thing he had forgotten that would have kept me from being in the state I now found myself in.

I let myself come back to reality and looked again at the pregnancy test. What was I going to do? I knew absolutely nothing about babies. In fact, I'd never even been around one except for Mitch's niece Diana. Although I had seen her on several occasions, I'd never held her and actually had no physical contact with her other than a gentle caress on her head or a soft kiss on the cheek. Those gestures were hardly enough to make me mother-material. Then there was Mitch. How was he going to take this? I was sure he would be upset. In fact, he would probably be downright angry. He had made it clear to me on more than one occasion that he didn't want a baby this soon. He wanted us to be married for a while first and to have time to adjust to each other before we thought about starting a family. No, he definitely wasn't going to be happy about this. Not one bit.

I stuffed the wand and the instruction sheet back into the package and hid them behind a bottle of liquid hand soap beneath the sink. That way, when Mitch got home, he wouldn't discover the evidence before I had a chance to tell him the news. Mitch. What was I going to say to him? I had absolutely no clue whatsoever. Then it came to me. If I was certain he'd be upset, I needed to find a way to soften the blow. Sort of ease him into the situation so to speak. Yeah, that was it.

I hurried to the kitchen and began to make a short grocery list. Soon I had written down exactly what I needed to make chicken parmesan—one of his favorite dishes. It was only three fifty-five, so I still had just enough time to head down to the corner market, stop at the bakery for a cherry cheesecake, and get everything ready for his arrival home from work around five-thirty. I was grateful that he'd told me not to come down and help out at the bistro today thinking I'd be better off coming home right after school to rest. The arrangement had bought me some much-needed time to make arrangements of my own.

Rushing through the motions, I managed to run my errands and get back home by four-twenty. I quickly put together the entrée, placed it into the oven, and set the table in elegant fashion—complete with a candle at both ends. In the center and slightly off to the side, I placed a bud vase containing two single red roses that I'd picked up at the market. Feeling satisfied with my work, I hurried off to freshen up before Mitch got home.

Promptly at five-thirty, I heard his key in the lock. After lighting the candles and pulling the food from the oven, I placed myself next to the door to greet him as he stepped inside.

"Hi, honey," I said as cheerfully as I could.

"Hey, beautiful," he greeted in return as he gave me a soft kiss. He hung his jacket on the rack by the door and inhaled deeply. "Mmm, smells great. And take a look at that table." He turned back to me, took me into his arms, and lowered his voice to a sexy tone. "Someone in the mood for a little romance tonight?"

"Oh, maybe," I said as I ran my finger along his jaw line. He smiled sweetly, and I could already see the desire beginning to burn in his eyes.

"How long until dinner?" he asked as he began to kiss my neck.

"A few minutes. I still have to make the salad."

He began to nibble my ear. "Good. Just enough time for an appetizer."

Before I knew it, he had covered my mouth with his. I was lost in the pleasure of his kisses as I let our passion detract from the unsettled mood I had been feeling just moments before. He led me to the couch and lay me back on it, continuing to kiss me as he removed his tie and began to unbutton his shirt. He moved away from me slightly as he laid his glasses on the coffee table. Moving back in, he began to kiss me again while he let his hands move over me seductively—every inch of me responding to his touch. Reluctantly, he started to stand up; and I reached out to grab hold of his shirt.

"Where are you going?" I asked longingly.

"To the bedroom. I'll be right back."

"No, don't go."

He gently removed his shirt from my grip, stood up, and looked down at me—his eyes shining with love. "Well, love, before I can continue here, I need something from the nightstand. So, I have to go." He held out his hand. "But, you can go with me if you want."

I decided to play along and buy myself a little more time. "Okay, I can do that."

Once in the bedroom, we took up where we had left off and let our desires take control. As Mitch reached to open the nightstand drawer, I grabbed his arm.

"No, don't," I said softly.

He gave me a puzzled look. "Come on, honey, stop. You know it's necessary."

"Not this time."

He moved a little further away, furrowed his brow, and now looked completely perplexed. "What are you talking about? Why would this time be different than any other?" He began to bite his lip. "Wait a minute. Are you trying to tell me you want to have a baby? Sweetheart,

I thought we discussed this, and we both agreed that we wanted to wait a while. Am I right?"

I shrugged and moved closer to him. I began to make circles on his chest with my finger. "Well, yeah, we did, but don't you think it might be nice to have a baby now?"

He snickered. "No, not really."

"Why not? I don't think I'd mind if we had one sooner than we planned."

Mitch rolled completely away from me and sat up. "We've already discussed this, Dana, and you agreed with me. Why the sudden desire to be pregnant?"

I lowered my voice and softened it as much as possible. "Because I already am."

A look of complete shock came over him as he closed his eyes and dropped his head. "Please tell me you didn't just say what I think you just said. Tell me you didn't just say you're pregnant." He lifted his chin, opened his eyes, and stared directly into mine.

I grimaced as I saw the look of fear emerging on his face. "I can't."

His face lost all color, and he began to shake his head emphatically. "Oh, no. No, no, no...."

I reached out to touch his arm. "Mitchell, don't be upset...."

"Don't be *upset*?!? What do you mean 'don't be upset'? How can I *not* be upset?" He jumped out of bed, pulled on his boxers, and began to pace the floor. "Here I am, all set for a nice romantic evening with my wife, just minutes—no, more like seconds—away from making love to her; and she springs this on me." He paused in the middle of the room, closed his eyes, and looked up as he exhaled loudly. "I can't believe this. I just can't believe this. The one time, the *only* time I forget, and this happens." He opened his eyes again and began to bite his lip, one of his traits I affectionately called a 'Mitchism.' "How long have you known? When did you find out? Have you seen a doctor?"

"Honey, please calm down."

He sighed loudly and clenched his jaw. "Just answer the questions, Dana."

I pulled my robe from the back of the chair, wrapped it around me, and moved to sit on the side of the bed that faced him. "I've only known for a few hours. I picked up a pregnancy test on the way home from work, and I took it as soon as I got here."

"And it was positive."

"Yes, it was positive. Would you like me to show it to you?"

He shook his head. "No, I don't want to see it." He sat down in the chair, ran his hand over his face, and then looked directly at me.

"Are you sure you did it correctly? Maybe it's not right. Maybe it's one of those false positives, you know, what you get when something is messed up."

I rolled my eyes at his attempt to grasp at straws. "Mitch, I doubt that I messed it up. It doesn't take a rocket scientist to know how to pee on a stick."

"You don't have to be condescending. I was only asking."

"I wasn't being condescending. And you need to calm down."

"I'll calm down when I'm ready to calm down. Right now, I'm not ready."

He stood up and walked to the closet, pulled a pair of jeans and a sweatshirt off their hangers, and threw them on. He took an old Phillies cap down from the shelf and placed it on his head, picked up his shoes, and walked back to the chair.

I watched as he sat in silence for a moment and stared at the floor. I could tell by the look on his face that he was trying his best to deal with the information I had given him and was having a rough time with it.

He brought his eyes up to meet mine. Their usual sparkle was replaced with confusion and what I perceived as a twinge of anger. "Dana, if you found this out two hours ago, why am I not finding out until now?"

I started to approach him, but the look on his face made me think better of it; and I sat back down on the bed. "I thought it might be nicer if I waited until you got home. I thought we could have a nice romantic dinner, maybe cuddle up on the couch afterwards, and then I was going to tell you. I didn't think it would be a good idea to come to the bistro and interrupt you while you were working."

He sighed heavily. "Well, you thought wrong."

I decided to try a different approach. "Honey, why don't you shower and unwind while I finish dinner? Then we can eat and afterwards, if you feel like talking...."

"I need to get out for a while," he said as he finished tying his shoe. He placed his wallet in his back pocket and looked at me as he began to bite his lip once more.

"What about dinner? I made chicken parmesan for you...."

"I'm not hungry. I'll be back later." A moment later I heard the door close behind him.

Deciding to take a drive, Mitch started his car to let it warm up and turned the heat up all the way against the cold he was feeling. As he began to drive, thoughts of Dana and this new situation consumed him. This was definitely not news he had expected to hear tonight. How could she think for even one instant that his reaction to it would be calm and amicable? He was angry, yes, but not with her. She hadn't done anything wrong, but he had. He'd let his impatience get the best of him. How could he have been so selfish and so irresponsible to allow this to happen in the first place? He thought back to their wedding night and the eagerness of his desire for their union. In his desperation to fulfill his need, he had totally neglected to complete the one simple act that would have prevented all of this. They were barely used to the idea of being married, and now they were preparing to become parents. He sighed. It wasn't supposed to happen this way. They were supposed to be married for a few years first, buy a house, maybe even a minivan and a dog, and then decide together when the time was right to start a family. No, it wasn't supposed to be like this. It was too soon—far too soon—and he wasn't ready. He needed more time to prepare, more time to get to know Dana as his wife and partner, more time for her to get to know him as well. But, there was no more time. It had been stripped away from him in one moment of passion, and there was no getting it back.

He couldn't help the smile that tugged at his lips as he thought of Dana and the way she'd tried to calm him down. What a little trooper she was. She was trying so hard to accept this and be happy, but he knew she was probably more terrified than he was. He remembered that once she had mentioned in conversation that she knew nothing about babies. How was she going to know what to do? He'd had some experience with his nieces and nephews, but not enough to teach her everything she would need to know. He assumed that a lot of it had to be instinct just like anything else. He was sure that his mom and the girls would help, too, as well as her best friend Kayla.

His thoughts took him in another direction; and he began to ponder his new responsibilities not only to his wife, but also to his child. As for Dana, he needed to help her through this as best he could, to show her that he supported her, and that he would take care of her in spite of his own feelings about the situation. He had to forget about how he felt. Whether or not he was ready for it didn't matter. Now, he needed to put her first knowing that the smallest act of kindness, such as letting her have a peaceful nap or even holding her when she got emotional, would mean the world to her. And his child. *What was that going to be like*, he thought, *to be a father?* Well, in reality, he already was. He'd earned that title at the moment of conception. But a dad? He had never taken the time to picture himself in that role—at least not this soon. There were so many things he would need to be able to do: just little things like hold the baby when it cries or change a diaper or take it for a walk in the park. Of course, there were the bigger things, too, like being a good provider and making sure that he took care of his responsibilities at the bistro as well as maintaining the shows with the band. The band. Soon, he would have to rethink all that. He thought back to that day four months earlier when much to his surprise his old college buddies had shown up at Gartano's. Needing a front man to fill in, they asked him to play a New Year's Eve gig with them. He had been reluctant; but Dana had encouraged him, believed in him, and now he was having the time of his life reconnecting with a part of him each weekend on stage that he'd thought was gone forever. Would being a part of the band and being a husband and father work for him? He didn't know. Dana had become such a part of all that, too. Once the baby came, she wouldn't be able to join him at the club or for the rehearsals the way she could now. How would she handle those changes? Would she feel left out? He wasn't sure, but he decided that was something he'd worry about later.

Not sure exactly where he was going, he turned the car around and started to head toward home. On the drive back, he thought about his bride once more. Most likely, she was sitting alone on the couch wondering where he had gone and if he was ever going to come to grips with this news. He allowed himself to dwell on that idea. A baby. *Sure it was happening soon, but so had everything else*, he thought, chuckling to himself. He'd fallen for Dana the first time he saw her, married her only three months later, and now they were expecting less than eight weeks after the wedding. Maybe it wasn't exactly the way he'd planned, but evidently, there was a reason for that. After all, he couldn't go back and change the circumstances. What was done was done. He had to accept the cards they'd been dealt and help Dana do the same.

As Mitch re-entered town, his eyes focused in on Reynolds's Toy Store. *Funny*, he thought. He had always known it was there, but it never registered with him until that moment. Smiling to himself, he found a parking spot near the door and went inside.

I heard Mitch's key in the lock and the soft sound of his voice calling out to me. However, what I first saw come through the door wasn't him.

"Honey, I'm home," he called from behind the biggest teddy bear I had ever seen!

"Mitchell, what on earth is *that?*" I said amidst my bursts of laughter.

A bright, childlike smile radiated from his face as he stepped inside and closed the door behind him. Setting the giant toy in the chair, he placed his hand atop its head and gave it a friendly pat.

"I decided it's never too soon to start spoiling my child," he replied gleefully. "What do you think of Mr. Bear here? I wanted something bigger, but the salesclerk said this is as big as they come!"

Still laughing, I stood up to do a closer inspection and ran my hand through the shaggy brown fur. "It's great, honey. I'm sure the baby's going to love it."

The smile slowly faded from his face, and his eyes filled with worry. "Gosh, you don't think he'll be afraid of it, do you? I hadn't thought of that."

I rubbed his arm reassuringly. "No, I don't think so. But, what do you mean 'he'?"

He straightened his spine and pulled back his shoulders as he puffed out his chest in a prideful stance. "He, as in male gender. You know, a son."

I shook my head at him and began to laugh again.

"What's so funny?"

"You are, you goof! I can't believe you're already worrying about what gender this child is going to be. Besides, you do understand that you don't have much say in the matter."

"Well, it is the man that determines the sex; and if I was able to get you pregnant on the first shot, then it's possible I could have produced a son as well."

I doubled over with hysteria. "I swear, Mitchell Tarrington, if that ego of yours gets any bigger, it's going to explode."

I could see the evidence of the dimple on his right cheek starting to emerge. "Ego? Baby, I'm not bragging. I'm stating a mere fact."

Managing to compose myself a little, I moved to place my arms around him; and he looked down at me, smiling sweetly, his bright blue eyes shining like a sun-filled sky. "What if we have a little girl? Will you be disappointed?"

"Of course not," he replied. "But, a boy would be nice—someone to carry on the family name."

"Let's leave that up to God," I said as I moved even closer to him. I brushed a stray hair off his forehead. "I'm glad to see that you seem to be okay with this now. When you left here, I was thinking I was going to have to put you in therapy."

"Well, my love, don't rule that out just yet. This is a pretty big pill to swallow."

I began to play with a button on my sweater. "I'm trying to swallow the same one, you know."

He sat down on the couch, pulled me down on his lap, and placed an arm around me. "Yeah, I know. Think we can do it?"

I shrugged. "I'm not sure, but I guess we're going to find out, aren't we?"

I felt the tenderness of his soft kiss on my forehead. "Yeah, baby, I guess we will."

The smell of fresh coffee and the sound of Mitch singing and softly playing his guitar awoke me early the next morning. I yawned and stretched and then padded wearily into the bathroom to splash some water on my face. Gazing into the mirror at my reflection, I decided that I definitely was not a morning person. I paused for a moment to listen to my husband. He had the music in his blood just as our friend, Joseph, said at our wedding reception. I wiped my face dry, ran a quick brush through my hair, and went off to say hello.

Mitch looked up and smiled as I approached. "Good morning, beautiful. How're you feeling this morning?"

"Tired," I replied as I fell onto the couch next to him.

He smiled sweetly. "Well, I have a feeling that just comes with the territory," he said as he gently patted my stomach. "At least you aren't having any morning sickness."

I grimaced. "I hope I continue not to have any."

He patted his hand on his guitar. "I hope I didn't wake you. I just saw my guitar sitting in the corner and thought I'd play for a while."

"No, you didn't bother me," I smiled. "What's that you were playing just now?"

"Oh, nothing special. Just goofing around actually. Sometimes I'll come up with these tunes off the top of my head, and they really aren't anything other than something I made up; songs without words, that's all."

I picked up his coffee cup and took a sip while I held it for a moment to take in the warmth between my hands. "Why don't you take one of the tunes and write words to go with it? You wrote a song for me. That proves you know how to do it."

He leaned the guitar against the chair and walked into the kitchen to pour himself another cup of coffee. "Who knows? Maybe I will," he replied. "You keep that cup. I'll just drink this one." Pulling two bowls from the cupboard, he filled them both with cereal and milk. "What's the game plan for today, my love? It's going to be nice to have an entire day to ourselves. Jimmy was great to agree to handle the bistro today; and with the club being closed for the remodeling, it all worked out perfectly."

I took another sip of coffee and shrugged as I joined him at the table.

"I don't know. Other than going to your parents' for dinner later, I don't have a clue. There are tons of ways to spend a Saturday. What do you think?"

He looked at me. "Dana, I asked you first. You need to tell me, love." He smiled. "Need a few choices?"

I put down my cup and turned to face him. "Sure, that would be helpful."

"Let's see—we could go for a walk in the park, catch a matinee, go to the art museum, go to the zoo, head down to Penn's Landing, take the train over to Peddler's Village and do some window shopping...." My husband had suddenly transformed into the head of the travel bureau.

"Hold on, honey. You said a few choices. Now I'm even more confused than I was before." Feeling a little overwhelmed, I sighed heavily.

Mitch laughed. "I'm sorry, sweetheart. I guess I got carried away. Did any of those sound like fun to you?"

"That's the problem, Mitchell. They all did. I can't decide," I whined. "Why don't you just tell me what you'd like to do?"

"Because, it's your day off, too. Why don't you decide how we spend the afternoon, and I'll pick where we go for lunch, okay?" He took a sip of his coffee and then sat back in his chair and began to play with his wedding ring.

I gave him a look. "Okay, let's go to a matinee. I'm sure there's a movie playing that we can both agree on. We can have lunch and then head over to the theatre."

Mitch got a look of shock and surprise on his face. He placed his hand on his heart and pushed his chair back slightly. "My gosh, did Dana actually make a decision on her own? I'm not sure how to handle this," he teased.

"Very funny. I'm quite capable of making decisions, I'll have you know. I don't want to disappoint you, that's all," I explained as I took a bite of my breakfast.

"Not possible, love. You could never disappoint me in any way, shape, or form," he said with a bright smile.

"Now, don't go making me out to be perfect. I'm far from it."

He took a bite and then spoke with emphasis. "I didn't say you were perfect. I said you don't disappoint me. You have annoying little traits like everyone else."

I put down my spoon and looked at him curiously. "I have annoying little traits? Like what? Please enlighten me." I sat back and folded my arms.

Mitch took a drink of his coffee and put up his hand to me, the hint of a smirk forming on his lips. "No way. If I say one word, you are going to get upset; and I'm not going to spend our day off arguing with you."

I stared at him sitting smugly on the other side of the table. "Mitchell, if you weren't going to share with me, tell me why you even brought it up?"

"I didn't. You did. You're the one who said you weren't perfect. I only agreed." He wiped the corner of his mouth with a napkin. "Anyway, I know I'm not perfect either."

I looked down into my bowl. "That's for sure," I muttered just loud enough for him to hear me.

Mitch pushed his bowl away from him and placed his napkin on the table next to it. He sat back in his chair and folded his hands neatly in his lap. "Just what is that supposed to mean?" he asked with a hint of annoyance in his voice.

I placed my napkin on the table as well and took the last sip of my coffee. I looked up to give him a mischievous smile. "Nothing, sweetie. I don't want to spend our day off arguing with you either."

Mitch laughed as he stood up and placed his bowl and cup in the sink. He walked to my chair and leaned down close to my ear. "You're such a funny little girl, you know that? It's okay though. I still love you." He kissed me on the cheek and retreated to the living room while I proceeded to clean up the kitchen.

A few minutes later I joined my husband who was positioned comfortably in the chair leafing through the morning newspaper. I sat down on the couch and watched as he turned to the last section, folded it over, and straightened it out. He placed his finger on the page and slowly began to move it down each column stopping every now and then to study whatever was at the tip of it at that moment. After a few minutes of observing this activity, my curiosity got the best of me.

"Mitch, honey, what are you looking for?"

He never took his eyes off the page. "Houses."

Now he had *really* aroused my curiosity. "Houses? For what?"

He lowered the paper just enough to look at me over the top of it. "For us. We're having a baby, remember? We can't expect to stay here. There's not enough room."

"I really don't think we need to worry about that yet. We only found out about the baby yesterday. There's plenty of time."

I heard him sigh, and he placed the newspaper on his lap. "Seven months, my dear. We only have seven months to prepare for this child. Who knows how long it will take to find a place we like? Then there's the subject of waiting for the financing to go through, and then we have to move in...."

"I don't think that will take seven months. Besides, we have plenty of room here for a baby—at least for a while. In fact, we could easily stay here another year or two."

He looked at me as if I had just lost all sense of reason. "It's a one-bedroom apartment. Where do you expect the kid to sleep—in the bathtub?"

I rolled my eyes at him. "We can move a few things around in our room and put the crib in there. What about that?"

He began to chuckle and shake his head emphatically, waving his hand for effect. "No, no, Dana. No way! I'm not having the baby in our room!"

"Why?"

He suddenly seemed at a loss for words. "Well, uh, because you and I, because we...."

"What, Mitch? Because we what?"

"Well, because we...because we're the parents, that's why. We need our privacy. There are certain things a child shouldn't witness, that's all."

I caught on and began to laugh. "Honey, I don't think you need to worry about that. The baby isn't going to have a clue. You're just being silly now, and besides, it's not like that happens every night."

"Yeah, how well I know that."

His words struck a chord with me, and I sprang to my feet. "Oh, so now I don't keep you happy, Mitchell? First, you call me annoying, and now you say this? Well, gee, thanks a lot!" I turned toward the hallway and began to stomp off.

I heard Mitch sigh and mutter something under his breath before he started after me. "Dana, come back here. Come on, sweetheart. I didn't mean anything by it."

I reached the bedroom right before Mitch, slammed the door in his face, and locked it as I did. *How could he be so mean*, I thought? I crawled back into bed and pulled the covers up around me tightly. If this was how he wanted to treat me, I would just spend the entire day right there and be perfectly happy doing it. Unfortunately for me, I'd forgotten the key which was stashed at the top of the doorframe; and the next thing I knew, he was sitting on the bed next to me.

He reached out cautiously and began to stroke my hair with the palm of his hand. "Pregnancy hormones, huh?"

I pushed his hand away and turned to glare at him angrily. "Is that what you're going to do for the next seven months? Blame everything that happens between us on my 'raging hormones'? Did you ever stop to think that maybe it could be *your* fault?"

He placed his hand on his chest, and I could hear the irritation in his voice. "My fault? All I said was that I wouldn't mind if we got together a little more often than we do; and you took my head off, ran into the bedroom, and slammed the door in my face. Now, tell me that wasn't hormone induced."

I sat up, threw back the covers, climbed out of bed, and headed toward the bathroom. "That isn't what you said at all. You said that I'm not 'willing' enough for you and that I also annoy you, which tells me clearly that you aren't as happy with me as you say you are."

He smiled and tried to sound convincing. "I'm perfectly happy with you, and no, that isn't what I said. That's just the way you perceived it."

I was in the bathroom now, and Mitch was standing inside the doorway leaning against the frame. Taking the tube from the drawer, I squeezed a dab of toothpaste on my toothbrush and began to brush my teeth; I had decided to ignore my husband's presence for the moment. He simply stood there, his arms crossed in an obstinate fashion, his eyes fixed on my reflection in the mirror. I rinsed my mouth, then walked to the shower, pulled back the curtain, and turned on the water. Taking a towel from the linen closet, I placed it on the vanity and began to undress, but not before I shot another remark at Mitch.

"I perceived it that way because that's the way you said it."

He sighed and shook his head as he walked away.

I was exiting the shower as Mitch re-entered the bathroom wiping his sweaty face on the t-shirt he'd been wearing earlier. I assumed he'd been lifting weights as he did each morning; and he glanced at me long enough to give me a naughty little smile as he dropped his shirt in the middle of the floor much the way a defiant child would toss a cup of milk off his high chair tray. I decided not to satisfy his attitude by showing my annoyance at his behavior. I moved to the mirror, took out my hair dryer and brush, and began to dry my hair. Obviously annoyed by my nonchalance, he stepped slightly in front of me and began to lather up his face with shaving cream. He paused to look at me and cleared his throat.

"Excuse me, but I'd like to shave. Could you please move over?"

I took one step to my left, and he gave me a look. "Uh, possibly a little more?"

"I need some of the mirror, too, you know. This bathroom isn't very big."

He pointed toward the door. "Then why don't you step out and let me have it for a few minutes?"

I moved back into my original position. "I was here first, and I have to dry my hair before it frizzes. So, why don't you step out and let me finish up?"

He gave me a disgruntled look and began to splash water on his face to rinse off the shaving cream. "Fine, I'll shave after my shower." He stepped past me, pulled back the shower curtain, and turned on the water.

I kept my focus on the task at hand. "Good, because that's where your razor is—in the shower."

"Dana, you didn't use my razor to shave your legs again, did you?"

I decided my vindictive grin in his direction was enough of an answer. He muttered something about women being a pain and stepped into the shower.

Finishing up in the bathroom, I retreated to the bedroom and pulled out a favorite pair of jeans and a sweater. Removing my robe, I proceeded to slip on the jeans I had worn countless times in the past month. However, for some strange reason, this time they wouldn't fasten. I sucked in my stomach and tried again; but try as I might, one side just wouldn't meet the other. *Maybe I could start by zipping them first*, I thought. That seemed to be working until the zipper stopped halfway. Disgustedly, I shimmied them off and pulled out another pair, this time barely managing to pull them over my derriere. As I stood there sporting nothing more than my undergarments with a pair of jeans hanging halfway off my hips; my husband walked into the closet, gave me a once over, and began to snicker.

"Interesting look, sweetheart. I kinda like it myself, but I don't think you can go out in public like that."

He turned his back to me and began to search for his own outfit. I placed a hand on my stomach and glanced down at the telltale bulge forming at my waistline. I couldn't believe it. Only eight weeks' pregnant, and I was already starting to show. In fact, I didn't know how I hadn't noticed it sooner. I stood like that for a moment and glanced at Mitch as I wondered what he must have thought when he looked at me: probably that his slender new bride had morphed into 'The Blob.' Although I knew he'd never say it, I was sure that's what he was thinking. He finished dressing and turned back to me, his eyes moving over me once again. His smile faded as he noticed the tear trickle down my cheek, and he took me into his arms and kissed me softly on the top of my head.

"Maybe we should skip the movie and go shopping for some maternity clothes. What do you think?"

I was right—he, too, had noticed my new physique. I decided to try to change his mindset.

"I don't need maternity clothes. I still have plenty of things in here that will fit me."

Defiantly, I moved away from him, shed the jeans, and tossed them out of the closet along with the first pair I had tried. Mitch finished dressing and obviously thought it best if he left the room while I continued my search for something—anything—that might still fit me without making me look or feel like a hippo in a wetsuit. Try as I might, however, I realized that most of my wardrobe had indeed become uncomfortably small. Within a few minutes, I had a pile of clothes lying around me on the closet floor and another slowly forming just outside the door. Finally, I found at the very back of the rack my biggest, baggiest pair of pants and sweater—the ones I only wore on my 'fat' days and even then only if I wasn't going out of the house. I stared at them for a moment and was reluctant even to reach for them. Glancing at the row of hangers I'd just emptied and realizing I had no other choice unless I wanted to stay in my underwear all day, I took them down and began to slip them on. Just as I had suspected, the pants fit perfectly. Sighing heavily, I slowly pulled on the sweater; and it too fit, perhaps even better than the pants. I tugged on it to stretch it out a bit; and sighing again, I trudged out the bedroom door and almost ran right into my husband.

He pointed to my outfit and tried to hold in his smile. "Is that what you plan to wear today?"

I looked down at my attire. "Why? What's wrong with it?"

He placed a hand on my shoulder, turned me enough to look at my backside, and then faced me again. "Looks a bit snug to me, love. In fact, it looks like it may burst at the seams. Don't you have anything that might be a touch bigger?"

I ran past him, threw myself into the middle of the bed, and began to cry. I heard him say something to the effect of "not again"; and soon he was lying on the bed next to me, pulling me into a comforting embrace.

"Don't cry, honey. It's okay," he said soothingly. "I didn't mean to make you feel bad. I was only trying to tell you that you shouldn't squeeze into the tightest outfit you own just to prove to me that you can, that's all."

I began to cry even harder. "Why are you being so mean to me today?"

"What'd I say?"

My clueless husband turned slightly toward the closet and caught sight of the mound of clothing I had rejected in my quest for the day's ensemble. He turned back toward me, and his face told me that he finally understood the reason for my emotions.

"Oh."

I simply nodded, wiping my eyes with the back of my hand.

He sat up and pulled a tissue from the box on the nightstand, handing it to me. I dabbed my eyes, blew my nose, and sat up as well. He climbed off the bed and reached out to me.

"Looks like we do need to do some shopping after all, huh? Come on. We'll spend a couple of hours at the mall and have some lunch. If you feel up to it after that, we can still catch that movie this afternoon. Okay?"

"You said I looked awful. I can't go out like this! Everyone will think you brought your pet hippo to the mall." I placed a hand on my stomach, glanced at it, and then looked up at him. "Just look at me, Mitch. I'm huge! If I'm this big now, imagine what I'll look like in a month."

He snickered. "No, you aren't huge, and you don't look awful. You never look awful. In fact, I'm not even sure you're *capable* of looking awful. Now dry your eyes and let's get moving, shall we?"

"Are you going to stop making fun of me?"

He adjusted his glasses and gave me a rueful look. "I wasn't making...." He sighed heavily. "Yes, love, I won't do it anymore. I'm sorry."

"Apology accepted."

He smiled and shook his head as he ushered me out the door.

As we stepped inside the mall, I suddenly felt as if all my cares of earlier dropped away; and my mood lightened. Looking around gleefully, I kicked into shopaholic mode and hooked my arm through Mitch's as he smiled down at me.

Like a kid at Christmas, I glanced blissfully from window to window and marveled at the bright cheerful colors of the spring clothing on display in each one. Shades of pink and blue, yellow and green, adorned the mannequins therein—the vibrant hues in everything from shorts to sundresses. Adding to the appeal, fun accessories in the same colors worked to pull the looks together. As we journeyed along, I suddenly spotted the most adorable sundress in a bright blue boasting a pattern of tiny white daisies. On the mannequin's arm was a tote in the same color as the dress, and at its feet were strappy white sandals. Squealing with delight, I pulled my husband in the direction of the store window.

"I take it you see something you like," Mitch smiled as we approached the store.

"Oh, honey, isn't it the cutest thing you ever saw? I've got to have it!"

"Precisely what I thought when I saw you for the first time," he said with a dreamy look in his eyes.

"Oh, silly, I mean the dress," I replied as I totally ignored his attempt at romance.

"Come on, let's go in."

I tugged on his hand, but he stood firm. "What's the problem? Let's go in. I want to try on that outfit."

He twisted his jaw and pointed up to the sign on the front of the store that said Petite World. I knew what he was thinking, and I was determined that I would prove him wrong.

"Mitchell Tarrington, if you think for one minute that I came here to shop for maternity clothes, you're dreadfully wrong. I'm only eight weeks' pregnant, and I may be getting big already; but all I need to do is buy some things in a size or two larger than what I wear now. I won't need maternity clothes for at *least* another month, maybe two. Now, are you going in with me or are you waiting out here?"

"Dana, if you go into that store and try anything on, you'll only be disappointed when it doesn't fit you. Why don't we go to the maternity store? I'm sure you can find something there more suitable."

I let go of his hand and stubbornly walked into Petite World. Mitch decided to follow; but whether it was to prove me right or wrong, I didn't know.

I found the rack containing the sundresses and searched through until I found one that matched the dress in the window. Suddenly, something occurred to me that I hadn't considered. I glanced at Mitch and then back at the rack. What size would I need? I was normally a six, but my closet expedition of earlier had proven that my waistline had obviously expanded beyond that point. If I still had a few months to wear it before succumbing to maternity attire, then I would have to get something that would allow for some growth. Taking a few steps forward to the other side of the rack, I found a size twelve and cheerfully handed it to my husband who was standing silently just behind me. Beckoning him to follow, I located the shoe display, found my size in the sandals, and handed them to Mitch as well. Before heading to the fitting room, I had added two more dresses, a pair of jeans, and a sweater. Stopping just outside the door, he managed one last plea before handing over the goods.

"Are you absolutely sure you want to do this?"

I nodded. "Oh ye of little faith, you'd better get your wallet ready." He snickered as I took the items from his arms and headed into the fitting room.

Excited about the possibility, I eagerly pulled off the frumpy outfit and pulled on the jeans. *Why won't they button? They're three sizes larger than what I normally wear. Maybe they run small*, I thought. *Yeah, that has to be it.* I sucked in my stomach and managed to get them fastened. Turning toward the mirror, the smile quickly left my face. I looked just as I felt—as if I had tried to stuff myself into them. Sighing, I took them off and decided perhaps I'd have better luck with the daisy sundress. After all, that was the reason I'd gone into the store in the first place. Facing the mirror once more, I decided that it didn't look that bad, except for the fact that in another week or two it would be at least three inches shorter in the front than in the back due to my growing stomach. Glancing at the items still hanging there, I decided it wasn't even worth the effort. The shoes were probably a lost cause as well. Mitch had been right. Feeling rather defeated, I got dressed and headed out to face him.

"Well, where are the outfits?" Mitch asked with a smirk.

"Let's go, Mitchell," I simply replied.

"Aren't you even going to get the sundress? I thought you liked it." His smirk grew even larger.

"Would you please be quiet and for once in your life not rub it in, okay?" His teasing was starting to irritate me although it was obvious that he was having too much fun to notice that fact.

"I didn't say anything. Why are you snapping at me?"

"I wasn't snapping at you. Now, please, just drop it."

"There—you did it again. And what is it that I'm supposed to drop? I don't have a clue. Is this because I tried to tell you not to go into that store? Of course, you wouldn't listen...." That impish little grin of his was spreading all over his face.

"Mitch, I said let it go." I defiantly stuffed my hands into my coat pockets.

"Fine, I won't say anything else even though I didn't do anything wrong. All I tried to do was keep you from getting yourself upset. But, you're too darn stubborn to ever listen to me. You get something in that head of yours and...."

I stepped in front of him, stopped dead in my tracks, and threw up my hands. "Are you actually that dense that you don't know when to stop talking? You're really starting to make me angry."

"Oh, so now I'm dense? Well, I'd say you better stop to think about what logic motivated you to try on an outfit in a petite store when we're supposed to be here shopping for maternity clothes!" He folded his arms across his chest and took on a smug expression looking as if he had just won the Presidential Debate.

What a time for the hormones to kick in again, I thought. Here I was trying to stand up to him, and I could feel the tears welling up in my eyes and my lip beginning to quiver as I stared into his face. "I only wanted to see if I could.... I was just hoping I could fit...."

He looked at me sympathetically, took my hand, and led me over to a bench where we could sit down. Taking me into his arms, he kissed the top of my head as I tried to fight my tears. "It's all right, honey. I'm sorry. I didn't mean to make you cry."

I sniffled. "Can we go home now, please? I don't want to shop anymore."

He moved away and wiped my tears with his thumb. "I know you really don't want to leave, do you?" I shrugged. "All right then, dry your eyes and let's go see what else we can find. I told you I'd take you shopping, and that's what I plan to do." He stood up and reached out for my hand. "Come on, beautiful," he said. "Let's find you some new clothes. Anything you want."

About an hour and almost two hundred dollars later, my husband's usual sweet, cheerful demeanor was slowly becoming anything but. I didn't quite understand why because he'd told me to get anything I wanted, and I was only taking him at his word. Attempting to diffuse the ticking time bomb I had seemingly created, I sent Mitch to buy a cold drink; and I scurried off to the men's department in Jacy's Department Store. I located a shirt in an awesome plum color thinking it would look great on him and decided to double my chance at brownie points by picking out another in a medium blue pinstripe—as well as two coordinating ties. Making the purchase as quickly as possible, I returned to maternity wear. He reappeared a minute later with an orange smoothie and did nothing more than glance at the bag I was holding and sigh. I assumed he thought I had found more things for myself during his absence, so I left him with that mindset and decided I would surprise him with his gift later on. We resumed our expedition; and as we passed the shoe department, I was certain that I heard a pair of loafers calling out to me. I veered off the main aisle to answer them, but Mitch continued on and had taken about twenty steps before he realized I was no longer next to him. By the time he spotted me and started in my direction, he looked less than pleased. I was still having fun, however, and sent the clerk off to find not only the loafers but a pair of sneakers and pumps in both black and beige, size six and a half.

When I took a seat to wait for her return, Mitch appeared in front of me. His arms were loaded with bags, and his jaw was clenched in disciplinary fashion. I smiled up at him as he glanced in the direction of the door the clerk had disappeared behind and then down at me. He didn't say a word as he stood there and stared at me. As the clerk piled the shoeboxes next to me, she asked in a pleasant tone if there was anything else I'd care to see. Before I had a chance to answer, Mitch turned toward her and simply said, "She has enough." She gave me a sympathetic smile and hurried off to another customer.

Mitch sat down and watched as I shed my sneakers, plunged into the first shoebox, and eagerly slipped on the loafers. I stood up to inspect them in the mirror a few feet away. I turned this way and that as I pulled up my jeans to put the shoes in full view. Liking what I saw, I thought I'd try to lighten Mitch's mood by getting him involved in the process.

"Honey, what do you think of these?" I asked pointing down to my shoes. "I like the way they look, don't you?"

He shrugged, not showing much interest at first. Then a mischievous grin started to pull at the corners of his mouth. "What does it matter what they look like? In a few months, you won't be able to see them anyway."

I kicked off the shoes, missed his shin by inches with the first one, and made a direct hit to his left knee with the other. I stepped back into my sneakers and stomped out of the store. I glanced back just enough to see him scramble to gather up six shopping bags and hurry after me.

"Hey, wait up," he called as he quickened his step to catch up.

"I want to go home, Mitchell," I said as we approached the entrance to the mall.

"We can't go home yet. You haven't hit the other fifty stores in the mall, and I still have some available credit left on my card. Heaven forbid we should leave before you have the chance to max it out!"

I wrinkled my face in an angry expression and glared at him. "You're the one who told me to get whatever I wanted. I was only doing what I was told."

He threw up his hand and pretended to look shocked. "Well, I didn't actually think you'd listen to me. You don't listen to anything else I say to you."

I stopped and folded my arms stubbornly. "I thought I'd better take advantage of the situation while I could. You're such a cheapskate most of the time."

He held up the bags as if I needed a visual. "Cheapskate? Dana, I dropped two hundred dollars here today. If I hadn't said anything back there, I'm sure you would have added another hundred or two in shoes. And you're calling me a cheapskate? Give me a break!"

I turned and started away from him again. "I am. Right now. Take me home."

"Fine, if that's what you want."

"It is."

We drove in total silence. I stared out the window; and Mitch, at the road ahead. Whenever he would glance my way, I'd be sure to catch his eye and then turn away and ignore him. I knew it was mean and probably even a bit childish; but in a vindictive sort of way, I enjoyed it. He tried to reach out for my hand at one point, but I pulled away. He sighed heavily and placed his hand back on the steering wheel. Finally, as we approached the edge of the city, Mitch decided to speak.

"Are you hungry?" he asked, his voice sounding a bit apprehensive.

"I'll get something at home," I snapped, not bothering to turn away from the window. "After all, I did spend quite a bit at the mall. I wouldn't want to risk exhausting all your resources by eating out, too."

"I was trying to be nice; but if you want to continue acting like a spoiled brat, then fine. I'll just take you home."

I slowly turned my head in his direction, and I was certain that smoke was beginning to come out of my ears. "*Excuse me?* Who exactly do you think you're calling a spoiled brat, Mitchell Jacob Tarrington III?"

The light turned red, and he slowed the car to a stop. Puffing out his cheeks, he blew the air out slowly and then cocked his head toward me. His expression indicated that he thought I wasn't exhibiting much intelligence at that moment. Obviously deciding that gesture wasn't enough, he clarified by saying, "Well, my dear, let's see—you and I are the only ones in the car; and since I don't make a habit of talking to myself, who does that leave?"

"You're mean."

"No, I'm not, and I wish you'd quit saying that." He focused his eyes back on the road as the light turned green. "Oh, and just so you know, I was only joking back there at Jacy's. I didn't mean for you to get mad at me."

"Well, I didn't find your little comment very amusing."

"At least you didn't call me mean again," he muttered softly.

We made it home; and as Mitch retrieved the bags from the car, I headed upstairs and into the apartment. Sloughing off my shoes and coat, I collapsed onto the couch. I closed my eyes and lay back on the pillows in an attempt to ease out of my melancholy mood. So much for not spending the day arguing. Could it be that I really *was* being saturated with an overabundance of extra hormones that he didn't know how to handle, or was he simply in a mood of his own? I didn't know exactly what was attributing to his attitude, but I knew that I could be perfectly happy staying on that couch the rest of the afternoon and not interacting with him at all. Bearing that thought in mind, I began to sink into a peaceful bliss until I felt a soft kiss fall on my cheek. A moment later, I felt his hand on my face as he leaned in for something more deliberate than just a peck, his breath warm against my skin. I slowly opened my eyes as he moved in next to me and slid his arms around me as he brought me closer to him. I remained silent and unresponsive to the moves he was putting on me, and he whispered softly in my ear.

"We've been at each other all morning, love. Why don't we call a truce? I really want to make up with you."

Men. What pigs, I thought. I gently pushed away his hands and stood up.

"I swear! Is that the *only* way you know how to make up with me? Or, communicate with me for that matter? I'm not a rabbit, you know, but I'm beginning to think you are."

The look on his face made it apparent that I had caught him off guard with my comment. He popped up off the couch and stomped toward the kitchen. "Fine, Dana. If you don't want me to touch you, I won't. Not a problem."

He began pulling things from the cabinets, slamming doors closed, and banging jars onto the counter until he finished gathering all the fixings for his lunch—a peanut butter and jelly sandwich. I watched as he angrily went about his work of smearing peanut butter on one slice of bread and jelly on the other. Squashing them together, he took a rather large bite and threw the knife into the sink. He poured himself a glass of milk, snatched the bag of potato chips off the counter, and walked back into the living room to park himself on the chair. Paying no attention to me, he placed his fare on the coffee table, picked up the remote, and turned on the TV.

"You could have asked if I was hungry, too, you know," I told him.

He glanced at me out of the corner of his eye. As he turned his attention back to the basketball game he'd found, he grunted, "I asked you in the car, remember?"

I waved him off with both hands as I headed off to make my own lunch. *What was it about men that made women so crazy*, I wondered? I'd always heard the saying that you couldn't live with them and couldn't live without them. Right then, I was certain that I fully understood what the former part of that statement meant.

I finished my lunch and decided I wasn't going to let Mr. Grumpy ruin my entire day. I thought I'd be productive by going through the stack of mail lying on the table which was two days old and yet unopened. Slicing open the first envelope with a kitchen knife, I removed the paper inside and unfolded it. An application for a credit card. Not something we needed, so I placed it off to the side and reached for envelope number two. Soon I had formed a pile of things to be tossed out, a pile that needed to be kept, and one comprised of those items that needed to be inspected a bit further. About that time, I noticed my husband glancing my way, and I made eye contact for an instant before turning my attention back to my work. Finding something of interest in what I was doing, he approached me.

"I was going to go through all that later, but I guess I could help you now if you want me to."

I handed him the next envelope on the stack. "Open it up, see what it is, and then place it in the appropriate pile."

He looked at me curiously. "Appropriate pile? Gee, I didn't know there was a protocol for opening mail, but okay. I don't want to mess up your procedure."

"Can't you just help without being sarcastic?"

"I wasn't being...oh, just forget it. You were doing better on your own." He tossed the envelope on the table; and as he started to storm away, he added, "Oh, and by the way, you're still acting like a spoiled brat."

"If anyone's spoiled here, Mitchell, it's definitely not me. I'm not lucky enough to have the owner of a big company like Tarrington Industries as my daddy. I'm certain you never did without a thing in your life," I muttered as he walked away.

Hearing my comment, he stopped and wheeled around to face me. "I'm sorry you're jealous of my family's wealth. I didn't choose my upbringing any more than you chose yours. If you could have, I'll bet you would have opted to live with a younger family after your parents died. I'm sure that would have been much better than spending your days eating fried chicken with an old lady and talking to goats on a farm in the middle of nowhere." He changed the tone of his voice to sound very prideful and let out a chuckle. "You should thank your lucky stars that you found me, too. Heaven knows that hick town boy you came to Philly with certainly wouldn't have given you half of what I have. Had I not come along when I did, who knows where you would've ended up."

I threw down the envelope I was holding and stood up slowly, glaring at him with fire in my eyes. "How *dare* you, Mitchell Tarrington!"

He took a step closer to me, his expression one of complacency. "How dare I what, Dana? How dare I tell the truth?"

The truth? Is that what he thought? He didn't know anything about my childhood. He had no idea what it was like to have your parents one minute and in the blink of an eye have them taken from you forever. I remembered as if it were yesterday—the look on my Grammy's face when she came to me with the news—the news that the plane Daddy and Mom were in had gone down. He'd taken her up in his new Cessna promising me that they would fly over the house, and I could wave to them. I never had that chance. The next time I saw them was at their funeral. Barely twelve years old, I had never experienced death. I certainly didn't know what to think or how to feel. I was hurt, angry, and confused all at the same time. Had it not been for Grammy, I would have been completely alone in the world; but with her love and God's grace, I grew stronger day by day. I learned to smile again. I learned that I could love and be loved; and when I met Eddie Williams my senior year, I fell hard and fast. It didn't take more than a moment's thought to say yes when he asked me to move to Philly with him on graduation day; and for five long years, he was everything to me. However, that night in Gartano's, October 4 the previous year to be exact, he confessed his love for another. With Grammy gone and nowhere to turn except to my best friend Kayla, I found myself alone again. Little did I know Mitch was watching me that night as he worked behind the counter there, and he fell in love with me the first time he looked into my eyes. A month later, I realized I'd done the same thing with him. Three months later we married, and now here I was, staring into the eyes that told everything his heart was feeling. Right then, they were cold and angry, and I had to wonder as I looked even deeper if he truly believed what he was saying. Did he really think he saved me from some terrible fate? I counted it a blessing that I had him in my life; but if God had chosen to send me down a different path, I knew I would have made it. I was glad He hadn't, but I knew I would have been all right. Life had made me strong. Therefore, I decided that Mitch was the one who needed the dose of reality.

I walked to where he stood and took my place directly in front of him, took a deep breath, and looked him squarely in the eyes. "You might want to think you're my knight in shining armor, Mitch, but guess what? You aren't. I'm here because *I* chose *you*, NOT because you saved me from the depths of poverty and despair. As for my childhood, you don't have a clue. My Grammy didn't have to take me in, but she did; and I thank God for that every day. In fact, I wish she were still here so I could show her how grateful I am for raising me and teaching me how to be a responsible adult. She taught me that it's the people in your life that are important, not how much money you have or what you can do with it. That's more than I can say for the way you were obviously raised." I moved past him and started down the hallway, turned around, and walked back toward him to make my final point. "Just for the record, Eddie Williams does quite well for himself. Had I married him, I certainly wouldn't be living in a one-bedroom apartment with mismatched furniture eating peanut butter sandwiches for lunch!"

Mitch stood staring at me as I walked into the bedroom and slammed the door behind me. For the first time all day I had rendered him speechless; and in a somewhat malicious way, I felt good about it.

I rolled over, opened my eyes, and wiped them sleepily with the back of my hand. Glancing at the clock on the nightstand, I realized that two hours had somehow escaped me and that I had slept so soundly I had almost forgotten about fighting with Mitch. Almost, but not quite. Just as I was letting the thoughts of earlier creep back in, I heard a faint knock and the door eased open.

Mitch quietly entered the room, looking rather guilty, his eyes glued to the floor. He stopped by the bed and bringing a hand from behind his back held out to me a single red rose. Slowly he looked at me, his eyes pleading for forgiveness. I sat up as he took a seat next to me and cautiously reached out to take my hand.

"Are you still angry with me?" His voice was very soft, and I thought I heard the hint of a quiver in it as he spoke.

I took a deep breath as I looked down at my hand in his and then lifted my eyes to look into his face. "You really hurt me with what you said, Mitch."

He rubbed the top of my hand with his thumb. "Yeah, I know. I'm sorry," he replied. "I know how much you loved your grandmother, and I was way out of line. In fact, I've had the last two hours to think about what a heel I am."

I could feel the tears welling up in my eyes. Though I tried to hold them back, they had a mind of their own. As they began to splash against his hand, he looked up at me sympathetically, reached out, and pulled me in close, letting his arms encircle me in a protective embrace.

"Oh, honey, please don't do that. You know I hate it when you cry," he whispered. He placed his cheek against the top of my head, and I heard him inhale deeply almost as if he was fighting his own emotions.

He moved away from me, smiled sweetly, and then wiped my tears with his hand.

"I'm sorry, too," I said with a sniffle. "I really do love your family, you know. And I love this apartment. And peanut butter and jelly sandwiches."

He simply nodded as he tucked a strand of hair behind my ear. I smiled at him and placed my hand on his cheek. I gazed into his eyes and noticed that the sparkle in them was starting to return, so I moved a little closer and put my arms around him.

"What time is your mom having dinner?" I asked.

"She told everyone to be there by five."

I glanced briefly at the clock. "Hmm, let's see. It's three-thirty now, so that gives us at least another hour before we have to head out. Just enough time to make up. What do you think?"

He spent the next hour showing me that he wholeheartedly agreed.

Chapter 2

Mitch pulled up in front of the Tarrington Estate and put the car in park, turned off the engine, and snatched the keys from the ignition with a smile.

"Ready to do this?" he asked as he looked at me.

I smoothed my sweater over the little paunch on my stomach. "It's really obvious, isn't it?"

"What's obvious?"

"That I'm pregnant, you goof."

He chuckled and leaned toward me to give me a quick peck on the cheek. As he reached for the door handle and stepped out of the car, I heard him say, "I'm not answering that."

I stepped out of the car myself and stood my ground. "What do you mean you aren't answering that?"

He tucked his arm around my waist and gently prompted me toward the house. "Because if I say yes, you're going to become self-conscious and be worried about how you look all night. If I say no, you won't believe me anyway." He gazed down at me—that adorable dimple prominent in his smile. "Now, come on, and let's go tell our family it's going to grow."

I stopped again. "Which one of us is going to tell them?"

He shrugged. "We both are, I guess. What does it matter?"

"How can we both tell them? That would mean we'd have to say it at exactly the same time, and we haven't practiced that. It would take some doing, but I suppose we could...."

He sighed and moved around to face me. "Honey, what's the matter? Are you nervous about this for some reason?"

"Aren't you?"

He shook his head. "No, not at all. Why should I be?"

"Because we've only been married eight weeks, Mitch. Eight weeks today, in fact. Don't you think that...don't you think that everyone is going to think that's *why* we got married so quickly?"

I watched as he squinted his eyes and seemed to look very confused. "You mean they're going to think I got you pregnant and decided I should marry you?" He began to laugh which annoyed me just a tad. "Dana, that's absurd. My family knows me better than that, sweetheart. I don't know where you come up with these silly notions."

Now he was bordering on annoying me *and* making me angry. "It's not silly, and you don't have to be so crass about it. If your son brought his new bride of two months home and announced that she was pregnant, not to mention already showing, what would *you* think?"

"That he got a little too eager on his wedding night just like his dad. Now, cut this out and let's go inside, okay? You're worrying for nothing."

Before I knew it, I was stepping inside the front door, Mitch holding tightly to my hand as I was still trying to convince him that I had a valid point. There was a possibility, however remote it might have been, that at least one person in his family was going to believe I was already pregnant when we got married. As Mitch helped me off with my sweater and handed it to Alexander, the butler, I took a quick moment to analyze the situation. In the less than two months of our engagement, we changed the wedding date three times, each date sooner than the one before. Engaged on Christmas Eve, we had gone from getting married on October 4 the following year to February 18. Although I knew Mitch's family policy was 'no secrets,' I doubted he would be brazen enough to share the secrets of our intimacy with anyone, let alone that we were both virgins when we married. Without that knowledge, I could see where it would be very easy for them to make assumptions about a pregnancy announced only two months into the marriage. Suddenly, I felt Mitch's fingers wrap around mine bringing me back into reality.

"Everyone's in the dining room. Come on—and please, stop worrying, would you?" He kissed me softly on the cheek. "I love you, you look beautiful, no worries." He led me down the hallway toward the dining room, and I could have sworn I felt my stomach turn completely over.

No one noticed us enter the room at first, and Mitch let go of me and moved his hand to my shoulder. I would have been fine letting the whole thing unfold on its own, but I had temporarily forgotten that my husband was a front man in a band as well as the owner of a restaurant. He was used to taking charge. He cleared his throat rather loudly and drew everyone's attention our way. I thought I felt thirteen pairs of eyes suddenly drop to my stomach, but I shook my head and told myself I was only imagining things. After all, we hadn't said a word yet.

"Hey, newlyweds!" Mitch's brother Chris stepped to the front of the room and folded his arms, his lips curled in a broad grin. "It's about time you got here. Ready to share why you asked all of us to come?"

I felt Mitch draw me closer to his side. "I suppose so," he said as he glanced down at me. Then he started to smile. "You know, sweetheart, why don't you tell them? After all, it's more about you than it is me anyway."

I slowly lifted my eyes to meet his ornery expression and narrowed my gaze to show him clearly that he'd stepped over the line. He knew I was nervous. He knew I'd been worried about his family's reaction the past few moments; and yet, in front of everyone, he'd put me on the spot. I decided I wasn't going to cave.

"Oh, no, honey, since you're the one responsible, I think you should tell them."

He returned my less-than-amicable expression, and I patted his back mischievously as if to say, "Gotcha!"

He took a deep breath. "Well, all right then. I guess I'll tell you. Over the last couple of weeks, Dana hasn't been feeling well. Uh, well, it's not exactly that she hasn't been feeling well, just sort of tired—actually, a lot more tired than usual—and a little emotional here and there. Then a few nights ago, she almost got sick after dinner...."

I sighed and rolled my eyes. I was naughty, but not that naughty. I couldn't stand to sit idly by and watch the poor guy squirm. I decided to throw him a line.

"Mitch, why don't you spare them the details, dear, and just come out with it?"

He gave me that less-than-amicable look again, and I gave him a big smile. Perhaps the line I'd tossed him didn't do much to save him completely, but at least it got him a little closer to the shore.

"Okay, I will. We're having a baby. I mean, Dana's having a baby, not me. Oh, you know what I mean!"

There was complete silence in the room at that moment, not even the sound of anyone breathing because I believed the news knocked the wind right out of them. Suddenly, everyone began to talk at once; and we were swept up in their hugs, kisses, and congratulations. As I stood in the midst of Mitch's family, I suddenly felt the wave of uncertainty rise in my stomach once more. They *seemed* happy, but I still had to wonder what they were thinking. Could the silence after the announcement mean they were all asking themselves that question—just *when* was this baby conceived? I knew to some, possibly even to my own husband, that to worry about such a thing didn't make sense. After all, had it been any of the others, I certainly wouldn't be standing there judging them. In spite of that, I knew in my heart that the last thing I wanted was anyone thinking that Mitch only married me to give a child a name, or worse yet, that I got pregnant to trap myself a husband from a prominent family. I felt as if I somehow needed to let them in on the truth, but I didn't have to. Mitch did it for me.

He held up his hand to silence everyone. "We want to let you all in on something else, too. Just for the record, Dana and I were planning to wait a few years before starting a family. This all came as a real surprise. Tonight we're going to celebrate the news of the pregnancy; and seven months from tonight or thereabouts, we can celebrate the birth of yet another little Tarrington!"

I noticed Chris and Jake smile at one another, and Chris nodded as he turned back to his brother. Seven years Mitch's senior, he had always felt the need to act as his mentor, but rarely saw reason to pass up the opportunity for some friendly ribbing.

"Someone was a little too hasty after the reception, 'eh? And I'm guessing the someone *wasn't* Dana, was it, Mitch?"

He received his answer in his younger brother's blush of embarrassment which caused the rest of the family to laugh.

Shortly after dinner, everyone gathered in the family room. Mitch took his usual place on the piano bench and seated me in the chair next to him. As the rest of the family settled in various locations around the room, he leaned close to me and whispered in my ear.

"Still harboring those silly notions you were earlier?"

"They weren't silly notions, Mitch; and no, I'm not. You and Chris did a good job of clearing all that up."

He snickered. "Yeah, remind me later that I need to clock him one for that comment."

"I must say, this is quite the surprise," Mitch's father said with a twinkle in his eye. Mitchell Jacob Tarrington, Jr., or 'Jake' as he preferred to be called, was a wonderful example to his family of what a loving father and husband should be. Despite the fact that he was the founder and CEO of one of the largest medical products companies in the eastern United States, he wasn't the kind to flaunt his wealth or his position to anyone. In their forty years of marriage, he and Mitch's mother Olivia had built their home around strong family values and the principles of love and respect—passing those same disciplines on to each of their four children. From the first moment Mitch introduced me, they had made me feel welcome; and I had no doubt that our child would receive that same type of love and acceptance.

Mitch took my hand in his, brought it to his lips, and kissed it softly. "Absolutely!" he quipped. "I mean, we both wanted kids, but we certainly weren't figuring on it this soon."

"Well, little brother, you never were a patient one," Chris teased.

Mitch smirked playfully and shot a glance my way. "Uh, well, yeah, I think we already established that's how this happened. My lack of patience." Everyone chuckled, and I blushed.

"I think it's wonderful news," Olivia smiled. "There's always room for another baby in the family."

"Dana, I know it's soon, but have you considered any names yet?" Mitch's sister Julia asked.

"No, not really. There are a few names I've always liked, but we haven't talked about it."

Mitch chimed in. "I do know one thing for sure. If the baby's a boy, his name definitely *won't* be Mitchell! That one stops right here," he said pointing to himself.

"Why's that, son? Don't like your name?" Jake asked with a crooked grin.

He smiled. "Well, it could get confusing for the poor kid. You go by Jake, I go by Mitch, and a lot of the time I'm called Mitchell as well. What would we call him? We've kind of run out of possibilities."

"How about 'Little Mitch'?" Mitch's other sister Angelina suggested.

Mitch looked at her and shook his head. "Sorry, sis, but that sounds goofy. Besides, what do we do when the kid's twenty years old and taller than I am? It won't fit very well. No, I think we'll just come up with another name."

"Well, you'll have plenty of time for all that," Chris's wife Trudy interjected. "There are a lot of other things to worry about besides what you're going to call the baby."

"Like what?" Mitch asked curiously.

Trudy launched into a ten-minute dissertation on all the aspects of pregnancy. She touched on everything but conception, and I believed the only reason she left that out was because she figured we already had that part down. Along the way, the others jumped in here and there with their own comments and advice; and by the time everyone had finished, I felt a bit dizzy.

As nine o'clock rolled around, I felt my eyelids getting quite heavy. After another round of hugs and kisses and a dinner invitation from Chris and Trudy for the following evening, Mitch and I headed for home. Starting down the long drive from the house, I yawned sleepily and lay my head back against the seat and closed my eyes. All the conversations of the evening's visit with the Tarrington's began to permeate my thoughts; and I suddenly came to the realization that at least two things were blatantly true: one, that I had no idea before tonight that pregnancy was going to be this complicated, and two, that I was totally clueless about babies. Given these facts, if I had no idea how to get through this pregnancy in one piece, how on earth was I going to know what to do once this child was no longer inside me? I opened my eyes and glanced over at Mitch. Catching me out of the corner of his eye, he smiled and then turned his attention back to his driving. I had to wonder if he had any more knowledge about all this than I did or if indeed we were entering parenthood as the blind leading the blind. I wanted to believe that his experience with his nieces and nephews would be helpful, but I was sure that any knowledge he might have was limited at best. I wasn't sure exactly how we would pull all this off, but I had to think that we weren't the only expectant parents who had ever felt that way. I surmised it was a touch of instinct mixed with a helping of the experience of those who had already gone through it and a heaping dose of faith to pull everything together.

We pulled up to the building and got out of the car—Mitch hitting the door lock button on the keychain, then taking me by the hand. Once inside, I turned to him as we walked up the stairs.

"Mitch, do you think we're going to make good parents?" I asked.

He gave me a funny look. "I don't know, Dana. I think we will. All we can do is our best, love. Beyond that, it's really out of our hands." We reached our apartment, and he paused to give me a little hug before unlocking the door. "Now, stop your worrying, okay? I love you, and everything's going to be fine."

I only hoped he was right.

We stepped inside, and Mitch took my coat and hung it on the rack with his own. Tossing his keys on the table, he grabbed me into a tight embrace.

"This was an awful day, in the beginning anyway. But, it turned out all right in the end, didn't it?"

"Yes, it did," I replied. "I like having things like this much better than the way they were. I really don't like to argue."

"Neither do I," he said leaning down to kiss me. "How about we change and just hang out for a while. What do you say?"

"Okay, but I am pretty tired." I glanced at the clock. "It's going on ten. Care if I go ahead and turn in?"

Mitch rubbed my back with his hand. "No, that's okay, if that's what you want to do. Maybe I'll grab a book and read in bed. Would that bother you?"

I shook my head. "No, that's fine."

I wandered off to the bathroom to wash off my makeup, took off my clothes, and tossed them into the hamper. I brushed my teeth and stood before the mirror to stare at my reflection. Something about me definitely looked different, I decided, and began to inspect my physique more thoroughly. I poked gently at the bulge that proved the evidence of our child, then brought my face in closer to the mirror and moved it from side to side as I checked out the laugh lines that had begun to form around my eyes. Concluding that my eyebrows looked like two overgrown caterpillars, I grabbed a pair of tweezers from the drawer and began to neaten them up as I plucked out one painful hair after another until they looked sane again. I pulled out my jar of cold cream, smeared some on my face and rubbed it vigorously, then splashed myself with some water to rinse it all off. I peered into the mirror again. *Funny what makeup can do to hide all those little imperfections*, I thought. Then I noticed my hair, its mousy brown hue looking almost dull and worn. *Maybe I should try some highlights*, I thought, *in a soft chestnut or even something a little bolder like a darker blonde to contrast.* I gathered it all up in my hand and placed it on top of my head. I pursed my now pale lips and turned from side to side as I let it all fall down again.

As I watched it fall, I noticed how tiny my breasts looked, not quite filling up the bra I was wearing. *What did Mitch find so appealing there*, I wondered. I knew they would grow larger throughout the pregnancy; and since I'd never been well blessed in that area, I tried to imagine what that was going to be like. Taking several tissues from the box on the back of the vanity, I stuffed them into my bra and stepped back for inspection. Wow, I could live with that size every day! I was sure Mitch would like it and wondered if I should save up and get enhancements done in order to stay that way after the baby was born. That would be a nice surprise for him. Might even make a few heads turn, coupled with the highlights in my hair. Maybe a little bigger wouldn't be so bad either. I grabbed a few more tissues and stuffed them in, then pushed in and up to simulate cleavage. I thought that looked even better as I turned from side to side to inspect my profile. My fantasy ended with Mitch's laughter.

"Dana Tarrington, what on earth are you doing?" he asked, still laughing.

I could feel the warmth of my blush as he stepped closer to me and stared at the tissues sticking out here and there. He started to laugh even harder.

"Is this what you do when I'm not around? Kind of weird, honey," he teased.

"Stop laughing at me, Mitchell. I was doing this for you," I said as I began to remove the tissues.

He looked perplexed. "For me? Why would you be stuffing your bra for me?"

I pulled out more tissues and threw them on the vanity. "I just wondered what I might look like a few months from now, that's all. I was thinking I might save up and get enhancements done after the baby's born. Would you like that?"

He smiled and watched as I pulled out the last few tissues which caused me to return to my normal state.

"No, because I think you're beautiful already," he replied.

"What about some highlights in my hair, you know, to brighten it up a bit? I was also looking at my little baby paunch here. I'd better go out tomorrow and pick up some of that cocoa butter cream Trudy was telling me about. If I start using it now, maybe I won't get any stretch marks...."

Mitch turned me around to face him and pulled me close. "Maybe you need to stop spending so much time inspecting yourself in the mirror. I think you worry way too much." He gathered up the tissues and tossed them into the wastebasket. "You won't be needing these anymore. Now, come on, love. Let's go to bed."

I sighed loudly. "Okay, but I'm still going to seriously consider those enhancements!"

I heard Mitch laugh as he walked away.

A few minutes later we settled into bed. I cuddled up securely under the covers; and Mitch, armed with his book. I rolled over to face him and lay there quietly staring at him until finally he felt my eyes upon him.

"Is there something you want, dear?" he asked.

"What if I just got the highlights?"

He laughed and placed the book next to him, scooted down beneath the covers, and pulled me into his arms. "You are such a funny little girl." He gave me a playful peck on the forehead. "What makes you think you need to change anything? I feel quite blessed to have such a beautiful woman as my wife. I think you're perfect just the way you are."

"That isn't what you said this morning," I reminded.

He rolled his eyes and sighed—a crooked grin starting to tug at his lips. "Okay, maybe not *perfect,* but close enough for me. How's that?"

"Fine, I guess, but how about a month from now when I'm all big and fat? Will you still feel that way then?"

"Absolutely," he quipped, "especially when you're all big and fat. Know why?"

I shook my head, not exactly sure I wanted to hear his answer.

"Because that's when you'll need me the most. And do you know why *that* is?"

I cocked my head to one side and gave him a look. "No, but I'm sure you're going to tell me."

His eyes gleamed with mischief. "Because you'll need me around to help you do all those things you won't be able to do yourself: like tie your shoes, pick things up off the floor, help you fit through the doorway...."

He laughed and turned away as I walloped him with my pillow.

"Mitchell Tarrington, you're...."

Still laughing, he pulled me into his arms and wrapped them tightly around me. "I know—terrible. But, I know you love it."

He was right—I did.

Sunday came as usual with church, lunch, and a lazy afternoon. Mitch vegetated on the couch in front of the TV watching sports, and it amazed me how he was able to flip through the channels between six different games and know exactly what was happening in each one. I guessed it had something to do with testosterone and decided it best not to ask questions. Instead, I sat in the chair curled up with a good book.

Around five o'clock I decided it was time to get ready for our date with Chris and Trudy, so I marked my page and started toward the bedroom. Still glued to the TV set, Mitch never noticed my departure until twenty minutes later when I reappeared before him with a dress in each hand.

"Mitch, which one do you think I should wear tonight?"

He was staring at the TV as if I wasn't even standing there.

"Hello? Earth to Mitch—which one?"

Shaking the cobwebs out of his head that I was sure had formed there during the afternoon, he pointed to my right hand without as much as a glance in my direction. "That one."

I picked up the remote, turned off the TV, and held up the dresses again. "You weren't even looking. Now, tell me which one you like better."

"What, baby, did you say something?"

"Just forget it." I returned to the bedroom deciding that his opinion probably didn't matter much anyway. A minute later, I heard the TV once more.

Ten minutes passed, and I was standing in the bathroom putting the final touches on my makeup when Mitch burst into the room like he'd been shot from a cannon.

"Dana, why didn't you tell me what time it was? They're going to be here in fifteen minutes!"

I didn't feel like debating the fact that I'd stood before him just ten minutes earlier asking for his opinion on my outfit. I thought that might have given him some indication that I was preparing for our evening out; but apparently, I had been wrong.

"I'm sorry. You still have time, honey. Don't worry about it."

I moved away from the mirror and watched as he frantically pulled out his shaving supplies mumbling something all the while about not wanting to be late and how he hated to keep people waiting. I sighed softly and retreated to the bedroom to put on my jewelry and shoes.

Deciding I'd try to soothe my frazzled husband, I located the Jacy's bag from the day before and pulled out the plum colored shirt. I heard Mitch turn on the shower as I began to iron it, and I finished just as he walked into the bedroom sporting nothing more than a panicky expression. As he shot past me toward his dresser, I unplugged the iron and turned to face him.

"Sweetie, don't finish dressing yet," I said.

He slipped his t-shirt over his head and gave me a grin as he raised one eyebrow. "Baby, we only have about five minutes before they get here. That's not much time...."

I rolled my eyes at him. "Put away the ego, Mitch. That isn't what I was talking about. I bought you something yesterday, and I ironed it so you can wear it tonight."

His eyes lit up, and he stepped closer to me. "Really? Something for me?"

I handed him the shirt and watched his happy expression do a complete turn around.

"What's wrong? You don't like it, do you?"

He stared blankly at the shirt in his hands. "It's purple, honey," was all that he said.

"It's not purple, Mitchell. It's plum," I replied as I folded my arms in front of me.

He slowly lifted his eyes to meet mine. "Tell me, Dana, are plums not purple? Besides, isn't purple a darker shade of pink? You know how I feel about wearing pink."

I turned stubbornly and sat down in the chair with my arms still folded. "Fine, Mitch, just forget it. I'll take it back."

He placed the shirt on the bed and crouched down in front of me. "Ah, come on, love. Don't go getting mad about it. It's nice, but purple's just not my color, that's all." He caught a glimpse of the blue pinstriped shirt sticking out of the bag and took it out for a closer look. "Oh, now, here we go. This one's really nice. Much more 'me.'"

"So is the other one if you'd give it a chance. I thought you were into trying new things."

"I am, sweetheart, but it's purple. You know—the whole pink thing relived?"

I stood up and marched to the closet, snatched one of his shirts off the hanger, and delivered it to him. I thrust it toward him angrily. "Here, just wear this then. I don't care."

I kept my arms at my sides still clutching the shirt as he reached out and pulled me to him. "Please don't be upset with me. I love you for thinking of me, but it's...."

"Purple. I know. You already told me that five times. I told you I'd return it, so why are you creating an issue here?"

"Because I know you're upset, and I don't want you to be. When you saw this shirt, I know you thought I'd look nice in it, didn't you?" I nodded. "You're disappointed that I don't like it, aren't you?" I shrugged. "Tell you what," he started as an impish grin began to emerge. "Remember that teddy the girls got you for your bridal shower? You wouldn't wear it because you said it was too big for you. Well, with you being pregnant and all, it should fit you now. If you wear that for me, I'll wear the purple shirt for you."

I made a disgusted face. "Forget it, Mitchell. The shirt goes back." I heard him laughing as I left the room.

Just as Chris and Trudy knocked on the door, Mitch appeared behind me donning the plum colored shirt and adjusting the tie I'd purchased to go with it. I smiled, and he shrugged, as if saying I'd won; and I was quite satisfied with that. I started to reach for the doorknob, hesitated, and turned to plant a long, passionate kiss on my husband. I thought that since he'd been kind enough to wear the shirt for me, a steamy kiss was the least I could do. He pulled away breathless which was exactly the effect I had been going for.

"Hi, come on in," I said as our guests stepped inside. Mitch said nothing, and I guessed he was still trying to catch his breath after the kiss.

"Greetings," Chris quipped with a smile. He turned to Mitch and gave him a once over. "My, my, don't you look the part tonight. New shirt?"

Mitch glanced at me and then down at himself. "Yeah, Dana bought it for me yesterday. What do you think?"

Chris nodded approvingly. "Nice. Color looks good on you, too. I'd say your wife has good taste; but she picked you, so maybe that statement wouldn't be completely honest." He laughed as Mitch smirked and punched him on the arm.

A short while later we arrived at Chandler's, a fancy little restaurant on the other side of town. We piled out of Chris and Trudy's van, Mitch offering his arm to me in a chivalrous fashion as we walked inside. After checking our coats, we followed the Maitre 'D to a quaint little table in the corner of the dimly lit restaurant. We ordered drinks and appetizers, and then Trudy and I excused ourselves to the ladies' room which gave the men a chance to chat alone.

"You've had that ring a couple of months now, Mitchell. How's married life treating you so far? You two getting along okay?" Chris asked.

Mitch took a sip of water and smiled. "We do most of the time—I'd say about ninety-eight percent. But, she can really be stubborn; and when she gets on the jealousy kick, it drives me insane. I'm learning how to handle it though. I just wish she'd believe me when I tell her I'm not interested in anyone else." He shot a quick look from side to side as if he were trying to make sure no one else was listening, and then he leaned toward his brother. "Like I told you before, Chris, the woman is absolutely amazing. She's sweet, and she's fun; and man, oh, man is she sexy!"

Chris chuckled. "By that I take it there are no problems in the romance area?"

"Are you kidding? No complaints from this guy as far as that's concerned." Mitch smiled. "You know, funny thing about it all is she always puts me first. As long as I'm happy, she doesn't care about anything else. She's not the least bit selfish with her affection. That just makes me want her even more. Sometimes, I just look at her, and I want to be with her."

Chris looked at his brother affectionately. "That's how it should be, little brother. Remember what I told you? The love is what makes it special. If you don't have that kind of attraction to her, then you shouldn't be together. Even after ten years, I still feel that way about Trudy, too. It's a good feeling to know that you have that in your life."

"Yeah, it really is," Mitch replied with a dreamy sort of look on his face. "I honestly don't know how I ever got along without her." Then he chuckled. "Then again, there have been a few times when I've honestly wondered what planet she's from. For instance, she thinks that she has to look perfect every time we leave the house. I was shocked that tonight it only took her twenty minutes to get ready. She can do it when she wants, but most of the time it takes her forever. And when she gets her mind set on something, don't even try to reason with her. It's like talking to a brick wall."

Chris laughed knowingly. "She's a woman, Mitch. That's how it is. Trudy can be the sweetest girl on the face of the earth until she determines to do something, and then it's her way or no way. I've learned the best thing to do is to just give in. If it's not going to hurt anyone or make a major difference any other way, then I let her take control."

The dinner salads arrived, and Mitch picked up his fork to take a bite. "Well, all in all, Chris, I'm really happy. Happier than I ever thought I could be."

"I know you are, little brother. There's no doubt in my mind about that—none whatsoever."

Off in the ladies' room, Trudy and I were engaged in our own conversation.

"Okay, Dana, tell me. What's it like to be Mrs. Mitch Tarrington?" Trudy asked taking a seat on a little bench while I checked my makeup.

"Fabulous! Mitch is the sweetest, most loving man in the whole world!" I smiled and looked at her in the mirror. "Well, most of the time anyway."

Trudy giggled. "Now, I can't imagine Mitch would have any negative qualities," she said sarcastically.

"Oh, please! I've seen mules less stubborn than that man at times. And what a flirt! I'm telling you, Trudy, women are drawn to those good looks, and he loves it. He tells me he's just being friendly, but I know flirting when I see it. That's probably the one thing about Mitch that really bugs me." I turned to face her. "But, I can understand why other women would want him. He is so sexy that it's all I can do to control myself most of the time when I look at him! Put Mitch in a t-shirt with those muscles just showing enough to tease, and I'm gone!" I pretended to fan myself with one hand and placed the back of the other on my forehead in a swooning fashion.

Trudy laughed. "Okay, I guess I don't have to ask if things are all right in *that* area."

"Better than all right, Trudy. 'Unbelievable' is more the word if I had to give you one! I still find it hard to believe I'm the only woman he's ever been with. He has this way of putting my needs above his own, always worried about my happiness. Because he's that way, I just want to give him that much more. I can honestly say I'm more than satisfied with Mitch in every way. I couldn't be happier!"

"That's easy to see, Dana. Just the way you look when you talk about him tells me that." She smiled sweetly. "I'm glad. That's how I feel about Chris, too. I don't know what I'd ever do without him. He's my world."

As we walked back to the table, we could see our husbands' bright faces lost in conversation.

"Talking about us?" Trudy asked as we sat back down.

"Of course, but only good things," Mitch said with a smile and placed his arm around my shoulders.

Trudy decided to have a little fun. "Well, we were talking about you boys, too; and gee, Mitch, I didn't know Dana could have so much dirt on you in only two months. Wow!"

Mitch gave me a dumbfounded little grin. "What's she talking about, love? What kind of 'dirt'?"

"Oh, nothing that needs to be brought up now, sweetie," I said with a smile. I patted his leg under the table, spread my napkin across my lap, and took a bite of my salad. I looked across the table at Trudy and winked.

Chris placed his elbow on the table and leaned toward me with a smile of his own. "Sure you don't want to share, Dana? Sounds interesting."

"Oh, I don't know. I really don't want to embarrass him or anything. You know how sensitive he can be," I said with a smirk.

Chris almost choked on his bite of salad. "Mitch Tarrington sensitive? That'll be the day! Come on, Dana, let's hear this."

Mitch sat back and placed his napkin on the table. "Yeah, Dana darling, let's hear this."

"Ok, let's see." I thought hard to try to conjure up a good story, one that was both believable and yet, unbelievable. "You remember the night the band took him out for his bachelor party? I found out he went to a strip club. Seems our innocent little Mitchell wasn't so innocent after all."

Mitch's mouth dropped open, and his fork fell into his plate. His face was full of shock and surprise, and he could hardly believe what he was hearing. "Dana, uh, how did you know about that?" he asked. It seemed as if his voice was shaking just a little.

I grinned. "Know about what, honey?" I replied still playing my little game with him.

"That the guys took me to a strip club," he said. I thought it was adding to the fun that he was playing along with me for the sake of Chris and Trudy.

"Oh, I have my ways, Mitchell," I said, glancing at Chris who was grinning from ear to ear. Then I laughed.

"Really, now, Mitch? And you didn't invite me along?" Chris pretended to be disappointed. "Some brother you are!" Trudy gave him the look of death.

"I had no idea we were going there; honestly, I didn't. I was just along for the ride." Mitch was sounding convincingly guilty, and I concluded that he was having fun with this, too.

"Tell me, little brother, what was that experience like? I've only heard about such things." Chris was still grinning and glancing sideways at Trudy who was still giving him the look of death.

"I'm sure he really enjoyed it. I mean, what man wouldn't? You're all just animals anyway when it comes down to it," I said.

Mitch was getting very uncomfortable with the whole conversation. How could she possibly know about the strip club? He hadn't told her, and he was sure the guys wouldn't have either. Maybe someone saw him there, someone who knew Dana. The question was, who could it have been? His thoughts ended with the sound of Dana's laughter.

"Oh, come on guys, Mitch at a strip club? He's too good a guy for something like that. I was only joking." I smiled and took him by the hand. "Actually, I don't have anything at all bad to say about him. He's as close to perfect as you can get." I turned to Mitch. "Sweetie, that was pretty convincing the way you were playing along with me."

Mitch breathed a giant sigh of relief and chuckled somewhat nervously. "Yeah, me at a strip club. That'll be the day!"

Our dinners arrived; and although we were all sharing in lighthearted conversation, Mitch still seemed to be a bit uncomfortable with things. A few minutes into the meal, he stood up.

"If you'll all excuse me for a minute, I need to use the men's room. I'll be right back," he said pushing in his chair. He gave Chris a desperate look: one of those secret code things they shared. A second later, Chris was on his feet as well following Mitch. As they entered the men's room, Mitch stopped and put his head down, taking a deep breath.

"Something wrong, buddy? Are you okay?" Chris asked him.

"I just saw my life flash before my eyes out there, Chris," Mitch replied He placed a hand on his forehead and closed his eyes.

"I'm not following you, Mitch. What do you mean?"

Mitch turned and faced Chris. "I know Dana was only teasing me just now, but I thought I was in major trouble there for a minute or two." He leaned against the sink. "The night the guys took me out, we really did go to a strip joint."

Chris stared at his brother in disbelief. "You're kidding, right? You actually went to see strippers?"

Mitch nodded. "Yeah, we did. Totally not my idea though. The guys were just out for some fun, and they thought I'd get into it, too. All I could think about the whole night was how Dana would kill me if she ever found out. Just now, I was preparing for my death later tonight."

"I gotta ask," Chris said with a grin, "did you enjoy it?"

Mitch smirked at him and shook his head, not at all surprised that his brother would ask that question. "I'm not sure, Chris. I mean, it wasn't like anything I'd ever done before. You know—the innocent little virgin boy and all. Sure, I'll admit I've looked at a few magazines in the past. But, these were *real* women, half naked, right there in front of me. I guess I could say in all honesty that it was, well, interesting."

Chris laughed. "Come on, Mitch, you saw beautiful women without their clothes on, close enough for you to touch; and all you can say is it was 'interesting'? Man, have you got a lot to learn."

Mitch looked at him and cocked his head. "Where's your sense of responsibility, Christopher, not to mention your morals? You're a married man with four children. Enjoying a striptease from anyone other than your wife should be the farthest thing from your mind."

Chris sighed. "Look, Mitchell, I'm totally dedicated to Trudy and the kids. I would never do anything to risk losing them. But, I'm also a man; and I'm sure that if I were whisked off to a strip club by some of my buddies, I'd probably allow myself to enjoy it just a little. Doesn't mean I'd ever go there on my own, and it doesn't mean I'd ever even entertain the thought of cheating on Trudy. Looking isn't a crime, little brother. Think about this. If the girls had taken Dana to see male strippers, do you think she would have covered her eyes?"

Mitch looked up and sighed. "No, but she wouldn't have lied to me about it. She would have told me everything that happened. I know that much. However, I'm not Dana, and I *did* lie to her. Now, it's really eating at me. I had allowed myself to forget all about it. Now, it's back, and I don't know how to handle it."

Chris stared at him for a minute. One thing he had never known Mitch to do was tell a lie. Even when he knew it would get him into trouble, he had always been painstakingly honest about everything. Now, here he was telling him he had been dishonest with the one person that meant the most to him in the world. And he was looking to his big brother for advice.

"Not telling her about going there isn't the same as lying to her, buddy. You just withheld the information. That's not wrong, not really."

Mitch put his hands in his pockets and began to pace nervously. "No, Chris, I *lied* to her. She asked me where the guys took me, and I told her to a club. When she pushed the issue, I looked her square in the eyes and I lied. I told her I didn't go to a strip club, that I wasn't near any women, that nothing happened. The worst part is she believed me. She trusted me, and I betrayed her trust and then lied about it."

Chris shrugged. "Okay, so you lied to her. Something you shouldn't have done, granted, but it was only one time. As long as you don't make a habit of it, don't beat yourself up over it. Let it go. Just keep your mouth shut, and no one's the wiser. Besides, where's the harm in your watching some girls dance? It's not like they were all over you or anything."

Mitch sighed again and bit his lip gazing right at Chris. Chris knew his brother well enough to know what the look meant. "Oh, man, Mitch, did you do something with one of them? Please tell me you didn't."

Mitch put up his hand. "No, I didn't do anything; but one of the girls found out it was my bachelor party, and she did a striptease just for me. She stood right in front of me and took off everything right down to a g-string. Then she sat down on my lap and kissed my cheek." He smiled. "The guys were practically climbing over me to get closer to her. I felt so guilty, Chris. I knew I shouldn't have been there, and I didn't bother doing a thing about it. I know most guys would've been in seventh heaven, but I felt guilty; and I still do. I remember smiling at her after she told me I was cute or something like that. She was pretty, but again, all I could really think about was how Dana would feel if she found out. I mean, I threw out my sports magazine swimsuit issue because she found it, and it made her uncomfortable. Imagine how she'd feel if she knew her husband was kissed by a half-naked stripper!"

Chris walked over to Mitch and put his arm around his shoulders. "Look, little brother, you need to let it go. Dana has no clue about any of this. Her choice of what subject to tease you about just now was pure coincidence. Why would you want to start trouble? My advice, if you want it, is to just go back out there with that famous Mitch Tarrington smile and pretend we never had this conversation. The strip club is in the past, man. Leave it there."

Mitch nodded. "Yeah, I guess you're right. I mean, I haven't lied to her since then, and I don't plan to ever do it again. The only reason I did it that time was to keep from upsetting her. I was actually afraid if she knew she might not marry me. She's a very jealous woman, Chris. I know she wouldn't have understood that by staying there I was only trying to keep from offending the guys."

"Well, she never has to know about any of it. It's over. Now, they're gonna think we fell in if we don't go back out there. Come on, little brother." Chris reached for the door handle, but then stopped and turned back to Mitch. "Do you feel better having told me all this?"

Mitch nodded. "Yeah, thanks. I was really starting to get uncomfortable."

"Put it behind you now. Let's go. And smile, okay?"

The men returned to the table, and I put my hand on Mitch's arm as he sat down. "Everything okay, honey? You were gone for a long time. I was getting worried."

"Oh, uh, yeah, everything's just fine, sweetheart. We just got a little sidetracked."

"Sidetracked? How?" I asked curiously.

Mitch looked at Chris, and Chris thought fast. "I thought I left the lights on in the van, and we went out the back way to check. Sorry we didn't come and tell you first."

Mitch took a bite of his dinner and looked over the top of his glasses at Chris who just sighed.

We enjoyed the rest of our dinner and conversation with Chris and Trudy. We shared stories about our honeymoon and all the things we'd adjusted to in our first few months of married life. The evening ended all too soon as Chris pulled up in front of our apartment building.

"You guys want to come up for a while?" Mitch asked.

"Thanks, but I really think we'd better get home to the kids," Chris answered. "Maybe another time though."

"Well, okay, thanks a lot for dinner. It was great," Mitch said.

"Yeah, thanks a lot. We'll do it again soon, okay?" I added.

"Sounds good. Catch you guys later." Chris smiled and waved as they pulled away.

Mitch took me by the hand and turned me toward him. He looked right into my eyes. "Dana, I love you, more than anything."

I wasn't sure why, but there seemed to be something different in the way he was saying it—something deeper and more heartfelt than ever before. I smiled and put my arms around him.

"I love you, too, honey. More than anything."

He leaned down to kiss me—a long kiss full of love and emotion—the kind that told me he just wanted to display his feelings and nothing more. He pulled away and took me by the hand once more.

"Come on, beautiful, let's go inside. It's a little chilly out here tonight."

Once inside, we headed to the bedroom to change into more comfortable attire. I noticed Mitch out of the corner of my eye just watching me as if he were seeing me again for the first time. I turned to him and smiled, and he smiled back sweetly with his eyes full of affection. Pulling on his sweats, he walked over to me and smiling again drew me into another loving embrace this time just holding me close. Letting me go, he kissed me softly on the cheek and exited to the living room.

A few minutes later I joined him, and he was lying on the couch flipping through the channels on TV. He smiled as he saw me and patted the spot next to him offering me a place. "Come over here and let me be close to you, okay?"

I hesitated. "Can I trust you not to start anything?" I asked.

"Like what?"

"You know," I said back as I moved just a little closer to the couch.

"I'll do my best, promise. I'm actually feeling pretty wiped out all of a sudden."

He scooted as far back as he could, and I lay down next to him. He put his arm around me and kissed my cheek. "You were certainly in the mood before we left, I mean, at least that's the impression I got from that kiss. Why not now?"

I yawned. "Because I'm feeling pretty wiped out, too, and the kiss was only to thank you for wearing the shirt. Besides, can't we just be near each other without doing something more? We used to be able to."

He smiled and turned me so I was facing him. "Sure, sweetheart, we can still do that. In fact, I like to do that." He kissed me softly as he grinned playfully. "However, the option is available should you choose to take it."

I smiled and rolled my eyes. "Men," I muttered disgustedly.

Mitch began playing with my hair, pushing it back from my face and tucking it behind my ear, then brushing away the strands that were falling onto my forehead. "Honey, can I ask you a hypothetical question?"

I shrugged. "Sure, I guess so. What is it?"

Mitch's face grew serious. "If you did something, say, that you knew would upset me or that might even damage our relationship, would you ever lie to me about it to spare my feelings and avoid a conflict?"

I looked at him suspiciously. "Mitch, why are you asking me something like that? Is there something you need to tell me?"

He managed a smile. "No, love, it's purely hypothetical. Honest. Now, answer me, would you lie about it?"

I sighed deeply and gave the question a moment of deep consideration. "No, I don't think I would. I believe that, when you're in a committed relationship, you should always be honest with the other person. Trust is a delicate thing, and you shouldn't play around with it."

Fabulous, Mitch thought. *Definitely not the answer I was expecting or wanting to hear from her.* Looking into her eyes right then, he knew that she actually would do just as she was saying. She would never lie to him about anything. He knew in his heart that her willingness to always be honest was a good thing and would keep that bond between them sacred. Her answer, however, was making him feel even guiltier about the lie he had told her. *Should I just go ahead and come clean?* He looked at her again. *No, Chris was right. She has no clue about anything that happened, and she doesn't need to. Why stir up the bees when you already have the honey?* Deciding to leave well enough alone once again, he kissed her on the forehead.

"That makes sense," he answered. "I was just wondering—no particular reason."

I kissed him softly and then cuddled up as close as I could get to him. My eyelids were beginning to feel very heavy. Mitch gently brushed the hair back from my forehead and rested his cheek there. "Baby, why don't we go to bed? We'll just fall asleep if we stay here, so we may as well."

"Yeah, okay," I said sleepily as I headed into the bedroom with Mitch close behind.

He turned on the lamp on the nightstand and pulled off his sweats while I pulled down the covers on the bed. I crawled under, pulled them back up tightly around me, and curled up into a little ball. I heard him chuckle softly; and he slipped in next to me, took off his glasses, and turned off the light. I lay there for a few moments thinking about his question and wondering why he had asked. Could it be that there really was something he felt guilty about: something that he was afraid to tell me? If so, I couldn't imagine for the life of me what it might be. He had said the question was purely hypothetical. Deciding to dismiss it as nothing of importance, I rolled over to kiss him goodnight and drifted off to sleep.

Chapter 3

Monday morning came, and the beginning of another week was upon us. As was the case most mornings, I awoke to an empty bed which indicated that Mitch was already up, most likely nursing his second cup of coffee and getting his daily dose of current events from the newspaper. Unlike myself, he was very much the morning person; and I knew that soon he'd come bouncing into the room, crawl onto the bed next to me, and tell me it was time to get up for work. Also like most mornings, I'd turn over, pull the covers over my head, and tell him to go away.

I opened one eye and looked at the clock—six thirty-five. His usual wake-up call came around six-forty giving me just five minutes to slip back into hibernation and be at least half-asleep when he came in. I was sure by now he knew it was all a game—I would pretend to be asleep, and he would play along, shaking me gently a few times before kissing me and allowing me to open my eyes slowly and grumble about how tired I was. Then he would tell me I needed to hurry and ask what I wanted for breakfast. I'd mumble an answer, and he'd pretend that he understood, prepare me whatever he was having himself; and I'd let on that it was exactly what I wanted. I didn't know why we did it; but it was our routine, and it worked for us. In an odd sort of way, I believed that if I ever did even part of it differently, it would throw off his entire day. So, I figured, why take that chance?

I glanced at the clock again. Six thirty-nine and fifty-seven seconds. Three, two, one....

Right on cue, the door opened; and I felt the bed move and then his hand on my shoulder.

"Dana, sweetheart," one shake, two shakes, "time to wake up." Now for the kiss....

I rolled over, peeked at him, pulled the covers over my head, and grumbled, "I'm tired Mitchell, please let me sleep. Just five more minutes."

"Can't love. You'll be late. Now, come on, get yourself moving." He climbed off the bed and headed toward the door. "What would you like for breakfast?"

"Hmm, a bagel and a cup of tea," I said knowing the words were barely audible.

"Oatmeal it is. You go wash up, and I'll get that ready, okay?"

Oatmeal? How on earth did he get oatmeal out of that? Oh, well, at least I wasn't going to starve.

I rubbed my eyes sleepily, threw back the covers and shivered, already missing the warmth I had enjoyed just moments earlier. Slowly, I started to climb out of bed as I did every morning; but as I sat up, I noticed right away that something was different. Dreadfully different. My stomach did a flip-flop and then another, and I suddenly felt very lightheaded. I sat very still for a moment thinking perhaps I'd just moved too quickly in one way or another, but the flip-flops started becoming increasingly stronger. *No, this can't be happening*, I thought. *I was fine all weekend—heck, I was fine for the past eight weeks! Why now? Why today?* I rushed to the bathroom as quickly as I could, and I made it just in time.

A few minutes and a few episodes later, I sat in the middle of the bathroom floor too weak to stand. I heard Mitch go back into the bedroom, and not finding me there, he called out to me; but I was even too weak to answer. Finally discovering me, he stopped in the doorway and just stared at me with a horrified look on his face.

"Mitch, I'm sick," I whined, "very sick. I can't get up. I tried, but I was too dizzy."

He shook his head sympathetically and knelt down beside me. "Ah, man, honey, I thought you were going to be lucky and not have to go through all this. You were doing so well."

I nodded as he gently helped me to my feet and secured his arm around my waist for support. "Yeah, me too," I replied. "I was fine until I started to get out of bed, and then it just kinda hit me all at once."

I moved to the sink, splashed some cool water on my face, and rinsed out my mouth with some mouthwash as Mitch stood protectively beside me. After finishing my task, he secured an arm around me once more and helped me back to bed.

Mitch pulled the covers up around me and placed a wastebasket by the side of the bed "just in case" before heading off to call Carrie and report that a case of 'morning sickness' was going to keep me home for the day. As I lay there waiting for him to come back, I said a silent prayer that this wouldn't be my sentence every morning for the next seven months. I'd heard about women getting morning sickness; but since I'd never really been around any pregnant women, I didn't have the inkling of an idea as to how long it lasted. I turned just slightly to readjust my pillows, and my stomach did another flip; so I decided to just lie very still and pray it settled down. I closed my eyes and swallowed hard against the feeling that was starting to rise in my throat again. Just as Mitch reappeared in the doorway, I hurried past him to the bathroom for round two.

Saturating a washcloth with cold water, Mitch wrung it out, folded it in half, and handed it to me to place on my forehead. He placed the lid down and took a seat on the toilet as he gazed at me with love and concern. I heard him sigh quietly, but he said nothing. He just sat there stroking my hair, and every once in a while he would tuck a strand behind my ear. I couldn't imagine right then how anyone could say they enjoyed being pregnant. Throwing up, gaining weight, acquiring stretch marks, and experiencing aches and pains in places I hadn't known existed wasn't exactly my idea of a good time. As I glanced down and placed a hand on my stomach, it was as if I suddenly understood. I didn't know this child. I didn't know anything about it, and I certainly didn't know how I was going to take care of it; but I did know that I already loved it. As strange as that may have seemed to me after only a few days of knowing about it, it had become a part of my life; and I felt a love for it like nothing I had ever known. Somehow I knew that as each day passed, that love would only grow stronger. Sometimes you make sacrifices for the people you love the most, and I guessed that was what I was doing. I was making a few sacrifices for my child. Our child. Looking at it from that perspective, it made everything seem just a little easier to bear.

Placing his hand on top of mine, Mitch smiled sweetly, and his eyes were full of affection. "Still a little hard to believe, isn't it?"

I nodded as I looked down at our hands resting on my abdomen. "Yeah, a little." I lifted my head, and my brown eyes met his of bright blue. "But, you know, I don't think I'd trade it for anything. Would you?"

Mitch hesitated a moment with his answer, not exactly sure what to say. He had thought he was okay with all this, that he'd accepted the circumstances and was ready to deal with whatever they brought along. However, seeing her there a few minutes earlier—the sickness taking control of her, the lack of color in her face, the sparkle gone from her eyes—confirmed in him just the opposite. He wasn't ready. Not now, not yet. However, as he stared into her eyes, he knew he couldn't say those words to her. Evidently, she'd come to grips with the situation, and it would crush her to know that for some reason he couldn't. Therefore, he simply sat there as she waited patiently for his answer.

"Mitch? Is something wrong?"

He shook his head and smiled. "No, love, everything's fine. I was just thinking, that's all."

"About what?"

He decided to tell her what he knew she needed to hear. "Your question. My answer is no. I wouldn't trade it either, not for anything in the world."

I looked up at him with a smile as he rose to his feet and pulled me gently to mine. "Come on, let's get you back to bed where you can rest. Then I'm going to call Jimmy and tell him I'll need him to take over for me today. I want to stay home with you."

"No, you go to work. Jimmy gave you Saturday, and you promised him the day off today. I'm sure he's already made plans."

We were back in the bedroom now, and he pulled back the covers on the bed. "Well, I'll give him two days off, but I need today with you. It's okay. He'll understand. Jimmy's a good guy."

I slipped under the blanket but didn't lie down. "Yes, he is, but you can't keep asking him to work for you. You're the owner of Gartano's now, Mitch, not Jimmy. He sold the place because he didn't want to be there all the time. He wanted to step back and let someone else take over, and that someone is you. Now, stop fussing over me. Get ready and go to work."

"Did I ever tell you that you're stubborn?"

"Yes, you have. Quite a few times in fact. But, so are you, and I can tell that you aren't listening to me at all, are you?"

He reached for the phone on the nightstand. "Did you say something?"

"Smart aleck."

He began to dial the phone, paused, and clicked down the receiver. "I just remembered. Jimmy said he was taking his son fishing today, and they were leaving at some ridiculously early hour like four or five o'clock. I guess that idea's out."

He rested his elbow on his knee and placed his chin in his hand as if he were contemplating his next move. He sighed heavily and looked at me sadly. "I suppose I don't have any other choice but to go in for a while, huh? I know Kayla and the others can handle things this evening, but I don't expect them to do it all day."

I gave him a gentle push off the bed, and he stood up and looked at me again. I waved my hand toward the door in a motion for him to go, and reluctantly, he obeyed.

A few minutes later, Mitch reappeared with a towel wrapped around his waist, his hair wet and mussed from his shower. Without a word he began to dress, and I lay in bed, silent as well, watching his ritual. Although he would never admit it, he was definitely a creature of habit—first his boxers, then his t-shirt and socks, next his shirt, and then his pants, belt, and shoes. He placed his glasses back on so that he could see to tie his necktie, placed his collar down over it, adjusted the knot, and turned to the mirror to run a comb through his wavy dark hair. He turned to face me, his expression solemn, his eyes sad and distant. I knew he didn't want to leave and that knowing he had to do so upset him. He managed a smile for me—although I could tell it was forced—and ran a hand down his shirt to smooth it out.

"Well, all ready to face the world," he said softly. "I guess I'd better get going. I have to do some paperwork before we open today, and I want to put in a supply order." He walked to the side of the bed and placed the back of his hand on my cheek as he caressed it gently. "Can I get you anything before I go?"

"No thanks, sweetie. I'm fine. You just go and don't worry about me. Maybe I'll feel better later; and if I do, I'll pop down to the bistro and say hello. After all, I haven't told Kayla yet, and this isn't something you share with your best friend over the phone."

He bent down to deliver a loving kiss. "I'll go, but I can't promise I won't worry. You get some rest now, understand?"

"Yes, master," I said, and he smiled.

The sun was blindingly bright in a cloudless blue sky as Mitch walked out the door that Pete, the doorman, held open for him. He inhaled deeply to fill his lungs with the crisp morning air and pulled the zipper on his jacket just a little higher. As he headed down the sidewalk the three blocks to Gartano's, all he could think about was Dana. He hated leaving her alone knowing that she wasn't feeling well, but he knew it was necessary. There was no other choice. He needed to make sure that things continued to run as usual at the bistro and that he did what he could to keep business strong. To falter in that responsibility would be to falter in his responsibility to his family, and he couldn't let that happen, no matter what. His family. That thought made him smile, remembering the love in Dana's eyes as she'd looked into his, her hand resting beneath his on their unborn child. He couldn't imagine what she must be feeling knowing that inside her grew the evidence of the love they shared, a love that was stronger and more real than anything he had ever known. When he had met her, he never imagined his heart could hold that much love for another human being; and he'd believed that she filled it completely. Evidently, his heart was bigger than he had thought because somehow, despite the fear and uncertainty he felt, his child had found a place there; and the seed was planted for a whole new love to grow.

As he reached Gartano's, Mitch pulled the key from his pocket and unlocked the door. He stepped inside, closed the door behind him, and stood for a moment just taking in his surroundings. Back in December when Jimmy had approached him about buying out his share of the place, he took very little time to make his decision. He had known in his heart that it was the right thing to do. In turning around again to relock the door, he couldn't help but notice the plaque hanging next to it which he'd received as a Christmas gift from Jimmy and the rest of the crew. With pride, he read the inscription: *"Gartano's Italian Bistro, Established 1987, Mitchell J. Tarrington, III, Proprietor."* He chuckled to himself as he recalled the little surprise party Dana had pulled together in celebration of his new venture and the pocket watch she'd given him inscribed with the promise that she would always love him. Two days later, he returned that promise to her with an engagement ring, and now here he was. He had so many blessings in his life, so many reasons to be thankful. With that thought in mind, his spirits lifted, and he began to whistle a happy tune as he walked down the hallway to the office to start his day.

I didn't remember falling asleep, but evidently I had because the clock was now telling me it was almost ten. I rubbed my eyes and sat up slowly not certain if the uneasy feeling I'd encountered earlier would return. For a moment, I kept very still almost anticipating that it would, but much to my delight my stomach felt settled. I yawned and stretched, stepped out of bed, and headed to the kitchen to greet the day. I wasn't used to having a day to myself, not during the week anyway. As I poured a cup of coffee, I thought about what I might do with this free time. I could spend it right there, curled up on the couch beneath a blanket, doing nothing more than watching TV all day. On the other hand, I could peruse the ad circulars from the Sunday newspaper and do some shopping. Now, that sounded like a plan to me! Quickly, I rescinded that idea knowing Mitch would probably blow a gasket if I spent any more money. However, he did keep me from getting that pair of loafers at Jacy's and only because he was being a wise acre. I wanted those shoes. No, I *needed* those shoes. They fit me well, they were cute, and they went with practically everything I owned. Besides, I didn't have to charge them to his card; and if I brought them home, didn't wear them for a couple of days and then eased them into my wardrobe, he probably wouldn't even notice. Pleased with my reasoning, I grabbed a cherry Pop Tart from the cupboard and gobbled it down as I headed off to shower and dress.

Thirty-five minutes later I found myself inside the shoe department at Jacy's Department Store trying on the loafers a second time. Stepping up to the mirror, I made a final inspection, took them off, and asked the clerk to ring them up. I determined that would be my only purchase of the day, that is, until I made the mistake of passing by the maternity department. During my excursion with Mitch on Saturday, I had passed up a cute denim jumper opting for a pair of black pants that he had thought would be 'more practical.' *Well, he isn't here to persuade me today*, I thought. I located the jumper in my size as well as a white long sleeve t-shirt with tiny pink and blue flowers and another in bright yellow. Passing by a sale rack on my way to the checkout, I found a green cable-knit sweater that was a steal at thirty percent off. No woman alive who was sane would pass that up, I decided.

Pleased with my purchases, I intended to leave the store at that moment until I saw a great leather handbag that would match the loafers perfectly. If I got a new handbag, I would definitely need a new wallet to go with it and searched the display until I found just what I was looking for. Paying for everything, I quickly made my exit before I had the chance to find anything else.

On the way home I felt my stomach rumble a little telling me that my choice of breakfast cuisine apparently hadn't been enough now that I was 'eating for two.' Spotting a pair of Golden Arches just ahead, I swung into the parking lot and cruised into the drive-thru line. After studying the menu board, I pulled forward and placed my order for a cheeseburger, an order of fries, and a chocolate milkshake. Reaching the window to pay, I felt the rumble again and told the young man taking my money to make that cheeseburger a double.

I made it back to the apartment building right around one-fifteen. I sucked down my milkshake and half my fries as I fumbled up the stairs with the remainder of my lunch and an armload of packages. Somehow, I managed to get the key in the lock and opened the door to find my frenzied husband waiting on the other side.

"Mitch! What are you doing here?"

"Wondering where in the heck you were, that's what!" The tone of his voice was a combination of panic and irritation. "I tried to call; and when you didn't answer, I didn't know what to think. I've been looking all over for you!"

I glanced down to see the portable phone in his hand and concluded that he'd probably been calling everyone he knew trying to determine my whereabouts—either that or he'd placed a missing person's report with the local police. Based on his reaction, I wasn't sure which was true.

I placed everything down by the door and went to give him a reassuring kiss and a hug.

"I'm sorry, honey. I didn't mean to worry you. I was feeling better so I went out for a while. I was going to eat my lunch and then come to see you at the bistro."

"You know, Dana, I wish you wouldn't have gone out without letting me know. Here I was thinking I'd come home to find you passed out on the floor or something, and all the while you were just out gallivanting around and spending money!"

I couldn't believe his attitude. "Gosh, Mitchell, are you disappointed that I'm all right?" I asked as I stepped away from him.

"Of course I'm not disappointed."

"You're sure acting like it. Besides, since when do I have to check in with you before I go somewhere? You aren't my father, you know."

"You knew I was worried about leaving you this morning. I hated the fact that I couldn't stay home and take care of you. The least you could have done was let me know you were okay."

"Well, you can see that now, so why don't you just go back to work?"

He sighed heavily and stepped away, the look in his eyes telling me my words had stung. "Fine, if you don't want me to show any concern for your well-being, then I won't. Just handle it your way. I can't deal with the hormones anyhow." He grabbed his jacket off the back of the chair and hurried out the door.

"Mitch…. Oh, that's just great," I sighed as I fell onto the couch. As I sat there in the silence, I began to feel guilty knowing that I had hurt his feelings when all he was trying to do was show me that he loved me. *I should be thankful*, I thought, *that I have someone in my life who does love me that much.* I decided that I'd make it up to him. I grabbed my coat and headed off to Gartano's to do just that.

When I walked into the bistro, it was as if I were walking into a haven of comfort; and I felt the shroud of discontent slowly lift off my shoulders. Glancing around, I didn't see Mitch and concluded that he must be in the office. I began to head in that direction, only to get intercepted by Kayla.

"Hey, girly, what are you doing here? Aren't you supposed to be at school?" she asked as she gave me a friendly hug.

I nodded. "Yeah, but I got sick this morning, and Mitch thought I should stay home."

She gave me a puzzled look. "Now, that boy never mentioned a thing to me about your being sick. If you were bad enough to take the day off, what made you come down here?"

"I need to talk to you about something. Do you have a minute?"

She glanced around the dining room and laughed. "A minute's about all I've got judging by this crowd, but you just take your time and tell me what you need to. I'm all ears."

"Remember how I told you that Mitch thought I was coming down with something? Well, he was right."

Kayla's smile turned to a look of genuine concern. She reached out to take my hand. "What's wrong, Dana? Is it serious?"

I gave her a wide smile. "I'm pregnant."

First, she stared at me, then a smile spread across her face, and she grabbed me into a hug. "Pregnant? Oh, my girl, that's just wonderful! My baby girl's having a baby!" She pulled away from me with a questioning look. "Does Mitch know? He didn't say anything."

I nodded. "I told him not to. I wanted to tell you myself."

She grabbed both of my hands, her face brightening once more. "This is wonderful news, Dana. Are you happy?"

I nodded again. "I'm really happy. Just shocked. We definitely weren't planning for a baby this soon, but I guess God had other ideas."

"Yes, He did, and His ideas are always right on. Is Mitch happy?"

"I think so—at least he said he is. We're both pretty scared, too, Kayla. Neither of us really knows that much about babies. I mean, he's had a little experience with his nieces and nephews; but as for me, I've never even held a baby before. I don't have a clue what to do or even where to start!"

She smiled her confident smile. "Don't you be worried about a thing, now, you hear me? Kayla's here to help you, and you know that I will." She gave me another hug. "Now, I mean it; don't worry."

I returned her smile. "Thanks, Kayla, I'll do my best." I pointed toward the office. "I'll let you get back to work now. I need to go talk to Mitch."

Kayla looked confused. "Mitch? Honey, he's not here. He said he had to run out for something, and he hasn't come back yet."

Now, I was the one who was confused. I relayed the story to her about our encounter at home just a short while earlier.

"I don't understand," I said as I finished giving her the details. "I assumed he was coming back here." I sighed and took my coat down from the rack. "Well, maybe he had another errand to run or something. I guess I'll just go back home and see him when he gets there later."

Kayla held open the door for me. "I'll tell him you stopped by when he gets back, okay?"

I nodded and waved as I stepped outside, and Kayla closed the door behind me.

I thought about Mitch while I walked along. Where could he have gone? He did his banking on Fridays, so he wouldn't be there; and we hadn't taken anything to the dry cleaner, so he'd have no need to go there, either. Did he go out for a bite of lunch, perhaps? No, not likely. He usually ate something at the bistro. I dug a little deeper into my brain. He was upset when he left home, so maybe he just went for a little walk to clear his head. I knew he didn't like to let personal issues interfere with his work and probably decided it would be best if he calmed down before he tried to finish out his day. Thinking that was the most logical answer, I reached the apartment building deciding that I wasn't going to concern myself with the issue any longer. He was a big boy, and he could take care of himself.

The weather was unseasonably warm, and I sat down on a bench in front of the building deciding I would enjoy what was left of the afternoon there rather than going back inside. Daffodils were poking their bright yellow heads out of the earth nearby as tulips of every color seemed to be growing tall enough to touch the sky. I smiled as I turned my face to the sun and closed my eyes while I inhaled deeply to take in the fresh clean air. I listened to the birds chirping around me and felt the whisper of the soft breeze on my face. Absorbed in myself, I was almost startled when I felt a gentle hand touch my shoulder.

"Hey, beautiful, mind if I join you?"

I opened my eyes to see Mitch looking down at me, the corners of his mouth raised in a sweet, soft smile. I nodded and scooted over just enough for him to take a seat next to me.

"Where were you?" I asked. "I came to the bistro to find you, but Kayla said you weren't there. I thought that's where you went when you left here."

He shook his head. "Well, it started off like that, but I got about halfway there and realized that I didn't want to leave you the way I did. When I came back, you weren't here."

I giggled. "I guess we both had the same thought in mind, huh?"

His smile grew even brighter, and his eyes sparkled. "Yeah, I guess so," he answered as he took my hand.

His attention diverted for a moment to a sparrow that had landed on the lawn just a few feet away. Its beak was filled with twigs and grass, the remnants of what would soon be weaved into a nest. It was preparing to build a home for the offspring that were most likely soon to be born. It flew off, lighting in a tree close by, busily and almost frantically going about its work. I glanced at Mitch as he watched it intently, his expression telling me he was deep in thought.

"What are you thinking about?" I asked.

He pointed to the tiny bird. "I was thinking, Dana, how that little bird over there is really no different from me. He's trying to build a nest for his mate and family, and he's got to provide for them and take care of them just the same way I do mine." He sighed and turned back to me. "Well, I guess there is one difference between us. He seems to know exactly what he needs to do. I don't."

I squeezed his hand and looked deep into his blue eyes feeling as if I could almost see into his very soul. "Mitch, is there something bothering you?"

He nodded. "Dana, I love you more than anything in this world. I love our baby, too, but the truth is...." He stopped, unable to bring out the words.

I touched his cheek softly. "You aren't happy about this pregnancy, are you?"

He dropped his eyes from mine, his voice barely audible. "I don't know. I mean, I think I am—happy that is—but I don't think I'm ready. This isn't the way it was supposed to happen. We were supposed to be married for a few years first. We were supposed to talk about it and decide together that we were ready for a baby and then work on making it happen. Instead, it just happened." He stood up and placed his hands in his pockets as he began to stare off into the distance. "I'm afraid, Dana. I thought that when it came time for us to have kids that we'd have more time to prepare for it. I mean, a baby is a big step. Probably the biggest step we'll ever take. I just don't see how we can go into this totally blind and be totally ready in just seven months. I don't want to mess this up. If you mess up with a kid, it's not like you can do it over again." He kicked a pebble and watched as it bounced down the sidewalk. "I shouldn't have been so careless. If I hadn't been, we'd be okay."

I took a deep breath in an attempt to make my tone more soothing to him. "We're still okay, Mitch. You know, maybe this was all a surprise, and maybe we weren't planning for this just yet; but for some reason this is what is meant to be. We can't go back and change it, and we shouldn't question it. We need to just accept it and go on. I've done that, and you need to do it, too." I placed my hand on his arm hoping he would turn to face me, but instead he kept his focus straight ahead. "As for messing anything up, honey, I don't want to do that either. I'm really afraid this baby's going to come out of me, and I'm not going to know what to do with it when it does. I guess we're just going to have to figure it out as we go along." I didn't get up, but I leaned my body toward him as if it would somehow help me get my point across. "Now," I continued, "I want you to stop blaming yourself and acting like you've committed some hideous crime that you should be punished for. The only thing you're guilty of is loving me. Last time I checked that wasn't against the law."

Mitch helped me to my feet and slowly placed his arms around me pulling me to him. "You're right, sweetheart. I do love you—so much it hurts sometimes. Not in my wildest dreams did I ever imagine I could feel this way about another human being, and it amazes me that each day it only gets stronger." He pressed his face against the top of my head and breathed deeply as if to take me in. "I hated to see you get sick this morning especially knowing that I couldn't do anything about it. I don't want you to ever hurt, or cry, or feel sickness, or anything bad. To think that I could be even remotely responsible for causing any of those things for you hurts me more than you know. I guess that's another part of all this that bothers me. I know it's just part of the process, but it still bothers me."

I lifted my face and looked at him again. "Well, you have to let that go. What are you going to do when I go into labor? I would imagine that's going to be a lot worse than having morning sickness."

He shrugged. "Yeah, but they can give you things to take that pain away, can't they? There's not a lot you can do to keep yourself from throwing up when the urge strikes."

"True, but what I'm trying to say is that we just have to put up with it, honey. As much as you may want to and as much as I may want you to, you can't make it go away."

He nodded. "I know. Guess it's just the man in me wanting to be in control of the situation, huh?"

"Yeah, I guess that's probably what it is," I replied as I brushed a stray hair from his forehead.

"If I can't make it go away, at least tell me what I can do to help you through it. I want to take care of you, but I don't know what to do. This is all new to me, you know."

I smiled. "Just be there for me. That's all I need."

He placed his hand on my face and drew me to him gently. "Okay, I promise you can count on me. I won't let you down." Mitch kissed me softly as I wrapped my arms around him once more and held him tightly.

I poked his chest playfully with my fingertip. "Oh, yeah, big guy, one other thing."

He took a step back but kept me in his embrace. "What's that?"

"You have to promise that you'll let me be there for you, too, and that you'll stop feeling guilty. God's given us a precious gift, Mitchell. Just think—in seven months, we'll have a little Tarrington. You should be happy about that."

As he looked into my eyes and smiled, I thought I could see the clouds of doubt and fear drifting away from him. "You're right, sweetheart. I should be happy. I'm having a baby. Can you believe that?"

I giggled. "Actually, honey, *I'm* the one having the baby. You get to stand there and watch."

He laughed and pulled me to him once more and rocked me gently in his arms. "I have to watch? I thought my part was finished."

I was laughing now as well. "Oh, so is that what you thought? You thought that you got your hour of fun, and I get nine months of agony, not to mention however many hours of labor? I don't think so, buddy! If I have to go through it, you have to be there to watch."

His eyes were dancing with mischief. "Well, all right, if you insist. But, if the Eagles have a game on TV that day, you have to be finished before kickoff time. Deal?"

I rolled my eyes at him and shook my head as his face beamed. "I'll do my best."

I sent Mitch back to work; and feeling the urge to be productive, I spent the next few hours tidying up the apartment. Noticing that we were running low on a few things, I made a quick trip to the grocery store and then stopped off at the bakery to satisfy a craving for a custard filled doughnut. Arriving home about thirty minutes later, I wearily climbed up the stairs to the apartment suddenly feeling a strong sense of fatigue come over me. I hadn't done anything of real physical merit that day other than running the vacuum, and yet I felt as if I'd put in forty hours of hard labor. Kicking off my shoes just inside the door, I put away the groceries, trudged off to the bedroom, and fell on to the bed.

The longer I lay there, the more relaxed I became. Realizing the fear that I might fall asleep and miss cooking dinner for Mitch, I made myself get up and head to the kitchen.

I pulled out the cookbook and flipped to the page for a beef casserole. I figured it would be something Mitch would probably like, so I read over the recipe; and it didn't seem that difficult to me. I pulled out all the ingredients deciding that I would go ahead and start so that I would have plenty of time to get everything ready before he walked through the door. Smelling everything made me a little hungry, so I pulled out a bag of pretzels and munched while I prepared all the ingredients. I managed to put it all together and place it in the oven by four-thirty. Feeling a sense of accomplishment, I decided to reward myself by vegetating on the couch in front of the TV. The next thing I knew, I had drifted off into peaceful slumber.

I must have fallen into a deep sleep because I didn't remember hearing the timer go off about thirty minutes later indicating that the casserole was done. However, I did hear the smoke alarm.

"What the…oh, no!" I jumped up as fast as I could; and grabbing an oven mitt, I pulled the casserole out of the oven and threw it on top of the stove. Climbing up on a chair to reach the alarm, I pulled off the cover and disconnected the battery, then scrambled down and began to open as many windows as I could as well as the balcony doors to let the smoke out. Then I returned to the couch and began to cry. I had hoped that dinner would be a nice way to make up for my earlier behavior, but I had blown it. It just didn't seem fair. Today had started on such a sour note, and I wanted to surprise Mitch—to be able to have him come home to a hot meal and a kiss at the end of a long day. Now that wasn't going to happen and all because I had been careless.

I heard Mitch's key in the lock; and when he saw the smoke, he quickly threw open the door and stepped inside. He stood still in the doorway for a moment, pushed the door closed and looked at me, then at what should have been his dinner. A slow smile came across his face as he struggled to hold in his laughter.

"I see you made dinner for me, sweetheart," he said snickering. "Let me guess—steak, well-done, right?"

"Don't make jokes, Mitchell. It's not funny," I said sadly as the tears rolled down my cheeks.

Mitch took off his jacket and came over to sit next to me. He put his arm around me and pulled me close to him. "Ah, baby, don't cry. It's okay. What happened?" he asked.

"I fell asleep, and I didn't hear the timer go off on the stove. When I woke up, the whole place was filled with smoke."

"Well, I'm glad you woke up. It might have caused a fire," he said as he began to stroke my hair. Although his comment was meant to soothe, it caused me to feel even worse.

"Oh, that would have been great. Dana not only burned dinner, but she burned down the building as well!" I began to sniffle again.

Mitch couldn't help his smile. "Sweetheart, stop crying. It's all right. That didn't happen. We can have something else for dinner." He placed a hand on each of my shoulders and looked into my eyes still brimming with tears. "Why don't I take you to Charley's for a burger? Or, we can go down to the bistro for some spaghetti and a big piece of apple pie. How's that sound?"

"I wanted to make dinner for you tonight to kinda make up for the way I was acting earlier today. I wanted you to come home to me and a nice hot meal," I whined. "Once again, Dana ruins everything."

Mitch gently moved away from me and wiped my tears with his hands. "Now, you know why I don't cook. The place would always look like this." He glanced over at the dish on the stovetop. "Anyway, that still looks better than it would if I'd attempted it." Once again, he'd made me smile. "Come on, love, dry your eyes and go fix your makeup. I'll change, and we'll go grab something before we meet the guys, okay?" I nodded as he pulled me to my feet and kissed me. "While you get ready, I'll call the neighbors and let them know that the smoke is only from our dinner, and they don't have to evacuate the building," he teased in yet another attempt to make me smile.

"Yeah, okay," I muttered.

I stood rubbing my eyes for a minute while Mitch stretched a little and replaced the smoke alarm. "How did you get that down? You climbed up there, didn't you?"

"I didn't have a choice. I didn't want anyone to call the fire department, and I couldn't reach it."

He sighed. "Okay, but please don't climb anymore. There's a stepstool right here in this closet." He opened the door and pointed to it. "Use that if you need to, understand? I don't want you to risk falling and getting hurt."

I nodded and was starting to feel a little better until I saw the casserole again, and the tears started to flow.

Mitch looked at me sympathetically and then walked over and put his arm around my shoulders. "Honey, it's all right. Why are you still crying?"

I pointed to the charcoal-broiled pan sitting there looking quite pathetic. "Just look at that, Mitch. That was supposed to be our dinner, and now I couldn't even feed it to a dog. I just can't get anything right, can I?"

He sighed and hugged me to himself as he gave me a kiss on top of my head. "I know you're capable of making whatever that was supposed to be and doing it quite well. You're a great cook, sweetheart. Accidents happen. Don't beat yourself up over it." He bent down and looked into my eyes. "I'm not upset with you. Now, let's go get ready, and I'll take you out for dinner tonight. Come on now. Stop being sad."

I took a deep breath and let it out slowly, wiped my eyes, and started into the bathroom. Mitch stood watching me, and I heard him chuckle softly to himself before starting to follow.

"Just leave a few windows cracked open while we're gone to take the rest of the smoke out. It's going to be a little cold in here when we get back, but we can turn up the heat and snuggle up," Mitch called to me from the bedroom. I didn't answer because I had decided to start crying again.

A minute or two later Mitch appeared in the doorway in his jeans and t-shirt pulling on his oxford. He saw me, sighed, and then put his arms around me once again.

"Dana, tell me what's wrong. Is there something else bothering you besides the burnt dinner?" I shook my head. "Then why are you being so emotional?" He paused and looked down at me. "Wait, is this another one of those pregnancy hormone things?"

"I don't know. I just feel like crying, that's all," I replied sniffling.

He pulled a tissue out of the box and handed it to me. "Well, okay, but how long do you think you're going to want to cry because I'm really kind of hungry?"

I pushed him away and wiped my eyes. "Gee, aren't you sympathetic," I said sarcastically as I tossed the tissue into the wastebasket.

Mitch looked dumbfounded and put up his hands in question. "What'd I say?" he asked actually quite clueless. Then he looked at me, and his tone and expression softened. "Look, I'm sorry, baby, but you are awfully moody this evening; and well, I'm not up on all this hormonal stuff. It's kind of new to me, don't forget."

"How long have we known each other, Mitchell? Five months? I've done it every month, dear, when I've had PMS, so you have to have some idea." I pulled out my makeup bag. "Besides, you have sisters, remember?"

He didn't answer but instead just kissed me on the cheek. "I'll wait for you in the living room."

I finished my makeup and walked back into the living room. By now, most of the smoke had cleared, so I closed and locked the balcony doors. Mitch was sitting on the chair leafing through the newspaper. He put it down and stood up.

"All ready to go?" he asked.

"I suppose. I think I am hungry for spaghetti. Let's just go to Gartano's."

He smiled. "Whatever you want, pretty lady," he said. "Lead the way."

We got to the car, and Mitch opened my door for me and then went around on the other side to get in. Once on the road, he took my hand and smiled. "So what were we going to have for dinner?"

"It was a beef casserole. I really thought you'd like it, and I was going to make some rolls and also have applesauce. I know you like applesauce, and I bought the kind with cinnamon." I could feel my voice starting to quiver again.

Mitch squeezed my hand. "Don't you go getting all sad on me again, okay? I don't want you worrying about it anymore. I love taking you out. Gives me a chance to show the world what a beautiful wife I have." He pulled me over to lean on his shoulder and kissed me softly on the forehead.

We pulled into the bistro, and Mitch parked the car. Shutting off the ignition, he turned to me and placed his hand on top of mine. "You know, I was just thinking about all those bags sitting by the door earlier today and wondering how much more money you spent. Makes me glad you decided on Gartano's for dinner. That way, I don't have to worry about going completely broke."

I smacked his arm lightly as he laughed. "You're really the comedian tonight, aren't you?"

Once inside, Kayla greeted us at the door—her demeanor bright and cheery as usual. "Well, hello! Didn't you just leave here?" she said teasingly to Mitch.

"I told Dana we should probably come back and make sure you're working. We both know how you like to goof off on the job."

She snickered. "You know me too well."

We sat down at a little corner table where Kayla took our order with a smile and hurried off toward the kitchen. Mitch gazed around the room with a bright smile of his own and then looked at me.

"I can't believe this, Dana. When I left here forty minutes ago, this place was just as packed as it is now. It's always like this. I think I'm going to have to seriously consider hiring at least one more waitress, maybe two."

I started to answer but was quickly distracted as Kayla brought our drinks and salads, and I began to shovel it in, feeling quite ravenous. Mitch paused and looked at me with a grin.

"Didn't you eat anything today, love?"

"Yeah, I ate. Why?"

He picked up his fork again and turned his attention back to his plate. "No reason, just wondering."

I placed my fork down and looked at him across the table. "Mitchell, you had a reason for asking. Tell me."

He continued to eat without looking at me. "You just seem to have quite an appetite this evening, and I thought perhaps you didn't feel like eating all day. I know you didn't eat anything before I left for work this morning."

"No, but I had a Pop Tart before I went out shopping; and for lunch, I had a double cheeseburger, some fries, and a chocolate shake," I replied as I watched him chuckle a little. "Oh, yeah, I had a custard-filled doughnut, too. And some pretzels. But, that's all."

Now he looked up at me as he shook his head, and his eyes were shining with mischief. "That's *all?* Well, maybe you should have ordered something a little more filling than spaghetti. I don't want you to starve yourself during this pregnancy." He began to chuckle again.

"You aren't funny, Mitchell."

"I thought you said I was quite the comedian earlier."

"Yeah, well, don't quit your day job," I said snidely and turned back to my salad.

He laughed and reached across the table to pat me on the hand. "You're so much fun!"

Kayla arrived with our meals, and Mitch dug right in. However, thinking about what he had said made me hesitate to eat my own. The last thing I wanted was for him to start seeing me devouring everything in sight and gaining more weight than Dumbo, the elephant. Noticing I wasn't eating, he placed his fork on his plate, wiped the corner of his mouth with his napkin, and reached out for my hand.

"What's wrong, honey? Did I upset you? I was only teasing."

"I filled up on the salad. I'm just not that hungry now, that's all."

"Why don't I get you a box for it then? Maybe you'll be hungry for it later, and we can warm it up at Mom's." He gave me a knowing look.

"Or, maybe you can stop worrying that I think you're eating too much and enjoy it now like I know you want to."

I hated when he did that. He knew me far too well. "I was just thinking that you were right, that's all. I did have a lot to eat this afternoon, and I should really try to watch how much extra weight I gain."

He cocked his head and gave me that look that told me he thought I was being irrational. "Sweetheart, you know you're going to gain weight. You're pregnant, for crying out loud. It's inevitable. I don't think worrying about it every time you eat something is going to be healthy for you or the baby." He reached across the table, picked up my fork, and handed it to me. "Go on and finish your meal. If you don't hurry, I'm going to get to the dessert before you do, and you may not get any."

No matter what my mood, he always found a way to say just the right thing. Taking the fork from him, I began to indulge and savored every bite.

The rest of the spaghetti and a piece of apple pie later, Mitch and I set course for his parents' house to meet his band mates for rehearsal. I thought it somewhat interesting that two conservative adults in their early sixties would play host to six rambunctious, overgrown boys in their twenties, allowing them to enter their home each evening of the week to make a bunch of noise. However, in reality, what might have been noise to some was music to most. The band, or 'Ace' as they were known, was a very gifted group of individuals who not only took their talents seriously, but also knew how to have fun with them. Each Saturday evening at Studio 14 in town, they played as the house band to a standing-room-only crowd who would dance, sing, and laugh right along with them. They all loved what they did, and they did it well. I had often commented to Mitch that they should consider going professional, but he would usually tell me they were only in it for the fun, not the prestige. Therefore, I decided as long as they were happy then so was I.

We pulled up to the Tarrington Estate, and Mitch parked the car. He turned to me, and his face held a curious look.

"That's Chris's car. Wonder what he's doing here," he said as he pointed to the sporty BMW sitting next to us.

"Why don't you ask him?" I replied and nodded toward Chris as he came out the front door.

We got out of the car, and he greeted us with a smile. "Hey, there are the parents," he said gleefully. "Here to rehearse, I'm guessing.

If not, there are some guys in there pounding on instruments that shouldn't be."

Mitch snickered. "No, they belong there. What are you doing here?"

"Trudy took the kids to some birthday party at Fun Time Pizza, so I came over here...."

"To sponge a meal off Mom, no doubt," Mitch said finishing Chris's sentence.

Chris gave his brother a playful shove. "Actually, no, I came over to give Dad a business proposal I'd been working on so he can review it before our meeting tomorrow." Then he grinned. "Mom insisted that I stay for dinner."

"You're so spoiled," Mitch said with a sideways grin of his own.

Chris began to laugh. "Me? Oh, give me a break, Mitchell. If anything, you're the one who's spoiled, little brother. The baby always gets his way in everything."

Mitch joined in the laughter as the two headed toward the house. Seeming to forget that I was behind them, they continued their friendly banter.

Chris reached the door first and held it open for Mitch as he stepped inside. They continued on as I grabbed the handle myself before it slammed closed in my face.

Mitch stopped and turned to his brother. "What'd you have for dessert?"

Chris looked at him curiously before he answered. "Well, she had Alexander whip up some chocolate mousse when she knew I was staying. Why?"

Mitch tapped a thoughtful finger on his chin and smiled. "Ah, chocolate mousse, you say? Funny, but isn't that your favorite? Spoiled. You're spoiled."

Chris folded his arms across his chest and pretended to prepare for debate. "Hold on here, little brother. Do you remember the time Mom and Dad took all of us to Hershey Park, and we stayed at Grandma and Grandpa's for the night? Who told Mom that Grandma's guest bed was lumpy and got to sleep in between her and Dad all night? Wasn't the girls or me. Face it, kid, you're spoiled."

"Chris, that doesn't count. I was six years old, for crying out loud!"

Chris waved his hand as if he were wiping away that example. "Okay, I'll give you another one. What about that time a couple years ago when you had the flu? You called Mom whining that you didn't have any clean clothes because you were 'too weak' to do your laundry.

As I recall, she not only washed and ironed your clothes, but she cleaned your apartment and cooked you enough meals for a week!"

I decided to chime in. "Mitchell, you actually did that to your poor mother? Shame on you!"

He turned around looking like he knew he was losing the argument. "I didn't ask her to. She did it on her own. Besides, I was sick."

Chris and I exchanged a smile and said in unison, "Spoiled!"

Just then, Olivia appeared and looked at the ornery expressions filling her sons' faces. "What are you boys up to?"

Mitch placed an arm around his mother's shoulders. "Mom, who's more spoiled here, me or Chris?"

Olivia smiled. "I'd say it's about even." She started down the hallway toward the family room, and Chris began to follow her. Mitch just threw up his hands and shook his head.

Chris continued his protest as he stayed at Olivia's heels. "Even? No way, Mom, Mitch is definitely much more spoiled than I am. Remember that time...." Olivia rolled her eyes, and we watched as she kept walking with Chris's voice trailing off as they moved farther away.

We made our way through the family room where Olivia and Chris were now lost in idle conversation and found Mitch's band mates waiting in the rec room. They all stopped playing when we walked in, and Shep was the first to speak.

"Hey, Trip, we were beginning to think you got abducted by aliens or something. What's up, dude? What took you so long?"

I smiled at his use of the nickname they had given Mitch years before. Finding out he was actually Mitchell Tarrington III, they called him a 'Triple Tarrington,' which quickly became shortened to Trip. Then again, Shep was actually Todd Sheppard; and their drummer, Aaron Newsonberg, donned the handle of Newbie. Somehow, Zach, Ty, and Ash had escaped the wrath of a pseudonym, but I wondered if it was only because the others had yet to come up with anything suitable for them.

"Sorry about that, guys," he replied. "Chris and I were having a little discussion about which of us is more spoiled."

The five men exchanged playful grins. "I'd say you win hands down on that one," Ty said.

Mitch chuckled. "Okay, you losers, let's see what you've got."

I sat down at the back of the room while Mitch took his place at the front, strapped on his guitar, and led the guys through the first two songs. I watched in awe as they played. Their talents never ceased to amaze me, and they sounded as if they had been making music all their lives. Mitch's voice was as strong as ever, each note in perfect pitch, and right on key. I was feeling quite content as I sat there as well as pleased that my stomach had been calm since that morning. Just as that thought crossed my mind, I realized I may have been a bit premature with my happiness. As Mitch cued the band to replay the last song, I felt the unpleasant churning begin to take place telling me that my dinner was about to make an encore performance of its own. Oblivious to the fact, I heard my husband beginning to sing once more as I raced out of the room.

Halfway through the song, Mitch's eyes scanned the back of the room, and he stopped playing.

"Not again," he muttered as he undid the strap on his guitar.

The others stopped playing as well. "What's wrong, Mitch? Are we off again?" Ash asked.

Mitch leaned his guitar against the amplifier and started toward the back of the room.

"Uh, no, you're fine. I just have to check on Dana. Keep going without me."

"What's her problem, Trip?" Newbie called out.

"Me." Mitch picked up his pace as he got to the door and disappeared into the hallway.

He sighed heavily as he reached the doorway of the bathroom and found me leaning against the sink with one hand on my stomach and the other splashing cool water on my face.

"I was hoping this wasn't what you were doing," he said.

"I don't think our baby likes Italian food. He sent it back out."

Mitch smiled. "Well, we can't have that, now can we—especially since his daddy's half Italian." He placed a hand on my shoulder, and his smile grew even brighter. "Oh, and by the way, you said 'he.'"

I reached for the mouthwash in the medicine cabinet, took a capful, rinsed, and spit. "Purely a figure of speech. I wasn't meaning to imply that I'm having a boy. Anyway, you said 'he' as well."

"Only because you did."

I turned to him, and he reached out to take me into a gentle embrace. He held me there for a few moments just letting me feel the comfort of his arms around me and then slowly moved away looking into my eyes.

"Is there anything I can do, sweetheart? Anything I can get for you?"

I shook my head and pulled him to me again just wanting to be close to him. "No, this is enough," I replied softly. I felt his kiss like a whisper on the top of my head.

Returning to the rec room, Mitch found the most comfortable chair he could, moved it into the middle of the room, and then sat me down in it. He stroked his chin for a minute in thought; then he moved a small coffee table over in front of the chair and propped up my feet. He sat down next to them and pulled off my shoes as he began to gently rub my feet. He looked at me with an affectionate smile, and I began to melt as I gazed into his bright blue eyes filled with love. *Maybe I could get used to this pregnancy thing*, I thought. The extra pampering was kind of nice especially if he'd always look at me that way when he did it.

"Hey, lover boy, are we going to finish this set or are you going to kiss up to your wife all night?" Zach called out teasingly.

Mitch turned just enough to see him. "Give me a minute to think about it, and I'll get back to you," he replied. He stood up and leaned down to kiss me softly once, then again, and headed back to the front of the room.

Ty and Zach looked at Mitch curiously as he took his place next to them once more.

"Hey, Trip, Dana doesn't look so good, dude. Is she okay?" Zach asked as he shot a glance my way.

Mitch smiled and glanced at me as well before turning back to the guys. "Well, I kinda wanted to talk to all of you about that." He beckoned the others to come closer to him in a sort of huddle. "Things are going to change for us a lot in the upcoming months—for me and Dana, that is. I'm not sure yet how, or if it's going to affect the band, so I wanted you guys to know so that you could be prepared in case anything happens."

Ash looked at Mitch with concern. "What's the deal, Mitch?"

Mitch smiled brightly. "Dana's pregnant."

The guys all exchanged looks and broke into happy shouts of congratulations, each of them shaking his hand and patting him on the back. Shep gave him a friendly hug.

"I thought you said you two wanted to wait a while to do the baby thing, Trip. This is kind of a surprise."

"Yes, it definitely was!" Mitch answered. "Not at all what we were expecting this soon, but, hey, things happen." He looked my way with a smile. "I'm definitely not disappointed."

"Well, when's the blessed event taking place?" Ash asked.

"We aren't sure of that just yet. We only found out day before yesterday," Mitch answered. "She's about eight weeks along, so we're guessing in seven months or so."

Ash smiled. "Wait a minute, dude. Eight weeks, did you say?" Mitch smiled as the guys all looked at each other with bright faces. "Couldn't curb the passion, huh?" Ash gave Mitch a playful little shove.

"Yeah, something like that," Mitch blushed. Then he turned to me. "Look at how beautiful she is. Can you blame me?"

"Not at all, man! Not at all." Ash smiled.

The guys all looked at me and then at each other. Suddenly, I found myself surrounded by handsome young men all giving me hugs and congratulating me as well.

"Hey, Mrs. Trip. This is all cool," Shep said with a smile.

"You'll be a great mom, Dana. I just know it," Ash said. He gave me a kiss on the cheek, and then he laughed. "Let's all hope and pray the baby doesn't look like Mitch!" The guys and I laughed with him.

"I heard that, dude. To be honest, though, I feel the same way," Mitch grinned.

"Well, I think he's adorable even if all of you don't," I said with a smile of my own.

Mitch came to stand beside me and put his hand on my shoulder. "See, somebody loves me." He pretended to pout.

"Ok, pretty boy, let's get back to work here," Ash said as he prompted Mitch to the front.

The guys obviously decided it was time for some friendly teasing.

"Pretty boy? I'm not the one who looks like a girl with that little earring going on there. Does Cindy let you borrow one of hers sometimes?" Mitch gave him a little shove and was smiling all the while.

"Hey, chicks dig this," Ash replied. He placed his fingertip on his earring. "In fact, Cindy told me she thinks it's sexy."

"Yeah, well, she doesn't want to hurt your feelings, that's all," Mitch chided.

"It's really the mustache that chicks dig," Ty chimed in. "Makes you look masculine, you know."

"Well, you do need all the help with that you can get," Newbie teased.

"At least I can grow one," Ty retorted.

All the guys were still laughing as they got into position. Mitch cued up the first song, and they played through it transitioning right into the second and third. When Mitch finally noticed that I was no longer sitting in the chair, I heard the music stop. Soon, my husband was standing in the doorway of the bathroom smiling and shaking his head at me again.

"Somehow I knew I'd find you in here," he said.

"As bad as it sounds, I'm actually starting to get used to it," I replied weakly as I leaned against the sink.

Mitch put the bottle of mouthwash back into the cabinet and then took me by the hand. "It's going to get better. I know it will," he said quietly. "Come on, let's get this rehearsal over with and get you home. Or, would you like to go now? I can cut it short."

I smiled. "No, sweetie, it's all right. You go on and finish what you need to. I'll be okay."

Mitch pulled me to him in a gentle hug. "You're a little trooper, Dana Tarrington. I sure hope our baby turns out like you."

"Gee, I was hoping it turns out like you—except for one thing," I smirked.

He put his arm around me as we walked back into the rec room. "And what would that one thing be?"

"I'm not sure I can deal with another as stubborn as you are!" I laughed.

"Me? Honey, you take the prize when it comes to stubbornness!" he laughed back. He gave me a kiss on my forehead. "You sit tight, pretty lady. We'll be done soon."

"Is she okay, Mitch?" Ty asked as Mitch went back to the band.

Mitch smiled. "Yeah, she's okay, thanks. Just the morning sickness thing—only it looks like she's going to get it at night, too. That part of the deal just started today. In fact, she had to stay home from work." He looked at me and smiled, and I smiled back. "I just really hate seeing her like that especially when I know I'm to blame for it."

Ash patted Mitch on the back. Being the only other married man in the group, he and his wife had two small children. "I can sympathize. Cindy was like that when she was pregnant with Jonathan. I hated it every time she got sick. The good news is that it doesn't last forever. Before you know it, you'll be looking for an all-night store trying to satisfy some weird craving she has!"

"Oh, gee, something to look forward to," Mitch said sarcastically but with a bright smile.

Almost an hour passed before the guys said goodnight and went merrily on their way with the promise of repeating the entire routine the following evening. Taking my hand as we closed the door to our friends, Mitch turned to me and gave me a soft kiss.

"Let's go say goodbye to everyone, and then I'll take you home, love. I'm sure you're pretty wiped out."

Walking down the hallway, Mitch detected the faint smell of something coming from the kitchen. He stopped and inhaled deeply.

A dreamy look came over him. "Oh, Dana, I think Mom made chocolate chip cookies. I don't know how I didn't notice it when we were walking the guys to the door."

He grabbed my hand and practically dragged me to the kitchen. Chris and Jake were sitting at the table, mulling over some paperwork and indulging in Mitch's favorite treat.

Noticing his younger brother's expression, Chris turned toward him with a half-eaten cookie in his hand and pointed to the plate in front of him.

"Mom didn't want you to feel left out since I had that chocolate mousse, little brother, so she made these for you. Better get some before Dad and I eat them all."

Mitch let go of me, pulled out a chair, and eagerly took a cookie—stuffing the entire thing into his mouth. He closed his eyes and smiled as if letting the taste seduce him. Opening his eyes again, he reached for the plate and pulled it toward him.

"Hey, what do you think you're doing there?" Chris asked.

"You said Mom made them for me, so I'm just claiming what's mine," Mitch replied and snatched another cookie from the plate. Jake lifted his eyes from the paper he was reading and looked at his young son with a smile, shook his head, and went back to his work.

I smiled at my husband's childlike manner and gave his shoulder a friendly rub. "Would you like a glass of milk with those?" I asked leaning close to his ear.

In an almost startled fashion, Mitch jumped up from his chair and placed his arm around my shoulders as he took the last bite of the cookie he had been holding. "Oh, baby, I'm sorry," he said with true remorse. "I promised to take you home to rest, didn't I? Come on. Let's get going."

I placed my head against his shoulder and put my arm around him, giving him a gentle hug. "We can wait a little while. I wouldn't want you to miss out on those cookies. They look pretty good."

That boyish grin came back to his face, and his eyes sparkled. He pointed to the cookies. "If you'll get us a glass of milk, I'll share with you," he said.

I placed a hand on my stomach. "I'm not sure the baby wants any cookies and milk, but I'll sit with you while you have some," I replied softly.

I poured a glass of milk and then joined the others. I took a seat next to Mitch and watched as he smirked at his brother and pushed the plate back into the center of the table. Chris and Jake both took another cookie, and I smiled as I studied each one of the men for just a moment. Of the three, Jake was the largest in stature, followed by Chris and then Mitch; but Mitch was the most muscular, and I concluded it was because he lifted weights almost daily. While Chris resembled his father with sandy blonde hair and soft hazel eyes, Mitch looked nothing like the two—his wavy dark hair and piercing blue eyes matched those of his mother. While the three men may not have shared many physical attributes, they did share a deep love and admiration for each other which was the glue that helped hold the family together.

I sometimes found myself jealous of Mitch and the closeness he shared with his parents and siblings as well as his ability to interact with them almost daily. I had grown up as an only child and what family I did have was now gone. Most of the time, however, I was glad that he had all these people in his life because since I married him, they were a part of my life, too.

Jake placed down the paper he had been studying, leaned slightly forward in his chair, and folded his hands. He smiled at his youngest child across the table.

"Mitchell, I hear business is booming down at Gartano's. One of my colleagues stopped in there a few days ago and said it was almost standing-room only."

Mitch beamed. Upon his graduation from high school eight years earlier, Jake offered him a position at Tarrington Industries hoping to help his young son secure a future. Much to his surprise, Mitch turned him down—his ambition to find his own way without relying on the security net his father's wealth could provide. Jake thought him foolish at the time, young and naïve to the ways of the world, and he concluded that Mitch would learn quickly that he had been wrong in making the decision that he had. To further drive home his point, he rewrote Mitch's trust fund so that he could not receive the money until he turned twenty-five. Although Jake was angry and hurt, he secretly prayed that his son would somehow prove him wrong, and that was exactly what he had done. Sometimes working two jobs to get by, Mitch paved the road to his future with his own sweat and blood. He had made it, and now sat before his father with the pride of his accomplishment evident on his face.

"It's been outrageous, Dad. In fact, I think I'm going to run an ad for a few more waitresses and a cook or two. I figure that will take the pressure off the ones who are already there. A few of them have been pulling double shifts, and I certainly don't want to burn anyone out."

Jake nodded in agreement. "Sounds like you have your head on straight there, son. If you start overworking your employees, it not only harms them physically, but it drops their productivity. You may even lose one or two, and you don't want to do that." He reached out for another cookie, thought twice, and pulled back his hand. "Did you say you're going to start interviewing soon?"

"Well, I need to place an ad first, so I guess it'll depend on how much of a response I get to that. Then I'll start having people come in and go from there." He gave me a sideways glance and moved a little closer to me. He brought his hand from under the table and placed it on my shoulder. "Besides, I don't know how much longer I can have Dana working with us. She needs to take care of herself, and I certainly don't want to risk anything happening to her or the baby. That's for sure."

Jake looked at Chris, who seemed to be watching me for a reaction, and then back to Mitch, his expression clearly showing his pride for his son's compassion. "Yes, I agree with you, Mitch," he said. "It's wise to look out for her the way that you do."

Mitch glanced at me again, but I refused to look at him. Granted, I did appreciate his concern; but at the rate he was going with his protectiveness, he would have me on complete bed rest within the week!

Chris turned to me. "How do you feel about that, Dana?" he asked.

I shrugged. "Personally, I don't see any reason why I can't continue to help out down there as long as I'm feeling all right," I replied. "But, if Mitch wants to let me go, I guess there's not a lot I can do about it. After all, he is the boss." I shot him a smug look, and he rolled his eyes at me.

Apparently afraid a fight was about to ensue, Chris decided to step in and change the subject.

"Hey, little brother, you guys sounded great tonight. I've heard you sing at least a thousand times, and you still amaze me. You have a true gift."

"I guess so, but I'm nothing without the rest of those guys."

"It's great that you're a team player, Mitchell, but you could very easily make it on your own without a problem. I'm sure of that."

Mitch seemed to be lost in thought, and I began to wonder what else he was about to divulge.

"Thanks, Chris, but I don't plan to do anything more than what I'm doing now. I'm perfectly happy with doing the gigs every weekend and just hanging out with the guys." He smiled at me. "Besides, I may quit the band altogether once the baby comes."

I shot him a look of disbelief, surprised at what he'd just said. "Mitch, what are you talking about? You can't quit the band. It means too much to you."

He nodded. "Yes, it does, Dana, but you and our baby mean more. If it gets to be too much to handle with everything else, I'm not going to stay. That was the understanding from day one, remember?"

"Mitchell Tarrington, I know how much you love your music, and you are *not* quitting the band. Do you hear me?" I folded my arms and looked at him defiantly.

He was fighting hard to keep the smile off his face. "Listen, my love. I make my own decisions, and I'll do what I feel is best for my family. In fact, we don't even need to be discussing this now, do we? I'm not entirely sure my brother and father want to witness an argument." He glanced at Jake and Chris who were just watching us with a smile.

"You are so stubborn," I muttered angrily.

Mitch chose to ignore the comment. "For now, I'm just going to keep things the way they are and wait to see what happens. If business down at Gartano's keeps on the way it is now, I may have to start spending more time there, which is going to mean less time for everything else. If I have to do that and need to choose how to spend the rest of my time, you can bet it'll be with my family."

"What will you do to unwind, Mitch? You know your music is an outlet for you. If you give that up, what then?" I asked, once again full of defiance.

Mitch let out a heavy sigh and turned to me. "I can still have my music without being in the band. I did it before I met you, and I can do it again. Now, let's move on, okay?"

"I know you enjoy being with the guys, too, and if you give up the band, you won't get to see them anymore. Sure, maybe you'll keep in touch for a while, but eventually...."

Mitch set his jaw which sent me a clear message that he was about to lose his temper. He sat silently for a moment as if trying to collect himself before he spoke. Then he looked me directly in the eyes.

"Dana, I'm not up for discussing this any further right now, and I'd appreciate it if you'd just drop the subject. We can talk about it later."

I gave him a disgruntled look, and he slowly reached for my hand. However, when he squeezed it, I didn't reciprocate.

Olivia, who had been reading in the front room, came into the kitchen just then and smiled at her husband and sons contently munching away on their snack. I took a moment to look at her as well—her dark hair falling neatly just above her shoulders and her soft blue eyes radiantly bright. Still very attractive, time had been kind to her, gracing her with an appearance much younger than her sixty years.

"I see you three found those cookies," she said with a grin. "I didn't think it would take long for you to finish them off. Maybe I should have baked a few more."

Mitch waved his hand at her and shook his head. "Oh, no, Mom. This is plenty. Thanks," he muttered through a full mouth.

"Mitch, swallow before you speak," she scolded, and he chuckled.

She sat down on the chair next to Jake, and she looked at me sympathetically when she noticed I was empty handed.

"Dana, wouldn't you like something, dear? If you don't get some, these boys will have them all gone in the blink of an eye."

"No, thanks," I said rather quietly. "The baby didn't like dinner, and I'm not so sure it would want a snack right about now."

Mitch dropped a hand below the table, and I felt it on my leg. I placed my hand upon it and gave it a gentle squeeze.

"She hasn't been feeling quite up to par today," he said. "The morning sickness thing kicked in just as she woke up, and it came back tonight as well. But, I'm sure she'll be past all that in a few weeks and back to her old self again."

Olivia bit her lip, and I wondered if Mitch had inherited that trait from her. "Gee, I hope so, honey, but I was sick the entire time I carried you. Some days were worse than others, but it didn't end until the day you were born."

Chris leaned toward his brother with a twinkle in his eye. "Wow, Mitchell, you were a pain from the very beginning. Shame that you never outgrew it." Mitch gave him an icy glare as Chris laughed.

"You mean it can really last that long?" Mitch asked rather mortified.

"It can, but every woman is different. Some women have it for a few weeks while others have it for months. It can also differ from pregnancy to pregnancy. With Julia, I was only sick for about three weeks; with Chris, off and on for three months; and with Angelina, I wasn't sick at all." She smiled. "However, with you for some reason, it was relentless. You made up for it, though, after you were born. You were a very good-natured baby. Hardly cried at all."

Mitch sat back, crossed his arms, and gave Chris a very smug look. "See, I wasn't such a pain after all."

I laughed. "Have these two always taunted each other like this, Olivia?" I asked.

She laughed as well. "Oh, Dana, I could sit here all night and tell you stories!"

Mitch took that as his cue to move things along. He stood up and moved to stand behind my chair, pulling it out just slightly. "Well, maybe another time, Mom," he said with a grin. "I'd better get this lovely lady home and in bed."

Chris couldn't resist one more stab at his younger brother. "Uh, Mitch, haven't you learned anything? That's kinda how she got in that condition."

Jake and Olivia laughed as Mitch gave his brother another icy glare. I simply blushed.

After saying our goodbyes, we had barely made it down the drive from the house when Mitch reached out and took my hand.

"Dana, I'm sorry if you're upset or mad or whatever else you might be about my considering getting out of the band; but if that is what's going to be best for all of us, then it's what I'm going to do. The last thing I want to do is spread myself so thin that I don't give you and the baby what you need from me." Although he was speaking softly, I could hear the decisive tone in his voice.

I placed my other hand on top of his. "All we need is your love, and staying with the band isn't going to affect how much of that you can give us, is it?"

I noticed a slow smile come to his face, and he squeezed my hand. "I'm glad to hear that you feel that way; and I love you for saying it, but I know in my heart there's a lot more to being the head of a family than just loving them. I need to not only work and provide, but I need to have time to give to them. If I have too much on my plate, I may not be able to handle it all. That's all I'm saying."

I settled back into my seat and turned away from him with a sigh. "Maybe so, but I know you. You handle everything now without a problem, and you'll be able to handle things after we have the baby just as well. I just don't want your entire life to be me and this child. You need to do something for yourself, too."

Mitch was staring intently at the road ahead which clearly told me that he was pondering my train of logic. He sighed and turned to glance at me just slightly.

"Well, like I said earlier, we'll just have to wait and see how things go, okay?" He fixed his eyes back on the road. "I love you. I just don't want to let you down by not being there when you need me."

I leaned against his shoulder and took his hand, giving it a squeeze. "Mitch, since I've known you, you haven't let me down one time. I really don't think it's something you're even capable of doing. Why are you worrying about it so much?"

He smiled. "Because I've never been a dad before, sweetheart. This is probably the biggest thing that's ever happened to me. Like I told you before, I just want to make sure I don't mess it up."

"You won't, honey. This baby is going to have the best daddy in the whole wide world."

We were silent the next few minutes; and as we pulled into the parking lot of the building, he turned to me again.

"You are really something else—you know that?" His eyes were shining with a soft affection as he kissed me. "Stay put. I'll come around and help you out." The next thing I knew, Mitch was opening my door and taking me by the hand to help me out of the car. "Hang on to me, ok?" He grasped my hand tightly and hooked it through his arm as if securing me even more.

Inside the apartment, we hung up our coats and headed toward the bedroom to change.

"Tired, love?" Mitch asked as he turned on the lamp.

"A little," I replied. "Why? Is there something you wanted to do?"

His face lit up as he raised his eyebrows at me and flashed that dimple that I loved so much. "No, but I'm open to suggestions."

"I don't know what you mean," I said, playfully.

"Why don't you come here and let me show you?"

I finished pulling on my pajamas and walked over to my husband who took me into his embrace. "Now, are you ready to hear my proposal or would you like to make one of your own?" he said as he lowered his voice to a sexy tone.

I traced his jaw with my fingertip, and he smiled—his eyes filling with desire. I slowly slid my arms around his neck and drew him toward me. Leaning close to his ear, I said in my softest, most seductive voice, "Let's cuddle up on the couch…."

"Uh-huh…."

"We'll pull the blanket over us…." I continued, now kissing his cheek.

"Yeah…."

"And then…." I pulled him closer, giving him a soft kiss, letting my lips lightly brush his. I opened my eyes to look at him—the anticipation on his face more than apparent.

I could hear his breath coming quicker. "Go on…."

"We'll watch some TV."

Mitch dropped his head and began to laugh. "You little brat. That wasn't very nice. Here you got me all hot and heavy just to tell me you want to watch TV?" His faced glowed in a radiant smile.

"Well, yeah, what'd you think I was going to say?" I touched him on the cheek as I gave him an ornery grin and trotted off toward the living room. When I noticed he wasn't following, I called back to him. "Aren't you going to join me?"

He popped his head around the corner, and he was still smiling. "Maybe after I go and take a cold shower!"

I laughed. "Get out here, you!" I called, and a few seconds later Mitch was sitting next to me on the couch.

He picked up the remote from the coffee table and turned on the TV as I pulled the blanket off the back of the couch and wrapped it around us. He smiled as he placed his arm around me and pulled me close.

"You know, love, this is the best—just the two of us here together like this." I leaned my head on his shoulder, and he kissed my forehead. He glanced away for just a moment: his expression curious.

"What are you thinking about, Mitch? I can see those gears turning in your head."

He turned back to me with a smile and moved just slightly so that my head was now resting on his chest. "I was just thinking about our conversation on the way home, that's all," he replied. "You really are assertive."

I lifted my head to look at him. "In what way?"

He sighed softly as he began to stroke my hair. "Just the way you told me in no uncertain terms that I was *not* quitting the band. I was just thinking that it made me realize how strongly you feel about my happiness and, well, it touched me."

I ran my hand over his chest and stopped to rest it on his heart. "It's just that I know how much you love your music and how happy it makes you when you're with the guys, whether it's a rehearsal or a show. It's your passion. I know it is. If I stand by and just let you walk away from all that, I'll feel as if I had a part in helping you give up a piece of who you are. I can't do that."

He rubbed his eyes beneath his glasses and twisted his jaw as he thought about my words. "What if I told you that I'll stay with the band, but only if you make me a promise?"

I glanced up into his eyes. "And just what might that promise be?"

He brought his hand down to rest on my arm and began to rub it as he pulled me toward him even more. "You have to promise me if you ever feel like I'm neglecting you or the baby, or I'm not doing my share around here to help, you'll tell me, ok?"

I nodded. "Ok, Mitch, I promise. I'll tell you."

He put up his hand. *"And,* if that should happen, or I feel like I can't handle everything, you'll let me make the decision as to what to do from there. Agreed?"

I looked up at him, and he gave me a disciplinary sort of look as he waited for my answer.

"Agreed," I said, and he smiled.

Chapter 4

Somehow, we managed to make it through the next few weeks, and it was during this time that I began my pre-natal care. I soon found that being a Tarrington had its advantages. The family seemed to have connections to the best resources available, and I was more than pleased that I knew people who carried that kind of clout. Physicians were no exception, and Angelina's husband Jim was invaluable in this area. Having been on the staff himself for over a year, he directed us to Dr. Mark Bradley, the Head of Obstetrics and Gynecology at Mercy Hospital. On the day of my first appointment, I left Mitch in the waiting room nervously perusing a copy of *'Parents'* magazine while I met with Dr. Bradley in the exam area. Happily, I received the confirmation of my self-diagnosis—I was indeed 'with child' and told we could expect our new bundle of joy sometime in late November.

Other than this news, life went on—each day seemingly blending into the next—as far as I was concerned anyway. Every morning I would awaken at some ungodly hour, get sick, splash water on my face, and return to bed, only to repeat the process a few hours later. Then Mitch would appear like an angel in waiting, tuck me safely back into bed, call me off work, and head out to put his time in at the bistro. I was beginning to feel as if my life was becoming one giant case of déjà vu, and I sadly conceded that it wasn't going to change anytime soon.

Early on a Friday, I sat bolt upright in bed and looked at the clock. Four thirty in the morning. At least I got to sleep for a little while. I sat very still for just a moment hoping the feeling would go away; but it only started to build, so I quickly grabbed my robe off the chair as I ran to the bathroom. *Thus, it begins,* I thought. A few minutes later, Mitch was standing in the doorway.

"Not again," he said solemnly as he handed me a cold washcloth.

I looked up and nodded. "I think I'll just bring my pillows in here and sleep. Might as well. Something tells me I won't be spending much time in bed the next couple of hours."

"You poor baby. I really wish I could do something to make you feel better."

"You can," I said sarcastically. "Get a vasectomy."

"Look, Dana, I...." Mitch took on a sad look and left the room.

A few minutes later, I felt well enough to try to return to bed. When I walked into the bedroom, instead of finding Mitch sleeping peacefully, he was sitting up with the light on, his eyes downcast, twisting his wedding band.

"Mitch, what's wrong? Why aren't you sleeping? You have to go to work later."

"Yeah, I know," he said softly. Then he looked up at me. "You know, I feel badly enough watching you get sick twenty times a day without you making me feel even more guilty about it." His tone held just a hint of irritation.

"What do you mean? When have I made you feel guilty?"

He pointed toward the bathroom. "Just now—in there. You basically told me not to get you pregnant again and that would make you feel better."

I crawled into bed next to him. "Honey, I'm sorry. I didn't mean to hurt your feelings. I didn't mean anything by it. I was just spouting off." I reached out for his hand. "I love you. Now, let's try to get some sleep before this child of yours wakes me up again."

He chuckled as he turned off the light. "Let me guess—it's going to be my child when it's naughty and your child when it's good, right?"

"You are such a smart man," I said and snuggled up to him.

Mitch once again awoke to the sound of the alarm and an empty bed. He reached for his glasses on the nightstand and went in search of Dana. Just as he had suspected, he found her once more in the bathroom sitting on the floor clutching a washcloth. Smiling, he went to her and gently began to stroke her hair.

"My poor, sweet Dana," he said softly. "Is there anything I can do?"

I looked up at him, and my eyes began to fill with tears. "Call work and tell them I won't be coming in today." Nodding, he walked out of the room.

I managed to wash my face and brush my teeth, pulled my hair into a ponytail, and then joined Mitch in the kitchen. He smiled sweetly as he saw me and reached out to pull me to him.

"Still feeling a little rough, huh?" he asked.

"Yes, I am. But, I can't keep missing work. I have to find a way to fight this thing and get on with my business."

"Well, honey, you can't go to work and be there throwing up all morning either, now can you?" he said, pouring a cup of coffee.

I could feel the tears starting to drip down my cheeks. "I've only worked four hours in the past three weeks, and even then I had to leave early each time. If I keep missing work, they're going to fire me. Then what will we do?" I said sadly as I plopped down in a chair.

Mitch sighed. "Dana, they won't fire you. They understand that you've been sick. Why don't you call and talk to your boss? Maybe they can arrange a different schedule for you. There are only about five or six weeks left of school. I'm sure it wouldn't be a big deal."

"Yes it would, Mitchell. School lets out at three o'clock. I doubt they would agree to letting me work from noon until three everyday. I don't really start feeling up to doing anything much before that."

He smiled in an attempt to ease my concerns. "Sweetheart, if it's the money you're worried about, don't. I'm a rich kid, remember?"

"No, you aren't. You used to be, but you chose to give all that up—now didn't you?" I retorted.

"I still have connections, love. All it takes is a phone call or two." He was still smiling.

I stood up and trudged toward the couch, falling onto it with a heavy sigh. "Mitch Tarrington, how can you possibly make jokes at a time like this?"

"At a time like what, Dana? You have morning sickness—not the bubonic plague. You'll get over it in a month or so, and life will go on. Now, stop feeling so down. I'm going to go get dressed." He headed off to the bedroom, and I decided to follow.

I sat down on the side of the bed and watched him as he walked into the closet, selected an outfit, then returned to the center of the room and began to put it on. Suddenly, something struck me. "Mitch?" I said getting his attention.

"Yeah, what?" he replied.

"What if this doesn't go away, and I can't go back to school? What if I'm like your mom was with you, and I'm sick through the entire pregnancy? Then what?"

He let out an exasperated breath. "It'll go away, trust me. You just need to learn how to handle it, you know, what times of day it's the worst and when you can still function pretty close to normal. Once you get that down, you'll be fine until it's gone completely."

"I'm glad one of us is confident of that," I replied sarcastically.

Mitch walked over and sat down beside me. "Honey, it's going to be okay, I promise. Millions of other couples face this stuff every day. But, just think. In the end, won't it all be worth it when we get to hold our little Tarrington?"

I managed a weak smile. "Yeah, our little Tarrington."

"What if I call Jimmy and tell him I'm taking the day off, too? I've yet to do that for you; and if I catch him right now, it shouldn't be a problem. I'll stay right here with you all day. If you want, we don't even have to leave the bedroom." He raised his eyebrows impishly.

"I really think you should go to work, Mitch. One of us has to bring home some money. We're going to have a lot of expenses in the days ahead."

He stood up. "That's why I also have medical insurance, dear." Thrusting his hands into his pockets, he turned to me. "I don't feel right leaving you at home alone all day especially when I know you're not feeling well. I feel terrible about it each time I walk out that door."

"Didn't you just tell me I have to learn to deal with this? I can't do that if I have you here waiting on me and doting over me all day. Please go to work."

He sighed. "I can't take care of you now? Fine, I won't try anymore," he said, sounding rather dejected. He gave me a quick peck on the forehead. "I'll see you a little after five." He left the room.

I fell back onto the bed. *Why is that man so stubborn*, I asked myself. As I heard the sound of Mitch closing and locking the door, I closed my eyes and lay very still in an effort to fight off the feeling that was creeping up on me again. It only took a minute or two for me to realize that ignoring it wasn't going to work, and I headed off once more to take care of business.

Finally feeling half-human a few minutes later, I retreated to the kitchen thinking I would try to eat. Mitch had told me that keeping something light on my stomach might help to alleviate the nausea and keep up my strength. I decided on a bowl of oatmeal and a cup of hot tea thinking that might sit a little better on my stomach than coffee. As I poured the water into the cup, I heard Mitch's key in the lock once more.

"Hi," he said quietly as he closed the door behind him.

I smiled a soft smile. "Hi. Why'd you come back?" I asked.

"Because I didn't feel right leaving you that way, and I wanted to tell you that I'm sorry for snapping at you."

I walked over and put my arms around him. "It's all right. I didn't think a thing about it. Anyway, I'm the one who needs to apologize. I wasn't very nice to you."

He smiled. "Well, I think we're both a little on edge about all this, aren't we? It seems like since we found out, the tension around here is so thick you could cut it with a knife. You gotta admit, love, this is a lot for us to handle especially this soon."

I nodded and looked into his eyes. "I know it is, but I also know if anyone can handle it, you can. I'm going to need you to help me."

"I'll do my best. You know I will," he replied. "Well, are we all right now?"

I answered him with a long, wonderful kiss.

Around twelve-thirty I showered and dressed, tidied up the apartment, and sat down on the couch. I wasn't used to being at home during the day, and I felt almost at a loss as to what to do with my time. I could go to the mall, but somehow shopping for maternity clothes wasn't nearly as much fun as picking out a sexy, form-fitting dress or a pair of tight blue jeans. I could go for a walk in the park, but that wasn't much fun alone; and roller skating and bowling were out of the question given my current physical state. There was only one thing left to do. I grabbed a lightweight jacket and my purse and then headed out the door to Gartano's.

As I walked in, the warmth and familiarity of the place made me smile. As usual, the dining room was filled with customers, and the waitresses were busily flitting from table to table. I could already feel some of my melancholy mood fading away as I hung my jacket on the rack, and I felt a smile creeping onto my face. When I turned around, however, that smile quickly faded away.

In the middle of the room a table hosted two young ladies, both of their pretty faces bright with smiles. Obviously lost in cheerful conversation, they were laughing giddily at the handsome young man who had joined them. He was apparently telling them a story and being quite animated about it. The man was straddling a chair with his back to the door, and he hadn't seen me come in. I stood silently still and watched my husband entertain these lovely women.

The longer I stood watching him, the more depressed I grew. Why was he there, and why did he seem like he was enjoying himself so much? I looked down at myself, and I had the answer. He'd noticed the changes in me—the bulge at my waistline now fully visible and a sure sign to all onlookers that I was indeed expecting. Perhaps as he'd helped me to my feet in the bathroom that morning, he'd noticed I was slightly heavier than I had been previously. I knew he had liked my body; he'd told me so on several occasions. But, not this body. This wasn't the body he'd married. This was something entirely different. The women at his table were beautiful and built with not an ounce of fat anywhere on them. When I'd looked at myself the mirror earlier that day, I had seen it all beginning to take place. I realized I was pregnant and that I would inevitably get larger in the stomach as the baby grew; but why did I have to gain everywhere else and why so early in the game? It was far too soon. Feeling even more depressed as I took down my coat, I turned back toward the door and reached for the handle. Just as I did, Kayla noticed me.

"Hey, girl, where do you think you're going? You just got here!" She walked over to me and gave me a hug. "Did you leave work early or something?"

"No, I took the day off. I was thinking maybe this wasn't such a good idea. I think I'm going to go home."

Kayla gave me an odd look. "You came here for a reason, Dana, and I'll bet that reason was Mitch. Why would you leave before you even had a chance to see him?"

I nodded in the direction of the table where he was sitting. "Oh, I've seen him," I replied. "He just hasn't seen me yet."

She smiled. "Come on now, girl. He's only talking to the customers. That's all."

I sighed. "Well, call it what you will." I turned to her and forced a smile. "Anyway, I think I am going to go home. I'm starting to feel a bit woozy again, and I'd like to take a nap." I reached for the door handle once more. "I'll see you later, Kayla. Oh, please don't tell Mitch I was here, okay? I, uh, don't want him to worry."

Somehow making it back home and into the apartment, I locked the door and went straight into the bedroom. Lying on the chair was a stack of maternity clothes from the laundry that I'd folded earlier but had yet to put away. Glancing from them to my bulging waistline, I lay down on the bed and began to cry. Letting my emotions take control, I cried myself to sleep.

Around five I woke up and decided I would try to make dinner for Mitch. Even if I didn't feel much like eating myself, the least that I could do was try to have a hot meal ready for him. Retreating to the kitchen, I pulled out some pork chops, a few potatoes to bake, and a bag of frozen broccoli. Within a few minutes I had everything well on its way. Feeling quite content, I went to sit down in the living room. As I approached the chair, I saw the giant teddy bear in the corner, and I smiled. *He is going to be such a good father*, I thought. I had no doubt in my mind that our child would never want for anything as long as Mitch felt he could provide it.

A few minutes later I heard Mitch unlock the door, and he stepped inside—his face glowing. "Well, hello beautiful!" he chirped as he hung up his coat. Throwing his keys on the table, he came to sit down next to me and gave me a kiss. "Feeling a little better?"

I nodded. "Yeah, a little I guess. Dinner will be ready in a few minutes."

He inhaled deeply. "Smells great. What're we having?"

"You're having pork chops," I told him. "I'm having a salad."

He gave me an inquisitive look. "Aren't you hungry for pork chops? I think it sounds wonderful."

I sighed. "Well, I think I'm better off with the salad," I replied, "considering that even my maternity clothes look tight on me."

He smiled. "Dana, you're pregnant. You have to eat normally so you and the baby will be healthy. You can't be concerned about gaining weight, honey. You're going to do that no matter what."

I stood up to go and check on dinner. "I certainly don't have to help it along now, do I?"

Mitch followed me into the kitchen. "That's fine, dear. Do what you want. But, I think you're overreacting just a tad."

"No, I'm not. The less pounds I contribute to myself, the less I'll have to lose once the baby comes. Besides, maybe the sight of me won't turn you off so much."

He cocked his head to one side and furrowed his brow curiously. "What?"

"You heard me, Mitchell. I saw how you were acting around those girls today. You wish I was all thin and gorgeous like that again, don't you?"

He looked surprised. "What girls?" Then it dawned on him. "Wait a minute. Were you at the bistro today? Why didn't you say hello to me?"

I placed the broccoli into the steamer. "You were busy."

"I was busy? Busy doing what?"

"Flirting. And, you didn't answer my question."

"I wasn't flirting with anyone. What question is it that I'm supposed to answer?" He pointed to me and then to himself. "You didn't answer my question either."

"Yes, I did. I said you were busy."

"Flirting."

"Yes."

He was beginning to become defensive. "I don't believe you. Why is it that every time I talk to another woman you accuse me of flirting with her?"

I pulled a plate from the cupboard and began to fill it with his dinner. "Because you do. You don't even realize when you're doing it."

I placed the plate on the table, poured him a glass of milk, and set it down next to his plate. "Those women were beautiful, Mitch; not like me. I know you've noticed how big I am already, and I'm sure you miss the fact that I don't look like they do anymore."

Mitch sighed loudly. "For crying out loud, Dana, you're *pregnant*! And no, I haven't noticed anything different about you, not at all, except that you've gotten into this mode of feeling sorry for yourself."

I turned around to face him. "Oh, so is that what you think I'm doing? Feeling sorry for myself? A little hard not to when I come to the bistro and see my husband sitting with two women pretty enough to be models, laughing and talking and having a good old time. And, may I mention, they were checking you out, too, my dear. I was watching."

He shook his head and allowed his dimple to show just slightly. "Obviously, you didn't look close enough to recognize who the one lady was, did you?" I shook my head, and he let his smile come out all the way. "Remember Eric Tallmadge, my dad's business colleague that we met at our reception? It was his wife Vanessa, and the lady with her was her sister Judy. She said she'd been eager to check the place out; so when Judy suggested they have lunch together, Vanessa suggested Gartano's." Mitch reached out for me and took my hand. "So you see, my love, no one was checking out anyone. We were talking about the reception. Vanessa was mentioning that little show I put on during dinner when everyone was clanking their glasses for us to kiss. I was simply adding the finishing touches, and that's all."

I suddenly felt lower than a snake's belly. "Really? That's what you were talking about? Our reception?"

Mitch folded his arms and looked very smug as he nodded. "Yes, dear, that's what we were talking about. Nothing more."

I turned away from him, not exactly sure what to say. "I'm sorry, Mitch. When I saw you there talking with them the way you were and looking so happy, naturally I thought…."

"That I was flirting with two attractive women because for some reason you don't think I'm happy with you. Dana, if that was the case, why would I even still be here?"

I sighed. "I don't know. Maybe you feel obligated. I am pregnant with your child, you know."

Mitch turned away from me. He was clearly upset, and his smile was now replaced with a look of anger. "You know, I'm not wasting any more precious time with this ridiculous conversation. I'm going to go and take a shower." He walked off down the hall muttering to himself under his breath.

A few minutes later he reappeared after he'd showered and changed into jeans and an oxford. He gave me another displeased look as he walked back into the kitchen and sat down at the table. He picked up the salad from my place, put it in front of himself, and placed his plate of food in front of me. "You and the baby need more to eat than a salad. This is my dinner tonight," he said taking a bite.

I looked at him. "Why'd you do that? I want the salad. Please give it to me."

He placed a piece of lettuce, a carrot, and a cucumber slice on the side of my plate. "There, you have salad. Now, eat your dinner." he replied sternly as he took another bite.

I stared at the plate of food in front of me. "You are so stubborn," I stated.

"Yep, you're right. I am. Get used to it."

Knowing there was no sense in arguing, I began to eat the pork chops. They did taste good; but the more I ate, the guiltier I felt. I had made that dinner for him with the thought that a hot meal would comfort him at the end of a long day at work. Now, he was eating cold lettuce with a glass of milk. I stood up and took another plate from the cupboard, placed half the food on it, and sat it down in front of him. "Give me the rest of the salad, and we'll be even," I told him.

He handed me the salad and started to eat the other food. "Talk about stubborn," he replied with a smirk.

After we finished and Mitch cleared the dishes from the table, he took me by the hand and positioned me so that I faced him. "Dana, listen to me, okay? I love you. You are beautiful. I want you to stop worrying, and I want you to stop feeling sorry for yourself, got it? You and this baby mean everything to me."

I looked deep into his eyes, shining with emotion. I nodded, and he smiled. Placing his hand on my face, he gently drew me to him and kissed me softly. As I started to pull away, he drew me to him again and this time kissed me with more passion and purpose than he had before. He placed his arms around me and held me tightly, softly whispering into my ear. "I'm not going anywhere, sweetheart. I promise. I'm here forever."

As we drove to the Tarrington Estate to meet the band, I stared out the window in silence. Mitch turned the radio on low and was singing along with it, so I closed my eyes and let myself drink in the sweet sound of his voice. Almost unconsciously, I placed a hand on my abdomen and began to rub it gently as if I were sending some sort of soothing message to the child within me. I began to think about the baby and wondered if it would inherit its father's talent for music or if it might be more like me, the quiet observer—admiring those like him who had been blessed with such abilities that I didn't possess myself. Bringing an image of Mitch into my mind, I wondered what this child would look like physically. Would it be a boy, born with lots of dark wavy hair, his eyes a piercing blue like his father's? Or, would they be a coffee-brown like mine, his hair more straight with soft hints of red that only shown in the brightest of light? Perhaps we'd have a little girl—one not resembling either of us fully—a strawberry blonde with hazel eyes: a picture of the grandmother she'd never know. Those questions were yet to be answered although in reality the answers really didn't matter. I would love my child no matter what. He or she was a product of the love I shared with Mitch—an extension of everything we were separately and together.

I felt the car come to a stop, and I opened my eyes for a moment to watch a mother raccoon and her baby scurry across the road ahead of us. Mitch turned to smile at me, and I knew he was thinking the same thing I was. Soon, we, too, would be a family. In essence, we already were. Nothing that happened from the time I read the pregnancy test to the day I died would be just about Mitch or me anymore. Every breath, every step, every thought or deed would somehow involve our child whether directly or indirectly. It was now a full and evident part of my being, a full and evident part of our lives; and forevermore, after God, our top priority.

Pulling onto the long drive leading up to his parents' house, Mitch glanced over at me and reached out to touch my shoulder. Seeing my hand still resting on my abdomen, he put his there as well, gave it a little rub, and snickered softly. I smiled at him, and he flashed his dimple at me as his eyes sparkled. I melted at the love I saw shining there. Leaning against him, I hugged his arm and kissed his cheek as I heard him softly whisper that he loved me. Everything I wanted, everything I needed was right there in that car at that moment in time; and somehow, I felt as if all was right with the world. I knew Mitch was going to be a wonderful father simply because he was a wonderful husband.

As we walked hand in hand to the door, Mitch paused for a moment and stood very still listening to the sound of the music coming through the open windows of the house.

"Hear that, Dana?" he asked. "Those guys are terrific. They don't need me to make it work."

I gave him a stern look. "Yes, they do, and don't you dare start that talk again," I warned. "We've already been through all that."

"Yes, dear," he answered while leading me toward the door once again. "I was only making a point."

"So was I," I replied as we stepped inside. I greeted Alexander and handed him my jacket as Mitch started toward the rec room. He disappeared around the corner of the family room. A minute later, I heard his voice ringing out as he began to sing with the tune the guys were playing. Alexander smiled and shook his head. I returned the gesture and then began to follow the sound of my husband's voice.

"You amaze me, Trip," Shep commented as they finished playing. "You come in on the middle of a tune, pick it right up, and everything is perfect with you, man."

I could see the pride shining in his eyes, but I knew he'd take the compliment modestly. "Hey, give yourself some credit. I was listening to you all outside before I came in, and I told Dana that you guys have talent. You could easily make it without me, no doubt."

Zach stepped forward and placed a hand on Mitch's shoulder. "That's where you're wrong, dude. Without those pipes of yours, we're just a bunch of noise."

Mitch glanced toward the back of the room, and our eyes met. I gave him an I-told-you-so look, and he smiled.

"Well, let's make some more of that noise, shall we?" Mitch strapped on his guitar, and the six of them began to do what they did best.

I settled into my chair and sat somewhat self-absorbed. My eyes closed against that all-too-familiar feeling that was beginning to creep up on me once again. Thinking that perhaps I could somehow control it, I cleared my mind and placed my focus on nothing more than the sound of Mitch's voice as he sang. No matter what the song, his tone was almost angelic, soothing me in a way that nothing else could. I could feel myself starting to relax, and I sank down into the chair just a little more. The next thing I knew, Mitch was gently prompting me to wake up.

I opened my eyes to see him kneeling down before me with an affectionate glow about his face. "Hey, baby, you must have really been tired to sleep through all that. The guys had this place rocking tonight!"

I rubbed my eyes, sat up, and glanced around to see that everyone had gone except the two of us. "Where are the guys?" I asked.

"They left about fifteen minutes ago. They all said to tell you goodnight," he answered as he slowly reached out to touch my cheek. "I've been sitting here just watching you since then. You looked so peaceful I didn't want to disturb you."

I placed a hand on my stomach and smiled at him. I realized that, although I hadn't intended to fall asleep, I had managed to combat my queasiness.

"Guess what?" I said as he rose to his feet.

"What?"

"I didn't get sick tonight," I announced cheerfully. "I was starting to earlier, but I closed my eyes and concentrated on listening to you sing. I felt so relaxed that I forgot all about feeling nasty."

He chuckled. "And everything else, too, it seems." He reached out for me, and that adorable little dimple began to come out in his crooked grin. "Did you know that you snore?"

I let my mouth fall open. "I do not!"

He tucked an arm around my waist, and we headed into the family room where Jake and Olivia were relaxing. "Yes, you do. That's why I woke you up. I was afraid you might cause an earthquake or something."

He didn't seem to care that we were now standing in the midst of his parents, and they were both intently listening to our conversation. I could feel the heat of my blush rising in my cheeks. "Stop it, Mitch. That's not true!"

"It is true. Dana Tarrington snores when she sleeps and quite loudly, I might add. I never realized that kind of noise could come from such a tiny little thing like you." He was still grinning that crooked grin of his as he pretended to inspect the ceiling and the walls. "Well, at least you didn't crack any of the plaster. Everything still looks intact."

I was sure I resembled a cherry about then. "Mitch, stop. It's not very nice to accuse me of things."

"Well, I'm just paying you back for earlier; that's all."

"For what?"

"For accusing me of flirting with Vanessa and Judy. Only difference is I'm innocent. You really do snore."

I caught Jake out of the corner of my eye and saw him snicker. I guessed Mitch didn't really care about embarrassing me either as long as he was having fun.

I decided to redirect the conversation and try to save at least a touch of my dignity. "Olivia, would you mind if I made myself a cup of tea? I think it might help settle my stomach."

She smiled. "Mitchell, why don't you go and get it for her? Let her sit down and rest."

His eyes began to sparkle, and I could see mischief written all over his face. "I'd better take her with me, Mom. If I leave her here, she might fall asleep again; and I wouldn't want you to have to get out the ear plugs or anything. I'm surprised you couldn't hear her above the band tonight."

"I'll go and get the tea myself, thanks." With that I headed off.

I placed a cup of water in the microwave; and as I waited for it to heat up, I pulled a teabag from the canister on the counter. As I stared blankly at the cup twirling slowly inside the appliance, I felt a set of arms come around me and a cheek softly rub against mine.

"Did I embarrass you, love?" Mitch asked.

The timer on the microwave sounded, and I moved away from him to retrieve my cup of water. "Yes, you did. Not that you care."

He turned me toward him and put his arms around me again although I didn't return the gesture. "If I didn't care, I wouldn't have come out here. I was only having fun, Dana. I'm sorry."

I stepped away from him and pulled the string on the teabag which caused it to bob in the cup. I turned toward him and pretended to pout. "Well, you don't have to tease me all the time especially in front of people."

He started to smile. "Well, what *am* I allowed to do? In the last few weeks, I've learned that I'm not allowed to take care of you, give my food to you, comment on your clothing, talk to anyone outside the family who's a female, or concern myself in any way with your well-being. Now, I'm not allowed to tease you, either. Is it all right for me to breathe?"

"I don't know. I'll have to think about it," I replied with a smile of my own.

Laughing, he took the cup from my hand, placed it on the counter, and bent down to deliver a long, lingering kiss. He certainly made it difficult to stay mad at him especially when he was melting my insides into putty...not that I was really ever mad anyway.

Later that evening, I lay in bed listening to the sound of Mitch sleeping, his soft and steady breathing the only sound filling the room. The moonlight through the window was casting a soft glow on his face, and I marveled at the handsome man lying next to me—the man that meant more to me than anything in the world. As if he could sense my thoughts, he rolled over in his sleep and reached out for me; and I wrapped my arms around him and pulled him as close as I could. Overcome with the strength of my desire, I began to kiss him softly, slowly arousing him to full consciousness. As I felt his arms encircle me, I moved closer to him still and let his kisses bring my senses alive in the way that only he could do. I could feel my hunger for him increasing as our emotions took control, and our hearts pounded wildly for each other. Whispering that I loved him, he returned my words and held me so tightly that I felt as if I were truly a part of him. Kissing me softly once more, he moved slightly away from me and smiled.

"Uh, sweetheart, what was that all about?" he asked while he stared somewhat blankly toward the ceiling.

"I just needed to feel close to you, that's all," I answered.

I heard him snicker softly. "Well, I suppose you can't get any closer than that, can you?" He rolled to his side and reached out for me and then gave me another soft kiss on my cheek. "Why don't we just stay close all night?"

"Sounds good to me," I said as I snuggled up to him. Feeling safe and secure in his arms, I drifted into a peaceful sleep.

The sound of rain lightly tapping against the windowpane awoke me the next morning. Much to my surprise, I rolled over to find Mitch still sleeping soundly next to me, contently rolled into a ball, and clutching his pillow as if it were somehow going to run away from him. I smiled and kissed him on the side of his head, and he stirred a little but didn't awaken. Glancing at the clock, I saw that it was almost eight and happily realized that somehow I'd escaped my routine round of morning sickness. I sat up and didn't move while I waited for the feeling to come; but much to my delight, I felt quite normal. Resisting the urge to shout with glee at the top of my lungs, I grabbed my robe from the back of the chair and headed out to greet the day.

I started a pot of coffee and pulled out two frying pans, a half dozen eggs, and a pound of bacon. Soon the apartment filled with the mouth-watering aroma of our breakfast. My husband appeared out of nowhere and paused as he pulled a t-shirt over his head and attempted to rub his eyes at the same time. Once his glasses were in place, he yawned and stretched, trudged wearily over to me, and stood very still. I noticed that he looked a bit surprised.

"What's wrong?" I asked.

"I'm just not used to seeing you in the kitchen first thing in the morning. Aren't you supposed to be sitting in the middle of the bathroom floor?"

"I know. Kinda weird, huh? Not to mention, it's pretty sad that we've come to get used to that scenario."

He poured each of us a cup of coffee and took a long drink of his. "Well, I for one like this scenario much better." He took two plates from the cupboard, placed them on the counter next to me, and then inhaled deeply. "See, maybe you are going to get over the morning sickness thing."

I filled the plates, handed one to him, and we both sat down together. I took a bite of the scrambled eggs and savored their fluffy texture. "You know what's even stranger? I actually feel like eating. This is pretty good."

Mitch arched his eyebrows playfully. "So were you. You can wake me up like that any time you want."

I blushed as I watched him snicker. "Mitch, you're terrible!"

He put down his fork and pretended to pout. "Gee, honey, I'm sorry. I guess I'll have to try harder the next time."

He began to laugh as I rolled my eyes at him. "Would you just close your mouth and eat, please?"

He laughed even harder. "How on earth am I supposed to do that? If I close my mouth and try to eat, I'll drop my food all over the floor. I'm sure you don't want to clean eggs and bacon off the floor, do you?"

Smiling at my mischievous husband, I shook my head and turned my attention back to my meal. "I swear, I don't know why I put up with you."

He tapped the tip of his finger on my wedding rings. "Because you married me. You have to."

"I suppose so."

As Mitch proceeded to indulge in his daily weight lifting routine, I moseyed off to shower and dress. Just as I was emerging from the bedroom, he was coming down the hallway, wiping his face on a towel. Seeing me, he stopped and gave me a curious look.

"You have your work clothes on. You aren't planning to go to the bistro with me today, are you?"

"Sure, why not?"

He bit his lip and twisted his jaw. "Uh, no reason, only that I assumed you'd stay home like you have the past couple of Saturdays. What will you do if you get sick while you're working?"

I placed a hand on my stomach. "I really don't think that's a concern today. I feel pretty good, and I'd like to give it a try, okay?"

He placed a gentle hand on my shoulder, and his expression softened. "Are you sure? I mean, maybe you should make sure you really are over the sickness thing before diving back in. I'd really hate for you to be there ready to take someone's order and be overcome with nausea or something. I honestly think it would be best if you stayed at home at least one more week."

I let my eyes meet his and tried to see if I could read a deeper reason behind his reluctance. "Mitch, is there some reason you don't want me at Gartano's today?"

He tilted his head upward and let out a loud, exasperated breath. "For crying out loud, Dana, don't start that. I'm only trying to look out for you. Someone has to take these things into consideration, you know."

"Well, I already have, and I want to go to work with you. I feel fine, and I don't want to spend another Saturday all alone at home."

He draped the towel over his shoulder and turned to walk into the bathroom. "Fine, you do what you want." He gave me a quick peck on the forehead. "I'm going to get ready."

A short while later we were in the car on the way to work. The rain poured out of the sky in buckets, and I was doubtful that it would end anytime soon. Mitch was unusually quiet, and I concluded that for some reason he was upset about my decision to join him at the bistro. I didn't know exactly why; and if anything, I had thought he'd be pleased that I felt well enough to do so. Then another thought occurred to me. He wanted me to quit. He didn't think I could handle it being pregnant. He'd said as much to Chris and Jake and having me stay at home those past few weeks was his way of easing me out without a fight. Granted, once the sickness had taken hold of me, I had shared his concern about my ability to make it through a full day of waitressing. However, although I'd never said so to him, my intent had always been to return to my duties once I was past that stage of the pregnancy. I pondered it all for another moment. Yes, that had to be it. It made sense. By coming along with him, I'd foiled his plan. Now, there was no way he could make me quit, at least not with a clear conscience. I had proven him wrong, and there was no man in the world that liked that especially when it was a woman doing the proving.

Mitch pulled the car close to the door of Gartano's and put it in park. "Go ahead and get out. Stay under the awning so you don't get wet."

I obeyed his command, opened the car door, and hurried out as quickly as a pregnant woman could. I hovered close to the building as I watched Mitch park the car, step out with his umbrella, and jog to my side—still unable to escape being soaked from top to bottom. He unlocked the door as he ran a hand through his hair and sloughed off the water, held open the door, and stepped in behind me. Without a word, he closed the door behind us, relocked it, and turned to walk toward the office. I hesitated for a second or two before I followed.

Reaching around the corner to turn on the light, he stepped inside the office, hung up his jacket on the rack, and took a seat at the desk. I hung up my coat as well and took a place beside his chair. He ignored me as he leafed through a stack of papers. After placing them down, he sat back, folded his hands, and looked directly at me.

"Mitch, you haven't said more than five words since we left home. I'm feeling like you're sorry that you told me I could come with you today."

He sighed. "Honey, I don't have a problem with you being here. What I have a problem with is your overdoing it simply because you're feeling better than normal today. I just don't want anything to happen to you."

I attempted to sit on the corner of the desk, but realized I was no longer able to boost myself up enough to do so. Instead, I repositioned myself a few steps closer to him. He tried not to smile as he noticed and reached out to pull me onto his lap.

"Dana, promise me. Promise that if you get tired today or start feeling sick or anything else that you'll tell me."

"I'm not an invalid, Mitchell. I'm pregnant. Stop worrying. I'm fine."

"Promise or I'm taking you home right now."

I looked into his eyes and took notice of the stern, yet loving, expression on his face. "Mitch...."

"Come on, Dana, I'm waiting."

I sighed deeply. "Okay, I promise. Happy?"

He pursed his lips and nodded. "Yep."

"Now, can I go out and get started setting up the dining room? I'm sure some of the salt shakers need filling, and I can take the chairs down from the tables."

"No, I'll do that. You concentrate on the salt shakers and replace the flowers on the tables. You don't need to be lifting."

I stood up and turned to walk away from him. "For Pete's sake, I think I'm capable of lifting a five-pound chair."

He started after me. "What if you accidentally hit yourself in the stomach with one? I said I'll handle the chairs or leave them for Kayla. She should be here soon."

I spun around so abruptly that he almost ran into me. "What if a meteor comes crashing through the roof and hits me? What if I walk outside and get run over by a five-year-old roller skating down the sidewalk? What if we have an earthquake, and I fall into a big crack in the earth?"

He shrugged. "Well, if any of those things happened, it would be unfortunate. However, that's out of my control. The chairs in my dining room aren't." He smirked and stuck his tongue out at me playfully. "So there."

I turned toward the dining room once more. "Such a stubborn man." I heard Mitch's laughter behind me.

Kayla's smile widened as she peered through the window and saw me, and I hurried to unlock the door and let her inside. *At least someone is happy to have me here*, I thought. She shook out her umbrella and pulled me into a hug.

"Well, well, it's good to see you here this morning! How are you feeling?"

"Better than I have in a long time," I replied cheerfully. "I can't believe I haven't had any sickness since yesterday morning."

"You don't say!" she responded. "Maybe you're gonna get over it." She turned to hang her coat on the rack. "Just make sure you don't overdo it today."

"Oh, that's great. Not you, too."

She looked puzzled. "What do you mean?"

I pulled out a chair and sat down at a nearby table. "That's precisely the same thing my husband said to me earlier. I feel as if he didn't want me to come here today for some reason, and he's trying everything he can to make me look and feel like a total invalid."

Kayla reached out and patted my hand in her motherly sort of way. "Now, girly, he's just trying to take care of you, and you need to let him. You know how important that is to him. That boy has a heart of gold, and you are going to hurt his feelings something terrible if you don't give in at least a little."

I stood up and pushed in my chair. Picking up the box of carnations from the neighboring table, I proceeded to replace the slightly wilted ones filling the bud vase. "It's one thing to take care of me, Kayla, but he's taking it to the extreme. Can you believe that he actually told his brother and father that he needs to hire another waitress? Do you know why? Because he doesn't think I can handle it now that I'm pregnant." I smoothed my hand over the tablecloth and placed the vase in the middle of the table. "I'm as capable now of doing whatever I could do before all this happened. I just have to find a way to convince him of that."

The rest of the crew arrived shortly after Kayla did; and by eleven o'clock, a small crowd was beginning to form outside the door. No one seemed to care that it was still raining; and when Mitch unlocked the door, they filed in—umbrellas and all—shaking the moisture from their clothing and welcoming the opportunity to warm up and dry out. We all set about our work. As the pace quickened, so did I, and somehow managed to keep myself right in tune with the other waitresses. Mitch stayed behind the counter for the first few hours, and every once in a while I would catch him watching me as if he were anticipating that I might slow down. Much to my delight I didn't; and when he caught my eye and winked, I knew that was his way of saying he was proud of me.

Lunchtime flew by, and mid-afternoon crept up on us before we knew it. The crowd began to thin out, and we all welcomed the chance to breathe a little. Mitch was making his rounds from table to table, his lighthearted nature captivating each customer he met. It wasn't surprising to me why business was booming. He always took the time to make sure everyone was satisfied; and that not only brought in new diners, but it kept the old ones coming back. I cleared a table in the corner, started into the kitchen with my tray full of dirty dishes, and left him to do his work.

"Thanks for coming in today. Glad you enjoyed everything," Mitch said to the young couple seated at the table. "I hope you'll come back soon."

With a bright smile, he moved in almost unconscious fashion to the next table. When the attractive young lady smiled back at him, he felt his knees buckle. He placed a hand on the back of her chair to steady himself.

"Hey, blue eyes, remember me?"

Mitch stood in silence just staring at her. *How on earth could I forget you?* he thought. *You danced half-naked not three inches from my face a few months ago!*

"Honey, are you okay? You look a little pale." Gloria pushed out a chair and pointed. "Maybe you should sit down."

Mitch nodded. "Yeah, thanks." He took a seat next to her. "I guess I'm just a little surprised to see you, that's all. Here, I mean."

She laughed. "We 'entertainers' do eat, you know." She gave him a once over. "Uh, uh, uh, you sure are a handsome devil. You were awfully cute the night I first met you; but, sweetie, you clean up real nice." She noticed his wedding band and took hold of his hand to inspect it. "I see you took the plunge. Congratulations."

"Thanks." Mitch glanced around the dining room hoping not to see Dana and breathed a sigh of relief when he didn't. The last thing he wanted to do was try to explain why he was sitting at a table with a buxom blonde who was holding his hand—and now rubbing the top of it with her thumb.

"So you work here, huh?"

"Well, actually, I own the place." He pointed to the plaque on the wall directly behind him. "I bought it shortly before I got married."

Gloria smiled. "Wow! I'm impressed. This is the first time I've actually been in here myself, but I heard the buzz around town and thought I'd check it out." She let go of his hand and gave his arm a gentle squeeze. "I'm really glad I did. It's nice to see you again."

Just then the door opened, and Mitch turned to see Gloria's friend Kandy. *This is just great,* he thought. *Just when I thought I could escape unscathed, the other half of the tag team shows up.*

"Hey, Kandy, look who I found! Remember our shy little bachelor Mitch?"

"How could I forget?" Kandy placed a hand on his shoulder and gave it a little rub. "Would you like to join us for lunch?"

Mitch did another scan for Dana and again breathed a sigh of relief when he didn't spot her anywhere. He took Kandy's invitation as his cue to move on. He stood up, pushed in his chair, and cleared his throat nervously. "Thanks, but I have to get back to work. Only an hour or so before I'll be heading out, and I still have tons to do."

Gloria glanced at the clock on the wall just above Mitch's head. "I noticed that you open at eleven, and you get to leave at three? You must bring in the dough to get to keep those kinds of hours."

Mitch couldn't help his smile. "I do all right, I guess, but this isn't my only job. I'm also a musician."

The two women looked at each other, and their faces lit up. "A musician? No kidding!" Kandy exclaimed. "Your girl got a rare find in you, sweetheart. What do you play? Are you, like, in a band or something?"

Mitch's pride began to show in the way it always did when he talked about the band. "Yeah, I'm the front man for Ace. We're the headliners down at Studio 14 on Saturday nights. I'm lead guitar and vocals primarily. I can play keyboards and drums, too, although I usually don't." He suddenly realized he was starting to babble, so he decided to try once more to make his escape. "Well, it was good to see both of you. Enjoy your lunch." He started to move away when he felt someone grab hold of his arm.

"Whoa, not so fast there. Can't a girl give you a little hug goodbye?" Mitch must have blushed because Gloria giggled. "Now, come on, Mitch. Don't be shy. We do 'know' each other after all!" Gloria stood up and gave Mitch a tight squeeze.

Mitch pulled away as quickly as he could without appearing rude and said goodbye once more. Instead of turning to talk to the customers at the next table, he made a beeline for the office.

Mitch closed the door and sat down at the desk, tilted his head back, and released every bit of air filling his lungs. Holding his glasses in one hand, he ran the other hand through his hair, stopping to rest it on top of his head as if the thoughts filling it up had given him a headache. He closed his eyes and said a silent prayer of thanks that Dana hadn't witnessed the scene with Gloria. He had no idea how he would have explained things to her, and he couldn't have told her the truth. She wouldn't have understood that. Once again, fate had played in his favor. Although he could think of reasons he needed to return to the dining room, he opted for staying where he was and finding something to keep him occupied long enough for Gloria to leave.

Ten minutes passed, and his mind wouldn't let go of Gloria. It wasn't so much her, he surmised, but what she was and what she stood for. It bothered him to think that he let himself be a part of it when he'd known in his heart it was wrong. On the night the guys took him to Caroway's, he could easily have expressed his discomfort, asked them to go somewhere else, and been done with it. Instead, he sat there with a smile on his face and allowed himself to enjoy the erotic ritual performed for him by a total stranger. That thought, as it had that night, made him feel guilty. In reality, he actually did nothing more than watch a woman dance. At least that's what his brother and friends wanted him to believe. However, he knew the source of his guilt didn't lie simply in that fact. It was rooted in the untruth he had told to the woman he loved, the lie that he still held deep within himself to that day, and it had come all too easily. Well, that was at least part of it. The other part was Dana thought she was the first and only woman he had ever seen naked. To her as his wife that was special, even sacred. That's why he knew in his heart that telling her the truth about that night would have crushed her. To him, Gloria meant nothing, and he could barely even remember what she looked like. Dana was beautiful, sensual, and real. The visual stimulation she provided for him was so intense that he could barely breathe sometimes even when she was fully clothed. He loved her that much. But, he'd seen Gloria first, not to mention the other dancers on stage that night. She'd never understand it was nothing more than a night out with the guys to him. The girls just happened to be there.

He pushed the pile of papers to the corner of his desk and picked up the picture sitting there of Dana and himself on their wedding day. He smiled at her smile: the way her eyes lit up, the beauty that radiated from her face, how happy she looked with him. Looking at himself, he could see the happiness there as well. It was how he felt with her, so true and so right. Again, he gave thanks for the fact she hadn't seen him with Gloria that day and for not having to make painful explanations. He also gave thanks for the fact that he would never have to.

He set the picture back in its place, stood up, and adjusted his tie. He glanced at the clock and decided that it was time to move on and let go of the past once more. Opening the door, he headed back into the bistro to find Dana and take her home.

"It's only two-twenty. Why are we leaving now?" I asked as Mitch helped me on with my jacket.

"Because I want to. I just feel like I need to get out of here."

I placed my purse on my shoulder and gave him a questioning look. "Why? Did something happen?"

Mitch started to usher me toward the door in a somewhat urgent fashion. "No, I just want to go. It's been a hectic day, and I'm tired."

He opened the door and held it for me; but just as I was about to step out, I remembered our umbrella propped next to it. "Oops, almost forgot this." I picked it up, and then I turned back toward Mitch just in time to notice his gaze fixed on two women sitting at a nearby table. One of them caught his eye, smiled, and waved daintily.

"Bye, Mitch! Nice to see you again," she called out as we stepped out the door.

Although the rain had stopped, Mitch took the umbrella from my hand and began to fumble with it nervously in an attempt to open it up.

"Mitchell, what are you doing? It's not raining now," I said looking at him strangely.

He paused and looked up at the sun beginning to peek through the clouds above. He looked at the umbrella and forced a smile. "Oh, uh, yeah, right. Guess we don't need this after all."

He took my hand and started down the sidewalk in the direction of the apartment. After a few steps, he stopped and turned toward me as I hesitated and let go. "Aren't you coming?"

I walked to where he stood and placed a gentle hand on his arm. "We drove today, honey. Don't you remember?"

He hit himself lightly on the side of the head and chuckled. "Oh, yeah. Man, I'm losing it, huh?"

"Sweetie, what's wrong with you? You're acting very strangely." Then a thought occurred to me. "Mitch, who was that girl? Do you know her?"

He took my hand once more and started toward the car. "What girl?"

I sighed loudly thinking he wasn't really serious. "The one that just said goodbye to you."

He cleared his throat and gripped my hand a little tighter. "No one, sweetheart. Just a customer."

I glanced up at him and could swear I saw beads of sweat forming on his brow. "Why did she say that it was nice to see you *again*?"

"I don't know. Maybe she's a repeat customer or something. I don't have a clue."

We reached the car, and he walked to my side and unlocked the door. I looked at his face, and it held an expression tinged with guilt and fear. I decided to try again.

"Are you sure you don't know her? She seemed to know you. If not, why did she call you by name?"

He clenched his jaw, and there was an edge to his voice. He seemed unusually disturbed by my question. "Why are you interrogating me, Dana? I already told you that I don't know who she is. Why don't you want to believe me?"

He opened the car door, and I got in. "I just wondered, that's all."

He went around and got in the driver's side, placed the key in the ignition, then turned toward me. "Listen, I'm sorry. I'm just tired, and I didn't mean to snap." I nodded in response and turned toward the window. I felt him take my hand. "Hey, you aren't mad at me now, are you?"

I looked at him, and his eyes seemed almost sad and distant as if my answer was truly going to affect him. I gave him a soft smile. "No, I'm not mad at you."

Inside the apartment, Mitch headed straight for the couch and fell onto it with a yawn. Shoes fell to the floor along with his tie, and shirttails escaped the confines of trousers. He settled down and pulled the blanket off the back of the couch to cover him. He laid his glasses on the coffee table, pulled the blanket up, and closed his eyes.

"Mitch, don't you want to go and lie on the bed with me? I thought I might take a nap, too."

He barely shook his head, and I wondered if he might already be almost asleep since he didn't open his eyes. "No, I'll just stay here, baby. You go ahead," he replied almost in a whisper. "Wake me at four-thirty, and I'll take you to dinner, okay?"

"Okay," I replied. I touched him softly on top of his head as I turned to walk to the bedroom. "Sleep tight, honey. I love you."

"Uh, huh, love you, too," he mumbled sleepily.

I closed the bedroom door, kicked off my shoes, and grabbed a blanket from the closet. Lying down on the bed, I pulled it over me and turned to stare up at the ceiling. Thoughts of the mystery girl from the bistro began to fill my head. Mitch said he didn't know her, but I wasn't sure I bought that story. If he didn't, how did she know his name? Why would she say that it had been nice to see him again? That obviously indicated that she had met him at some point in the past. I considered his explanation that perhaps she was a repeat customer.

Maybe there was a chance he'd talked to her during a previous visit and had told her his name. He usually did make it a point to introduce himself to the patrons. I decided there was the possibility that he had been telling the truth. Now, the choice was mine—I could either lie there all day and question his sincerity, or I could believe him and save my sanity. Choosing the latter, I set the alarm for four twenty-five and drifted off to sleep.

Chapter 5

At four-thirty as requested, I gently shook my husband awake. He opened one eye, looked at me sleepily, and smiled.

"Hey, beautiful, come here." He pulled back the blanket as if to invite me to join him beneath it. I smiled back in acceptance and lay down next to him. He covered us up and pulled me close. "Let's just forget about everything else and stay right here, okay?"

"That sounds nice, but what about the show tonight? I don't think the guys would be very happy if their front man didn't come."

He kissed my cheek. "Yeah, you're probably right. Guess I should go get ready then, huh?" He started to sit up, pulling me up with him. "I was thinking that we could grab some dinner if you feel up to it, and then I'll just drop you back off here before I head to the club."

I gave him a strange look. "Why would you do that? I'm going with you tonight."

He returned the look. "You are? I just assumed you'd stay home again like you have been. You know it's going to be hot and crowded, and if you get sick...."

I sighed loudly. "I'll run to the bathroom. I haven't been sick all day though, and I made it through work just fine. I'm feeling pretty confident that tonight won't be any different."

"I hope you're right, but what if...."

I started into my spiel about the meteors, roller skating five-year-olds, and such, as he folded his arms and pointed his eyes toward the ceiling.

He sat there listening to me until he must have finally decided he wasn't going to win the argument. "I don't think it's a good idea, but all right. I know there's no sense trying to reason with you." He stood to his full six-foot-two and stretched. "Where would you like to go for dinner?"

I stood as well and followed him toward the bedroom. "How about The Mark? I'm thinking that a steak and baked potato sound pretty good right now."

"That's fine. Let's change, and we'll head out. I want to get to the club a little early tonight and run through number four in the set if we have time. There's that one note at the end that I can't seem to get."

I walked into the closet to select an outfit for the evening. "What are you talking about? I've never heard you miss a note."

He laughed. "Well, those pretty little ears of yours just aren't trained to hear it, love. Trust me. I do from time to time."

"Well, I'll bet if you miss any tonight no one will know but you."

"And the guys and anyone else who might happen to be there who knows anything about pitch, range, and key. That's enough to make me want to get it right."

I patted him on the cheek. "Such a perfectionist, aren't you?"

Walking back into the bedroom, I quickly changed clothes and turned to the full-length mirror. "Fantastic," I grumbled as I gazed unhappily at the dark grey suit I had chosen. "All I need now is a trunk, and I'll make any zookeeper proud."

Mitch noticed me as he tucked his shirt into his jeans which were just tight enough to show off his slender physique. I was jealous.

"Are you almost ready? It's close to five, and I'd really like to get to the club no later than seven."

"Give me ten minutes. I need to change and fix my makeup."

"What do you mean, 'change'? You already did that. What's wrong with that outfit?"

I turned toward him. "If I wear this, people will be trying to feed me peanuts all night!"

He laughed and pulled me into a hug. "Oh, my sweet Dana, what am I going to do with you? You look beautiful. Now, stop fretting, and let's get going."

I stepped away from him and turned to the mirror again. "Mitch, I need to change. I refuse to leave the house looking like Dumbo!" I began to undress as I headed into the closet.

Mitch thrust his hands into his pockets—as far as they would go anyway—and stood in the middle of the room watching me search through my wardrobe. "Why are you so self-conscious? You have absolutely no reason to be."

I gave him a disgusted look. "That's easy for you to say, Mr. Rock-Hard-Body-of-the-Gods. You don't have to worry about people trying to harpoon you if you get too close to any large bodies of water."

He smirked. "Rock hard, huh?" I caught him out of the corner of my eye checking himself out in the mirror.

I shook my head at him as I pulled a top from the rack, looked it over, and placed it back. "Why do I open my mouth?"

Almost twenty minutes later I was dressed and heading out the door although still not completely satisfied with my selection. Mitch was slightly agitated by this time and afraid that we would never possibly make it to the club in time for him to rehearse before the show. Hoping to ease his tension just a little, I opted to trade my steak and potato for a burger and fries at Charley's—thinking the service there might be quicker. Pleased with the idea, we arrived, ordered, and had our food all within half an hour.

"Still feeling well?" Mitch asked as I plunged into my burger.

I wiped a dab of ketchup from my chin and nodded. "Yeah, amazingly enough, I do," I replied. "I honestly can't believe I've gone an entire day without getting sick even once!"

He snatched a fry from my plate and grinned. "I hope things stay this way. I really do."

Those had to be the famous last words. No sooner had we arrived at the club about forty minutes later when I began to feel my stomach turning over within me. I placed my hand there and glanced at Mitch as we started to walk inside, and I took a deep breath just as we reached the door.

"Are you okay?" he asked with concern.

I didn't want to tell him that I was starting to feel poorly because I knew he'd insist on taking me home. "Yeah, I'm fine," I replied. "Just a touch of indigestion—nothing to worry about." By the expression on his face, I wasn't sure he believed me; but he nodded and held the door open for me anyway. Once inside, we found the guys all busily setting up the stage doing sound checks and the like, and Mitch smiled.

"You know, these guys do all this stuff each week before I even get here. I really should start coming early and helping them with it," he said.

"You have another job on the weekend, too, Trip. We don't," Zach said as he walked up behind him. "It's not a big deal, man. You're the front. You do most of the work anyway."

"Yeah, but I'm also a team player, Zach. I shouldn't stick you with all this."

Zach looked at me with a smile. "He doesn't know when to shut up, does he?" he asked. I shook my head with a grin as Mitch smirked at me.

"Hey, guys, I'd like to run through number four a couple of times if we can. I still don't feel right about my pitch, and that last note's a killer."

"Cool, let's do it," Ash said, and they all got into position.

I took my seat in the usual place and listened as the band began to play. Mitch was belting it out as usual, his voice strong and sweet. They ended the song, and he stood silently for a moment. Then a slow smile came upon his face. "I got it," he said confidently. "I finally got it."

"Cool deal, Trip! Want to do it again?" Newbie asked.

"Yeah, two more takes. I want to be sure," Mitch replied.

The guys did the song twice more, and Mitch hit it perfectly. With his confidence restored, he instructed the guys to take a breather as he joined me at the table.

"See, honey, I knew you could do it," I said praising him as he sat down next to me.

He let out a long breath, and his face beamed. "Oh, you don't know how happy that makes me. I could picture myself getting up there and totally blowing it tonight. It's really a relief to know I finally got it down."

I gave him a strange look. "Uh, Mitch, speaking of down, I don't think my dinner is going to stay there." I got up and started toward the ladies' room.

"Oh, Dana, not again, sweetheart. Not here," Mitch said as he started after me.

At least five minutes and three episodes later, I came back out to find Mitch standing next to the door waiting for me. "I don't think the baby likes burgers and fries either," I said halfheartedly. "I should have known I wasn't going to be lucky enough to make it through a whole day feeling well."

Mitch looked at me sympathetically. "Would you like me to take you home, love? I can ask Ty to take the show tonight. It's really not a big deal."

I smiled at his concern. "No, it's all right. Maybe I'll get a glass of ginger ale to sip. That might help."

He put his arm around my shoulders. "Are you sure? I can take you right now."

"I'm feeling better now, and I want to stay. Please don't worry about it anymore. I'll be fine."

By the time we got back to the table, Mitch's family had arrived and greeted us cheerfully.

"There you are. We were wondering if you were here yet," Paul said.

"The baby decided it didn't like what we fed it for dinner," I sighed as I sat down.

"Still not feeling well, Dana?" Jim asked.

"You know, she was doing really well most of the day. We ate lunch at the bistro, and she was fine. Then we went to Charley's for dinner, and she came here and got sick. I don't get it," Mitch stated and began to rub my back.

"Could just be the time of day. Many women get sick in the morning and around the same time every night. Don't worry, buddy. We'll take care of her," Jim said. Then he turned to me. "Dana, if you want to go home, Ang or I can give you a ride," he offered.

I smiled. "Thanks, but I would like to stay. I've been looking forward to this all day, and I really don't want to spend another evening at home by myself."

Mitch sat down next to me with his hand still on my back. "You could rest, baby, and be more comfortable. It's going to get hot and crowded here; and if you have to get to the bathroom quickly, you may not make it with all the people."

I looked at him stubbornly. "Then that's a chance I'll just have to take. I'm not leaving," I said.

Mitch looked at the others and shrugged as he stood up. "Guess that's that. You know where to find me if you need me." He smiled and kissed me. "You relax, sweetheart. I love you."

"I love you, too. Now, go on and stop worrying about me," I told him.

"I'll go, but I won't stop worrying. I'll probably never do that," he said with that adorable grin of his. "See you all a little later." With that, he disappeared backstage.

About half an hour and a few trips to the ladies' room later, I headed back to our table to wait for Ace to take the stage. Much to my surprise, I found Mitch sitting in my seat.

"I came back to see how you were feeling, and everyone told me you've been making a path to the ladies' room. I honestly think you'd be better off at home. We can always try it again next week if you feel up to it."

I sighed deeply. "Mitch, I told you earlier I don't want to leave," I replied firmly. "I'm going to be fine."

He took my hand, helped me up, and escorted me a few steps away from the table so the others couldn't hear our conversation. "Look,

Dana, I know you're miserable. I can see it in your face. Why don't you let me take you home, and I can be back before the show starts? I can even stay home with you and let Ty handle everything here tonight. What do you say?"

"I say that I'm beginning to feel like you're trying to get rid of me for some reason," I answered looking right into his eyes.

"Don't be ridiculous, Dana. You know I love having you here, baby, but I hate to see you suffering just for me. You can go home, get into your pajamas, and watch TV, or even go to bed if you want."

I crossed my arms stubbornly and turned to walk back to the table. "I said no, Mitchell, and that's the end of it!"

Mitch followed me back to the table and pulled out a chair for me to sit down. Then he leaned down close to me. "You are such a stubborn little thing, but I still love you." He kissed me on the cheek. "You relax, and I'll see you in a little while."

"Yeah, whatever," I replied smugly.

He sighed. "What? Are you mad at me now?" he asked softly.

"No, but I don't know why you're pushing me to leave. I'm tired of locking myself up in the apartment every time I'm not feeling well."

"I just want to take care of you, sweetheart, and make sure you're comfortable; that's all. But, I'll leave you alone if that's what you want." He stood up and looked at the others. "You guys take care of her for me, okay?"

"Don't worry. She'll be fine," Jim reassured. "You go and have a good time."

As Mitch walked away, I looked at his family. "Has he always been this persistent or is it something he only exhibits with me?" I asked.

Chris laughed. "No, it's not something new. He's concerned about you, Dana. Let him take care of you. It'll make him feel good."

I sighed. "He thinks that simply because I'm not feeling well that I should stay home all the time. I have to learn to deal with this sooner or later. Might as well be sooner."

Just as I got up to head off again, the lights dimmed and the club manager Rob Winslow appeared on stage to announce the band. I fought back the feeling for as long as I could until I saw Mitch. As they launched into the first song, I waved at him and quickly made my little side trip once again.

I found the ladies' room a little more crowded this time, and a line was forming just inside the door. I weaved around everyone and walked quickly into the first stall that opened up to take care of things. I heard a woman mutter that I needed to wait my turn; but immediately following her comment, I heard someone else say that perhaps I was sick. *Good,* I thought. *At least I won't have anyone ganging up on me for taking cuts in line.*

Finishing up, I took a deep breath and walked out to the sink. Noticing disgruntled looks from a few of the women still in line, I turned toward them. "I'm sorry I went in front of you; but I'm pregnant, and I was sick," I said determining that might help them to understand a little better.

One of the women toward the back smiled. When she spoke, I recognized her voice as the one who had defended me earlier. "Don't think a thing about it. I hope you feel better." A few of the others nodded in agreement.

"Thanks," I said weakly. I splashed some cool water on my face and rinsed my mouth out a little. After I dried off, I took a couple more deep breaths and started toward the table again.

The band was still going strong; and as I approached the table, Mitch noticed me and smiled sympathetically. Something about the way he looked just then caught my attention, and I stopped and watched him for a moment. He was still smiling, playing his heart out, but he was almost looking distracted for some reason. I wasn't sure what that could be about but decided perhaps it was just my imagination.

As the song ended, Mitch placed the microphone back in the stand and smiled brightly. "How's everyone doing tonight?" he asked as the crowd cheered. He put up his hand as if to silence everyone before he continued. "As I'm sure a lot of you already know, about three months ago I was blessed with a beautiful new bride." Everyone applauded again. "Much to my surprise, I found out recently that's not the only blessing that occurred that day." He smiled and chuckled a little. "In about six months or so, I'm going to become a dad!" The room suddenly filled with applause and cheers. Mitch pointed to me and stood still for a moment while everyone calmed down again. "She hasn't been able to make it here the past few weeks, but she's here tonight. Any other time I'd put her on the spot and make her come up here; but let's just say the baby's been keeping her busy, so I'll let her sit this one out. Dana, this is for you."

The crowd once again applauded loudly as Mitch strapped on his acoustic guitar and pulled a stool into the middle of the stage. He sat down as the lights dimmed and adjusted the microphone. He smiled sweetly at me as he began to sing, his voice soft and soothing as always. I was starting to feel a little queasy again, but I closed my eyes and tried hard to fight the feeling and concentrated on listening to Mitch's voice as he sang. Just then, I felt a hand touch my shoulder lightly, and I opened my eyes to see Chris looking at me with concern.

"Are you all right, Dana?" he asked.

"I'm trying to be. I don't want to run away while he's singing to me," I said as I turned toward Mitch and forced a smile.

"Take a deep breath," Chris said, and I did.

As Mitch ended the song, he grinned at me again; and when he turned to switch back to his electric guitar and cue the next song, I headed off once more. Just as I got to the restroom door, I heard Angelina's voice behind me.

"Dana, wait up a minute." She caught up with me and placed a hand on my arm. "Jim wanted me to check on you."

I smiled and nodded to her but didn't speak as I hurried into the restroom and found an empty stall. Angelina positioned herself outside the door. "We're all getting really concerned about you tonight, Dana. Have you been sick each time you've come in here?"

I opened the door and nodded weakly as I exited and walked to the sink. "Yeah, I have. This is the worst it's been yet. I'm really beginning to wonder if it may have been something I ate."

"Could've been," she answered. "Mitch just came down for the break, and he asked me to drive you home. Jim can catch a ride with him after the show is over."

I shook my head defiantly. "No, I don't want to go home. I've been a part of this ever since Mitch started, and I don't plan to change that now. I feel bad enough that I couldn't be here these last few weeks. I'm staying tonight. I'll be fine." Then I turned to her and thought perhaps I'd sounded a little too harsh. "I'm sorry. I know he's concerned about me, but I really wish he'd back off."

She smiled. "I know how you feel, but don't expect him to. He's very headstrong. Always has been."

"You aren't telling me anything I don't already know. I live with the man, remember?" I said with a smirk.

"My condolences," Angelina said teasingly. "Come on. Let's go back and watch the rest of the show. I'll buy you a soda."

"Sounds wonderful," I said. Suddenly, I noticed that I didn't have my purse. "Oh, Ang, I left my purse in the restroom. You go back to the table, and I'll be there in a minute."

"Okay," she answered. "I'll go ahead and get that soda for you."

I returned to the stall I had just exited; and much to my relief, my purse was still hanging on the back of the door. I retrieved it and headed out toward the table. I didn't hear the band, so I assumed Mitch would be sitting with the others. I was eager to talk to him about pushing me to go home. I would somehow convince him that I was feeling better—even though I really wasn't—and persuade him to allow me to stay. As I filed through the crowd, I could see him standing there, his face bright, and the sight of him warmed my heart. However, the closer I got that feeling quickly disappeared.

Mitch was standing a few steps away from the table, and in front of him was a beautiful young woman. She looked to be around his age or perhaps slightly younger with long, flowing blonde hair and a figure that would make any man sit up and take notice. I noticed that the skirt she wore came about mid-thigh and really showed off her long, shapely legs. Her top dipped into a deep V, and her generous bust line practically spilled over it. I strategically made my way a little closer to them; and suddenly, I realized who she was. It was the mystery girl from the bistro! I stopped just out of their sight but made sure I was close enough to hear their conversation.

"I'm glad I got to come and see you here tonight, Mitch!" the girl said as she placed her hand on his arm and gave it a little rub. "When you mentioned earlier today that you played here, I told Kandy that I had to check it out especially since I have the night off. You really put on quite the show."

Mitch grinned. "Thanks. I'm glad you're enjoying it, Gloria."

"Yeah, I am having a lot of fun watching you perform, but not nearly as much fun as I had performing for you." She moved her hand to rest on his cheek. "I still can't get over what beautiful blue eyes you have." The girl reached up and carefully took off Mitch's glasses. "It's a shame you hide them behind those glasses." Mitch blushed as she put them back on. The girl smiled. "Oh, I didn't mean to embarrass you, but I do remember you are a little shy, aren't you? Well, I hope you weren't too embarrassed the night we met. I know I enjoyed it, and I hope you did, too."

Okay—what was this girl talking about? I wasn't sure, but I did know that I didn't like what I was hearing. Just when, or better yet, *how* did she 'perform' for him? And Mitch, shy? Not a day in his life! That brought me to whatever it was they 'enjoyed' together. From the looks of her and the way she was coming on to him, I could only imagine. I decided to remain out of their sight; but the more I heard of the conversation, the more I wanted to tear into her—actually, into *both* of them. I fought to keep myself still as I listened to them continue.

"Yeah, I guess I did," Mitch responded. He blushed again. "Actually, I enjoyed it a little more than I thought I would. You do, uh, perform well." Mitch knew his comment sounded stupid, but he decided to try to be nice. He was getting very uncomfortable talking to her and was really hoping she would disappear before Dana returned.

"I'm happy to hear that." She moved a little closer and put her hand on his arm again. "Well, I'm glad we got to chat a little. Maybe after the show I can buy you a drink or something to celebrate that baby you have coming." She moved in even closer. "Have fun up there, blue eyes. I'll catch you later." She gave him a kiss on the cheek and placed her hand on his face once more before she walked away.

As I watched her leave and my husband's eyes following her, I took a deep breath and decided it was time to move in. As Mitch spotted me, I saw him take a deep breath as well, and he forced a smile.

"I was wondering where you were, sweetheart. Angelina said you went back to get your purse, but it took you a long time. Did you get sick again?"

I ignored his question. "Mitchell, wasn't that the girl from the bistro today?" I asked and pointed in her direction.

Mitch's face lost all expression, and he suddenly became pale. "Oh, yeah. She came here to watch the show," he replied. "I guess she must have made the connection."

I looked right into his eyes. "I asked you today who she was, and you told me you didn't know her; so, I'm going to ask you again. Who is she, Mitch?"

He took another deep breath. "Dana, I told you. I don't know." He timidly placed his hand on my arm. "You never answered my question. Were you sick again?"

I pulled my arm back, and he looked at me strangely. "No, I wasn't sick again. But, I would like to know why you won't tell me who she is, and why you were talking to her—or better yet, why you were letting her paw all over you."

Mitch closed his eyes and sighed deeply before he opened them again. "For the last time, she's just a girl who happens to eat at Gartano's and also came here to watch the show. Pure coincidence. She heard me say we were having a baby, and she wanted to congratulate us. That's it. Now, let it go, please."

I glanced over at the table and noticed that it seemed Mitch and I had become the center of attention, but I didn't care.

"Mitchell Jacob Tarrington, you're lying to me. You'd better tell me the truth, and you'd better tell me now!" My voice was getting louder, and a few people looked my way; but I didn't care about that, either.

Mitch tried to remain calm and kept an even tone to his voice. "Dana, I already told you...."

"I don't want to hear what you already told me, Mitch. I want to hear the truth! I was listening to that entire conversation, and I heard the two of you call each other by name. I know that you know who she is. It's highly unlikely that she'd act that way if you didn't. Why won't you tell me?"

Mitch looked dumbfounded. "What do you mean *you were listening*? I didn't see you anywhere. What in the heck were you doing—hiding out and spying on me?"

I decided to ignore this question as well. "I'm waiting. Tell me who that girl is and how you know her."

Newbie was approaching the table now obviously coming to talk to his girlfriend Janine. With an impish grin, he walked up to Mitch and tapped him on the shoulder. The way Mitch stood in front of me apparently blocked me from Newbie's view.

"Hey, Trip, wasn't that your friend from the strip club? Maybe we can get her to give another special performance after the show," he snickered. Mitch clenched his jaw and pointed to me. Newbie instantly turned red. "Oh, hi, Dana. Feeling better?" he asked.

"Aaron, Mitch seems to be having some difficulty telling me who that girl is. Can you help him out?" I asked.

Newbie looked at Mitch with uncertainty as Mitch's face filled with fear. "Not really, Dana," he replied nervously. "I'd better go say hi to Janine before she gets upset with me. Gotta stay on her good side, you know." With that, he hurried off.

Suddenly, Newbie's words registered with me. "Wait a minute—did he say she was from a strip club? What's going on, Mitch? Is that girl a stripper? And if she is, how does she know you?"

Mitch took my hand, and led me a few steps further away from the table. He sighed loudly, then took off his glasses, and rubbed his eyes. Putting them back on, he looked up as if to collect his thoughts before he looked back at me.

"Dana, I don't know where to start, so I'll just come out with it." Nervously, he began to relay the story to me about his experience at Caroway's the night he'd met Gloria. He gave me all the sordid details and paused every few sentences to take a deep breath or bite his lip guiltily. I stood there in shock as I listened to him—the anger and pain intertwining within me to create a volcano of emotion that took everything I had to hold back. He reached out for my other hand, but I pulled both of them back and folded my arms tightly across my chest. I didn't want him to touch me. In fact, I wasn't even sure at that moment that I wanted him near me. He came to the end of the story and interjected one final piece of information.

"The night Chris and Trudy took us out to dinner and you were teasing me about going to a strip club, I thought you'd found out.

That's why I was going along with you. I should have told you then, but I didn't."

I could feel my emotional volcano slowly beginning to erupt. "Why not, Mitch? Did you think it would be better to lie so you could be free to see her again if you wanted? Is she the reason you've been so intent on getting me to go home tonight? Is she the reason you didn't want me to go to work with you today? Did you know she would be coming in for lunch?"

"No, Dana, that's not true at all...."

"Then why didn't you tell me? You looked me right in the eyes, Mitchell, and you lied to me! How could you do that?" I was getting louder, but I still didn't care. I was angry and decided I wasn't going to hold back.

"I knew you'd be upset, and I decided it was better if you didn't find out about what happened that night."

I was glaring at him with fire in my eyes, my anger level rising even more. "What did happen, Mitch? Did she touch you?"

He didn't speak—just nodded—his eyes still downcast. "She touched my cheek with her hand and ran it down my chest like you do sometimes. Then she sat down on my lap and kissed my cheek before she walked away. That's all."

I felt the floodgates open, and tears began to flow freely down my cheeks. "I'm not sure I believe you. You lied to me before. How do I know you aren't lying to me now?" He reached out for me again, but I backed away. "I saw how she was all over you just now, and you weren't making any attempt to get away from her. You were enjoying it, like I'll bet you were enjoying her that night. I saw the attraction, and I'm sure everyone else did, too. Now I know why you've been pushing for me to go home all evening. You knew she was going to be here, didn't you? Now that I'm getting larger with the baby and I'm not as appealing to you, are you planning to hook up with her? Is that why she came into the bistro today, so you could plan your get-together tonight?" I took a deep breath and tried to gain my composure a little. "What else did she do for you besides dance, Mitchell? Did you sleep together?"

"Dana, stop it!" Mitch said firmly. "You don't know what you're talking about! You don't trust me at all, do you? I have never cheated on you. You're the only woman I've ever been with."

"Then why didn't you tell me about all this before? When you came over the day after it happened and I asked you where you went, why didn't you tell me the truth? You lied to me, Mitch. You looked me right in the eyes, and you lied to me. You told me you didn't go to a strip club. You told me there were no naked women, and you only played pool. All the while, you were lying. Then you lied at the restaurant. Now today, you lied to me again when you said you didn't know her." I looked at him—the fire of my fury drying the tears of pain. "Then you have the audacity to stand before me and question my trust for you? I don't see how I can trust someone who doesn't love me enough to be honest with me."

"No, you have it all wrong. I lied because I didn't want to hurt you *because* I love you. I know it was wrong, but I had to. I couldn't let you know."

"Do you really think I'm that shallow? Do you really think I'm going to believe that you kept the truth from me to spare my feelings? Get real. I'm not that stupid. You're just like Eddie, Mitchell Tarrington. You can't settle for only one woman. The way you flirt all the time and the way those eyes of yours are always wandering, I don't know why I didn't see this coming. Or, maybe this is your way of getting out of the responsibility of being a father. You've already told me that you aren't ready for this baby. If you hook up with her and let me go, you don't have to worry about it. Is that what this is all about?" I threw my hand up and waved it in her direction as if motioning for him to follow her. "Well, go on. You can have her. Maybe if you're lucky, she brought her friend; and you can have her, too."

I started to walk away, but Mitch caught me by the arm. "Dana, don't compare me to Eddie. I'm nothing like him. I have always been faithful to you. The thought of cheating on you or leaving you has never even crossed my mind." His voice softened, and he sighed deeply. "Look, I know I was wrong, and I'm sorry. Believe me, I'm sorry. I wanted to tell you, and I almost did a couple of times. In fact, I thought about telling you today after she came into Gartano's, but I was afraid. I know how jealous you are, and I was afraid if I told you that it would destroy what we have. I couldn't take that chance."

"What chance, Mitch? That I'd leave you? That would be tragic for you, now wouldn't it, to have your plan foiled? To think that you couldn't have me at home to take care of you after you got done with your little plaything at the club? What a terrible thought!"

I could see by the look in his eyes that I had made him angry with my comment, and the irritated tone of his voice confirmed it. "That's enough! I'm sick and tired of you accusing me of wanting another woman, or worse yet, being with one. I have absolutely no interest in anyone but you, and I'm sorry if you don't want to believe that. I lied, Dana. Yes, I'm guilty of that, and I'm ashamed of it; but I won't let you continue to accuse me of things I haven't done. I didn't plan to be untruthful. I had every intention of coming over after my night out and telling you that I had gone to a club to play pool. That statement would have been one hundred percent accurate. When you kept pushing the issue, I panicked; and the lie came out. It wasn't premeditated, and it certainly wasn't something I wanted to do. It just happened."

I could feel the rage bursting forth, and I couldn't control myself. "No, Mitch, you lied because you thought you could get away with it. It was your way of being able to do what you wanted and justify your actions then and now. I don't believe you when you say you haven't cheated on me. You probably have all along. Who knows? Maybe you were lining this whole thing up with her tonight to do it again. You've never been able to keep your eyes where they belong—not from the very first time we went out." I stepped closer to him. "I honestly thought I could trust you. I thought I'd found someone that I could rely on to be different than Eddie was, but I was wrong. You're just like him. If you lied to me about this, what else have you lied to me about? You're nothing but scum!" I said as my hand caught Mitch's right cheek. I turned and stormed toward the exit of the club.

Mitch stood in shock—the sting of Dana's blow still strong on his face. He put his hand up to it and pulled it away to look for blood. Not finding any, he slowly dropped his hand and still stood motionless. Coming to his senses, he realized what he needed to do. He couldn't let this happen and risk losing her again. He'd almost done that once after their fight on Christmas Eve. That time he hadn't gone after her, and that had been a mistake. Fate had given him a chance this time to do things differently, and he was going to take advantage of it.

Mitch slowly turned back toward the table where his family was sitting, and all of them were seemingly as shocked by the incident as he was. He looked at Chris; and without a word Chris nodded, grabbed his jacket, and headed toward Mitch. Jim stood up as well.

"I'll tell the guys you had an emergency. They can handle it from there. You go and don't worry about a thing," he told Mitch.

Mitch simply nodded. Noticing that Dana had left their jackets hanging on her chair, he grabbed them both and headed with Chris out into the night.

Just outside the door, Chris turned to him. "I'm assuming all that had to do with that girl you were talking to. Am I right?"

Mitch nodded. "She was the girl from the strip club. Now Dana knows everything. I was so stupid. I should have told her earlier. I'll be lucky if she even wants to see me."

"Don't worry, little brother," Chris said reassuringly. "She's just angry right now. Give her a few hours, and she'll be over it."

Mitch looked at his brother as if he were insane. "Christopher, she *hit* me, for crying out loud! This is definitely not something she's going to get over within a few hours!"

They got into Chris's car, and Mitch turned toward the window in silence. His heart overflowed with a whirlwind of emotions, and his mind was working overtime trying to sort them all out. Despite the fact that he had hurt Dana, he didn't regret telling her what had happened. He felt as if a two-ton weight had been lifted off his shoulders. Even though she didn't understand right now, he hoped he would find a way to make her see that he had done what he had for her.

He looked back at Chris. "Do you think she even went home?"

"I'm sure she did, buddy," Chris replied. "Where else would she possibly go?"

Mitch sighed and began to fidget nervously, turned toward the window, and then back to Chris again. "I don't know. I just want to find her and straighten all this out. I hope she'll give me the chance." He took off his glasses and rubbed his eyes. Before he spoke again, he took a deep breath to fight his emotions. "I can't lose her, Chris. I almost let it happen once. I can't let it happen again. I love her more than life itself."

Chris glanced at his younger brother; and even in the dim light of the car, he could see the expression of pain and fear that covered his face. He reached out and gently patted Mitch on the leg. "It'll be okay, Mitch. Don't worry. I know it'll be okay."

Mitch replaced his glasses and turned to stare out the window. His mind was racing—his heart breaking in two. He slowly reached up to touch his cheek as he remembered the sting of Dana's anger against it. How could he have let things come to this? How could he have been so senseless to believe he could keep the secret of his bachelor night and Gloria from her forever? He thought back to the day after when she'd asked him what he'd done with the guys, and he lied to her telling her they'd only gone to a club to play pool. Had he stopped right there it might have been all right. However, he didn't. He went on to say that he had not been to a strip club and that he hadn't had contact with other women. He remembered the way she'd looked at him, her eyes filled with love, and drank every word he'd told her with absolute trust. She believed him, and all the while he'd been telling her a lie.

Then he thought about the night at the restaurant with Chris and Trudy. He felt once again the fear that had gripped him when he thought she'd found out. At home later that night, he'd wanted to tell her, but still he kept silent. Now, he'd lied to her again and pretended that he'd never encountered Gloria before that day even though Dana had known better. He knew what she was thinking: the one person in this world she trusted completely had betrayed her just like the one before. She thought he was just like Eddie—telling her one thing to her face as he was doing something else behind her back. In his heart, Mitch knew he was nothing like him. Yes, he'd lied to her, but not to be malicious. He'd done it to protect her feelings and to keep her from feeling like she did right then. *Funny how plans sometimes seem to work against you that way*, he thought.

It seemed like forever to Mitch, but only a few minutes passed before they were pulling into the parking lot of the apartment building. His eyes scanned each spot looking for the evidence that Dana was indeed there. Not seeing his car, he anxiously turned to Chris.

"Chris, my car's not here. Dana didn't come home."

Chris looked puzzled. "Are you sure? I mean, where else could she have gone?" He paused a moment to think. "Maybe to Kayla's?"

Chris pulled up next to the door and put the car in park. Mitch put his head back against the seat, closed his eyes, and tried to collect his thoughts. "No, Kayla and Joseph were going to visit her family for the weekend. They were leaving after she got off work today. She isn't home." He took off his glasses and rubbed his eyes. "I don't know where she might be. I just hope that she's all right."

Chris looked at his brother sympathetically. "I'm sure she is, little brother. Don't worry. Maybe she's driving around a little to clear her head. Why don't you go upstairs and wait for her? If she's not home in, oh, say half an hour or so, call me. I'll go out and help you look for her."

Mitch put his glasses back on and nodded. "Yeah, okay. I'll call you if I don't hear from her in a little while." He opened the door and stepped out into the chill of the night. "Thanks for the ride, Chris."

Chris smiled lovingly. "Don't mention it. Good luck." Mitch closed the door and watched as his brother drove away.

Mitch trudged up the stairs and paused just outside the door of the apartment. He put his forehead against it and closed his eyes again. Where could she have gone? He thought about her being all alone—a beautiful, young, not to mention pregnant woman driving around in the city at night. How vulnerable she would be to someone who might want to do her harm and even more so given the fact that she was also in a poor emotional state right then. He stood back up and started down the stairs as he shuddered at the thoughts that tumbled inside his head. He needed to try to find her. Then he stopped. She'd lived in that city for almost five years and had gone out plenty of times by herself at night. She'd always been okay and would never venture into any area that she felt was unsafe. What if he left and she came home to an empty apartment? She'd think he stayed behind at the club to be with Gloria, and that would ruin any chance he had left with her for sure. He turned around and went back up the stairs to open the door and then stepped into the lonely darkness.

I could barely see the road in front of me through the tears that were streaming down my face. My head and stomach were beginning to ache from all the emotions that were churning inside me. As I thought about Mitch and all that had taken place that night, my heart felt as though it would surely stop beating from the pain he had caused. I had never thought, not even for a moment, he would ever lie to me or that he would ever betray my trust in him the way he had. I never thought he'd have the nerve to look me in the eyes and tell me things that weren't true—let alone do it with a straight face and not so much as a twinge of guilt. If he was trying to learn to perfect his technique, he was off to a good start.

Then there was Gloria. She was a beautiful woman, no doubt—the kind that any man would love to spend time with. The more I thought about her, the more I believed that she may have done just that with Mitch. He had lied to me about going to the strip club, so what was there to make me believe he hadn't lied about cheating with her as well? What was it about the men I attracted that made them find it so difficult to remain loyal to me? Was I too difficult to get along with, too boring a conversationalist, not desirable enough physically? Or, were all men so caught up in their own little worlds that they needed more than one woman to satisfy their ego trips? Did it make them appear more masculine to their peers? I didn't know.

As I pondered those questions, the hurt was still strong; but the anger was beginning to grow stronger. Who did Mitch Tarrington think he was that he could treat me this way and get away with it? Did he think that I was some little peon that would allow him to carouse around with other women, and then come home to me and expect me to fulfill his every manly whim? If he did, he was in for a rude awakening. It was at that moment I realized the perfect way to do that to him.

I knew I couldn't drive around forever, so I turned down the street that would take me home. I didn't want to talk to Mitch—or even see him for that matter—but I had to take care of business. As I arrived at the building, I slowly headed inside and up the stairs. I opened the door to total darkness, so I assumed Mitch wasn't there. *Not surprising*, I thought. *I knew that once he got rid of me, he would take the opportunity to spend time with Gloria.* As I turned to lock the door, I heard Mitch's soft voice.

"Thank God. You're home. I was worried about you."

I turned on the light and saw him sitting on the couch. His face was covered in an expression of relief and yet his eyes were filled with sadness.

"What are you doing here?" I snapped. "I assumed you'd still be at the club. Your girlfriend will be wondering where you went."

Mitch stood up and started to approach me. "Stop it, Dana. She's not my girlfriend or anything else to me for that matter. I couldn't care less about her." He took a deep breath and softened his tone. "I think we need to talk about all this. Just give me a chance to explain things to you, okay?"

I put up my hands, and he stopped where he was. "You've already said enough, and I have nothing more to say to you. Therefore, as far as I'm concerned, that means we're through talking." I headed into the bedroom and proceeded to retrieve a large suitcase from the back of the closet. Mitch followed me and stood motionless in the doorway while he watched me intently.

His voice was full of fear. "Dana, what are you doing? Are you leaving me?"

I went to his dresser, removed the belongings, and then threw them into the suitcase with disarray. "No, I don't have anywhere to go. I have no family here remember. You do."

His expression was a mixture of shock and disbelief. "What do you mean? You're asking me to leave?"

I walked into the closet, pulled several items off the hangers, and walked back out to throw them into the suitcase as well. "No, I'm telling you to. I don't want you here, Mitch."

"What…what do you mean you don't want me here? I don't understand…."

I pushed the suitcase closed, zipped it up, and then tossed it as best I could in his direction. He took a step back and stared down at it lying by his feet.

"I don't think it takes a lot of intelligence to figure that out, Mitchell. I don't want to be around you. I want you to leave." I sat down on the side of the bed and watched his eyes slowly lift to meet mine. "Now, take your suitcase and go."

Mitch cautiously took a step closer to me. "Honey, please listen to me. I lied to you, and I'm sorry. But, that's all I did. You have to believe me." He swallowed hard. "I love you, Dana."

The look on his face at that moment tore the heart right out of me, but I knew I needed to stand my ground and be strong. I took a very deep breath and let it out slowly.

"I said go."

He started to walk toward me again; but I turned away, and he stopped. "Dana, come on. Don't you think this is a little extreme? We can work this out, baby. All we need to do is talk about it. Please let me talk to you…." This time I didn't answer, and I heard him sigh. "I love you, sweetheart, only you. Please don't do this."

I reached deep within myself and pulled up every ounce of courage that I had. I turned and looked right into his eyes. "You've hurt me for the last time, Mitchell Tarrington. Now, go and leave me alone."

"Dana…." Mitch sighed loudly as he realized there was no use in pursuing the issue any further. He knew he could stay there all night just pleading with her, but she wasn't going to budge. Her anger was still too strong. He paused for a moment to consider his options but concluded that since most of them involved resisting her wishes, they would only anger her more. He looked at her face covered in hatred and pain, her eyes swollen, and her makeup streaked from her tears. She was pale, and he knew that had to be from the sickness she'd been fighting all night. He yearned so badly just to take her into his arms—to hold her and take care of her. Yet he knew right then she'd never let that happen. As much as he wanted to fight it and stay, he feared that making her any more angry might in some way have an ill effect on the pregnancy. That was something he simply couldn't risk. If anything happened to the baby because of him, there was no way she would ever forgive him; and he knew that he'd never be able to forgive himself.

Feeling backed into a corner, Mitch reluctantly picked up the suitcase and looked at her once more. His wounded heart ached intensely.

"If you change your mind, I'll be at Chris and Trudy's. I love you, Dana." With that, he was gone.

As I heard the door close gently behind him and his key as he locked it, I fell onto the bed and began to sob.

As Mitch pulled into Chris's driveway, he noticed his parents' car still parked there. They must have been babysitting tonight and hadn't left yet, even though Chris was now at home. What would they think about the situation he was in? He shut off the car and sat for a moment. *Perhaps I should go to a hotel,* he thought. *That would probably be better than intruding on Chris and his family, and more so, facing Mom and Dad.* He wasn't quite ready to do that just yet. However, before he had a chance to make his decision final and leave, the front porch light came on. In an instant, Chris was out the door pulling his coat on as he walked as if he had been anticipating Mitch's arrival. Mitch opened the car door and got out to meet his brother halfway.

"Since you're here, I'm assuming she didn't come home. Let me get the car out, and I'll go help you look for her," Chris said.

Mitch put up his hand. "No, Chris, we don't have to do that. She's home."

Chris gave Mitch a confused look. "If she's home, Mitch, then what are you doing here? Shouldn't you be there trying to work things out with her?"

Mitch sighed, dropped his eyes from Chris, and thrust his hands into his pockets. "Well, that's what I think, but she doesn't want me around. She told me to leave."

Chris looked up and let out a long, loud breath. He turned back to Mitch and shook his head. "You're kidding me. She actually kicked you out of the house? All you did was lie to her about some stripper. It's not like you slept with the woman or anything. Wow."

Mitch leaned his back against his car and looked at Chris. "Well, you and I know that's all that happened, but try telling her that. In Dana's mind I not only lied to her, but I did it so I could spend more time with the stripper and perfect my qualities as an adulterer. Oh, and I should mention that I'm doing all this because my wife of three months is now unappealing to me because she's pregnant with my child; and I don't want the responsibility of being a father. Although *I* was unaware of it until tonight, I've obviously been cheating on her all along which must also mean she's not really the one I lost my virginity to. So, I lied to her about that as well. Apparently, all I know how to do is flirt with other women, and I'm just like Eddie Williams." Mitch sighed. "The man poisoned her mind into thinking she can't trust anyone of the male gender and that we're all womanizing pigs, and I have to pay for it." Mitch turned toward a passing car and watched until its taillights were out of sight. He sighed heavily and pointed toward the house. "Now, I'm here. If it's not too much to ask, I need a hot shower and a place to sleep for the night."

Chris watched as his brother bit his lip nervously and fought back the emotions that had clearly started to form in his eyes. He managed a smile for him and nodded.

"Sure, little brother, come on in. You know you always have a place here." Chris started to walk toward the house. When he noticed that Mitch wasn't following, he turned back around.

"What's going on, Mitch? Aren't you coming?"

Mitch pointed to his parents' car. "I was just thinking. Mom and Dad are here, Christopher. I can't let them know what's going on, and I know they'll ask questions and want to know why I'm here. I'm not ready to handle that. Maybe I'll go downtown and stay somewhere tonight. Just tell them I stopped by to let you know Dana was all right."

Chris reached out to place his hand on Mitch's shoulder and looked him right in the eyes. "Mitchell, it's all right, buddy. I don't want you to be alone tonight. Besides, Mom and Dad already know what's going on—well, kind of."

Mitch gave him a curious look. "What do you mean, 'kind of'?"

Chris folded his arms. "Well, when I came home early, naturally they wanted to know why. You know it's next to impossible to get anything past Mom. I just told them Dana got upset with you and left the club, and I gave you a ride home. I told them that she wasn't home when you got there, so I promised to be on standby in case you wanted me to go and help you look for her. They decided to stick around just in case since Trudy's still out."

"You mean Trudy isn't home yet? It's kind of late for her to still be out, isn't it?"

Chris looked at his watch. "It's only a little after ten. The show started at eight, and we were only there about an hour or so before everything happened. She should be home soon." He pointed to Mitch's trunk. "Get your things and come on inside. Don't worry. Everything's going to be fine."

Mitch retrieved his suitcase from the trunk of the car, hit the door lock button on his keychain, and followed Chris inside. Mitch assumed the children were in bed already as the house was unusually quiet. The only sound came from the ticking of the grandfather clock in the foyer. He placed his suitcase down; and as he took off his coat, his mother approached him.

"Mitch! This is a surprise. What are you doing here? Is Dana all right, honey?" she asked.

Mitch gave her a hug. "Yes, Dana's fine. She's at home. I just needed to, uh, get out for a little while, that's all. You know—to let things cool down a bit."

Olivia stepped aside as Jake walked up to his son. Noticing the handprint on Mitch's cheek, Jake reached out and gently touched it. "That's quite the mark there, son. Did Dana hit you?"

Mitch nodded. "Yeah, Dad, she did, but I deserved it. Actually, I deserved much more than that," he sighed. "But, if you don't mind, I'd rather not talk about it right now."

Jake looked at his young son and saw the pain and uncertainty on his face. "I'm not sure that's such a good idea. Come with me, Mitchell. Let's go for a little walk."

Mitch looked at Olivia. "Go ahead, honey. Go with your dad," she persuaded.

The two men walked in silence down the hallway to Chris's den. Jake motioned for Mitch to sit down, closed the door, and then took a seat opposite him.

"I've always thought it best not to meddle in my children's personal affairs, but I think I might like to know what happened tonight, Mitch."

Mitch sighed heavily and dropped his eyes from those of his father. He proceeded to tell him everything from start to finish beginning with the night at the strip club and ending with the events of that evening with Dana. Jake sat silently and listened intently to the things Mitch had to say. As he finished, Jake stood up and turned toward a picture on the wall with his back to Mitch.

"Why did you lie to her, son? Your mother and I never taught you to be dishonest about anything." Jake didn't look at him as he spoke, but the tone of his voice told Mitch that he was anything but pleased.

"I was afraid that if I told her the truth I might lose her again, and I couldn't take that chance. I figured if she never knew that everything would be okay."

Jake turned around slightly. "What do you mean—lose her 'again'?"

Mitch hadn't realized what he'd said. He really didn't want to share the ordeal with Jake, but his words were now forcing him to tell the story.

"Well, I'm reluctant to tell you, Dad. I'm not sure what you'll think of me if I do." He couldn't help but smile a little. "Then again, I just told you that my wife slapped me because of an encounter with a stripper now, didn't I?"

Jake sat down again, leaned forward a little, and patted Mitch on the knee. "Try me, Mitch," he said.

Mitch began to bite his lip nervously. "Well, it started with that fist fight Chris and I had on Christmas Eve. The entire reason I hit Chris to begin with is that he took a comment I made about Dana and twisted it. He made it sound like she wasn't as innocent as I was making her out to be. He also insisted that we were sleeping together, and he didn't believe me when I told him both of us were still virgins. He said that he couldn't believe that to be true about Dana especially after seeing the way she kissed me when I proposed. Although he knew I was getting upset, he went on to say that the reason I hadn't been with her was because I was too afraid to let her teach me how to be a man."

Jake sat back and fixed his eyes on Mitch. "So, you punched him."

Mitch nodded. "Precisely. I wasn't about to let him get away with those comments."

Jake sat quietly for a minute and absorbed Mitch's words. "That's all well and good, son, but it still doesn't quite tell me how you lost Dana. Did she get upset about the fight?"

Mitch shook his head. "No, Dad. In fact, I never told her what it was about. To this day she doesn't know. However, as I was sitting alone afterwards thinking, I convinced myself that maybe Chris was right. After we left your house that night, I took Dana back to my apartment with the excuse that I wanted her to see the place since she'd never been there. I put the moves on her, and one thing led to another. She told me she wanted to wait until we got married, but I kept pushing the issue. When she wouldn't give in to me, I got mad and said a lot of very mean things to her including that I didn't know why I had ever fallen for her. She was hurt and angry, so she left." Mitch paused and stood up, thrusting his hands into his pockets as he began to pace nervously. "That's not even the worst part. To make a long story short, I went to the bistro thinking I could get my mind off things for a while. While I was there, Jessica Radcliff showed up. She said she was in town for the holiday and wanted to see me. I tried to get rid of her, but before I could, she kissed me. I didn't know Dana had come down there to try to make up with me. She saw me with Jess; and not knowing who she was, thought I'd found someone else. Although it wasn't at all what it appeared to be, she got upset and ran out of the bistro. Instead of going after her, I was stupid and just let her go." He sat back down and took off his glasses to rub his eyes. "To continue on that note—the stupidity, that is—I took three bottles of wine from the stockroom, went home, and got myself very drunk."

Jake stared at Mitch and slowly shook his head. "You're right. That wasn't a wise thing to do, son," he said, "especially for a man who isn't a drinker to begin with."

Mitch sighed. "I know, but I thought I'd lost her forever, and I didn't know any other way to get rid of that pain. I can't remember ever hurting like that before, and I thought I'd just drink until I couldn't feel it anymore. Apparently, Jimmy came to check on me; and when I didn't answer, he called Chris. Chris called Jim and Paul, and the three of them came over to stay with me. While I was sleeping, Chris called Dana over, and she stayed, too. Thank God, we worked it all out. That's why when this thing with the strip club happened, I was afraid to tell her for fear she wouldn't marry me. I knew she'd never believe I was innocent a second time." Mitch could feel the tears forming in his eyes. "Now, because I screwed up again, my wife's at home all alone thinking I've cheated on her with a stripper, that I don't find her attractive, and most likely, that everything I've ever told her is a lie." Mitch took off his glasses and wiped his eyes. He replaced them and looked at his father sadly. "She deserves so much more than I've given her, Dad. All I can seem to do is break her heart. I won't blame her if she never wants to see me again."

Jake's heart was breaking for his young son. He reached out for him and pulled him to his feet in a tight embrace. To Jake, he was just a boy, hurt and confused, afraid that the one person who meant the most to him in the world hated him. As he had when Mitch was a child, he wished he could hold him until the pain went away; but he knew he couldn't. As a father, his first instinct was to scold him for his wrongdoings and lecture him, but there was no sense in doing that now. What was done was done, and hopefully, Mitch had learned from his mistakes. Mitch looked down and removed his glasses once more to wipe away the tears he'd allowed to form there. Replacing them, he looked at Jake again.

"I'm not the wonderful person you all think I am. Now you can see that for yourself."

Jake shook his head. "Yes, you are wonderful, son. You have many admirable qualities. We all make wrong decisions in life and do things that we regret. The important thing is that we learn from our mistakes, and we move on." He smiled. "In spite of everything that's happened tonight, I can guarantee that Dana still loves you with everything she has. She may be hurt and angry, but she still loves you."

Mitch shrugged. "I'm not so sure about that. She's never hit me before, and she's certainly never told me I was scum. She doesn't think she can trust me anymore, and she thinks I've cheated on her." He sighed. "She doesn't even want me around her. I'm here because she kicked me out of the apartment."

Jake smiled a little. "I know, son. I saw your suitcase by the door. But, Mitch, she's upset. You know yourself from what you just told me that people say things in anger that they don't mean. You did betray her trust, and that's something you'll need to work hard to restore. She already had a man do that to her, and now she feels as if you have, too. The problem is she wasn't married to that other man. Not only are you her husband, but you are also the father of that child she's carrying. I'm not going to tell you it won't take some doing, but I will tell you that it isn't anything you *can't* do."

Mitch looked at his father. "Then you think I still have a chance with her? I love her, Dad, more than anything in the world. You know that, don't you?"

Jake nodded. "Yes, I know that; and deep down, Dana does, too. And yes, I know you still have a chance with her. It'll all work out, trust me." He stood up as well, placed a hand on each of Mitch's shoulders, and turned him so that the two were face to face. "Listen to me, Mitch. Give her a little space, a little time to think things through, and to clear her head a bit. Don't rush back in and force the issue. Stay here tonight and try to rest. Wait for tomorrow. Maybe by then she'll be ready to talk."

Mitch nodded. "I'll stay, but I won't rest. I know that much." He sighed deeply. "Why does this relationship stuff have to be so darn difficult? Leave it to me to fall for the most stubborn girl on the planet!"

Jake laughed and gave Mitch a playful shove. "No, son, you're wrong. That would be your mother!" Mitch couldn't help but laugh a little himself.

Jake's expression changed to one of love and compassion. "Mitchell, you have a lot of people in your life who really love you. I know that you're hurting right now, and you're afraid. But, if you need us—if you need me—I'm here for you. I promise you everything will work out."

Mitch bit his lip and nodded. "Yeah, I hope so. I wish I were with her right now. I miss her so much. I really do love her."

Jake smiled. "I know you do, Mitch. I know you do."

The two returned to the living room where Trudy was now sitting with Olivia and Chris. She smiled as Mitch approached her and stood up to give him a warm hug.

"Don't you worry. Dana will come around. She just needs to put her thoughts together. She's upset right now."

"I hope you're right, but I can't say that I blame her at all for feeling the way that she does." He looked soulfully at his mother and brother. "If you'll all excuse me, I think I'm going to catch a quick shower and turn in. I'm pretty beat."

"I was just going to get us all a cup of coffee, and Trudy made some chocolate chip cookies earlier," Chris said as he pointed toward the kitchen. "Don't you want to stick around and have some with us? I know those are your favorite."

Mitch lowered his eyes and shook his head. "No thanks. I'm really not very hungry." He looked up at Chris. "I'll crash on the foldout in the den if that's okay. I don't want to be any trouble."

Chris smiled at him. "No, you go ahead and take the guest room. You'll be more comfortable there, and you'll have a little more privacy. There's an extra blanket in the closet if you want it."

Mitch forced a smile. "Thanks. Goodnight, everyone."

With a heavy heart, Mitch collected his suitcase and made his way up the stairs to the guest room. He stepped inside and closed the door behind him. The full moon outside was casting a soft glow about the room. He walked to the window to look up at it taking its place in the night sky surrounded by an endless sea of stars. *I shouldn't be here*, he thought. He knew he should be at home with his wife, holding her close, observing that scene from his own bedroom window. He should be drinking in the beauty of her smile, the warmth of her touch, the taste of her kisses. He should be telling her how much he loves her, how she completes him, how she makes his life worth living. Even if he were there, even if he was telling her all the things that were now piercing his heart, she wouldn't believe him. Because of one act of stupidity on his part, she felt that she *couldn't* believe him. His mind took him back to that night when he had asked her if she would ever lie to him about anything. She had answered by telling him no—that she felt trust was a delicate thing not to be toyed with. Now he understood fully what that meant. It took years to build but only moments to destroy. He had found that out the hard way, and now he was paying for it.

He moved to the nightstand and turned on the light—then placed his suitcase on the bed and opened it up. His heart sank again as his mind replayed the scene of Dana angrily throwing his belongings into it and the look on her face as she'd told him to leave. He understood her rage, but he never thought in a million years that she would ever tell him to go. Perhaps she thought he wanted to leave. Maybe she thought that if he was having an affair she would make it easier for him and give him an out. Perhaps she'd decided that she didn't want to be with him anymore because he couldn't be trusted. None of those things were true, and he wanted to tell her just that; but she wouldn't talk to him. He had so much he wanted to say to her and so many things she needed to know. He sighed heavily and took a pair of boxers, sweatpants, and a t-shirt from the bag, then placed it on the floor at the foot of the bed. He stared at it for a moment and hoped that the next time he picked it up it would be to go home.

He headed toward the bathroom to take a quick shower, but then turned around as if something were pulling him back into the room. Laying everything down, he went to the phone on the nightstand and picked it up. Maybe she wouldn't talk to him; but if he left a message, she'd have to listen. He began to dial, but thinking twice, pressed his finger down on the receiver and placed the handset back on the cradle. His father's advice was running through his head now. "Don't force the issue; give her time," he'd said. Mitch knew that he was right. Collecting his things once more, he went off to get ready for bed knowing in his heart that it was going to be a long, lonely night.

Chapter 6

It began around midnight. At first, I thought I was in a horrible dream until I felt it gripping me again, taking me to my knees as I stepped out of bed. Something wasn't right. This wasn't like the sickness I had been feeling the past few weeks. This was different, worse. I grabbed hold of the nightstand and pulled myself slowly to my feet; but the pain cut through me again, so sharp and intense that I audibly cried out. I called Mitch's name—forgetting for just a moment—and when he didn't answer, the memory of the night's events came flooding back to me. Suddenly, fear overcame me like a dark cloud and surrounded me as the pain grew more intense with my panic. What was happening? Was God making everything final? Was this His way of taking the only thing still connecting me with Mitch? I placed my hand on my stomach and began to call out to Him as I pleaded in agony, the tears rolling down my cheeks. "Please, not my baby, not my baby!"

My hands trembled as I reached for the phone. I tried to take a deep breath, but the pain wouldn't allow it. It felt as if I had swallowed shards of broken glass; and with each breath they cut me—tearing into me until I could barely stand it. I looked at the keypad on the phone unable to see it clearly through the swollen creases that were now my eyes. I needed help, but there was no one to help me, no one to turn to. I couldn't call him. My pride wouldn't let me. The hurt was still too strong, too fresh. I didn't want him there anyway. As far as I was concerned, he was no longer a part of my life. Yes, I did love him, but why should I want someone who only wanted me when it was convenient for him? I'd witnessed the scene between Gloria and him—there was definitely an attraction. No matter what he said in his defense, I didn't know how I could believe otherwise. With him I no longer knew what was true and what wasn't. I had found out that night what Mitchell Tarrington was all about. I'd been burnt once by a lying cheat, and I wasn't about to let it happen again. I was not willing to play second string. It was all or nothing, and right then I was choosing nothing.

I started to dial Jake and Olivia's number but thought better of it. I didn't want to face them and to have to explain why I was alone or why I had made their son leave his home. Knowing I would have to do the same with any other member of his family, that left me with few other choices. By now, the guys in the band were all heading home, and they all lived too far away to really be of assistance anyway. Granted, Newbie did live in town, but most likely he was with Janine. I realized then that I didn't even know her last name let alone her number. Kayla was gone. I was truly alone. As the pain tore through me again, I decided I had no other choice. As much as I hated to do so, I dialed the number.

The sound of the late-night news droned in the background as Chris settled into his favorite recliner—a light sleep overtaking him. He thought he heard the telephone, but he wasn't sure. It sounded too distant to distinguish whether it was real or if he was dreaming. He heard it again, but then the ringing ended as quickly as it had begun. Perhaps someone else had picked it up—probably Trudy. Dismissing it, he allowed himself to slip fully into peaceful slumber.

An hour later and now in bed, he heard it again. The ringing pierced the silence like a distant scream. This time he knew it was truly happening. Chris turned on the light and answered sleepily, "Yeah, hello?"

"Chris, it's Jim. There's been an accident."

The hallway was dark, but he had traveled it often and knew it well. Not bothering to turn on the light, he reached the room at the end of it only to find the door standing open. *Perhaps he went to the bathroom,* he thought, *or he's downstairs.* He walked back down the hallway, ruled out the first possibility, and hurried as quickly as he could to the floor below.

The light of the moon shining through the curtains in the front room was the only light throughout the house. His eyes were now accustomed to the darkness, and he moved from room to room in his search softly calling his brother's name. He didn't answer. *Where could he possibly be? Surely he didn't go out at this time of night without telling someone.* He took his jacket from the rack and headed out the front door.

Mitch's car was still there. Chris ran around the yard calling for him in vain. His eyes combed the street and the neighboring yards, but still he saw nothing. Maybe Dana had decided she wanted to talk and had come to pick him up. Maybe he had been sleeping too soundly to hear them leave. Panic suddenly gripped his heart. Had Mitch been the one in the car with her?

Jim said they didn't know who the man was. He hadn't seen him, and the staff who had taken him in couldn't find a wallet or any ID. He was unconscious, as was Dana, so at that point they had no way of knowing. As part of the trauma team, Jim couldn't leave Dana's side to find out. However, Jim's fear was alleviated when Chris told him that Mitch was there with him. Now that fear brought the taste of bile to Chris's mouth. Perhaps the mystery man was Mitch after all. If he had been eager to meet with Dana, it was possible that he had left in such a hurry that he neglected to take his wallet. Perhaps they started to argue again, he got distracted, and the accident occurred. Chris didn't have the answers. It was all speculation which right now he didn't have time for. He keyed in the code for the automatic opener, and the garage door lifted. Quickly getting into his car, he headed off to Dana.

As he approached the intersection, Chris noticed a figure standing on the corner just under the streetlight. He wasn't close enough to tell whether it was a man or woman, but he saw the person step off the curb and into the street unaware that he was approaching. He slowed down and sounded his horn. The person jumped back to the curb and into the light. As Chris approached, he pulled over and rolled down his window.

"Mitchell! What in the heck are you doing? Trying to get yourself killed?" He felt a wave of relief come over him just seeing him standing there and knowing he was okay. But, that fact brought back the question: if the man in the car with Dana hadn't been Mitch, who had it been?

"Actually, I was just trying to clear my head. I couldn't sleep, so I thought a walk might help."

Chris unlocked the door. "Get in, little brother. I have something I need to tell you."

The bright red letters pointed to the entrance of the Emergency Room at Mercy Hospital. Mitch's heart pounded wildly in his chest as he ran through the double doors, and his eyes frantically searched for any sign of her. Behind a small metal desk sat a middle-aged woman unconsciously shuffling through a stack of forms lying in front of her. He ran up to her and paused just long enough to catch his breath and her attention.

"May I help you?"

"Dana Tarrington. Where is she?" he asked—his voice filled with anxiety.

"What is your name, sir?"

"I'm Mitchell Tarrington, her husband. Where is she? Where's my wife?"

The receptionist sifted through a few papers. "The doctors are with her right now in Trauma, sir. You'll need to wait here."

Mitch could feel every nerve in his body stand on end. "I want to see her. Where is she? Where's Trauma?" His fear was beginning to take over.

Just then, Chris arrived and approached Mitch. "I'm sorry I took so long. I couldn't find a spot close by to park. What's going on?" he asked.

"They have her in Trauma, and this lady's telling me I can't see her!" Mitch exclaimed. "I want to know where Trauma is, and I want to see my wife!"

Chris placed his hand on Mitch's shoulder. "Come on, buddy. Calm down. The doctors need to be able to take care of her. I'm sure they'll come and tell you what's going on shortly."

Mitch turned back to the receptionist. "Are you going to tell me where my wife is or am I going to have to go back there and find her myself?" His tone was very agitated, and he was getting loud.

The receptionist stood up and tried to keep a soothing tone to her own voice. "Mr. Tarrington, I'm sorry, but I can't permit anyone but staff to go back there. If you'll have a seat, I'll let someone know you're here."

Mitch began to shake his head, and he was biting his lip to hold back his emotions. "I'm *not* sitting down, and I'm *not* going to until I see my wife!"

Chris placed a hand on his arm. "Mitch, come on. Let's sit down. It's okay," he said as he attempted to calm him down. However, it wasn't working. He had another thought. "Come with me to the payphone. I know Kayla's not there right now, but she'll be hurt if we don't have a message waiting for her when she gets home. Dana would want her to know what's going on." Mitch wasn't moving. "Hey, little brother. It's all right. Jim's back there with her, and he'll take good care of her. Come with me. I don't know Kayla's number."

Mitch sighed and reluctantly followed Chris. He stood with his head down and his hands thrust into his pockets. His eyes were filled with hurt. Every so often, Chris would see him look up at the Emergency Room doors with a blank stare on his face. He gently touched Mitch's shoulder.

"Mitchell, what's her number?"

Mitch shook his head. "Uh, I think it's 555-698...oh, man. It's...I can't remember. I'm sorry, Chris."

Chris smiled. "It's okay. Why don't you sit down for a minute? I'll dial information and get the number." He put the coins into the phone and watched Mitch as his eyes now moved toward the doors of the Trauma Unit as if waiting to see Dana emerge from behind them.

Chris left his message, then hung up, and put a few more coins into the phone. He began to dial another number. "Who are you calling now?" Mitch asked.

"Mom and Dad," he answered. He reached into his pocket and pulled out two quarters. "Go and get us each a cup of coffee from the machine over there." He handed Mitch the coins and gently prompted him in the right direction. Mitch looked at him and nodded as he slowly walked away.

Olivia answered the phone. "Hello?"

"Hey, Mom, it's Chris. I only have a minute here, but I wanted to call to let you know. Dana's been in a car accident. We're at the hospital. Jim was here when they brought her in, and he called me."

"Oh, my, Christopher! Is she hurt badly? Is Mitch okay?"

"Mitch wasn't with her. We don't have any details yet. We just got here, but I wondered if you and Dad could come down? Mitch is an emotional wreck, and I really think he could use some support from you right now. The kid doesn't know his left from his right."

"Of course, honey. I'll get Dad, and we'll be there right away." She paused. "Tell Mitch that we're coming and stay with him, Chris. Try to keep him calm."

"I will, Mom. I just left Kayla a message. I'm sure she'll want to know what happened. I also told Trudy to call Julia and Angelina. Angie can drop Megan by our house on the way down here, so Trudy can watch her. I'll see you all when you get here. Bye."

Chris looked across the room at his younger brother and noticed how lost he seemed to be. He was thankful for the fact that he could be with him. He knew that if Mitch had come alone, it was possible security might have thrown him out for causing a raucous. He couldn't help but smile at that thought. Mitch was a stubborn man, and he loved Dana more than anything. If he hadn't distracted him with the phone call a few minutes ago, he was certain Mitch would have forced his way back into the Trauma Unit causing trouble for everyone. He walked toward him now as Mitch took the second cup of coffee from the machine, and he tried to give him a confident smile.

"Thanks, little brother," Chris said, taking the cup from him. "Mom and Dad are on their way. Come on now. Let's sit and wait. It's all we can do."

"No, it's not. They have to tell me something, Chris. I'm her husband, for Pete's sake! I'm going back over there...."

Chris grabbed Mitch's arm. "You're too upset, buddy. Let's just stay here for a few minutes. I'm sure Jim or another doctor will come out soon."

As if he had been listening, a distinguished-looking, older man approached the pair. He was holding a clipboard in one hand, and he smiled as he got to them.

"Is one of you Mr. Tarrington?" the man asked. "I'm Dr. Prescott."

"Well, yes—actually we both are—but I think my brother's the one you want," Chris replied, pointing to Mitch. Dr. Prescott turned to Mitch and extended a hand.

Mitch returned the handshake and began to bite his lip nervously. "How is she, doctor? Can I see her?"

The doctor glanced at his clipboard as if he had to remind himself of Dana's condition. "All I can tell you at this time, Mr. Tarrington, is that she suffered multiple injuries. Fortunately, none of them were extremely serious. We're still waiting for some of the test results. I don't know any of the details of the actual accident, but it appears that your wife took the brunt of it." The doctor glanced at Chris; then he looked at Mitch again and sighed. "She's still unconscious, and I do know she has a concussion; so, we plan to keep her sedated until we have a more definite diagnosis with everything else. At this point, we're doing what we can to keep her as comfortable as possible."

Mitch sighed heavily. "What about the baby?"

Dr. Prescott took a deep breath and blew it out determinedly. "Dr. Bradley immediately began monitoring as soon as it was possible to do so. It appears that your wife may have been having some mild contractions. As a precaution, we administered medication, and thankfully, got at least that problem resolved. He thinks it may be possible that the contractions began prior to the accident, but he isn't completely sure about that just yet. There was also some mild bleeding; but fortunately, she didn't miscarry. Along with everything else, we are investigating possible trauma to the fetus, and if so, to what extent."

Mitch stood silently for a moment and let himself absorb the doctor's words before he spoke again. "Is that still a possibility? Could she lose the baby?"

"I wish I could tell you more, Mr. Tarrington, or that her prognosis was more positive. However, for now, all we can do is wait."

Remembering that the doctor had not answered his question, he decided to ask again. "Can I see her, please? I really want to see my wife."

Dr. Prescott laid a gentle hand on Mitch's arm. "We're getting her settled in a room right now. Due to the pregnancy, we've opted to place her in I.C.U. at least for now." He glanced toward the E.R. doors and then back to Mitch. "I understand that you're Dr. Macklin's brother-in-law, right?" Mitch nodded. "Then I'll have him come and get you in a few minutes." He gave Mitch a sympathetic look meant to reassure, but it had little effect on Mitch's true feelings. "Don't worry, son. We're going to take good care of your wife and baby." Mitch looked down and nodded as the doctor turned to walk away.

Chris rubbed his brother's shoulder lovingly before starting after the elderly physician. "Dr. Prescott, can I ask something, sir?"

The doctor turned with a soft smile. "What can I help you with?"

"I didn't tell my brother there was someone else in the car with Dana. I won't go into detail, but a lot has happened tonight. I didn't think he needed that tidbit to deal with just yet." The doctor nodded as if he understood completely. "Can you tell me who was the driver of the vehicle?"

Before the doctor had a chance to respond, the doors opened to Jake and Olivia, Julia, Angelina, and Paul following close behind. Chris looked at Dr. Prescott, and the doctor looked toward the door as if to tell Chris to join his family. Chris nodded in response and returned to his brother's side.

Mitch looked up, and his parents took him into their arms. It was the safest and most loved he'd felt all night, and he didn't want it to end. He held on to them tightly and fought with all he had to keep from falling apart. Slowly, they moved away from him, and his mother took hold of his hand.

"It's going to be all right, honey. You know that," she said with reassurance.

Mitch looked down, took a deep breath, and brought his eyes up to meet hers. She could see the pain in his face and not even a faint remnant of the sparkle his eyes usually held. Right then, they glistened with the tears he was struggling to keep in, and her heart ached knowing his was doing the same.

He breathed in deeply again and then let the air escape slowly and silently. "If I hadn't upset her, she would never have left the club. I'd be home right now holding her in my arms. Now, because of me, she's lying here in this hospital hurt and alone thinking I don't love her. What's more, my baby may never get a chance to be born."

Jake brought Mitch's chin up to look him squarely in the eyes. "Mitch, don't go blaming yourself for this, son. The fact that she was upset has nothing to do with the accident. It's just an unfortunate set of circumstances."

"That's right, Mitchell," Julia said as she wrapped her arms around him. "Keep your chin up. Say a prayer and have faith. We'll all do the same."

Jim thrust his hands into the pockets of his lab coat as they stepped off the elevator. The floor was quiet as they walked past several rooms—most dimly lit or completely dark—the occupants long since asleep. Mitch could feel the thickness of tension surrounding him. The air seemed filled with a kind of desperation that told him nothing was to be taken lightly there. I.C.U. Jim had briefed him downstairs of Dana's condition; and until they felt comfortable enough with her stability, she would be a patient in that unit. She would receive the best care possible, and she and the baby would be monitored around the clock.

The fact that Dana's room was just outside the nurse's station set Mitch's mind at ease a bit. He knew that if anything happened to her—that if she was in even the slightest bit of distress—a highly-trained medical team would be summoned to respond immediately. They approached the desk, and Jim stopped to address the nurses there.

"Caroline, Mona, this is Mr. Tarrington. This is the first he's seen his wife since they brought her in, so I told him he could stay for a short while." He touched Mitch's arm and led him gently to the doorway of Dana's room. "Now, remember—we have her sedated to keep her comfortable, so she'll be sleeping while you're here. It's important that you don't try to wake her, all right? It's imperative that she get as much rest as possible."

"I understand," Mitch replied softly. "I won't bother her. I only want to see her, that's all."

"Well then, I'll go down with the others for now. I'll be back for you in a few minutes." He watched as Mitch glanced into the room where Dana lay. "Will you be okay, buddy? Would you rather I stay?"

Mitch shook his head. "No, thanks. I'd really like some time alone with her."

Jim gave him a reassuring smile as he walked away.

A soft light was shining near Dana's bed—just bright enough for Mitch to see her clearly. He slowly entered the room, and his heart ached at the sight of her tiny body lying there—wires hooked to her everywhere—or so it seemed. He stepped closer to the bed and reached out to touch her gently. He began to stroke her hair and bent down to kiss her on the forehead. In spite of everything, she seemed to be sleeping peacefully, oblivious to the fact that he was even there.

He wondered if she had any idea about what had happened or where she was. Pulling a chair close to the side of her bed, he sat down and reached out for her hand. He sat there staring at her and then spoke softly.

"My sweet Dana, I'm so sorry. I love you so much. Please forgive me." He bent down to kiss her again and kept his cheek against hers to let himself get lost in the warmth of being near her. Closing his eyes, he said a silent prayer for her and for their child, and he looked up at her once again. Unable to hold in his emotions any longer, the heartache consumed every ounce of strength he had left. As he sat in the silence, he finally let go of everything he had been suppressing that night. His shoulders heaved under the power of his sobs, and the tears of pain fell steadily down his cheeks. Tenderly placing his other hand on top of Dana's, he turned his face to the ceiling and opened his heart to the only hope he had left.

"Lord, forgive me for not taking care of the blessings You gave me. I've failed miserably in being the husband that I know You want me to be to her. I've failed in so many ways. I shouldn't have lied to her. I know that now. I shouldn't have done any of the things I did. I'm truly sorry even though I know sometimes sorry isn't enough. I know I don't deserve to ask anything of You. But, if you'll just let her get well, I promise I'll be the kind of man she needs. I'll take care of her and love her. I'll do everything in my power to make sure that she never doubts how I feel, not even for a second. All I need is one more chance to show her. Please give me one more chance." He swallowed hard as he tried to choke back the tears that were splashing onto the bed next to Dana. "It can't end this way, Lord. She's my life, my everything. I can't make it without her. Please, I'm begging You. Don't let it end."

Just then, Mitch noticed the monitor strapped to Dana's swollen abdomen, and he smiled for a moment as he listened to the faint sound of his child's heartbeat. "You hang in there, little one, you hear? Your mama and I love you very much, and we both need you." He gave Dana's stomach a loving pat, wiped his eyes, and turned them toward Heaven once again.

"Lord, please take care of my baby. I'm so ashamed that I was ever angry about it, and I'm even more ashamed that I ever thought it was a mistake. I know that You don't make mistakes; and if You let this happen, then You must have a good reason for it. I love this child, and I want nothing more than to hold it, and love it, and help it grow. I want to be a father, Lord. I want us to be a family. Please, let us have a chance to be a family. I'll take care of them both, I promise. I won't let You down."

As Mitch finished his prayer, he felt a presence in the room as if someone were standing right behind him. Turning slightly, he detected nothing more than a faint shadow as it disappeared down the hall. He brought his attention back to his wife and child. Suddenly feeling a sense of peace come over him, he kissed Dana on the cheek, lay his head on the bed, and drifted off into dreams of her.

A short while later, Jim returned and gently shook Mitch to wake him. "Hey, Mitchell, it's time for you to go. Come on. I'll drive you home."

For an instant, Mitch didn't remember where he was; but when he opened his eyes and raised his head off the bed, it all came back to him like a nightmare that wouldn't end.

"Mitch, you need to go home now and try to get some rest," Jim repeated. "You can come back in the morning."

Mitch rubbed his eyes beneath his glasses and looked up at Jim. "I'm not going home, Jim. I'm not leaving her."

Jim sighed deeply. "How did I know you were going to say that?" he said with a slight smirk. Then his face grew serious. "Look, I know you want to stay, but it's against regulations. This is I.C.U., and they're a little more strict up here about things. Besides, I've already let you stay longer than I'm supposed to. You have to go."

Mitch looked at Dana, then down to the baby monitor, and finally back to Jim. "You must not have heard me. I said I'm not leaving. Now, you can either go and leave me alone or try to force me out of here." His tone was very firm and matter-of-fact. "If you haven't noticed, I'm a bit stronger than you are. I can bench almost three hundred pounds, so I really don't think you stand much of a chance."

Jim shook his head. "Please don't do this. Please don't make me do something I don't want to do."

"Then don't make me do something I don't want to do. Let me stay here with her. I won't bother her, and I won't wake her. I'll just sit here next to her. That's all I want, Jim. I want to be with her." He looked back at Dana once more. "If you want to call security to try to make me leave, then go ahead. Do what you feel you must. I'm telling you right now, though, it's not going to work."

"Mitch, please try to understand. I could lose my job. I have to ask you to leave." Jim tried to keep his voice calm in order to persuade Mitch to see his side of things, but he knew in his mind that he was fighting a losing battle.

Mitch looked up at Jim defiantly. "Well, you did ask me, and I've given you my answer." Mitch turned back to Dana and noticed her stir just a little. "It's okay, baby. I'm here. Just rest," he said to her soothingly and reached up to gently stroke her hair.

Jim knew there was no use in pursuing the issue with him any further. He glanced at the nurses' station. "All right, I'll see what I can do." He turned to exit the room and sighed in defeat.

A few minutes later, Mitch was starting to nod off again. When he heard footsteps behind him, he looked up to see Jim and another doctor standing there.

"Mr. Tarrington, I'm Dr. Braden, Chief of Staff here," he said as he shook Mitch's hand. "Can we talk for a few minutes?"

"Sure," Mitch replied, "but I'm still not leaving."

Jim and Dr. Braden both smiled. "Well, Mr. Tarrington, Dr. Macklin filled me in on the details of the situation here. First, I have to tell you that it is against hospital regulations to allow you to stay with an I.C.U. patient overnight. I'm sure Jim already informed you of that. However, under the circumstances, I'm going to make an exception in your case." He paused and looked up at Jim, then back at Mitch. "There are a few conditions, however, that you will need to agree to before I give the final okay."

Mitch nodded. "Anything."

"There will be someone in position at the nurses' station at all times. If your wife begins to awaken or seems in distress in any way, they'll know. However, you'll have to leave the room if our staff needs to assist her. Do you understand?" Mitch nodded. "In addition to that, you have to allow her every opportunity to rest. She's been through a lot, and you mustn't wake her. Do you understand that as well?"

"I won't bother her, doctor. I only want to be with her," Mitch replied softly.

Dr. Braden smiled. "How long have you two been married?" he asked.

"Just around three months," Mitch replied.

Dr. Braden glanced at the chart hanging on the end of Dana's bed and gave Mitch a crooked grin. "Honeymoon baby, huh?"

"One better—wedding night," Mitch replied, smiling a little himself.

"Well, congratulations." He looked at the monitors surrounding the bed. "Looks like everything's stable right now. The baby's heartbeat could be a little stronger but let's just wait it out, okay?" He walked back to Mitch and extended his hand. "I'll fill in the nurses so they won't give you any grief. If there's anything you need, let one of them know."

"Thanks," Mitch said as he shook his hand.

As Dr. Braden left the room, Jim turned to Mitch. "You know, I never thought I'd see the day where you actually threatened me," he said with a little smirk.

"You've never pushed me to that point before, Jim. Now you know," Mitch replied. "I'm sorry that I had to act that way, but I wasn't about to go home and leave my wife and child here. I couldn't do that."

Jim smiled and placed his hand on Mitch's shoulder. "No need to apologize. I understand completely. You try to get some rest. I'll go tell the others what's going on so they can all go home, too. I'll be back in around seven or so."

"Thanks, Jim. I really appreciate everything," Mitch said softly.

"Not a problem. Glad to help." As Jim looked into Mitch's eyes, he could see the sadness and concern there and the uncertainty of what was to come. He tried to offer one last word of encouragement. "Dana strikes me as a fighter, Mitch. I know things may not look good right now, but I'm sure tomorrow will be much more positive."

Mitch nodded and tried to muster up a smile, but it wouldn't come. "Well, I'll just be sitting here waiting for tomorrow," he replied. Just then, Mitch remembered the old saying that 'tomorrow never comes.' This time, however, he hoped he'd be wrong.

Mitch turned back to Dana. She seemed a little more restless now than she had before, and he wondered if perhaps she was trying to wake up and starting to feel the pain of her injuries. He reached out for her hand once more, stood up, and moved a little closer to the side of the bed. He began to stroke her hair and sing to her very softly hoping that if she could hear him at all it might relax her. He bent down to kiss her on the forehead. "It's okay, beautiful," he said softly. "Don't worry. Everything's okay." He watched as she seemed to settle down again as if she could hear him and understood. "That's right, sweetheart. You rest. I'm right here." Kissing her again, he sat back down and nodded off once again.

Early the next morning, the sound of Jim's voice and the light of the sun streaming in through the curtains awakened Mitch. "Good morning," Jim said.

Mitch took off his glasses and rubbed his eyes. "What time is it?" he asked.

"Around seven-ten. I wanted to stop in and see how things were going before I start my rounds. Did you sleep well?"

"About as well as can be expected in a chair," Mitch replied. He glanced at Dana. "She was a little restless last night, but," he smiled at her and rubbed the top of her hand lightly with his finger, "I sang to her; and she seemed to relax after that."

"Ah, yes, the soothing tones of Mitch Tarrington. Doesn't surprise me."

Jim looked at Dana's chart and did a quick check of the monitors. "Well, it looks as if this little one of yours decided to fight a little harder, Mitchell. The heartbeat seems a bit stronger this morning."

Mitch smiled. "Yeah, well, we kind of had a little talk last night," he replied.

"Dr. Bradley's on his way up here right now. I ran into him downstairs a minute ago. When he comes, I'd like you to go get yourself a cup of coffee or something so he can have a few minutes to check things out, okay?" Jim smiled at the look of despair on Mitch's face. "Don't worry; when you get back, we'll give you a full update."

Mitch looked at Dana still sleeping peacefully. Finding a clear spot between the cuts, scrapes, and stitches that graced her cheek, he touched it lightly and caressed it with his thumb. "I'd rather stay here, Jim. I won't get in the way."

Jim placed a hand on Mitch's shoulder. Remembering their near-confrontation the night before, he conceded. "Okay, if that's what you want."

Dr. Bradley extended his hand and gave Mitch a friendly grin. "Good morning, Mr. Tarrington. Dr. Macklin tells me you spent the night. It's not the Ritz by any means, but I still hope you were able to rest well."

Mitch rubbed his neck and twisted his shoulders a bit. "I'm a little stiff, but it'll work itself out," he replied.

The doctor took the chart from the foot of the bed. He shuffled through the first few pages, glanced at the monitors, and made a few notes. Replacing it, he walked to the side of the bed and gently pulled down the blanket. As Dana's delicate frame was revealed, Mitch noticed for the first time the bruises on her collarbone as well as the edge of a large bandage peeking out from beneath the neckline of her hospital gown. Very carefully, the doctor placed the stethoscope against her chest. Mitch held his breath and waited to hear what he had to say.

"A bit of a wheeze, but not much," Dr. Bradley said. "Most likely those few cracked ribs are causing some discomfort. Her lungs actually sound clear to me."

"Cracked ribs?" Mitch inquired.

Dr. Bradley gave him a strange look. "You act as if you didn't know that. Didn't anyone go over her injuries with you?"

Mitch shook his head. "No, all I knew for sure was that she had a concussion. Other than that, I'm clueless."

"Well then, we need to chat, don't we?"

Dr. Bradley pulled the chart from the end of the bed once more and positioned himself next to Mitch. He launched into a list of conditions ranging from minor cuts to major ones requiring stitches, bruises to cracked ribs, a concussion, a fractured left leg, and a dislocated right hip. To top off the list, he added that her left arm appeared to have a small break between the elbow and the wrist; but they wanted another set of x-rays before they made the final diagnosis. Her right kidney was bruised as well, but luckily, not severely.

Feeling a little shaky, Mitch pulled up a chair and sat down to absorb what the doctor had just told him. He began to bite his lip nervously and looked up with questioning eyes.

"What about the baby?"

Dr. Bradley sighed. "The heartbeat seems to be a bit stronger this morning which is encouraging, but I'm afraid to say that I don't think we're out of the woods quite yet. All I can say at this point is that I'd like to keep monitoring things and see where we are in a few hours. I may go ahead and order an ultrasound to check everything out a little further."

Mitch reached out for Dana's hand. The motion caught the doctor's eye and caused him to smile. "Are they going to be okay?"

The doctor nodded. "Your wife is strong, and the fact that she's young and has otherwise been healthy is on her side. My main concern with the baby is that it appears Dana was having contractions prior to the accident occurring. Although we were able to stop them, I'm not sure of the basis from which they began or if they really had any ill effect on the fetus itself. I don't have all her test results back, but once I do I'm going to reevaluate everything. If there are still pieces missing to that puzzle, I'll delve in a bit further until we have it all in place."

He looked up as if in deep thought, made a note on the chart, and then turned to Jim. "Let's allow her to wake up this morning. We'll keep her closely monitored; and a little later, we'll get that ultrasound. If you'll let the nurses know to back off the sedative, I'll take care of everything else." He turned back to Mitch and smiled sympathetically, deciding he would try to put the young husband's mind at ease. "Let's go ahead and see exactly what's happening. Then we can talk a little more about what to expect. Does that sound good to you, Mr. Tarrington?"

Mitch looked into the face of the woman he loved more than life itself. "That sounds fine."

Dr. Bradley shook Mitch's hand and started to exit the room but made an about-face. "Oh, I just thought you might like to know. I ran into Dr. Ryan, our E.R. physician, downstairs just as I was getting on the elevator. The young man who was in the car with your wife was treated and released early this morning. Said he only suffered a few cuts and bruises along with a nice bump on the head, but he should be just fine. Lucky man."

Mitch looked dumbfounded. His eyes darted from Dr. Bradley to Jim and back again. "What are you talking about? What man in the car?"

Dr. Bradley seemed at a loss for words and looked to Jim for a sign as to how to handle the situation. Jim approached Mitch somehow knowing what was to come. "Mitchell, didn't Chris tell you that Dana wasn't alone?"

Mitch stood up. "No, he didn't. Who was in the car with her, Jim?"

Now it was Jim's turn to seek answers from Dr. Bradley. "Well, when he first came in, we didn't know because he had no identification on him; and since he and your wife were both unconscious, we had no way to find out. He told us later that he left his wallet in his car."

Mitch was growing a bit impatient with the doctor's lack of attention to the question at hand. "Who was he, doctor?"

"I believe he said his name was William…no, wait, that's not right. William was his last name." He pulled at his chin, lost in thought. "Oh, yes. Edward Williams. That was it."

Mitch felt faint and collapsed into the chair as a sick feeling came over him. "No, you're kidding me. Eddie Williams was in the car with her?"

The two doctors now looked as perplexed as Mitch was. Jim's expression told Dr. Bradley that it was time for him to make an exit. "I'll go put those orders in and catch up with you a little later." With that, he was gone.

"I can't believe it. Eddie Williams. Why would they be together?"

Jim pulled a chair next to Mitch and sat down. "Mitch, who's Eddie Williams?"

Mitch sighed heavily. "Dana's ex-boyfriend, the guy that dumped her the night I first saw her at Gartano's." He lifted his eyes to meet Jim's. "I don't get it, Jim. The guy left her for another woman. He *cheated* on her, for Pete's sake! Why would she be with him?"

Then another thought entered Mitch's mind, and it was something he didn't want to think about. Perhaps the reason Dana had been with Eddie was to get back at him. That train of thought carried some logic, especially since she thought he had cheated on her with Gloria. Perhaps Eddie acted as a means for her to tell him that she was letting him go— that she was moving on with her life by hooking back up with her ex. Then again, the more he thought about it, the less he believed it. She didn't like Eddie. In fact, she actually despised him. Why would she want to be with someone that admitted his guilt in being adulterous? No, it didn't make sense. Yet another riddle that he couldn't solve at least not for the moment.

His face was now filled with questions, and he turned back to Jim. "Jim, if you knew that Dana was in the car with someone else, why didn't you tell me? Not only that, but why didn't you tell me *whom* she was with?"

Jim pursed his lips and shrugged. "I thought Chris told you. I had no idea; and to be honest, I really didn't think about it. I was too involved with Dana and everything happening with her—not to mention trying to keep you calm about the situation. As to who the guy was, Mitchell, I didn't know myself until just now. In fact, like Dr. Bradley just said in the initial scheme of things, no one knew. I never checked into it after I got you settled in here last night. I'm sorry."

Mitch sprang to his feet and began to pace. "Did Chris know? Did he know who it was?"

"I don't know."

Mitch walked to the side of the bed and looked down at Dana. He stared at her with eyes that reflected hurt and confusion. "Why, baby? Why him? Do you really hate me that much?"

Not knowing what else to say, Jim left Mitch alone with his thoughts.

Chris and Jake stepped off the elevator and rounded the corner that would lead them down the hallway to Dana's room. They knew of the restrictions on visiting I.C.U. patients, but those restrictions didn't matter when weighed against their knowledge of Mitch's emotional state. As they approached the nurse's station, they spotted Jim. He glanced nervously into Dana's room and then began to walk toward them.

"Look, guys, before you go in there, I need to brief you on something." Jim explained the scene that had occurred only moments before and relayed the words of despair that Mitch had spoken to his sleeping wife. Chris looked into the air and exhaled loudly.

"I should have told him," he said guiltily. "With everything else he was trying to deal with, I didn't think he needed to be trying to figure out who the person was or why she was with him. I knew he'd be upset and blame himself even more." He turned to his father. "Let me go in first, Dad. I'll see what I can do."

Jake nodded, and Chris paused for a moment before entering the room.

Mitch was standing over Dana with his hand resting on top of her head and a distressed look on his face. He was biting his lip and just that gesture alone told Chris that he was upset and struggling with his emotions. Chris touched him on the shoulder, and he turned. His expression changed from hurt to anger which caused Chris to withdraw his hand and take a step back.

"You knew, didn't you, Christopher? Why didn't you tell me? Why didn't you tell me she was with Eddie?"

"Mitch, I didn't know. Honest. I didn't know who it was until just now."

"You did know she wasn't alone. Why didn't you tell me that?"

Chris sighed and walked to the window. Although he wasn't facing Mitch, he could still feel his eyes upon him. "You were dealing with a lot, little brother; and I didn't think you needed anything else to worry about—at least not last night. I knew you'd start blaming yourself thinking you drove her into the arms of another man or something crazy like that. I know you. I know how you operate."

Mitch sat down and leaned forward to rest his elbows on his knees. He placed his chin against his folded hands. "What am I supposed to think, Chris? Out of the clear blue, that stripper showed up at my restaurant for lunch, and I was totally shocked. I tried to dismiss it as coincidence, but then she came to the club on the same day. Naturally, Dana wanted to know what my connection was. I tried to deny any, but she found out that I really did know her—somewhat personally I might add—and concluded that she's my lover. She kicked me out of the house, told me she wanted nothing to do with me, and then ended up in the hospital as the result of a car accident that occurred while she was in the company of her ex-boyfriend. Tell me, if it were you, what would you think?"

Chris turned around to face his younger brother. "That there has to be a logical explanation."

Mitch cocked his head and stared blankly at Chris. "I doubt that."

Chris leaned his back against the wall. "Come on, buddy, you don't honestly believe that she'd hook up with that lowlife again, do you? You told me yourself that she compared you to him and not in a positive way at all. She didn't have anything kind to say about him." Chris puffed his jaws and blew out the air. "No, little brother, there's no way she'd want to go back to him—not if she's sane anyway. There has to be some other explanation. There has to be."

"Then I'd sure like to know what it is."

Mitch felt that presence behind him again—the same one he had felt the night before. Only this time when he turned around, he saw his worst nightmare staring back at him.

"I can answer that."

Eddie Williams stood in the doorway with his gaze fixed upon Mitch. His eyes moved for a moment toward Dana, and he wrung his hands nervously in front of him. Meeting Mitch's icy stare once more, he stepped cautiously into the room and stopped about a foot away from him.

"What are you doing here? What's more, what were you doing with my wife last night? I thought I told you before to stay away from her."

Chris took a step closer to his brother as Mitch stood up and took a few steps toward Eddie. Chris decided to stay a few inches behind him hoping to keep him in check.

"I came to see how Dana is. I don't remember much after the accident, but I feel responsible somehow. I didn't think you'd be here."

Mitch tightened his jaw and slowly clenched his fists at his sides. Chris noticed the gesture and moved even closer to his brother. "Why wouldn't I be here? She's my wife, and she's carrying my child. Where else would I be?"

Hearing the tone of Mitch's voice, Jake stepped into the room. "What's going on here, Mitchell? Who is this?"

Mitch chose not to answer. Instead, he kept his focus on Eddie. "I asked you a question. Why were you with Dana last night?"

Eddie swallowed hard and put up his hands as if he were trying to ward off Mitch's potential attack. "Cool down. I wasn't *with* her. I was out with a couple of buddies of mine down at Kirby's, and she came wandering into the place. I was surprised to see her in a bar because I know that's just not somewhere Dana would ever go. When I looked closer, I noticed she looked sick. I heard her ask the bartender if she could use the phone to call someone, and then she just collapsed." Eddie glanced down at Mitch's hands, and his voice suddenly became shaky. "They were going to call an ambulance, but I told them that I knew her and that I could probably get her to the hospital quicker than the paramedics could get there. Kirby's is only a ten-minute drive from here. So, I carried her to my car and headed out. It was like twelve-thirty, almost one, and the streets were dead; so I didn't bother stopping for any lights. I just slowed down a little; and if nothing was coming, I went through. The truck came out of nowhere...." Eddie sighed as he glanced at Dana again and then back to Mitch before lowering his eyes. "That's all I remember until I woke up downstairs."

Mitch took off his glasses; and after rubbing his eyes, he replaced them. His expression was cold and heartless as he glared at Eddie standing before him. "You said you were at Kirby's. Obviously, you were drinking. You put my pregnant wife in your car and attempted to drive her somewhere when you'd been drinking?" Mitch's temper was beginning to show, and his voice was getting louder.

Eddie took a cautious step back. "Hey, dude, take it easy. I threw back a few, sure, but I wasn't drunk."

"How many is a 'few'?"

"I don't know—maybe four or five and a couple shots. I knew what I was doing."

Mitch could feel the heat of the fire that was now burning in his eyes. Before his older brother had a chance to step in, Mitch had Eddie's shirt in his hand. His fist was drawn and ready to strike. "Look at her! If you knew what you were doing, why is my wife lying in that bed? Why don't I know if my child is even going to survive? Why did you try driving her here when you'd been drinking?"

Eddie put his hands up. "Look, man, I was only trying to help her. I had no clue she was pregnant." He gave Mitch a snide smile. "Wait a minute—I get it now. I knew there was more to the story besides what I'd been told. I could hardly believe she could fall for a guy for real and want to marry him after only three months. She *had* to marry you because you knocked her up, didn't you?" He chuckled. "Five years, and she never gave in to me. Guess money *can* buy you love after all."

The accusation was the final straw for Mitch. He tugged on Eddie, pulled him closer, and got right in his face. "I thought you must be an idiot the day you left Dana, but now I know it for a fact. You'd better be glad you're in I.C.U., you jerk, because when I'm finished with you, you're going to need it!"

Just as Mitch drew back his fist, Chris grabbed it and placed his arm around his brother's chest to pull him back. Jake did the same with Eddie, releasing him from Mitch's grip and turning him toward the door. "If you know what's good for you, young man, you'll leave now and never look back." Eddie pulled his shirt back into place and started to walk away. Just as he reached the door, he turned and glared at Mitch.

"You might think you're all tough, rich boy, but you'd better watch your back. Be warned—no one threatens Eddie Williams and gets away with it!"

It took every ounce of strength Chris had to hold Mitch in place and keep him from following Eddie down the hallway. Once Eddie was out of sight, Jake stepped in front of Mitch and placed his hands on his shoulders. "Let him go, Chris." Chris obeyed his father, and Jake tightened his grip as he watched Mitch's eyes still staring into the hallway. "It's all right, son. Settle down. He's gone now."

Mitch freed himself from his father and fell into the chair again. He took off his glasses and laid them on the table next to Dana's bed and placed his face in his hands. As they had the night before, the tears refused to stay inside. He let them come not caring who saw them or what they would think. His father stood beside him, pulled him over to lean against him, and let him have his cry.

I opened my eyes slowly. The pain in my head was almost more than I could bear. "Jim, is that you? Where am I?"

Jim stepped closer to the bed and smiled. "You're in the hospital, Dana. You had an accident last night. Do you remember?"

I tried hard to think back, but my mind was blank at that moment. "No, not really," I replied as I looked around at the machines surrounding my bed. "What are all these things?"

"We're monitoring a few things, dear. This one controls your IV; the one to your immediate right monitors your heart rate, and this one is for the baby," Jim replied as he pointed to each one.

I glanced down to the monitor strapped to my stomach. "Is the baby okay?" I asked.

"Well, the heartbeat is a little stronger than it was last night, but Dr. Bradley wants to run a few more tests this afternoon to see exactly where things stand. Apparently, you were having some contractions last night, but we were able to administer some medication to stop them. Do you remember having the contractions, Dana?"

Unfortunately, that pain was still very fresh in my mind. "Yes, that part of things I do remember. It was the worst pain I think I've ever had in my life. I tried to make it to the hospital, but the pain kept getting worse and worse; so I looked for somewhere to stop so that I could call someone to come and get me. The only place I could find was a bar on the corner of Franklin. All I remember after that was asking the bartender if I could use the phone. Then everything went black."

Jim started to relay the details of the accident but thought better of it. "Well, we're going to take good care of that little one. Don't you worry."

I nodded. "What about me? My head really hurts. In fact, all of me hurts. It feels like it's hard to breathe."

He smiled. "I'm sure you will hurt for a while considering all the bumps and bruises you have." He listed my injuries one by one. By the time he finished, I was flabbergasted. "In spite of all that, I'd say you were actually pretty lucky."

Just then, another thought occurred to me. "Where's Mitchell? Does he even know I'm here?"

Jim gave me a strange look. "Yes, he does, Dana. He's here. In fact, he's been here all night. He refused to leave and," Jim paused and chuckled a little, "he actually threatened to take me on if I didn't let him stay. It took a heavy dose of persuasion to even get him out of the room right now."

"Guess he must be feeling guilty, huh?"

Jim decided to ignore the comment. "I asked him to step out for a few minutes while I got things situated in here. I think he went down the hall to the lounge for a cup of coffee."

"Well, he can take his time. I'm not much interested in seeing him," I replied.

At that moment, I saw Mitch step into my line of vision just outside the door of the room. He turned slowly; and when he saw through the window that I was awake, he smiled. Noticing that I wasn't returning his expression, his smile faded; and he looked at Jim as if to ask if he should enter. Jim looked at him and then at me.

"Dana, is it okay if I have him come in?" Jim asked.

"I told you before that I really don't care to see him," I replied softly. I closed my eyes and sank back into my pillow.

Jim glanced back at Mitch whose face was now filled with disillusion. "I know you're upset with him, dear, but the man has been worried sick about you all night. Will you at least let him come in and say hello? I know it would make him feel better. He's very upset by all of this."

I sighed deeply. "What about the way I feel? Don't you think it upset me to know that my husband looked me in the eye and lied to me, not just once, but at least three times? Don't you think it upset me to watch him allow another woman to put her hands all over him? Don't you think it upset me to see the smile on his face while she did it? If he wasn't attracted to her, why was he letting her come on to him like that? Tell me, why should I give a rat's tail about how he feels? He certainly didn't take my feelings into consideration, now did he?"

Jim looked dumbfounded by my comments. "Dana, I don't really know about all those things. What I do know, however, is that Mitch really loves you."

"You couldn't prove that by me right now," I said. "Not after last night. I had the wool pulled over my eyes once, Jim. I'll be darned if I'm going to stand by and let it happen again. I know what I saw, regardless of whatever excuse he wants to make. I didn't recognize it with Eddie, but I'm smarter now."

"Dana, how do you know he wasn't telling you the truth last night?"

I couldn't believe he was asking that question. Was this guy for real?

"You're right, Jim. How do I know? Well, I guess the only way I can answer that is by saying that he wasn't truthful to me about the whole ordeal from the beginning. Why should I think he's being truthful now? She was being way too friendly to be just an acquaintance. I can hardly believe that he wasn't enjoying the attention. Mitch loves being the center of attention." I closed my eyes once more. "Please tell him to go and leave me alone. He can be free to do whatever he wants."

Jim lowered his eyes and sighed. "Fine, Dana. I'll tell him you'd rather be alone right now. I'll come back a little later." He turned and exited the room.

Mitch glanced at Dana through the window. "I was close enough to hear the last part of that. Just as I suspected. She doesn't want to see me."

"Unfortunately, you're right. Perhaps it wouldn't be such a bad idea if you went downstairs and joined Chris and your dad for a cup of coffee. That'll give her a chance to think things through before you get back, and maybe she'll be more receptive then."

Mitch sighed heavily. "You know, the more I think about this, Jim, the angrier I'm getting. She's constantly accusing me—wrongfully I might add—of either cheating on her or wanting to cheat on her. Maybe I should just go in there and deal with it."

Jim placed his hand on Mitch's shoulder. "Actually, I don't know if that's such a wise idea right now, Mitchell. She's upset and hurt by what's happened between the two of you, not to mention that she's also trying to deal with everything involving the accident. Why don't you come with me and leave her alone for a while? I think you'll be better off if you do. Come on. I'll walk with you."

Mitch dropped his head and then brought his eyes back up slightly to look at Dana. "All right, Jim. I'll go," he said softly.

The two men walked silently to the elevator, and Jim pushed the button to summon it. "You know you are doing the right thing, Mitchell. I really believe you are."

Mitch glanced back toward Dana's room and hesitated before he stepped onto the elevator behind Jim. "I don't know what's right anymore."

Engrossed in his thoughts, Mitch began to search his soul for the confidence he would need to take the next step into his future.

Chapter 7

Her name was Eleanor Compton, R.N., or so the nametag read anyway. She was an older woman probably in her late 60's, and I assumed she'd been a nurse most of her life. She seemed a bit harsh at first impression by the way she carried herself, but her smile was warm and welcoming. When she spoke, her tone was soft and soothing which convinced me that she was truly a kind soul. Eleanor placed a warm hand upon my forehead much the way my Grammy used to do when she was checking me for a fever. She pushed a few buttons on one of the monitors and turned to me.

"Is there anything at all I can get for you, Mrs. Tarrington? Would you like to try eating something?"

I offered a smile in response. "No, thank you. I'm really not very hungry."

"Maybe later then." She glanced around the room as if she were expecting someone else to be there. "Where did that handsome young husband of yours run off to? Didn't think he would step one foot out of this room. The little sweetheart was here all night long right next to your bed. Dr. Macklin said he refused to leave you." She patted my hand. "Bless his heart; he was so worried about you. I started to come in last night, but he was sitting there holding your hand and offering up some words to the Good Lord. He looked like his heart was breaking with those tears coming down his cheeks. I didn't want to interrupt him, so I waited until he fell asleep. Might have embarrassed him had he known I saw. I didn't want him to think I was spying on him or anything like that. I heard him singing to you, too. He has a pretty voice." She pulled the blanket up around me and smoothed it out. "I'm sure he wasn't too comfortable sitting in that chair all night, but I guess it was more important for him to be near you." She smiled sweetly. "You should count yourself blessed, dear. You can definitely tell that one loves you. I'd say he's a keeper."

I turned away from her, not wanting her to see the tears starting down my own cheeks. I felt a lump come up in my throat, and I choked it back down. Somehow, Eleanor's words spoke to my heart in a way that I just couldn't explain. Maybe it wasn't guilt that he felt after all. Maybe it really was love.

Mitch took a deep breath and poised himself for the inevitable. He tried hard to battle the thoughts that were racing into his mind. He couldn't allow himself to think about anything but right here, right now.

Their life together up to that point didn't matter. All that mattered was Dana and her happiness from here on out. If that meant letting her go, then that was what he had to do.

He stepped into the room, and I turned my head to look at him. His eyes were so filled with hurt and pain that they had no sparkle left in them. He was biting his lip and breathing deeply—I imagined in an effort not to break down in front of me. He straightened his shoulders and took a few steps, stopping at the foot of my bed.

"What are you doing here? I thought I told Jim to tell you to go away."

"I know you don't want me here, but I need to talk to you. I need for you to please listen to what I have to say." He paused, took another deep breath, and continued. "Just now I was downstairs thinking about everything that's happened and wondering how I might be able to come up here and make it right with you. Then I realized that no matter what I might say, you won't believe me anyway. You'll never believe that I never meant to hurt you, that I've never cheated on you, or that you are the only woman I truly love and desire. I'm to blame for that mistrust, Dana. If I had been honest with you from the beginning, if I had told you about the strip club and everything that happened that night when I had the chance, things might have been different. I was a coward, and I took the coward's way out by lying to you instead. I destroyed your trust in me, and now I have to live with the consequences of my actions." He closed his eyes for a moment, and I could see the internal struggle starting to emerge on his face. He opened his eyes and looked right at me. "I love you, and I want nothing more than to live all the days of my life with you. But, more than that, I want you to be happy. I want you to have the kind of life you deserve and to have someone who will love and care for you and treat you the way you deserve to be treated. I don't think...." He swallowed hard, and I heard his voice crack. "I don't think that person is me. All I seem to be able to do is bring pain into your life. I don't want that for you; and I know after last night, you don't want that either. Therefore, I've come to say goodbye. I've come to tell you that I'm going to give you the chance to find the happiness you desire and deserve. I'm giving you the chance to have the things you want out of life." He closed his eyes again as he struggled to bring out his words. "I will always love you, and I hope you find what your heart desires."

He turned to walk away, paused, and turned slightly toward me. His voice was very soft. "You don't have to tell the baby about me if you don't want to. However, I would like to know when it's born and that you're both all right, if it isn't too much for me to ask."

Somewhere in the innermost part of my soul where all things I held precious dwelled, I felt a stirring like nothing I had ever felt before. Eleanor had seen it; and now through his words, I was seeing it as well. Despite anything I might have believed to the contrary, his love for me was real. Just then he had proven it to me. He was selflessly giving me the chance to live the kind of life that he thought I wanted to live. It didn't matter what he wanted or how it might affect him in the end. He was willing to sacrifice a life with me if he thought I would be happier without him. I felt the tears start to flow down my face and fall softly onto the blanket.

"Don't you remember? I told you that you have to be there to watch."

He had started to walk away, but my words caused him to stop and turn around with a questioning look in his eyes. "Do you want me to be?"

"More than anything."

Mitch came to me and took me gently into his arms, holding me as tightly as he could without causing me discomfort. "Don't cry, sweetheart. It's all right. Everything's all right," he said soothingly. He held me for what seemed like a lifetime, just letting us be near each other, allowing our hearts to reconnect, and our pain to disappear. Finally pulling away, he wiped my tears with his thumb and softly placed his hand on my cheek.

"I was so afraid, Dana. I was so afraid you'd just let me go," he said as he struggled to hold back his own tears.

"In my heart, I never really wanted us to be apart. When I saw you with Gloria last night, I thought that's what *you* wanted; so I decided to give you a way out. Besides, after I watched the two of you standing together at the club and the way she was coming on to you—not to mention the fact that you seemed to be enjoying it—I was of the mind that something was definitely going on. There was no way I was going to stand by and let myself go through the pain again that Eddie had caused me." I choked back the tears that were threatening to spill out of my eyes. "I thought you didn't love me anymore. I didn't know what I had done wrong, but I really believed you didn't want me."

Mitch shook his head. "No, baby, you did nothing wrong. Honestly, you didn't. Everything that happened was my fault. I should have been honest with you from the beginning, but I was so afraid that I'd lose you if I told you the truth." He took my hand and rubbed the top of it gently with his thumb. "Gloria means nothing to me. You are the only woman I love and the only woman I have any desire to be with. I mean that."

I lowered my eyes from his. "If that's true, then why were you enjoying her company so much last night? Your smile could have lit up the entire room!"

He gently tilted my chin up and looked deeply into my eyes. "Honey, listen to me. I wasn't enjoying her company at all. In fact, I was hoping she'd go away so I could come and find you. I didn't know how to get rid of her, so I just stood there like a total idiot and let her do her thing. I'm sorry that I made you feel the way you did." He placed his other hand on top of mine and held it tightly. "I have loved you from the moment I first saw you, Dana, and that has only grown deeper with time. I know I haven't done a very good job with showing you how I feel, but I hope you'll let me try to make it up to you. I promise, sweetheart, I won't let you down again." His face held a soft smile, but his eyes reflected a hint of the guilt and shame that still lingered in his heart.

He brought my hand to his lips and kissed it tenderly. "I know you think you can't trust me, but I want the chance to prove otherwise. Will you give me that chance, Dana? Can you forgive me?" His expression changed, and he looked like his entire future hung on my answer.

I smiled at him, and the tension left his face. "Yes, I can forgive you, but only if you can forgive me. I'm sorry that I acted the way I did, but I don't want to lose you, Mitch. That's why I got so upset when I saw you with Gloria. It really scares me to see you with someone else. I'm afraid you're going to find someone who's more appealing to you, and you're going to leave me."

He shook his head. "I understand, baby, but you don't have to worry. I'm not going to. I promise." He gripped my hand a little tighter and leaned closer to me. "Dana, there's something you need to understand. In both of my chosen professions, I'm in the public eye. I'm going to encounter a lot of different people—many of them women—and some who may even be attractive. Just because I talk to them amicably doesn't mean I'm attracted to any of them or that I want to run off with any of them and have a torrid affair. I will never cheat on you. I could never live with myself if I did that to you, and I would probably shoot myself if I ever even thought about it. You're the only girl for me now and always. Nothing can change that." He rubbed the top of my hand with his thumb. "As for my forgiving you, there's nothing to forgive. I deserved everything I got. All I want to do is to move on from all this. Are you willing to do that?"

"Yes, I am," I replied. "But, there is something I need to know."

Without letting go of my hand, Mitch pulled the chair over and sat back down. "Anything, love. What is it?"

I was somewhat embarrassed by my question, but I needed to ask. "When you saw Gloria naked, Mitch, did it turn you on?"

He smiled at me with love in his eyes and shook his head. "No, not really. Not the way you do." Then I saw that old familiar smirk coming out. "I have to say, I believe parts of her aren't even real, if you get my drift. Oh, and technically, she wasn't naked. She was wearing a g-string."

I gave him a look. "My mistake," I said sarcastically.

He laughed and then leaned over and placed his cheek against mine. "I won't lie and say that I don't think Gloria's pretty because she is. But, no one comes as close to being as beautiful to me as you are." He pulled away just far enough to look into my eyes. "The whole time I was at Caroway's, all I could think about was you. In fact, you were the only thing on my mind the entire night. I started to come up and see you when the guys dropped me off to get my car, but I didn't want to wake you. I even picked up the phone to call you as I climbed into bed that night. I honestly don't know sometimes how I manage to function because you are constantly on my mind, day and night, night and day. That's how much I love you. I can't exist without you."

My heart melted as I looked into his eyes, and I watched as the old familiar sparkle began to return. "I can't exist without you either. And I never want to try."

He bent down to kiss me softly and let his lips linger near mine for a moment before moving away. As he did, I caught a glimpse of my reflection in the lens of his glasses. I placed a trembling hand on my cheek, lightly fingering the line of stitches adorning it. The way I looked at him must have gained his attention because he looked at me with a panicky expression.

"Honey, what's the matter? Is something wrong?"

"Mitchell, what happened to me? How did I get in an accident, and how did I get here?"

Mitch pulled the chair close to my bed and took my hand in his. He began to explain everything that had happened with regard to Eddie—taking extra care not to leave out any details. As he spoke, I could feel that bitter taste in my mouth that came whenever I thought of Eddie Williams, which thankfully wasn't that often. I had to smile at the animated way Mitch told of their confrontation in my room that morning and replayed the scene for me step by step. I listened intently and absorbed every word. As he ended his story, he clenched his jaw as if just talking about it brought back the anger.

"I really wanted to deck him, Dana. If Chris hadn't stopped me, I would have flattened him right there. He could have killed you!" He took a deep breath and softened his tone. "There is one other thing I would like to know. Why didn't you call me last night when you started having the pain?"

I cast my eyes down from his and felt somewhat ashamed. "At first, I didn't want to. I was so angry and hurt by everything that had happened that the last place I wanted to be was around you. I'm sorry to say that now, but it's true. When the pain got worse, I realized that I needed to do something. I did try to call you at Chris's, but no one picked up the phone; so I decided to drive myself to the hospital. The pain was too much for me to bear, and I didn't know if I could make it there on my own. I stopped at that bar to ask if I could use the phone because I wanted to try calling you again. That's all I remember."

He smiled in an understanding kind of way. "I would have been there for you. You know that, don't you?" His voice became very quiet. "I'm sorry I wasn't. If I hadn't screwed up the way I did, maybe none of this would have happened." He took a deep breath, and the irritation returned to his tone. "I still can't believe that creep did this to you. What's worse is that he doesn't seem to feel the least little bit of remorse about it. You don't know how hard it was to keep from punching his lights out!"

"You know, as much as I hate violence, I think I would have enjoyed seeing you do that," I replied smugly. "As far as that threat, I wouldn't worry about it. Eddie's a wimp. He was only trying to see if he could scare you."

He chuckled. "Well, all I know is that I was pretty hot. In fact, I still am."

I smiled into the eyes that captured my heart. "Yes, sweetie, you certainly are."

A short while later, Eleanor returned to my room and greeted me cheerfully. "How about a little breakfast now, Mrs. Tarrington, and then I'll help you get freshened up so you feel better." She turned to Mitch and offered him a smile as well. "There you are. I wondered where you'd run off to earlier when I popped in here. How are you this morning?"

"I'm fine, thanks," Mitch replied softly. He glanced my way with a twinkle in his eyes. "Actually, I'm great."

"That's wonderful." She leaned down close to me and shot Mitch a glance out of the corner of her eye. "He certainly is a cutie, isn't he?" I smiled and nodded as Mitch blushed. "Now, what can I get for you? I hear the pancakes are pretty good, and I see you don't have any restrictions on your diet."

I gave her an unsettled look. "I'm really not feeling very hungry right at the moment. In fact, I'm starting to feel a little queasy. I thought this child was going to give me a break this morning, but I guess I must have been wrong."

She smiled at me sympathetically. "I understand, but it really will help if you try to get something in your stomach. How about some cereal and toast?"

I nodded. "I'll try," I said reluctantly.

She left the room, and I looked at Mitch. He was unshaven, and his shirt was slightly wrinkled from trying to sleep in the chair all night. His hair was slightly messed up, and he looked tired. Yet to me, I couldn't imagine a more wonderful sight in the world at that moment. He yawned and stretched and then settled down into the chair just a little more. Noticing my eyes upon him, he smiled.

"I'm sure I look quite disheveled right now," he said.

"You look adorable," I replied. "You always do. I'm sure you must be tired though. I can't imagine that you were able to sleep very well sitting up in a chair last night." I reached out for his hand. "Why don't you go home for a while and get some rest? You don't need to stay here with me all day. Other than hurting like the dickens, I'm all right."

"Well, for starters, it might be a little hard to get home without a car. Chris drove me here last night," he said. "I feel fine. I would much rather be right here with you."

"I know, honey, but you need to shower and shave. I'm sure you haven't eaten anything, and you can't go without sleeping. Why don't you call someone to pick you up on the way home from church? You can come back to see me later after you clean up and take a nap."

His face took on a stubborn expression, which was becoming all too familiar to me. "Dana, I said I'm fine, and I don't want to go anywhere. I don't want you to be here alone. Now, you rest until they bring your breakfast. When it comes, I want you to eat. You can't expect to get well unless you keep up your strength."

"I thought I was the assertive one in this relationship," I said. I put a hint of a whine into my voice.

"Not anymore. Now, it's my turn," he said with a grin. "Somebody has to keep that rebel spirit of yours in line. If I know you—and I'd say I do—you'll go home thinking you can do everything you did before."

"Why wouldn't I be able to? I still have plenty of parts that work just fine."

He chuckled. "Sweetheart, that's not fair. Now, you have me thinking...."

It took me a moment to understand him, but I caught on and giggled. "Mitch, you're terrible!"

"But, I know you love it!"

An hour or so passed by, and we found ourselves inside a dimly lit exam room. The technician was carefully applying a warm gel to my stomach as Mitch watched her intently. He stood by the side of my bed, and he held my hand tightly. I smiled up at him; and he returned my look, shifting his eyes once again to the technician.

"Will this tell us if there's anything wrong with the baby?" he asked.

"It will definitely be a help to the doctor in making that diagnosis," the technician said. She smiled and turned to look at us. "Ready to see some pictures of your baby?" she asked.

Mitch's smile could have lit up the world. "Absolutely!" he quipped happily.

She carefully began to move the wand over my swollen abdomen, and then stopped to move the monitor so that we could both see it. She pointed to what looked like a tiny speck on the screen inside a perfect circle. "That's your little one there, and this is the amniotic sack. It helps protect the baby," she said. "I'll print out a few pictures for you to take along."

"What's the little dot that seems to be flashing right there?" I asked.

"That's the heart beating," she replied.

Captivated by what he was seeing, Mitch fixed his eyes completely on the monitor. "I can't believe it, Dana. Look at that. It's so amazing," he said.

"It's a miracle, Mitchell. Nothing less than a miracle." I felt him squeeze my hand.

She moved the wand around some more, printed out a few pictures, and handed them to Mitch. "Here you go, Daddy. You can put these in your wallet," she teased.

"No, I'm planning to frame them," he said proudly. "That's after I show them off to everyone first."

"I need to show these photos to the doctor so I'll have you wait here for a few minutes and rest. If you need anything at all before Dr. Bradley comes in, just press the red button above the table there."

Mitch was still staring at the ultrasound pictures he was holding—seemingly lost in his own little world. "Honey, did you hear what she said?"

He shook his head, bringing himself back to reality. "Uh, oh, I'm sorry. What was that?"

I smiled. "Never mind."

Dr. Bradley stepped into the room and shook Mitch's hand. "Hello again, Mr. Tarrington."

"Hi, and please call me Mitch," he replied.

"Fine, Mitch. I just had a look at the ultrasound, and I have to say I have some mixed feelings about things."

I reached out for Mitch's hand and held on tightly. "Is something wrong, doctor?" I asked.

He sighed. "Well, I'm not exactly sure how to tell you this...."

Mitch looked down at me and placed his other hand on top of mine. "Go ahead and tell us please," he said.

I watched as a slow smile came to the doctor's face. "Let me say first that—in spite of all you've been through, Dana—everything looks just fine," he started. "However, I picked up something on the third picture that the technician wasn't sure about at first, so she didn't want to say anything until she spoke with me."

I gripped Mitch's hand even tighter. "Please, doctor. Tell us what the problem is," I pleaded.

"The problem is I think the two of you need to start preparing yourselves for double trouble. Dana, you're pregnant with twins."

The color drained from Mitch's face, and Dr. Bradley caught him just before he hit the floor.

"Mitch, can you hear me? Come on. Stay with me," Dr. Bradley said as he waved a capsule of smelling salts under Mitch's nose.

Mitch shook his head and started to sit up. "What happened?" he asked.

"Guess I shocked you a little more than I thought I would," the doctor said with a smile.

"Honey, are you okay?" I asked. "Say something, Mitch."

He looked at me, then to the doctor, and back to me. "Twins. We're having twins."

"That's what it looks like. Here, let me show you how I made that determination." Dr. Bradley pointed to something on one of the pictures—slightly to the right of and behind the other baby. "What I'd like to do is take a listen to see if we can pick up that heartbeat. I need to make sure that little one didn't suffer any trauma." He picked up a phone and dialed an extension. "Gina, Dr. Bradley. Set up a room on maternity for Mrs. Tarrington, special care. I'd like her up there instead of here in I.C.U. Set up for a monitor as well. We'll be up there in about ten minutes." He hung up the phone and turned back to us. "Don't worry about a thing. We're going to make sure everything is fine."

He came close to Mitch once again and touched him on the shoulder. "Feeling better?"

"Yeah, I guess so," he replied slowly. He still seemed a little out of sorts.

"You sit there until I come back, okay? I won't be long." With that, the doctor exited the room.

I turned to Mitch. "Mitchell, we're having two babies—not just one—two. I don't believe this. Pinch me to make sure I'm not dreaming."

He shook his head. "If you are, I'm in the dream with you," he said. "Twins. Totally unreal."

"I guess that might explain why I've been so sick." I turned to him with a smile and tried to lighten the mood. "You really don't do anything small, do you?"

He began to smirk. "First time and I produce twins. Wow!"

"Give me a break," I said sarcastically.

He continued his little ego trip. "What? Are you questioning my role in this?" he asked.

"Didn't you ever take biology? In case you don't know, the determination of twins has nothing to do with the father. The mother makes that happen. You know, when the egg splits, dear?"

The smile slowly left his face. "Yeah, that may be, but I still had to be there to make it happen, now didn't I?"

I rolled my eyes at him as Dr. Bradley came back in. "How're you doing over there, Dad? Are you all right now?"

"I think I'm still in shock," Mitch replied. "Are you sure you didn't misread that thing?"

Dr. Bradley smiled. "That's always a possibility, but I really don't believe so."

Mitch started to get up from the chair, but thought better of it and sat back down. "I just can't believe all this. We've only known each other for six months, been married for three, and now here we are preparing to become the parents of twins. I know I have to be dreaming."

"Seems like a lot in such a short time, I'm sure," Dr. Bradley started. "However, there are plenty of resources available here at the hospital to help you. From what Jim's told me, you have a rather large family to support you as well. I have the utmost confidence that the two of you will be remarkable parents. Two children really aren't any more difficult than one child. No need to worry."

Mitch and I exchanged looks; and if I read his face correctly, he wasn't totally convinced either.

Mitch stared out the window trying to sort the thoughts jumbled up inside his brain. Twins. Why did that word bring about such a sense of fear in him and yet so much joy? He didn't have any explanation for it other than the fact that somehow the addition of a second child changed his entire outlook on things. Suddenly, many of the decisions they had already made were no longer going to work. Although Dana was convinced that they could easily accommodate a child in their current home, there was no way a one-bedroom apartment was going to be sufficient now. He'd been reluctant about one crib in their bedroom, but he downright refused to allow two of them. He made a mental note to start perusing the newspaper again for houses or at least a two-bedroom place to get them by for a while longer.

As he turned to look at Dana resting peacefully, he couldn't help but wonder how this turn of events would affect her in the upcoming months. She had already been enduring relentless sickness, and now she was facing recovery and rehabilitation from the accident. She certainly wasn't going to heal overnight. Although he had only been teasing her about having a "rebel spirit," in reality, it was very true. There was no doubt that she would try her best to keep going and retain her independence despite any continuing illness, pain, or restrictions that might be placed on her as a result of the accident. He wondered as well if Dr. Bradley might put her on bed-rest due to the contractions she'd experienced. He tried to perish that thought. Just trying to get her to slow down now was hard enough—let alone trying to keep her in bed for the next six months. He was certain that he'd have to call for backup if that happened. Perhaps he could get his mom to come over for a few hours every day to sit with her and arrange with Jimmy to take some of his hours at the bistro for a while. As far as rehearsals, well, he might have to give those up altogether. In fact, he may have to give up the band itself altogether. He turned back toward the window with a sigh. That wouldn't go over well with her either. She'd already made her feelings on that subject perfectly clear to him. What was he supposed to do? His top priority was to make sure he took care of her and the babies. Yes, he'd promised her that he wouldn't quit the band, but he'd promised God he'd take care of his family. In his mind, the decision of which promise he needed to keep was a no-brainer. He would just have to make her understand his reasoning the best that he could and let that be good enough.

He stepped away from the window, pulled a chair up next to her bed, and sat down to watch her sleep. She looked like an absolute angel to him. Just a few hours earlier he had prepared to let her go and to forsake a future with her in order to give her the kind of life he thought she desired. Much to his surprise, she expressed that she had done the same thing for him; in telling him to go the night before, she had thought she was giving him the chance to be happy. He pondered that thought for a moment, and it caused him to smile. It was clear to him now that she loved him as much as he loved her. If that was true, then it was a love that would never die.

Dana began to stir slightly, and it startled him because he had started to drift off himself. His first inclination was to glance at each of the monitors surrounding her and to make sure there was no cause for alarm. Seeing nothing disturbing, he stood up and adjusted her blanket, kissed her softly on the forehead, and began to stroke her hair lovingly.

"Mitch?"

"Yeah, baby, I'm right here. You just rest."

"I had a dream—about the babies," I said softly.

"Was it a nice dream?"

I nodded weakly, and my head began to throb again. "Yeah, it was. I saw them, Mitch. They were so tiny, so delicate, so...."

Mitch smiled as he listened to her words trailing off telling him that she had drifted back to sleep. "Go back to them, love. Have sweet dreams. You deserve them."

Keeping a hand on top of her head, he used the other to move the chair closer to the bed and then sat back down. The room was almost completely silent. The only sounds came from the faint beeps of the monitors and Dana's slow and steady breathing. As he sat there, his mind drifted back to days gone by and the memories of many nights his mother would sit by his bed comforting him by softly stroking his hair—much the way he was doing for Dana right now. He smiled as he remembered the lullaby she would often sing to him as a small boy. Placing one hand on Dana's stomach, he began to sing.

"Hush, little baby, don't say a word. Daddy's gonna buy you a mocking bird. And, if that mocking bird don't sing...."

"You know, I never quite figured out why someone would buy a mocking bird for a baby. Kinda dumb, if you ask me." Mitch looked up to see his brother standing in the doorway.

"It's only a song, you knucklehead. And what are you doing back here anyway? You should be spending the afternoon with your family."

"I am. You and Dana." Chris walked to where his brother sat and playfully gave him a gentle shove. Pulling up a chair, he sat down and handed Mitch a small brown paper bag. "Here. Trudy made you some lunch. We assumed you hadn't left this room long enough to eat anything today."

Mitch smiled and eagerly plunged into the bag, withdrew an egg salad sandwich, and took a large bite. "This is great. Thanks."

"No problem. I brought your car and your suitcase back, too. I figured I could hitch a ride home with Jim later. Or, maybe you can just drop me off on your way." He only pointed his eyes in Mitch's direction and gave him a sideways grin.

Mitch opened the can of soda Trudy had packed and took a long drink as he shook his head. "Sorry, but I'm staying right here. Guess Jim's your ticket out of here today." He pointed to Dana. "I'm not leaving her, Chris. Nice try."

Chris sighed as he gazed at the obstinate look on his brother's face. He tried to soften the tone of his voice with the hope that he might be more convincing. "You need to get some rest. And a shower and a shave don't look like they'd be out of the question either. Don't you want to be at your best for your girl?"

Mitch took another bite of his sandwich and looked smugly at Chris. "That's the beauty of true love, Christopher. You don't have to be at your best all the time. She doesn't care what I look like. All that matters is that we're together." He took another drink of his soda and wiped his mouth with the back of his hand. "And besides, now that I have my suitcase, I'll ask Jim if I can use a shower here to clean up a little."

"Mitchell, it'll be okay if you leave her for a little while, buddy. I'm sure she won't mind."

"She might not, but I will." He stood up and placed the back of his hand tenderly on her forehead. "This morning I was all set to let her go. I thought she'd be happier without me; and even though it was the last thing I wanted, I told her that I'd go and leave her alone. But, you know what?" He smiled softly at Dana. "She told me to stay. She wants me. Me—the total screw-up who can't ever seem to get it right. I don't deserve that kind of love, Chris, but she's willing to give it to me anyway. She sees something in me that I just can't see myself. Because of that—because she loves me that much—I'm not leaving her side. It's my fault that all this happened. I've let her down one too many times, and I'm not going to do it again. When she walks out of here, then so will I. Until then, my place is right here." He took a deep breath and swallowed the lump that had come up in his throat, not wanting to show his emotions again in front of Chris. "I love her more than anything, and I want to make sure that she never doubts that again."

Chris listened to his brother's words. Knowing there was no sense in pushing the issue, he nodded in response. "Okay, little brother.

Have it your way." He settled back in the chair and crossed his arms. "There is one other thing I brought along with me— something I think you might be interested in seeing." Reaching into his back pocket, he withdrew a folded piece of paper and handed it to Mitch. Mitch took it and studied it intently before raising his eyes to look at Chris.

"Where did you get this?"

"It pays to have legal connections in the family. Paul asked me to pass it along to you. It seems as if Mr. Williams won't be getting the opportunity to cause any more accidents—for the next couple of months, at least."

Mitch tapped his finger on the police report and clenched his jaw. "His blood alcohol level was almost three points over the legal limit, and he 'knew what he was doing'?" He shuddered at the thoughts beginning to sink into his mind. "My God, Chris. He could have killed her. He could have killed all of them! What in the Sam Hill was he thinking?"

"That's just it, Mitch. He wasn't. Paul said the police chief was actually on the scene, and he's the one who ordered the blood test. I guess they were going to pay Eddie a visit this afternoon and make the arrest. Not only did they get him on DUI, but also for reckless operation of a vehicle, failure to control, and running a traffic light. Apparently, this is his second DUI." He reached out and placed his fingertip at the bottom of the paper as if to point out the fine print. "Take a look at what he's facing: thirty days in jail, suspension of his license for six months, and A.A. Paul said the best Eddie can hope for here is that the judge will trade the jail time for community service or a hefty fine. As I understand it, the rest is non-negotiable." He patted his brother on the leg and smiled. "At least we'll have the satisfaction of knowing that he's getting some justice."

Mitch nodded slowly and turned his face toward Dana. His heart ached for her. "Some—but in my book, not nearly enough."

Chris suddenly tilted his head to one side and gave Mitch an inquisitive stare. "Hang on, little brother—you said 'all' of them. Don't you mean 'both' of them? Or...." He began to let a little grin surface. "Is there something you haven't told me?"

Mitch sank back in his chair; and although he tried to act nonchalant, his pride was more than evident in his tone. "Oh, I must have forgotten. We found out this morning that we're having twins."

Before Mitch had a chance to take his next breath, Chris had him out of the chair—and about three inches above the floor—with his arms locked tightly around him in a bear hug. "For crying out loud, little brother! That isn't something you just forget! Congratulations, man! This is fantastic news!"

"Thanks—now could you put me down, please? I can't breathe!"

Chris laughed and set Mitch down again as he released his grip. "You are really something else, Mitchell Tarrington. Married with twins all in less than a year. Unbelievable!"

Mitch chuckled and stretched out his arms with the palms of his hands facing upward. "Hey, when you got it, you got it!"

Chris grabbed Mitch in a headlock and rubbed his knuckles over the top of his head as the two grinned, and their eyes shined with the brotherly love they shared.

The next week passed slowly, and the days and nights seemed to blend in endless succession. Although everyone who stopped by to visit, as well as Mitch, did their best to keep my spirits up, I realized during this time that I was tired. Not so much in the physical sense of the word, but rather I was tired of lying in bed, tired of watching the days come and go through the window, and most of all, tired of feeling like I'd been run over by a freight train. I wanted nothing more at that point than to get well and go home.

After convincing my husband on day seven that I couldn't live another moment without a copy of *Glamour* magazine and a *Kit Kat* bar, he agreed to take a jaunt to the hospital gift shop for the objects of my desire. His departure gave me a few minutes alone to conjure up some confidence and a whole lot of courage.

I turned slightly to take into view the walker standing next to my bedside table. In an earlier attempt at helping me regain mobility, Dr. Bradley had placed it close to my bed and tried to convince me that I was now strong enough to stand and possibly even move a few feet forward to a wheelchair sitting in the middle of the room. Reluctantly, with the help of the doctor and Mitch, I sat up, moved to the side of the bed, and allowed myself to slide forward until my feet touched the floor. Once my hands rested firmly on the walker, I looked toward my husband and said only six words: "I think I'm going to fall."

"No, you aren't, sweetheart. We've got you."

"It's all right, Dana. Just go slowly. Put your weight against the walker and let it support you. The cast is stabilizing the break on the left, and your right hip is healed enough to take a little pressure. Although you'll have the use of a wheelchair when you go home, I still want to be sure you can get around a bit on your own without an issue." Dr. Bradley placed a comforting hand against the small of my back. "I know you feel weak right now, but it's time to get you moving again so we can get you out of this place."

As I began to move, I grimaced against the pains that shot like fire up both arms from wrist to shoulder. The pressure of my upper body pushing into the apparatus seemed to be more than they could bear. Taking a deep breath to combat the feeling, I was quickly reminded of the tight bandages binding my torso and the cracked ribs stinging like a thousand bees attacking my body. I wanted to cry, but instead I swallowed hard against the emotion and tried my best to push forward. A few steps seemed like a thousand on legs that were heavy and yet as wobbly as pieces of wet spaghetti. Two minutes felt more like an hour as I inched closer to the chair. Mitch's hand was placed firmly against my back, and Dr. Bradley stood as close as possible on the other side. Suddenly I stopped, my legs gave out, and the two men scrambled to keep me from going all the way down.

"Grab the chair, Mitch," Dr. Bradley ordered.

A moment later, I was wheeled to the side of the bed where Mitch carefully lifted me and placed me back beneath the blanket. I could feel every inch of my body trembling and my muscles struggling to regain their stability. I lay back against the pillow and closed my eyes. My breath was coming as rapidly as if I had just run a marathon. Taking my wrist between his thumb and two fingers, Dr. Bradley checked my pulse and then touched my forehead. He gave me a gentle smile.

"Don't be discouraged, Dana. You did very well. Get some rest now, and we'll try again later, okay?"

I opened my eyes and nodded weakly. Patting Mitch on the shoulder, he turned and exited the room.

Mitch bent down and softly kissed my cheek. His eyes filled with sympathy. He took my hand and offered a sweet smile.

"I'm proud of you, sweetheart," he said. "I know you'll make it all the way the next time."

I wasn't feeling the confidence he was trying his best to instill. "What if I don't? What if I'm stuck in this stupid bed for another week? At this rate, I'll be here until these kids are born!"

His smile broadened as he listened to my self-pity. "Honey, relax. You have to expect that you're still going to be a bit weak. You haven't used any of those muscles for a while. Perhaps trying to make you go that far was a little too much for the first time." He glanced behind him at the wheelchair, now only about three feet away from the bed. "If we keep this beast where it is right now, I'm sure you can get there without a hitch. What do you think?"

I shrugged. "Maybe," I said without much enthusiasm.

Mitch tousled my hair. "Well, let's not worry about it now. Would you like to watch some TV or maybe take a little nap?"

I set my lip in a pout designed to make him give in to my every whim. "What I'd really like," I began with just enough whine in my voice to be convincing, "is a little massage. Everything aches."

"Sure thing, love. I'll do the best I can, but I don't want to hurt you." He began to let his hands gently glide over my neck, shoulders, and upper arms, applying just a hint of pressure so as not to cause me discomfort. After a few moments, I began to relax; and he finished by offering a loving kiss. "There you are, Mrs. Tarrington. Anything else?" he asked.

It was then that I sent him off to the gift shop. Now here I was, contemplating how to make it from Point A to Point B without killing myself.

If I can just get the IV bag off the stand, I can place it on the pole attached to the walker. Then I'll just take myself on over to the chair....

The first task proved to be a touch harder than I had anticipated, but I managed to accomplish it with the right amount of extra effort. Securing my right hand around the IV pole on the walker, I slid myself slowly off the side of the bed, letting my hand slide down the pole to the walker at the same time. When both hands were firmly in place, I took a deep breath—as best I could—and started on my journey.

I felt a sharp pain pierce my right hip, and I stopped for a moment to let the discomfort subside before prodding on. "You can do this, Dana," I said to myself aloud. "If you ever want to go home, you *have* to do this."

Wincing with every step, I started on again, gritting my teeth and doing my best to ignore the pangs of discomfort that were taunting my extremities. Finally, in a moment of triumph, I transferred the IV bag to the pole on the wheelchair, turned myself completely around, and eased down into the seat—a feeling of pride and satisfaction sweeping over me. Exhausted from my feat, I closed my eyes and concentrated on steadying my breathing to help me relax. Meditating in the quiet stillness, I was almost startled when I heard Mitch's voice.

"Honey, how did you get there? Tell me Dr. Bradley helped you. Or, someone else. Anyone else."

I opened my eyes slowly and smiled up at him. "Nope. I did it myself."

"You *what?!?*"

"I said I did it myself."

He placed the items he'd purchased on the foot of the bed and walked to where I was, crouching down in front of the wheelchair to put us at eye level. "I heard what you said." He reached out to touch my face. "Dana, you shouldn't have done that, sweetheart. You're still weak. What would you have done if you'd fallen again? You could have hurt yourself or the babies. That wasn't a very wise thing to do without someone else here to help you."

I searched his eyes for even the faintest hint that he might also be proud of my accomplishment. However, all I saw was disappointment, and that disappointed me.

"I didn't want anyone else to help me, Mitch. I wanted to prove to myself that I could make it, and I did. I took my time, and I was careful. Other than being a bit tired and sore, I'm fine." I sighed and turned away from him. "I don't know why you want to make me into some fragile little invalid. I had an accident. Big deal. I have to get over it sometime, don't I?"

He stood up and peered down at me. He said nothing, but instead simply stared at me in disbelief. Slowly, the corners of his mouth began to lift into a broad smile that took over his face, his eyes sparkling and full of love.

"You are really something else, you know that? I said you had a rebel spirit, and I was right." He knelt down in front of me, turning my chin so that I was facing him again. Taking both my hands in his, he rubbed the tops of them with his thumbs. "That's why I love you. You always keep me guessing."

"Well then, you won't be shocked to find out that I plan to walk on my own by tomorrow."

He laughed. "Let's not push it, okay?" Leaning forward, he kissed me with all he had.

Determined to get my life back, I worked hard over the next few days; and midway through the week, Dr. Bradley presented the paperwork that spelled the end of my hospital sentence. Mitch hung on his every word as he carefully went over my discharge instructions. Shooting a look of discipline in my direction, he gave his word that I would follow them to the letter. It seemed as if I could do nothing more than eat, sleep, and breathe; but as long as I was doing it at home, I didn't care.

As I signed the discharge form, I began to feel giddy knowing that soon sweet freedom would be mine. While Mitch took a final sweep around the room making sure we had all my belongings, I glanced out the window in eager anticipation of feeling the warmth of the day outside. A few minutes later as we finally drove away, I watched in the side mirror as Mercy Hospital grew smaller and smaller and finally faded out of sight.

"Now, my love, just because you're going home doesn't mean you have free rein to do whatever you want," Mitch began. "I know you're feeling a lot better than you did even a week ago, but you still have a lot of recovering to do. You heard what Dr. Bradley said—a lot of rest for at least two weeks and restricted activities after that while you go through the physical therapy."

I turned my face to the sun, closed my eyes, and breathed deeply to take in the fresh morning air through the open window. "Yes, I heard," I replied. "Don't forget, Mr. Tarrington, that those 'restricted activities' involve you, too."

I glanced over enough to see his dimple through a little smirk. "Yeah, I know. I'll behave myself." I felt his hand touch the few inches of exposed skin just above the cast on my leg. I turned my head toward him completely and watched as his dimple emerged full-force. "But, I'm telling you, love, I've really missed you; and it's not going to be easy."

"Just pretend we aren't married," I replied as I moved his hand to rest on his own leg. "That should make it easier for you."

"Hmm. Let me think about that," he said as he twisted his jaw. "You're almost four months pregnant with my children, we're both wearing wedding bands, and you'll be lying next to me in bed each night. Yet, somehow, you think that I'll be able to pretend we aren't married. Highly unlikely."

"Well, there's always the option of having you stay at your parents' house."

He shot me a look out of the corner of his eye. "Guess I'll be learning how to pretend—that and taking a lot of cold showers!" he answered decisively. I laughed.

Entering the apartment, I felt a wave of emotions sweep over me as my eyes scanned my surroundings. In the middle of the kitchen table was a vase filled with the most beautiful bouquet of flowers I'd ever seen. Next to them was a small box wrapped in pink and tied with a blue ribbon. In the corner of the room next to Mr. Bear was his equally-large stuffed counterpart. I began to giggle with delight as I looked up at my husband's radiant smile.

"Mitchell, what is all this? More so, when did you do it? You never left the hospital the entire time I was there," I asked as he continued to beam.

He bit his lip, looking like the cat that swallowed the mouse. "Oh, contraire, mon ami`," he replied with his best French accent. "Yesterday evening when you fell asleep after dinner, I slipped out for a while. I told the nurses that if you woke up before I got back, they should tell you that I went down to the cafeteria. I figured that would be believable enough."

"Oh, so *that's* why you didn't eat with me last night, huh? You told me you weren't hungry yet. And to think I believed you."

He grinned, and his eyes twinkled with boyish mischief. "How could you not believe a face like this?"

He pushed the chair toward the table, carefully brought the vase close to me, and allowed me to inspect the flowers and take in their sweet aroma. Placing it back, he handed me the box and then pulled out a chair from the table and sat down.

"Since I don't know if we have boys or girls or both, I had the salesclerk use pink and blue," he began. "Go on, sweetheart. Open it."

I smiled and began to fumble with the ribbon. Still having limited motion of both arms due to the injuries, Mitch held the box in place as I ripped the paper off and lifted the lid. Seeing the object inside, my heart filled with love as tears of joy trickled down my cheeks.

Mitch reached into the box, removed the delicate crystal frame, and placed it gently in my trembling hands. Inside each of the two small hearts was one of the ultrasound pictures Dr. Bradley had given us of the twins. I allowed my fingers to trace the outline of each heart, and then I lifted my eyes to look at Mitch. His bright blue eyes shined with the strength of the love he'd put into the gift. He reached out to touch the frame.

"When the babies are born, we can replace those pictures with actual ones," he said softly.

With tears still flowing, I leaned toward him and kissed him tenderly. I pulled away just enough to look into his eyes. "I love it, Mitch. It's so beautiful. And I love you. More than anything."

"You don't know how much it means to hear you say that," he replied. "I love you, too. More than anything." Not wanting his own tears to flow, he stood up quickly and excitedly gaited across the room, picked up the teddy bear, and returned to my side.

"Dana Tarrington, I'd like you to meet Mr. Teddy, Mr. Bear's brother." He plopped the toy down next to me as I laughed. "I know how kids fight over toys, so I thought it best for each of them to have their own."

I reached out and entangled my fingers in the soft, shaggy fur. "I have a feeling Daddy's going to spoil these kids rotten, isn't he?"

Mitch pretended to ignore me as he whistled a little tune. Then he looked at me with a grin and placed a finger on his chest. "Who? Me? I would never think of doing such a thing!"

We both laughed as Mitch bent down and gave me a loving hug. "Welcome home, Mommy," he said.

Chapter 8

Over the weeks that followed, between countless doctor's visits and hours of grueling physical therapy, I was able to regain enough strength and mobility to return some normalcy to my life. Much to my delight, I was finally able to shed the casts that had once held my limbs captive; and much to Mitch's delight, many of my 'restrictions' were lifted. Throughout my recovery, Mitch was always by my side and quite the protector, never allowing me to be alone for more than an hour at most. Thrilled with the news that yet another Tarrington would be joining the lineup, his family was more than supportive and did everything from running errands for us to tidying up the apartment and bringing in meals. Because Mitch could do little more than boil water, I was especially grateful for this and the fact that it kept carryout food from becoming our way of life.

Mitch returned to work a week after my release from the hospital; and on most days while he was there, I was in the care of his mother, one of his sisters, or Trudy. He told me that it made him "feel better" about leaving me, but I knew the truth of the matter was that he was afraid I wouldn't follow the doctor's orders given the chance to be alone and do as I pleased. I wasn't sure why he was so worried; even after the casts were removed, I moved with the grace of a duck caught in an oil slick thanks to a limp left over from the dislocated hip. Due to the contractions I'd suffered—which Dr. Bradley determined were caused by stress, excessive vomiting, and slight dehydration—my pregnancy was labeled high-risk, even though the threat of a miscarriage was actually low at that point. Mitch took this very seriously and made sure that I did nothing to cause myself even the most remote possibility of soreness or fatigue. His caring nature not only touched me, but it concerned me as well. In addition to carrying out his duties at the bistro, he resumed his rehearsals and shows with the band. Many nights he would come home afterward to tackle a few loads of laundry or another task before going to bed. I could often see the exhaustion in the way he carried himself, but he would always insist with a smile that he was fine and tell me not to worry. I did anyway.

When I could finally stand with only the support of a cane, I insisted that he at least allow me to cook dinner; and he was agreeable as long as I made a solemn vow not to do anything else around the apartment. Although I felt somewhat helpless, I gave him the satisfaction of acquiescing to this arrangement to avoid causing strife between us.

With each passing day, I not only became stronger, but I became larger as well. It seemed that the moment the doctor had said 'twins,' I began to double in size as if my body suddenly realized that there was a second child and needed to make up for lost time. Mitch would often send glances my way and wasn't completely sure what to make of the new shape I was taking. Whenever I would happen to catch his eye, he would simply smile at me and tell me how beautiful he thought I was. Sometimes I believed him, and other times I wondered if he was only saying it to cover up what he was really thinking: *who are you, and what did you do with my wife?*

Other than recovering from the accident, the best part of all was that somewhere around the beginning of my fifth month we felt our children move for the first time. We were cuddling up on the couch engrossed in an old movie on TV when I felt something 'jump' just below my navel. Slightly startled by this strange new sensation, I placed my hand in that spot and waited. This time I not only felt the jump, but also a gentle poke on the palm of my hand. Not bothering to say why, I grabbed Mitch's hand, lifted my top enough to reveal my lower abdomen, and placed his hand where mine had been. He looked into my eyes with a questioning expression on his face. Suddenly, the baby kicked again, and Mitch's mouth slowly curled upward until his entire face was beaming. Placing my hand on top of his, we moved closer to one another and sat there for several minutes engulfed in the wonder of the lives within me—the lives our love had created.

In the blink of an eye, yet another month passed. Finally, I felt the sense of relief associated with the fact that the morning sickness had become nothing more than an unpleasant memory. I was overjoyed that I could now enjoy a meal and be able to hold it down for more than an hour. The only downside was that the illness had replaced itself with what I deemed as a voracious appetite. It seemed that I was eating just about anything in sight and at just about any time of the day or night. Whenever I would become self-conscious about it, my husband would smile sweetly, remind me that I was "eating for three," and jokingly say that if the kids were anything like him they were probably hogging most of the food anyway.

One morning around two, I sat up in bed and looked at the clock realizing I'd only been there for about three hours. I glanced over at Mitch sleeping soundly, lost deep in his dreams. *Why am I awake*, I wondered? My stomach growled just then in answer to my question. *This is crazy*, I thought. I had eaten two slices of pie at Jake and Olivia's after rehearsal as well as enough roast beef at dinner to sink a small battleship, and yet I was hungry. I lay back down thinking that if I ignored the feeling I would fall back to sleep. It growled again—only this time louder than before. I turned over and closed my eyes tightly trying to concentrate on relaxing; but the longer I tried to fight it, the stronger the feeling grew. I decided that the only way I would get back to sleep was going to be to satisfy my appetite. I moved slowly to the side of the bed and slid out from beneath the covers as I did my best not to disturb my husband. Succeeding at the attempt, I pulled the blanket back up over him, slipped on my robe, and tiptoed to the kitchen.

I turned on the light and opened the refrigerator door. My stomach growled again, and I daintily placed my hand on my mother load. "Hold on there, little ones. I'm getting something for you," I said as if I knew my unborn children could hear and understand me. I stared into the refrigerator, not certain what it was that I was hungry for. There was some leftover chicken from the night before last, but that didn't appeal to me. I moved it out of the way to reveal two containers of yogurt, a package of bologna, and three slices of pizza Mitch had brought home from the bistro. Sighing heavily, I opened the first drawer. A few oranges, some grapes, and fixings for salad. Next drawer. Some cheese, half a slab of bacon, and some smoked sausage. I made a 'yuck' face and moved to the freezer. Suddenly, I heard angels singing. Chocolate chip pistachio ice cream! The heavens were smiling on me, I decided.

Excitedly, I grabbed the container and pushed the freezer door closed. Grabbing a spoon, I took a seat at the table. In eager anticipation, I pulled off the lid and poised my spoon to dig in—only to find it was empty! *What's up with that*, I wondered? The only logical explanation was that Mitch had eaten it; and instead of throwing the container in the trash, he'd placed it back into the freezer. Now, what was I going to do?

"Sorry, babies. Your daddy's a piggy," I said as I glanced down at my stomach. As I sat slowly wasting away from hunger, a sleepy Mitch appeared at the end of the hallway. I could tell he'd gotten up quickly as he was without his glasses, and his boxers were sitting somewhat off-kilter on his hips.

"Dana, what are you doing?"

I put the spoon on the table and placed my chin in my hands. "Well, I was going to have some ice cream, but it appears you ate it all," I said as I glanced at the container.

He shook his head to clear out the fog. "Honey, it's two-thirty in the morning. Why are you eating ice cream now?"

I placed the spoon back in the drawer and threw the container into the trash as he walked toward me. "I'm not," I replied. "You ate it all.

And just for the record, empty containers belong in the trash and not in the freezer."

"Sorry," he said as he rubbed his eyes. "Come on. Let's go back to bed."

He began to walk back toward the bedroom; but noticing I wasn't following, he stopped and turned around. "What's the matter? Aren't you coming?"

"I can't sleep. I'm hungry."

"Then eat something."

"We don't have anything."

He sighed and trudged over to the refrigerator, opened the door, and pointed. "If we don't have anything, what's all that?"

"I'm not hungry for any of that. I want chocolate chip pistachio ice cream."

"We don't have any."

"I know. You ate it all."

He closed the door and turned to face me. "What do you want me to do about it now, dear?" he asked.

I smiled.

He caught on and began to shake his head. He threw in a wagging finger for effect. "Oh, no! There is no way I'm going out at this time of night for ice cream. Eat something else, and we can get some tomorrow."

"I don't want anything else. I want ice cream, Mitch," I whined. I gave him my best puppy dog eyes. "I think Miraldi's over on Bell Street is open all night...."

"Dana...."

I sat on the side of the bed as Mitch pulled on his shoes. "I can't believe I'm doing this," he muttered almost to himself. He looked up at me with a lopsided grin on his face. "Either I'm nuts, or I really love you," he said as he rose to his feet.

I walked over to where he was standing and gave him a kiss on the cheek. "Maybe a little of both," I replied.

"Yeah, maybe." He ran a hand through his hair and gave me a sweet, soft smile. "Okay, Mommy, you sit tight. I'll be back as soon as I get what you want."

As Mitch pulled onto the road, he had to smile as he thought of his sweet Dana and her beautiful smile that caused him to melt like putty. How could he possibly refuse her anything when she looked at him that way? He couldn't, and he was sure she knew that. But, he didn't mind. He didn't mind that it was two forty-five in the morning, the hottest night of the year; and he was going to the store for—of all things—chocolate chip pistachio ice cream. He didn't mind because he loved her more than anything, and he would do anything he could if he thought it would make her happy. Absolutely anything.

Arriving at the store a few minutes later, Mitch found a parking spot and got out of the car to head inside. Catching a glimpse of himself in the glass door, he paused for a moment to stare at his reflection and chuckled softly at what he saw. His faded t-shirt, donning the logo of his college alma mater, was now tight across the chest reflecting the muscular changes in his physique over the years. The track shorts were just the opposite: big and baggy—not the thing he would usually wear in public. The stubble on his face was thick and dark; and although he'd made a minor attempt to smooth it out, his crown was sporting a serious case of bed hair. He shrugged and pulled the door open as he stepped into the bright fluorescent light. After all, he wasn't there to make a fashion statement. He was there on a mission to satisfy the woman he loved.

Heading straight to the freezer section, he positioned himself in front of the ice cream cases to search for Dana's object of desire. Triple walnut crunch, chocolate fudge supreme, rocky road, strawberry swirl—it all seemed too complex. *Whatever happened to just plain chocolate or vanilla*, he wondered? Shrugging off the thought, he took a step forward to get a closer look. Pecans and cream, mint marshmallow, mocha pecan cluster. *What was it I came here for again? Chocolate chip pistachio. Or, was it chocolate chip **and** pistachio?* Oh, great. He couldn't remember. *Think, Mitch, think*, he told himself. He closed his eyes for a moment, conjuring up an image of the empty ice cream container in his mind. *Let's see now*, he thought; *she said I'd eaten all of it...chocolate chip pistachio. Yes, that was it.* Feeling pleased, he opened his eyes and moved down the line of freezers until he located the brand and then stopped to allow his eyes to scan through all the flavors. He didn't see it. *No, it has to be here.* He'd probably just missed it. He moved his eyes over the containers again, and he took extra care to look at each and every one. Chocolate chip pistachio. Again, he didn't see it. *This can't be happening. Maybe one more look....*

He stood still for a moment to think out his plan. They didn't have what she wanted. He could just pick out something else and hope she'd be happy with his selection. However, she'd made it very clear that she didn't want anything else. He could go home without anything, but that would only make matters worse. She was emotional enough already without him giving her another reason to exhibit it. Suddenly, the light went on, and he smiled. He reached into the freezer case and pulled out a pint of plain pistachio ice cream. If he bought that and a bag of chocolate chips, she could mix them together herself. He'd score a few extra points for his intuitiveness, her craving would be satisfied, and all would be right with the world. Feeling prideful and triumphant, he headed to the checkout.

The cashier smiled pleasantly as Mitch placed his items on the counter. He noticed her eyes do a quick once over him, and she snickered.

"Let me guess—frat party just ended, and you decided you were hungry, right? I've had more than one of you boys in here tonight."

Mitch looked down at himself and snickered as well. "Oh, no, I'm way beyond that, trust me. I have a pregnant wife at home who wanted chocolate chip pistachio ice cream."

"And you're thinking since we don't have any she can mix these things together and make it herself. Smart man and what a good husband you are to come out for her in the middle of the night." As Mitch handed her a twenty-dollar bill, she finished out the sale and gave him his change. "Is this your first baby?"

He nodded and flashed her a prideful smile. "Yes. It is. Well, actually, I should say *they* are. We're having twins."

"Well now, congratulations!" she said as she handed Mitch his bag. "I hope your wife enjoys her ice cream."

"Thanks. So do I."

Arriving back home, Mitch placed his key in the lock, opened the door, and stepped into the apartment. Not noticing that I was waiting by the door, he turned suddenly and almost ran into me. I grabbed the bag from his hand and hurried to the kitchen.

"Hey, baby, I'm home," he chuckled as I took up my spoon once more and sat down at the table. "Guess you've been waiting for me, huh?"

"I've never wanted anything so badly in my life," I said as I opened the bag. Eagerly, I removed the container of ice cream and pulled off the lid. My eyes slowly lifted to my husband who had parked himself in the chair across from me.

"What?" he asked.

"What is this, Mitch? I asked for chocolate chip pistachio. I'm *craving* chocolate chip pistachio. This is just pistachio."

He pointed. "The chocolate chips are in the bag."

"They aren't supposed to be in the bag, dear. They're supposed to be in the ice cream."

He reached for the bag, pulled out the chocolate chips, and handed them to me. "Well, honey, they didn't have that kind of ice cream. I thought you could make your own." He grimaced. "I was wrong, wasn't

I?" He stood up and pushed in his chair. "I'm sorry. I thought it was better than not bringing you anything at all."

The look of disappointment on his face was more than I could take. I opened the bag of chocolate chips and threw a few into the ice cream. "It's okay. I'm sure it'll taste just fine."

I watched a sense of relief come over him, and he smiled as he sat down next to me again.

"Mind if I have a bite?"

I smiled and handed him the spoon. He dug deep into the container and scooped up a rather large portion but not before he threw in a few more chocolate chips. "Hey, that's pretty good." He thrust the spoon back in but noticed just then that I was looking at him and paused.

"I'll get another spoon," I said. He nodded and flashed me a glimpse of that dimple I loved so much.

Twenty-three minutes, a pint of ice cream, and half a bag of chocolate chips later, Mitch and I were curled up next to one another in bed once more. He rolled over, placed his arm around me, and pulled me close as he rested his hand on my stomach.

"Feel better?" he asked as he began to lightly rub his hand across me.

"Much," I yawned. "Now I think I can actually get some sleep."

He kissed my cheek and rested his face there. "Sleep, huh? Well, I'm wide awake now, and I thought it might be nice if we stayed up a little longer. What do you say?"

"I say *is that all you ever think about?*"

He laughed as he kissed me again, inhaling deeply. "Well, no—sometimes I do think about eating."

I rolled over to face him. "I know, and I'm the one who has to satisfy that feeling, too."

"Yeah, but I did go out at two-thirty in the morning to get you ice cream. Doesn't that count for something?"

I ran my finger down his chest, and he smiled. "It was two forty-five, and yes it does." I kissed him softly. "You're the most wonderful husband in the world. Thank you. Now, roll over and go back to sleep."

"That isn't exactly what I was thinking, but okay. Have it your way." He pulled me close, and together we drifted off into peaceful slumber.

The alarm sounded at seven. Mitch rolled over and slapped the snooze button, turned back over, and then hugged his pillow to him. Wearily, I wiped my eyes, sat up, and gazed at him.

He opened one eye. "What?"

"You need to get up and get ready. My appointment's at eight-thirty."

"I don't want to get up right now. I'm tired. Someone sent me out at two-thirty in the morning for ice cream."

I bent down to snuggle up to him and gave him a kiss on the cheek as I ran a hand through his hair. "Two forty-five, and I'll love you forever for doing it. Come on. I'll go wash up and make us some breakfast."

"I would hope you'll love me forever regardless." He yawned. "I want pancakes and sausage. You owe me, lady."

"Oh, is that so?"

"Yeah, it is. In fact, I want blueberries in mine."

I tousled his hair and stepped out of bed. "Demanding, aren't we? Okay. I'll talk to the cook and see what I can arrange."

Mitch sat down at the table a short while later with a cup of coffee in one hand and the morning newspaper in the other. He took a long drink, then placed his cup down, and tapped his finger on the page.

"Hey, honey, check this out," he said as he excitedly handed me the paper. "Right there. The ad on the bottom left side."

I placed his breakfast down in front of him and took the newspaper from his hand. "Oh, cool! Shoe Town is having a 'buy one pair, get the second pair half-price.'" I patted him on the head in a teasing fashion. "Thanks for pointing that out."

He smirked at me. "You are such a funny girl. I'm not looking at that. The ad next to it for Hallmark Homes."

I glanced at him—then back to the ad. "Lovely three-bedroom colonial, formal dining room, two-and-a-half baths, living room, family room with fireplace, sun room, and laundry. Full basement could be easily finished for an enjoyable family fun area. Open today from two until four at 137 Fireside Lane. Listed at $130,000."

"Sounds great, doesn't it? I think we should go take a look," Mitch said as he took a huge bite of his pancakes.

"Sounds like a lot more than we need at this point. What's wrong with …."

"We aren't staying here, Dana. We've been through this already, and we both agree that we need more room. If we make the investment in a house now, we'll be all set when we're ready to have the next baby. With three bedrooms we can put each of the twins in their own room, or we could put them together and make the other a guest room until we need it ourselves. It has a basement, too, so we could make a playroom down there if we want. Let's at least go take a look."

I handed the paper back to him and sat down to my own meal. "I don't know, Mitch. Do you think we can afford it?"

"Yes, we can. Even if you quit working after the babies come, we can easily swing the payment on my salary. Besides, you never pay what they're listing it for. It's called the art of negotiation. Most of the time you can whittle the price down by five grand or more. The list price is really just a starting point."

"Then why even bother listing a price? Why don't they just say 'taking offers'?"

He smirked at me again. "Cute. Now, seriously, what do you say? After your appointment, I'll head into work. You can meet me there around three, and we'll go over to the house." He stood up to pour another cup of coffee. "I'll even take you to dinner afterwards."

I lowered my fork and gave him a sideways glance. "You really think this is something we should do? You don't think it's too soon?"

He sat back down, placed his cup on the table, and leaned toward me. He took my hand and smiled that sweet smile of his—the one where his dimple came out in full force and his eyes filled with love and understanding. "I know it seems like our lives change by the second, but for me that's part of the joy of being married to you. Each day is like a whole new adventure. No one can ever say our lives are boring by any stretch." He placed his other hand on top of mine. "We're in this together, love. Whatever comes our way, we'll handle it. Everything will be fine."

I felt my insides turning to putty the way they always did when he looked at me that way. I smiled. "Then count me in."

With breakfast finished and cleared away, Mitch headed for his weight bench; and I headed for a soothing shower. Although it was still early, the sun peeking through the blinds was foretelling the promise of another hot and steamy day. Being six months' pregnant was one thing, but being six months' pregnant in August on a ninety-degree day was quite another. Secretly praying for rain—or a freak snowstorm—I headed toward the bathroom.

Right around eight, we made our way to Mercy Hospital where we would meet Dr. Bradley. Today, both of us were more than ready to see him. At my previous visit, Dr. Bradley had scheduled another ultrasound—the last one I would have before the twins were born. He had promised that the babies were now big enough that, if positioned correctly, we would most likely be able to determine their sexes. While the prospect of knowing whether we had boys, girls, or one of each enticed me, Mitch took an opposite view. "Let's just be surprised," he said. "Adds to the excitement."

"I've had quite enough excitement during this pregnancy, thank you," I retorted. "Besides, if we know what we're having, I can start shopping for things."

He shot me a sideways grin. "Oh, I get it. Anything to use as an excuse to shop. Not that you ever need one of those anyway."

That remark earned him an elbow in the ribs. "Come on, Mitchell. I'm sure you'll want to have plenty of time to gloat if you find out one of them is a boy."

He twisted his jaw in thought and then nodded approvingly. "Okay, let's find out."

Now, here we were, replaying the scene from just three months ago. Only this time, there were no wires strapped to me, no fear of the outcome of the testing, no worries that something dreadful might occur. It was a joyous occasion, to say the least, and one we had been eagerly anticipating for the past three weeks.

"Okay, Mom and Dad," the doctor began, "this is the big moment. I'm sure you're going to see a major difference in things from three months ago." He looked from Mitch to me. "Did you decide if you want to know the sexes?"

I gazed up at Mitch, and he hesitated with his answer as he looked back at me. Then he smiled. "Yes, we want to know."

"Very good. Let's see if your little ones will cooperate."

As he had before, Mitch fixed his eyes on the monitor; and the expression on his face was one of true awe. As the doctor moved the wand across my stomach, images of tiny hands and feet, perfectly formed fingers and toes, and faces with little button noses came into our view on the screen. The doctor would stop every so often to point something out to us, and each time Mitch's eyes would move to meet mine only temporarily before returning to the pictures in front of him. Pausing for a moment, the doctor looked at both of us again.

"I'm just asking to be certain—you want to know what you're having, right?"

"What? You mean we aren't having babies?" Mitch joked.

"Ignore him," I said sarcastically as Dr. Bradley laughed. Mitch bent down and kissed my forehead.

The doctor placed another glob of warm gel on my abdomen and moved the wand downward until it almost disappeared completely below the giant mound on my torso. Suddenly, Mitch's face lit up, his eyes widened, and he placed a finger on the monitor screen. "Is that what I think it is?" he asked.

"Yes, I believe so. Looks like this one's a boy," Dr. Bradley said gleefully.

I looked at Mitch, and I wondered if the smile would ever leave his face. I decided if I had to look at it every day—all day—I would gladly do so forever.

Moving the wand just a bit to the right, Dr. Bradley moved it back and forth, up and down, and in an almost circular motion. We could see ears, eyes, hands, and arms—but nothing else. "Well, we can see who's going to be the defiant one of the two," he said teasingly. "Those legs are closed tight. Sorry, but you'll have to find out about this one the old fashioned way."

This news didn't seem to bother Mitch. His face was still saturated with that prize-winning grin.

"It's all right. We'll take whatever we get," he said proudly. I translated that to mean, "As long as I know I have my boy, it's okay if the other kid's a girl." I had to giggle.

Dr. Bradley smiled. "Okay, Dad, it's time for you to go take a seat in the waiting area. I'm going to let Mom here clean up a little, and then I'm going to check a few other things. From what I've seen so far, I'm quite pleased with how things are progressing, folks. No repercussion from the accident whatsoever, and everything is just as it should be at this point." He turned to face me. "I do want you to continue taking good care of yourself, however; and if you feel like you're getting tired, don't push it. Use a level head, all right?" I nodded, and he turned back to Mitch. "When I'm finished with her, I'll send her out to find you. Then we'll talk about setting you up for childbirth classes."

Mitch was still smiling. "Sounds good." He helped me sit up on the table and gave me a loving kiss. "I'll see you soon, sweetheart. I love you."

"Love you, too—and you'd better watch before your face freezes like that." I heard him laugh as he walked away.

Mitch slipped a quarter into the machine and watched as a paper cup dropped and filled with liquid, seeming to know just where to stop before running over. Lifting the door, he removed the cup and brought the piping hot coffee to his lips, carefully taking a sip so as not to burn his mouth. It wasn't the greatest brew in the world, but for now it would do. Slipping into a chair in the far corner of the room, he found an outdated issue of *Time* and aimlessly began to flip through it. He hoped that he wouldn't get interested in any articles that he wouldn't be able to finish before Dana came to find him.

That concern proved irrelevant as he reached the back cover ad boasting an executive toting a large *American Tourister* suitcase. Tossing the magazine onto the round table in front of him, he took another sip of his coffee and settled down into his chair to wait.

"Mitch? Is that you?"

The feminine voice behind him held a familiar tone. Turning just slightly, he smiled and stood up. The young woman welcomed him into a friendly embrace.

"Casey! My gosh, what are you doing here? I thought...."

She smiled warmly. "I did, but I'm back. Chicago just wasn't all it seemed chalked up to be. So, I decided to come home. Got here about three weeks ago."

Mitch motioned to a chair, and she sat down. He took the chair opposite her. It had been over a year, but she hadn't changed at all. Her face glowed in a radiant smile, and her emerald eyes glistened beneath long, curled lashes. Flecks of light were catching in her strawberry blonde hair, bringing out the natural highlights and adding a sparkle to her appearance. He'd always found her especially attractive, and that hadn't changed over the time they'd been apart. What had changed, however, was that now his heart belonged to someone else. Completely.

The two sat for the next few minutes reliving times past and catching up with times present. Finally, Casey stood and pulled her purse strap over her shoulder.

"Well, I'd better get going. I'm here to see my niece. She's having surgery in about two hours."

Mitch stood as well. "Oh? Nothing serious, I hope."

Casey smiled. "No, just a tonsillectomy. She'll be going home this evening, but I promised I'd stop by."

Mitch nodded and Casey offered another hug. "You know, I never thought I'd see you again, Mitch. I hoped to, but...." She stopped mid-sentence, as if completing her thought would be too painful. She conjured up a grin. "Hey, I have an idea. Why don't I take you out tonight, on me? Dinner and dancing, if you're up to it. I was always impressed with those moves of yours. We can catch up."

Mitch had to chuckle at the thought. He could only imagine what Dana would say about that!

"Thanks, but I really can't. I'm sorry."

Casey's smile faded. "Oh, it's okay. I guess I shouldn't have been presumptuous. Forgive me."

Mitch looked at the dejected expression on her face. "No, it's not that. I'm married."

Her expression now changed to shock. "You're *married*? When did that happen? I haven't been gone that long, and I didn't hear that you were seeing anyone after I left."

Mitch placed his hands in his pockets. "It's all kind of funny actually," he started. "She came into my restaurant back in October. I took one look at her, and that did it. We got married in February."

"Wow! Love at first sight! That's wonderful! Congratulations!" Then she realized what he had said. "Wait—did you say *your* restaurant?"

"Yeah. I bought Gartano's—that little Italian bistro downtown. Took over a couple of months before I got married."

"I'm impressed! You've been quite the busy guy, haven't you?"

Oh, if you only knew, he thought.

Suddenly, a look of concern came over her, and she touched him lightly on the arm. "By the way, what are you doing here? Is someone ill? Not you, I hope...."

He felt that old familiar tug at his heart—the same feeling he always got when he thought of Dana. But now, it seemed a little stronger, and he knew it had to be because of the twins.

"Oh, no. I'm waiting for my wife to finish up her appointment. Just a checkup," he replied.

Casey glanced at her watch and smiled again. "I really have to go, Mitch. It was great to see you again."

He simply nodded as she walked away, and then he sat back down to wait for his wife.

"Hey, handsome!" I greeted as I approached my husband.

Mitch stood up, placed an arm around my shoulders, and kissed my cheek. "You know I love you, don't you?"

I pulled my head back enough to look at him suspiciously. "What'd you do?"

He laughed and pulled me to him as we began to walk back toward Dr. Bradley's office. "Nothing. Can't I even tell you I love you without your thinking there's a motive behind it?"

I settled into the crook of his arm. "Well, I guess so. It's just that you asked whether or not I knew that you loved me. You didn't just say it."

"Okay. I love you. Is that better?"

"Yes."

Mitch glanced briefly in the direction Casey had gone. *That was then; this is now,* he thought to himself. Turning back toward Dana with a smile, he knew that "now" was exactly where he wanted to be.

A short while later, we were back in the car and heading for home, filled with delight at the news regarding our children and uncertainty about the impending childbirth education classes we'd just scheduled.

"I don't get it," I began. "How on earth do they think that the way you breathe is going to control excruciating, gut-wrenching agony? Must be some man who came up with that one. Probably didn't know how else to make it look like he really cared about his wife's comfort through the ordeal. Truth be known, he probably didn't want to hear all the names she was calling him, so he tried to give her something else to do."

"Hey! You aren't going to call me names, are you?"

"I don't know. Guess you'll just have to get good at all this breathing stuff yourself so you can coach me. Then you can keep me focused, and I won't be able to call you anything."

He shot me a sideways glance. "I don't need to learn anything. I already know how to breathe—did that during the conception phase of things if you recall." He began to grin and gave his demonstration of heavy breathing to which I promptly smacked him on the arm—hard. He just laughed.

Pulling into a spot close to the building, Mitch instructed me to sit still as he came around to open my door. "Let's get you all tucked away upstairs, and then I'll head over to the bistro for a while. You bring the car at three, and we can go look at the open house. How's that sound?"

"Why don't I go with you to work today? I have nothing else to do, and I know you could use the help."

He stopped midway through the parking lot, turned to me, and took both my hands in his. "Dana, you need to take care of yourself. You've been through a lot, and waitressing is hard work. That's why I've been insisting that you stay home, sweetheart. It's not that I don't want you…."

I let go of his hands and started toward the building without him. "Yeah, right."

I heard the cadence of his footsteps on the pavement as he tried to catch up with me. "Come on. Let's not go through this again. You've been doing so well these past weeks since the accident. I don't want to risk anything happening to you, that's all. You need your rest."

I swung around to face him. "You heard Dr. Bradley. He said everything looks fine. There are no repercussions from the accident whatsoever. Sure, I still have a bit of a limp, but it's not that bad. I don't even have to use the cane anymore. Therefore, I don't have to lie around like a zombie doing nothing. I can start being useful again." I placed my palm on his cheek. "Please let me come with you today."

As he stood there gazing into her eyes, he thought back to the times she'd insisted on joining him when she was sick and how he had always tried to persuade her otherwise. On most of those occasions he'd lost the battle, and he knew today was going to be another one of those times.

He bit his lip, and finally he nodded. "Fine. You aren't waiting tables, however. I'll find some light work for you. Nothing too demanding, got it?"

I knew it was the only way he'd concede my point, so I readily agreed.

Mitch tapped on the window of the bistro to get Kayla's attention, and she quickly opened the door, an anxious grin on her face.

"Well, girly, tell me—what did the doctor say? Did you find out what you're having?"

"He said I'm just fine and that everything looks normal with the pregnancy."

"And...."

I looked at Mitch as if to ask if I should tell her, and he nodded in approval. "Well, one of the babies wouldn't cooperate. So, that one's still a secret," I said. Then I smiled at my husband whose face began to beam as it had when he first heard the news. "I'll let Mitch tell you about the other one."

He didn't have to answer because his smile gave it away. "You got your boy, didn't you?" Kayla asked.

He nodded as she hugged us both. "Well, well, congratulations!" she chimed. "I'm so happy for the two of you!"

"Thanks, Kayla," Mitch answered. "I guess I'd better go have a little chat with my wife here before we open. Seems she has her mind set on helping out today, and we need to work out a game plan."

Kayla smiled. "Don't worry. I'll be out here, and I won't let her do too much!"

"Oh, fantastic. A conspiracy," I said as the two of them laughed.

Mitch closed the office door, took a seat at the desk, and pulled me onto his lap. "I'm glad that you got a good report today. The three of you mean everything to me. I mean that."

I began to run my fingers through the back of his hair. "You mean everything to us, too."

He encircled his arms around me and interlocked the fingers of his hands in such a way as to fence me in. "I'm glad to hear that. Now, we need to talk about what you are *not* going to do today."

"Mitchell...."

"Listen to me. I'm serious. I don't want you doing any bending, lifting, stooping, carrying, climbing, or anything else that's going to make you tired, sore, or otherwise. Understood?"

"I have no restrictions on my activities, Mitch."

"Yes, you do. I just made restrictions. Either you abide by them, or I take you home. Besides, Dr. Bradley told you not to push it. I'm here to make sure you pay attention. Any questions?"

"You're mean."

"I'm not mean. I'm taking care of my family. Now, are you going to listen to me or not?"

"Do I have a choice?"

"Not really."

I managed to wriggle free from captivity and stood up. "Fine. Am I allowed to go to the bathroom?"

He glanced upward and pretended to ponder my question. "I suppose I can allow you to do that."

I stuck my tongue out at him as I exited the room.

Returning just about three minutes later, I caught the tail end of a phone conversation. I stood quietly off to the side until he hung up. Then he reached out for me and placed me back on his lap.

"What was that all about?" I asked.

Once again he caged me inside his arms and gave me a peck on the forehead before he answered.

"That was Marjorie from the classified department at the newspaper," he began. "I've decided it's time to place that ad for another waitress."

I moved away from him as much as I could and stared into his face. "Why did you do that? You heard the doctor. I can help out now. You don't have to think about hiring anyone for at least another three months. Even then, there's really no need. I'll only be off on maternity leave for six weeks. It's been longer than that since I've worked due to the accident, and the girls have handled it just fine. Surely they can handle six weeks!"

He sighed and gave me that disciplinary look once again. "Yes, love, I heard the doctor. But as I said earlier, you heard me. I'm not allowing you to wear yourself out here and that's that. As for the girls being able to handle things, they have done well; but it hasn't been easy. I should have placed this ad a lot sooner than I did. I was just so consumed with everything else that I didn't want to worry about interviews and all that. With things getting back to normal, I can take the extra time I need to find someone. I don't want to wait until you're in labor to get extra help in here."

"I can handle it, Mitch. I really can. Why put out the expense for someone else when you have me?"

He glanced down at the evidence of his children and placed a gentle hand there. "Sweetheart, I don't mean to offend you at all, but the more things progress, the slower you're going to be. I need someone who can handle the pace around here. Besides, I don't think you'll have much time to consider working here once you have two little ones who'll need you at home. Who would babysit?"

He was trying to outwit me with logic, but I wasn't having any of it. "We can bring them to work with us. As I understand it, babies sleep a lot; so we can set up a little crib in here for them. I'm never here more than four or five hours anyway. Since we'd both be here, we can both take care of them."

Mitch started to grin. "What do we do when we're swamped, we're both caught up in other things, and the babies need attention? We can't ignore the patrons, and we definitely can't ignore our kids. Anyway, this is a restaurant, not a daycare center. Babies have no business here." He kissed my forehead again and patted my stomach.

"You aren't even trying to see my side of this, are you?"

"No more than you're trying to see mine. I need to hire a waitress. I've placed the ad, and it's a done deal. You can help with other things but not waitressing. I just think it would be a bit too tiring considering everything you've been through. Once the babies come, I'd love to see you here only for brief visits. Then it's back home where they need to be." He placed me on my feet and pulled his chair closer to the desk. "I have some things here I need to take care of. You go on out there and remember what I told you."

I moved toward the door as Mitch delved into his work. Once he was absorbed in his task, I headed out toward the bistro seemingly unnoticed. If I could prove to him that I could easily resume all the duties I had performed prior to the accident, perhaps he wouldn't be so reluctant to allow me to keep helping out. The bistro—like the band rehearsals and shows—had become a part of who I was and a way that Mitch and I could connect. Giving up any of those things would be like giving up a chance to share my husband's life with him. I didn't want to be the wife in the background. I wanted a piece of the action.

Reaching beneath the counter, I grabbed an apron and began to tie it on. Opening the drawer next to the cash register, I took out a booklet of order tickets, located a pen, and started toward a table when I felt a hand on my arm.

"Where do you think you're going?" I turned around to face Mitch, a stern look on his face.

"No one's waited on table six yet. I'm going to take their drink order."

"No, you aren't. I said no waitressing."

I prepared for debate. "Everyone else is busy, and it's rude to make them sit and wait. Let go of me so I can get over there."

He took the pen and pad from my hands, intercepting Phyllis as she hurried by to pull an order. "Hey, can you get drinks for six? No one's helped them yet."

She looked almost irritated by his request. "The group at six will have to wait a minute, Mitch. The guys on ten still need salads, and fourteen doesn't have a bread basket—not to mention that these calzones are getting cold because I had to take care of seating three other tables before I could come and get them."

He sighed deeply and began to bite his lip, turning in desperation to Kayla. Having heard his request to Phyllis, she raised a hand. "Sorry, honey, but my hands are full right now, too. I'll get to them as fast as I can."

As he watched Katie, who was filling a glass with soda, he decided it wasn't even worth the effort. He stood looking quite lost for a time as he watched the others moving frantically about the dining room. I thought he might concede that I was the only hope that table six wouldn't die of thirst, but instead he placed a hand on my shoulder and pointed toward the door.

"You go seat the guy that just came in. I'll handle table six." Without giving me a chance to answer, he hurried away.

"Oh, Mitchell, I swear, I don't know how much more of this I can take," I muttered under my breath as I walked toward the door. "Why don't I just ask the doctor to put me on a ventilator for the next three months? That way you won't have to worry that I'm getting too tired from breathing!"

After scanning the room to find an empty table, I let my eyes go back to the man standing near the door. A feeling of relief swept over me as I reached him.

"Chris!" I exclaimed as I hit him full force with a hug. "Thank goodness you're here. You have to help me!"

Looking completely perplexed, he slowly raised his arm to return the hug and then gently placed me at arm's length. "What's wrong?" Suddenly the light came on, and he began to smirk. "Okay, what did Mitch do now?"

I grabbed his hand and pulled him a few steps away from the door. "He's become a tyrant, that's what. I can't take it anymore!"

Chris laughed. "A tyrant, huh? I've heard him called a lot of things, but never a tyrant."

I moved closer to him and lowered my voice so that no one else could hear. "Oh, believe me, he is. I went to the doctor this morning, and he told me I have no restrictions. None. Zero. Zilch. Nada. Yet, 'Mr. Authority' won't allow me to lift a finger to help out around here." I made a sweep of the dining room with my hand. "You can see how busy we are, Chris. It's always like this. The girls are exhausting themselves! And here I am, perfectly capable to pitch in and give them a little relief; and all I'm allowed to do is stand at the door and point out empty tables. It's as if he thinks anything else is going to be too strenuous for me."

Chris gazed at me thoughtfully and said something I never thought I'd hear especially from him. "I'm afraid I have to agree with Mitch on this one, Dana."

I stepped back and turned my head just slightly to give him a one-eyed stare. "You what?"

Chris dropped his head for a minute and let out a long breath. Raising his eyes to meet mine once more, he stated, "I know that's not what you wanted me to say, and I'm sorry. Mitch is only trying to look out for you. You've been through a lot. Why take a chance on causing something else to occur? Waitressing isn't an easy task. Help out in other ways." Seeing the look of despair on my face, he smiled. "Dana, he loves you. Humor him, okay? Take it easy. It's only a few more months."

I threw up my hand. "I don't believe this! Why is everyone against me here? I'm pregnant, not dying. Most pregnant women continue all their normal activities right up to delivery time. You of all people should know that. Your wife was pregnant four times."

He tried to smile softly. "Sweetheart, you aren't most pregnant women. You just recovered from a major accident. You had contractions. You're carrying twins. You're considered high-risk." He reached out and touched my shoulder in what I assumed was an attempt to comfort me. "You have a husband who thinks the world of you and those babies. I really think you need to listen to him."

I saw him lift his eyes to look directly above my head, but he brought them back quickly to focus on my face which was now harboring an expression of disgust. I thought he'd be the one person I could count on to side with me. Obviously, that had been a wrong assumption on my part.

"You aren't willing to try to talk to him? You won't ask him to let up on me at least a little?"

He shook his head slowly. "Nope, not this time. Sorry."

I threw out one last plea. "Chris, I know he loves me and that he's trying to take care of me. I appreciate that. But, he's being totally unreasonable. I've gone through the therapy; I've gone through the healing, and I'm fine now. There's no reason why I can't go back to the way things were before all that."

Chris's eyes lifted above my head again; and when I felt hands on the upper part of both my arms, I realized why.

"So, Christopher, how evil has my wife been making me out to be? Better yet, what has she been trying to convince you to do about it?"

I turned around to face him with a scowl. "Don't worry, Mitchell. He agrees with you. He thinks I'm a helpless little weakling, too." I shot Chris a quick glance over my shoulder. "I suppose pig-headedness must run in the family—at least in the men anyway."

The two shared a laugh at my words which only managed to make me angry.

"That's fine. You two go ahead and have your fun. Enjoy a laugh at my expense." I turned toward Mitch completely. "If you refuse to let me even take an order—simply because you think I'm too weak to handle it—then I guess I'm also too weak to do anything else. I'm going to go sit in the office—unless, of course, you think sitting might tire me out too much." With that I started toward the office.

Mitch took a step to follow, but Chris took hold of his arm. "Let her go cool down, little brother. She'll be okay." He pointed toward an empty table. "Mind if I take that? I was actually here to get a pizza, but I got a little distracted." He gave Mitch a sideways grin as he reached the table.

Mitch looked in the direction of the office as he pulled out a chair and sat down next to Chris. "Yeah. Sorry about that, man. I'm not sure what she said to you, but I doubt that she was professing her undying love for me."

Chris smiled. "Not unless 'tyrant' is one of your pet names."

Mitch looked toward the office again and then back to Chris. "Tyrant? She actually called me that?"

Chris nodded as he picked up the menu off the table. "Yeah, she did. Could've been worse though." He turned the page and glanced up at Mitch. "Want to share a pizza?"

"No, thanks, I'm really not hungry." Mitch sat back in his chair and brought his hands up in front of his mouth, covering his nose. Dropping them slightly, he tapped the fingers of his right hand against those of his left. "I feel like I'm walking uphill with a boulder strapped to my back when it comes to her. The woman just went through six weeks of physical therapy. She doesn't understand that simply because the doctor lifted her restrictions that it's still too soon for her to go back to her normal routine. She's so darn independent. I don't mind her helping out. It's just that I want her to ease back into it slowly." He leaned forward and began to play with the wrapper Chris had taken off his straw. "I tried to explain that I'm only looking out for her, but she thinks I'm trying to be mean."

Chris placed his order with Phyllis. He laid his menu on the table, leaned back, and took a drink of soda. "Actually, 'unreasonable' is the term she used. I suppose 'mean' would cover it, too."

Mitch reached across the table and took a drink of Chris's soda himself. "Gee, aren't you a haven of comfort," he mocked.

"Ah, come on, little brother. Don't take it so hard. Ninety percent of her little tirade just now was hormonal. Trust me on that one. I went through it enough with Trudy to know. The rest of it was simply the fact that she knows you're probably right about things, and she doesn't want to admit it." He balled up the straw wrapper and tossed it at Mitch, bouncing it off his shoulder. "Let it go. I'm sure she'll come around." He folded his hands on the table—a thoughtful look on his face. "In her defense, though, you have to try to realize that she probably just wants some normalcy back in her life. These last three months certainly haven't been a joy ride for her." He took another drink of his soda—this time toying with the straw for a moment before setting it back down. "You know, Mitch, maybe you *should* ease up on her a little. Let her find out for herself what her limits are. When she sees that she truly can't do it all, you'll have more of a leg to stand on with your argument."

Mitch glanced toward the office once more and nodded slowly. "Yeah, you're probably right." He leaned back again and slouched down a bit in the chair. "I guess she's been building up for that little outburst all morning." He gave Chris a brief account of Dana's reaction to his ad for a waitress. As he finished the story, he added, "I'm just afraid of how she's going to react when I give her the other news."

Chris looked at Mitch inquisitively. "What other news?"

"I'm quitting the band."

Chris sat silently and absorbed his brother's words before he spoke. "I thought you decided to stay. What changed?"

Mitch exhaled loudly. "Everything."

Chris started to smile. "That's pretty vague, Mitch. Care to expound a little?"

Mitch pushed his chair away from the table, leaned forward, and clasped his hands in front of him with his forearms resting on his knees. "For the last three months, in addition to heading up the band and working my job, I've been a nurse, housekeeper, cook, chauffer, and husband. Soon, I'm going to be adding father to that as well. I'm exhausted, Chris. Literally and thoroughly exhausted. Something has to give, and the only thing I can rationally let go is the band." He moved his chair closer to the table and turned over the coffee cup sitting there as he summoned Katie to fill it for him.

"You need to remember that you had extenuating circumstances forcing you to take on those extra roles. Those circumstances are pretty much gone."

Mitch took a sip of his coffee and held the cup between his hands. "Some of them may be, but they're only going to be replaced with new ones. Dana knows nothing about babies. She's never even held one—let alone take care of one. I know a little, but I'm far from being an expert in the field myself. Once these kids get here, she's going to need me as much as, if not more than, she did while she was recovering from the accident." He placed the cup on the saucer and looked his brother squarely in the eyes. "When she was in the hospital that first night, I promised God that I would take care of her and the babies no matter what. Part of doing that is being able to be there whenever they need me. If I'm off at rehearsals or shows every night, that can't happen." He leaned back in the chair again. "Like I said, I made a promise, and I have every intention of keeping it."

Chris looked thoughtfully at his younger brother and saw the decisiveness on his face. "Sounds like you're pretty serious about this, little brother. What did the guys have to say about it?"

Mitch sighed deeply. He dropped his head and then began to bite his lip as he brought his eyes up to meet Chris's. "I haven't told them yet. I was thinking I'd break it to them tonight after rehearsal or maybe tomorrow after the show. My plan is to stay through September as far as the shows. I'm thinking by that time they should have someone to replace me. Heck, for that matter, Ty can take over as front. He's got the know how—that's for sure. They don't need me to survive."

"Are you sure about that? They seem to think a lot of you."

Mitch nodded. "Yeah, I'm sure. Those guys are a plethora of talent. I'm just one man. I can be replaced. Trust me."

Chris reached out and patted Mitch on the arm. "Well, if you really feel this is what you need to do, then you have my support." Phyllis appeared with the pizza which Chris promptly pushed toward Mitch. He picked up one piece and then stood up and pushed in his chair. "Here—go find your wife and share the rest with her. I'll just take this one to go."

He started to open his wallet, but Mitch stood and covered Chris's hand with his own. "It's on me. I'll even cover the tip for you."

Chris smiled. "Gee, I'll have to come here for lunch more often."

I sat with my elbow resting on Mitch's desk, chin in my hand, twirling a straightened paperclip in the other. Tossing it into the wastebasket, I placed my other hand under my chin as well and stared blankly across the room.

"Why does he *always* have to be right?" I asked myself aloud as I pondered the situation at hand. "Why can't I win an argument for once?"

In the fifteen minutes since I'd stormed out of the dining room, I had tried my best to convince myself that I was just as capable as ever to manage all the duties the other waitresses were so expertly performing right at that moment. I tried to tell myself that in spite of all I had endured those past three months that I still had the strength and energy to take on everything I had before. Try as I might to wrestle with the truth, however, the truth kept winning out. Times had changed. *I* had changed. I was somewhere in the neighborhood of thirty pounds over my normal weight; and according to those who knew anything about it, I was 'carrying low.' Besides that, I still had a slight limp and compensated for the imbalance by shifting my weight to the other hip. When put together, this meant that more than two hours on my feet at any given time resulted in the need for a heating pad to my lower back later that evening and/or a massage from Mitch. I could easily perform most tasks around the apartment—those my over-protective husband wouldn't try to take over himself, that is—but found that I often welcomed a few minutes on the couch if not a cozy cat nap afterwards. It was happening. I was succumbing to the final trimester aches and pains—the ones that were the result of children who were growing larger, gaining strength, and repositioning within me in preparation of their birth. As much as I loved them and as much as I understood, I wanted just a piece of the old Dana back. The old Dana: full of energy, full of strength, full of.... I yawned and reached down to pat my stomach with a smile. Well, I supposed I could get used to the new Dana, too. After all, the unpleasant parts of her were only temporary. And the new Dana had something the old one didn't—twins. That made it all worthwhile.

Mitch stopped in the doorway of the office taking in the sight before him. Dana was sitting back just slightly in the chair, and her hand was on her stomach moving in a slow, circular motion. He smiled. He'd caught her doing that more and more lately: rubbing her abdomen as if she were consoling the children within her. Although she sometimes seemed uncertain about it herself, he had no doubt that she would be a good mother. He knew the twins would never be lacking in love because love was Dana's nature. She'd proven that to him on more than one occasion simply by enduring all the trials he knew he put her through. She might get angry. She might even give him the what-for, but in the end she always made sure he knew how much she loved him. As he stood there watching her, he could clearly see that her love for the twins was already in place; and once they arrived, she would do everything in her power to see to it that they never had reason to doubt it.

He stepped into the room and reached over me to place the pizza on the desk. I lifted my eyes to look at him, and he smiled.

"Are you okay?" he asked.

I shrugged. "Yeah, I guess so. I was just thinking, that's all."

"Still think I'm an unreasonable tyrant?"

"You've been talking to your brother."

Mitch chuckled. "You mean the pig-headed one? Yes, I have. But, don't be too hard on him, love. He gave us a pizza." He walked around the chair and took a seat on the corner of the desk. His expression softened, and he looked into my eyes with compassion.

"Dana, the night of the accident, as I was sitting next to your bed in the hospital, I felt something I've never felt in my entire life. I felt helpless. Totally and completely helpless. I looked at you, and everything within me wanted to take you from that bed and make you well; but I knew there was absolutely nothing I could do. I made a promise right then and there that if...when...you got well I'd do everything I could to keep you that way." He paused and took a deep breath. "I suppose in my attempt to do that I took it a bit too far, and I'm sorry. I do hope you understand that I only had your best interest in mind. That's all that matters to me."

I nodded. "Yes, I know. I love you for that, Mitch. I really do. However, I'm the one who should be apologizing. Instead of trying to see your reasoning and being grateful that you cared so much, I let my independence take over." I cast my eyes downward and almost felt ashamed for my actions. "The more you tried to protect me, the more I wanted to prove you wrong and show you that I could do all the things I did before. Sitting here now and having a chance to think it over, I realized that you're right. I'm not the same as I was before everything happened. I'm a lot bigger. I'm a lot slower, and I'm not quite as, well, 'spunky' as I was."

He smiled. "Well, I don't know about that last one. I don't think there's much that can get rid of your 'spunk.'"

He stood up, moved toward me, and pulled me against him in a warm hug. "It sounds like we need to strike a compromise. What do you say?"

"What sort of compromise?"

He moved away and knelt down before me. "I'll back off on you if you promise not to push yourself just to prove to me that you can. Deal?"

I gave it a moment of thought before I nodded. "Deal. But, you have to trust me to know what I can handle, okay?"

"Okay, but you have to trust me and let me take over if I feel I need to step in."

I reached out my hand as if to shake, but Mitch shook his head. "That may be the way you settle a deal, but not me." Placing a hand on each side of my face, he leaned in for the most wonderful kiss he could possibly deliver.

Chapter 9

A few hours later, we found ourselves pulling into the driveway of 137 Fireside Lane. Mitch turned off the car, and we sat for a minute to take a closer look. Four tall windows framed with black shutters on the front of the champagne-colored home were nestled at the back of a white railed porch that spanned the entire length of the house. Scanning the beautifully landscaped yard, we noticed two small saplings planted near the front. Although not yet old enough to bear fruit, I recognized that one was an apple tree—reminding me of the one I had at home as a child. As we got out and made our way up the walk, a small garden gnome sitting on a rock amongst a vibrant display of flowers greeted us with a smile. We knocked on the door; and when we heard a faint voice tell us to come in, we stepped inside.

"Welcome." The realtor greeted us just inside the door with a pleasant smile and extended her hand. "Tricia Trenton with Hallmark Homes. And you are?"

"I'm Mitch Tarrington, and this is my wife Dana," he replied as he shook her hand.

Tricia shook my hand as well. "Mitch and Dana, very nice to meet you. Why don't I take you on a little tour of the house? I'll point out some of the features, and then you can go back through on your own at your leisure. How does that sound?"

"That sounds fine," Mitch replied.

Hand in hand, Mitch and I followed Tricia through every room of the 2,400-square foot home including the basement. By the time we reached our starting point once again, I was ready for a nap.

"Why don't you have another look if you'd like, and then I'll be happy to answer any questions you might have. I'll be out in the dining room."

"Thanks," Mitch replied as she walked away.

He turned to me with a smile. "Well, baby, what do you think? Pretty nice, huh?"

I took a seat on a rocking chair right next to me and looked up at him with a sigh. "Pretty big, too."

He placed a gentle hand on my shoulder and gave it a rub. "Is that your way of saying you don't like it?"

"No, that's my way of saying it's pretty big. It's a lovely home; but by the time I got from the bedrooms to the kitchen, I was ready to go back up and crawl into bed! See, I told you I've lost some of my spunk."

Mitch laughed and extended a hand to help me out of the chair. "Well, would you like to take another tour, or would you rather go home and rest?"

"I suppose we could take another look if you want to," I replied halfheartedly as I placed both hands on my lower back.

For once I was grateful that he could read me the way he could. "You know, on second thought, maybe it is a little more than what we need right now. Why don't we talk to Tricia and see if she has anything else available on a smaller scale?"

I gave him a hug. "My back and I thank you," I said, and he laughed.

Joining Tricia in the dining room, we spent the next half hour going over prospective floor plans and looking at pictures of other homes on the market more suitable to our needs. Before leaving, we made an appointment to meet with her again the following afternoon to tour a few more houses in the area. As we pulled out of the driveway, Mitch glanced over at me with a smile.

"You know, this is pretty exciting—shopping for our first house."

I leaned over against his shoulder. "Yeah, it is. You know, I wasn't sure this morning that I was quite ready for this yet; but after going through that house and seeing how it was decorated, I started getting some ideas of what I could do with a place of my own."

He gave me a sideways grin. "Oh yeah? Like what?"

I sat back up. "Well, first of all, I'd want our bedroom to be done in pinks and blues—not real bright—more in pastels like we had for the wedding," I began. "I think that would be really pretty, and we could get a new comforter with a floral pattern on it or even a quilt. Then we could add a lacey dust ruffle around the bottom with curtains to match." I glanced at Mitch, and I could see him raise his eyebrows in a 'you've-got-to-be-kidding' sort of way. "Or, if we're going to do pink and blue in the twins' room, then we could do yellow in ours. That would be nice, don't you think? Something bright and sunny. No, maybe not. Bedrooms are supposed to be more tranquil, aren't they?" I paused for a moment to think. "Maybe the pink and blue would be better for the bedroom, and we could do yellow in the kitchen. Sunflowers maybe. Or fruit. I've seen a lot of kitchen items with fruit motifs."

Mitch kept his eyes straight ahead, not offering any comments or even answering my questions, so I continued to ramble on excitedly.

"As for the living room, what about mauve? I saw these awesome drapes at Carlson's a few weeks ago with a floral pattern that would go so well with that color. We'd have to get a new sofa, though, because ours really wouldn't match. We could keep the chair, I guess, unless you want to get a new one. What about a sofa table? They had a really cute lamp there, too, that would look great on a sofa table. I actually started to buy it, but we don't have anywhere to put it right now. And as far as the third bedroom, since we won't be needing that for a while, you could make it into a little den if you want. I'll let you decide how you want to decorate that since it would be your space."

Mitch chuckled. "Oh, so I do get some input, huh? For a while there I was beginning to wonder. Seems like you have it all worked out already."

I gave him a strange look. "What's that supposed to mean? Of course you get input. It's going to be your house, too, after all." I shrugged him off. "What do you think about everything I said?"

He hesitated for a moment before answering. "I think I'll be spending most of my time in the den."

"Why?"

He smiled. "Honey, come on. Pink and blue? Sunflowers? Mauve with floral curtains? Sounds like I'll be living in Princess Palace."

I crossed my arms. "Okay then, what would *you* like?"

He grinned. "How about we paint all the walls white—it's easier to decorate when you start with a neutral color—and we stick with the primaries? You know: blue, green, red...."

I sighed. "I know my primary colors, Mitch. I'm a kindergarten teacher. Remember?"

"Oh, yeah, of course. Anyway, plain curtains in the living room, and we can keep the sofa we have since anything goes with white walls. We can get a plaid comforter for the bed, and I was thinking about mirrors on the ceiling. Maybe even one of those disco lights to add a little ambience."

I gave him a look. "You can't be serious."

"Sure, why not?" His face began to light up with mischief. "Since you didn't mention any theme for the bathroom, I was thinking about frogs. Frogs live in water; there's water in the bathroom—you get it, don't you?" By this time I was quite mortified. "Oh, and if you want sunflowers in the kitchen, that's fine. After all, you'll be spending most of your time out there anyway."

I cocked my head toward him. "Oh, is that so?"

"Uh-huh. I plan to keep you in the kitchen—barefoot and pregnant."

He began to laugh as I gave his shoulder a gentle shove. "You really are terrible."

"Maybe. But, I know you love it!"

Deciding on dinner at The Mark, we settled into a cozy corner booth; and Mitch moved in as close to me as he could get. Not seeming to care who else was watching, he put both arms around me and held me against him protectively as he rested his cheek against the top of my head,. I allowed myself to feel the warmth of his embrace and inhaled deeply, taking in the scent of his cologne. He moved away and tilted my chin up with just one finger, kissed me softly, and smiled into my eyes.

"I wonder how much we'll be able to do things like this after the twins are born," he said.

"I don't know. I would imagine it's not easy to go out with two babies in tow."

He picked up the menu lying in front of him and began to study it. "Well, we don't have to take them everywhere with us you know. There *are* babysitters. Besides, I'm sure there will be plenty of times that by the end of the day you'll be practically running out the door to get away from them."

I reached for my own menu but paused instead to respond to my husband. "Why? Don't you think I'm going to enjoy being a mother?"

He lowered his menu and looked at me with a smile. "Sure, honey, I think you'll love being a mom."

I picked up my menu and glanced over it though my mind was really on what Mitch had said. I placed it back on the table and turned toward him. "Then why would you say that I'd be eager to get away from my children? Do you think it's going to be that stressful for me?"

Mitch had to smile at Dana's innocence. As hard as it was for him to believe her naïveté on the subject, he knew she didn't have a clue as to what caring for an infant entailed. Like anything else she did, he knew she'd give it her all and master the task. He also knew that she'd become tired or even frustrated at times and would welcome the chance to just be Dana without having to be Mommy at the same time. Looking at the questions in her eyes, he wasn't sure how he could explain the meaning of his words without causing her to start worrying about her lack of knowledge on the subject. Rather than try, he decided to answer her in the simplest way he knew how.

"No, love, I don't. I think you'll be just fine."

At that moment the waitress appeared to take their order, and Mitch was grateful for her presence knowing that it meant he could move the conversation in another direction.

As she walked away, he turned toward his wife and noticed her once again unconsciously rubbing her stomach.

"Do you think they know what you're doing?" he asked as he pointed to the motion.

I glanced down to see my hand resting on my abdomen—unaware that I had even placed it there. "Oh, I don't know," I replied. "I think it's just a habit I've developed. It's a little hard to ignore this huge bulge in my middle. It seems like every time I look at it, it's larger than it was the time before."

Mitch laughed. "I think you're exaggerating a bit. I haven't noticed much of a difference in the last month or so."

I gave him a look of shock. "Then you haven't been looking very closely, Mitchell. I've gained eight pounds since my last visit to Dr. Bradley. I've *definitely* gotten bigger."

He placed a hand on the middle of my back and gave it a gentle rub. "I do look closely, and maybe you have gotten bigger; but all I'm saying is that I haven't noticed it. Besides, doesn't the baby grow most rapidly in that last few months anyway?"

"I think so. At the rate these two are going, they'll each come out looking like four-year- olds!"

"If that's the case, I'm not sure you'll want to opt for a natural delivery."

I grimaced at the thought of that. "I'm not sure I want to opt for a natural delivery regardless. If what everyone is telling me is true, I want to be knocked out cold!"

Mitch's face took on an expression of sympathy, and he leaned over to kiss me on top of my head as he continued to rub my back lovingly. "Don't listen to other people, sweetheart. Everyone has a different experience, and just because someone else's delivery wasn't the greatest doesn't mean yours won't be." Mitch took a roll from the basket the waitress had placed in the middle of the table, sliced it open, and began to spread butter on one half. "Besides, I think they found out it was actually dangerous to have the mother unconscious during delivery. But, I hear they have some pretty hefty drugs that will take care of the discomfort." He patted my shoulder. "I'll be right there with you. I know you'll do fine."

He handed me the piece of bread he had buttered, and I took a bite. "That's easy for you to say. All you have to do is tell me to breathe."

He turned toward me and looked directly into my eyes with a lopsided grin. "Did I ever tell you that you worry way too much?"

"Yes."

"Good. I was just checking."

The late day sun beat down on us as we made our way toward the Tarrington Estate for rehearsal. Turning my face upward as if to mock it, I let the cool breeze wash over me; and I realized right then just why Mitch had chosen a convertible. He was almost too tall to fit into it with any real amount of comfort, but the rush from driving with the top down on a day like today was worth it. Glancing his way, I noticed how right he looked sitting there: his left hand on the wheel, his right resting on the gearshift, and his sunglasses giving him that James Dean sort of coolness and appeal. Apparently feeling my stare, he moved his right hand to my stomach, patted it gently, and then took my hand.

"Did little Waldo and Wilhelm get enough to eat?"

I scrunched up my face, pulled my head back slightly, and stared at him. "Little Waldo and *what?* Wilhelm? Oh, no, Mitchell. There's no way we're calling our children that!"

I could see the orneriness shining in his eyes even though he wasn't looking directly at me. "Yeah. You're right. One of them might be a girl. How about Waldo and Wilhelmina?"

"No way! I would never do that to my child."

"Oh, like you can come up with something better," he teased.

"Megan's only three, Mitch, and I believe even *she* could come up with something better than that!"

"Well, if you don't like my suggestions, let's hear yours. I've been throwing out names right and left for two weeks now, and you shoot them all down; but yet I haven't heard anything from you."

I sighed, sat back in my seat, and turned to look out over the countryside. "I know. It's just that picking a child's name is a big responsibility."

He took my hand again and gave it a little squeeze. "Baby, you're making this a lot more difficult than it has to be. Simply pick out a couple of names that you like; and if we agree on them, it's a done deal."

"First of all, a name is something the child has to live with for the rest of his or her life. You can't use the first thing that pops into your head. Second, we both have to like the names we pick."

He nodded slowly, and I could see the gears turning. "Okay, here's an idea. I'll pick one name, and you pick the other. That takes half the pressure off, and we both have input. What do you think of that idea?"

"There you go again. Just like decorating the house. You're implying that I'm not going to give you any input. You helped make these babies. You're going to help raise them; therefore, you have input, Mitchell."

He started to speak but must have thought twice because he closed his mouth tightly and sighed. Pausing, he took a deep breath and continued. "Yes, dear, you're right. So how about it? I choose a name, and you choose a name. I'm sure we can each come up with at least one good one."

I wasn't sure I was totally keen on his idea, but I supposed it was worth a shot. I just hoped his idea of a good name was something other than Waldo or Wilhelmina.

"Okay. You go first. What name do you like?" I asked.

"For a boy or girl?"

"Doesn't matter. Pick one."

"Well, I don't want to pick a boy's name if that's what you are going to pick or a girl's name if you want to name the girl."

I closed my eyes and sighed again. "Fine, Mitch. You name the boy."

I saw him twist his jaw in thought. "Okay. I think I like the name Theophilus. Theophilus Tarrington. Kinda has a ring to it, don't you think?"

"Theo...what?"

He repeated the name—this time very slowly—and with a smile from ear to ear.

"Yes. I heard you the first time. I was just trying to figure out how you came up with such a name."

"What's wrong with it?"

"What's wrong with...Mitch, come on. You wouldn't really name a child Theophilus, now would you?"

"We could call him Theo. Or Phil."

"How about let's not?"

He snickered. "Let's not? You're telling me my names are weird, and you come up with 'let's not'? Honey, I don't think...."

"I don't think I want to continue this discussion with you." I crossed my arms and turned away from him in a huff. If he wasn't going to be serious, I decided I wasn't going to talk to him.

He began to laugh. "Sweetie, come on, I was just having fun. Don't go getting mad at me."

"You tease me way too much, Mitchell."

He caressed my cheek with his thumb. "You're right. I'm sorry. Why don't you tell me a name you like?"

I thought for a moment. "Pamela."

"Pamela. Pam. That's nice. I like it."

My face lit up like a Christmas tree. "You do? Really? If we have a girl, we can call her Pamela?"

"Fine with me. In fact, I've liked that name from the very first time I ever heard it."

I was afraid to ask. "When was that?"

"Back in high school. First girl I ever went out with had the name Pamela. Pam Barrone. Really pretty: long dark hair, great legs, big...."

"Stop right there, buster. I withdraw the name from the running."

"Why? Because I used to date someone with that name?"

"That and the fact that I don't want my daughter's name to make you think of some girl with big...big...oh, you know!"

"Big brown eyes?" He snickered. "What did you think I was going to say?"

"Mitchell Jacob Tarrington, you really make me crazy sometimes."

He pulled me against his shoulder and gave me a kiss on the cheek. "You're such a funny little girl. You know that? I love you."

The rest of the band had yet to arrive when we got to his parents' house, so Mitch and I decided to join Jake and Olivia on the back patio for some cold lemonade. As I looked out across the back lot, I understood why the pair had chosen that location to make their home so many years before. The view was nothing less than breathtaking. The rolling hills were dotted with trees of every kind, and their foliage displayed a kaleidoscope of colors that reflected the autumn that was quickly approaching. There was nothing but countryside as far as the eye could see—no other houses and no signs of life other than an occasional hawk gliding on the breeze or a tiny woodland creature foraging for a meal. I could only imagine the number of hours the Tarrington family had spent right there just basking in the beauty around them.

I turned slightly to my left to see the sunlight dancing on the soft ripples of a small lake nestled just beyond a row of hearty evergreens. Their branches cast shadows on the water like arms reaching to grab the rays of light. I concluded that it had to be where Mitch and his siblings had swam during the hot weather and skated when it turned cold. It reminded me of the one near my Grammy's house where I used to play. While not quite as big, it provided hours of entertainment for a young girl growing up without the company of brothers or sisters. Although I was a proficient swimmer, Grammy would never allow me in the water alone. I would often sit on the makeshift dock dangling my feet in the crisp, cool water as I soaked up the warmth of the summer sun. When evening fell and supper had been cleared away, I'd take a large flashlight from the broom closet and head back to the edge of the lake to scout for bullfrogs. Though I'd never actually caught one, I'd had fun trying; and Grammy would never scold me for the mud that would usually be caked on my clothes and my skin or the countless pairs of sneakers I ruined in the process.

I smiled at the memories filling my mind and allowed myself to get lost in the innocence of days gone by. I missed her more than ever and wished that she could be with me to celebrate the birth of my own children, to give me advice, and to fill me with the wisdom to be the kind of mother I longed to be. Unfortunately, all I had were the lessons she had instilled in me through the years and the love that filled my heart knowing the sacrifices she made for me each and every day. In my eyes Grammy had been a saint, and I knew that God had to give her an extra special place in Heaven because of it.

"Honey, are you okay?"

Mitch's words and his gentle hand on my arm stirred me back from my daydream, and I smiled.

"Yeah, I'm all right," I answered softly. "I was just thinking."

He breathed a little sigh of relief and smiled back at me through loving eyes. "Well, you had me worried for a minute. Mom asked you a question. She was wondering when would be a good time to plan your baby shower."

I turned to her a little surprised—both at the thought of a shower and that I had been so wrapped up in myself that I hadn't noticed she was even speaking to me.

"Baby shower? Is that like a wedding shower, but for the baby?"

Mitch chuckled and seemed surprised by my ignorance. "Yeah, sweetheart, that's exactly what it is. Didn't you know you'd be having one?"

Feeling slightly embarrassed, I dropped my eyes from his. "No, actually I didn't. I just assumed we'd have a lot of shopping to do."

He laughed and placed an arm around my shoulders, pulled me toward him, and kissed the top of my head. "I have little doubt that won't be happening regardless," he said, "knowing the way you like to shop."

"Dana, dear, unless there's someone else you'd like to add to the list, we can use the same one we used for your bridal shower," Olivia began. "I was thinking it might be nice to have it within the next few weeks. That way if there is anything you don't receive that you still need, it will give you and Mitch plenty of time to pick it up before the babies are born."

"That sounds fine," I replied. I wasn't really sure how to respond.

"Since Mitch shared that at least one of the babies is a boy, we can put that on the invitations if you'd like; or we can leave off the information and that way the guests won't be partial to purchasing everything in blue. Maybe that would be best. What do you think?"

I turned to Mitch hoping he'd provide an answer or at least a clue, but he only shrugged.

"Whatever you think is best, Olivia," I answered timidly.

"Now, where have you registered? I can list the names of the stores on the invitations as well."

"Registered?"

Thankfully, Mitch was sensing my impending panic. "Oh, we haven't done that yet, Mom. Can we get back to you with the info?"

Olivia smiled. "Of course, honey, that's fine." She turned to me again. "Dana, the girls suggested Sunday, September 11, after church. Does that sound all right with you?"

I looked at Mitch again; and he smiled softly, giving me a reassuring nod. I looked at Olivia and smiled. "Sure, that's fine."

Just then we heard the clamor of our friends behind us, and Alexander appeared to announce the arrival of the band. Mitch stood up to greet them and then sent them off to the rec room where he promised to meet them in a few minutes. He came to stand next to my chair, reached out, and brushed the hair back off my forehead with a smile.

"Baby, why don't you just stay out here and relax with Mom and Dad for a while? I have some important business to go over with the guys before we go through the set."

I looked at him curiously. "What kind of 'business,' Mitch?"

He began to bite his lip somewhat nervously and shifted his eyes to his parents before looking at me again. "Nothing, love. Just business. I'll talk to you about it later, okay?"

Although my first inclination was to delve deeper into the mystery, I decided to concede and wait until I had him alone before I grilled him for information. A captive audience is always easier to deal with anyway, I concluded.

"Well, okay, I'll just hang out here," I replied.

"Thank you," he said as he leaned down to kiss me. "I'll see you a little later."

As he disappeared into the house, I turned to Jake and Olivia. "Do either of you know what that was all about?"

They exchanged a look, and then both shook their heads. "Not a clue, Dana," Jake said. "I wouldn't worry about it though. Probably just a bunch of musical mumbo-jumbo you wouldn't understand anyway."

"I'm sure you're probably right," I said as I glanced toward the house. "Most likely nothing of any importance to me."

Now, if I could only convince myself of that, I thought.

Mitch paused for a moment in the family room to collect his thoughts. Glancing through the door to the rec room, he could see his band mates gathered together in the front of the room. They were tinkering with instruments and sharing in lighthearted conversation while waiting patiently for him to arrive. His heart sank in his chest as he thought about the news he had to give them tonight—the 'business' he needed to discuss as he had put it to Dana. The past eight months with them had been like reliving a part of his past that he thought he'd never experience again, the joy of doing what he loved to do with the five men who had become as close as brothers to him. He would miss them it was true, but he knew that they would be fine without him. They were talented and dedicated to their task; and as he'd told Chris, he was just one man who could easily be replaced. He had to keep telling himself that—*he could be replaced.* Making himself believe that was the only way to make the ordeal more bearable—that and the knowledge that it was going to be the best thing for his family. In his heart, he knew he was doing the right thing. He swallowed the lump rising in his throat, took a deep breath, and put a smile on his face.

"Hey, Trip, what's happening?" Shep greeted him with a bright smile.

"Not a whole lot, man," he replied. He sighed heavily; and feeling his confidence waning, he forced another smile and decided he'd better get it over with before he lost his nerve. "Well, actually, that's not exactly true. There's something I have to talk to you guys about before we get started."

The five moved in closer to their front man—all of them with concerned expressions. Ash placed a hand on his shoulder. "Is something wrong, Mitch?" he asked.

Mitch picked up his guitar and absently began to run his hand along the neck. Beginning to bite his lip against his emotions, he placed it back down and turned back to his friends.

"This is really hard for me, guys, so I'm just going to come out with it," he started. "You know that Dana and I have been through a lot these past few months, and it's made me realize that, well, I'm no Superman. I've really done my best to keep everything together; and I've managed, but it hasn't been easy. I know when the babies come she's going to need me even more than she did during her recovery, and I have to be there for her. I know now that, as much as I want to, I can't do everything. Something's gotta give."

Mitch knew they were all reading between the lines—he could see it on their faces—but Newbie was the only one brave enough to ask. "What are you trying to tell us, Trip? Are you quitting the band?"

Mitch dropped his eyes and nodded. "Yeah, that's what I'm trying to tell you. I'm sorry, guys, but I have to put my family first. I have to take care of them. I'm sure you can understand that."

The silence was deafening for only the next minute, but it seemed like an eternity to Mitch. He lifted his eyes to glance at each one of them and noticed that their expressions reflected disappointment in what he had told them. Finally, Shep stepped forward and looked him squarely in the eyes—his voice filled with anxiety and desperation.

"You can't do that, Mitch. You can't quit. Not now."

Mitch gave Shep a questioning look. "Why not? What's so important about *now?*"

Before he had a chance to answer, Zach placed a hand on Shep's arm and stepped slightly in front of him almost as if he were blocking him from Mitch's view. "He just means that we don't want to lose you, man. You're our rock. We need you."

Mitch smiled and shook his head. "No, you don't. Every week you come here, and you give 150 percent. Just when I think that's all there is, you step on that stage and give the crowd 150 more." He looked toward the instruments for a moment as he gathered his thoughts before looking at his friends once more. "I thank you for the wonderful gift you've given me—the chance to have some good times and reconnect with a part of my past. More than that, I've had the chance to reconnect with all of you; and even if I'm out of Ace, I won't let you out of my life." He chuckled. "I love you guys even if you are a bunch of losers."

Shep was standing slightly behind the others now with his head down and his eyes cast toward the floor. It was taking everything within him to remain quiet and to keep from blurting out the news they had been hoping to surprise Mitch with themselves tonight. What they had planned as a night of joy and celebration had turned into everything but. Realizing suddenly that their eyes were upon him, he lifted his head and stepped up to his friend.

"We're gonna miss you, dude."

Mitch reached out, and the two exchanged a hug as he fought back his emotions once more. Pulling away, he gave Shep a smile. "Hey, you aren't getting rid of me that easy. I'm staying on until the end of September at least, and I'll do what I can to help you find a replacement...."

"Whoa—did you say a *replacement?*" Ty chimed in. "Listen, Trip. At some point there may be someone standing in front of that main mike, but that person will never be a replacement. He would only be filling in until *you* decide to come back. Got it?"

Mitch nodded. A warm smile glowed on his face, and his heart filled with the strength of the bond between them. "Got it." Ready to break the melancholy mood settling over them, he picked up his guitar and placed the strap over his shoulder. "Now, how about we make some music? We still have a gig to pull off tomorrow night."

For the next two hours, they played like they had never played before.

As we turned onto the main road leading away from the Tarrington Estate, Mitch pointed toward the horizon.

"You know, it's a shame to waste such a beautiful sunset. If you aren't too tired, I know the perfect place to watch it from. Are you game?"

"Sure," I said as I gazed past the end of his finger at the bright orange ball sinking behind the clouds.

A long winding road took us up into the hills, and soon we came to a clearing overlooking the edge of the city. Lights on the distant buildings glittered like fireflies as the sun painted streaks of red and pink, blue and purple against the twilight sky. Pulling a safe distance from the edge of the cliff, Mitch turned off the ignition and turned toward me.

"Welcome to Fantasy Ridge," he said with a smile, "where the girls fantasize about life in the city below, and the boys fantasize about... well...*other* things."

I giggled. "Is that what *everyone* calls it or what *you* call it?"

"No, everyone—not just me." He moved closer and placed his arm around my shoulders. "I can't say I haven't had a fantasy or two up here myself. In my younger days, of course."

"Oh, so I'm not the first girl you've brought up here, huh?"

He brushed back my hair and began to kiss my neck. "No, but you're the only one that matters."

"Why? Because we're married?"

I heard a soft snicker as he began to nibble my ear. "Well, yes, and with the others it really was just a fantasy. With you it can be reality."

Just then, I glanced around us and noticed several other cars parked within a few yards on either side. I gently pushed against Mitch's chest causing him to sit up enough to look at me.

"What's the matter?"

"If you haven't noticed, Mitchell, there are other people here—other people who are *watching* us."

He laughed. "Yes, love, there are other people here. But trust me, they *aren't* watching us."

He started in again, and again I pushed him away. "I thought we came up here to watch the sunset, not to make out."

He sat up, turned slightly toward the overlook, and then back to me. "Nice. Well worth the drive up here. Now, where was I?"

"No, Mitch. If you want to give me a kiss, that's fine. Anything else will have to wait until we get home."

"You sure?"

"Of course, I'm sure. I'm not going to be the free entertainment for all these people."

He sat up completely and settled back into his seat. "You wouldn't be—they have their own entertainment." He folded his hands and placed them neatly in his lap. "That's fine. I'll respect your wishes."

"I didn't say I wouldn't neck with you."

He started to smirk impishly. "No, no, you can't go changing your tune now, sister. You said I wasn't allowed to do anything more than kiss you, and I already did that." He turned his eyes toward the horizon. "Let's watch the sunset. After all, that's why we came up here."

Grabbing hold of his shirt, I pulled him toward me and gave him a long passionate kiss. Moving away for just a moment, he smiled brightly; and his eyes danced with love. Then he moved back in to return the gesture, times two. Or maybe three.

The stars were settling in above us as we sat hand in hand gazing at the city far below. Mitch had become quiet after our little kissing session. Looking at him just then, I tried to read the distant expression on his face. I reached out to run my fingers through the back of his hair, and he glanced at me for a moment before turning his attention ahead once more. He sighed deeply, and I touched his cheek lightly with my index finger, caressing it softly.

"Talk to me, Mitch. Tell me what's on your mind."

Mitch continued to stare into the distance. His thoughts were focused on finding the words he needed to say. The reason he had brought her there was to tell her he'd quit Ace. The sunset had only been an excuse. He thought the beauty of the surroundings and a touch of romance on his part would be enough to put her into a more accepting mood. He'd been able to complete the first part of his plan, and now he needed to follow through on the second. But, he didn't want to. It had been a long day filled with a roller coaster of emotions; and now here they were, together and relaxed, feeling nothing more than the love between them. She needed this time. He couldn't take that away from her. He decided to keep things to himself for a while longer. He concluded there would be other opportunities as he let the one before him slip away.

He brought her hand to his lips and kissed it softly. "Nothing, love. I was just enjoying the moment."

As I had earlier, I wanted to dive in feet first and pull it out of him; but I chose to remain silent instead. Whatever he was keeping from me—and I knew there was something—seemed to be causing turmoil within him. I decided I would give him another day or so to work it out for himself; and if I was still in the dark, then I would ask.

Night turned to daylight, and morning quickly changed to afternoon. At one o'clock we said our goodbyes to the crew at Gartano's and made our way to the offices of Hallmark Homes. Once there, we would meet with Tricia who would lead us to the properties we wanted to tour. The first, a four-bedroom split-level, was nestled in a quiet neighborhood just a street away from Chris and Trudy. Mitch told me he had always liked the area, and I secretly knew he was hoping the home would have what we were looking for. The other was a three-bedroom ranch closer to the downtown area, thus being a bit more convenient for Mitch's commute to work. We decided to look closely at both and then take the weekend to discuss the pros and cons of each. If neither suited our tastes, Tricia assured us there were more on the market from which to choose.

At 1:30 pm, we found ourselves pulling into the driveway of the first home. Parking next to Tricia's minivan, Mitch turned to me with a smile.

"First the house and then one of those," he said as he pointed his thumb in the direction of the van.

I laughed. "Let's not get the cart before the horse, dear, okay?" I pointed discreetly toward Tricia who had moved back the front curtains on one end enough to peek out at us. "Come on, my handsome husband. Let's go have a look."

Stepping inside the house, I had to place a hand over my mouth to keep from gasping audibly at my surroundings. Elegantly embroidered floral drapes framed the large bay window surrounded by walls painted in mauve. I took a few steps forward to run my hand lightly across a sofa table—its polished surface adorned with frames of every shape and size. Gingerly lifting one to look at the photograph, I smiled at the two little girls, obviously twins, smiling back at me. Placing the frame back, I lifted my eyes straight ahead toward the doorway leading to the kitchen. Although the living room wall blocked most of my view, I could see enough to notice the bright yellow placemats accenting the small round dining table, and I smiled. This was already feeling like home, and I hadn't moved more than five steps from the front door.

"Would you like to see the rest?" Tricia asked and broke the silence that had settled over us.

I'm not sure I need to, I said to myself. To her I replied, "I'd love that."

She led us into the kitchen, and again my eyes widened as I gazed around me. *This just couldn't be happening*, I told myself. No, I had to be dreaming, or hallucinating, or something. Sunflowers were everywhere—on the curtains, on the accent rug, on the canisters that lined the countertop. As Tricia rattled off something about the appliances staying with the house, I don't believe Mitch and I were even paying attention. Slowly, I turned my head toward him, and his eyes were as large as mine were. His face clearly showed we were thinking the same thing. This wasn't merely a coincidence. This was meant to be.

As our tour continued, the more I saw the more I was convinced. The master bedroom, done in varied shades of blue, boasted a walk-in closet that was every girl's dream come true. As I stepped inside and turned around to marvel at the size, my ornery husband commented, "Gee, honey, this is only big enough for all your clothes. Where would I put mine?" Tricia laughed as I simply smirked and rolled my eyes.

After viewing the other rooms upstairs, we followed our guide to the lower level of the home. Just off to the left of the stone fireplace in the spacious family room was a smaller room that the residents used as a playroom for their children. "It could easily be transformed into a fourth bedroom if you wanted or even a cozy home office," Tricia offered. We went on to find a half bath and a large laundry room with a fold-down ironing board and built-in shelves to hold laundry products. Taking the three steps back up to the main level, Tricia led us through the kitchen to a small entry way with a door that opened to the attached two-car garage. Retracing our steps through the kitchen, we followed her through the dining room and finally out sliding glass doors to the brick patio at the back of the house. Pointing toward the back of the yard, Mitch turned to her curiously.

"What's that building used for?" he asked.

"That's a workshop," Tricia explained. "I guess Mr. Tanner, the owner, likes to do woodworking as a hobby. Apparently, he didn't want to take up the garage with it, so he put up the outbuilding."

Mitch smiled and nodded approvingly. "Cool. A place I can escape to," he said.

"Or, a place for the band to rehearse," I countered. "Just think, Mitch. Your parents can have their house back."

I could have sworn I saw him cringe at my comment. "Yeah, I suppose," he replied quietly.

Mitch glanced back at the workshop as he stepped into the house once more. *I sure hope it's heated,* he thought to himself. *Once she finds out I won't be needing it for rehearsals, she just may make me live out there.*

"Would you like to go through again on your own or are you ready to go to the next home?" Tricia asked as she closed and locked the sliding doors behind us.

Mitch looked to me for an answer, and I shrugged. "Personally, I don't think I even want to look at the next house. I like this one."

Mitch placed a hand on my shoulder and gave it a gentle rub. "Me too," he replied. "I honestly think this is just what we're looking for."

Tricia looked first at Mitch, then at me, and then at both of us as if we were insane. "You really don't want to look at anything else? You may find something you like better."

Mitch glanced down at me with a smile. "I know it has to sound a little odd for us to settle on the first home we look at. That's just how Dana and I operate. We see something we like, and we go for it. I think we'd like to put in an offer."

Tricia shrugged and followed it up with a warm smile. "Well, who am I to argue? Let's head back to the office. I'll call and cancel the other viewing, and then we can talk about what we need to do from here."

Soon we were settled back in the car and heading out. I turned to Mitch and started to speak, but he interrupted.

"You don't have to say it, Dana. I knew the minute we walked in there. It's perfect, isn't it?"

"Mitch, it's more than perfect! It's like we were supposed to find it."

He reached out for my hand. "Well, love, I agree. We'll know for sure if they accept our offer."

The rest of the afternoon we spent with Tricia on the other side of an oak desk at the Hallmark Homes regional office going over the details of a contract and discussing price negotiations. With an asking price of $130,000, Mitch felt that an offer of $120,000 would be the place to start, and Tricia agreed. She mentioned that she would use our social status as a dickering tool—first home, newly married, and expecting twins. I hoped that the couple would go for that since they were parents of twins themselves. She also thought that the fact they needed to sell quickly (the man was relocating for his job) would work in our favor.

With Tricia's promise to call us as soon as she had any news, we left her to do her work and headed for home.

A short while later we found ourselves at home once again. Exhausted from the day, I headed straight for the couch and fell onto it as I grabbed the blanket off the back and repositioned the pillow under my head in one fluid motion. Mitch took a seat on the coffee table in front of me and folded his hands looking quite serious.

"What?" I asked.

"Are you all right?"

"I'm fine. Just a little tired. Why?"

He reached out with his left hand to stroke my hair. "I was hoping we could talk for a little while. No big deal. You go ahead and rest."

I had closed my eyes with the intent to take a nap but opened them now to look at him. Perhaps something was suddenly prompting him to share his secret with me. I didn't want him to lose his nerve, so I tried to look a little more alert.

"I'm listening. What did you want to talk about?"

He stood up, straightened my blanket, and leaned down to kiss my forehead. "Nothing that can't wait until later. You stay here and relax. I think I'll walk down to Cutman's Deli and pick up a couple of sandwiches for dinner."

Before I had a chance to protest, he was out the door. I could hear the sound of his key as he locked it behind him.

Sighing in defeat, I closed my eyes, surrendered to the fatigue, and drifted off to sleep.

The blazing heat was taking its toll on Mitch as he started his walk to Cutman's. Unrolling the sleeve on his shirt so that it fell just past his right elbow, he used it to wipe the perspiration from his face and brow. Rolling it back up, he then loosened his tie, pulled it off, and stuffed it in the pocket of his trousers. He silently cursed himself for being so hasty in his departure that he hadn't taken the time to change from his work attire into something cooler. But, he was certain that had he allowed himself even those few extra minutes, Dana would have begun to ask questions. He knew he needed to tell her and get it over with—he'd psyched himself up to do so all the way home from Tricia's office—and he'd planned to come clean the minute they got home. However, as soon as she'd mentioned that she was tired, it gave his mind the excuse it needed to put things off a little longer. He'd never been one to procrastinate, so why was he doing it now? The only answer he could give himself was because he knew she'd be upset, and he didn't want to face her reaction.

When did you turn into such a coward, Mitch Tarrington? he asked himself. *Just tell her and get it over with. Would you rather she find out from someone else and make matters worse?* That was something he really hadn't considered. What if they went to the club tonight and one of the guys let it slip? He knew he could trust Chris not to say anything, and no one else in his family was aware of the information. *What's the big deal anyway? It's not like you're telling her you want a divorce or anything. After all, you're giving up the band so you can be a better husband and father. She should appreciate that.* She might if he hadn't made her a promise to the contrary. When someone gave Dana their word, she took it to heart—especially when it was him and especially after everything they had been through in the past few months. How could she ever learn to trust him again if he was constantly keeping secrets from her? *So much for the 'no secrets' ethic of the family,* he thought. These days he wasn't very good at upholding it.

He wiped his forehead again—this time with the palm of his hand—and cleaned off the moisture on the leg of his pants. Spying a hot dog vendor on the opposite corner, he decided to cross the street and buy a cold drink to keep him from succumbing to the unbearable temperature. Once at Cutman's he would sit for a few minutes inside to cool off before making the trek back home. Dana had enough to deal with without having to help him recover from heat exhaustion, too.

Mitch shook the cup and moved the straw within it to suck up the last remnants of the soda. Removing the lid, he threw it into a trash receptacle and began to chew on the ice, savoring the sensation as the cubes melted to send a trickle of cool liquid down his throat. As he finished the last few pieces, Cutman's was in sight; and he quickened his pace, welcoming the blast of refreshingly cold air as he opened the door to step inside.

Not certain what Dana might be hungry for, he ordered the first two items listed on the menu, paid the server, and took a seat to wait for his food. Only a few other patrons occupied the dining room of the small establishment, so he didn't feel odd about taking a table all for himself. He gazed out the window into the streets buzzing with Saturday afternoon activity. He chuckled to himself as a father passed by with his young son. The child was frantically licking an ice cream cone oblivious to the fact that his melting treat was covering his face and dripping mercilessly down both arms. His heart warmed to know that in just a few years he could do the same with his own children. He smiled as he thought of how Dana would most likely scold him for giving them snacks before dinner knowing all the while that it probably wouldn't be the last time she would have to do so.

The server called him back to the counter to pick up his food, and he hesitated before opening the door to the midday heat once again. He would tell her as soon as he got back home, he decided. That way she could get angry or cry or whatever she was going to do, and hopefully the storm would blow over before he stepped onto the stage later that night.

"Hey, beautiful, time to wake up."

Mitch kissed me softly and ran the back of his hand down my cheek. My eyelids struggled to open against the light streaming in through the balcony doors opposite me. I yawned sleepily and stretched as my husband smiled at me and offered his hand to help me to a sitting position. He took the seat next to me, and I fell against him with my head landing on his chest.

"Why am I so tired?"

"Just part of the process, love," he replied. "Besides, we have had a busy day so far between work and taking care of all that house business. The fact that it's somewhere around 92 degrees outside doesn't help either." He pressed his cheek against the side of my head and spoke to me tenderly. "Would you like to stay home tonight and rest? You can take a nice bubble bath and curl up here on the couch for the evening. If you want, I'll even stop by the Tasty Twist on the way home and pick up a couple of root beer floats. How's that sound?"

I brought my hand up and ran it across his chest. My fingertips lightly grazed the rippling muscles hidden beneath his shirt. He tucked a strand of hair behind my ear, and I moved my hand to meet his as our fingers intertwined.

"Thank you for thinking of me, but I really would like to go with you. I may not be able to go much after the babies get here—especially this winter—so I want to take advantage of it while I still can."

Okay, man, here's the golden opportunity. She's given you the lead in—all you have to do is handle the follow up.

I heard Mitch take a deep breath, and he brought his arm around me and pulled me closer.

"Honey, about that—there's something I need to tell you."

The serious tone in his voice caused me to sit up, and he moved his arm from around me to take my hand. He paused for a moment before he started to speak again.

"Dana, I know that you're probably going to disagree; but I've made a decision, and I hope that you'll take into consideration why I'm doing it. I...."

The sound of the phone ringing caused us both to jump.

I started to stand, but hesitated. "Should I just let the machine get it?"

He looked a little dejected as he shook his head. "No, it might be something important. Go ahead and answer it."

At this rate I'd never find out what he was hiding. I gave him a quick peck as I stood up and made my way into the kitchen.

"Oh, hi, Carrie! I didn't expect to hear from you today. What's up?"

That was all Mitch needed to hear—to know that once again his plan would have to wait. Glancing toward Dana as he rose to his feet, he headed toward the bathroom, hoping somehow that a shower would wash away his melancholy frame of mind.

Mitch stood in front of the bathroom mirror quieting himself enough to listen to his wife's seemingly endless chatter as she spoke to her friend on the telephone. *How do women find so much to talk about*, he wondered. Had the call been for him, his conversation would have been over within five minutes if it had even lasted that long. He smiled to himself at the bubbly sound of her voice and became curious as he heard his name interjected once or twice into the conversation. He didn't know what she was saying about him, but knowing Dana it was most likely something good. If it wasn't, he didn't want to know anyway.

I hung up the phone and went to seek out my husband who was just emerging from the bathroom.

"Finished talking already?" Mitch teased as I followed him into the bedroom.

"That was Carrie, my friend from school, remember? She just called to tell me they found a substitute to take my class this fall."

"Really? Who's that?" he asked with feigned interest as he pulled a t-shirt over his head.

"Erica Carlisle. She just received her teaching degree a few months ago. She visited the school last fall and spent a few days with me in the classroom. She's really a nice person, and I'm sure the kids will get along well with her." I sat down on the side of the bed as Mitch finished dressing. "I suppose the kids will get so used to her they won't warm up to me at all when I finally go back," I was unable to hide the disappointment in my voice. "I really wish I could at least start the fall and just take a month or two when the babies get here. That way the kids would know who I am, and it would make things easier later on." I perked up as a thought came to my mind. "Hey, maybe I could just go in for a few hours a day, or just a few days a week. That way, when I take my class back, it won't be a shock to anyone."

Mitch finished tying his shoes and looked up at me with a soft smile. "Dana, you know that Dr. Bradley suggested you wait to go back. Your idea isn't bad, but you don't want the kids to get used to you popping in and out and then become disappointed when you don't do it for six or eight weeks. I think you should listen to the doctor." He stood to walk to the dresser but paused to give me a kiss. "Don't worry, honey. It'll all work out in the end. You'll see."

Then another thought occurred to me. "Mitch, you don't think they brought her in to replace me, do you? I mean, she's newly graduated, and she probably needs a permanent job. With all the school I've already missed, maybe they're going to fire me and hire her instead."

He was standing in front of the mirror now combing his hair, and he paused to speak to my reflection. "No, I don't think that at all, and neither should you. Your boss understands everything you've been through. I have no doubt that your job is as secure as it ever was."

"I hope you're right."

He laid the comb on the dresser, put on his glasses, and turned to reach out for me. "Come here and let me give you a hug. Then we need to go eat our sandwiches. It's getting late."

I moved into his arms and let the comfort of his embrace surround me knowing that I could always count on him.

And Mitch knew he could always count on yet another opportunity.

Zach and Ash greeted Mitch as we arrived at the club. They immediately whisked him away to help them attend to some 'urgent' matter involving a faulty amplifier, so I parked myself in the usual place and waited for the rest of the family to arrive. As I watched Mitch and his band mates, something seemed different about the way they were interacting with one another; and it was piquing my curiosity. They were talking and joking as they normally did. Every once in a while, however, I would catch one of them glancing my way with eyes almost sad and distant—as if pleading for me to help solve a problem— a problem unknown to me. At one point Shep approached Mitch from behind and placed a hand on his shoulder prompting him to take a few steps away from the rest of the group. Mitch started to lead him toward the front of the stage; but spying me out of the corner of his eye, he turned him around, and the pair stepped off stage completely. The action made me even more curious. Could it be that the band was in on Mitch's secret too? Was it some sort of surprise they were putting together to spring on everyone during the show? I wasn't sure; but the longer I sat there observing them, the more I wanted to find out.

Chris was the first of the Tarrington crew to arrive, and he greeted me with a warm smile and a hug.

"Hey, Dana," he said as he pulled out his chair and sat down. "Trudy's not going to make it tonight. Kyle's a little under the weather, and she thought she'd better stay home with him."

"Oh, I'm sorry to hear that," I replied. "I hope it's nothing too serious."

"I don't think so. Probably one of those strange bugs kids pick up from other kids. I'm sure he'll be fine in a day or two."

I turned toward the stage again just in time to see Mitch and Ash engaged in conversation. When Ash noticed me looking, he cupped Mitch's shoulder and turned him so that their backs were facing me.

I leaned slightly toward Chris and discreetly pointed my thumb in their direction. "Speaking of strange, Mitch and the guys have been acting that way since we got here. I have no clue why though."

Chris looked toward them for a moment and then turned back to me. "They're probably just trying to come to grips with things. I'm sure it's all still sinking in."

I looked at him strangely. "What's still sinking in?"

He turned pale. "Oh, uh, whatever it is that they're trying to come to grips with I guess."

I leaned toward him again. Giving him a stern look, I spoke slowly and placed emphasis on every word.

"You know something, don't you, Chris? You know what Mitch is hiding from me."

"I don't think Mitch would hide anything from you, Dana. He's not that kind of guy."

"Stop trying to protect him. You know he's hiding something, and *I* know that *you* know what that something is. Spill it."

Chris dropped his head and blew out a long breath. "Look, I think he should be the one to tell you. I thought he already did, or I would have kept my mouth shut."

"Tell me, Chris."

"Dana, I can't. I can't squeal on him. He's my little brother."

"And, I'm his wife. I'm the woman who lives with him, and the one who's pregnant with his children." I raised my thumb and forefinger, bringing them as close together as I could without touching. "Since Mitch *chose* me for those roles, I think that outranks your big brother status just a little."

Chris sighed heavily. "Okay, but you have to promise you won't get mad. It's not good for a woman in your condition to get herself too worked up."

I placed a hand on his arm and looked into his eyes so that he knew I was serious. "Quit stalling and forget about my 'condition.' I want to know what's going on."

"Mitch quit the band."

"He *what*?!?" I said with my voice a little louder than I wanted it to be. Angrily, I pushed out my chair and started to rise. "I'm going up there right now and find out exactly what he thinks he's doing!"

Chris stood up and gently but firmly took hold of my arm. He prompted me to sit back down. "Wait, Dana. Don't do that."

"Give me one good reason why I shouldn't."

Chris released his grip on me and sat back in his chair. "Because you'll upset him. You really don't want him to be on stage when he's upset, do you?"

"Well, I'll be sitting out here, and I'll be upset. What's the difference?"

"Because he'll be performing. All you'll be doing is watching. You know he likes to be at his best when he's up there. If you get him all uptight right now, he won't be."

Glancing briefly in the direction of the stage, I settled back into my chair and turned to Chris. "Why, Chris? Did he give you any idea why he decided to quit? He promised me that he'd stay with them. I don't understand what made him change his mind."

Chris slid down in his chair, folded his hands, and placed them on the table. "In his words, Dana, *everything*."

I was confused. "Everything? What *everything*? I don't get it."

Chris sat back up but kept his hands in place except to run one through his hair before he spoke. For the next few minutes, he replayed the conversation he and Mitch had at the bistro a few days earlier. By the time he finished his rendition of the story, I had started to feel guilty.

"You mean he quit because of me?"

"Not *because* of you, Dana. *For* you. And for the babies." He leaned forward. "You know that right after God that family comes first to Mitch. He's not about to let anything get in the way of him being the kind of husband and father he feels he should be—not work, not the band, not anything. Since he can't give up work for obvious reasons, he's eliminating the only other thing that he can."

I turned to look at Mitch myself, smiling and laughing with his friends, looking as if there was no place in the world he'd rather be at that moment. I caught his eye, and he smiled at me. His glow faded away as he studied my face and watched as I was unable to keep a tear from running down my cheek. Keeping his eyes fixed on me, he said something to Zach and started toward me. I quickly turned away, wiped my eyes, and tried hard to muster up a smile before he got to the table.

I felt a gentle hand on my shoulder. "Sweetheart, is something wrong? Why are you crying?"

I turned my face upward to look into his eyes. I was sure that mine were glistening with the tears that still threatened to fall from them. "I'm not crying. I just had something in my eye. It was watering a little."

He didn't look convinced. Now, instead of looking concerned, he was beginning to look angry.

"Chris, I'd like to see you for a minute. Outside."

Oh, great, I thought. *He's figured it out.* I placed a hand on his arm, and he paused to look at me as Chris rose from his chair.

"Mitch, please don't," I pleaded.

He gently removed my hand and looked into my eyes, but only for a moment before turning to glare at his brother once again. "It's all right, Dana. I won't give him anything he doesn't deserve."

"Mitch...."

He pointed toward the door; and with the obedience of a trained animal, Chris started in that direction. "This is between him and me. Let me handle it."

I sat helpless as I watched him follow Chris out the door.

Outside the club the pair of brothers moved around the corner of the building to escape the line of patrons waiting to get in. Mitch set his jaw and with angry eyes stepped close to Chris.

"You told her, didn't you?"

"Yeah, I did Mitch. I ratted you out, but only because she figured out that I knew what you've been hiding from her the past two days." Mitch looked a bit stunned by Chris's comment, and Chris took notice of the expression. "Uh-huh, Mitchell, that's right. She knew you had a secret. She just didn't know what it was."

Mitch took another step toward Chris, but Chris stood his ground. "I was going to tell her. You had no business butting your nose in where it doesn't belong."

"I wasn't trying to butt into anything. I assumed she knew. You told me at the bistro that you were going to tell her that night."

"Well, I didn't."

"Obviously. But, I did. I tried to keep quiet, but she wouldn't back down. I really didn't have a choice." Chris stepped up to Mitch until the two were almost touching noses. "Now, are you going to hit me and get it over with or are we going to stand here all night debating whether or not I should have opened my mouth?"

Mitch turned away, exhaled loudly, and took a few steps away from Chris. He stood with his head down for a moment and then turned and faced his brother. Most of the anger had left his face, and he softened his tone. "No, I'm not going to hit you although I probably should. I'm surprised she didn't storm up on stage and start World War III when you told her."

Chris began to smile. "Oh, trust me, little brother, she wanted to. I wouldn't let her.

Mitch chuckled, and a little smirk came to his own face. "Guess I should thank you for that, shouldn't I?" His expression turned serious again. "Of course, I wouldn't be surprised if she doesn't talk to me the rest of the night for breaking my promise to her. I'm sure she thinks I'm just one big lie after another. First that whole thing with Gloria and now this."

Chris leaned his back against the corner of the building and crossed his arms. "Why didn't you tell her the other night, Mitch? Why'd you wait?" Then he began to laugh. "Didn't feel like sleeping on the couch, huh?"

Mitch couldn't help but join in himself. "Yeah, something like that. I hate having her upset with me. The girl's beautiful, but she has one ugly temper." He grew serious again. "I just keep remembering what happened the last time I really upset her, Chris. I don't want that to happen again. In fact, just the thought of it scares the living daylights out of me. I could never live with myself."

"Do you honestly believe the solution is to hide everything from her that you know she won't be happy about? I don't think that's going to help matters much in the long run." He walked up to Mitch and lightly tapped his jaw with the palm of his hand. "She loves you, little brother; and if it helps at all, she knows why you decided to leave the band. I filled her in. Sure, she's upset, but you'll work it out." Chris moved his hand to rest on Mitch's shoulder. "Mitchell, you've conquered greater things than this in the past six months, and you'll conquer bigger things in the next sixty years. I understand your fear, but I think it's time to put that to rest and reopen those lines of communication."

Mitch nodded. "You know, I really hate it when you're right. Makes me feel like a stupid kid."

Chris laughed and pushed Mitch playfully. "That's because you are."

"Watch it, buddy. I can still throw that punch, you know."

"I don't think you want to do that because then I'd have to hit you back. We'd get into it, and you'd probably end up getting hurt. I don't think it would be good for your professional image if you went on stage sporting a black eye and a bloody nose."

Mitch laughed. "Actually, you'd be the one getting hurt, Christopher, but I'll let you think what you want."

"Thank you."

Unlike moments earlier, the two were all smiles as they headed back into the club.

"I don't want you to do this, Mitch."

We were standing in a corridor leading to a fire exit at the back of Studio 14. The band was still making last-minute adjustments to the stage, performing sound checks, and taping down set sheets next to each instrument. My husband stood across from me with his back against the wall and his hands stuffed into the pockets of his jeans. In response to my plea, he placed the top of his head against the wall and closed his eyes as he sighed heavily. Bringing his chin back down, he looked directly into my eyes.

"Dana, we've been through this a thousand times in the last ten minutes. I've already made my decision, and I'm not changing it. This is something I feel I need to do. Please try to understand that."

"I do understand. You think you have to do this because I was in that stupid accident, and you have to take care of me. Besides that, you don't think I'll be able to handle these twins on my own. Well, you're wrong on both counts. I'm quite capable of taking care of everything for two hours a night and three on Saturday."

Mitch walked over to me and brushed the hair back from my face, leaving his hand resting on my cheek. He spoke soothingly as a gentle smile graced his face.

"That's not the point, love. I know you are. I *want* to take care of you. I always have since the very first day I met you. I want to take care of our children, too. When they're grown, I want them to remember a father who took the time to be there for them—not one who was so caught up in his own pleasures that he was never around." He lifted his other hand and held my face tenderly between them. "Your accident was like a wake-up call for me. If I had been there for you as I should have been, it never would have happened. I vowed that very night that I would take care of you from then on, and I don't intend to break that promise. It's sacred. I made that promise to God." He smiled. "It's the least I can do to thank Him for giving my family back to me."

I felt a tear trickle down my cheek, and Mitch moved his thumb to follow it down the contour of my nose before he gently wiped it away.

"I know you're going to miss all this, and it's breaking my heart to think that I'm responsible for you letting it go." I sniffled and wiped a tear from the other cheek. "Will you at least agree to stay with the guys until the babies are due instead of leaving in September?"

He sighed. "You aren't going to let me just bow out gracefully, are you?" I shook my head, and he laughed. "Okay, love, I'll think about it. Emphasis on *think*. That doesn't mean I'll agree."

"I suppose that's all I can ask," I replied as I put my arms around him. But, all the while I was thinking, *it's not over yet*.

Giving me a quick kiss, Mitch took hold of my hand and led me back to the table. By now the other family members had arrived, and everyone turned our way as we approached. I didn't want to assume that Chris had shared the news with them, but the way they were looking at us made me think that they were sensing something wasn't quite right. I decided that if Mitch was going to do this he needed to let his family in on it. After all, the policy was 'no secrets,' right?

Instead of sitting down when he pulled out my chair, I moved closer and put my arm around his waist before getting the family's attention.

"Everyone, Mitch has something he wants to tell all of you."

All eyes were on Mitch, and suddenly he looked like a rabbit staring down the barrel of a shotgun. He leaned close to me with his own eyes fixed on his family and whispered in my ear, "Uh, no I don't."

I gritted my teeth in a forced smile and leaned his way. "Oh, honey, I think you do. You don't want to keep secrets from your family, do you?"

He cleared his throat and strategically turned his head to look behind me, grazing close to my ear again in an attempt to be discreet. "Dana, don't do this. I'll tell them in my own time, okay?"

Before I had a chance to answer, Julia chimed in, "Mitchell, tell us. What's the big secret?"

Mitch sent a disgruntled look my way and took a deep breath before addressing his sister's question.

"I wanted to wait until tomorrow when everyone was together after church, but since my wife thinks I should tell you now...." He gave me another look as he continued. "After some careful consideration based on recent events which I don't need to explain, I've decided that I'm quitting the band."

Their faces filled with shock as they exchanged glances and then focused their attention back to Mitch. Angelina started to say something, but Mitch lifted his hand; and she stopped.

"I know what you're all thinking; and I also know that you probably don't agree with my decision, but I'd appreciate your support rather than you all trying to talk me out of it. I feel this is what I need to do. My family has to come first, and they can't if I'm caught up in everything else."

Silence fell over the table as Mitch's eyes darted from one family member to another seeking some sort of approval. Finally, Jim nodded and gave him a smile.

"Knowing you the way I do, Mitch, I can safely say that even if we tried, we couldn't change your mind on this anyway. With that being said, I give you my support."

The others nodded in agreement, and Mitch smiled.

"I'm staying on at least another month, maybe longer," he said, glancing at me out of the corner of his eye. "It's not over just yet. But hey, thanks a lot for understanding. That's important to me."

Excusing himself to return to the stage, Mitch turned away and started in that direction with me tagging close behind. As he reached the backstage door, he wheeled around to face me.

"Look, Dana, I know you aren't happy with me right now, but what you did out there wasn't very nice. You put me on the spot in front of my entire family."

"I'm sorry, but I didn't see any reason for you to wait. Besides, I'm sure either Chris or I would have let it slip sometime during the evening anyway. Better for them to hear it from you than from one of us."

He sighed heavily. "My reason to wait, my dear, was because my parents aren't here. I really wanted to tell everyone at the same time." He dropped his eyes, and his voice became very soft. "It's hard for me to give people news I know they won't be happy about. I'd rather just do it once instead of having to repeat myself. Waiting for tomorrow would have been a lot easier."

I stepped up to him and offered a hug. It was then that I realized how difficult this whole ordeal was for him. As much as he felt he *needed* to do this, I still believed that in his heart he really didn't *want* to do this.

I brought my eyes up to meet his. "Can you forgive me?"

He smiled as he shook his head and chuckled softly. His eyes filled with a soft affection. "You know I can't stay mad at you for very long—not when you look at me like that." He moved closer and bent down, letting his lips lightly brush against mine. "You are just way too beautiful, Mrs. Tarrington." I leaned toward him, and his kiss deepened as he placed his hands flat against my back and pulled me closer. Wrapping his arms around me tightly, he brought me to him even more and moved his face away enough to look deep into my eyes.

"You don't know what you do to me, love," he whispered.

I smiled as I traced my finger down the line of his jaw, settling on his dimple. "Oh, I think I might have an idea," I replied. "Unfortunately, this isn't the place or time to do anything about it."

He kissed me again and sighed. "Yeah, I know. Bummer, huh?"

Now I let my fingers glide down his biceps—feeling every inch of strength in his embrace. "Yeah, but there's always later."

He took a step back and rocked me gently in his arms. "That's not fair. Now, every time I look at you tonight, I'll be thinking about later."

"Me, too."

Mitch pulled me to him again; but just as he leaned in for his kiss, Newbie and Ty walked up next to us. Newbie cleared his throat, and Mitch moved his head just slightly to look at them.

"What do you two losers want?" he said teasingly. "Can't you see I'm busy?"

"You're something all right, but I'm not sure 'busy' is quite the word for it," Newbie replied.

The three of them chuckled, and Mitch gave me a quick kiss. Stepping away, he took hold of my hand, gave me a flash of his dimple, and winked as Ty reached out to open the door. "Until later." Letting go of his hand, I watched the door close behind them—my heart filled with the man I loved.

Chapter 10

In the week that followed, Mitch and I found ourselves barging head first into a completely new chapter of our married life. After gaining his parents' support regarding his decision to leave Ace, Mitch ended all discussion on the topic and went about his rehearsals as if nothing had changed. I went along with him and didn't bring it up. I figured this was his way of settling things in his own mind. However, like the rest of the family and I agreed, I was certain that he was going to miss that part of his life once it ended. Because of this, I made a vow known only to God and myself that if I could find a way to keep that from happening, I would. But for now, I chose to leave well enough alone rather than stir up any discontent between us. I decided it was a project I would work on later.

On Tuesday we received a call from Tricia regarding the offer we had made on the house. Although very pleased with our interest, the owners made a counter offer of $128,000. Having expected this, Mitch agreed to meet them in the middle and countered with his own offer of $125,000. By late Wednesday afternoon, we were sitting in the office of Hallmark Homes with Tricia going over the paperwork necessary to purchase our first home. The family had already started moving some of their belongs as Mr. Tanner was to begin his new job the following Monday. We were told that once financing had been approved, we could begin moving in within the next two to three weeks. Tricia assured us that she didn't foresee any difficulties, and in his excitement Mitch brought home three empty boxes from work the next day and had them packed within two hours. Feeling some of that same excitement myself, I made a trip to Carlson's Department Store on Friday morning and purchased the sofa table and lamp I had seen on my previous visit. When Mitch saw them, he just laughed and said that he was surprised I hadn't done that the minute our offer was accepted.

Friday held another surprise for us. Our first childbirth education class was scheduled for seven o'clock that evening. Mitch had arranged with his band mates to meet for a quick rehearsal at the club just before the show on Saturday allowing us to accommodate the change in our schedule. He also insisted that I take the day for myself rather than working with him at the bistro. He explained that in doing so it would give me more of an opportunity to rest and be ready for whatever the class would bring our way. Although I knew that the Friday lunch crowd at Gartano's was one of the biggest of the week, I complied with his wishes but made him agree first that he would at least let me stop by for lunch. With a smile and a kiss, we sealed the deal. At noon I met him there to share a pizza before going home for a well-deserved afternoon nap.

Later that evening after a quick dinner of chicken and rice, Mitch helped me clear the dishes and then retreated to take a shower. I went to the bedroom to change into my 'Lamaze attire'—a lightweight pair of cotton stretch pants coupled with a t-shirt Olivia had gotten me that said "Mommy's Little Angels" on the front with an arrow pointing to my stomach. Mitch chuckled when he saw it and made the comment that if they were indeed angels they must take after him. I simply shook my head at him and laughed.

An hour later we arrived at Mercy Hospital and made our way to the room where our classes were being held. Several couples had already arrived and greeted us with warm smiles as we entered. We found a vacant floor mat near the back of the room, and Mitch carefully helped me lower myself onto it. He took a seat next to me as our instructor took her place at the front of the room.

"Good evening, parents-to-be! My name is Kathy Sherman. I'm an R.N. here at Mercy as well as a Certified Childbirth Instructor, and I will be teaching you the techniques of natural childbirth or 'Lamaze' as many prefer to call it. Since this is our first time together, let's begin by going around the room and introducing ourselves. Also, I'd like to know a little about you, when you are due, and whether or not this is your first child."

As the introductions began, Mitch leaned close to my ear and whispered as he began to chuckle softly, "I never realized there were so many pregnant women in this city. Must have been a really cold winter."

I elbowed him in the ribs. "Mitchell, behave yourself, would you?" He responded with a soft kiss on the top of my head.

Finally, our turn arrived; and since the female half of the other couples had been dominating the introductions to that point, Mitch sat silently, smiled, and turned to me.

"Well, I'm Dana Tarrington, and this is my husband, Mitch," I began. I tried to base my introduction to what the others had said about themselves. "I'm a kindergarten teacher at Lincoln Elementary, and Mitch is the owner of Gartano's Italian Bistro and also the front man for Ace—the house band at Studio 14. We've been married since February, and our babies are due around the end of November."

Suddenly, I felt every eye turn our way; and as I had the day Mitch and I announced the pregnancy to his family, I wondered if these people were thinking I'd conceived out of wedlock. Thankfully, however, as Chris had saved me that day, Kathy saved me right then as she addressed the class.

"That's wonderful—extra love from your honeymoon and twins, too! Congratulations!"

"Thank you," I said timidly.

A woman about three mats away from us, who looked like she was ready to deliver any minute, spoke up.

"I'll bet that was a surprise for you, wasn't it?" she asked with a smile.

Mitch and I glanced at each other and nodded. "To say the least," Mitch replied. "But, a nice surprise." I couldn't help but smile at the love radiating from his face at that moment.

As the introductions moved on to the remaining couples, I took the opportunity to study my surroundings a little closer. The floor was covered in exercise mats neatly placed in three rows of five mats each. All of them were occupied by an expectant couple. Each mat was a bright red or yellow in color which gave a rather cheery contrast to the dull eggshell of the walls. At the front of the room was a large whiteboard partially covered by a projection screen that had been pulled down from the ceiling. Just a few feet away and directly in front of the screen, a small movie projector suggested some sort of film was on the evening's agenda. At the back of the room were two long tables filled with refreshments for the group. One table hosted pitchers of iced water and tea, a large tray of fresh cut vegetables, and another of fresh fruit. A box of donuts and a large urn were on another table. The aroma from the hot brewed coffee filled the room. I felt a little grumble in my stomach as I studied the fare, but I patted it gently as if to say we'd have to wait just a little bit longer to satisfy the cravings the sight had provoked.

Kathy moved to the front and center again to address the group. "It's certainly nice to meet everyone, and you'll all have the opportunity to mingle amongst yourselves a little later during our break. We have some refreshments at the back of the room you can help yourselves to at that time as well." All heads turned in that direction, and my stomach grumbled again. Mitch heard it this time and smiled.

"Since all of you are in your final trimester, we're going to take this week to discuss the changes that will occur between now and the time you deliver as well as some of the complications and conditions that can show up during this time. We'll start off with a general classroom-type discussion, take a break, and then finish out the evening with a film which will outline what to expect during labor and delivery. I placed the film at the end in case anyone wishes not to view it for whatever reason." She smiled. "I'll let you know ahead of time that an actual birth is shown, and it's not for the squeamish."

I couldn't resist leaning toward Mitch and whispering, "Honey, we'd better leave during the break. I don't want you to pass out again."

"Not funny," he whispered back.

For the next half hour, we listened intently as Kathy touched on topics ranging from the increased frequency of prenatal visits to preeclampsia and premature labor, the signs and symptoms, and what actions the doctor might take to stop it from occurring. *Been there, done that*, I thought. In tune to my feelings as always, Mitch pulled me close and held me protectively as he rested a hand gently on my abdomen. Knowing that Kathy's words were causing both of us to feel a little reminiscent about all we had been through to that point, I placed my head against his chest and let myself feel the security of his arms around me. I closed my eyes for a moment and said a silent prayer of thanks that the procedure had worked for us and hoped we could look forward to a normal delivery and healthy children.

Kathy moved away from the whiteboard and turned to face the class completely. "When you registered for this class, you were given a short questionnaire to fill out and bring to class with you tonight. If any of you have that, you can turn it in now; and I'll go through them during the break." She held up a stack of papers lying on the desk next to her. "If you forgot it tonight, you can fill out another one here and bring it back with you the next time." She glanced at her watch and then back to the class. "Let's take a twenty-minute break and then meet back here for the film. If you wish to leave at this time, please feel free."

The room filled with soft chatter as the couples began to rise slowly from their places and move around. I noticed most of the women exiting toward the restroom while the men were beginning to congregate around the coffee and donuts. Mitch stood, stretched, and then reached out to help me to my feet. I twisted from one side to the next in an attempt to loosen up my muscles and then placed my hands on my lower back and began to rub it.

"I'm not sure I could have taken another minute on that floor," I said to Mitch as he began to rub my shoulders. "I wasn't sure I was going to be able to get up!"

"Good thing I came along then, huh? You might have been stuck down there for the next three months," he chuckled.

"See, you do serve a purpose in my life," I chided.

"Oh, so that's the only reason you keep me around, huh?" He moved to place his arm around my shoulders as he led me toward the refreshments.

"No—you're good at *other* things, too."

Sure that I was about to feed his ego, he raised his eyebrows and shot me a sideways glance. "Is that so? Like what?" he asked with interest.

I paused for a moment and smiled. "Well, you run a mean vacuum; and when you do laundry, no one can compete with how white your whites are! And your dusting abilities—second to none. Shall I go on?"

He smirked. "No, I get the picture. I'm just your servant."

"Yeah, basically," I giggled.

We reached the table; and Mitch took a napkin, placed a small cake donut on it, and handed it to me. Taking a large cinnamon roll for himself, he moved to the urn and poured himself a cup of coffee.

I glanced down at my hand and then at what he held in his. "Wait a minute! Why do you get a huge roll and a cup of coffee, and all I get is this tiny little donut?"

He grinned playfully. "I figured if you're going to continue to use and abuse me, I'm going to need all the energy I can get!"

I laughed. "Why do I bother to ask?"

A few minutes later the class resumed as Kathy took her place at the front once more.

"I'm happy to see everyone decided to join us for the movie," she began. "This is a short film—only about twenty minutes. Then we'll use the last ten or so for questions."

On the screen before us, a young married couple arrived at the hospital looking quite calm and collected as they anticipated the birth of their child. Meeting them at the door, a nurse placed the woman in a wheelchair. Her husband lovingly held her hand and carried her small suitcase in the other. With a hand on her stomach, she announced the onset of a contraction, and her husband released his grip from hers to look at his watch. Telling him it had subsided, she smiled sweetly as they disappeared into the elevator.

These people have to be actors, I thought. *There's no way she'd be that calm during a contraction. I know that pain, and it certainly isn't something you smile through unless you have an unusually high pain threshold.* I leaned against Mitch—who had positioned himself behind me—and waited for the next scene hoping it would be a little more realistic.

Soon the camera was panning a labor and delivery room. The woman was all safely tucked into bed with an IV already started, her husband by her side, and both still surprisingly calm. The nurse was strapping a fetal monitor to her swollen abdomen as the doctor prepared to examine the woman's progress. As he placed her feet into the stirrups, the nurse finished her task and handed the husband a set of scrubs to put on over his clothing. As the camera began to move toward the bottom of the bed, my husband turned to me and whispered, "I really hope they aren't going to show this."

He got his wish as the camera focused in on the doctor's face. "You're about eight centimeters right now, Mrs. Lane," he said. "Since you're membranes haven't ruptured, I'm going to take care of that for you right now...."

The doctor removed a long instrument that resembled an oversized knitting needle from a sterile tray and turned back to the woman. Every female in the class cringed. I backed a little closer to Mitch.

"Now, you just relax, and Suzanne here will get you all prepped and ready for delivery. I'll be back to check on you shortly."

The doctor left the room, and the commentator began to explain just what "prepping" Mrs. Lane was going to encounter. I looked around the classroom and saw all the females cringe again as the commentator said the word 'enema.'

My husband decided to make his own comments. "Sweetheart," he said in hushed tones, "I love you, but I've gotta say I'm glad I'm not going through that."

"Gee, thanks a lot," I replied sarcastically, moving a little away from him.

After a few minutes of commentary, the camera found Mrs. Lane in the middle of a contraction; and this time she didn't look quite so relaxed. Her forehead glistened with beads of perspiration, and her face contorted in pain as her husband instructed, "Breathe, honey." Her eyes moved in his direction, and she huffed and puffed in a rhythmic fashion until at last the contraction subsided. She was panting for air, so he lovingly placed an oxygen mask over her nose and mouth and held it in place for a few seconds. Just as he pulled it away, she announced the onset of yet another contraction and began to squeeze his hand in a grip so tight I was sure she had to be breaking every bone within it. I saw some of the men cringe at this scene, and I smiled.

After a few more contractions, the doctor reentered the scene; and after examining Mrs. Lane, he announced that she was fully dilated, effaced, and ready for delivery. Seemingly, out of nowhere a medical team appeared, and the doctor positioned himself for the baby's birth.

"I want you to push with the next contraction; and Mr. Lane, I'd like you to help by supporting her head and shoulders."

Obediently, Mr. Lane moved into position; and as the contraction peaked, Mrs. Lane screamed out in pain.

Now, that's more like it, I thought. *Doesn't feel so good anymore, does it?* A satisfied smile came to my face, and I almost felt a little guilty.

As Kathy had promised, the next few minutes of the scene definitely weren't anything I'd ever want to see on primetime. The camera focused in on the baby's head as it crowned; and the background was filled with Mrs. Lane groaning, her husband telling her to breathe, and the doctor giving a play-by-play. I glanced at my wide-eyed husband with his gaze fixed on the scene before him and his expression a mixture of wonder and disgust. Glancing around the room, I could see that it appeared as if most of the other men shared this same expression. The women, on the other hand, were a mixed lot—some smiling, some looking disgusted, and others looking just plain terrified. Turning back to the screen as Mrs. Lane expelled one final blood-curdling scream, I decided I fit into the latter group. Mrs. Lane and the others in the class only had to do this one time. I had to do it twice.

"Congratulations! It's a girl," the doctor proudly announced as he laid the newborn infant on her mother's chest.

Ooh's and aah's filled the classroom, and most of the parents held smiles on their faces. I was still feeling terrified.

At this point we witnessed the cutting of the umbilical cord of little 'Emma' Lane and the procedures involved in her initial exam. We were all relieved that we didn't have to witness the delivery of the placenta although the commentator thought the procedure worth mentioning.

The film ended with a shot of the happy family, and Kathy turned the lights back on. She then began to lead us in a short summary of the film and opened the floor for questions. Only one woman spoke up to ask what type of pain relief was available and how soon after arriving at the hospital someone could have it. I tuned in and filed the information away because I somehow knew I was going to want to bring it back out later.

The class ended, and Mitch once again helped me to my feet. We walked silently to the elevator and somehow managed to get a car to ourselves. Once inside, I turned to him.

"There's no way, Mitch. I can't do that. I can't have these babies—not like that anyway."

Mitch laughed as he pushed the button for the ground floor. "Uh, sweetheart, as far as I know, that's the way babies have been born for centuries. I don't believe you really have much choice."

"Stop being silly. You know what I mean. If it's even half as terrifying as that movie made it look, you had better ask them to knock me out!"

He smiled down at me as the doors closed. "I told you, every woman's different. Besides, I'm sure that 'Mrs. Lane' lady was playing up the pain a little for the sake of show."

I looked at him in shock as my mouth fell open. "Excuse me, but where were you when Kathy said the film was showing an 'actual' birth?

The pain was real. Have you ever had a contraction? I have, and it hurts. It hurts a lot. And I wasn't even in labor at the time. I can only believe it's going to be worse when I actually am."

"Okay, so it hurts. No one ever told you it wasn't going to. I believe that's why they call it *labor*." The elevator doors opened, and he motioned for me to step out ahead of him. "They have drugs that will help you, sweetheart. Worrying isn't going to make things any easier, so you may as well not even do it."

We made our way to the car. Mitch held open the door for me and then went around and got in himself. He started the engine and reached up to push the button which would lower the convertible top.

"That's easy for you to say. Like you commented in there, you don't have to go through it."

He dropped his arm on the back of my seat and turned to look behind him as he backed out of the parking spot. "I only said that because I'm not sure I could handle that prepping part of things. Just the thought of it makes me squirm." He patted my leg. "I'll admit—I don't like doctors poking around me, especially in 'certain' areas."

I didn't comment on his statement but instead threw out another thought that suddenly popped into my mind. "You know, Mitch, Kathy brought up some things tonight that I hadn't even thought about. She said that multiple births run a greater risk of experiencing things that single ones don't."

"Yeah, like having more than one baby."

I sighed heavily and smirked at him as he laughed. "Come on. Be serious. What if I go into premature labor or something happens to me or one of the twins while I'm delivering?"

"What if you go in right on time, pop the kids out in two minutes flat, and all three of you walk out of the hospital two days later in perfect health?" He reached for my hand, brought it to his lips, and kissed it tenderly. "Why are you so uptight?"

"I've never had a baby before, and this class tonight has me thinking about things. I think I have the right to be a little nervous, don't you?"

He smiled. "Sure, but keep in mind that you were nervous about 'making' the baby, too; and you got through that with no problem. In fact, I'd say we both mastered that task quite well." He patted my stomach, and his smile widened. "Hey! I just got kicked!"

I ignored his sentiment. "If you'll recall, 'making a baby' wasn't what we were trying to do."

His voice softened. "Maybe, but I have no regrets. It was a beautiful experience for me, and this will be, too. It means even more because I get to share it with you." He placed his hand on my shoulder and began to rub it gently. "Everything is going to be fine, love. I promise."

I took his hand and ran my finger over the top of it. "How can you promise when you don't know?"

"Because I'm confident, that's how. You and the kids are healthy, we have the best obstetrician in the city, the entire maternity staff knows us, and we're getting educated so we'll be able to spot any potential problems before they happen." He put his arm around my shoulders and drew me to lean against him. "Honey, I know this pregnancy hasn't been easy for you, not in the least. Fortunately, we're past that now. There's nothing at this point to suggest that you'll experience any complications during the delivery. Now, I want you to relax and enjoy those two little acrobats that are bouncing around in there, okay?"

I placed my right hand on my abdomen and felt the gentle pokes of little kicking feet on my palm. I began to rub gently, and their activity seemed to increase as if my gesture was stimulating them even more. Mitch glanced down and smiled at me as he rubbed my arm, and I closed my eyes as I inhaled deeply to take in the scent of his cologne. Feeling safe and secure against him, I started to relax. I didn't know what the next few months were going to hold in store for us. But I knew that whatever it was, I could depend on Mitch to help me through it.

A few hours later I lay in bed, Mitch stretched out next to me reading a book. The open window beside the bed was allowing a cool evening breeze to drift over us, and I pushed down the blanket as if to welcome its gentle touch against my skin. Mitch glanced my way and chuckled softly at my choice of nighttime attire—a pair of cotton shorts and one of his old stretched-out t-shirts. Placing the book on the nightstand, he turned toward me, leaned up on his elbow, and put his other hand on my stomach.

"They're going crazy in there tonight, aren't they?"

I laid my hand next to his. "I'll say! They haven't quieted down much since we left class." I looked at him thoughtfully. "Do you think I had too much sugar this evening? Maybe that got them going."

"You only had a donut and a little ice cream cone at the Tasty Twist. I don't think that's going to have much effect on them."

I pulled the t-shirt up enough to reveal my belly and watched as the skin rippled with the movement of my children. "I don't know. Maybe they're going to be sensitive to sweets. We'll have to watch giving them too much."

Mitch grabbed both my hands, rolled me toward him, and then locked me in his embrace. A radiant smile graced his face, bringing out that dimple that I loved so much. "Maybe you're worrying too much again. Would you cut it out, please?"

"Well, someone has to be concerned about these things." I reached out to run my hand along his arm. "That someone is probably going to always be me; because if I know you, you'll slip them sugar every chance you get. You'll have them spoiled rotten in no time."

"What's the problem with that? That's what daddies do."

"The problem is I'll have to be the bad guy all the time."

He snickered mischievously. "Absolutely! It's all part of my plan. Daddy's the nice one; Mommy's the meanie."

He laughed as I walloped him with the pillow. "You're terrible, Mitchell Jacob Tarrington."

"You still love me, don't you?"

I looked into his bright blue eyes sparkling like the moon outside our window. "Oh, I suppose."

Taking off his glasses, he laid them on the nightstand, turned off the lamp, and then lay down and placed an arm around me.

"I love you," I said softly, and soon I drifted into a peaceful slumber.

Mitch pulled her as close as he could. He cherished the warmth of her body next to his and the sound of her slow and steady breathing as she lay lost in her dreams. He hoped they were pleasant. She deserved that. When he thought about all she'd been through during the last three months, it almost made him angry. Life just wasn't fair sometimes, and it seemed that it always sought out the best people to lay its biggest burdens on. Remembering the conversation they had after the Lamaze class, there was no doubt in his mind that she was nervous about the impending birth of their children. However, as she'd stated herself, she had a right to be. He knew that recent events had ingrained in her the impression that every ache, every cramp, every twinge of pain no matter how large or small should be a cause for near panic to her. Everything she didn't fully understand about what to expect brought relentless concern. It was going to be an even tougher road for him now than it had before; it was up to him to provide the extra ounce of reassurance she would need to remain at least remotely calm through the next few months. He could only pray that her fears would be unfounded when the day finally arrived.

"I love you, too," he whispered. "More than anything." Kissing her softly, he joined her in blissful sleep.

Early the next morning I sat on the couch with a 'Baby World' catalog open on my lap and a black fine-point *Sharpie* poised above it in my right hand. Page by page I carefully scanned each item, circling those of particular interest, much as a child would circle their favorite toys in the Christmas 'Sears & Roebuck.' Mitch sat nearby in the chair reading the sports page of the newspaper and nursing his third cup of coffee seemingly oblivious to the fact that I was even there. Turning the page of the catalog, I gazed at the assortment of cribs, bassinettes, and bedding gracing the pictures before me. One in particular caught my eye—a Jenny Lind style painted white with the picture of a teddy bear holding bright balloons on the headboard. I glanced to the corner of the living room where Mr. Bear and his brother had taken up residence; and thinking they would go well with the design, I started to circle it as my selection. As I lowered the marker to the page, however, another picture two lines down jumped out at me—a crib that could be converted into a toddler bed. I brought the *Sharpie* up and tapped the cap lightly against my chin in thought. Unable to decide, I thought I'd get Daddy involved in the process. I fixed my eyes on him for what seemed like forever before he looked my way and lowered the paper to acknowledge me.

"Something you need, love?" he asked.

I pointed to the catalog. "I can't decide which of these two cribs I like the best. What do you think?"

Placing the newspaper on the coffee table, he took the catalog from me and studied both pictures. "I don't know. They're both nice." He handed the catalog back to me, picked up the paper, and resumed his previous position. "Just pick whichever one you like."

I sighed and gave him a disgruntled look. "I like them both. That's why I asked for your opinion."

"Then get one of each," he replied without even bothering to look at me. "We *are* having two kids, so it all works out."

"I can't do that!"

"Why not? We need one for each kid, don't we? You can't decide, so just get them both."

"For heaven's sake! We can't have a nursery with furniture that doesn't match."

"We have mismatched furniture in our bedroom." He lowered the paper just a little. "This furniture isn't a matched set either. It's actually just stuff my family gave me."

I placed the book next to me and crossed my arms obstinately. "That's fine, but I'd like the nursery to match. I don't think it would kill you to help me decide. Or, is this going to be like our wedding where you want me to make all the choices?"

Apparently, something I said struck a chord. He placed the paper on the coffee table again and turned to me with a pointed finger. "Now, hold on there. I helped with every detail of our wedding—except for your dress—and that's only because I wasn't allowed to see it beforehand."

"You only helped because you felt guilty after I told you that I didn't think you cared. Otherwise, everything would have been entirely up to me."

He began to smirk. "That's because you're so much better at these things than I am, dear."

"No, that's because you don't want to be bothered with it. You aren't even making time to go shopping with me today."

He sighed. "That's not true. I would much rather see you be happy and get what you want than throw in my two cents and have you think you have to please me." He stood up and came to sit next to me. He took the catalog from me and placed it in his lap. "And I already told you the reason I'm not going shopping with you is because I have a lot to do today. I have to get through those applications so I can start interviews on Monday, and then the guys are coming by for dinner before we head to the club to rehearse for the show. It has absolutely nothing to do with me not wanting to be 'bothered.'" He picked up the catalog, quickly leafed through the pages I'd already scanned, and made a mental note of the items that were circled. "Anyway, if you *really* wanted my input, you would have consulted me before you went and circled all this other stuff. Why doesn't my opinion count on all that, but it's so detrimental on which crib to buy?"

I didn't have an answer, but I thought I should come up with something that sounded at least halfway logical. "Uh, well, because a crib is a major purchase, and all those other things are just 'fluff.' It's kinda like my picking out the curtains but asking you to help pick out the sofa."

He smiled. "We'll still end up getting what you like in the end anyway."

I began to smile myself. "That's not the point. At least we can say we both contributed to the process."

"Oh, so my opinion is just a technicality, huh? I get it." He smiled as he pointed to the crib with the teddy bear. "I like that one. I'm partial to teddies, you know." He raised his eyebrows. "The bears are kinda cute, too."

I caught on as he laughed and kissed my cheek playfully. "Mitchell Tarrington, you are so ornery."

"But, you wouldn't want me any other way, now would you?"

"Let me get back to you on that."

As I absorbed myself in the catalog once more, Mitch moved to his weight bench and sat down facing me. "If you don't want to go shopping alone, why don't you invite Kayla to tag along? I'm sure she'd enjoy that."

"She has to work. You know that. You make out the schedule, remember?"

He removed his t-shirt and lay back on the bench. I stood staring at him for a moment admiring his masculinity. Something about the way his muscles flexed under the weight of the barbell always seemed to catch my attention. He must have noticed the drool puddle forming at my feet because he chuckled.

"You've seen me without a shirt every day for the last seven months, and it still turns you on? That's nice to know." He brought the bar to his chest and slowly pushed it up a second time. Then he repeated the action as I watched in awe. I believed he may have been showing off just a little to pay me back for the stroke to his ego.

Finally, I shook my head to come back into reality. "I suppose I'm destined to go alone."

He placed the bar back on the stand and sat up. "Tell Kayla that I'll switch her to evening shift today, so she doesn't have to be in until five. Unless she has other plans, that should give you two plenty of time to shop. How's that sound?"

I assumed that knocking him over with my kiss was enough of an answer.

About forty minutes later, a faint knock on the door signaled Kayla's arrival. I hurried to greet her as Mitch followed close behind and attempted to manipulate his tie into a knot as he walked.

"Hey, girl, good morning!" she quipped cheerfully as she stepped inside. "All ready to shop 'til you drop?"

"You bet!" I answered. "I have the Baby World catalog here, and I circled all the things I want to look at when we get there. Then I can decide which things I want to put on my registry and which ones I want to go ahead and buy. Anything they don't have in the store I'll just see about ordering." Mitch was now in front of the mirror that hung over the entertainment center, and he shifted his eyes my way. "When we're finished at Baby World, I thought we could grab some lunch, head over to the mall, and check out the sales. What do you think?"

"I think it sounds like I'll be broke by the end of the day!" my husband chimed in, smiling all the while. "Maybe you should give me back my credit card."

"No way, buddy. You handed it over willingly. You'll just have to live with the consequences."

He pushed the knot up on his tie and walked over to where I stood. Placing his hand on my back, he offered a gentle rub. "Guess I'll have to put in a couple of extra hours at work to make up the cash you're planning to spend, huh?"

"More than a couple, I'd say. Should I bring your pillow when I drop off the change of clothes?"

He laughed and kissed me on my cheek. "I certainly hope I don't have to stay there *that* long!" He turned to Kayla. "You'll keep her in line, won't you, Kayla?"

"Don't count on me to do much good, honey. You know she has a mind of her own!"

Mitch nodded emphatically. "You can say that again!"

I turned and lightly poked my husband's chest with my finger. "Now, isn't that the pot calling the kettle black! You're as stubborn as I am—probably even more so!"

He smiled and drew me to him. "Let's hope little Romeo and Juliet don't turn out that way."

"Oh, my goodness! You aren't planning to name those little babies Romeo and Juliet, are you?" Kayla asked with surprise.

I looked up at Mitch's impish grin and shook my head. "No, we aren't. We also aren't calling them Rocky and Bullwinkle, Lucy and Ricky, or Sitting Bull and Pocahontas!"

Kayla laughed heartily as Mitch pointed to me. "She doesn't like any of the names I come up with, but yet she won't suggest anything herself."

I turned to Kayla. "I'm still thinking about it, that's all. You can't call a child the first thing that pops into your mind." I glanced at Mitch. "At least that's the way *I* feel about it."

"Let's not be critical here. I gave a lot of thought to all those suggestions. If I were simply trying to throw out names, I would have suggested something like Thing One and Thing Two or maybe even Green Eggs and Ham."

He laughed as I shook my head and looked at Kayla again. "Perhaps while we're at the mall, we can stop by the book store and pick up a book of baby names. Otherwise, I may have children who will have to suffer ridicule for the rest of their lives because of some ridiculous name their father stuck them with!"

He gave me a hug. "You do what you feel you must. I have to get to work." I followed him to the door, and he opened it and turned to give me a kiss before stepping out. "Have fun, sweetheart. I love you."

"I love you, too," I replied as I watched him disappear down the stairs.

Mitch smiled as the older gentleman walked toward him. Taking a seat in his usual spot at the counter, he greeted Mitch with a smile of his own as Mitch filled a cup with coffee and placed it in front of him.

"This place never slows down, does it, Mitch?" the old man asked as he glanced around the dining room. Joe was somewhat of a fixture at Gartano's, and he spent the better part of his days there sipping coffee and sharing conversation with anyone who would take the time to sit with him for a moment or two. The employees and patrons of Gartano's had become a substitute family for the widowed gentleman; his only true family, a son, lived hundreds of miles away. Mitch had grown close to Joe over the months he'd worked at the bistro and looked forward each day to the few minutes they would share at that counter.

Mitch absentmindedly wiped a spot on the counter in front of Joe and fixed his eyes on the crowded room before him. "Nope, not really. Guess that's a good thing, though, isn't it?"

Joe took a sip of his coffee. "I'd say so, but those girls might tend to disagree by the looks of things. Seems they're running themselves ragged." He pointed toward Mitch. "Speaking of girls, how's yours doing?"

Mitch smiled as he placed the towel under the counter and then turned sideways to lean against it. "Overall, she's doing just fine," Mitch started. "Take away the mood swings, the weird cravings, the huge appetite, the self-consciousness, all the little aches and pains, and the fact that everything that happens at home now is my fault—whether it really is or not—she's the same old Dana she's always been."

Joe laughed knowingly. "Sounds like you have your hands full there, my friend."

"I'll say! Along with all those other things, the closer the delivery gets, the more nervous she's becoming. We watched a movie in Lamaze class last night of an actual birth, and you can only imagine what I had to deal with afterward. Scared her to death. She's got herself convinced that something's going to go wrong when she goes into labor." He sighed heavily. "I guess if I'd been through all she has over the past few months, I'd be worried, too. I keep telling her she'll be fine, but...."

Joe held his cup in place as Mitch topped it off with hot coffee. "She tells you that you're not the one who has to do it, right?"

Mitch gave him a half smile. "How'd you know?"

"My wife was the same way. I'd tell her not to worry, but it didn't do a lick of good." He took a long drink and settled the cup back on the saucer. "All you can do is keep reassuring her, Mitch. At least you can be there when the time comes and hold her hand. Back when my boy was born, they wouldn't even let me in the room until an hour after the fact, and the first time I saw him was through a nursery window. You'll get to hold your little ones the minute they're born."

Mitch smiled and his heart warmed at the thought of seeing his children for the first time. "Yeah. That'll be great." He nodded smugly. "She'll be okay, Joe. I know she will. She has to be."

Joe lightly touched Mitch's arm and gave it a gentle pat. "I'm sure you're right."

On the opposite side of town, Kayla and I were engrossed in our shopping expedition and having a wonderful time just being together. With the Baby World catalog strategically balancing on top of my purse in the front of the shopping cart, we were standing in the midst of a sea of sleepers, dressing gowns, and clothing so small it almost seemed impossible that anyone existed who could actually fit into it. Glancing to my left, I spotted a miniature Phillie's cap and giggled excitedly as I headed in that direction. Holding it with both hands, I turned back to Kayla, and she nodded because she knew exactly what I was thinking.

"Mitch's boy will *definitely* have to have that!" she said.

"Oh, Kayla, isn't it adorable? Mitch is going to love it! It looks just like the one he has." I turned back to the rack and picked up a little baseball uniform. "Oh, my goodness! Would you look at this?" I grabbed another and looked at her inquisitively. "Should I get two? Or, don't you think it would be appropriate for a girl?"

She shrugged. "Girls and boys nowadays wear a lot of the same kinds of clothes. It wouldn't hurt a thing to put a little girl in a baseball uniform. Besides, you don't know for sure the other baby is a girl anyway."

I nodded decisively and placed the items in the cart. "You're right, I don't. We could end up with two boys." I had to giggle at the thought that crossed my mind at that moment. "Can you imagine what a stroke to Mitch's ego that would be, Kayla? He wouldn't come down from that high for months!"

She laughed in agreement. "That's for sure! He's already as proud as a peacock that you're having one boy—let alone thinking it may be two."

We slowly made our way down the aisle stopping every few feet to fawn over a tiny pair of bib overalls or a lacy dress with matching ruffled panties. Some things I would scan with the handheld device given for my use by the gift registry; other items I would simply admire and pass by, and some would be added to those things in the cart that I just couldn't wait to buy. Finally nearing the end of the clothing department, I paused for a moment to stretch a little. Unconsciously placing both hands on the small of my back, I began to gently rub it. Noticing the gesture, Kayla smiled sweetly and laid a hand on my arm.

"Are you getting tired, Dana?" she asked.

I straightened up and shook my head. "No, I'm fine, really. I never realized shopping for the babies was going to be this much fun. Besides, you and I don't get to do this very often. I plan to take full advantage of this opportunity." I smiled playfully. "Who knows when that grouchy boss of yours will give you another morning off!"

Kayla laughed. "Then we'd better keep shopping, hadn't we?"

"You bet!" I replied, and we spent the next three hours doing just that.

Mitch tossed the stack of papers on the desk, removed his glasses, and sat back in the chair to rub his eyes wearily. *Who would have known that screening applications would be this grueling,* he thought to himself. Sighing heavily, he placed his glasses back on and stared at the two piles before him—one consisting of applications from those he didn't think were qualified enough to interview and another of those he would start calling in on Monday. Raising his eyes to look across the desk, he saw Dana's picture. It reminded him of the time she'd sat across from him enduring an interview of her own. He smiled as his mind drifted back to that day.

She had wanted him to hire her to help wait tables; and feeling it would be too much with her full-time teaching job, he had promptly and firmly refused. Deciding she wouldn't take no for an answer, she presented him with an application and insisted that she would go through the 'formalities' if need be in order to change his mind. In an effort to derail her desire, he took her words to heart and put her through an interview. Much to his surprise, she passed it with flying colors. Seeing no way around the situation, he agreed to let her work only for tips; and it was probably one of the smartest moves he'd ever made. Not only was she a strong part of his staff, but it also gave him the opportunity to share a very special part of his life with her. As he glanced at the stack of applications again, he sighed. He knew having someone take her place was going to be difficult for her. She had grown to enjoy being a part of things at the bistro, and he knew she'd miss being there every day. She didn't know it was going to be harder on him.

Taking two empty file folders from the drawer, he labeled them accordingly, placed one in the filing cabinet, and the other in the middle of his desk. Placing the palms of both hands on the edge of his desk, he pushed his chair back until his arms became fully extended, and then he stood up and proceeded to stretch. Feeling mentally fatigued, he began to look forward to dinner with Dana and his friends and the chance to reenergize on stage later that evening. No matter what his physical or mental state, performing always seemed to bring new life to him as nothing else could. He glanced at Dana's picture again. *Yeah, beautiful, you're right—I do love being part of the band,* he thought. *I'm gonna miss the shows and hanging out with the guys. But, it's going to work out just fine. I know it will.*

He turned around with a smile which broadened as Dana walked into the office. Her own smile was as bright as the sun outside.

"Hey, handsome! Your posse followed me in, and they look hungry," I said as I placed the bag with his change of clothes on the desk chair. "Are you ready to eat?"

"Gee, don't I even get a kiss? I haven't seen you all day, you know."

I rolled my eyes and smiled as he welcomed me into his arms and bestowed me with a long, warm kiss. "Mmm, I kinda liked that. How about another one?" he asked as he gazed into my eyes.

"If I do that, you'll want another and another; and we'll be back here all night. You'll miss dinner and the show, and you'll have five guys who will be very upset with you."

He leaned his forehead against mine and sighed. "It was a long day, and I missed you. I was working so hard. I'm all tired and achy," he said with a little whine to his voice.

I hugged him a little tighter and rubbed his back soothingly. "My poor baby. Does that make it better?"

"A little," he pouted, "but I think another kiss or two would help even more." I could see his dimple starting to come out.

I ran my hands over his shoulders and then stepped away from him and took him by the hand. "Later, sweetie."

He shook his head as I attempted to drag him out the door. "Why is everything 'later' with you? What's wrong with 'now'?"

"Because 'now' we have people waiting for us. Come on."

As we walked down the hallway and into the bistro, he was playfully lagging a few steps behind and sporting a pouty little smirk. As we reached the table, Ty looked at him suspiciously.

"What's wrong with him?" he asked.

"She wouldn't kiss me," Mitch replied. He pointed at me and still pretended to pout. "I had a hard day, and she doesn't even care."

"I don't blame her," Ty said with a smile as he grabbed a roll from the basket. "If I was a girl, I wouldn't want to kiss you either."

The others chuckled, and Mitch gave him a look. "That's good to know because I wouldn't want you to anyway. Besides, you'd probably be a pretty ugly girl."

"Oh, I don't know," Ash replied teasingly. "He'd have to shave the mustache, but otherwise, I'd say he could pull it off."

Newbie chuckled and reached over to pull up a few strands of hair on the back of Ty's head. "Yeah, I can see it. Put a few extensions in back here, maybe add some highlights and curl it a little...."

In an attempt to shift the teasing away from himself, Ty moved away from Newbie and pointed to Mitch. "Hey, why are you picking on me? Tarrington's the pretty boy of the group, remember?"

Shep nodded with a little bit of a laugh. "Yeah, but he's got a wife. You can't even get a date. Maybe you'd have better luck if you *were* a girl, and you could find some poor, desperate guy to take you out."

Ty's mouth fell open, and the others now roared with laughter. Suddenly, a slow smile came to his face, and he turned to look directly at Shep. "Desperate, huh? You mean someone like *you?*"

We all laughed as Shep grinned at Ty and promised, "I'll get you later for that one!"

For the hour that followed, I sat next to Mitch and watched as he enjoyed the company of his friends—laughing and talking about nothing of particular merit—but instead just basking in the camaraderie they shared. As he had the week before at the club, he looked as if there were no place else in the world he would rather be at that moment. I knew he loved these men, and I knew that I had to keep them together. The question was how? Suddenly, I had an idea—it was a long shot but an idea nonetheless—so I decided to give it a try.

I waited a moment for a lull in the conversation before jumping in. "Hey, guys," I started, between bites of salad, "did Mitch tell you we got the house?"

Ash nodded. "Yeah, he did, Dana. That's really great. Congratulations!" He then turned to Mitch. "When are you moving in, Trip? You know you can count on us to help."

Zach grabbed a roll from the basket in the middle of the table and bit a large chunk of it off in a rather barbaric sort of way. "Sure, we'll help—but only if there's food involved," he said with a smile.

Newbie decided to chime in. "Don't listen to him. We'll be there regardless."

Mitch smiled affectionately at all of them, and I could easily see he was touched by the offer. "Hey, thanks guys. That means a lot." He looked at Zach and grinned. "I suppose we could probably arrange some sort of meal, too. I wouldn't want anyone to starve on my account."

I finished my salad and took a roll from the basket. "Did he tell you about the outbuilding? It's huge! Mr. Tanner, the previous owner, used it as a workshop. I thought it would be a perfect place for you guys to rehearse. Our realtor said it's heated, so you won't have to worry about getting cold out there this winter. I'll even make sure Mitch keeps a path shoveled so you won't have to tromp through snow to get back there."

I smiled and put even more excitement into my voice. "We can look into getting it soundproofed, too, so you won't disturb the neighbors. I'm not sure if it's air conditioned, though. If not, we can always get a wall unit and stick in there next spring. It's also closer to the city, so you won't have to drive as far as you do now to get to Jake and Olivia's." I glanced at Mitch, and he was beginning to bite his lip which told me he was starting to catch on.

As I finished my last sentence, an awkward silence fell over the group; however, no one wanted to admit that it made them uncomfortable. Newbie, always bold and straightforward, turned to Mitch and looked him squarely in the eyes.

"Does that mean you've changed your mind about staying with us, Trip?"

Mitch forced a smile meant to ease the disappointment he was about to deliver. "No, dude, I'm sorry. Nothing's changed." He tried to lift the tone of his voice to sound more cheerful. "I guess we could use the building for the next couple of months. It just might get cold enough to use the heat, too. You never can tell." Feeling the silence settling in again, Mitch picked up a menu off the table and pointed to it. "Make sure you guys save room for dessert. We added a few things to the menu. The canolli's excellent. If you've never had it before, it's well worth a try."

They all nodded in response and took the change in subject as Mitch's cue that he was ready to end the discussion about the band. I sighed in defeat and tried to avoid eye contact as he gave me one of his 'we'll discuss this later' expressions.

Later came sooner than I expected. After finishing dinner, the guys headed out to the club with a promise from Mitch that we would be there as soon as he changed clothes and had a brief chat with Jimmy. Although I would have preferred waiting at the table, Mitch insisted that I join him in the office while he changed. He closed the door, turned the lock, and then he turned to me with just the hint of a smile.

"Did you really think putting me on the spot with the guys was going to work?" he asked.

I shrugged. "I don't know," I answered softly, "but I had to try. You won't listen to me any other way."

He pulled a short-sleeved oxford from the bag, put it on, and left it open over his t-shirt. "I'll gladly listen to you, Dana, but only when we aren't discussing issues that are already settled. I've made up my mind, and I'm not changing it."

I walked to the couch and sat down. "You already did change it. You told me you'd stay with the band, and now you aren't. We made an agreement, and you're breaking it."

He finished tying his shoe and came to sit next to me. He took my hand in his and sighed deeply before he began to speak. "No, I'm not. If you'll recall, part of our agreement was that if things got to be too much that I would decide how to handle it." He brushed a wisp of hair off my forehead and smiled. "Now that I've exercised my right to do that, this really sexy woman I know won't back off. She's already talked me into staying with the band two months longer than I think I should."

"I have?"

"Yes, but that's *all* you're talking me into!"

As Mitch stood with a smile and reached out to help me to my feet, I couldn't help the thought that crossed my mind: *Congratulations, Dana. You just bought yourself two more months to figure things out.* And I planned to use them.

Chapter 11

Like the whisper of a cool breeze on a hot summer day, the atmosphere of Studio 14 rejuvenated Mitch the minute he stepped through the door. Only a few employees meandered about—they were still over an hour from opening to the public—but he could already detect a feeling in the air that was almost electrifying. He couldn't explain why, but something deep inside told him that this night would be one of their best yet. Maybe it was the fact that every rehearsal during the week had been remarkable. The guys had learned the songs quickly and could now play them flawlessly. Their talent never ceased to amaze him. In his heart he knew they really didn't need this rehearsal tonight, but he had decided to schedule it anyway. As the front man, he knew that overconfidence could be just as damaging as the lack thereof. While he wanted them to be proud of their accomplishments, he didn't want them thinking they were perfect. Keeping them levelheaded would keep them working their hardest. It would also ensure that they would continue to live up to the reputation they were rapidly attaining as one of the best club bands in the city. Ultimately, it would prepare them to remain in that light long after he moved on.

Itching with the urge to get the evening underway, Mitch settled Dana into her seat at the table, kissed her softly, and made his way onstage where the rest of the band was waiting. Seeing him approach, they instinctively moved to huddle around him as he greeted them and began to address any last-minute issues they had. With everything squared away after just a few minutes, they took their places at their instruments. Mitch cued the first song, and they played it through with ease, transitioning effortlessly into the second and third. Knowing the patrons would soon start to arrive, he had the band play only two more songs before wrapping it up and allowing them a chance to rest and regroup before the performance. Pleased with what he had heard, he left them to make the final adjustments and went to join Dana.

"Mind if I take this seat, pretty lady?" he asked as he pulled out the chair next to mine.

"No, I don't mind at all," I replied playfully. "Just be careful not to let my husband see you sitting there. He's very jealous."

Mitch sat down with a grin. "Well, I'm not worried about him. I'm sure I could take him in a fight any day. He's not all that tough."

I reached out and ran my finger down the side of his face, and his eyes lit up. "Oh, now you wouldn't want to start a fight. You might mess up that pretty face of yours."

He snickered. "Pretty, huh?"

I leaned toward him and looked deep into his bright blue eyes. "Yeah, pretty."

He smiled, and I could feel myself melting at the way he was looking at me. "I might get upset if anyone else said that; but since it's you, I guess it's all right." He gave me a kiss that warmed me from head to toe. "Sure hope your husband didn't see that. Even if he did, I don't care. In fact, I just might do it again."

"Would you?"

"Thought you'd never ask," he answered as he delivered another sweet kiss.

"I have something to show you," I told him with a bit of enthusiasm. He watched curiously as I reached into my purse and withdrew a small book.

"What's that?" he asked.

"Baby names. I thought we could go through it together, and *maybe* we can find a couple of names we can *both* agree on."

"Still don't like my suggestions, huh?"

I held the book up. "Does the fact that I even bought this book do anything to answer that question?"

He grinned and moved his chair closer to mine. "Oh, all right then. We'll pick something from your silly old book. But, personally, I think Bonnie and Clyde are much better names."

"Yeah, if you plan on teaching them how to rob banks!"

I reached into my purse again and pulled out a yellow highlighting marker as well as a ballpoint pen. "We'll mark anything we like in yellow; and the names we both like, we'll also circle with the pen, okay?"

"Sounds pretty complicated, but all right. Let's do it."

"Don't criticize, Mitchell. I'm only trying to be organized."

"I wasn't.... Fine, dear. Open the book and let's see what the choices are."

Leafing through the pages, it took us less than ten minutes to realize that there were very few names we both found agreeable. We covered almost twenty pages, highlighted ten names, and circled only three. It seemed as if every name I suggested either reminded Mitch of someone he knew, someone he used to know, or someone he used to go out with. I couldn't believe that one man had encountered that many people in only 26 years of life. Then again, I had to consider that he was a Tarrington, and I almost believed they knew everyone in the eastern United States. Beginning to feel frustrated, I snapped the book closed and almost caught Mitch's finger inside as he pointed to a name.

"Hey! What was that for? You could've cut off my finger!"

I laid the book and pens on the table and then sat back and folded my arms in front of me. "We're going to have the only children in the world who don't have names because we'll never be able to agree on anything."

Mitch picked up the book. "Dana, love, there are one thousand choices in this book. I'm certain that we can find at least two that we like."

I looked at him stubbornly. "Well, as far as girls' names go, I absolutely refuse to name my child after one of your old flames and have you get all google-eyed thinking about her whenever we say it. No thank you!"

Evidently finding my attitude somewhat amusing, he responded with a laugh. "Sweetheart, I'd never do that. Besides, none of those women have crossed my mind in years." He pointed to the book saying, "At least not until you mentioned them a few minutes ago."

"Well, you can just put them out of your mind completely. Should we have a girl, we'll name her Renee. That's my mother's middle name." I saw him start to smile, and he tried to bite his lip to hold it in.

"Don't tell me you went out with a Renee, too!"

He simply nodded.

"I give up!" I finally stated.

He laughed again and reached over to hug me although I didn't return the gesture. "Come on, baby. You're acting as if every girl's name in that book is off limits. If half the remaining names in there are boys' names, that gives us over 400 girls' names we can still pick from. I don't think I know that many."

"I wouldn't doubt it," I whined.

He sat back up and gave me a smug look. "What if I told you that the name of any guy you dated was off limits?"

"That would only eliminate three—Kevin Payne, Eddie, and you. As it was, Kevin and I only went out twice. It didn't take that long for me to figure out I really didn't like him. I wasn't the 'social butterfly' you were."

He smiled. "Trust me, I was no 'social butterfly.' Most of those girls were just like your Kevin Payne—one or two dates max—just someone to have on my arm at one of the many social events my parents forced me into attending before and after I dated Jessica. It doesn't look good for the son of a prominent businessman to show up at those things without a date. So you see, it was more of a 'have to' sort of thing."

"Excuse me if I don't share your pain."

Mitch laughed which caused me to smile myself. "That's okay. I'll forgive you. And don't worry, love. These kids won't go through life nameless, I'm sure."

A short while later, Mitch's family filed in along with what seemed like an endless succession of other patrons: all fired up and ready to watch Ace make music. Mitch rejoined his friends backstage, and the six engaged in their weekly 'pep talk,' said a short prayer, and then hit the stage with an energy that brought everyone to their feet. The smile on Mitch's face and the strength of his voice were undeniable indications that he loved every minute of being on that stage. He finished the first song breathless but took a drink of water and cued the band into the second and third. As he wound down the number and moved back toward the mike, he had to stand for at least three minutes before the crowd quieted enough to let him speak.

"Wow, do we have a rowdy group tonight or what?" he said as everyone began to cheer again. "That's fine because the guys and I are in a rowdy mood tonight, too! I need to catch my breath a little, so let's slow it down some. Grab somebody and get close."

Strapping on his headset, he hurried down from the stage toward me. Normally, I'd welcome the chance to dance with my husband; but since I'd grown so large over the past few months, I'd only done so in the privacy of our apartment. Although Mitch would make every attempt to hold me close, we soon learned that my belly made things a little less 'snug.' As he reached me, he smiled and extended a hand. I hesitated, and his eyes told me that he understood what I was thinking. Deciding that a little prompting couldn't hurt, he spoke directly into his mike.

"It's not every guy who gets to dance with his entire family at once," he quipped, drawing a chuckle from the crowd. "Guess I'm pretty lucky, huh?"

He cued the band as he began to sing, and he pulled me to him—smiling into my eyes and making me feel like we were the only two people in the room. I closed my eyes and drank in the sound of his voice as I let myself get lost in the moment. As the song ended, he gave me a soft kiss and whispered that he loved me.

"Everyone, give it up for my beautiful wife, Dana," he said with a bright smile. He winked at me, and I blushed.

As he walked up the stairs to the stage, he added, "I'd introduce the kids to you, too, but they don't have names yet." He turned my way with an ornery grin. "For some reason, she didn't like my suggestion of Gumby and Pokey."

Everyone laughed as the band started into the next song, and I shook my head at my husband.

Fifteen minutes later the band took a break, and Mitch once again found his way to the table. His face was bright and his demeanor cheerful as he gave me a playful kiss. Turning the chair around to straddle it, he sat down next to me.

"You're really having fun, aren't you?" I asked with a little smirk.

"Yes, I am...." he replied with a smirk of his own, dragging out his response as if he was waiting for me to say more.

He knew me far too well. "And to think you're bringing all that fun to an end. I don't get it, but it's your decision." I shot him a sideways glance.

"Guess I'll have to find other ways to have fun then," he fired back. He let his eyes move over me as he raised his eyebrows and grinned.

"Oh, stop it, Mitchell."

"Hey, you started it."

Backstage, Ash, Ty, and Zach stood with their backs against a wall while Shep paced anxiously in front of them. Newbie stood close to the curtain, and his position served a two-fold purpose: to make sure Mitch didn't walk into their conversation and to strategically watch the man sitting in the back of the room making notes on a steno pad.

"Is he out there, Newb?" Zach asked as he tried to glance around his friend to see for himself.

"Yeah, and he's still writing stuff down. I'd sure like to know what he's putting on that paper," Newbie replied.

"Whatever it is, it has to be something good," Zach answered. "Man, can you believe Trip tonight? That dude's on fire! He's always good, but he's really smokin' tonight!"

"You're not kidding," Ty agreed. "To think he's pulling this off and doesn't have any idea what's going on."

Shep stopped his pacing and turned toward his band mates. "We need to tell him, guys. What good is it going to do to have him play a perfect show for this dude and then leave the band without a clue as to what we could have had? You know there's not a snowball's chance in July they're going to even look at us without Trip. He makes us. Maybe if he knows what's going on, it'll change his mind about things."

Ash approached Shep and laid a hand on his shoulder. "We can't do that, man. We already talked about all this. Mitch has bigger things on his plate the band. He needs to take care of Dana and his kids. That's where his heart is; and if we're any kind of friends at all, we can't stand in the way of letting him do what he feels is right." He placed his other hand on the opposite shoulder and looked squarely into Shep's eyes. "We're gonna go out there, and we're gonna keep playing like we have all night. Next week we'll do the same thing and the week after that and so on. When the time comes to let Trip move on, we can look back and know that giving up a shot at fame was a small price to pay for giving a man a chance to be a dad."

As Shep stared into Ash's eyes, he knew that no amount of coercing was going to convince him—or any of the others for that matter—to tell Mitch what was happening right under his nose. It would remain their secret, and they would watch their dreams fade away as they gave their main man an opportunity to fulfill his. Taking a moment to glance into the faces of his friends, he knew in his heart that in spite of how much any of them wished this could be, they were doing the right thing by letting it go.

Shep nodded and dropped his eyes from Ash's. Although he couldn't see it, he could still feel his band mate's reassuring smile as he softly whispered, "He's gonna be a great dad."

"Yeah, he will be. No doubt," Ash replied.

An hour later the band bowed to a standing ovation as the crowd's jubilant cheers echoed throughout the club. As the six men disappeared off stage, the enthusiasm of the patrons continued until Rob Winslow made the final thank you and bid everyone a safe drive home. As I careened my way through the usual throng of groupies trying to get backstage to the guys, I got as far as the entrance to the corridor when I spotted a man who seemed a bit out of place. Unlike most of the other guys who frequented the club sporting jeans or casual attire, he was dressed in tailored slacks with a starched white shirt and tie. Although it probably wasn't of any significance, he was slightly older than the 20-30-something crowd that generally made up the audience; and I probably would have just brushed him off had I not noticed the stenography pad he was carrying in his hand. He approached Rob, offered a handshake, and the two began to engage in deep conversation. My curiosity now aroused, I made my way around them and camouflaged myself with a large group of women who had started to congregate near the backstage door. I got as close as I could to them; not wanting to be obvious, I turned my back to the two men. If either glanced my way, I would look like nothing more than another patron. Although the corridor was noisy with the women's giddy chatter, I put forth an extra effort to pick up as much of the men's conversation as I could.

"Were they everything I promised?" Rob asked the man.

"Absolutely phenomenal! As for that front man, I haven't heard a voice like that in years," the man responded. "Why hasn't he ever gone professional? With that kind of talent, he'd sell millions!" I heard the rustling of paper and assumed he was leafing through notes in his steno pad. "What's the kid's name again?"

Rob smiled. "Mitchell Tarrington—well, he actually goes by Mitch. I've heard the guys in the band refer to him by some nickname, too—Trip, or something like that. Not really sure what that stands for, but they all have nicknames for each other. From my understanding, they used to play together at U of PA a few years back. Mitch left the group, and they looked him up to front again when I called them in to play New Year's Eve. I had such a positive response from the patrons that night that I signed them on as my house band." Rob made a sweep of his hand toward the multitude of people still milling around. "As you can see, they've been packing in a crowd every weekend since then." He chuckled. "Needless to say, the girls love them!"

The man laughed as well. "Another positive. If you have the looks to go along with the talent, sometimes it doubles your popularity, not to mention your sales. I'd say these young men have it all going for them. However," he paused for a moment, and I detected a hint of disappointment in his voice, "I don't make the final decision as you well know. I just throw out the line. Alex and Shawn reel them in."

I heard Rob sigh, but his tone was still positive. "Understood, but I know you've been doing this for a lot of years, Steve, and you usually don't have any trouble persuading them when you see talent. They trust your judgment."

Steve spoke with confidence. "Well, you're right there. If it were up to me, I'd skip the formalities and sign them tomorrow. But, I think we'll get better results if we stick to the process. With that being said, why don't we go and have a chat with Ace?"

"Sounds good. Why don't I buy you a cup of coffee or something first and let this crowd clear out a little more?"

Steve agreed, and the two headed back toward the club while I stood motionless in shock and did my best to process the information I had just gained. It didn't take a genius to figure out that Steve was some sort of talent scout or recording company executive, and he'd been invited to the club that night by Rob to listen to Ace. Evidently, he had seen the potential in them to become more than just a club band. From the way it sounded, Steve saw that potential as well. Trembling with excitement, I started to move toward the backstage door. I had to get to the guys before Steve did and let them know what I'd heard.

"Max, can you clear the extras out of here so I can talk to the band?" I asked the security guard stationed by the door. "I have some important business I need to discuss with the guys, and I can't afford for it to be leaked out by anyone."

"I'll do my best, Dana," was his reply, and I let him step in ahead of me. Within a minute or two—and much to the dismay of the single men standing backstage—the barrage of women was gone; and the band mates surrounded me with curious faces.

"What'd you do all that for, Dana? What's up?" Zach asked as he looked past me toward a curvy blond and motioned with his hand for her to 'call' him.

"Yeah," Shep added as he pointed to a tall brunette in a very short skirt. "I was just about to snag a date for tomorrow night."

"There will be plenty of time for you to exercise your hormones later, guys. This is much more important than that," I said, beckoning them to come closer.

"I'm not sure about that, but okay," Zach replied with a sigh. "What's going on?"

I started to speak but paused and looked around. "Where's Mitch?"

"Is *that* all you wanted—just to know where your husband is?" Ty asked.

"Forget him, Dana," Ash said as he waved off Ty and stepped forward. "Mitch went to the men's room. He'll be right back. What's up?"

I thought I'd surely burst from the excitement that was sweeping over me once more. I told them all about the conversation I'd overheard only moments before and took extra care not to leave out any details. As I finished, I was surprised at the reaction that I received.

"We knew Steve was going to be here tonight, Dana," Ty started. "When we were breaking down the instruments a few weeks back, Rob told us."

"We were planning on telling Mitch about it at rehearsal the night he told us he was quitting. After he broke that news to us, we decided to keep it to ourselves," Zach added.

I must have looked lost because Ash came and placed a hand on my shoulder and softened his voice before he spoke. "Dana, we know how much it means to Mitch to be able to be there for you and the twins. We knew if we told him about Steve he'd feel like he had to stay for us, and the last thing we want is to stand in his way of doing what he feels he should. We know where his heart is, and it isn't with the band."

As I searched their faces, I could see a mixture of emotions. In each set of eyes I could see the sadness of a dream fading away, and yet I could see pride and joy in knowing that they were giving Mitch a chance to live his dream instead. I could feel my eyes clouding with tears as I realized the sacrifice these men were making for us. I reached up to wipe away a tear that had refused to stay inside—my heart deeply touched by the love they were showing for their friend.

"Guys, why? This is what you've always wanted, and now the chance is here. Why are you letting it slip away?"

Before any of them had the chance to answer, I heard the sound of footsteps behind me; and although I didn't turn around, I could tell by the sound of the gait that they belonged to Mitch. I felt his arms come around me in a gentle hug and his kiss falling softly on top of my head. I gazed up at him with tears glistening in my eyes. He gave me a sweet smile, then turned to his band mates, his grin widening just a little, and shook his head.

"Who's going to be the first to explain what's going on here?" he asked as he looked from one of them to the other.

"Explain what?" Ty asked trying to sound clueless.

Mitch placed an arm around my shoulders and pulled me to him. "Let's see—you're huddling around my teary-eyed wife, and some decked-out dude with Rob just asked if he could 'have a word' with us." He made a quick sweep with his hand. "Also, the usual entourage of women generally swarming around back here is gone."

The guys exchanged glances, but no one said a word. Mitch turned to me. "How about it? I have a feeling you're in on whatever this is. Care to share with me?"

My eyes moved slowly over the men standing next to me. "I overheard a conversation between Rob and Steve. That's the man with him. They think the band should go professional."

Mitch began to snicker. "Okay, so some guy thinks we're good. We hear that all the time, so what's making this person's opinion cause all the tension I'm feeling back here?"

"I think he's either a talent scout or someone from a record company," I answered.

Mitch furrowed his brow and narrowed his gaze as he caught a guilty look on Ash's face. "You know something, don't you?" He looked around him, and I could see a curious smirk forming on his face. "All of you do. I can tell. What's going on?"

Just then, the backstage door opened, and Rob and Steve appeared with bright smiles on their faces. We all turned toward them as they stopped just a few feet from the group.

"Guys, I hope we aren't interrupting anything," Rob started. "I have someone here I'd like you all to meet."

Steve stepped forward and extended his hand to Shep who was standing closest to him.

"Steve Garrett with Remington Records. It's good to meet you," he said as he shook Shep's hand. "If I remember correctly, you're bass guitar, right?"

Shep smiled widely. "Todd Sheppard, and that's right."

Steve moved to each man and extended his hand in a warm greeting. Much to their delight, he stated their positions as if he'd been following their talents for years. Finally, he stood before Mitch: and although I was sure he'd seen many actual celebrities in his career, he almost looked star-struck.

"You, young man, are the glue that holds this outfit together. Mitch Tarrington, a pleasure to meet you."

A slow smile came to Mitch's face, and he glanced down at me as if he were hoping I'd tell him how to respond. All I could do was smile with pride myself.

"The pleasure's mine," Mitch answered. "This is my wife, Dana," he said as Steve shook my hand as well.

Steve shook his head. "No, it was definitely mine tonight," he said as he turned to face them all again. "When Rob invited me here a few weeks back, he said I would be impressed. 'Impressed' is an understatement for what I felt when I heard the six of you. 'Blown away' was more like it! It's literally been years since I've heard that kind of talent from a club band. Sure, some of them are good, but most of them don't measure up to anything close to the standards we set at Remington Records. I can safely say that Ace goes above and beyond!"

The guys couldn't hold back their prideful smiles as they exchanged looks. Steve turned back to Mitch.

"And you—I was pulled in the minute you opened your mouth! How much voice training did it take for you to get that sound?"

Mitch blushed as if he was embarrassed to answer honestly. "I don't have any training. I guess you could say it's natural."

Steve looked flabbergasted. "No training? No voice lessons—nothing?"

Mitch began to smile as he shook his head. "Nothing."

"Unbelievable, son. You have a remarkable gift. With your permission, I'd like to give you a chance to use it. I'd like to bring Ace into the studio within the week to cut a demo. Once we have that on hand, I'll present it to my producers and see what they think." He gave Mitch a toothy grin. "If it were my decision, I'd sign you immediately. Unfortunately, I have to go through the ranks. I will say, however, that my gut feeling is good. Real good."

The smile slowly faded from Mitch's face, and he began to bite his lip. I held my breath as I waited for his reply. Glancing around, I could see that everyone else was doing the same.

Then came the words no one was expecting to hear. "I don't know. I mean...this is so sudden."

Steve sighed and nodded. "You're right, Mitch. It is. Why don't I give you all some time to let it sink in—say, a couple of days? We can schedule the studio for later in the week and give you a chance to rehearse your material. You can do anything you want. Original material is better, but covers are fine if that's what you're more comfortable with."

Mitch was still biting his lip, and he looked up into the anxious faces of his friends. "Look guys, I just don't know. You know where I stand on things right now, and well...." He sighed heavily. "I just don't know. I'm sorry."

Steve looked concerned. "Is there a problem?"

Ash could sense Mitch's turmoil and decided to step in. "Steve, to be honest the band was considering some 'structural changes' within the next few months. I think I speak for all of us when I say that we're honored by the offer, but I'm not sure this is the right time for us to make this type of move."

Steve stood speechless, and Rob was clearly stunned by what he'd just witnessed. Both had been certain that the band's reaction—and especially Mitch's—would be much more positive. Looking at them now, it seemed as if they all wished somehow that the meeting had never occurred.

Rob decided it was his turn to step up to the plate. "Guys, I don't want to pry; but when I spoke with you a few weeks ago about all this, you were pretty excited. Has something changed since then?"

"A few things," Ash replied and gave Mitch a quick look.

I could see the change in Rob's expression which told me that he understood the issue wasn't with the band, but with Mitch. "I see," he simply replied.

Steve spoke up once more. "As I said, I don't see talent like yours very often, and I would truly hate to see you pass up this opportunity." He continued to speak to the group as a whole but turned and focused more closely on Mitch. "Tell you what. Why don't we put off the demo for another week, and the six of you can discuss things this week." He pulled several business cards from a holder he'd had in his pocket and began to pass them out. "When you come to a decision, give me a call and let me know. We'll take it from there."

He shook everyone's hand once more and paused a bit longer when he came to Mitch. Looking into his eyes, he said, "I'll look forward to your call." With that, he and Rob were gone.

Mitch's eyes followed the men until they were out of sight, and then he put his focus back on his friends.

"All of you knew about this two weeks ago. Why'd you keep it from me? I thought I was the front man here." Hearing the agitation in his voice, I laid a hand on his arm as if it might help calm him.

Newbie stepped forward. "We were going to tell you, Trip—the night you told us you were quitting. We got together and decided that if your heart was set on leaving, we weren't going to hold you back. We know how important Dana and your kids are to you."

"Yeah, dude. We didn't want you to feel like you had to stay because of this." Ty took a deep breath and let it out slowly. "We honestly thought we could get you out of here tonight before Rob or that Steve guy had a chance to get to you. Obviously, it didn't work that way."

"No, it didn't," Mitch stated. Suddenly, his attention turned to Shep who had been standing silently in the background to that point. "Hold on. That's why you were so adamant about my not leaving 'now,' isn't it?

You wanted to tell me, but these guys wouldn't let you." He began to smirk. "How close am I?"

Shep returned the expression. "Pretty darn close."

"I thought so." Mitch walked to a chair a few feet away and took a seat, placed his head against the back of it, and closed his eyes tightly. He let his mind drift back to the scene at Gartano's many months before when he'd been surprised by a visit from his friends. During that initial meeting, Ty had expressed with much emphasis that appearing at Studio 14 could lead to a chance for them to make it 'big.' Mitch had known the guys possessed the talent, but in his heart he honestly never believed it would actually happen. Now they were staring into the face of a possible dream come true. He opened his eyes and looked at the forlorn faces of his friends. He knew it was breaking their hearts to give up this chance, but his heart warmed with the knowledge that they were doing so willingly for him. Knowing what he had to do, he stood and headed toward the stage.

"Mitchell, where are you going?" I asked as I began to follow.

He paused for a moment and turned to me with a determined look on his face. "You stay here with the guys. I'll be right back."

"Mr. Garrett, wait!" Mitch called out as he saw the man heading out the door of the club.

Steve turned around and waited for Mitch to approach. "What can I do for you?"

Taking a moment to catch his breath, Mitch began to explain. He told Steve about Dana's accident, the twins, and his decision to quit the band. He expressed his concern over the ability to manage fronting Ace along with taking care of the bistro and his family. He also explained how his band mates had kept the news of Steve's visit from him in the hopes that they could keep him from second-guessing his decision. Steve listened carefully to Mitch; and as he spoke, Rob quietly stepped up behind him to listen as well. The pair of executives exchanged a look as Mitch made his final suggestion.

"These guys have waited a lifetime for a shot like this, and the last thing I want to do is keep them from that opportunity. Are you willing to let them come in and cut the demo without me? Ty Sanders has an excellent voice. In fact, I told him he should step in as lead when I leave. I'm sure you'd be just as impressed with him at the mike as you were with me."

Steve placed a hand on Mitch's shoulder. "Look, I sympathize with all you and your wife have been through, and I admire your desire to put your family before anything else. That's important." He let out a long breath. "However, I'm going to be blunt. I think Ace is a very talented group as a whole. You are part of that whole. Without your vocals, well, I'm not sure I could sell my producers on the idea of signing them. It would almost be like the Stones with no Mick Jagger—somehow, it just doesn't work. You need that front man to add the little something extra that gets the rest of the band noticed. Only then can you really appreciate the true talent of the group collectively. Sure, people might listen to the band without him, but *with* him, they're going to *remember* the band. Get it?"

Mitch dropped his eyes from Steve's and nodded. "Yeah, I get it. It's either all or none."

Steve nodded. "I don't mean to imply that Ty isn't an outstanding vocalist. But you—you, Mitch, possess a true gift. I consider myself lucky that someone hasn't snagged you up long before now." He smiled. "The six of you work very well together. It's easy to see you have an emotional connection to one another as well as the professional element. That's important. You play as much for each other as you do for the crowd. When people see that you're having fun, they'll have fun with you. I saw that going on tonight, Mitch. Imagine doing that for a crowd of 25,000 or more instead of 250."

Mitch had to chuckle. "Man, I don't know about that. I was a little intimidated by the size of the crowd at this place!"

Rob stepped up and laughed as well. "I would never have guessed that. If you have stage fright, you sure do a good job of hiding it."

Mitch's expression turned serious once more as Steve directed his attention to him. "I know this is a big step for you especially along with those other things you shared with me. It sounds like you have your mind made up as far as leaving the band, but I hope you'll at least give my proposal some serious consideration. I see a lot of potential in you; and although I can't make any promises, I have a good feeling that Ace may have a very bright future with Remington Records."

Feeling a bit unsettled, Mitch nodded and began to bite his lip. "I'll think about it," he said quietly.

Steve smiled and extended his hand. "Good. You have my card, and I'll be looking forward to hearing from you." After bidding Mitch and Rob a good evening, he went on his way.

Rob once again placed a gentle hand on Mitch's shoulder. "Mitch, no one wants you to feel pressured about this. Don't lose sleep over it. All we ask is that you give the whole thing some thought, okay?"

"I will," Mitch replied. Not wanting to engage in another awkward conversation, Mitch excused himself saying he needed to get Dana home to rest. As he walked toward the backstage area, he thought to himself, *Oh, no, guys. I don't feel pressured. I feel like I've been backed into a corner.*

Mitch didn't say much as he returned to his band mates except for a few solemn goodbyes before he took Dana by the hand and headed into the balmy night. Upon reaching the car, he opened the door for her and waited until she had settled into her seat before he closed it and walked around to get in on the other side. He placed the keys in the ignition; but instead of starting the car, he turned to her.

"They don't want the band without me, Dana. I asked if Steve would let them cut a demo with Ty as lead, and he said no. They're good. They don't need me, but he won't give them a chance to prove that."

I gently placed my hand on his leg, but said nothing in response. I knew that my words would do little to comfort him anyway. As much as I wanted to help, I knew he needed to work this out on his own.

The sound of thunder rumbling in the distance awakened me. I rolled over to look at the clock on the nightstand which told me it was 3:12 a.m. Sleepily, I reached out for Mitch only to find I was there all alone. Knowing that he wasn't usually one to be up in the night, a wave of concern swept over me; and I slipped out of bed to search for my husband.

Except for the occasional flash of lightning coming through the blinds and the soft glow of the nightlight I kept in the bathroom, the apartment was completely dark. Carefully, I wandered toward the living room softly calling his name.

"I'm here, honey," I heard him say faintly.

By this time, my eyes had adjusted to the darkness enough that I could see him lying on the couch with one arm covering his eyes and the other resting across his stomach. As I came into view, he sat up and patted the seat next to him and prompted me to sit down. He placed an arm around me, pulled me against him, and kissed my forehead.

"Did the storm wake you?" he asked.

I snuggled closer to him as a loud clap of thunder rattled the windows. "That and the fact that you weren't in bed with me. What are you doing up?"

He began to rub my arm. "Trying to figure out how I can become Superman."

"I don't understand, Mitchell. What do you mean?"

"I mean, how do I do it all? When you were recovering from the accident, I not only continued to run the bistro; but I maintained our home, took care of you, and kept up with the band. I did everything, and I didn't mind; but it was hard. I was exhausted. There were times when I honestly fell into bed at night and woke up the next morning not even remembering how I got there!" He sighed heavily. "It's unrealistic of me to think that I can do all those things and throw two babies into the mix as well."

"But, you want to, don't you?"

He took his arm from around me, leaned back against the couch, and folded his hands in his lap. "Yeah, I do." He repositioned himself to face me, and I could detect excitement creeping into his voice. "I had a tough day yesterday at the bistro. Nothing went wrong or anything like that—I just had a lot of work, and I was pretty beat by the time you and the guys showed up. The minute I walked into the club and especially when I set foot on that stage, it was like the old Mitch fell away; and a new one took his place. I swear these shows are therapeutic. I felt *alive*, Dana. I was happy, and I was full of energy." He took my hand in his and caressed it softly with the index finger of his other hand. "You were right when you said I was having fun. I was. I really don't want that to end. Like I said, though, I don't see how I can do everything."

I took both his hands in mine. "Well, there's one important element to all this that I think you've forgotten. I'm no longer recovering. You don't have to do 'everything' anymore. A lot of those things you took over I can now take back. You're off the hook. You now have no excuse to quit the band."

He didn't answer, and I knew he was letting that thought sink in. Finally, he spoke.

"What about rehearsals? I won't have any time to spend with you and the kids if I'm off doing my thing every night. When will I get anything done around the house—things like cutting the lawn, painting the fence, or fixing a leaky faucet?"

I smiled at the knowledge that I was armed and ready for debate. "Change your schedule a little. Cut down to three rehearsals a week—which I might add, will now be no further away than your own backyard. The guys are good, and you know they don't need any more than that. The rest of the time you can devote to doing anything else you need or want to do."

He laughed. "You're always so logical. How do you do that?"

"Even Superman didn't have all the answers, Mitch. That's why he needed Lois Lane."

I felt his arms come around me and he pulled me close and buried his face in my hair. I could feel the warmth of his breath and his smile against me. "I love you, Lois Lane," he whispered. We sat silently in the darkness holding each other—the only sounds being the rain outside and the beating of two hearts deeply in love.

Bright and early the next morning, Chris greeted us just outside the entrance to the church. "I wasn't sure you were coming, little brother. What took you so long?"

Mitch yawned as he reached for the door handle. "I'm a little sluggish this morning, that's all. Dana and I were up half the night."

With a mischievous grin on his face, Chris chuckled and patted his brother on the back. "I remember those days. Enjoy it while you can, buddy. Trust me, it all changes once you have kids."

Mitch rolled his eyes at his brother's words. "We were *talking*, Chris."

Chris paused and gave Mitch a half smile. "*Just* talking?"

Mitch returned the expression. "Yeah, just talking. Sorry to disappoint you."

Chris instructed Trudy and I to go inside and join the others while he had a word with Mitch. He held the door for us; and once I had stepped inside, he moved to the side and lowered his voice to avoid drawing attention.

"You don't have to tell me if you don't want to, but I'm guessing anything that you felt worthy of discussing when you could have been sleeping—or whatever else—must be pretty important. Is everything okay?"

Mitch smiled. "Everything's fine except for the fact that I married a woman at least ten times smarter than I am. That's fine with me, too." His grin grew even broader and his eyes sparkled with the excitement he'd felt the night before. "She showed me how to be Superman."

Chris chuckled and shot his brother an inquisitive glance. "I thought you said all you did was talk."

Mitch began to laugh and shook his head at Chris. "Regarding the band and everything else, you numbskull. She made me realize that I can stay with Ace and still take on all the new responsibilities that are heading my way." He gave Chris a brief replay of the conversation he and Dana had shared.

"Isn't that kind of what I told you at Gartano's a few weeks ago? Of course, you wouldn't listen to me...." Chris said with a smirk.

"When have I *ever* listened to you, Christopher?" Mitch smiled. "Maybe on some subconscious level I needed to hear Dana say it. It's as if having her okay on the situation and hearing that she's well makes all the difference. Doesn't mean I'm not still a little nervous about everything, but I don't feel quite as petrified as I did before. I think I can handle it now."

"Good to hear, little brother." He placed his hand on the top of Mitch's arm. "You know that no one in the family was happy about your decision to leave the band anyway. We were hoping Dana would bring you back to your senses. We all knew you wouldn't listen to any of us."

"Well, that's really not the only thing that did it for me." He told Chris about Steve's visit to the club, the offer for the demo, and the way the band had tried to keep everything from him. As he finished the story he added, "After finding out that they were willing to give up their dream for me, I knew I had to do something."

Chris grinned. "To think that my brother—the one who used to follow me around like a little lost puppy—might be the next superstar! Unreal!" He extended his hand to Mitch. "Congratulations, Mitchell. I'm really proud of you."

Mitch's eyes shined. "Thanks, Chris. Even coming from you that means a lot!"

Hearing the soft sounds of music coming from within, Chris moved toward the door of the church and held it open for Mitch. "Come on, Hollywood. Let's get in there and give some thanks for all this, shall we?"

"Absolutely!"

Following the service, Mitch's family gathered at the back of the church as the two of us made our way out of the pew to join them. Lately, it seemed like I was beginning to do everything in slow motion. Just lifting my body from a sitting to standing position required more effort than I thought most people used to mow an acre of land. Mitch stood by patiently and offered a hand for support as he stepped slightly to the side to let my big belly and me pass by. I glanced at him with an uncomfortable look on my face, suddenly reminded of one of the more unpleasant aspects of being almost seven months pregnant. He smiled and gently prompted me in the right direction.

"Go on, love. I'll wait for you in the back."

"I really wish these children would find somewhere else to lie other than on my bladder," I remarked as I trudged off toward the ladies' room. I heard my husband laugh as I walked away.

Completing my task, I returned to the sanctuary to find my husband and the rest of the Tarrington crew exchanging hugs and handshakes. Surmising that he must have told them of the news regarding the band, I quietly took my place beside him until they were finished with their congratulations. Noticing I had returned, he smiled down at me and tucked an arm around my waist.

"How would you like to go out tonight and celebrate, kids?" Jake asked. "It's been a while since I've had the chance to treat my family to dinner. Does Chandler's sound good to everyone?"

"You don't have to do that, Dad," Mitch said. "Nothing's happened yet. It's just a demo. We may never become anything more than we are now."

Olivia smiled at her youngest child. "We know we don't have to, Mitch, but we want to," she said. As if she wasn't going to take no for an answer, she turned back to the rest of the group. "We'll meet there around six." She paused and looked into the faces of her grandchildren. "Little ones, too. I'll call as soon as I get home and make the reservation."

Jim and Angelina's daughter, Megan, who had just turned three years old, tugged on her uncle's pant leg. Mitch smiled and scooped her up into his arms.

"Whatcha need, Meggie?" he asked as he planted a kiss on her tiny cheek.

"When we go eat, will you sit by me, Uccle Mish?"

Mitch smirked. "Well, that depends. What are you going to have to eat?"

The little girl looked at him as if that question wasn't anything out of the ordinary. "Macroni and cheese. And frech fries and milk," she answered matter-of-factly.

Mitch smiled and tried not to laugh at her mispronunciations. "Hmm. French fries, huh? Will you share with me? I like French fries, and they only give grown-ups baked potatoes."

She twisted her jaw and then nodded with a smile. "Yep. I'll share."

Everyone chuckled softly as Mitch held her close. "It's a deal then. You can sit next to me."

I stood in front of the full-length mirror on the back of our closet door and glanced at the dresses I held in each of my hands. Moving the one in my left hand in front of me, I studied it for a moment before switching to the one on the right. It really shouldn't have been much of a decision—both were essentially the same style, really only differing in color—but I needed to choose the one that made me appear smaller than I actually was. Even if Mitch claimed he hadn't noticed much of a change in my physical appearance over the past few weeks, gazing at my reflection just then I could easily see that I was growing at the speed of light—or so it seemed anyway. I looked toward the nightstand for a moment at a picture Jake had taken of Mitch and me soon after our engagement. Looking at the slender, shapely woman staring back at me, I had to wonder: once these babies were born, would I ever look like that again? Would my normally high metabolism kick back in or would the shift in hormones during the pregnancy cause things to slow down? Would I lose the extra pounds brought on by my maternal state or only add more pounds to them? If I didn't return to my previous figure, would Mitch find me less attractive? Sighing heavily, I turned back to the mirror and studied the dresses again. Mitch crept up behind me, pushed up the knot on his tie, and removed the dress from my left hand.

"There. Now, you don't have to decide. We need to get going, love. It's five-fifteen."

"I want to wear the purple one, Mitch. Dark colors are more slimming."

It was then, much to my surprise, that my husband secured his fate for the rest of the evening simply by opening his mouth. "Then maybe you should opt for your black pant suit. Covers more area," he said with a grin as he patted me and glanced at my backside. As if that statement wasn't enough, he happened to notice the picture on the nightstand as well and picked it up as he passed by. "Gosh, you were so beautiful in that picture. Such a tiny little thing."

Unable to believe he'd just uttered those words to me, my mouth fell open as I watched him innocently sit down in the chair to tie his shoes. I stomped past him, angrily threw the dress in the middle of the bed, and headed for the living room couch. He lifted his eyes to watch me exit the room. I was sure he hadn't realized what he'd said because it took at least two minutes for him to find me.

"Dana, what's wrong? We need to get ready. Why are you sitting out here?"

I chose not to answer. I knew how much he hated the silent treatment, and I also knew that if I spoke I'd probably take his head off.

"Did I upset you? Are you sick? What's happening? Will you please tell me?"

I didn't even bother looking his way.

He sighed heavily and moved to sit in front of me on the coffee table. I turned to stare out the balcony doors.

"If it's the dress, you can wear the purple one, love. I really don't care. I was just trying to hurry things along, that's all." He smiled. "It *is* the dress, isn't it?"

Close, buddy, but no cigar, I thought. I looked at him, and his eyes pleaded for some sort of sign that he may be right. I gave him nothing.

I sat for another moment before deciding I wasn't going to give up my steak dinner because my husband was being a brainless twit. Retreating to the bedroom, I quickly put on the blue dress and stopped to look in the mirror again before I headed to the bathroom to brush my hair. Mitch caught up with me again and stood staring at me as he bit his lip.

"If you weren't going to wear the purple one anyway, why are you making such a fuss over it?" He started to fidget a little. "Okay, Dana, this silent stuff is driving me nuts. Just tell me what I did—yell, throw things at me, whatever you want to do—so we can get past this and have a pleasant evening."

I threw a tube of dark pink lipstick into my evening bag and turned to face him. He tried to offer a soft smile.

"You look lovely. Now, are you ready to go? Do you need a sweater? I can get it for you."

I moved past him toward the front door. I heard him say, "Okay, I guess not," as he followed.

During the fifteen-minute ride to Chandler's, our conversation was rather one-sided. Mitch talked, and I remained silent. Despite his pleas to find out what he had done wrong, his attempts at holding my hand, and his emotionless 'just-trying-to-get-out-of- the-doghouse' apologies, I still held my ground. After all, the man had lived with me for almost seven months—the last five of them with the knowledge of my pregnancy and my sensitivity to the changes taking place with my body. He should have known that I wouldn't take well to him making comments about it.

Mitch found a parking spot near the door. After turning off the car, he closed his hand around the keys and stared out the windshield at the building in front of him.

"I don't know what I did, Dana. I told you I was sorry. Why won't you talk to me? This is supposed to be a happy night, and you're making me miserable."

I decided to give him something to think about. "How can you truly be sorry if you don't know what you did?"

"Oh, for crying out loud. Let's just go inside, all right? I'm hungry."

The others were waiting in the lobby as we approached. Olivia immediately zoned in on her son's solemn expression. She stepped quickly to his side and ushered him a few steps away from the group.

"What's the matter, Mitch? Are you and Dana having a spat?"

He shrugged. "I guess so, but I don't know what it's about. She isn't speaking to me. All I did was offer a suggestion about what she might wear tonight, and she got mad at me."

Olivia smiled. "What did you say to her?"

Mitch gave his mother a recap of the scene at home, and she immediately began to laugh.

"Mitchell Jacob Tarrington. You actually told your wife that she should cover 'more area'? The girl is seven months' pregnant. You just don't say things like that at this stage of the game. She's getting larger by the minute, and she's sensitive about it. Can you imagine the message you sent to her? You probably made her feel even more self-conscious."

Mitch turned his eyes from his mother to his wife and stood staring at her for a moment before answering. "I never thought of it that way. I honestly thought I was being helpful."

"Helpful? Honey, making comments about her size isn't helpful. When I was pregnant, I'd cry practically every time I looked in the mirror those last few months. It wasn't that I didn't want to be pregnant, and it wasn't that I didn't love my baby. It was simply that I didn't want to be larger than I'd ever been in my life, and I was afraid your father wouldn't love me anymore if I was. I wanted to be exactly the same Olivia he married—in size and every other way." Olivia smiled. "When I look back now, I realize how silly that whole mentality was; but at the time, it was very real." She looked at Dana and then to her son. "I can't say for sure, but I would guess that's pretty much how Dana feels."

Mitch looked into his mother's eyes and remembered a time a much younger Mitch would take everything she said with a grain of salt. He had wanted so badly for her to be wrong, but ultimately found out in most situations that she was right on the money. Now, an older—and wiser—Mitch contemplated her words, took them to heart, and stored them away for future reference. He smiled down at her; and as he bent down to kiss her cheek, he whispered, "Thanks, Mom. I'll try to talk to her again."

Mitch approached me timidly with a sympathetic smile on his face. Gingerly, he placed his arm around me. To save face with his family, I allowed him to keep it there. The Maitre 'D ushered us to a table, and Mitch held the chair for me before placing Megan on a chair and sitting down between us. Noticing my shiver from the chill of the air conditioning vent above me, he removed his jacket and gently draped it over my shoulders. I glanced his way, and he smiled before picking up his menu.

"Dana, we're almost set for the baby shower," Julia started. "Mom said the responses have been coming in, and it looks like we'll have a great turnout. Everyone's excited to see you."

"We have some fun games planned, too. It's going to be a good time," Trudy added.

"Am I allowed to participate or is this another one of those 'women only' things like the bridal shower?" Mitch asked.

"Sorry, baby brother. It's women only," Julia stated.

Mitch sat back, folded his arms, and pretended to be upset even though he was smirking. "Now, hold on. That's not fair. I fathered these children, so I should be allowed to be at the party. Why don't they have baby showers for the dad?"

Chris laughed. "Mitchell, do you really want to sit through two hours of listening to your wife divulge what a selfish pig you are for getting her pregnant in the first place and how she's never letting you near her again? Could be a real blow to your ego, buddy. Trust me."

"Oh, no, Chris," Jim interjected. "That doesn't happen until she's actually in labor. The baby shower is just for discussing the aches and pains she has and how her husband doesn't understand any of her feelings."

"Gee, maybe I *don't* want to be there," Mitch conceded. "You guys can all come over to our place. We can get some cheese steaks and just hang out. I have a big back yard, so maybe we can even get the band there; and we'll play some football. What do you think? You, too, Dad."

The four men nodded in agreement. "Sounds good," Jim said. "Better than any old hen party." He shot a crooked grin at Angelina.

"Oh, you guys don't have a clue," she retorted. "At least we won't clog our arteries full of greasy sandwiches and then get all sweaty and smelly trying to prove that we still have the agility of teenagers. We'll be acting like adults."

"Yeah," Mitch grinned, "but we'll be the ones having fun!"

The friendly debate was interrupted by a man who introduced himself as John and announced that he would be serving us for the evening. He seemed a bit out of sorts for the usual wait staff at Chandler's as he was much younger and definitely better looking than anyone else I'd seen there in the past. He seemed relaxed, yet professional, as he moved around the table taking everyone's orders one by one. When finally it was my turn, he smiled brightly; and for a moment our eyes locked which made me slightly uncomfortable. I quickly looked down at my menu and raised it in front of my face in the hope of hiding the blush I could feel rising in my cheeks. As I handed John my menu, he smiled again. I smiled back and thanked him. From the corner of my eye I noticed my husband glance first at John, then at me, taking in the friendly exchange between us. Only Mitch's expression wasn't one of friendship but rather of jealousy.

Jake was the last to order; and before John walked away, he said, "If there's anything at all you need, please let me know." I could have sworn he looked right at me as he said it.

Trudy poked me gently in the ribs with her elbow and whispered, "He's a cutie, isn't he?"

I shrunk down in my chair just a little. "I really didn't notice," I whispered back.

She giggled. "Yes, you did. How could you not? He smiled at you."

"Okay, I noticed," I shot back softly. "But, I shouldn't have. I'm married—not to mention almost seven months' pregnant."

She smiled. "Dana, honey, it's okay. Doesn't mean that you want to go home with him. It simply means you noticed. That's all."

"Hey there, Mrs. Tarrington. Quit drooling over the waiter and pass me the bread basket, will you?" Chris said playfully as he smiled brightly at his wife.

"Hold your horses," she replied. "Besides, that guy can't be over twenty years old. Way too young for me." She handed Chris the basket of hot rolls. "I suppose I'm destined to stay with you."

Chris snickered. "Gee, you don't sound very happy about it."

Trudy took Chris by the hand and gave him a kiss. "I am perfectly happy with you, Christopher. I've finally got you trained the way I want you. Why would I want to start all over with someone new?"

He kissed her again as he slipped an arm around her shoulders. "At least I know it's by choice that you stay," he teased.

John returned to the table carrying two bottles of champagne and a tray of glasses filled with ginger ale. Placing the champagne next to Jake, he began to pass out the ginger ale to the children. I raised my hand, and he smiled at me again. This time I tried not to blush.

"I'll take one of those, too," I said. "I'm pregnant, so I can't have the champagne."

"Of course," he replied and set a glass of the soda in front of me. "I'm sorry, miss. I didn't notice."

Oh, John, you're good, I thought. *I'm sitting three feet back from the table because of my mother load, and you didn't notice. Yeah, right.*

Mitch dropped his arm on the back of my chair and began to rub my shoulder. "Yeah, my wife is due in November," he stated with emphasis on the words 'my wife.' "We're having twins."

John smiled again as he began to pour the champagne for the others. "That's wonderful. Congratulations." He looked directly at me again. "If you don't mind my saying, you really don't look like you're that far along—let alone having twins."

"Thank you," I replied, and Mitch once again got that jealous look on his face.

As John left the table, Jake drew everyone's attention to him; and he stood with his glass of champagne.

"I'd like to propose a toast," he began. "To our family's future superstar: Mitchell. God has given you a wonderful gift in your musical talents, and I'm thrilled that you are finally getting the opportunity you deserve to share them with the world. I'm very proud of you, son, and I love you." He raised his glass high as he smiled lovingly at his child. "To Mitch—all the best!"

Everyone toasted Mitch, and he smiled. "Thanks everyone, but there's something I have to say, too." He turned to me and took me by the hand, his expression serious. "Dana, I know I'm not always the smartest guy around—I say stupid things that make you angry with me, and I can be pretty insensitive at times. Yet, you never give up on me. If it wasn't for you—loving me, believing in me, guiding me—this whole demo thing wouldn't even be happening. It doesn't matter if I make it big or not. As long as I have you in my life, that's all I need. You are the most beautiful, most special, and most precious thing in my world. I love you, sweetheart." Everyone applauded as he leaned over and kissed me softly.

As the family resumed their chatter, Mitch moved away from me and tenderly wiped the tears that had decided to trickle down my cheeks. "Come on, now, love. Don't do that."

"I can't help it," I sniffled. "Here I am all mad at you, and then you go and say all those sweet things about me." I sniffled again as I felt my lip tremble. "I'm sorry, Mitch."

He smiled sweetly, placed a gentle hand on my cheek, and wiped away yet another tear with his thumb. "It's all right. I'm sorry, too. I should really learn to think before I open my big mouth. I didn't mean to hurt your feelings."

"Does this mean we're making up?" I asked as I began to gain my composure.

"Sure," he said, "as long as you promise to quit making eyes at the waiter."

"Okay, I promise." I didn't bother to tell him that I was actually trying to avoid eye contact with John because it made me uncomfortable—Mitch's jealousy somehow felt kind of good to me. I felt loved, protected, and desired. I simply let him believe what he wanted to believe; and for the rest of the evening, I only made eyes at him.

Chapter 12

Mitch closed and locked the door behind him and decided to leave the dining room lights off for the time being as he made his way back to the office of Gartano's. Sinking down into the chair at his desk, he picked up the folder he had placed in the middle of it prior to his departure on Saturday, opened it, and began to leaf through the contents. These were the applications for the prospective waitresses he would contact today. If he could get some of them to agree to interviews right away, it would help speed up the process. If not, he would just have to work out something else. His plan was to have the interviews done by Wednesday at noon, give himself the rest of that day to set up second interviews for Thursday, and make his selection by Friday. If that meant a need for him to work late on any given day, he would rearrange his rehearsal schedule with the band.

Dana had insisted on being a part of the interviewing process. While he was interested in her input and valued her opinion, he was also fearful that if any of the candidates were young, attractive, or outgoing, she would let her jealousy interfere with her reasoning. He knew she wouldn't want anyone working with him that she could possibly view as 'competition.' He could tell her there was no need to worry until he was blue in the face; but most likely, it wouldn't do a bit of good. Therefore, he would let her sit in as he spoke with each person and hope that someone would come along they could both be satisfied with.

Knowing it was going to be a long day, he picked up his travel mug and took a drink of the coffee he'd brought from home. He'd made it a little stronger that morning than usual—somehow thinking it would provide an extra kick to get him through his workload. It tasted good to him, and he wished he'd filled his Thermos rather than just a mug. Perhaps he could ask Dana to bring him more when she came down to meet him later. Sure, he could just drink whatever the crew made when they arrived, but somehow he didn't think it would have quite the same effect.

The sound of the door opening and a cheery, "Good morning" summoned Kayla's arrival. Mitch called his greeting back to her; and less than a minute later, she was standing at the office door.

"How are you this morning, Mr. Tarrington?" she asked.

"Not too bad," Mitch answered. "How about you?"

"Fine and dandy. What's on the agenda for today? Anything special?"

Mitch pointed to the folder. "I'm planning to start calling in candidates for the waitressing position. What I think I may do is schedule one every half hour or so if I can. We'll hold a table open out front. That way, if someone arrives a little early, they'll have a place to wait. I'd like you to kinda oversee things for me on that level and play hostess. Is that all right with you?"

Kayla smiled her signature smile. "That's just fine. I'm happy to help." She moved to take a seat on the couch. "Is Dana going to be a part of all this or is she leaving it up to you? I know she's not very happy about your hiring a replacement for her to begin with."

Mitch shook his head in response—a half smile on his own face. "I think she's resigned herself to the fact that waitressing and trying to handle two infants don't go hand in hand. She's still a little sad because she has to leave. Therefore, I'm careful not to use the word 'replacement' when I talk about a new hire. I tell her it's someone who's going to take up the slack for me. I'll think of a way to make her fit in when the time comes and maybe teach her how to do the books or something—just enough so she feels important, you know." He chuckled. "As for the interviews, you can bet your sweet dollar she wanted to be in on that. You know how she is about my being around any woman she doesn't know. I figured it would probably be better anyhow if she was comfortable with the person I decided to hire. It'll be easier on both of us if she goes through the process with me."

"Good idea," Kayla agreed. "If you don't mind my suggesting, maybe it would help even more if you let her train the new girl."

Mitch smiled and nodded approvingly. "That's an excellent idea, Kayla. Now I know why I keep you around here!" he joked.

"See, I am good for something." Kayla's laughter echoed through the hallway as she walked away.

The parking lot was nearly full, but I found a place not far from the door and pulled in. The 'dog days' of summer were upon us, and the scorching heat of the noontime sun had discouraged me from walking the three blocks from home to the bistro—opting instead for the comfort of my air-conditioned vehicle. Mitch had called earlier to tell me that his first interview was scheduled for 1:00 pm, but if I would arrive a little before that, he would take time out for lunch with me. With eager anticipation, I opened the car door and hurried as quickly as I could toward the entrance of Gartano's.

I tucked my keys in my purse and stepped into the coolness of the bistro. As usual, the dining room was filled near capacity with only a few empty tables to be seen. I waved a quick hello to Kayla and Phyllis who were busily moving about, and I retreated to the office to find Mitch.

"Hey handsome! I brought your coffee," I greeted as I stepped into his view.

"Oh, hi, baby. Thanks. I really think I'm going to need it," he replied. He took the Thermos from my hand and gave me a kiss. "Why don't we grab something quick for lunch, and then we'll be ready for the first interview? Kayla's going to play hostess for me. She has a table out there that'll serve as a waiting area for the candidates, and we'll talk to them back here."

"Sounds pretty official," I replied. "Do you plan to grill them the way you did me during my interview?"

He placed an arm around my waist and guided me toward the dining room. "Of course not," he said with a flash of his dimple. "I'd never be that hard on a complete stranger!"

"Oh, so you reserve your mean streak just for me, huh?"

"Yeah, something like that."

We enjoyed a lunch of Chicken Alfredo and split a canolli for dessert. As we started back toward the office, a young woman came through the door looking quite lost. I turned to Mitch.

"Do you suppose she's our first interview?" I asked as I discreetly pointed in her direction.

"Could be," he answered. "Maybe I should go find out. You head back to the office and wait for me, okay?"

"Okay."

Mitch approached her with a warm smile. "Hi. Welcome to Gartano's. Can I help you?" He noticed she looked quite anxious.

Soft brown eyes met his with a shy smile. "Oh, hi. I'm Jennifer Dugan. I have an interview at one o'clock with Mr. Tarrington."

"That would be me," he said as he extended a hand. "Nice to meet you, Jennifer. And please, call me Mitch."

"Nice to meet you, too," she replied in a barely audible tone as she offered a weak handshake. Her eyes widened as she scanned the dining room. "Wow. Is it always this busy?"

Mitch shrugged and seemed to be unaffected by the question. "Most of the time. We do a good business here. That's why I need someone who's quick on her feet and not afraid of a little hard work." Noticing she looked apprehensive, he decided to move things along and hoped she'd be more comfortable after she talked to Dana and him. "Why don't we go back in the office and chat for a few minutes? I'll tell you about the position and see what you think."

He started toward the office, but Jennifer stood her ground with a deer-in-the-headlights expression on her face as she continued to gaze at the busyness around her.

"Jennifer? Is something wrong?"

She hesitated for a moment before answering with a trembling voice. "I'm sorry, but I don't think this would work out for me."

Mitch stared at her in disbelief. "I don't understand. We haven't discussed anything yet."

Jennifer fumbled for the door handle. "I'm really sorry I wasted your time, Mitch. I don't think I'm the person you're looking for. Have a nice day." With that she was gone.

Mitch watched through the window in shock as Jennifer hurried to her car and sped away.

"Wasn't she our interview?" I asked Mitch as he entered the office alone.

He still held a befuddled look on his face as he glanced back toward the dining room and then turned to me. "That was the weirdest thing I've ever experienced."

"What are you talking about?"

He sat down in his chair and chuckled softly. "She acted like she'd never been around people before, Dana. She seemed a little nervous when I introduced myself—which is pretty normal for anyone going on an interview—but when I told her that the place was usually busy, she practically ran out the door!"

"No kidding!"

"I guess the crowd must have scared her away—or maybe I did. However, I didn't say anything that I think would have frightened her." He sighed; and removing her application from the file, he made a few notes in the margin and placed it on the bottom of the pile. "Well, I guess we'll just have to see how candidate number two works out, huh?"

"I suppose so. If the poor girl was that nervous, she'll probably have a tough time getting a job anywhere."

Mitch and I chatted idly for the next few minutes before Kayla appeared in the doorway.

"Excuse me, Mitch, but your...." She hesitated and tried to stifle a laugh. "Your interview is here. Should I send her back?" She was having a difficult time keeping her composure, and her smile caused both Mitch and me to smile out of sheer curiosity.

"Before you do that, step in here and close the door," Mitch instructed.

Kayla did as she was asked and stood at the corner of the desk as a wide smile emerged on her face.

"What's so funny about our next interview?" Mitch asked her.

"Well," Kayla started, "you know that Boy George character all the kids listened to a few years back?"

"Yeah...."

"Well, he's sitting in your dining room, and he...I mean, *she*...says her name is Georgina Boyd. You know, *'Boy George,' 'Georgina Boyd'*? Get it?"

Mitch and I exchanged a look. "Nah, you're pulling my leg, aren't you?"

Kayla let out a giggle. "Honey, I wouldn't do that to you. Go have a peek for yourself!"

Both Mitch and I squeezed into the doorway and covertly poked our heads around the corner to see our faux celebrity applicant.

"Oh, good grief!" Mitch exclaimed. "Okay, Kayla, pull yourself together and go send him...her...back here."

Kayla nodded as she placed a hand over her mouth to stifle yet another giggle.

"Well, at least this one didn't run away," Mitch said with a sigh.

Georgina appeared in the doorway and was quite a spectacle to see. Her long, braided black hair was intertwined with beads and hung just past the shoulders of the black trench coat which extended almost to her ankles. Penciled-in eyebrows sat atop eyes outlined in blue, and the lids were adorned with varied shades of bright shadow that curled outward toward her temples. Dark blush covered her chiseled cheekbones, and her lips were painted in a dark rose. From the black fedora covering the top of her head right down to the short black boots at the bottoms of tight-legged pants, she was the spitting image of the popular performer she mimicked. Had I not known differently, I may have asked for an autograph.

Mitch bit his lip for a moment, cleared his throat, and extended his hand. "Hi, Georgina. I'm Mitch Tarrington, the owner of Gartano's; and this is my wife Dana."

"Hi," she answered as she took a seat across from us. Mitch cleared his throat again and picked up her application.

"Tell me a little about yourself, Georgina."

At first we thought her silence reflected her desire to formulate an answer before speaking, but then she gave us a puzzled look. "What do you want to know?"

Mitch and I looked at one another. "Anything you want to tell us," Mitch said.

She looked at me and still seemed perplexed. I decided to go with the obvious.

"I couldn't help but notice your outfit," I started. "Are you a big fan of Boy George?"

Her eyes glazed over, and I could swear she went into a trance. "Yes, I am," she said dreamily. "In fact, that's why I need this job."

"Why? So you can go to his concerts and buy his records?"

She found something amusing about what I said. "Oh, no," she laughed. "I want to have plastic surgery so I can look more like him. Then, I'm going to take voice lessons and try to develop an act—you know, as an impersonator. We already have names that are alike. Georgie Boyd—everyone calls me Georgie by the way—and Boy George. Pretty neat, huh?"

Mitch and I stared at one another. Was this person for real?

Being a true professional, Mitch somehow managed to keep things together. "That's very interesting...Georgie...and I'd love to hear more about that. However, I do have other ladies coming in this afternoon, so I think I'd better talk to you about the position. I don't want to take up too much of your time."

In the fastest interview I've ever witnessed, Mitch had asked his questions, summarized the position, and was sending 'Georgie' on her way within eight minutes flat. As he watched her depart through the front door, he turned to Kayla who had joined him there.

"Is number three here yet?"

Kayla pointed to a feeble-looking, gray-haired woman sitting at a table near the counter sipping a cup of coffee. "Yeah, Mitch. She's right there. Claudia Roberts."

Mitch closed his eyes for a minute, took a deep breath, and released it slowly. "Give me ten minutes to recoup, okay? Then you can send her back."

Kayla smiled. "No problem. And hang in there. You'll find someone."

After another hour and a half, Mitch became fearful that Kayla's statement wouldn't hold true. Claudia wasn't that 'someone.' Neither was Rebecca, Jackie, Kelly, or Ann.

Kayla appeared in the doorway one last time. "This is Miss Traci Miraldi," she stated as she introduced the pretty young woman standing next to her.

Mitch and I introduced ourselves and started into the routine. Traci seemed very poised as she answered our questions directly and intelligently. Seeming pleased that finally he was interviewing someone who might have merit, I could hear a spark return to Mitch's voice as he spoke; and the sluggishness of the six previous disappointments dropped away. In the standard method most interviewers use to measure the worth of a potential future colleague, Mitch asked the question of all questions: "Tell me why I should hire you."

Traci didn't hesitate with an answer. "Because I'm Ben Miraldi's daughter—you know—Miraldi's Supermarket over on Bell Street. Daddy holds a lot of clout in this city, and I know he could do a lot to help your business. I could surely put in a good word if things were to work out."

The smile left Mitch's face, and he stared at Traci. "Excuse me?"

"Aren't you familiar with my father?"

Mitch placed the application on the desk and sat back in his chair. He brought his hands up in front of him and began to tap his fingertips together. "Very," he answered smugly. "In fact, I believe he may purchase some products from *my* father's company, Tarrington Industries, to resell in his store. Have you heard of Mitchell Tarrington, Jr.—or possibly, 'Jake' Tarrington? That's *my* dad. I'm Mitchell, III."

Traci's mouth fell open. "I didn't know."

"It looks like we have something in common, Traci. We both have successful businessmen as fathers. Only there is one difference. I didn't use my father's 'clout' to get this job. I did it all on my own. I've found it's a lot more satisfying because of that fact." He stood up. "Thanks for coming in today. It's been nice talking to you; and should I feel we need a second interview, I'll contact you on Wednesday afternoon."

Traci thanked us both; and when Mitch knew she was out of earshot, he said softly, "I wouldn't hold my breath if I were you!"

Mitch sank half-heartedly into his chair and took off his glasses. "This day certainly didn't go anything like I'd hoped," he said. "If tomorrow is the same, what am I going to do?"

I moved behind him and began to rub his shoulders. "I'm sorry, honey," I said as I gave him a soft kiss on the top of his head. "I'm sure someone will come along that will work out."

He reached up to cover my hand with his. "I know. I'm feeling a little run down right about now." He swung the chair around and pulled me gently onto his lap. "Why don't we go home and just be together for a couple of hours before rehearsal? I could really use some peace and quiet."

"And a little TLC?" I added.

He smiled as he snuggled into me. "No, I need a lot of that."

"Kayla, we're heading out," Mitch called as we walked hand in hand toward the door. "You know what to do if you need me, but Jimmy should be here soon. Can you tell him I had a bad day, and I'll catch up with him tomorrow?"

"Sure, Mitch, I can do that. I'm sorry none of those ladies worked out for you."

Mitch shrugged. "Maybe tomorrow will be better."

Kayla offered a sympathetic smile. "I'm sure it will, honey. You two go on now and have a good evening."

I gave my best friend a hug. "Thanks, Kayla. You're the best."

The blinking light on our answering machine greeted us as we stepped into the apartment. Mitch pushed the button and stood with his back against the counter as he listened to the message.

"Hi, Mitch and Dana. This is Tricia Trenton. I have some good news—the Tanners are officially relocated, and the house is all yours whenever you want to move in. Please call me back at the office, and we can make arrangements for you to get the keys. I'll be here until 6:00 tonight. Thanks!"

Unable to hide the excitement I was feeling, I clasped my hands in front of me. "Let's go there, Mitch. Let's go now and pick up the keys. Can we?"

Mitch laughed at my childlike giddiness. "I suppose we could do that. Give me a minute to change clothes, and we can head over there."

I took a seat in the chair as Mitch went off to change. As I sat there looking around me, a sentimental stupor did its best to invade my excitement over the prospect of our new home. In the short time I had been there, the apartment had been a source of countless memories—both good and bad. It was the place Mitch and I came of age together on our first night as husband and wife. That night would be etched in our minds forever. Simply through the strength of our love, not only had we sealed the bond of our new life, but we soon found out that we had created two new lives as well. In that place I had felt the pain of betrayal, the fear of losing, and the joy of healing. We had laughed and cried there, argued, made up, talked, and debated. Most of all, we had called it home. As Mitch reappeared with a smile, it was then that I realized that no matter where we were it would be home as long as we were together.

After signing a document stating that Tricia had relinquished the keys to us, Mitch and I headed for our new home at 415 Redwood Place. As we pulled into the driveway, I felt the excitement return as Mitch looked at me with a bright smile.

"Come on, beautiful. Let's go check out our house."

Mitch unlocked the front door and pushed it open to reveal a now vacant living room. Tucking the key into his pocket, he swung around to me with a wide grin.

"I believe I'm supposed to carry you over the threshold, aren't I?"

I giggled. "Sweetheart, I don't think you need to worry about it. I'm a lot bigger than I was the last time you did that. You'll throw out your back trying to lift me!"

"Nonsense!" he declared, and in one swift movement he hoisted me into his arms, stepped through the doorway, and placed me down gently on the other side. He tried hard not to show that the gesture had left him a little breathless as he smiled brightly. "See, I'm not as weak as you think I am."

"No, but you can't breathe now, can you?" I laughed, and he took a deep breath of admission as he, too, began to join in. "You might bench 300 pounds, Mitchell, but it isn't often I see you walking around the house carrying the weights."

He gave me a kiss. "I'm sorry, honey. I guess I'm just tired or something." He took my hand. "Come on. Let's go look around. We can figure out where we're going to put everything."

I took a few steps forward and stopped in the middle of the room. "Well, the couch can go here with the sofa table right behind it. Over there we can put the chair, and the entertainment center can go against that wall." A sudden overwhelming thought occurred to me as I glanced toward the four steps that led to the family room on the lower level. "Oh, Mitch," I said half-heartedly as I pointed in that direction. "If we put all the furniture up here, what will we put down there?"

"I don't know," he answered. "Maybe we'll have to think about getting another couch and chair for this room and put what we have down there for now. What do you think?"

My eyes lit up, and I dove into him for a hug. "Really? That's great! Can we call off rehearsal and go shopping tonight?"

Mitch roared with laughter. "Slow down there, love. It doesn't have to be done right away. We'll get there."

I backed away from him and gave him an incredulous look. "We can't have an empty room, Mitchell. We're going to have to get something before we move in."

Mitch stared at his wife, hands on her hips, looking like she meant business. He knew there was no sense trying to change her mind, so the only thing he could do was strike a compromise.

He stepped toward her with a soft smile and took her by the hand. "It's really going to be a busy week, honey. With the interviews, the demo, and everything else, I'm not going to have much time to go shopping. I'm sure you'll want to come by here to do a little cleaning, and we still have to finish packing. Then we have to see if the crew can help us move. Let's try to get in by next Sunday, and I promise we'll go shopping right away. I'll ask Jimmy to cover for me on Monday, and we'll spend the day combing the furniture stores. All right?"

"It's going to look awkward with no furniture in here."

Hearing the hint of emotion filling her voice, he kissed her softly. He knew under other circumstances she would readily give in to his plan—but not when she had seven months worth of hormones raging within her. "Only for a day. All right?"

He smiled as she sighed in defeat. "All right."

Deciding he would ward off any additional emotional episodes, Mitch took Dana by the hand and led her upstairs and into what would become the nursery. The sun was playing peak-a-boo with the clouds outside and casting shadows in the room, so he turned on the overhead light and then wrapped his arms around his wife from behind as he placed his cheek against hers.

"Now, what are we doing in here, Mommy?"

Immediately, he saw her mood lighten with his question. He would never understand those pregnancy hormones.

"Since our bedroom is on the other side of that wall," I pointed to my right, "why don't we put the top of the cribs there? We can put them side by side with enough room in between for us to move around. If the twins cry at night, we'll be sure to hear them; and they'll have the security of being next to each another." I pointed toward the window. "We can put the dresser there and the changing table and rocking chair against this wall over here." I took a few steps to my left and waved my hand along the wall to provide a visual. I turned around and opened the double folding doors of the closet. "Do you think there's going to be enough room in here for everything, Mitch? I'm not sure."

"If you stop buying baby stuff every chance you get, there will be," he smirked. "With all that stuff you got at Baby World, you don't need to have the shower!"

I rolled my eyes and took his hand to lead him out of the room. "Don't start that again, you big goof. I didn't buy much at all considering I was shopping for two."

"I still can't believe you bought a warmer for the diaper wipes."

"Well, like I said last night, would you want someone putting a cold cloth to your delicate little behind?"

He snickered. "It's really not something I've given much thought to, dear. Trust me."

We spent the next half hour flitting around the house envisioning the rooms furnished and decorated with our belongings. As our self-guided tour wound up in the kitchen, Mitch unlocked the sliding doors off the dining area and stepped outside.

"This yard is huge, Dana," he said as he stood on the brick patio at the back of the house. "And I think you're right—that outbuilding will be perfect for rehearsals. I'll have to look into getting it soundproofed though. I wouldn't want any of the neighbors complaining."

I slid my arm around his waist and laid my head on his shoulder. "Are you kidding? Once these people hear you guys, they'll be barging their way in for free concerts!"

Mitch took his watch from his pocket; and noticing that it was already after five, he announced that we should be going. We made sure everything was locked tight and started the trek back home. Along the way we chatted about the day and what was ahead for tomorrow.

"I hope tomorrow's candidates for the waitressing job are better than the prospects you had today," I began. "I honestly have to wonder what planet a few of them were from."

Mitch gave me that ornery grin that usually meant he was out for some fun. "I don't know, baby. I thought Kelly was okay. Maybe I'll consider her."

I thought back to Kelly Madison: the tall, busty blonde whose skirt was as short as her top was low. Her high heels clicked against the tiled floor as she strutted down the hallway into the office—her stride giving a new meaning to the words 'back porch swing.' The moment she appeared in the doorway was the moment I began to decide that she wasn't a suitable candidate. My decision was locked in stone as soon as she sat down across from us and decided to cross her long, shapely legs as she directed a sexy smile toward my husband. A slow smile overcame him, and I swear his eyes never made it to her face during the entire interview.

I redirected my thoughts to the conversation at hand. "Consider her for what? A mistress?"

Mitch snickered. "Oh, come on now. You know I'm not that kind of guy. I think she'd make a fine waitress. After all, she does have experience."

I made a face at him. "Yeah, I'm sure she does—but not in waiting tables!"

He laughed and shot another impish grin my way. "You aren't being very nice. I didn't see anything wrong with her."

"I know. I was sitting next to you while you were making eyes at her."

He reached out for my hand and brought it to his lips for a tender kiss. "Don't be talking about making eyes, little miss. You were doing a pretty good job of it with that John guy last night at Chandler's!"

"I was not making eyes at John. I don't flirt with other men, Mitchell. However, I can't say the same about you and other women." I decided to be ornery right back. "Tell me—what color were Kelly's eyes?"

Mitch looked stupefied. "How would I know that?"

"You wouldn't because you never looked at her face."

Mitch broke into a hearty laughter, pulled me against his shoulder, and hugged me tightly with his right arm. "You are such a funny little girl. I love you so much."

"I love you, too, even if you are terrible!"

The late afternoon sky was growing ominously darker, and the trees rustled in the sultry breeze as jagged streaks of lightning bounded across the horizon. As we drew closer to the Tarrington Estate, my nerves settled knowing that soon we would be in the safety and comfort of the house and away from the impending storm. Mitch reached over to give my hand a gentle squeeze.

"Almost there, baby. Don't worry."

I nodded in silence—my eyes still fixed on the clouds which seemed to be closing in around us. Just as we turned onto the lane leading up to the house, the sky surrendered its bounty and sent the torrential downpour to the earth below. The bright headlights and racing wipers on the car were no match for the rain that fell in sheets before us. Mitch pulled the car to the side of the road near the old stable and put it in park.

"We'll sit for a minute or two and see if it lets up, okay? I really can't see a thing ahead of me."

A crash of thunder sent a chill up my spine, and I placed a trembling hand on Mitch's leg. "Please, honey, let's go on to the house. I really don't like being out here in this."

Mitch took hold of my hand and turned to me with a reassuring smile. "Dana, even with as many times as I've driven this lane, I don't want to try navigating it in this. I'm afraid I might miss a turn and send us down over the hill. I'm sure it'll ease off shortly."

Just as he uttered the words, the crashing sound of the raindrops against the roof of the car began to grow softer; and he put the car into gear and eased it slowly back onto the lane. Within a few minutes we were pulling up in front of the house, and I breathed a heavy sigh of relief.

"Wait right here. I'll run inside and get an umbrella," Mitch instructed.

Before I had a chance to protest, he was out of the car and running toward the house. I watched as he catapulted up the stairs of the porch, and I laughed as he turned toward me shaking off the rain much the way a dog would. A moment later, he was walking back toward the car under the cover of a bright green golf umbrella.

"Hang on to me. The sidewalk's a bit slippery."

Alexander met us just inside the door with two warm towels. As Mitch propped the umbrella next to the door, I noticed that it wasn't the only thing soaked. So was he.

"Mitch, you're going to catch cold if you don't get out of those wet clothes. Come on—let's get you undressed, and Alexander can put your things in the dryer. I'm sure your dad has a robe or something you can wear for a few minutes."

He gave me a mortified look. "I can't rehearse in a bathrobe, for heaven's sake! I'm not all that wet. I'll be fine."

I gave him a stern look. "What are you talking about? You're soaked to the bone. Stop arguing with me and go take your clothes off."

Mitch raised his eyebrows and stepped very close to me. A slow smile came to his face, and he lowered his voice to just above a whisper. "Gee, I kinda like it when you take charge. Very direct. Sexy, too."

I smacked his arm lightly as he began to laugh. "Cut it out, will you? I'm serious. I don't want you getting sick."

He took my face between his hands and kissed me. "Thank you for being concerned, but I'll dry out in a few minutes. Now, let's go greet the guys, shall we?"

"You are so stubborn," I muttered as I began to follow. Alexander smiled and nodded in agreement.

The guys were tinkering with their instruments when we walked in. Newbie looked up at his waterlogged pal and shook his head.

"Go take those clothes off, Trip," he suggested.

Mitch smirked and pointed to me. "Sounded better when she said it." Newbie laughed.

"Did you bring a set list?" Zach asked. "We didn't see anything when we got here or else we would've been working on it."

Mitch smiled. "Nope. No list this week, guys. We won't be needing it."

The five exchanged puzzled glances. "What do you mean? What are we playing Saturday night?"

"Well, if nobody has a major objection, I'm going to need Saturday night off. We got the keys to the house today, and we plan on trying to move in this weekend. I already talked to Rob. He said Ty can take the gig, or he'll just book in a DJ for the night."

"It'll be hard for me to play when I'm helping you guys move," Ty chimed in with a grin. The others mimicked the statement.

"Thanks, guys. We appreciate that." Mitch could hardly stifle the broad smile threatening to sweep across his face. "There's one other thing. You have to help me decide which songs we should use for the demo."

Again the men looked at one another as if they hadn't heard clearly what Mitch had said.

"What demo?" Shep asked. "I thought we were done with all that business. You know—your becoming a dad and all."

"How can we be done when we haven't recorded anything yet?" Mitch answered. "I'm gonna become a dad regardless. Now, are you with me or not?"

Ash pushed his way to the front of the group and placed a hand on Mitch's shoulder, looking him squarely in the eyes. "You mean you're staying?"

"Yeah, I'm staying."

The group practically knocked him over as they rushed at him, hugging him, shaking his hand, and patting him on the back. Through it all he just smiled as he felt that deep sense of camaraderie rush over him again.

"You're super, man," Zach exclaimed.

Yeah, Mitch thought as he cast a loving smile toward Dana. *Superman.*

Chapter 13

Tuesday's episode of *Find That Waitress* proved to be just as humiliating as Monday's, and Mitch left Gartano's that afternoon feeling distraught. Of the five women he'd interviewed that day, none seemed appropriate. As he started the walk home, he thought about the candidates: first was Juanita, a pleasant Hispanic lady whose sister, Marisol, assured Mitch that she would gladly act as an interpreter until Juanita finished her English lessons. Next came Belinda, an apparently happy young girl who giggled after every response; Josephine who was old enough to be his great-grandmother, and Connie with her blue Mohawk, spiked collar, and fishnet hose who stated firmly that she could never work on a weekend because 'that's when she hung out with her old man.' Finally there was Blanche, the mother of three high-spirited young sons whom she brought along because her babysitter had backed out at the last minute 'again.' As Mitch concluded her interview—interrupted countless times by cries of 'Mommm!'—he could fully understand why.

I'm a decent guy. I'm running a decent establishment. Why can't I find even one halfway decent person to hire? What's the deal? The only semi-logical answer he could fathom to that question was that he had simply picked the wrong people to interview. While most of them seemed pleasant, he needed more than that in a waitress. He needed someone who was not only easy to get along with, but quick, dedicated, neat in appearance, and trustworthy. *Gee, I need someone like Dana, Kayla, Katie, and Phyllis. I wonder if any of them would be up for cloning....*

Stopping at the corner to wait for a passing car, Mitch took a moment to place his thumb and forefinger to his throbbing forehead. He'd begun to feel a little woozy right around lunchtime, but his analogy that he was simply hungry proved wrong when the feeling was still with him after a bowl of pasta and two sodas. He was also beginning to feel achy but passed it off as nothing more than the result of a tension-filled day. As he crossed the street, the apartment building was in sight, and he welcomed the prospect of a short nap before dinner. Maybe if he was lucky, Dana might even be up to providing him with a back rub; and if the offer was made, he certainly wouldn't turn it down.

Mitch stepped through the door, a weak smile on his face, and greeted me with a less than enthusiastic, "Hi, baby. How was your day?"

When I began to study his flushed cheeks and glassy eyes, he quickly turned toward the kitchen as if that would stop me from saying, "Honey, you don't look so good. You aren't feeling well, are you?"

"You can't answer a question with a question," he replied as he popped two aspirin into his mouth and chugged the last of the orange juice directly from the carton.

"Okay, then I'll make it a statement. You aren't feeling well."

"I'm fine," he said. "I'm just a little tired. Do I have time for a short nap before dinner?"

"If you're fine, why did you take aspirin?"

"You did it again. You answered my question with a question."

"Sorry. Yes, you have time for a short nap. The roast isn't quite done. Now, will you answer my question?"

"What question?"

I sighed. "Why did you take aspirin?"

He gave me a funny look. "Why do people usually take aspirin, Dana?"

"Do you have a headache?"

He let out a long, exasperated breath. "I'm going to go lie down while I still have some time."

I watched in silence as he went into the bedroom and closed the door behind him.

Forty minutes later, I pulled the roast from the oven, set the table, and went to wake my husband. Creeping into the bedroom as silently as I could, I sat down next to him on the bed and gently began to rub his back. The moment my fingers touched his skin, I could feel the heat that told me he was fevered. I placed my palm against his forehead to confirm the diagnosis.

"What are you doing?" he asked in a sleepy voice.

"I came to tell you that dinner's ready, but I'm thinking maybe you should get undressed and crawl into bed. You have a fever."

He sat up and rubbed his eyes before reaching for his glasses on the nightstand. "I'm probably warm because I had the blanket all wrapped around me. I feel...I feel...*achoo!* Excuse me. I feel perfectly...*achoo!* fine."

"God bless you," I said as I handed him a tissue.

"Thanks. Just a little tickle. Must be some dust in the air. "

"Uh-huh."

He sighed heavily and gave me a reassuring pat on the back. "I'm okay. Go put dinner on the table. I have to go to the bathroom."

Mitch watched as Dana reluctantly moved toward the door, and he did his best to muster up a smile when she turned to look at him again before disappearing down the hallway. Feeling another sneeze building, he grabbed a tissue from the box, pressed it to his nose, and buried his face in his forearm hoping to stifle the sound.

"I heard that!" Dana called from the kitchen. *So much for that idea*, he thought.

Making his way into the bathroom, he paused for a moment to look at his haggard reflection in the mirror before he removed his glasses to splash some cool water on his face. He reached for the towel, patted his face dry, and replaced his glasses to look at himself once more. He looked almost as bad as he felt. This was the last thing either of them needed this week. Things were already stressful enough without a cold, the flu, or whatever it was he was coming down with. He sighed heavily. Why did these things pick the most inopportune times to crop up? He might not be able to stop the illness from running its course, but he could stop himself from letting it get to him. He would just have to keep going somehow. He'd have to play Superman again. Yeah, that was it.

"Mitch, are you okay?"

He straightened up, took a deep breath, and let it out slowly. The aspirin had managed to reduce the throbbing in his head to a dull annoyance, and for that he was grateful. However, the pain had migrated; and now he found it hard to move the limbs that felt like pieces of lead. *Come on, Superman. It's just a cold, not kryptonite. You can fight it.*

"Yeah, baby. I'll be right there."

Cutting a piece of my roast, I scraped it through my mashed potatoes as I anticipated the treat my mouth was about to receive. When I noticed that my husband had hardly taken two bites of his meal, I lowered my fork back to my plate and reached out again to touch his forehead. As I laid my napkin next to my plate and started to stand, Mitch caught me gently by the arm.

"Where are you going?" he asked.

"To get the thermometer. I want to see how high your temperature is. You look miserable."

He placed his fork on his plate, and it caused a rather loud 'chink' as it hit the edge. He was obviously annoyed by my perseverance in determining that he was indeed ill and not just suffering from 'dust in the air' and a tightly-wrapped blanket. He looked at me disgustedly and blew out a long breath.

"I told you that I'm fine. Now, I'd appreciate it very much if you would drop the subject."

I sat back down and refocused my attention on my dinner. "Forgive me for being concerned," I said with a hint of annoyance in my own voice.

"Did you get any boxes packed today?" he asked in an attempt to change the subject.

I decided to go for the short reply. "A few."

"Well, I can do some packing when we get home." He stood up, moved to the refrigerator, and removed the pitcher of cold water. "I'm really thirsty tonight for some reason," he commented as he poured his third glassful. "Guess I dried myself out doing all those interviews today."

I wanted to tell him to stop making excuses, but instead I said, "Did you find anyone you think will work out?"

His look was a mixture of frustration and disgust. "Actually, I think yesterday's lineup far outshined today's."

I returned the look. "No way!"

He nodded and proceeded to give me the less than admirable rundown of the day's candidates. He finished by stating, "I guess I'll either go back through the applications again and call in other ladies, or I'll run another ad and see what happens."

"Maybe that would be best," I concluded.

"Yeah, I think...." He quickly turned away from the table and put his forearm in front of his face. *"Achoo!* I think I'll probably do that." He turned back to the table and noticed that I was giving him 'the look.'

"Don't even try to tell me it's dusty out here, too."

He smirked and looked away from me. "It could be. You never know."

An hour later we found ourselves at Jake and Olivia's once again. I noticed that as soon as Mitch hit the inside of the house, he hightailed it to the rec room to avoid a confrontation with his mother. Given the strong connection she had with him, he knew she would inevitably ask about his condition. He also knew that she'd see right through his 'dust' story. For some reason it didn't bother him to make excuses to his wife—but to try to pull something over on Mom was a different story altogether.

"Hey, dudes, one thing before we start," Mitch announced as he approached his band mates. "Don't any of you tell me that I look like pond scum. I'm perfectly fine, and I've heard enough of it from my wife tonight to last me for a while."

The five looked at each another and grinned. "I wondered how long it would take before the 'oh, I think he's adorable' phase would wear off," Zach teased as he altered his voice to sound like a girl. "I do think, however, that 'road kill' suits you better than 'pond scum.'"

"Gee, thanks. I'm glad you cleared that up for me," Mitch replied.

I took my place in the usual spot and watched in silence as the guys did their thing at the front of the room. I could feel the movements of the babies as they awakened within me, and I wondered if they were somehow aroused by the sound of the music. I smiled as I placed my hand on my stomach and rubbed it gently as if to say hello. Suddenly, I realized that in just a few short months this entire scene would change. The guys would be occupying the outbuilding in our backyard, and I would most likely be inside the house taking care of the twins. Since Mitch planned to get the building soundproofed, I wouldn't be able to hear them rehearse anymore unless I actually went into the building. It would be winter by then, so venturing out there with the babies wasn't going to be an option. Soon I would be separated from something that had become a big part of my life—something that Mitch and I shared. The rehearsals and the shows would be his alone. As much as I wanted the twins, I had to wonder what other changes they might bring that could cause Mitch and me to go in different directions. I didn't know, but I secretly hoped that more than anything they would bring us closer together.

As I sat absorbed in my thoughts, Mitch crept up beside me and startled me when he spoke my name. "Dana? Could you please ask Alexander to bring us something cold to drink?"

"Oh, yeah, sure. What would you like?"

"Anything would be fine." I noticed a hoarseness to his voice but decided not to mention it.

Alexander appeared about five minutes later with a pitcher of iced tea, glasses, and seven pieces of carrot cake on a tray. "I brought some honey that you might slip into Mitchell's glass," he commented. "It will help soothe his throat." He gave me a sly smile and a wink.

"You noticed."

"Indeed," he replied. "The flush in his cheeks isn't always because of you, Dana, and I've known him long enough to tell the difference."

I gave him a smile as I touched him gently on the arm. "Thank you, Alexander. I'll be sure he gets a good dose."

Spying the dessert, the six swarmed toward the back of the room practically knocking one another over to get to it. Mitch seemed to be more interested in the tea than the cake, and I concluded that he was still feeling the effects of the fever. Before handing him a glass, I poured some honey into it and stirred it up.

As he brought the glass to his lips he looked at me suspiciously and then drank it down without stopping. "Can you pour me some more, please?"

I did as he asked and took careful note of his face. His cheeks were still flushed, and his eyes were glassy. I reached up to brush back a wisp of hair and strategically let my fingers graze his forehead. He was still very warm. I needed to figure out a way to get him home and in bed without him suspecting anything. Feeling a soft kick come from within me, I smiled and looked down.

"Thanks, guys. I owe you one," I said softly.

When he summoned the band to follow him to the front once more, I grabbed hold of his hand to gain his attention and faked a yawn.

"Mitch, do you think we could go home soon? I was pretty busy today, and I'm awfully tired and sore. I think I might like to turn in early." I yawned again to make it seem more convincing.

He smiled and nodded. "Sure, love. Can you give me another half hour to wrap things up?"

Certain that was the best I could do, I took the offer. "Okay, sweetie. That's fine."

I waited as patiently as I could for the next half hour as I listened to the beautiful voice of Mitchell Tarrington III transform into something that sounded more like Kermit the Frog with laryngitis. The guys decided to stay silent—that is, until Mitch attempted to hit his falsetto at the end of a song. He now sounded like Kermit the Frog caught in a vise.

"What the heck was *that?*" Ty said with shock. "Are you losing your voice?"

Mitch tried to retain his dignity. "I'm just a little dry, that's all," he replied as he stroked his throat with his thumb and forefinger. He glanced toward the back of the room. Seeing Dana there, he decided to use her as his out. The noise of the instruments had caused the pounding in his head to resume, and the rawness in his throat was slowly consuming what little bit of voice he had left. Turning to the guys, he pointed in her direction.

"Hey, let's call it a wrap for tonight, okay? Dana spent the day packing boxes for the move, and she's pretty worn out. I think I should take her home and let her get some rest." He wasn't sure if they could see through his facade as well as he'd seen through Dana's, but he didn't care.

"That's cool, Trip. We can take this up tomorrow," Shep said as the others agreed.

Mitch's voice was barely above a whisper. "Thanks. See you then."

The men made their way toward the front door with Mitch taking up the rear. As Ash paused to tell me goodnight, he whispered, "Make sure he takes care of that cold, Dana. Knowing him, he'll try to keep going and really get himself down."

"I know. He's as stubborn as they come."

Ash laughed. "Precisely what I mean."

For the next few days, Mitch exhibited that stubbornness to the fullest. After having Jim stop by to examine him on Wednesday morning and a diagnosis of a throat and ear infection, he was sentenced to two days of bed rest accompanied by ten to fourteen days of antibiotics. As if that wasn't enough to put him into a foul mood, Jim topped it off with restricting him from his two favorite things—singing, to avoid additional strain on his throat, and me, to avoid spreading his germs. Although he couldn't really speak above a whisper—when any sound came out at all, that is—he let it be known that he was thoroughly agitated by the entire situation. On Thursday morning he insisted that he needed to go to work. Feeling brave, he went as far as to shower and dress before I threatened to make him sleep on the couch for six months if he so much as put the toe of his shoe outside the door. With a long, loud sigh he relented and stomped back to the bedroom, threw his clothes in a heap on the floor, and crawled into bed. Even when I tried to make up by taking him homemade chicken noodle soup and freshly squeezed lemonade, he kept his back to me and ate only after I had exited the room. It was then that I decided taking care of the twins might not be so difficult after all. The way he was acting made me feel like I was already caring for a baby.

On Saturday, Mitch awoke early and quietly crept into the living room where Dana still slept peacefully. He stood for a moment and gazed down at her. She was so beautiful that he could have spent all day right there and never grown tired of looking at her. Unfortunately, today promised to be a busy day, and he was finally feeling almost human again. When his illness had set in, she insisted on sleeping on the couch in an effort to keep herself well. He'd tried to argue the point, but she would hear nothing of it; and reluctantly he gave in. Although they were only separated by a wall or two, he'd felt like they were worlds apart. Tonight, however, would be a different story. They would be in their new home, and of course, that would be a cause for celebration. Smiling at the thought, he blew her a kiss and went into the kitchen to make a pot of coffee—being as quiet as he could so he wouldn't wake her.

Stepping into the hallway, Mitch retrieved the morning paper. After pouring a cup of coffee, he returned to the bedroom and sank down into the chair to catch up on current events. As he turned the page, his eyes settled on an ad for Morgan Furniture; and he began to study it. Of particular interest was the sale on living room sets, and he found a few among the pictures that he thought Dana might like. Making a mental note to show them to her, he turned the page and moved on.

Absorbed in the moment, Mitch never heard me enter the room, and I slipped up behind him to drape my arms around his chest. He lowered the paper and stared up at me as a broad smile came to his face.

"Hey, handsome, what are you doing up? It's early. You need your rest," I stated as I placed a kiss on top of his head.

"I'm tired of resting," he replied. He stretched as far as he could and caught me around the waist, bringing me as close as he could toward the chair and himself. "I'm feeling much better; and besides, today is moving day. Everyone's going to be here in about an hour or so."

"Two," I corrected as I looked at the clock. "That gives you at least another hour to yourself. Now, come on—get back over there and relax."

"I am relaxed. And if I still have an hour to myself, then I should get to choose where—and how—to spend it, right?"

"I suppose so."

He stood up with a grin and pulled me into his arms. His eyes sparkled. "I've spent forty hours in that bed away from you. Now, I want to spend one hour *with* you—very much with you. How about it?"

"Mitchell...."

He took a step back but still held me in his embrace. "Mitchell, what?"

"You aren't over your illness yet. Not completely anyway. You don't want me to get sick, do you?"

"Come on, Dana. I'm fine." He pulled me to him again and gave me a quick, playful peck on the forehead. "I've missed you."

I began to laugh. "Missed me? It's not like we were miles apart, you silly boy."

"It felt like it to me. I hated sleeping in here all alone."

"Well, tonight you can sleep with me again, provided Jim gives you the all-clear. Okay?"

He simply smiled.

A few minutes before ten, the knock came at the door signifying the arrival of our moving team. Chris, Jake, and Paul were the first to arrive with Jim, Shep, and Newbie following close behind. By one minute after the hour, Ash, Zach, and Ty were joining the others to meet Mitch with armloads of boxes as he pulled the moving truck up to the front entrance of the building. I watched from the window as Jim and Mitch stood inside the edge of the truck, and the others handed them boxes to place inside. Soon the team came bounding back into the apartment, grabbed more boxes, and started the process all over again. Wanting to do more than fade into the background, I moved toward the bedroom with the thought that I could bring the lighter things into the living room and possibly save the men some unnecessary steps. Just as I appeared at the end of the hallway with a box, Mitch came through the door. Upon seeing me, he set his jaw and quickly moved in my direction, practically snatching the box from my hands.

"What do you think you're doing by carrying that? You know better," he scolded.

"I'm only trying to help. Don't even start that invalid stuff again because it won't work."

He turned to hand the box to Ty and then turned back to me. He took my hand and led me a few steps to the side. "Honey, please humor me today, all right? I know you want to help, but please leave the carrying to us. I don't want you lifting anything."

I sighed disgustedly. "Fine. Then what would you have me to do?"

He stood silently for a moment—biting his lip in thought. "Why don't you drive over to the house? That way you can be there to tell the guys where things should go." He smiled. "You can be the supervisor and bark out the orders. I know you're good at doing that."

"Ha, ha, Mitchell. Very funny," I replied snidely as I fished my car keys out of my purse.

"Go on, now, and I'll see you in a little while." He gave me a kiss on the cheek and started to move away.

"Don't forget about the boxes in the bedroom, Mitch. And you said you were going to stop by and make sure Mr. Sedgewick has both sets of our keys."

He nodded. "I'll take care of it, dear."

I headed toward the door but did an about-face as another thought crossed my mind. "Honey, please make sure you don't leave anything behind." I glanced out the balcony doors. "Did you get our little patio set?"

He turned around, cocked his head to one side, and gave me a lopsided grin to match. "I will and I did. Anything else?"

"I'm really going to miss this place."

His expression softened, and he moved toward me again and took me into his arms. Hugging me tightly to him, he whispered, "I know, love. Me, too. But, our new house is going to be great, don't you think?"

"Uh-huh."

He took a step back and smiled down at me. "I promise I'll take care of everything. You go on. I'll be there shortly with the first load." He leaned down, kissed me, and then pulled away slightly with an even bigger smile. "You know, I just realized how much I missed doing that, too." He kissed me again, this time in a more deliberate fashion. I decided right then that I must have missed him, too, because I was enjoying it as much as he was.

"Mitch, how about taking your hands off your wife and using them to help carry boxes?"

Ty pointed to us with a wide grin as he turned to Newbie. "Can you believe this guy? I swear he has a one-track mind."

"Yeah, I know what you mean. Seems like we've been breaking these two up a lot lately, doesn't it?"

"Well, they *are* newlyweds, so maybe that accounts for some of it," Ty said.

"Hey, give me a break," Mitch answered. "I just spent the last two days sleeping alone in bed with typhoid fever or something. I'm only making up for lost time."

"I'd better go now," I stated as I moved away slowly. Mitch started to kiss me again; but before he could, the pair grabbed his arms and playfully pulled him away.

"Hurry, Dana, or we'll never get any work out of him today!" Newbie laughed.

I pushed the button on one of the remotes Tricia had given us, and the garage door lifted. Once I had pulled inside, I pushed the button again to lower it, got out of the car, and opened the door which led into my new kitchen. *How nice that will be this winter,* I thought to myself. *I won't have to worry about going out in the nasty weather to get in or out of the car with the twins.* I placed my purse and keys on the counter and then walked into the living room to wait on the guys to arrive. Since there was no furniture in the house yet, I took a seat on one of the lower steps and looked around the room. On Thursday afternoon while Mitch napped, Julia, Olivia, Angelina, and I came by to clean while Trudy took the kids to the park for a few hours. I was grateful for the help they had provided and more than pleased with the results of their efforts. Everything in the house from top to bottom sparkled, and I had the satisfaction of knowing that it was one less thing I had to worry about. I couldn't wait to get everything in and put away so the rooms wouldn't look so empty. Mitch had shown me the ad for the sale at Morgan Furniture earlier that morning, and I was eager to head over there at the first opportunity to check out the merchandise. I didn't like the idea that the living room would be empty for a few days, but the thought of new furniture appealed to me so much that it almost cancelled out the disappointment.

The clamor of the truck backing into the driveway interrupted my thoughts, and I stood to open the front door. As I rose to my feet, a strange feeling overtook me; and I instinctively placed a hand on my stomach. It started just below my breasts and moved slowly downward—a squeezing sensation that made everything in my abdominal region tight and rock hard. It felt like a contraction, but the one thing that made me question it was that there was no pain. I stood still for a moment and took a deep breath as I tried to relax. Mitch saw me through the front window as he opened the back of the truck, and he smiled and waved before sauntering up the sidewalk toward the house. I met him at the door and tried to muster up a smile.

"Hey, love!" he greeted as he stepped inside. Noticing the placement of my hands, he inquired, "What's going on in there? Are those two turning somersaults again?"

"Uh, well, yeah—at least they were a minute ago. They're quieting back down now."

He smiled. "This time next year we'll probably be chasing them all over this place, won't we?"

I could feel the tightness slipping away, and I nodded. "Yeah, we probably will."

Mitch glanced out the window and saw that the others were arriving. "I'd better go out and get things underway. You just stand there and look pretty, okay? I don't want you lifting a finger."

Within a half hour, the first truckload of boxes were scattered around the house; and everyone had returned to the apartment for the second round. Since we only had the living room and bedroom furniture as well as the kitchen table and chairs, they assumed one more load would be enough to bring it all. I took another seat on the stairs to wait and hoped that I wouldn't have a recurrence of the strange contractions. Much to my dismay, however, I endured the situation twice more, although phase two and three were lighter than the first. By now I was becoming concerned and hoped whatever was happening wasn't a precursor to premature labor. I decided rather than worrying Mitch, I would find a way to get Jim alone and solicit some free medical advice.

As luck would have it, Jim was the first through the door with the sofa table. I gave him a somewhat desperate look and caught his arm as he placed it down.

He looked at me with concern. "Is something wrong, Dana?"

"I don't know. I think I'm having contractions. I've had about three of them since I got here, but they don't hurt at all. Everything just feels tight."

He nodded as if he already had a diagnosis. "Does it start just under your breastbone and move down, only lasting for a minute or so?"

"Exactly. What's wrong, Jim? Am I going into labor?"

He smiled reassuringly and shook his head. "No, I don't think so. Sounds like the Braxton Hicks."

"The what?"

"Braxton Hicks contractions. They're like practice contractions: totally painless and most of all, totally harmless. They may be a little uncomfortable at times, but they aren't a signal of anything more than your body preparing for the real thing."

"Am I going to be okay?"

He smiled. "I'd say so. If you do start having any pain or these change in any way, you might want to call Dr. Bradley. It probably wouldn't be a bad idea to mention it at your next visit with him anyway."

I breathed a sigh of relief. "Thank goodness. I really didn't feel much like giving birth today!"

"Who's giving birth today?" Mitch walked in and placed down the lamps he was holding. Having caught the tail end of our conversation, he looked quite concerned as he approached me and laid a hand on my arm. "Is something wrong, love? Are you all right?"

"Just some Braxton Hicks, Mitch. Nothing to worry about," Jim replied for me.

Mitch furrowed his brow. He looked first at Jim and then at me. "Braxton Hicks? What's that?"

"Practice contractions—perfectly harmless and perfectly normal at this stage of the game. She's just fine."

Mitch was looking a little pale. "You aren't in labor, are you?"

I smiled. "No, honey. No babies yet. I promise."

He looked at Jim as if he needed a confirmation of my statement. "She's right. No babies yet. Nothing to worry about."

Mitch let out a long breath. "Thank goodness. You had me worried there for a minute or two." He looked at both of us again and then took my hand. "Ash and Paul are carrying in the chair. Tell them where you want it, and then you sit down and rest, okay?"

"Sweetheart, I'm fine. I don't need to rest."

"Dana, please. Do this for me."

I gave Jim a defeated look, and he shrugged as if he knew his input wouldn't do much to alter the situation. As the men carefully maneuvered the chair through the doorway, I sent them to the family room and reluctantly followed. Mitch stood guard at the top of the stairs. When I sat down, he smiled and walked away.

A short while later I heard the sound of my husband's voice coming from near the front door. "Turn it a little to the right, Jim—no, my right—there. Now, ease it through." He laughed. "Whoa! Hold up. You're pinning Ash against the doorframe. Oh, well, if he gets hurt you can fix him up, can't you?"

Although it was driving me crazy not knowing what it was they were trying to carry in, I dared not move for fear of my husband coming unglued. The contractions—even though they were not a concern as Jim had explained—had placed Mitch into an overprotective mode. I appreciated the fact that he was trying to look out for me, but I didn't feel much like being coddled all day. Maybe if I tiptoed to the edge of the stairs, I could see them. I decided I would give it a try. Gingerly, I stood up and moved toward the stairs with the stealth of a cat. I peeked around the corner just as Mitch and Jake turned to go upstairs with our mattresses. I tried to move out of his eyeshot but temporarily forgot that pregnant women don't move very quickly.

"I saw you. Why aren't you resting?"

"I'm not tired, Mitchell. I only wanted to see what you were doing."

"You saw. Now, please go sit down."

"You're impossible."

I heard the four of them laugh as they ascended the stairs.

As I sat obediently in my husband-inflicted 'time-out' chair, I could hear the distant sounds of the guys as they attempted to carry in the remainder of the furniture, place it in the appropriate areas, and reassemble those few pieces that required it. I could hear them giving each other directions, laughing, joking, and occasionally grumbling at one another if something wasn't quite to their liking. I wanted so much to be a part of it all, but instead I remained in the background and waited until someone remembered I was there. Fortunately, that didn't take long. Ash appeared at the top of the stairs, leaned over the railing, and smiled.

"Hey, Mrs. Trip, your hubby would like to see you upstairs."

"Are you sure? He's the one who told me I needed to rest."

"I think he wants to make sure things are placed to your liking. He told me to 'go get the boss'; and if your marriage is anything like mine, that usually means the *wife*."

I laughed. "Isn't that the way all marriages are? At least that's what I thought."

Ash allowed me to go up ahead of him, and I entered the bedroom to see Mitch leaning against the bed. He looked quite exhausted, but he sported a huge smile just the same.

"Hello, my queen. Is everything in here to your satisfaction?"

Much to my amazement, he had not only placed the furniture, but he had also managed to find the bedding in one of the boxes and placed it on as well. Simply seeing everything in place made it start to feel more like home.

"You did everything, Mitch! It looks wonderful!"

"Well, not everything," he replied with an ornery grin as he pointed up to the ceiling. "I still have to install the mirrors above the bed and put in the disco light."

Ash, Jake, and Jim joined in his laughter. I just shook my head. "You are terrible, Mitchell Tarrington."

He moved across the room and gave me a big hug. "But, I know you love it!"

As the noonday sun took its place in the sky, the crew settled down for a feast of pizza, pasta, and soda—compliments of Mitch and Gartano's Italian Bistro. Much to my surprise, the women of the family arrived to assist in unpacking boxes; and as I sat there looking around at everyone, I was grateful for the love of family and good friends. Mitch and I were truly blessed. Although our lunch seemed a small payback, we knew they would be more than grateful for the gesture.

After everyone's bellies were full, Mitch took the men to inspect the outbuilding while the women and I worked to make our new house look more like a home. Before long we had the kitchen completed and had moved downstairs to the family room. Since I personally had little flair for decorating when it came down to it, I decided to enlist the talents of my team to help me out. Each lady was to take a box, open it, and place the contents around the room in any fashion of their choosing. Then each time I would observe the decor, I would see those personal touches; and they would serve as a reminder of the special people in our lives.

Angelina opened the box closest to her and smiled as she lifted our wedding picture out of it. It was definitely a favorite of mine that I felt deserved a place of distinction in our home. Obviously, she had the same idea as she placed it in the middle of the wall directly above the fireplace mantel. We all stopped working for a moment to admire it.

My mind drifted back to our wedding day and the time the picture had been taken. Just before leaving the church for our reception, Mitch and I found a moment alone in the foyer. He had placed one hand on my shoulder, the other on my face and tenderly kissed me, his thumb gently caressing my cheek. The photographer had been on the ball and captured the moment perfectly on film—so perfectly that we had the print enlarged and framed. As we all stood there gazing at it, the men came back inside and broke the serenity of the moment as they filed noisily into our space.

"What's the attraction?" Mitch asked as he embraced me from behind.

"We were admiring your wedding picture, Mitchell. It's so beautiful," Angelina answered.

He smiled a broad smile and placed a hand on my stomach. "Well, it was a beautiful day from start to finish," he said as he softly kissed my cheek.

Before long all the boxes were unpacked, and Mitch and I bid farewell to our guests. Exhausted from the day, I collapsed into the chair as Mitch sunk back into the cushions of the sofa. Turning to his side, he glanced around the family room and smiled.

"You ladies did a fine job of decorating," he commented. "It's nice to know you don't have to rely on me to help you. I don't have much of a knack for stuff like that."

"Well, you better learn fast because I'll need your help with the nursery. Don't forget—I'm the one who's 'baby illiterate.'"

Mitch laughed. *"Baby illiterate?* Now, there's a term for you!"

"It's true. I was the only one in Lamaze class last night who didn't know how to change a diaper, Mitchell. It was a good thing your mother was there filling in for you, or I may have put it on the wrong end of the doll!"

He chuckled, but his eyes were filled with love and understanding. "Honey, it's not a big deal. Those are the kinds of things you're there to learn. I'm sure you're the only one who thought a thing about it."

I slouched down in the chair just a little. "No one likes to feel inadequate, you know."

"Sweetheart, you aren't inadequate. You're simply new to all this. Don't be so hard on yourself, okay? I have no doubt that you'll be a terrific mom."

As always, he knew just what to say to bring a smile to my face. "You really think so?"

"Absolutely!"

Chapter 14

The rest of the weekend passed by quickly, and it was nice to see Mitch feeling well and back to himself again. On Monday morning after breakfast, we made our way to Morgan Furniture to check out the living room sets. After much debate, we settled on a beige sofa and loveseat as well as a coffee table and end tables to match the sofa table I had already purchased. After arranging to have it all delivered on Thursday, we headed to Baby World. Since Mitch had actually helped me choose between the two cribs I'd seen in the catalog, I wanted to gain his final approval by letting him see the winning item in person before making the purchase. I took his hand in mine as we walked inside; and as I had done the day Kayla and I had gone there, he stopped in awe the minute he was through the door.

"Good grief! No wonder it took you two half the day to go through this joint! How on earth do you know where to start?"

"That's easy," I said with a smile. "First, you go over to that desk marked 'Baby Registry' and you sign in. Then you take the little scanner, go into the store, and pick things out in each department." I pointed casually to the bed and bath area to our left. "Kayla and I decided to start there, and we moved into each department. It was a blast!" Suddenly, a thought occurred to me. "You know, maybe we should go and get a scanner in case we see anything else we want to add to the registry." I started to lead him in that direction, but he stopped midway.

"No, I think not. I know you brought a truckload of stuff home with you, and I'm fairly certain you put at least that much on the registry. I think that should suffice for now."

I sighed and stuck my tongue out at him. "Party pooper."

"Somebody has to keep the budget under control," he replied with a shrug and a smile.

I led him to the crib display and stopped in front of the one we had seen in the catalog. Letting go of my hand, he walked around it as he carefully inspected it and ran his hand along the top railing. He bent down to look underneath and then stood back up, turned to me, and smiled.

"Looks pretty sturdy. What do you think?"

I giggled. "I think you looked like you were inspecting a car instead of a baby crib. The twins are only going to sleep in them, not drive them!"

He grinned. "I'm just thinking of their safety, that's all. They have to sleep in these things until they're at least two years old. You don't want to put them in something that's going to fall apart the first time they stand up at the side and start to shake it, do you?"

I gave him a strange look. "What makes you think they'll do that? They're children, not caged animals."

He laughed, put his arm around my shoulders, and pulled me against him as he planted a kiss on the top of my head. "You really are 'baby illiterate' aren't you? Trust me. In about a year or so, they are going to be fighting you tooth and nail when you put them in that thing; and they will most likely stand up, grab the side, and shake it while they scream for you."

My eyes grew wide. "How am I supposed to handle that?"

He smiled as he headed toward the area where the bedding was sold. "You'll learn."

"Sounds like I'll learn a lot of things, won't I?"

"We both will, love," he replied tenderly. "I'm not 'all-knowing' either. I just happen to have had the advantage of babysitting for nieces and nephews a few times. I've seen them in action. Kids can really do some crazy things!"

"I'm glad you have that experience, too, sweetie. All I can really relate to are the five-year olds I teach. Any age less than that is a total mystery."

Mitch and I reached the display of bedding and began to scan the various comforters, bumper pads, and blankets they had to offer. During my previous shopping trip, I had opted not to purchase or register for any of these items. Although I had seen a few ensembles in the catalog that I liked, I had decided instead to wait and let Mitch help me with the final selection. To go with the cribs, we chose a teddy bear theme for the nursery overall and purchased the bedding along with a few appliqués for the walls. Rather than pay extra delivery charges, Mitch opted to ask for the use of Chris's van to pick the items up and thus have an extra hand to help assemble them as well. He would call Chris later that evening and make arrangements.

We left Baby World feeling quite satisfied with the day's endeavors, and decided to pay a visit to Olivia. On Saturday, she had asked me to supply her with a few baby pictures of myself that she and the others could use at the baby shower. I wasn't sure what her plans were for them, but I had managed to pull some from my album that I thought she could use. As we made the drive, I pulled the envelope from my purse and looked through them once more.

"Mitch, who do you think our babies will look like? You or me?"

He glanced over at me and smiled. "If we're lucky at all, you."

"Why do you say that? You're very handsome. I'm hoping they look like you."

"Maybe they'll be the perfect combination of both of us. Guess we'll just have to wait and see, huh?"

"Yeah, I guess so—but I still hope they look like you!"

Olivia was wandering through the small flower garden at the side of the house with her hands full of freshly picked blossoms in an array of bright colors. Hearing the car coming up the lane, she turned to us with a smile and a wave as she walked closer to the front of the house to greet us.

"Well, isn't this a nice surprise! Mitch, didn't you work today?"

"No, I took the day off. I promised Dana I'd take her shopping today. Now, we're visiting you."

"I'm glad you are! Have you eaten? Alexander's just finishing lunch. I believe he was making sandwiches of some sort."

Mitch smiled and took my hand as we began to follow Olivia toward the house. "That sounds great to me. How about you, sweetheart?"

"Wonderful!"

And wonderful it was! We enjoyed a fine lunch of ham sandwiches with freshly baked cherry pie for dessert and washed it all down with tall glasses of iced tea. Sufficiently filled, we went into the family room to relax and enjoy each other's company.

"I brought the baby pictures for you, Olivia," I said as Mitch and I took a seat on the couch. "I only brought six. If you need more, I can bring them by tomorrow or something."

"Not rehearsing tonight?" she asked Mitch.

"Not yet. Jim thought I should take a few more days and rest my voice. I'm eager to get back into it though. We really need to practice up for that demo."

"You'd best take Jim's advice. You don't want to jump back in too soon and maybe cause yourself more pain." She smiled as she turned to me. "Dana, let's have a look at those pictures."

Taking them from me, she took a seat in the chair next to us and smiled brightly as she glanced at each photo. Suddenly, her expression softened as she studied the picture she held in her hands. Lifting her eyes to look at us, she turned the picture around so that we could see it.

"This must be your mother holding you, Dana, and I'm guessing the other lady is your grandmother. What a lovely family. I'm sure they would be so happy about your babies." She handed the picture to Mitch; and as he looked at it, so did I. "It looks like they really were a close family and that they loved you very much."

"I loved them, too," I said quietly. "I still do." As I stared at the picture in my husband's hands, a wave of emotions swept over me. Olivia was right. They would have been happy about my babies. They would have loved Mitch and my children as much as they loved me. I knew they would have been there when the day arrived to welcome them into the world with us, and they would have stayed close to me for as long as I needed them to help me and teach me the ways of motherhood. I knew that even when the day came that they had to go home, a simple phone call would have brought them close again. Unfortunately, none of that was possible. They had gone home already—to a home where I couldn't touch them or talk to them or pick up the phone and call them. They couldn't be there with me when my twins were born; and they would never hold them, kiss them, or spoil them the way grandparents do. My heart began to ache, and it was all I could do to hold back the tears filling my eyes. I swallowed hard against the lump in my throat and knew that I had to get out of the room before the flood of emotions took control.

"I think I need to step outside for some fresh air. Excuse me." The last words came out in a trembling tone as I hurried out the front door.

Olivia gave Mitch a dumbfounded look. "Mitchell, did I say something wrong? Maybe I should go and talk to her."

Mitch stood and shook his head—his expression sympathetic. "No, it's okay, Mom. I'll go."

I stood at the front porch railing, and the tears flowed freely down both cheeks. I heard the door close gently behind me, but I didn't turn around to see who it was. A moment later, Mitch stood beside me and tenderly touched my shoulder.

"I miss them. I miss them so much."

He pulled me to him in a protective hug. His arms wrapped tightly around me as he held me close. "I know you do, love. It's okay. I'm here. I'm right here."

For the next few moments he held me and rested his cheek on the top of my head as he tenderly rubbed my back in an attempt to soothe me. As much as I loved him and was grateful that he was there, at that moment I wished it was my mother or Grammy holding me instead. But, I would never tell him that. Because he had never experienced the pain himself, it would only hurt his feelings to try to explain it to him. Instead, I let myself bask in the comfort he provided and did my best to pull myself back together.

Finally, I stepped back from his embrace and wiped the tears from my cheeks. "I'm sorry. I didn't mean to run out like that."

He pulled me to him again. "Honey, it's all right. I know you wish your family could be here with you in a physical sense. Do you remember what I told you a long time ago? As long as you have them in your heart, they're always with you in spirit."

I looked into his bright blue eyes that were shining with love and affection. "It's just not the same. They'll never know these babies, Mitch. These are their grandchildren—the very first grandchildren they would ever have—and they will never know they exist. I could feel the lump rising in my throat again. "And our kids will never know them."

Mitch took me by the hand and led me to the porch swing. He sat down beside me. "I know that's what you may think, but I don't believe that."

"What do you mean?"

He smiled a soft, sweet smile. "I believe that babies come from Heaven and that every child is a gift from God. Therefore, those who live in Heaven know the babies before we do. They know all about them, and they love them." He brushed a strand of hair off my face and tucked it behind my left ear. "When the children are sent to us, they already have the seed of that love growing within them. We nurture that, and they come to know those people by the things we tell them." He took my hand and looked into my eyes. "Your heart is filled with so much love, Dana, for your parents and for your grandmother. They live on within you—through the love you have for them and the love they had for you. You'll look at those pictures with the kids, and you'll tell them stories; and they will become familiar with those people through you. Maybe they will never touch physically, or maybe they won't ever talk on the phone or share an ice cream cone; but when *you* do those things with our kids, a part of your family will be there, too."

I took a moment to think about his words. As I did, a peace began to surround my heart. I felt a soft kick come from within, and it caused me to smile. Mitch seemed to know what was happening although I hadn't said a word, and he reached out to place his hand on my abdomen. Feeling the kick himself, he also smiled; and I placed my hand on top of his. I leaned against his shoulder, and he kissed my forehead as he whispered softly in my ear.

"I love you—all three of you."

"We love you, too," I replied.

Olivia gazed out the window and smiled at the sight of her son and his wife as they cuddled on the porch swing. Their hands were resting on the evidence of their unborn children. Every once in a while one of them would laugh as they felt a strong kick—the other moving their hand to the spot where it had occurred. Finally, Olivia saw him kiss her—a soft and tender kiss full of the love she knew he felt for her—the love that she knew had been undeniable from the very first time he saw her. She remembered the night Mitch had come to her almost a year ago—excited, yet confused, by what he was feeling for a woman he'd never even met. "Mothers have this way of knowing things, Mitch," she'd told him, "and I believe tonight you fell in love." At first he was skeptical of her words, but it only took a moment before he admitted that she could be right. Now they were freely exhibiting that love. As Mitch stood and reached out for Dana's hand, Olivia moved away from the window so that they wouldn't know she had been watching them. She moved quickly toward the foyer and smiled tenderly as they walked through the door hand in hand.

"Is everything all right, kids?" she asked.

Mitch smiled. "Just fine, Mom. No worries."

Olivia approached me and extended her arms for a hug. "Dana, I'm sorry I upset you, dear. I didn't mean to, and I hope you'll forgive me."

I returned her hug and gave her a smile. "I know, and it's okay. I'm sorry I ran out the way I did. It's just that, well, you wouldn't think I'd still miss them the way that I do. I thought time was supposed to heal all wounds."

She looked into my eyes affectionately and took my hand. "It might heal the wounds, but it doesn't take away the memories. My parents and grandparents have been gone for many years. A few of them passed on even before Chris was born. There are times when something will make me think about them—especially when something special happens in my life—and I long for them to be here. It's okay, Dana. It just shows how very much they meant to you and the kind of love they gave you—the same love you give to everyone around you. That's what makes you so special."

She stepped away with a smile, and Mitch took my hand again. "I have an idea," she said with a twinge of excitement in her voice. "Why don't I get my album, and I'll show you some pictures of Mitch when he was a baby. How about that?"

I looked up at Mitch. and he smiled. "Okay, but only show her the ones where I'm fully clothed. I don't think it would be appropriate for her to see the others."

"Oh, Heaven forbid your *wife* should see you as a naked baby!" I laughed.

"Come on, you big clown. I'll need you to take the album down from the shelf in the closet," Olivia said as she prompted her son in that direction.

A short time later the three of us sat on the couch with Olivia in the middle and the photo album spread open on her lap. For the next half hour, we stayed there and relived Mitch's early years. Olivia's stories brought each picture to life. I watched as the infant became a toddler taking his first steps with his father lovingly encouraging him. I saw the toddler splashing happily in a bathtub full of bubbles, blowing out candles on his birthday cake, and waving to his siblings as they climbed onto the school bus. As I admired each scene that had been captured on film so long ago, the one thing that stood out the most was the bright smile Mitch always had, always happy, the world a place of joy to him. I glanced over at him just then and noticed that time hadn't changed him. He had a way of taking the rain and turning it to drops of golden sunshine. My heart warmed to know that each day of my life—no matter what I might face—he would be there to shine that light on me.

As we reached the end, Olivia closed the album and turned to Mitch with a sentimental gleam in her eyes. "It only seems like yesterday that you were the baby in those pictures, Mitchell," she started. "Now, you're all grown up and about to have your own babies. It hardly seems possible."

"There are times when it still seems impossible to me, too, Mom," he replied. He looked over her head at me and gave me a flash of that adorable dimple. " I'm blessed. I'm really blessed."

After visiting for another hour, Mitch insisted on taking me home to rest, and I didn't resist. It seemed that lately I had been getting tired much easier and after less activity than I had even a few weeks ago. At that moment, a nap sounded divine. During our drive, he announced that his plan was to make sure I was tucked safely away at home before heading into Gartano's for a few hours to catch up on things. When I mentioned that the idea had been for him to take the day off, he countered that he'd already been home since last Wednesday and felt like he needed to at least check in. I decided it wasn't a point worth arguing. Once I got out of the car in the driveway, I sent him on his way with a kiss and went inside.

Mitch drove slowly down the street and took in the scenery of their new neighborhood. Most of the houses were quiet right then, and he assumed that was probably because the occupants were at work. Those that did show signs of activity were reserved for small children or pets frolicking in the yard, and it reaffirmed to him that this was a place where he could feel comfortable raising his own children. He looked forward to meeting some of the neighbors. Since Chris and Trudy lived only a street away, they knew a few of the couples and had promised to introduce them. He was sure Dana would feel more at ease there once they had some new friends, but knowing Trudy was close by if needed did provide some comfort.

As always, the parking lot of Gartano's was filled near capacity, and Mitch smiled as he pulled in. Whistling a happy tune as he walked to the door, he stepped inside and was greeted by Kayla's bright smile.

"Why, hello there, Mitch!" she said as she offered a friendly hug. "You look like you're feeling better."

"I am, thanks. Looks like you've been keeping this place running like a fine-tuned engine. Just the way I like it!"

She laughed as she shot her eyes toward Jimmy who had come to greet Mitch as well. "I suppose I can't take *all* the credit. Jimmy helped a little."

Jimmy extended a hand and patted Mitch on the back. "Glad to see you up and around, boss, but I thought you were taking the day off. What are you doing here?"

Mitch looked around the crowded room and felt pleased. "You know me. I can't stay away for long." He placed a hand on Jimmy's shoulder as the pair walked toward the kitchen. "How are things going? Any issues?"

"Nope. Not a one," Jimmy replied cheerfully. "The girls have been working hard, and I've been hardly working!"

The men shared a laugh, and then Mitch greeted his kitchen crew before retreating toward the office. He sat down at his desk and leafed through the pile of mail that had been placed there for him. Seeing nothing that seemed urgent, he fished through the file drawer for the folder of applications and pulled it out. He started to open it, but then he hesitated. *What's the use?* he thought to himself. *I've already gone through this file four times; and I interviewed the best candidates, which didn't turn out to be all that great after all.* He turned back to the cabinet, opened the drawer, and replaced the file. Sinking back in his chair, he closed his eyes to think for a moment. Maybe he should consider rewriting the ad. If he was a bit more specific in mentioning the type of person he wanted for the job, he might draw in a better lot of candidates. He opened his eyes and pulled a legal pad from the drawer. He tapped the pen against his lower lip for a moment and then began to scribble down a few words. He paused to read what he had written:

"Waitress needed—hardworking, dependable person needed for fast-paced environment. Experience preferred, but willing to train the right candidate."

He stopped reading, chuckled, and added a line:

"Nervous individuals, those with screaming children, 'ladies of the evening,' and children of prominent businessmen need not apply."

He laughed aloud and crossed out the last line. *How nice it would be if I really could write it like that,* he thought. *How much nicer still if the perfect person would just walk in off the street, and I wouldn't have to pay for another ad.*

Little did he know his wish was about to come true.

The pretty young lady stood by the front door and clutched the newspaper clipping in her hands. Although the ad had appeared over a week ago, she was hopeful that the position hadn't been filled. She needed one more chance—one more opportunity to prove herself. This was something she needed to do and something she had been thinking about even before she saw the ad. It was as if destiny had spoken to her through the newspaper, and it had told her to follow her heart. Everything she had ever wanted could be waiting on the other side of that door. Taking a deep breath, she conjured up her courage and stepped inside.

"Hi there, welcome to Gartano's," Kayla greeted. "Dining alone today?"

The woman smiled. "Oh, no. I'm actually looking for Mitch Tarrington. Is he here?"

Before Kayla could answer, Mitch appeared in the dining room; and he and the young woman spotted each other at the same time.

"Casey? My gosh! What are you doing here?"

Mitch extended a hand, but instead Casey hugged him as she'd done the day at the hospital.

"What's with this formal stuff, buddy? You and I know each other too well for all that!" She pulled away with a smile. "I remembered your saying that you own this place, and I was in the neighborhood...."

Mitch pointed to a chair at a nearby table and prompted Casey to sit down. "Great—glad you could stop in. Why don't you make yourself comfortable, and I'll have one of the girls fix you up?"

She smiled. "Actually, I'm not here for lunch, Mitch," she said. "I saw this ad in the newspaper a few weeks ago, and I was hoping that I might apply for the job—that is, if you haven't already hired someone."

Mitch laughed. "You're kidding me, right?"

Casey seemed to be caught off guard by his reaction. "I'm sorry, but I don't understand what's so funny."

Mitch smiled. "I'm sorry. It's nothing personal. It's just that, well, I was back in the office a few minutes ago thinking about rerunning that ad." He gave her a quick briefing on the interviews the week before. "I was actually hoping someone would walk in off the street so I wouldn't have to go through all that again."

This is going to be easier than I thought, Casey said to herself. "Wow, that's really incredible! Call it fate—you need a waitress, and I need a job. I've been searching for three weeks and so far, nothing." She gave him a soft smile and leaned slightly toward him, touching his hand gently. "What do you think? Willing to give me a shot?"

Mitch hesitated with his answer. Thoughts of Dana began to flood his mind, and he couldn't help wondering what she would have to say about the situation. Well, that was a no-brainer. She wouldn't like it. She wouldn't like the fact that Casey was young, attractive, and a part of his past. However, that was the operative term—past. There was nothing between them anymore. Yes, he still thought she was pretty, but that was the extent of his feelings for her at that point. Actually, it was more of an observation. Anyone that looked at her could see that she was easy on the eyes. He began to reason the circumstances. He needed a waitress, and no one had been able to even come close to what he was looking for. He knew Casey had experience. She had been waiting tables at his father's country club when they met, and he knew that she had the right personality for the job. If she was anyone else with those credentials, he would hire her; so why should the fact that he used to date her stop him? Besides, he believed in his heart that after all they had gone through over the past few months, he'd more than proved to Dana that his love for her was true. He'd given her no reason to doubt it, and he felt that he could easily convince her that she had no reason to now. In fact, the more he thought about it, the more he decided that she would probably be happy that he'd found someone to fill the job—no matter who it was. He looked at Casey and nodded.

"If you can start tomorrow morning at eleven, the job's yours."

Casey squealed with delight and clasped her hands together in front of her. "Thank you, Mitch. Thank you so much! I know you won't be disappointed."

Mitch led Casey into the office where he had her fill out her paperwork and briefed her on the details of the position. Noticing the picture of Mitch and Dana sitting on the corner of the desk, Casey picked it up to take a closer look.

"This must be your wife," she observed. "She's really pretty, Mitch. I can see how she swept you off your feet."

Mitch's heart warmed as he took the picture from Casey and gazed at his beautiful bride. "She definitely did that," he replied. "I still can't believe it myself sometimes. I'm truly blessed."

"That's great. I'm glad you're happy." Casey decided it was time to delve deeper into what she really wanted to know. "What does she think about your being a musician and fronting a band? Is she very supportive?"

Mitch nodded and sat back in his chair. "Absolutely. In fact, she's the one who encouraged me to get back with the guys. I think sometimes she enjoys watching me perform more than I enjoy doing it!"

Casey smiled and looked right into Mitch's eyes. "Well, I'm sure you're enjoyable to watch no matter what you're doing."

The comment embarrassed him a little, and he quickly turned his eyes toward the pile of papers on his desk. "Do you have any questions for me? About the job, I mean."

"I can't think of anything right now," she replied.

"If you think of anything, I'll be here for about another hour or so. You can call me or just write them down, and we can talk tomorrow."

Casey took this as her cue to go. She stood up; and when Mitch was on his feet as well, she gave him yet another friendly hug.

"Thanks again. I know I'm going to enjoy working here. I can't tell you what this means to me."

Mitch stepped away and began to escort Casey toward the front door. "Don't mention it. You have no idea how much it means to *me*. I was beginning to think decent candidates for this job didn't exist."

They reached the front door, and Casey smiled brightly at Mitch. "I guess I'll see you bright and early tomorrow morning, boss," she said.

"When you get here, there will probably be a line waiting to get in. Come around to the delivery entrance, and I'll let you in there." Mitch held the door for her and pointed at her playfully as she turned to wave. "Eleven sharp—and don't be late!"

He closed the door with a smile and turned around just in time to see Kayla jump away from the window she'd been peeking through.

"I'm sure you want to know my association with her, don't you?" he asked with a sly smile. "Now I know why you and my wife get along so well. You're cut from the same mold. I saw you looking at her, and you were probably spying on us back in the office, too."

"Don't you go accusing me of anything," Kayla retorted. "I would never invade your privacy that way. You should know better than that, young man."

Mitch gave her half a grin and nodded. "You're right, Kayla. I'm sorry. But, you're curious, aren't you?"

She turned back to the table she had cleared and began to wipe it with a wet cloth. "It's none of my business how you know her. However, I would say it seems you know her pretty well."

Mitch walked to the table, turned around a chair, and straddled it. "We dated about a year and a half ago. She moved to Chicago for a while and has been looking for a job since she got back. She used to be a waitress at my dad's country club. Heaven knows I haven't been able to find anyone else to fit in here, so I figured why not?"

Kayla stood up straight and picked up the bus pan full of dirty dishes. "Now, see? Didn't ol' Kayla tell you the right person would come along?"

Mitch smiled. "Yes, you did. She's a nice girl, and I really think she'll work out well. She has one of those personalities that you just can't help but like."

"She did seem sweet," Kayla agreed. "Well, I'm happy it's all worked out. Now, you don't have to worry about it anymore. I'm sure that's a weight off your shoulders."

Mitch stood up and replaced the chair at the table. "Absolutely! I think it will make Dana pretty happy to know that I finally found someone who's worth having around here."

Kayla gave Mitch a playful grin as she put the pan back down and placed her hands on her hips. "Just what is that supposed to mean, Mr. Tarrington?"

Mitch laughed. "Guess that didn't come out quite the way I intended, did it?"

A little over an hour later, Mitch pulled into the garage and watched in the rearview mirror as the door came down behind him. Taking the keys from the ignition, he sat for a moment to collect his thoughts. He was excited to share the news about Casey with Dana but not so excited about how she might react. He had to think positive. He would give her all the details, reassure her that he loved only her, and pray that would be enough. He put a smile on his face and went inside.

The smell of freshly baked bread filled the air as Mitch opened the door, and he inhaled deeply. Dana was standing at the counter slicing a carrot into the bowl of salad, and he walked up behind her, encircled his arms around her, and kissed her cheek.

"Hey, beautiful! Something smells great—besides you, that is."

I turned my face toward his and smiled. "Flattery will get you everywhere," I answered, and he grinned as he raised his eyebrows playfully.

Kissing me again, Mitch moved to the sink and began to wash his hands. "Well, did you get a chance to rest a little? I hope so. I know you were tired."

"Yes, I did. I sat down intending to relax in front of the TV, and the next thing I knew I was waking up a half hour later."

He smiled. "That's good, love. You need your rest."

I carried the salad to the table, and Mitch followed close behind with our place settings. "How were things at the bistro? Anything new or exciting?"

Here you go, Mitch. Play it up. "Actually, yes there is. I finally found a new waitress!"

"Wow! How'd that happen?"

"It's kind of a funny story," he began. "I was sitting in the office trying to rewrite the ad, and an old friend of mine happened to come in. Casey Tomlin. She and I used to hang out together." He took some salad, placed it onto his plate, and smothered it with dressing. He was acting very nonchalant. "Anyway, she asked about the position; and the next thing I knew, we were filling out the paperwork. Talk about fate, huh?"

I gave him a curious look. "Uh, when you say you 'hung out together,' what exactly do you mean by that?"

He cringed a little but was still trying to come across as if it wasn't of any importance. "We used to go out."

Now my look was one of shock and disbelief tinged with a touch of anger. "Wait a minute—you used to *date* her? And, you *hired* her? What on earth were you thinking, Mitchell? Have you gone insane?"

He was about to take a bite of his salad, but he lowered the fork and looked at me. "I was thinking that she needed a job, and I needed a waitress. It was simply a matter of her being in the right place at the right time."

"For crying out loud, Mitch, you used to *date* her! Did you actually think I'd be all right with this?"

He placed his fork on his plate and sighed heavily. "In view of everything we've dealt with in the past three months, that's exactly what I thought. She's just an old friend, Dana. Nothing more."

I absently pushed a cucumber slice around the edge of my plate and refused to look up at him. "You used to date her, Mitch. You had feelings for her. That makes her more than just an old friend."

Mitch let out a long, exasperated breath and looked at me across the table before turning his attention back to his meal. "I can see that you're going to need some time to get used to this idea. That's okay. Take all the time you need."

We basically finished our dinner in silence, and afterward Mitch went upstairs to change clothes while I cleaned the kitchen. Upon his return, he announced that he was going to take a walk.

"Feel like tagging along?"

"Not really," I replied.

He gave me a soft kiss and brushed the hair back from my face. "Okay then. You stay here and relax. I'll be back in a little while." He turned around as he opened the door. "Lock this behind me, all right? I've got my key. I love you."

Mitch headed down the street with his mind once again focused on Dana. *Gee, that went over like a fly in a punch bowl*, he thought. *I really thought she was over all the jealousy stuff. Have I just set myself up for a heavy dose of hard living, compliments of my wife? There has to be a way that I can get her to feel more comfortable with all this. I mean, it's not like I have any desire to be with Casey again. It was fun while it lasted, sure—but that was over a year ago.* His mind settled on that thought as he remembered the day he and Casey had met. After a morning of working out at the club his father belonged to, he decided to stop in the restaurant for a bite of lunch before going home. Instead of eyeing the menu, however, he found himself eyeing the attractive young waitress standing next to him poised and ready to take his order. The charm on her necklace—a gold musical note—gave him the lead in to start a conversation; and he soon learned that she had a love of music much like himself. Her warm smile and cheerful demeanor drew him in, and he asked her to dinner that evening followed by a moonlit stroll through the park. That night became the first of many they would share together over the next five months.

Then one evening, Casey told Mitch that she had an opportunity to audition for a band in Chicago that was looking for a female vocalist. If she was chosen for the job, she would begin touring with them; and it could possibly open the door for her to be 'discovered.' She had heard about the audition through a friend of a friend. While she was very interested in the chance to pursue her dreams, she was also very interested in her relationship with Mitch. Although he was saddened to be letting go of someone he was beginning to care deeply about, he knew it would be selfish and wrong of him to stand in the way of her dreams. On the following Monday, a teary-eyed Casey kissed him one last time and turned quickly toward the boarding ramp to the plane that would take her to Chicago. Over the weeks that followed, Mitch quickly learned that besides the physical distance between them, their lives were heading in two different directions. Feeling that Casey would never take the initiative, he suggested they end their romance. Much to his surprise, she agreed. They had not communicated again until the recent day at the hospital. He chuckled. *Funny how things work out*, he pondered. *Here I am, about to get a possible break into a music career; and here she is, leaving hers behind. Guess whatever's meant to be will be.*

Rounding the corner of the next street, he walked the length of five houses and smiled as he spied Chris pulling into his driveway. Quickening his pace, he called out to him and waved. Chris waved back and stood next to his car until Mitch began to walk up his driveway.

"Hey, little brother. Out for an evening stroll?"

"Actually, I thought I'd come and bug you for a while. Why are you so late getting home?"

"Dad and I had dinner with one of our clients this evening." He ducked back into the car and withdrew his briefcase along with a bouquet of flowers. "We were going to bring him to Gartano's, but Dad said he'd rather do that when he knew you were there. We ended up at The Mark."

Mitch seemed more interested in the flowers than what his brother had to say. "Hey, do me a favor. Let me take those flowers to Dana. She's upset with me right now, and they might score some brownie points for me."

Chris gave him a shocked expression and then began to laugh. "Are you kidding? These are for *my* wife, buddy. Get your own."

Chris began to walk toward the front door as Mitch still pleaded his case. "Come on, Chris. Trudy's not mad at you. My wife may make me sleep on the couch tonight. You'll be cuddled up next to yours in bed."

Chris gave Mitch a sly grin. "Precisely why I'm bringing her flowers. I'm *definitely* in a cuddling mood."

Mitch moved in front of Chris and blocked his path. "You don't think she'll pick up on that without the flowers?"

"Call them a bit of insurance. And, why's Dana mad at you now?" he asked as he moved around Mitch and started toward the door again.

"I hired a new waitress."

"So?"

"Casey Tomlin."

Now it was Chris who stood firmly in front of Mitch. "You hired your ex-girlfriend to work with you? Are you insane?"

"That's what Dana wanted to know. I guess the vote on that one's unanimous, huh?"

Chris chuckled. "Mitch, I don't know what your logic was, but I gotta say I don't think the brain was engaged when you made the decision."

Mitch lowered his eyes, sighed, and brought them back up to meet Chris's. "I ran into her a few weeks ago at the hospital while I was waiting for Dana to finish her checkup. She moved back to Philly recently; and when she saw the ad I ran for a waitress, she decided to apply. I hadn't been able to find anyone else suitable for the job, so I hired her."

Chris shook his head. "And, when you told Dana, she blew up at you."

"Not exactly," Mitch replied as he replayed for Chris the conversation he and Dana had. "I guess she's not as far over the jealousy thing as I thought she was. It's not like I hired Jessica for the job. Sure, Casey and I cared about each other, but I wouldn't say I was in love with her or anything."

Chris resumed his walk and this time made it to the front door and opened it. Trudy was waiting just inside holding Diana. Chris kissed them both as he handed the bouquet to Trudy. "These are for you, sweetheart." He shot Mitch another sly grin and turned back to his wife. "You can thank me for them later."

Trudy gave her husband a light tap on the arm. "Christopher, behave yourself—especially in front of company."

"He's not company," Chris retorted. "He's only my little brother."

"Don't listen to him, Mitch. Come on in," Trudy said as she shot a playful look at Chris. "You're special to me."

"Thanks. At least there's one female in the family tonight who's still speaking to me."

"Oh, my," Trudy said. "Trouble in paradise I presume."

Mitch gave Trudy a rundown of the day's events and followed up by saying, "I have to figure out how to make this work. It wouldn't be right to tell Casey now that she can't have the job, but I also can't have Dana upset either over her being there. There has to be a happy medium somewhere."

The three of them sat silently for a moment before Trudy spoke. "Maybe if she has a chance to meet Casey before the two of you work together, she'll easily see that there's nothing to worry about. I'm sure that Dana's apprehensive because she doesn't know anything about her. A casual meeting might give her a chance to get to know her a little."

Mitch bit his lip and nodded. "That might be kind of tough given the fact that Casey's starting tomorrow morning. It is a good idea though. Maybe I can work something out."

Mitch looked at Chris who was shaking his head—the expression on his face clearly stating that he disagreed.

"Don't you think it would be better for Dana to meet her at Gartano's? I'm sure she's not going to be comfortable holding a one-on-one with your ex."

"Well, I think that they should get together, you know, for coffee or something," Trudy explained. "That way they can talk; and if Dana knows something about her, she might not be as worried about Mitch working with her."

"It wouldn't be a one-on-one either. I'd be there, too," Mitch interjected.

Chris stood up, loosened his tie, and started toward the kitchen. "You, my dear, have crazy ideas sometimes," he said to Trudy as he passed by her chair. Then he turned to Mitch. "And, I still think you're insane. Now, do either of you want something to drink?"

Mitch stood as well and thrust his hands into his pockets. "No, thanks. I'm going to head back home and see if she's ready to talk about this."

Trudy walked him to the door. "Don't worry. I still say once she gets to know Casey, she'll be more receptive. You have to remember that the two of you haven't even been together a year, Mitch. She's still getting used to things."

He smiled. "Yeah, I know. It'll probably take her a lifetime to get used to me!" Almost forgetting the main reason he'd stopped by, he turned back to Trudy. "Oh, yeah—would it be a problem to borrow your van tomorrow evening? We bought the baby cribs and need to pick them up."

Chris suddenly appeared behind Trudy with a can of soda in one hand and a cookie in the other. "I suppose you'll need me to help put the things together, right?"

"Well, you are an expert with four kids and all."

Chris smiled. "Fine. I'll pick you up at six."

I was upstairs folding a basket of laundry on the bed when Mitch arrived back home. I heard him call out to me, but I didn't answer. A minute later I could hear his hurried footsteps on the stairs.

"There you are," he said as he saw me through the doorway of the bedroom. "Why didn't you answer? I was getting worried when I didn't see you anywhere."

"Sorry," I replied. "Didn't mean to worry you."

He pointed to the laundry basket which was still half full. "How'd you get that upstairs?"

"I used my magic and floated it up here," I said sarcastically.

He sighed deeply. "Honey, please don't be lifting things like that. It's much too heavy. I could have carried it for you when I got back."

"Thanks, but I managed."

He sighed again; and after he moved a folded stack of t-shirts to the side, he sat down on the corner of the bed opposite me. "I know you're upset about my hiring Casey, but I'd like you not to be."

"Okay, I won't be."

He chuckled softly and shook his head. "It would be nice if it was that simple with you, but I know better."

"Are you saying I'm complicated?"

"Not at all. If you'll give her a chance, I think that you'll probably end up liking her."

I lowered the towel I was folding and gave him a look. "Like her? Mitchell, I know nothing about her! I didn't even know she existed until an hour ago. Is there some reason you never bothered to tell me about her?"

He bit his lip. "Nothing other than the fact that it simply never came to mind. So, don't go thinking that I'm trying to withhold information from you because I'm not."

I lifted my eyes long enough to roll them at him. He stood up, took the clean laundry from my hands, and prompted me to sit next to him. "Dana, I have nothing to hide from you. Yes, Casey and I were an item for a while—but a short while. We only dated for about five months, and that was over a year ago. It ended at least six months before I met you. Any feelings we might have for each another are simply platonic at best, and that isn't going to change. You have to trust me on that."

I looked deep into his bright blue eyes that pleaded for my approval. I wanted to trust what he was saying, and I fought hard against the thoughts in my head that were trying to persuade me otherwise. Finally I nodded, and he smiled.

"I trust you, Mitch, but that doesn't mean that I'm completely comfortable with this whole thing. Like I said, I don't know anything about this Casey person."

For some reason my statement seemed to spark something in him, and the bright glow of his face sent my trusting thoughts reeling completely in the other direction. "Well, let's see—she's twenty-five, a little taller than you with strawberry blonde hair and green eyes. She used to be a waitress at my dad's country club. That's actually how we met. She has this infectious personality that draws people in. You can't help but like her. I know the customers and the crew will get along great with her." I thought he was done until he added with a laugh, "I just thought of something the two of you have in common. She loves chocolate cake. It's her favorite, too."

I vowed right then I would never eat another piece of chocolate cake as long as I lived.

"Great. Maybe we can exchange recipes," I muttered.

Mitch chuckled and turned to kneel in front of me as he took my hand in his. "Give her a chance, baby. Okay? For me?"

I sighed. "Okay."

He gave me a soft kiss and smiled sweetly. "That's my girl."

Chapter 15

The next morning, Mitch awoke early and rolled over to put his arm around his sleeping wife. She stirred slightly and snuggled closer to him, and he smiled. He moved his hand to rest against her abdomen and felt the poke of a tiny foot against it.

"Good morning, little ones," he whispered. "It's too early for you to be up, but I guess that's what babies do, huh?"

He gently rubbed her stomach as he continued to feel the movements within it—some stronger than others but all telling him that the miracles they had created were happy and well. Patting her stomach tenderly, he gave her a soft kiss on the cheek and then crawled out of bed.

I awoke to the aroma of freshly brewed coffee and knew immediately that Mitch was already up and starting his day. I wandered downstairs to find him as I rubbed my eyes sleepily with one hand and unconsciously rubbed my stomach with the other.

"Good morning, beautiful," he greeted as I descended the stairs to the family room where he sat. He pointed to my stomach. "Did those two wake you up? They were doing some tricks up in bed a few minutes ago."

"No, they didn't wake me. I guess I've probably gotten used to the movements. But, I do have to wonder—if they're this active inside me, what are they going to be like when they aren't inside me?"

"Probably not much different," he answered as he started toward the kitchen for another cup of coffee. "Want me to make you some cereal or something?"

I began to follow him up the stairs and into the kitchen. "No, thanks. I was thinking I'd make you some scrambled eggs—if you're hungry, that is."

"That sounds great," he answered as he poured us each some coffee. "Does this mean you aren't mad at me anymore?"

I decided to play dumb. "About what?" I asked as I prepared the egg mixture and poured it into the frying pan.

"About my hiring Casey."

I began to push the mixture around the pan a little more aggressively when I heard her name. "Oh, that," I replied shortly. "Why should I be mad about that?"

Mitch placed the coffee cups on the counter and turned to lean his back against it. "You shouldn't. There's nothing to be upset about. It's all perfectly innocent."

I'll believe that once I get a chance to see her in action, I thought to myself.

I retrieved the bacon from the refrigerator, placed half of it into another pan, and turned on the flame beneath it. "I'm sure it is."

Mitch furrowed his brow a little and gave me a look. "Are you saying that to be sarcastic, or do you believe me?"

I decided to give him the answer he wanted to hear. "I believe you."

"Really?"

I was about to turn the bacon but looked up at him instead with the fork poised in the air. "Yes, Mitchell. Now, could you please hand me a couple of plates so we can eat? I don't want you running late for work."

He did as he was asked, and we sat down to our breakfast. Every once in a while he would glance up at me and give me a curious look as if he were having difficulty believing what I had said was true. I would pretend not to notice. The last thing I needed was for him to read the signs in my face revealing that it wasn't.

A short while later as I was making the bed, Mitch wandered in from his shower and headed into the closet to choose his attire for the day. I finished my task and paused for a moment to watch him as he shuffled through various shirts, pants, and ties trying to coordinate the perfect outfit. *Why all the effort in choosing your clothes today, Mitch?* I wanted to ask him. *Usually you just grab the first thing you come to and throw it on. Someone you're trying to impress?* Unfortunately, I thought I knew the answer to that question. I decided I was probably right when he turned to me dressed in the plum colored shirt and matching tie—especially since he hadn't worn it again after the night we went out with Chris and Trudy.

"How do I look?" he asked as he swept his hand over himself.

"Handsome as always," I replied, although I really wanted to ask why he cared.

"Thanks!" He gave me a kiss on the cheek as he brushed by me and went back into the bathroom, whistling a happy tune. I made my way to the doorway and watched as he removed his glasses, ran a comb through his hair, and splashed on the cologne he usually wore only for me. Replacing his glasses, he smiled at his reflection and turned around.

"Guess I'd better head out," he said as he walked toward the stairs. "I want to get there a little early so I can get some things out of the way before Casey arrives. I want to be available to show her how everything works."

You'd better be talking about the bistro when you say that, mister. I just smiled and nodded.

As we got to the door leading to the garage, he took his keys off the hook next to it and smiled at me. "Be a good girl today. I love you." He gave me a kiss as he reached for the doorknob. "See you later."

I walked into the living room and watched as he pulled out of the driveway and disappeared down the street. "Actually, my love, you'll see me sooner," I said aloud.

Hurrying upstairs, I showered, dressed, and took some extra time to make sure my hair and makeup looked just right. Pleased with my efforts, I took one last look in the full-length mirror before I made my way out to the car. As the garage door lifted, I put the key in the ignition and paused. What excuse was I going to give Mitch for coming down there so early? I didn't want it to be obvious that the only reason I was there was to check out Casey. I started the car and began to back out of the driveway. I wasn't sure yet what I would do, but I was determined to think of something.

As I approached the edge of town, I spotted Carlson's Department Store out of the corner of my eye and smiled. Since my baby shower was coming up on Sunday, I would need something new to wear. Most of my maternity clothes were casual, and those that weren't, well—they simply didn't seem appropriate for an occasion such as this. After all, there would be several people there that I hadn't seen since the wedding, and I wanted to look my best. My mind was working overtime as I swung the car in the direction of the store; and as I found a parking spot, I had my plan in place. I would purchase a new outfit and then stop by Gartano's on the way home to show it to Mitch and possibly convince him to have lunch with me. Casey wasn't due to arrive until eleven, so that gave me a little over an hour to shop and get to the bistro around the same time she would—if not before. Pleased with my idea, I cheerfully headed toward the door.

Mitch closed the ledger and smiled with pride. He knew business had been good, but the numbers truly reinforced the fact. According to his records, profits seemed to be increasing more and more each quarter; and as he walked toward the window and saw the line of patrons waiting to get in, he was confident that the pattern would continue.

As he finished helping Katie take the last of the chairs down from the tables in the dining room, he heard a faint knock on the delivery entrance door. He headed in that direction and paused to straighten his tie and smooth his shirt before he opened it.

"Good morning, Mitch! Here I am, right on time!" Casey playfully looked at her watch, and Mitch chuckled.

"Just what I like—punctuality," he replied with a wide grin. "Come with me and I'll get you signed in. Then I can give you a little tour of the place and introduce you to some of your new coworkers."

"Sounds great," Casey said as she followed him the few steps into the office.

Mitch showed Casey where to place her purse and sign in, and then he led her out into the dining room. Calling the other waitresses to the counter, he introduced her and instructed Kayla to go ahead and open the door. As the line of patrons streamed in, Casey's eyes grew wide—not with trepidation, but with excitement.

"This job's going to keep me hopping. I can tell already," she stated, "but that's how I like it."

"Good, because that's how it's going to be. Now, why don't I introduce you to the crew in the kitchen, and then I'll have one of the girls let you tag along on the floor for awhile."

As the two reappeared in the dining room, Joe was taking his place at the counter and smiled as he saw his young manager friend.

"Well, good day to you, Mr. Tarrington. Who might this pretty young lady be?"

"Hey, Joe," Mitch greeted as they approached. "This is the newest addition to our team, Casey Tomlin. Casey, this is Joe Purcell. He's our best customer."

Casey and Joe exchanged a handshake, and the elderly gentleman's eyes danced. "I don't know about all that, but I might say instead that I'm the best seat warmer in the place! My young friend here treats me very well. I think you'll enjoy working here, Casey."

Casey glanced up at Mitch with a smile of her own. "I'm sure I will. Mitch is a real sweetheart to give me this job." She placed a hand on his arm and playfully put her head against his shoulder. "But, he's a real sweetheart anyway."

I entered the front door of Gartano's not a moment too soon—armed with the evidence of my morning spree at Carlson's. As I spied the attractive female hanging on my husband's arm, I felt every part of my body tighten. I couldn't move. *What does she think she's doing?* I asked myself. *Better yet, what does he think he's doing letting her do it?*

As I stood staring at the pair engaged in cheerful conversation with Joe, I felt a gentle hand on my arm and Kayla's familiar voice.

"Now, don't you go speculating none, young lady," she warned. "They're just friends."

"Yeah, and I'd say she's taking it a bit too far, wouldn't you?"

Kayla gently took my elbow and guided me a few steps away from the door. "She's just playing around."

I gave her a shocked look. "I certainly hope it doesn't come to that!"

Kayla giggled. "Dana, now you stop that right now. You know how much that boy loves you. He'd never fall prey to something like that!"

Just then Mitch spotted me, and the smile that always melted my heart spread widely across his face. He said something to Casey as he pointed in my direction, and the two of them started toward me.

"Oh, fantastic," I said under my breath.

Kayla shot me another look. "Girl, you calm yourself down and be nice. Remember, she's only a friend and a coworker. Nothing more."

She'd better not be!

Mitch gave me a soft kiss and smiled. "Hey, beautiful! What are you doing here?" He spotted the bag in my hand and chuckled. "Let me guess—Carlson's had this great sale going on, and you wanted to show me the bargains you couldn't pass up."

I nodded as I slipped my arm around his waist—more for effect than anything. "Something like that. I also thought we could have lunch." I glanced at Casey out of the corner of my eye. "That is, if you aren't caught up with other things."

"I might be able to arrange that if you can give me a few minutes." As if he'd forgotten she was standing next to him, he got a guilty expression on his face. "Oh, I'm sorry. Dana, this is Casey Tomlin, our new waitress. Casey, this is my wife Dana."

Casey extended her hand with a friendly grin, and I couldn't help observing that she looked like she just stepped off the cover of a fashion magazine. Hair, makeup, clothes, nails—everything done to sheer perfection. But, of course, she'd dated Mitchell Tarrington, III, and I was certain that I was the first girl who had ever been anything less than perfect in his life. As I was noticing her, she was noticing my stomach.

With a look that almost resembled shock, she turned to Mitch and again placed her hand on his arm. "Mitch, you didn't tell me your wife was expecting!"

I glanced at Mitch, and now he really looked guilty. "I guess it must have slipped my mind. Sorry."

I gave him a look that would have melted an iceberg. "Seems you're forgetting a lot of things lately, Mitchell."

Casey must have decided that my pregnancy wasn't going anywhere because she finally lifted her eyes to look into mine. "It's so nice to meet you, Dana," she said in a syrupy tone. "Mitch told me that the two of you had kind of a whirlwind romance. That's so sweet." She glanced down again. "I had no idea you were pregnant. When are you due?"

I gave Mitch a stern look which told him I wanted the record set straight. "She's due in late November," he replied. "We definitely weren't thinking of having a baby this soon, but I guess you could say it was a great honeymoon."

Casey laughed. "I'll say! Do you know what you're having?"

"One is a boy, and we aren't sure about the other one."

Casey's mouth dropped open, and she once again grabbed Mitch's arm. "Twins? My goodness! How exciting!" She turned back to me with her hand still in place. I looked up at Mitch and saw him biting his lip.

"I'll bet you were really shocked, weren't you? I know I would be! Do you have names picked out yet?"

I wasn't exactly in the mood to play twenty questions with little Miss Touchy-Feely, so I made my answers as short as possible. "Yes, we were; and no, not yet."

"Well, I must say the two of you are going to have your hands full; that's for sure! Why, I can't imagine getting married after dating someone for three months and then having twins so soon." She looked up at Mitch. "To think I remember you as the guy who likes to take things slow. Guess people change, huh?"

I gave Mitch a desperate look that signaled him to get Casey away from me before the hormones kicked in, and before I ripped the red hair directly from her scalp. Fortunately for her, he picked up on it.

"Honey, why don't you have a seat over there, and I'll get one of the girls to let Casey shadow. You can go ahead and order for me if you want."

"Guess that's my cue to go," Casey said. "It was nice chatting with you, Dana. I'm sure we'll be seeing a lot more of each other."

I can hardly wait.

A few minutes later Mitch returned to the table and sat down. He reached across and took my hand as he glanced in the direction of Casey who had been left in the care of Kayla.

"I told you she had an infectious personality, didn't I? What do you think?"

Yeah, it was infectious all right. All that syrupy sweetness was enough to make anyone sick.

"She's okay, I guess," I responded. "But, I'll tell you this much—if she lays another hand on you, she'll be pulling back a stub!"

The smile that had adorned his face only seconds before quickly dissipated. "Sweetheart, don't do this. She's just a friendly person; that's all. She doesn't mean anything by it."

"Then she shouldn't do it. It's not appropriate especially since you *are* a married man." I opened the menu and pretended to read it although I knew that Mitch was aware that I had it memorized. "And tell me—how on earth could you forget to tell her that I'm pregnant, Mitch? It isn't something that's easily overlooked."

Mitch sighed heavily and stared at me as he began to bite his lip again. "It just didn't come up, Dana. For crying out loud, I didn't do it on purpose. I'm sorry I didn't mention it to her, but she knows now." He opened his own menu, and I knew it was only because he was trying to avoid eye contact. He *definitely* had it memorized. "By the way, I saw through your little charade. I know you came down here to check out Casey—not to show me what you bought at Carlson's." He glanced up with a smile. "But that's okay. I'm surprised you didn't insist on riding in with me this morning."

I laid my menu beside my napkin and looked at him across the table. His eyes were sparkling, and I knew nothing I could say would convince him otherwise. "Okay, so I wanted to come down and see her for myself. Wouldn't you do the same thing if the roles were reversed?"

"I think that if the roles were reversed, I might be a little nicer and try giving the guy a chance before I passed judgment on him."

As I was about to summon Katie over to take our order, Kayla and Casey started toward the table. I gave Kayla a desperate look in the hope that she would divert toward another table, but she only smiled.

"I'm going to pretend I don't know the two of you so I can show Casey how to handle things. Okay?"

"Sure, that's fine," Mitch answered.

Kayla went into her 'formal' table talk—not that Kayla was ever really formal—and a minute later she disappeared to retrieve our drinks and salads with Casey at her heels. I looked across the table at Mitch who was trying his best to hold in a smile. He raised his eyebrows at me, and I simply said, "Hmmph," and turned my eyes toward the door as he chuckled.

"You are such a funny little girl. You know that? But, I do love you, and I don't want you to ever forget it."

Casey returned to our table a few minutes later with salads, drinks, and a basket of hot breadsticks. "Is there anything else you need right now?" she asked in her syrupy tone.

I really wanted to say, "Yeah, for you to find another place to work," but instead I replied, "No, thanks."

"Well, if you do, please let me know, okay?"

Mitch smiled and nodded approvingly as she walked away. "I think she's going to work out well. She has the know-how, and she's friendly."

"You already told me that."

He shuffled the lettuce around in his bowl to mix it in with the dressing and took a large bite. He must have finally realized that I was tired of discussing Casey because he pointed to the bag I'd placed next to my chair. "What'd you buy at Carlson's?"

"A new outfit to wear for my shower on Sunday."

"That's nice, baby. Are you going to show it to me?"

"Maybe later," I replied half-heartedly.

He tried to remain upbeat. "Oh, okay. Did you pick up anything else while you were there?"

"Like what?"

"I don't know—anything."

"No, just the outfit."

Kayla brought our entrees; and Mitch glanced up at her, moving his eyes in my direction. She smiled and nodded as if she knew exactly what he wanted. He laid his napkin on the table, pushed out his chair, and stood up.

"I'll be right back, love. I need to use the men's room—drank a little too much coffee this morning."

As Mitch made his escape, Kayla took his place at the table.

I pointed my fork at her. "Don't even try to lecture me, Kayla Turner," I began. "I'll get used to her. What other choice do I have?"

"None, as I see it. Mitch likes her; and frankly, so do I. She really is a nice person. I think she's going to be a good waitress. You should be happy that Mitch found somebody. I know I am! You know how we've been busting our tails around here."

I sighed heavily. "Yeah, I know. I am glad that he hired someone. I just wish she wasn't who she is."

Kayla giggled. "Who else would you like her to be?"

"Anyone that he had never dated."

She nodded slowly. "Dana, that was a long time before he ever met you. If he still had feelings for her, don't you think they'd still be together?"

"It's not that. He never told me anything about her until last night, and you should have seen the smile on his face when he did." I looked up to see Mitch at the end of the hallway. When he spotted Kayla still seated at the table, he headed toward the counter to talk to Joe. I continued. "Not only that, but he took twenty minutes primping this morning to get ready for work. Then he wanted to know how he looked."

"So?"

"So he wanted to make sure he looked good for her."

She shook her head and reached across the table to pat my hand. "I don't believe that at all, and you shouldn't either. In fact, I don't think you should believe any of the things that are going through your head right now. If Mitch thought for an instant that Casey wanted to rekindle the flame, I know for certain he'd nip that in the bud. Think about all the things you two have been through since you got together. Hasn't he done his share to prove how much he adores you? Why, most women would give their right arm for a man like that!"

Gee, Kayla, I thought. *That's precisely what I'm worried about, especially after seeing them together today.*

She stood up, came to stand next to me, and placed a gentle hand on my shoulder. "He needs you to trust him. It will hurt him to no end if you don't show him that you believe he only cares for you. Can't you open up a little and put your faith in him?"

I glanced toward the counter, and Mitch caught my eye and smiled. I turned back to Kayla and let out a long breath. I knew she was right. No matter how much I hated the situation, it didn't appear as if it would change anytime soon. Over the past several months, Mitch had always come through for me. I had to trust him, but that didn't mean I would ever trust Casey. There was just something about her that didn't seem genuine, and I wasn't falling for her nicey nice routine at all. She may have had everyone else fooled into thinking she really was that sweet, but not me.

I was letting that sink in when another thought crossed my mind. Maybe I *should* give her a chance—not that I particularly wanted to become chummy with Mitch's old flame. Maybe getting to know her a little would be enough to show her that Mitch and I had a deep commitment—one that she couldn't and shouldn't try to interfere with. Perhaps I was going about this all wrong. I looked his way again; and this time, I smiled back.

"I know, and you're right. But, all I can promise is that I'll try, okay?"

She bent down to give me a hug. "That's all anyone can ask, baby girl. I know you'll do just fine."

Mitch took his place at the table once more and dug into his meal. "Did you and Kayla have a nice chat?"

"Yeah, we did. I owe you an apology."

He lowered his fork and looked at me suspiciously. "For what, love?"

"For getting upset about Casey. You were right. I really shouldn't jump to conclusions. And, just for the record, I do trust you."

I thought for a moment that he was either going to choke on his spaghetti or start to laugh and spit it across the table.

"You do?"

I smiled. "Yes, Mitch, I do."

His smile at that moment could have lit up the world. "That really means a lot to me, sweetheart. Thank you."

As he took my hand in his, I felt a special warmth come over me just knowing that I had made him feel more at ease. I knew it wasn't going to be an easy task, but I would have to put aside my feelings around him and believe I had nothing to fear. In the meantime, I would learn more about Casey Tomlin and make sure of it.

The rest of the day quickly passed by, and at seven that evening Mitch and Chris were arriving back home with the baby cribs. I excitedly opened the door and stepped aside to allow them the spare room to carry the items upstairs for assembly. A minute later Mitch descended the stairs, walked out to the garage, and returned with his tool kit and a smile.

"This is cool," he stated with childlike glee. "I've really never had the chance to use any of these things."

"Have fun, sweetie," I replied.

I busied myself with a crossword puzzle as the two brothers went about their work. Every once in a while, I would stop to listen to them. Sometimes they were laughing and sharing conversation. Sometimes the words spoken were more heated—typical of mild sibling rivalry. After one such exchange, my husband came downstairs in a huff and stormed toward the kitchen. From the look on his face, I decided to see if I could cool the fire a little and stood up to follow.

Thrusting open the refrigerator door, he grabbed a can of soda and slammed the door closed which caused a vibration. He let out a long breath and looked right at me.

"He acts like he knows it all, and I know nothing. I *hate* that, Dana. Just because I'm the younger one doesn't mean I'm stupid."

"I'm sure he doesn't think that, honey."

He popped the tab on the soda can and took a long drink. He began to speak again, flailing his hand in the direction of the stairs. "I had all but one side put together on the first crib, and Mr. Know-It-All took one look and said it wasn't right. When I showed him the directions, you know what he said? He said I read them wrong! Can you believe that?"

I decided not to answer but instead to just let him vent.

"Just because he has kids and I don't, he thinks he's the expert at crib construction. Well, if he thinks he can do a better job, let him. I'll just stay down here."

I walked to where he stood and put my arms around him. As I slowly felt his arm come around me, I began to rub his back soothingly. "Mitch, why don't you take a minute to calm down and then go back up and help him? I don't think he meant to make you feel the way you do."

I could feel him starting to relax. "He's got a big mouth."

"He's not the only one I heard exchanging words up there."

He moved back a little and looked into my eyes. "Yeah, I know. I can be a hothead sometimes, too, I guess."

I giggled. "Sometimes?"

He smiled. "Okay, a lot. But, he started the whole thing."

I moved away and took him by the hand. "You sound like a four-year old. Now, come with me, and let's go back up there."

He sighed heavily but didn't resist.

Chris was standing in the middle of the room trying to hold up part of the crib with one hand and maneuver a screw into it with the other. He glanced up momentarily when we entered the room and then turned back to his work.

"Chris, I know you and Mitch had an argument. I could hear the yelling all the way downstairs." I let go of Mitch's hand and placed my own on my hips as I gave them just the hint of a smile. "If the two of you can't play nice together, I'm going to have to separate you. Now, apologize to one another and stop this nonsense."

He turned around with a slight grin and looked at his brother. "I'll only say I'm sorry if he says it first."

"Why should I say it first?" Mitch said as he placed a hand on his chest. "You started the whole thing by implying that I didn't know what I was talking about."

"Your problem is that you can't accept that you just *might* be wrong sometimes, Mitchell."

"I have absolutely no problem admitting when I'm wrong. I don't go around pretending to know everything like some people in this room who shall remain nameless!"

I looked from one to the other and held up my hand. "I give up," I said. As I walked away, I heard Chris's voice behind me.

"Quit your whining and get over here. I only have two hands, you know."

"Oh, you admit that you *do* need my help then?" Mitch asked.

"Isn't that what I just said?"

I simply laughed as I went back down the stairs.

About an hour later, Mitch called to me from the top of the stairs. "Hey, Dana, we're finished. Come on up and take a look."

Upon entering the nursery, I found Chris and Mitch standing proudly in the middle of the room. Bright smiles adorned both their faces. They had not only put together the cribs, but they had also placed the bumper pads and comforters in them as well. As I gazed around the room, bright appliqués of playful teddy bears danced on the walls. Touched by their efforts, I felt tears welling up in my eyes. Mitch shot a look at his brother and then came to me and took me into his arms.

"What's wrong, sweetheart?"

"It looks so wonderful, Mitch."

He snuggled against me and softly kissed the top of my head. "Oh—so these are happy tears, huh?"

"Yeah," I sniffled.

I felt him rub my back, and he kissed me again before he let me go. Taking my hand, he led me to the cribs.

"I didn't put the sheets on because I'm sure you want to wash those first. We can wash the comforters, too, but I thought I'd put them on just to give you an idea of what it's all going to look like. Now, all we have to do is wait to see if we get the changing table and rocker at your shower. If not, we'll go and pick them up ourselves. Okay?"

Chris began to hum as a smirk crossed his face, and he playfully turned his eyes toward the window. Mitch laughed.

"Let me guess—you and Trudy got them for us?"

"I'm sworn to secrecy," he replied.

Mitch turned to me. "Act surprised on Sunday, love."

"No problem."

Later that night as I lay in bed, my thoughts kept turning to Casey. Although Mitch and Kayla seemed to like her, there was something about her that rubbed me the wrong way—something that even made me a little suspicious as to her motives. I wasn't exactly sure if it was only one thing or a combination of several, but it was something. I closed my eyes and allowed myself to contemplate possible reasons behind my feelings. This was more than just a simple case of jealousy. These feelings went deep into my gut. Could it be that I felt her 'sweetness' was more of an act than an actual personality trait? I had known people in my past just like her. They would pour on the sugar as a means to manipulate you into giving them anything they wanted. The minute you decided to go against them, the dam would break, and the sugar would turn to acid. I pondered that reasoning for a moment. It seemed strange to me that she—or any other woman for that matter—would willingly choose to work with her ex-boyfriend. I thought that would make most women very uncomfortable. The only reasonable explanation—to me anyway—was that it meant the woman either hoped to rekindle the flame; or the ex had something else she wanted. I took my thoughts in another direction. Mitch reassured me more than once that he and Casey were only friends. He'd told me that the end of their relationship was a mutual decision. Once they parted ways, they had no further contact until the day at the hospital. If I were to believe it to be true that she wasn't after Mitch, what *was* she after?

While I began to search for that answer, Mitch pulled me to him and began to softly kiss my neck as he sighed contentedly. His fingers lightly brushed against my arm, and he moved closer to me and began to nibble my ear. As he started to make his motives apparent, I was still contemplating Casey's. Mitch suddenly noticed that I wasn't responding to him and moved slightly away from me.

"Sweetheart, is something wrong?"

"No, I was just thinking."

I heard him sigh heavily. "About what?"

Knowing that I couldn't come right out and tell him what I was really thinking, I decided instead to give him the *Readers Digest* version.

"Casey."

He sighed even more heavily and rolled completely onto his back. "Dana, you told me you'd give her a chance. What's more, you said you trusted me. If that wasn't the case, why'd you say it?"

Be careful how you respond, Dana, I warned myself. *Any mishaps and it's only going to hinder your getting any information from him that might be useful. Play it cool.*

I placed a hand on his chest and began to rub it lightly with my fingertips. "I meant what I said. I do trust you."

"But, you don't trust *her*. Am I right?"

"I really don't even know her, Mitch. How can I know whether or not I trust her?"

Even in the dim light of the moon shining through the window, I could see the expression on his face; and it was one that told me he was conjuring up some sort of idea. I knew it for certain when I added in the fact that he was also biting his lip,.

"We can remedy that," he began. "Why don't I invite her to Mom and Dad's tomorrow night while the guys and I rehearse? That way, the two of you can chat and afterward maybe we can have dessert together or something. I'm sure they wouldn't mind at all. They always liked Casey. What do you think?"

That was an easy answer. *Dana, just what have you gotten yourself into?*

I had to think fast. "I don't know if that's such a good idea. I mean, it's been almost a week since you got together with the guys, and I was really hoping to watch your rehearsal. I miss hearing you sing."

He laughed. "Baby, you hear me sing all the time. Besides, most of what we'll be doing tomorrow night is trying to figure out our set for the demo. I don't know how much actual playing is going to happen."

I must not have thought fast enough. "Well, uh...your mom may want to talk to me about the shower. It is coming up on Sunday afternoon, you know. I wouldn't want Casey to feel left out because she wasn't invited."

I realized immediately that I'd said the wrong thing.

"Now, there's an idea. Why don't you invite her to the shower? I think it would be a really nice gesture, considering the other girls from the bistro are going. Afterward, maybe the three of us can go out to dinner somewhere. It would give you a chance to chat with her a little."

I couldn't believe how far my foot would actually fit into my mouth. Right then, I was sure I had it in past the ankle and almost to my knee. I had to keep thinking. Surely, I could come up with a way to get myself out of this.

"Don't you think she'd be uncomfortable? She wouldn't know anyone other than me and maybe your mom and sisters. Besides, if I know your mom and Alexander, they'll prepare such a spread that no one will be able to think about dinner!"

Mitch rolled back toward me and placed his arm around me so that my head was now resting on his shoulder. He kissed my forehead and placed his cheek against the top of my head.

"I know this isn't something you want to hear, but Casey actually had the opportunity to meet not only my family but a lot of their friends. She attended a couple of parties Mom threw while we were dating. I have to honestly say that I doubt she'd be very uncomfortable.

If anything, she'd probably be glad to see everyone again. Some of them are people she used to serve at the country club."

I was at a loss for words, so I just lay there silently trying to figure out how I could still wriggle my way out of this mess. As if a cold fish had been slapped across my face, the realization came that there was absolutely nothing I could say or do at that point that would change his mind. I was stuck—stuck with his ex-girlfriend at my baby shower.

He lifted his head slightly to look at me. "You're awfully quiet all of a sudden. Did I upset you?"

You just invited the mystery ex to my shower—of course, you upset me! "Not really," I answered softly.

He kissed me again and cuddled up close. "Good. Then it's settled. I'll mention it to Casey tomorrow—unless you'd rather do it yourself."

Please, spare me the gory details!! "No, that's okay. You can ask her."

He rolled back to his side, drew me in close, and began to nibble my neck again. "Okay. Now, where were we?"

Did he *really* think our conversation had put me in more of an amorous mood? I took a deep breath, let it out slowly, and got close to his ear. "Mitch, I'm pretty tired. I'd really like to go to sleep now."

He moved his lips to meet my mouth, but I didn't respond to his kiss. He pulled away, and I heard him exhale loudly. "You weren't too tired to talk about Casey a minute ago."

"I am tired now. I'm sorry."

He let out another exasperated breath and kissed me softly. "All right then, but know I won't fall asleep very easily tonight." He rolled away from me and turned the opposite direction. "Good night, sweetheart. Pleasant dreams."

As I closed my eyes and my mind began to race once more, I somehow knew that it was going to be a long night.

The next morning I awakened once more to an empty bed, but this time there was a note lying on Mitch's pillow. Sleepily, I wiped my eyes and forced them to focus on his words.

"Dana, You seemed to be sleeping so peacefully that I didn't want to wake you up. After you read this note, give me a call at work so I can say 'good morning' to you. I love you with all my heart. Love, Mitch."

At the bottom beneath his signature was a smiley face, but instead of a circle it was shaped like a heart. I smiled as I reached for the portable phone on the nightstand and dialed the number for Gartano's.

Three rings later the sound of his voice gave me goose bumps, and I suddenly felt like a giddy teenager. "Gartano's Italian Bistro; this is Mitch. May I help you?"

"Hi handsome! I miss you."

I could hear him chuckle softly. "Hey, baby. You miss me? You just woke up!"

"I know, but I don't like to wake up without you here. Why did you leave home so early?"

"It's not early, sweetheart. It's almost eleven. In fact, I was just telling Casey that I'm probably going to let her fly solo at some point today because it looks like we're going to have a full house again. I think she can handle it. She did really well yesterday, and Kayla said the customers all seemed to like her." He paused for a moment and cleared his throat. "You really must have been tired last night. When I left home this morning, you were sleeping like a rock! How are you feeling?"

Well, I was feeling fine until you mentioned Miss Touchy-Feely. Now, I think I have some nausea coming on.

"I'm okay, I guess. I can't really tell yet."

"Well, you just take it easy today and don't overdo things, all right? Chris mentioned something last night about Trudy having you and Ang over for lunch. I guess she's going to call you about it."

As I lay in bed the night before, I had concocted what I thought was a brilliant plan to spend time at the bistro and do some additional spying on Casey Tomlin. Just before the lunch crowd filed in, I planned to arrive at Gartano's and snag my husband before he had an opportunity to pair Casey with any of the other waitresses. I would explain that I had been 'thinking' and had decided that it probably wouldn't hurt to spend some one-on-one time with her. After all, if I was going to give her a chance, I had to get to know her, right? Then I would volunteer to train her myself. I really thought this was a plan Mitch would go for. I wouldn't be doing any actual waitressing, and I would be 'getting to know' Casey, thus proving to him that I was feeling more confident about the situation. I could subtly ask questions—as if I really wanted to befriend her—and little by little I could solve the mystery.

Now, Mitch's synopsis of Casey's progress at work, coupled with the potential luncheon at Trudy's, threw a monkey wrench into my scheme. First of all, if he thought she was doing that well and ready to be on her own, there wouldn't be any need for me to provide further training. I would be the proverbial 'third wheel'—totally not needed and in the way. Second, Mitch knew that even if I did have plans they wouldn't be anything so detrimental that they couldn't be altered in order to go to Trudy's. So, it seemed I'd spend another day in darkness. Or, *would* I? Suddenly, it hit me like a lightning bolt from the sky. Trudy and Angelina both knew Casey. Even if they hadn't spent a lot of time around her, they would know *something* about her. They would probably know enough to give me some clues into the how's and why's of Mitch's relationship with her. It might not be everything I was looking for, but it was a beginning.

"Honey, are you still there?"

"Oh, yeah, I'm here. Sorry. I got distracted for a minute."

"Okay. Well, I need to get going. That line outside is getting longer by the minute. Enjoy your day, and I'll see you later. I love you."

"I love you, too."

I hung up the phone and plopped back down against the pillows as I covered my eyes with my forearm. Thinking back on the whole waitressing fiasco, I almost wished at that moment he *had* hired Kelly. She may have looked like a harlot, but at least she wasn't an ex-girlfriend.

After taking a minute to freshen up, I meandered downstairs for a bagel and a cup of hot tea. I decided it would probably be best not to overindulge in case the luncheon did materialize. Just as that thought crossed my mind, the phone rang; and I received the official invitation. Angelina and Megan would be arriving at Trudy's around twelve-thirty, and I was welcome to come anytime I wanted with lunch to be served around one. I accepted and hung up the phone, glancing at the clock as I did. Eleven-twenty. That gave me about an hour or so to figure out Plan B, which I decided to name "Operation Grill and Fill." As I discreetly 'grilled' my sister-in-laws for info on Casey, I would be not only 'filled' with information but food as well. I knew it sounded corny, but it was the best I could do on such short notice. I sat down at the table with my breakfast and began to let my mind do its work.

Casey was filling a bus pan with dirty dishes as Mitch approached. She paused for a moment to look up at him with a smile.

"How am I doing so far, boss?" she asked playfully.

"No complaints from me," he replied with a smile of his own. "You're doing a fantastic job."

"Thank you. That's one thing about you that definitely hasn't changed. You are always so sweet, Mitch."

The way she looked at him caused him to blush; and hoping she wouldn't see, he turned away quickly.

"Well, I don't know about that. Go talk to Dana, and I'm sure she might give you a different story at times."

"That's just the way it is with wives, I guess. But, you know, she seems really sweet, too. I'm glad I had the chance to meet her yesterday. I still can't believe you didn't tell me you two were having a baby—whoops—I mean *babies*."

"Simply a blunder on my part. Hey, speaking of babies, my family's throwing Dana a shower on Sunday afternoon out at my parents' estate. I know it's short notice, but she asked me to tell you that she'd really like for you to attend. You'll know most of the people there, and afterward, I thought the three of us could go out to dinner. Dana would like the chance to get to know you a little better." He flashed her his irresistible smile, and this time she blushed. "What do you say?"

"Sounds great!" Then the smile slowly faded. "Are you sure I won't be imposing? I'm sure your mom already has everything planned."

"Nonsense! I'm sure Mom will be glad to have you there. Don't think any more about it because it's settled. I'll tell her tonight."

Casey followed Mitch with her eyes as he walked away, and she smiled. A year or so ago she never dreamed she'd see him again. Now, here she was working for him and rekindling their friendship. Friendship. When she met him again that day in the hospital, all the old feelings came rushing back; and she felt almost as if she'd never spent a day away from him—until he told her he was married. She recalled the feeling that had given her. It was as if someone had taken their fist and thrust it right into the pit of her stomach. Her mind had not allowed her any rest that night as she dwelled on it and cursed herself. Why hadn't she told him the truth the day they broke up? Why hadn't she said what was really on her mind instead of pretending that she, too, thought they should part ways? If she'd only been honest, maybe things would have been different—maybe it would have been her wearing his ring. There was no chance of that now. After meeting Dana and especially after seeing that she was pregnant, she now knew it for sure. She glanced up at Mitch again as he stood at the counter lost in conversation with Joe. He still had a way of making her weak in the knees when she looked at him. She turned away before he noticed her and let out a sigh as she returned to her work. She would think of something. She had to.

I was sifting through a stack of eye shadow compacts when the phone rang.

"Hi, Dana, it's Trudy," she began. She sounded a bit frazzled. "I'm sorry to do this, but I'm going to have to cancel our lunch date today. Alexis was feeling a little under the weather this morning, and I thought it was just a cold—until she came to me fifteen minutes ago and threw up in the middle of the floor."

"Oh, my," I remarked. "What do you think it is?"

"Probably just a case of the flu. She spent the night with my sister's little girl a few days ago, and Charlotte called last night to say that Annie was sick, too."

"Well, please tell her that I hope she feels better soon."

"Thanks, Dana. We'll try this again next week or something, okay?"

"Okay. Bye, Trudy."

I replaced the phone on its cradle and plopped down on the side of the bed. It looked as if yet another wrench had been thrown into my plan. As I checked the clock on the wall, I realized it was too late to instigate the initial scheme at Gartano's. With the luncheon being cancelled, 'Operation Grill and Fill' was now null and void as well. The only hope I had left was to try to interrogate Olivia tonight while Mitch was holding his rehearsal. Maybe she would be able to provide some sort of insight that would help me piece this whole puzzle together.

The evening didn't come soon enough for me; and as we made our way to Jake and Olivia's, I formulated in my head my method of questioning Olivia. I would have to be subtle. Mitch's mother was a very perceptive person, and the last thing I wanted was for her to catch on to what I was trying to do. Perhaps the way to approach this was to let Mitch bring up the shower, tell her about Casey, and see how she reacted. Then I could take it from there. I started to go over potential sets of dialogue that might take place and was deep in thought when Mitch reached out for my hand.

"You haven't said much since we left home, sweetheart. Something on your mind?"

"Huh? I'm sorry. What did you say?"

He chuckled. "I asked if you had something on your mind. Anything you'd like to talk about?"

Naturally, I wasn't about to tell him that I was planning to play 'Twenty Questions' with his mother. "No, not really." I faked a yawn. "I'm just a little sleepy, that's all."

"You didn't have to come with me. I wouldn't have minded your staying home to rest."

I leaned over against his shoulder. "I wanted to come. Remember I told you that I've missed hearing you sing."

"That's right. You did tell me that, didn't you?"

As we started to walk toward the house, Mitch stopped suddenly, swept me into his arms, and delivered a long, passionate kiss. I pulled away breathless, and he smiled.

"What was that for?" I asked.

"The mood struck me, that's all." He placed his arm around my shoulders and led me toward the house.

The guys were gathered in the rec room eagerly awaiting Mitch's arrival. As he entered the room, they applauded; and he took a playful bow.

"Hey, Trip," Zach greeted. "Feeling better?"

"Absolutely!" Mitch quipped cheerfully. "I hope you don't mind meeting here again, but I want to get the outbuilding soundproofed before we try playing at our place. I don't want to make a bad first impression on my neighbors by hitting them with all that noise."

Newbie laughed. "I take it that means none of them have heard you sing yet, huh?"

The other four laughed, and Mitch smirked. "Very funny. Now, are you losers ready to discuss this demo? I called Steve today, and he has us down for next Monday. That gives us less than a week to get things together." He gave them a confident smile. "But, I have no doubt we can make it work. I have a few ideas for songs, but I want your input, too."

Deciding they would probably be doing more talking than playing for a while, I slipped quietly out of the room to seek out Olivia and begin the questioning. As luck would have it, she was sitting alone at the kitchen table leafing through a stack of recipe cards. I glanced around to make sure Jake and Alexander were not close by, and then I took a seat next to her.

"Hi, Olivia," I greeted. "I'm not interrupting you, am I?"

"Of course not," she smiled. "I was just sorting through some recipes for the shower on Sunday. Maybe you can help me make a decision." She pulled two cards from the stack closest to her and held one up in each hand. "I can't decide between the Chicken Salad Supreme or the Seven-Layer Salad. Which do you prefer?"

I shrugged. "I don't think I'll be of much help because I like them both," I replied. "Which recipe makes more?"

She turned the cards toward herself and glanced at both. "I think I can make the chicken salad go further."

"Then go with that one," I suggested. "I'll be happy with anything."

She nodded and placed the card to the side. "Then it's settled. Chicken salad it will be." She sat back in her chair and focused her eyes on me as she smiled. "What's new with you?"

Olivia, you couldn't have asked a better question. "Well, not so much with me," I started, "but Mitch hired a new waitress. You might know her. Casey Tomlin."

"Oh, yes! Mitch called me from work today and gave me the good news. I don't think he could have picked a better girl for the job. She's so sweet and was always getting compliments when she worked at the country club. Everyone was so disappointed when she left."

"You do like her then?"

She looked a little surprised by my question. "Yes, Dana. I like her very much! Don't you?"

"To be honest, I only had a quick introduction. Other than that, I don't know a thing about her. Mitch never mentioned her until he came home the other night and said he'd hired her."

Now, she really looked surprised. "I find that strange considering how open Mitchell is about most things," she said. "He did tell you that the two of them dated for a while, didn't he?"

"Yes, he did mention something about that."

Her face seemed to light up the way Mitch's did the night he hired Casey. "I remember the night he first brought her home to meet everyone. Granted, most of us already knew her vaguely from the country club, but we didn't know she could sing. When Mitch sat down to play the piano and the two of them began to sing together, I swear I thought I was listening to a couple of angels! She has a beautiful voice ke he does. I think that may be why they got along so well together. They had something in common."

So that's the connection, I thought. "She sings?"

"Yes, she does. I believe she plays the piano, too. That's why she moved to Chicago. She was going to be in a band or something like that. I guess it didn't work out, so she moved back to Philadelphia—at least that's what Mitch told me on the phone this morning. I was surprised because she seemed to be very talented from what I remember."

I let Olivia's words sink in for a moment and pondered a few thoughts as they began to roam through my head. It seemed to me as if Casey and Mitch were the perfect match. Not only were they both gorgeous from top to bottom, but they shared a mutual talent and love for music. Top it all off with the fact that it seemed his mother adored her—what reason on earth did he ever have to break up with her? That was a piece of the puzzle I would still need to fit. Perhaps there was something deeper, and perhaps it was an answer only Mitch or Casey could provide. However, it wouldn't hurt to ask.

"Wow, that's really something. But, one thing I have to wonder about: if they had that much in common and got along so well, why didn't they stay together?"

She shrugged and offered a soft smile. "I can't really answer that, Dana. I suppose there are still some things even a mother doesn't know."

"What don't you know?" I looked up to see my husband entering the room with a half smile on his face.

Olivia glanced my way and winked. "A lot of things."

He walked to the refrigerator, withdrew a pitcher of cold water, and poured himself a tall glass. "I don't know, Mom. You always seemed to know what I was up to."

"Not always. I only wanted you to think I did so you'd stay out of trouble." She laughed. "That didn't always work, now did it?"

Mitch smirked. "Hey—I wasn't the bad kid. That was Chris. You must have us confused. We do resemble one another, you know."

"Yeah—like night and day!"

"Okay, okay, so I wasn't perfect as a kid. But, I grew out of it, didn't I?"

Olivia and I looked at each other and simply laughed.

"Okay, fine. I didn't." He came to stand behind my chair, leaned forward, and wrapped his arms around me. "Am I still lovable?"

I turned to look into the face that caused my heart to skip a beat. "I suppose," I said playfully. He smiled and gave me a kiss.

He stood up but kept a hand on my shoulder. "Mom, I told you that Casey's coming to the shower on Sunday, didn't I? She's really excited about seeing everyone again."

"Yes, you told me, and I think everyone will be excited to see her again. I haven't told the girls yet. I may keep quiet and let them be surprised when she gets here."

"That's cool," Mitch said. "Don't worry about sending her a formal invitation or anything. I gave her the time; and of course, she already knows how to get here. I told her Dana's registered at Baby World, too, so it's all taken care of."

Olivia smiled brightly. "Great! Be sure to tell her that I'm glad she'll be joining us."

Mitch gave my shoulder a little rub and leaned forward again to look at me. "Why don't you sit tight here with Mom for a while, honey? We're going to debate about a second song for the demo, and then we'll be starting the set for Saturday—maybe ten or fifteen more minutes."

I glanced at Olivia. She was replacing recipe cards into the box, so I decided most likely our conversation about Casey was over. I turned to Mitch.

"Well, considering these children have decided to lay on my bladder again, I think I'd better make a pit stop. As slow as I move, it'll take me ten minutes to do that."

I followed Mitch; and once we had cleared the doorway of the kitchen into the family room, he put his arm around my shoulders. "Did you and Mom have a nice conversation?"

"Yes, we did."

"What'd you talk about?"

I gave him a sideways glance. "Nothing really. She asked me what was new, and I told her." There was no way I was telling him we talked about Casey.

"What'd you tell her was new?"

"Nothing."

Now, he glanced at me. "You sat there for twenty minutes and talked about nothing?"

"Uh-huh."

He withdrew his arm and shrugged. "Okay. If you don't want to tell me, that's fine. I don't need to know."

I stopped and turned toward him. "There's nothing to tell, Mitchell. She asked what was new. I told her nothing. We decided on Chicken Salad Supreme over Seven-Layer Salad. That was it."

He resumed his trek toward the rec room. "Gee. Sounds exciting."

"You wanted to know."

Mitch rejoined his group, and I meandered in the direction of the bathroom a few doors down. After taking care of the matter at hand, I went to the rec room and settled into my chair at the back of the room. The guys were still in the midst of their discussion; so I leaned back, closed my eyes, and allowed my brain to rewind itself to a few days earlier. First, I thought about Mitch's reaction to my initial questions about Casey. Judging by the smile that had adorned his face, there was no doubt that his memories of her were all pleasant ones. He revealed nothing during the conversation that even resembled what I would see as a typical ex-boyfriend's point of view. The most obvious sign of this was the mere fact that he had hired her. As baffled as I was by her wanting to work with him, I was just as baffled by him wanting to work with her. This told me clearly that their parting was amicable and that they still had enough good feelings about each other to know that a day-to-day meeting wouldn't be an issue. If they'd had a bitter parting, this wouldn't be the case.

I now fast-forwarded to my conversation with Olivia. She, too, seemed to harbor happy memories of Casey and had only kind things to say about her. Of course, I had never heard Olivia speak negatively about anyone, but even the kindest mother would show some sort of distaste toward a woman who had hurt her son in any way. There was no way that same mother would openly welcome the woman back into her home. This again backed up my theory that the break-up had not been unpleasant. Given the fact Olivia went on to disclose Casey's musical talents—and with music being one of Mitch's true loves—it led me back to the question of just what *had* gone wrong between them. All of their commonalities and the positive regard they still seemed to hold for one another didn't add up to a separation. I needed to find out what had happened, and that might point me to why Casey wanted back in Mitch's life.

Finally, I jumped to yesterday and my own impressions of her. Within mere moments of meeting her, I had come to the conclusion that Casey Tomlin wasn't really who she wanted everyone to believe she was. There was something lurking beneath the surface of that pretty face. She was much too meticulous in her appearance—not a hair out of place nor a wrinkle in her clothing anywhere to be seen. Clearly, she was out to impress those around her. Granted, there was nothing wrong with wanting to look your best, but it seemed she took it a bit too far. It was almost as if she hoped the perfection on the outside would detract from the imperfection on the inside. Next was that sugary personality. I couldn't believe that even Mother Teresa—God bless her—was that nice *all* the time. All that said to me was that Casey was sucking up. But, to whom and for what? The only answer I could come up with for the 'whom' was Mitch. I still didn't know the 'for what.'

Not wanting to speculate until I had the chance to find out more, I decided it was time to turn my attention to other things. I opened my eyes and focused back on the front of the room where the six men were now gathered around their instruments. Mitch took a drink of water and positioned himself at the mike while Newbie tapped out the first few beats of the song on his cymbal. The other four joined in, and Mitch began to sing—his voice strong and pure. He saw me looking at him just then, and he smiled. As we locked eyes for that moment, I vowed that I would do whatever it took to keep him from falling prey to whatever Casey Tomlin might have up her sleeve.

As Ace wound down their last song for the night, Mitch turned to all of them with an expression that was nothing short of complete satisfaction.

"I don't know how Remington can refuse to take us if we go in there sounding like we did tonight," he said. "That was perfect, guys!"

"Let's hope we don't let our nerves blow it for us on Monday," Zach commented.

"Yeah, for sure," Newbie said.

Mitch shook his head. "That's why we're going to add these two to the set for Saturday, and we're also going to rehearse Sunday night.

We'll have it down so well that it'll be second nature. You'll be able to play that demo in your sleep."

My ears perked up at Mitch's words. Did he say they were rehearsing *Sunday* night? Maybe he'd forgotten about our plans with Casey. I could only hope.

My hope was short-lived. "Ah, no, I can't rehearse Sunday night. Dana and I have dinner plans." He sighed, but then his expression brightened. "Well, no worries. I'm sure they'll let us do a quick run-through at the studio before we record."

I liked the Sunday night deal better myself, I thought.

"Good. That takes care of that. Now, why don't we call it a wrap for tonight? I don't want to overwork the vocal cords on my first night back. I feel fine, but you never know."

"Makes sense to me," Newbie said. "Same time tomorrow night?"

Mitch nodded. "Yeah, sounds good."

Slowly easing myself to a standing position, I caught Mitch's hand and helped walk his friends to the door. After everyone had gone, I turned to him and pulled him into my embrace. Without saying a word, I kissed him—a long, slow, passionate kiss filled with all the love I could give him. He moved away and looked deep into my eyes. His expression was full of surprise.

"What was that for?" he asked.

I smiled. "Oh, let's just say the mood struck me."

Chapter 16

Over the next few days, I tried my best to downplay my curiosity about Casey and was careful not to ask too many questions. When Mitch would come home from work to tell me what a wonderful job she was doing, how well she was fitting in, and how much the customers seemed to like her, I didn't scream or throw things at him even though sometimes the urge struck me. Instead, I would sit quietly—usually with a forced smile on my face—and nod when I felt it was appropriate. If I was feeling particularly kind, I might even throw in a 'that's nice, sweetie' for effect. The last thing I needed was for him to figure out my plan.

On Thursday afternoon at two, the Morgan Furniture delivery team filled our empty living room; and on Friday evening at Lamaze class, we learned the how's and why's of colic, projectile vomiting, and messy diapers. I vowed to Mitch in a squeamish tone that if our children experienced any of those things I would be more than happy to let him handle it. He simply laughed and said he'd be glad to.

Saturday's show went without a hitch, and it was obvious to me and everyone else that Mitch was glad to be back on stage. The songs they had chosen for the demo sounded fantastic, and Mitch was certain that the guys would make Steve a proud man come Monday morning.

On Sunday morning, Mitch awakened me around seven-thirty, and I eased out of bed with a groan. Usually, Sundays were a pleasant, lazy day that Mitch and I could enjoy together doing nothing more than being in each other's company. However, not today. Today was going to be hustle and bustle from the word go: first church, then the shower, and then dinner with Casey. I'd barely taken five steps toward the bathroom, and already I felt like doing an about-face and jumping back into bed.

While I washed my face and tried to come to life, I could hear the cheerful sound of my husband singing downstairs. A moment later I thought I detected the aroma of some sort of food wafting up the stairs. Knowing that Mitch wasn't one to cook, I hurried to the kitchen to save from him burning down the house.

"What are you doing?" I asked as I approached.

He was standing over the toaster staring down into it with eager anticipation. "I'm making a couple of frozen waffles. Why?"

I breathed a sigh of relief that he wasn't attempting to use the stove, and I wouldn't be needing to call the fire department. "I was only wondering. I could smell them upstairs."

He inhaled deeply. "Yeah, they do smell pretty good, don't they? I thought a light breakfast was in order today since we'll both be eating a lot later on."

The toaster popped up the waffles; and Mitch tossed them onto a plate, smothered them with butter and syrup, and handed them to me. "Here. You take these, and I'll make more for myself. Do you want some coffee or a glass of milk?"

I knew I should avoid the caffeine, but today I also knew I'd need it. "Coffee, please."

I sat down at the table, and Mitch delivered my coffee to me. "There you are, love." He kissed my forehead. "Today's a big day for you. Are you excited?"

I wanted to ask him if I looked excited, but I didn't. "I guess so," I replied without much enthusiasm.

He gave me a curious look. "You don't sound like it." He smiled. "You aren't nervous about all the people being at the shower, are you? You've met them all before."

I shrugged. "No, not really."

He moved back to the toaster, placed two more waffles into the slots, and pushed down the button. "Well, I think you'll have a lot of fun. It sounds like Mom and the girls really went all out for this thing. I know Casey's looking forward to it. She said the last baby shower she went to was when her niece was born nine years ago."

"That's nice," I said.

"She's also looking forward to the three of us having dinner tonight. We decided that Charley's sounded good. She loves that mushroom burger they have, and she said she's been craving one. I told her you like to go there, too. What do you think?"

That you should have discussed it with your wife instead of your ex. "That's fine."

He prepared his breakfast and came to join me at the table. "I was thinking, too, that I can take you out to Mom and Dad's, and Casey can bring you home. I'll be ready when you get back, and we can go from there."

Oh, no. No way. Think fast, Dana. Think fast! "That would be kind of silly, don't you think? Casey's going to be driving her own car to Charley's, so why not have her go ahead and get us a table? Trudy has to come this way anyway, so she can drop me back along with my gifts."

I held my breath as I tried to study the look on his face. I wasn't sure if he was considering my proposal or preparing for a counterattack.

He nodded. "Yeah, I suppose that makes more sense. I'm sure she won't mind doing that." He took a sip of his coffee and smiled at me across the table. "Did I tell you that she got a $10 tip from some guy yesterday? I told her he was probably trying to hit on her, although he was old enough to be her father." He laughed. "She didn't believe me, but I caught him checking her out a couple of times when she wasn't paying attention. I wonder if he'll come in tomorrow."

"That's nice, sweetie," I replied again with little enthusiasm.

I surmised that my lack of interest prompted him to change the subject. "I'm glad we decided on Charley's for dinner tonight. I'm sure I'll be stuffing my face with the guys today, and I doubt I'll be wanting much more than a burger later."

I decided to show some interest as long as the subject wasn't Casey. "What are you having?"

"Well, Paul is bringing cheese steaks from Pat's. Jim is making his famous chip dip, and Chris said he's bringing a couple dozen cookies that Trudy made yesterday. Dad said he'd supply the soda. As for the others, they all said they'd pitch in something too; but I don't know what. I'm sure we won't be wanting for anything to eat today."

"Doesn't sound like it."

"It's okay, though. We're going to go out afterward and play some football, so I'll work it all off before you ever get home."

I stood and carried my plate to the sink. "You mean if you can move well enough to work it off."

He laughed. "I won't eat *that* much!"

"I'm sure I will. Then again, I can't move now, so it won't matter for me."

He laughed again and put his arms around me. "Don't you worry about it, love. I'll carry you wherever you need to go if I must."

"Thanks. It's nice to know I can count on you."

He smiled and looked right into my eyes. "Always."

We made it to church just as Pastor Michaels was addressing the congregation. Rather than trying to make me maneuver my belly past five people already seated in the pew, the Tarrington clan all slid down to the left. Mitch sat down, and I took the seat next to him on the aisle. This had become our routine for the past four weeks—the location allowed for an easy escape to the ladies' room if the children decided to kick my bladder during the service. Just as I'd begun to settle in, the pastor instructed everyone to stand for the opening hymn. I sighed, grabbed Mitch with one hand, the back of the pew in front of me with the other, and pushed myself back up onto my already aching feet. Mitch smiled and moved closer to me as he placed the hymnal where we could both see it.

After three songs, a word of prayer, and the passing of the offering plate, I was thankful for the opportunity to sit down again. Mitch brought his arm around me to rest on the back of the pew—his fingertips lightly stroking my shoulder. As the sermon began, I felt a wave of guilt come over me as I heard Pastor Michaels say something about being critical of others and how God will ultimately judge us the way we judge them. Mitch turned toward me slightly with that lopsided smirk of his and chuckled. I promptly elbowed him lightly in the ribs and sunk down into the pew.

The service ended, and I made my way to the ladies' room as I did each week while Mitch joined his family at the back of the church. By the time I returned, everyone had gone; and Mitch was holding his car keys and waiting patiently for me.

"Where is everyone?" I asked.

"They all had stuff to get done for this afternoon. Come on—I'll take you home to change, and then we'll head to Mom and Dad's."

Back at home I stood in front of the full length mirror as I studied the new outfit I'd purchased to wear to the shower. Mitch came to stand in the doorway, and a slow smile came to his face as he looked at me.

"Are you sure there won't be any men at this shower today?" he asked.

I straightened the collar on my blouse and turned sideways to inspect my profile. "No, only women. Why?"

"Because you look totally hot, and I don't want to have to worry about anyone hitting on you."

I started to laugh. "You're such a goof!"

He came to me and turned me to face him. "No, I'm not. You are beautiful, Dana." He gently brushed the hair back from my face. "I'm a very lucky man." He leaned down to kiss me, and I could feel the warmth of his love move through me from head to toe. He moved away from me and smiled softly. "We'd better get going before you get *me* going."

I turned toward the mirror once more. "Are you sure I look all right? I don't look like a blimp, do I?" I turned to the side again. "I swear I'm getting bigger every day."

"You're supposed to get bigger. You're pregnant, remember?"

"You never answered my question."

"I told you that you look beautiful. Stop worrying, and let's get you to your party. You don't want to be late."

I started away from the mirror, but as I did I caught a glimpse of my backside and stopped dead in my tracks.

I'd been holding Mitch's hand, and my motion caused him to jerk backward. "What's the matter?"

"No, Mitch. I can't wear this. It makes my butt look like the side of a barn!" I let go of his hand and headed into the closet. "I have to change."

Mitch promptly followed me, took my hand again, and gently but firmly led me out of the closet and toward the bedroom door. "No, you don't. That outfit is very nice, and you look fine. We have to go."

I glanced back again as he continued to usher me down the stairs and out to the car. As we pulled out of the garage, I made one last plea.

"I don't want to wear this outfit, Mitchell. Please take me back so I can change."

Once we had rounded the corner onto the main road, he took my hand. "Now, just settle down and allow yourself to have a good time, okay? You really do look beautiful. You'll be the prettiest girl there. You'll stand out in the crowd."

"Yeah—with a physique like this, how could I get lost?"

He chuckled and pulled me against his shoulder. "What am I going to do with you?"

A few minutes later Mitch was easing the car onto the lane leading up to his parents' house. I glanced down at my stomach and placed both hands there.

"Well, this is it. Prepare to be overwhelmed," I said to my unborn children.

Mitch gave me a strange sideways glance. "Honey, I don't think they're really going to know what's happening. Do you?"

I shrugged. "I don't know. But, why take the chance?"

He bit his lip. "Okay, dear. Whatever you say."

He came around to open my door; and once I was out of the car, he took my hand and led me inside. Olivia greeted us at the door and offered a hug.

"You look lovely, Dana," she said as her eyes moved over me. "Is that a new outfit?"

I nodded. "Yes, it is. I picked it up at Carlson's. They were having a great sale."

As if Mitch had disappeared, she placed an arm around my shoulders and began to walk toward the dining room as we continued to chat about the joys of shopping. Mitch cleared his throat loudly, and I turned around.

"Don't I even get a kiss goodbye?"

Olivia and I exchanged a smile, and I walked back to where my husband stood. His own smile brightened as he encircled his arms around me.

"Have fun today, all right? When Trudy brings you home, I'll be all set to go to dinner."

I gave him a soft kiss and a gentle push toward the door. "You have fun, too, and be good."

He smirked and raised his eyebrows in an ornery fashion as he pointed to my stomach. "Honey, if I wasn't good, there'd be no need for this shower today!"

"Oh, Mitchell, I swear...." I simply shook my head as he grinned from ear to ear, and Olivia laughed.

Mitch finished the last bite of his second cheese steak sandwich and washed it down with the final swig of root beer left in the can. "Is anyone up for a friendly game of football?"

Jim groaned. "At least let the food get into our stomachs, Mitch. Anyone ever tell you you're a bit impatient?"

"Their twins are proof of that," Zach teased as everyone laughed.

"No, the twins are proof of my 'superior masculinity,'" Mitch retorted.

Now, the troupe roared with laughter. Jake patted him on the back. "Sorry, son, but I really don't think you had much to do with that. The mother determines multiple births, not the father."

Mitch glanced at his father from the corner of his eye. "Come on, Dad. You're supposed to back me up here. Thanks a lot."

"Don't mention it."

A few minutes later Mitch led his family and friends to the backyard where they chose teams for what they decided to call the 'Baby Bowl.' Mitch, Shep, Newbie, Paul, and Jake headed up one team while Chris, Ty, Ash, Jim, and Zach formed the other. They set up the goals and began to play with Mitch and Ty acting as quarterbacks. Mitch threw the ball—a perfect spiral—right into Newbie's hands who ran it almost to the goal before being brutally tackled by Ash and Jim. The two exchanged a high five and got ready to stop the touchdown. This time, Mitch faked the pass and ran the few yards over the goal, spiked the ball, and did his little touchdown dance. But unlike the pros on TV, he really had the moves and played it to the hilt. He teammates cheered as the others laughed.

He pointed at the other team with a huge grin. "See, that's how you score points. But, don't worry. We aren't going to let you do that anyway."

Chris got in his face and playfully pointed his finger right back. "You're going down, little brother. Prepare to eat some dirt."

Ty faded back for the pass and tossed the ball—only to have it intercepted by Shep. Newbie blocked Chris, but Ash slipped around him for the tackle.

"Why to go, dude!" Zach called. "We are so bad!"

"You can say that again. So bad, you're going to lose!" Shep told him.

The ball was snapped again; and this time Paul was in control, maneuvering expertly to the goal. He spiked the ball and struck a little he-man pose. "Spare us," Zach said with a smile.

For the next hour, the ten played like a pack of overgrown boys—their cheeks flushed from the heat, their t-shirts, faces, and brows wet with perspiration. On the last play, Mitch threw the ball to Jake knowing that his opponents would be hesitant to tackle the senior member of the brigade. He ran it in for the winning touchdown, spiked it, and was greeted with hugs and handshakes from his teammates. The other team sighed in defeat but congratulated him as well.

"Nice play, Jake," Ty commented, "and very ingenious on your part, Trip."

"Hey, it takes more than that 'superior masculinity' to play the game well, dude," Mitch said.

"Must be why that was your only good play of the game," Chris retorted.

"Who asked you?" Mitch answered with a grin. "At least I didn't need oxygen after running down the field. Face it, Christopher. You're out of shape."

Chris laughed at his brother and positioned himself in front of him as if he were preparing to wrestle. "You think so? Come on, little brother. Show me your moves."

In the blink of an eye, the two were rolling around on the ground, taking turns trying to pin the other. In one swift move, Chris brought Mitch's arm behind his back, flipped him over, and slammed him into the ground. His glasses flew off, and his chin hit the corner of a rock, causing a deep gash. Chris, unaware of the situation, stood in victory and began to tease his younger brother.

"So wise guy, you want to take back what you said?"

Mitch uttered something inaudible and brought his hand to his chin as he slowly sat up. The others who had been standing by watching in fun all rushed to his side when they saw his hand covered in blood.

Shep handed Mitch his glasses as Jim bent down to take a closer look. "Wow, buddy, that's some cut. What'd you hit?"

Paul picked up the rock and handed it to him. "Looks like this is your culprit."

"One rock in the entire yard, and I had to find it," Mitch uttered.

Chris, who had disappeared at the sight of the injury, suddenly reappeared with a wet paper towel. "Man, Mitch, I'm sorry. I didn't mean to hurt you."

Jim took the towel and dabbed at the cut. "Looks like it might need a few stitches," he said as he helped Mitch to his feet.

Mitch shook his head. "Nah, it's all right. I just need to wash it out a little."

Fifteen minutes and five stitches later, Mitch winced again as Jim placed a dab of antiseptic cream on the wound and covered it with a

Band-Aid. "Here. You take this and apply it for a few days until that starts to heal."

Mitch sighed heavily and his stubborn side began to show. "Do you go anywhere without that stupid medical kit?" he asked.

"Not usually," Jim said with a grin. "I'm a doctor. I'm supposed to carry it with me for occasions such as this."

Chris sat down next to Mitch again—his face full of remorse. "I'm really sorry. I was only goofing around. You aren't mad at me, are you?"

Mitch shook his head. "No. It was an accident. No worries, man." Then he smiled. "I'll take it as a payback for that cut I gave you last Christmas Eve."

Chris patted him on the shoulder. "Sounds good to me."

I breathed a deep sigh of relief as Kayla's bright smile met mine. I rushed to her side and placed a hand on her shoulder.

"Thank goodness you got here when you did," I started. "If I have to listen to one more person tell me how 'big' I am and how I'm 'glowing,' I swear I'll scream!"

She laughed and hooked her arm through mine as she walked toward two empty seats at the head table. "There won't be any screaming today, baby girl—not unless you go into labor. And you better not do that because those two little buns still need time in the oven!"

We were about to sit down when our attention was drawn toward the clamor at the front door. We heard the sounds of Olivia and Trudy as they extended a giddy greeting to the newest guest, and a minute later we witnessed the 'hug exchange' between Julia, Angelina, and Casey.

I leaned close to Kayla's ear. *"Now* can I scream?"

"You be nice," she warned. "You knew she was going to be here. If you didn't want her, you shouldn't have invited her."

I sighed. "I didn't. Mitch did. It was all his idea, believe me. What's worse, I get to have dinner with her later, too. He thinks we should 'get to know each another.'"

Kayla gave me that tough love expression of hers that she knew I didn't like. "He's right. You should get to know her. She really is a nice girl, not to mention a friend of your husband's."

Poor Kayla. Casey has her fooled, too. "Ex-girlfriend. She's an ex-girlfriend; and frankly, I have no desire to get to know her. As far as I'm concerned, she can...."

"May I have everyone's attention? If everyone will take a seat, we can get started." Angelina was taking charge, and I was thankful that I could sit down and avoid having to greet Casey.

After some brief introductions, Angelina turned the floor over to me; and I struggled to my feet to make my 'opening remarks.'

"Hello, everyone," I started. "First of all, I want to apologize that this shower is taking place so soon after the first one; but you can blame that on Mitch." Everyone laughed, and I continued. "As of September 18, I'll officially be seven months' pregnant, which means the twins are due around the end of November. Some of you have asked about the sexes. Well, one is a boy for sure, and the other one wouldn't cooperate; so I guess we'll just have to wait and see. Mitch and I are still discussing names. We can't seem to agree on anything at this point—so we may end up calling them Baby 1 and Baby 2 for a while." Everyone laughed again. "Anyway, thanks for coming today, and I hope you all have a nice time." I sat back down, and Kayla smiled at me.

Olivia stood up and addressed the group. "I'd like to ask Glenda Michaels, our pastor's wife, to say grace for us; and we'll eat first. Then the girls have some games planned before Dana opens her gifts."

When Mrs. Michaels finished, I was instructed to take the lead and started to move toward the buffet that Olivia and Alexander had prepared. Once again they had outdone themselves, and I began to take my fill of the soups, salads, fruits, and vegetables laid out before me. Homemade rolls fresh from the oven were filled to capacity with the Chicken Salad Supreme we had chosen to serve a few nights before. Hot coffee, cold iced tea, and lemonade provided the perfect means to wash everything down. The large sheet cake, taking up a table of its own, would be our dessert. It was decorated with teddy bears holding bright balloons and the words 'Welcome Tarrington Twins' which caused me to smile.

With both hands full, I turned to go back to my chair—only to be stopped by Mitch's Aunt Katherine. Preparing myself for a full interrogation, I took a deep breath and forced a smile.

"Dana, I wanted to tell you that I was very relieved by your little speech a few minutes ago. I'm embarrassed to admit this; but when Olivia told me you were expecting so soon after the wedding, I naturally assumed that was the reason you two had gotten married so quickly. Of course, I didn't say anything to Olivia, but I'm happy to hear that wasn't the case. I hope you'll forgive me for thinking that way in the beginning."

I looked at her, and my mouth almost fell open in complete and total disbelief. How could one person be lacking so much tact? Not sure how to answer, I gave her the only response I could conjure up at the time.

"It's all right, Aunt Katherine," I said softly. I glanced down at my food and did my best to smile again. "If you'll excuse me, I'd better find my seat. I don't want to be the last one done. Nice talking to you."

As I walked away, I overheard another aunt say to her, "Really? I have to say that I wondered about that myself." I simply shook my head and went back to sit down.

I relayed the story to Kayla, and she also shook her head in disbelief. "That took a lot of nerve for her to say that to you. But, don't let it bother you, sweetie. Some people are just narrow-minded."

I glanced in the direction of the table where all the aunts were now seated, engaging in their own henpecking ceremony. "I suppose so; but to be honest, I've wondered all along when someone would display that mentality to me. I'm sure it does seem strange to a lot of people that we got married so quickly and then almost immediately announced a pregnancy."

Kayla gave me her confident smile. "Like I said, don't you worry about what other people think. Those who really matter know the truth."

I nodded and gave her a little hug. "You're right. Thanks."

She took a bite of her sandwich and winked. "That's what I'm here for."

Everyone finished lunch, and Trudy and Julia led us in some party games. The most interesting of all was "Name that Baby." Everyone was directed to a board displayed near the gift table where a multitude of different baby pictures of myself and the Tarrington family were posted. So as not to make it obvious which little boy was Mitch, the girls had brought along pictures of Chris, Paul, and Jim to add to the display. Everyone was to mark their guesses on a piece of paper, and the person with the most correct won the prize. Although I didn't play myself, I stood close to Kayla as she inspected each photo. Once we were seated again, she turned to me.

"I may be wrong, but I doubt that I couldn't pick out which one was Mitch," she said. "That dimple of his gives it away!"

I smirked. "Well, I don't know. Paul has dark hair and dimples, too."

She pretended to pout. "Here I thought I had it all figured out."

Once the answers were revealed, Kayla and Aunt Elaina were tied for the win. Kayla gave me a smug look.

"See, I was right after all. And anyway, Paul may have dimples, but Mitch only has one. In his right cheek."

"You are so observant," I teased.

Once the prizes were awarded, I was instructed to move to the gift table along with Trudy and Julia. One would hand me the gift while the other made a list of what it was and who it was from. My eyes grew wide as I took my place. Without opening even one gift, I had no doubt that every item on my registry had been purchased and then some. Knowing it would take a while to get through everything, I opted to only read the names of the givers and save anything else for later. Multitudes of tiny clothing, diapers, bottles, and blankets soon covered the table along with diaper bags, toys, and essentials. Olivia, Julia, and Angelina added a double stroller, two car seats, and a playpen to the mix as well. I thought back to Chris and Mitch as Trudy presented the rocking chair and changing table she'd purchased, and I did my best to fake a surprised expression. I only hoped she didn't see through me.

Finally, I reached the end of the pile; and after opening the last gift, I thanked everyone again. Before I had a chance to return to my seat, however, Julia and Angelina handed me another box.

"We have one that we wanted to save for last, Dana," Julia said as she glanced at her sister with a sly smile.

I looked from one to the other as I remembered the teddy and silk boxers they'd presented to me at my bridal shower. "Oh, no," I said.

"No, no, this is something we're sure you'll want. Go on and open it," she prompted.

Slowly, I undid the ribbon and carefully pulled the paper loose from the end of the box. Not sure what to expect, I hesitated before taking off the rest of the paper and lifting the lid. Pulling back the tissue paper, my eyes focused on a photo album with the words 'Our Story' embossed on the front. Lifting it from the box, I opened it to reveal pictures of Mitch and me starting as infants and ending with assorted shots of our wedding and more recent pictures of us over the past few months. Overwhelmed with sentiment, I looked up at the two who were smiling brightly.

"The last few pages are for the first pictures of the babies," Angelina said. "Then you can start each of them an album of their own."

"Mitch gave us the pictures of you that are in there. He said he had a heck of a time snatching them when you weren't looking."

I felt a tear trickle down my cheek. "It's beautiful. Thank you so much."

The sisters gave me a hug—followed close behind by Trudy and Olivia. Some of the guests began to move in for a closer look, and others inspected the gift table and mingled amongst themselves. Out of the corner of my eye, I saw Casey approaching and braced myself for a brief interlude. Before I had the chance to turn completely around, she was intercepted by Aunt Louise, Olivia, Trudy, and Julia who once again exchanged hugs with her. I watched as the five started into cheery conversation acting as if their reunion was the best thing that had ever happened to them. As I stood there observing the scene, a thought occurred to me. Casey had been someone of significance to not only the immediate Tarrington crew but the extended family as well. Could it be that this woman had been the clear choice for Mrs. Mitchell Tarrington, III, at one time? I was pondering that thought when I felt a soft touch on my shoulder.

"I hope you enjoyed the shower, Dana," Angelina started. "It seems like everyone had a good time." She paused for a moment as she noticed two more aunts join Casey's entourage. "I was really surprised to see Casey here today, too. I couldn't believe it when she told us that she's working with Mitch. I think that's great. She's a really sweet girl, and it was very nice of you to invite her."

Before I had a chance to formulate an answer, the Casey love-fest began to break up; and much to my dismay, she headed in my direction. I did my best to muster up a smile and reminded myself to be nice.

"Hi, Dana!" she said. "I've been meaning to talk to you all afternoon, but," she laughed a little, "every time I started to come your way someone would cut me off at the pass. I guess I've been away longer than I realized."

I took her line as a golden opportunity. "How long were you away from Philadelphia?"

"Almost a year and a half. I left in March of last year. I'm happy to be home again." She glanced around the room with a smile. "Anyway, thanks for inviting me today. It's been so great to see everyone again—and nice to see I was missed."

I sure wouldn't miss you if you went away, I thought. I tried to steer her back to the subject. "Now, you were in...where was it? Chicago?"

She turned her attention back to me. "Yeah, I was in Chicago. A friend of a friend of mine was auditioning female leads for his band, and I wanted to try out. It would have been an awesome opportunity, but things didn't exactly go the way I planned. I made a few more connections while I was there, but those didn't work out either; so I decided the best thing to do was come home." She smiled brightly. "I almost thought I was better off in Chicago because I really had a tough time finding a job here. But, fate led me to Gartano's, and here I am."

It was all I could do to keep from gagging on all that syrupy sweetness. "That's nice."

An awkward silence fell over us for a moment or two, and then Casey spoke again. "I'm looking forward to dinner with you and Mitch this evening. I was so excited when he suggested it! Athough I've been at the bistro a few days now, he and I haven't had much of an opportunity to really chat. I've been wanting to catch up on things with him." She paused for a moment and apparently decided she'd better put an addendum on her statement so as not to give me the wrong impression. "I really want to get to know you better, too, Dana. I think we can be good friends."

Controlling the gag reflex became even harder at that moment. I decided it was time to make an exit. "Well, Trudy's going to give me a ride home. I need to do a few things before we go out. Mitch and I were wondering if you would mind going ahead to Charley's and getting a table for us? We can meet you there."

She shrugged. "Sure, I'd be happy to do that."

"I see some of the guests are starting to leave. I'd better go say goodbye—don't want to be rude."

"Oh, okay. I guess I'll catch up with you once we get to Charley's."

"Yeah, see you there."

A short while later I bid Olivia goodbye and climbed into Trudy's van for the ride home. Although I was doing my best to engage in some sort of intelligible conversation with her, my mind was actually trying to formulate ways to get out of dinner with Casey. I could always go home and tell Mitch that I'd overeaten and wasn't hungry, but he'd simply instruct me to order a salad or something light from the menu just to go along. If I pretended to be sick, I'd have to keep that act up all night; and I didn't have the energy right then to pull it off. The tired routine was becoming overused to the point that I wasn't sure Mitch believed it anymore. Try as I might, nothing else came to mind; so I simply began to resign myself to the fact that our meeting was inevitable.

Instead of taking the time to unload my gifts right then, I gave Trudy my house key; and she promised that she and Chris would have everything in the house by the time we returned from dinner. I thanked her and trudged up the sidewalk.

Mitch was standing at the door looking sharp in his red alligator polo and khakis. He smiled brightly and offered a warm kiss as I stepped into the house.

"Hey, beautiful! How was your shower?"

I didn't answer because I spotted the stitches on his chin. "Honey, what happened? Are you okay?"

He chuckled. "I'm fine. Just a little wrestling injury—compliments of my brother. We were goofing around, and I fell on a rock." He twisted his back and rotated his left arm. "I didn't realize it until I was toweling off after my shower, but he did a number on my back, too. I'm feeling kinda stiff."

I gently lifted his chin to inspect it closer. The gash looked ugly, but the large purple bruise next to it looked even uglier. I placed a hand on the side of his face and stepped back hoping he wouldn't notice the light bulb that had suddenly come on over my head.

"Did you say your back hurts, too? Maybe we should cancel out on dinner. It sounds like you need to take some aspirin and lie down with the heating pad. I'm sure it's also going to hurt trying to open your mouth wide enough to bite into a hamburger."

He smirked at me, and I had to wonder if I'd been convincing enough with my concern. "Thank you for looking out for me, but I said I'm fine. Jim took care of it for me. Now, why don't you go freshen up a little, and we'll get going, okay?"

"Mitch, don't be so stubborn. You need to stay home and rest. I don't feel comfortable at all about us going out."

Now, he gave me the full view of his dimple. "I know you don't, but we're going." He gently prompted me in the direction of the stairs. "Go on and get yourself ready. I need to find another *Band-Aid* to put on this thing."

I touched up my makeup, ran a brush through my hair, and then stared at my reflection and sighed. No matter how much I didn't want it to, this evening's plan was going to take place; and there wasn't a thing I could do to change it. I would have to put on my fake smile, put forth my fake pleasant attitude, and fake interest in Casey and whatever she had to say. Then later when my husband rattled on about how nice she was and what a good time he had, I'd have to fake that I felt the same way. I didn't like dishonesty, and right then I felt very much that way. I sighed again and turned to see Mitch standing in the doorway—a soft, affectionate glow on his face.

Walking into the room, he reached out and pulled me into his arms. I laid my head against his chest and let myself savor the warmth of his embrace. "There's no need to be nervous about meeting with Casey tonight. All right?"

"I'm not nervous."

He pulled back enough to look into my eyes with a smirk. "You're sure about that?"

"Perfectly sure."

He kissed the top of my head as he stepped away from me. "I'm glad to hear that. Come on then. Let's get going. We don't want to keep her waiting there too long. She'll think we aren't coming."

Good—let's stall a few more minutes, and maybe she'll leave. I turned off the light and followed Mitch downstairs and out to the car.

Mitch offered his arm to me as we walked into Charley's, and he paused when we reached the door. "I love you, Dana. You know that, don't you?"

"Yes, I know that. I love you, too."

He tipped my chin up and caressed my cheek with his thumb as he kissed me softly. "Let's have a nice evening getting to know each other, okay?"

No problem—I plan to find out everything I can about Casey Tomlin. After tonight, the mystery will no longer be a mystery. I gave him a nod and a smile as he ushered me through the door.

About an hour into our quaint dinner for three, I began to realize that my plan wasn't going the way I'd anticipated. While I sat munching away on cheese fries, Casey and Mitch were taking a pleasant walk down 'Memory Lane.' I was beginning to feel like the chaperone on a date between two giddy teenagers the way they were reminiscing about the good times they'd had together. The only difference was a true chaperone would have quickly moved to sit between them in an effort to keep Miss Touchy-Feely from putting her mitts on him. I decided for something to do I would see how many times she placed a hand on his arm, hand, or shoulder; the count was now up to fifteen and steadily climbing. Glancing down at the spoon beside my plate, I thought about smacking Casey's hand with it the next time she touched him. However, I decided that might be a bit drastic.

By the time dessert arrived, I was no more informed about this woman than I had been before the evening began. The only new information I had was that her dog had died six months earlier. She remembered every detail of every date she and Mitch had gone on, and she still had the necklace with the music charm that she'd worn the night they met. The longer I sat there, the only thing that became clearer was that I was now even more baffled as to why the two ever parted ways—that and the fact it seemed they still had an attraction to each another. If not, they certainly weren't doing anything to convince me otherwise.

Finally, the check arrived, and my chivalrous husband volunteered to pick up the tab which earned him another 'you're so sweet' and a touch on the arm from Casey. As the three of us stood to leave, I moved in close to him and grabbed his hand in a firm grip that said both 'I love you,' and 'I'm making sure she knows to whom you belong.' The look I got from him clearly told me he understood.

Once outside, the three of us paused by the door to exchange goodbyes, and Casey gave me a smile.

"I really had a great time today, Dana. Thanks so much for letting me be a part of it." She glanced at Mitch with a flirtatious smile. "Make him take care of that nasty cut, too. I know how men can be about things like that." Turning back to me, she offered a hug which took me by surprise since I'd thought she reserved all those for Mitch. As I pulled away, I faked a smile and watched as she and my husband embraced as well. I stood silently and held my tongue as his eyes moved slowly over her as she stepped away and an approving smile came to his face. Taking Mitch's hand once more—firmly—I pulled him in the direction of the car before she had a chance to grab him again.

"Baby, can you let go so I can start the car?" Mitch asked.

I glanced out the windshield and watched as Casey's car disappeared from the parking lot. "I guess it's safe now. She's gone," I muttered.

Mitch started the car and turned to me with a baffled look. "What's that supposed to mean?"

I sighed. "Nothing, Mitchell. Absolutely nothing."

Leaning back against the seat, I closed my eyes and tried to allow myself to unwind. I felt Mitch take my hand and then the warmth of his tender kiss against it.

"I had a good time tonight. Did you?"

"I guess so."

"I'm glad you and Casey got to know each other a little. See, she's not so bad after all, is she?"

"I guess not."

"You know, it's too bad things didn't work out for her in Chicago. I know how badly she wanted that deal, but I suppose there's a reason for everything, huh?"

"I guess so."

He chuckled. "You're kinda short with your answers there, love. Don't feel like talking?"

"I guess not."

He laughed and kissed my hand again. "All right. You just relax, and we'll be home shortly."

As Dana settled into her seat, Mitch glanced at her and silently let out a heavy breath. The evening, planned as a means to squelch her jealousy, had apparently done just the opposite. He knew why she didn't want to talk: she was stewing over Casey. He'd noticed the looks she'd shot her way each time Casey mentioned one of their dates or paid him a compliment. He'd believed that at any minute the fire in his wife's eyes would surely turn the girl to a pile of ash, but the conversations had been perfectly innocent. All they had done was relive some old times. Actually, he'd hoped Dana might learn more about Casey—and even himself—through it all. But, instead of sharing in the camaraderie, she'd chosen instead to sit back and be the silent observer. He wondered what she'd been thinking as she listened to the two of them go on the way they had. He chuckled at the thought. Then again, maybe he didn't want to know.

He exhaled again—this time a little louder—and Dana opened one eye to peek at him. When she closed it again, he looked her way and smiled as he took his right hand off the wheel to flex it. *She and her death grip,* he thought. *Yeah, she noticed—no doubt about it.* He knew she had. That's why she'd grabbed his hand that way and wouldn't let go even once they were inside the car. She'd seen him notice Casey. He'd tried not to—he'd tried his hardest to turn away—but his eyes won the battle and focused back in on that tight blue dress. It hugged every curve of her body. She was right there, and he couldn't help but look. Unfortunately, his wife saw him. To him, it didn't mean a thing. It was the same as looking at a beautiful painting in a museum. It was pleasing to the eye, but there was no emotion attached to it whatsoever. But, he was sure Dana thought otherwise. Not only was Casey an attractive woman, but she was also his ex-girlfriend who had just spent three hours on a tour of the past with him. He was sure that in Dana's mind the affair had already begun—or was at least being contemplated.

Hearing her sigh, he reached over to take her hand, rubbing the softness of it with his thumb. He wished there was some way to convince her that she had nothing to fear. His heart swelled with love for her; and when he looked at her, it flooded with emotion so strong he could hardly control himself. Casey might be attractive, but it was only Dana who could move him that way—no one else, not now, not ever. To him her beauty was breathtaking, and he loved her in a way that he could never express to her in words. Maybe someday she'd understand and truly believe it, but for now, all he could do was his best to keep moving her in that direction. As for tonight, he'd just let it slip away; and should she bring anything up, he'd deal with it then.

My house key was lying on the kitchen table along with a note from Trudy that said all of my shower gifts were in the living room with the exception of the changing table and rocker which Chris had placed in the nursery. After reading the note over my shoulder, Mitch turned the corner into the living room; and his eyes grew wide.

"Holy cow! I think those ladies must have bought out every store in the county!"

"No, just Baby World," I replied. "Everything here was on my registry. Unless there's something we want to buy for the twins, we won't need to get anything else."

He smiled as he took a seat on the couch and began to survey the goods. "It's gonna take us until they're born to put all this stuff away. Maybe we should have bought a bigger house!"

I giggled. "No, I think we'll store some of these things in your outbuilding. Guess you and the guys will have to find another place to rehearse."

He shot me a smug little smirk—the boyish mischief gleaming in his eyes. "Well, after the demo tomorrow, we'll be the property of Remington Records; so we can rehearse at the studio every day."

"Is that so?"

"Yep."

I eased myself down beside him and snuggled into his shoulder. "I sure hope you're right, sweetie."

He sighed heavily. "In all honesty, Dana, I'm not sure what to expect from all this."

"Are you nervous?"

He shrugged. "A little. I don't want to mess this up for the guys. This really means a lot to them." He smiled as he thought of his band mates. "To think a few weeks ago they were going to give it all up for me. What a bunch of losers," he said affectionately.

I gave him a kiss on the cheek and wiped off the lipstick smear I'd left behind. "You won't mess it up. You'll be great." I grinned. "I think it's going to be kind of neat to be married to a famous musician."

I saw that sparkle returning to his eyes. "Yeah, and you know, it might not be so bad being one. Money, fame, lots of slender, curvy women...." He gave me an impish grin.

I playfully put both hands around his throat as he laughed.

Chapter 17

"Good morning, Mitch!" Steve greeted him with a firm handshake. "Ready to do this?"

"I think so," Mitch replied. He stuffed his hands into his pockets to keep them from shaking.

"Great! Your band's already here, and everything's set to go. If you want fifteen minutes or so to run through your songs before we record, that's fine. Then I'll go over how this is all going to work, and we'll get started."

"Sounds good."

Steve led Mitch down a long corridor to a room filled with soundboards, speakers, and at least a dozen recording devices. Steve smiled when he noticed that his younger counterpart had stopped to gaze around the room in awe.

"This is obviously our mixing room," Steve told him. "In a few minutes I'll introduce you to Jerry Patterson—the best sound man known to mankind. You boys just sing it, and Jerry will make it sound like gold."

"Cool" was all Mitch could say.

Steve pointed to a large window in front of the main board, and Mitch noticed his friends milling nervously around their instruments. "That's the live room where you'll be playing. The ceilings are twenty-four feet, and you won't hear better acoustics anywhere. When you get in there, we'll do a few sound checks; and if you need to tune up at all, you can." Steve turned to his left; and after he withdrew a key from his pocket to unlock it, he pushed open a heavy door to a small room hosting only a few speakers and a large microphone. "This is the voice room. The band will record a few takes without vocals, and then we'll put you in here. The music will be dubbed in through your headset for you to sing along with. After you finish, we'll put it together out here."

This time Mitch didn't answer. He was still in awe of everything around him.

"In all you'll do about six takes total that we'll put on tape: two of the entire group and then two each separate that we'll mix. We'll be able to hear you the entire time; so if you need anything, you just give us a signal. Don't worry about time. I have you booked through three, but I doubt we'll need that long."

Mitch was finally escorted into the live room, and the guys swarmed in on him like chicks to a mother hen. Their faces shown with a mixture of nerves, pride, and excitement. Mitch grinned, let out a heavy sigh, and began to bite his lip.

"Are any of you as uptight as I am right now?"

"I've been to the men's room six times since I got here, and I haven't had a thing to drink this morning," Newbie answered.

"My stomach's in knots," Zach chimed in. "I totally skipped breakfast for fear I'd throw up."

"I hope I can stop shaking long enough to play," Shep added.

Ash, always the strong one, stepped in. "Come on, guys. It's not that big a deal. Save the nerves for our first sold-out concert at the stadium. All we're gonna do today is play like we always do. Only difference today is someone will be recording it."

Mitch took a deep breath and let it out slowly. "He's right. Let's just forget where we are and play the tunes, okay? We're good. Let's prove it to them."

An hour and three takes later, Steve was singing the praises of Ace; and Jerry was adding his own comments—all to the effect of 'unbelievable' and 'one of the best I've heard in a while.' All the guys could do was smile.

Feeling more relaxed, Mitch readjusted the strap on his guitar. At Steve's prompt, the band began to play through the tunes once more but this time with no vocals. Upon finishing, they were brought into the mixing room while Mitch was ushered into the voice room to record his part. Jerry reiterated that he would dub the music in through Mitch's headphones, and all he had to do was sing along. Once he was in place at the mike, the door was closed. The red light above it indicated that the recording was in session. Suddenly, Mitch's voice began to radiate through the speakers in the mixing room, and a smile came to every man's face within earshot. Ty looked at Mitch through the small window of the room and shook his head.

"I thank God for my singing abilities, but I'll never come close to that," he said. "The man amazes me every time I hear him."

Steve nodded in agreement. "When I heard him sing at the club, he pulled me in the minute he opened his mouth. The guy's phenomenal. It's rare to find a natural talent like that."

Once Mitch had finished, he reentered the room to a rousing round of applause. Blushing, he smiled shyly at his friends.

"Come on, guys. You've all heard me before. You're embarrassing me."

"Not like that. You outdid yourself, Trip!" Zach said.

"Well, guys, let's allow Jerry a little time to work his magic, and we'll see how everything sounds. If you aren't happy with something, we'll put you back in the studio for another take." He noticed the nervous energy flowing through the group and grinned. "Tell you what—let's head next door to the diner, and I'll treat for lunch. What do you all say?"

Everyone agreed, and a few minutes later the troupe was situated around a table inside Margie's Diner. After placing his order, Mitch excused himself in search of a payphone so that he could call home. He found one in the hallway near the kitchen doors, fished a few coins from his pocket, and dialed the number. Three rings later he heard the sweet sound of her voice, and he smiled.

"Hey, beautiful! What's going on?"

"Hi, sweetie! I was just thinking about you. Have you had your recording session yet? How'd it go? Were you nervous?"

Mitch laughed. "Slow down, love! I can only answer one thing at a time."

"Sorry. I'm just eager to hear about everything, that's all."

"I know. We're actually finished cutting the demo, and now we're waiting on the sound guy to mix it all for us. Right now, we're over at Margie's Diner. Steve's treating us to lunch. When we go back, we'll listen to the reels; and if it's not the way it should be, we'll go in for another take or two. But, from what I observed, they seemed pleased so far."

I could hear the excitement in his voice, and it made me smile. "I knew they would be. You guys are great. See, I told you a long time ago you should go professional, but you wouldn't listen to me." I giggled. "I suppose that's nothing new, is it?"

"Hey, I always listen to you," he replied playfully. "I may not always *do* what you want, but I always listen."

"Okay, point taken," I said.

Mitch watched as two waitresses came out of the kitchen with loaded trays. Recognizing one of them to be the one who took his group's order, he sighed. "Well, honey, I see the food is arriving, so I'd better go. Before I do, are you okay? What have you been doing this morning?"

I glanced at the stacks of baby items surrounding me. "Just trying to sort through all the shower gifts. You were right. We did get a lot."

"Okay, love, you keep at it. Don't tire yourself out too much, all right? I love you."

"I won't. I love you, too."

He hung up the phone and stood for a moment with his hand on the receiver as if that would keep him connected to her for a moment longer. He knew that his last bit of advice would probably go unheeded. Since her recovery from the accident, she had been bent on proving that she wasn't an 'invalid' as she called it. But, she wasn't 'fully capable either, especially at seven months' pregnant. He was surprised—actually more shocked—that she had agreed to give up her place at the bistro. Although he'd tried to convince her that the workload had become too much, it wasn't until she found out on her own that the final decision was made; and she accepted it. He supposed she'd have to learn on her own her limits for other things as well. However, he'd probably continue to try to tell her because he loved her, and, she'd probably continue not to listen.

As he reached the end of the hallway and spotted his band mates engaged in cheerful conversation, he thought of Dana again. If not for her, he wouldn't be here right now. There would be no band, no fronting shows every week at the club, and no chance at a contract with Remington Records. While he cherished her and his children most, life now without Ace would seem incomplete. He would forever be grateful to Dana for convincing him to take that first step so many months ago and rejoin the band. He owed her so much, and yet he knew she would never ask for anything. She was content just to be in the background. He loved her so much.

After lunch and three more hours at the studio, the members of Ace bid Steve and Jerry goodbye. As they gathered outside on the sidewalk, none of them could hold in their excitement any longer. Passersby probably thought them odd as they exchanged hugs, whoops, hollers, and handshakes full of pride and accomplishment. Once it seemed everyone had settled down again, Shep turned to his friends with a wide grin.

"I don't know about the rest of you, but I think we're gonna be famous!"

"I'm with you, man. I don't think we ever sounded that good," Newbie added.

Although Mitch shared their feelings, he decided it best to keep the men grounded. Steve had expressed confidence in their future with Remington Records, but there was always the possibility of the producers turning them down. After all, they had the final say. Steve was only the scout. Mitch smiled at his comrades and beckoned them closer.

"I agree—we were awesome. But, let's not get ahead of ourselves. Steve told us it would be at least three weeks before we know anything. It's probably best if we don't set our sights too high for now."

"Why are you trying to bring us down, Trip?" Zach asked. "You're usually the most confident one of the bunch."

Mitch shook his head. "I'm not trying to bring you down. I'm trying to be realistic." He sighed and glanced around the group. "It doesn't matter how good we think we are or how good Steve or Jerry thinks we are. What matters is what the producers think."

Ty sighed and stepped up to the plate. "Yeah, guys, he's right. We should be proud of what we did in there today, but we shouldn't be buying houses in Malibu just yet."

A silence fell over them as they contemplated the words. Finally, they all nodded in agreement. After chatting for a few minutes longer, they exchanged more handshakes and went their separate ways.

Mitch climbed into his car, and a feeling of satisfaction settled over him as he began to make his way toward Gartano's. The guys had been justified to feel as proud as they had. They had worked hard, and it had truly shown in their performance today. He could honestly say that in all the time they had been together he'd never heard them sound better. He didn't know if fame and fortune paved the road ahead for the band, but they would soon find out. He only hoped the others wouldn't make themselves sick with worry until then.

Although not every table was filled, the dining room was still bustling when he arrived at the bistro a short while later. Before he had a chance to extend a greeting to his staff and head to the office, Casey intercepted him.

"Mitch! How'd it go today?"

"It was great," he said with a prideful grin. "The band was at their best, and the studio guys seemed really impressed. I honestly think we have a decent shot at something." He chuckled. "Of course, I can't share that opinion with the others, or they'll just get big heads. There would be no living with them for the next three weeks!"

She laughed. "Typical men—overloaded with ego, huh?"

Mitch smirked at her as she followed him toward the office. "Now, hold on a minute. I'm not egotistical. I'm very centered and modest, thank you!"

Casey rolled her eyes. "Of course you are," she answered sarcastically. Then her tone changed completely. "In fact, I'd say you're as close to perfect as a man can get."

She did it again—that same look she'd given him a few days ago when he'd invited her to Dana's shower. Again, it caused him to blush. If he didn't know better, he might think she was flirting with him. He quickly turned his face toward the desk and pointed toward a stack of mail lying next to the telephone.

"I'd better go through that stuff and see what I need to worry about. I'm sure the girls are wondering where you are, too."

Casey glanced toward the dining room. "I don't have any tables right now, but I probably should let you get to work." She turned to make her exit as he walked to the desk and sat down, but then she paused. "Oh, yeah. Thanks again for dinner last night. It was fun to have the chance to catch up on things."

"Yeah, it was nice," Mitch said.

She smiled. "I guess I'd better get back to work. I'm happy to hear that everything went well for you today. If anyone deserves to make it big, it's you."

"Thanks," Mitch quietly replied as she walked away.

Hearing the sound of her footsteps as they disappeared down the hallway, he glanced toward the door. His mind settled on her words. *No, she's only being nice, Mitch. Take it for what it is.* He shrugged and turned back to his work.

I opened my eyes and tried hard to get them focused enough to see the clock on the wall. Six-fifteen. I shook my head to clear out the fog and sat up. I remembered sitting down with the book of baby names after I finished mopping the kitchen floor, but I didn't remember falling asleep. My plan had been to scan ten pages or so, then take a shower, and surprise Mitch by joining him for dinner. Since he'd spent the better part of the day at the recording studio, his plan was to cancel rehearsal and stay late at the bistro. He'd told me that he'd probably work right through his dinner break and grab something quick at his desk. Because I knew that his idea of 'quick' could be anything from a few burnt breadsticks to a candy bar he found stuffed in his desk, I felt it was my duty as his wife to show up and make sure he had something of substance.

Thirty-two minutes, a shower, and a change of clothes later, I turned the corner onto the main road. It had been over ten hours since Mitch left home this morning; and since we'd been married, that was the longest we'd been apart. As I drove along, I let my mind drift to thoughts of him. My heart began to fill with longing. I could hardly wait to wrap my arms around him and give him a long, warm kiss. Smiling in eager anticipation, I continued on my way.

Mitch removed his glasses and stood up, extended his arms above his head as high as they would go, and stretched. Rubbing his eyes, he yawned and suddenly felt as though he was completely drained of all energy. He'd only been at work a little over three hours, but it felt like at least ten or more. He was sure that the fatigue was simply the after effects of all the nervous excitement he'd experienced earlier in the day. He sat back down, replaced his glasses, and started to work once more. His stomach growled, but he chose to ignore it for now. There was too much to be done: more mail to sort, daily ledgers to balance, schedules to work out. The list seemed endless. He could always eat a slice of pie and grab a bite at home later. It growled again, and he vowed he'd handle it as soon as he made out the supply order. He set his mind to his task and continued to ignore the feeling.

Absorbed in his work, he didn't hear the sound of her footsteps as she walked down the hall toward the office. In fact, the first thing that told him she was there was the smell of the food.

"Mr. Tarrington, dinner is served."

Lowering his pen, he turned slowly in his chair to see Casey standing behind him with a piping hot pizza, a soda, and a bright smile.

"Wow! Is this for me?" he asked.

She entered the office and placed the pizza in the middle of the desk. "I don't see any other Mr. Tarrington around, do you?" She pulled a few napkins and a straw from the pocket of her apron and laid them next to the pizza. "You haven't left the office since you got here, and I thought you might be getting a little hungry."

Mitch moved his paperwork off to the side and took a drink of his soda. "That's really nice of yo. Thanks."

Casey hesitated for a moment before starting toward the door. "Well, you enjoy that. I'm going on my dinner break now, too. If you need something else, just let me know; and I'll get it for you."

Mitch glanced at the pizza, hesitated himself, and then turned toward the door. "Hey, Casey—this is a pretty big pie. Why don't you help me eat it?"

She stepped back into the room. "Oh, I don't know. I don't want to interrupt your work. Besides, I know a sausage and mushroom is your favorite."

Mitch smirked at her. "Get yourself a soda and I'll pull out a chair."

By the time I arrived at the bistro, the dinner crowd had begun to file in; and the waitresses were busy with customers. I slipped in virtually unnoticed. When I didn't see Mitch anywhere, I concluded that he was in the office hard at work. As I entered the hallway, I slowed my pace so that I could sneak up and surprise him. Little did I know that I would be the one getting the surprise.

The sound of laughter greeted me as I approached the office door. Mitch was sitting at his desk, and his back was to me with Casey on the other side. As I stepped closer, I noticed the pizza on the desk between them that they were obviously sharing. *I thought he was working through his break today. At least, that's what he told me,* I said to myself. *Guess I didn't know the proper way to persuade him otherwise.* While I stood there observing the two, I could feel my temper building. *What's going on here,* I wondered? *Didn't he get enough of her last night?*

My first inclination was to bound into the room and give my husband a piece of my mind. Just as I was preparing myself for that confrontation, Casey spotted me standing in the doorway. Her eyes upon me caused Mitch to turn around, and his expression was a mixture of guilt and pure surprise. But then he smiled, and the little voice inside my head spoke to me loud and clear. *Look at him, Dana. You can't do this. You told him you trusted him. Keep your cool. Try a different approach.* I took a deep breath. Sometimes I really hated that little voice.

Mitch put down his pizza, wiped his mouth on a napkin, and then stood to approach me.

"Hey, sweetheart! I wasn't expecting to see you here tonight!" He gave me a quick kiss and placed a hand on my back.

That's obvious, I thought. I glanced at Casey again, who simply sat there and tried to look innocent as she munched away on her pizza. I wasn't buying it. I thought I would give her something to think about.

"Surely you can do better than that, Mitchell. I've missed you today." I took hold of his tie and gently pulled him down to me again for a long, slow kiss. He pulled away looking rather stunned, and I smiled as I slid an arm around his waist. "There's more where that came from," I whispered just loud enough for Casey to hear. Mitch shot me a bit of a befuddled glance.

I traced the outline of the designs on his tie with my fingertip. "I was thinking I'd come down here and convince you to have dinner with me—even though you said you wouldn't have time—but it looks like I'm too late." This time Casey looked guilty.

Mitch delivered a peck on my forehead as he slid out of my embrace and sat back down. He pointed to the pizza. "Well, there's still a little here that Casey didn't eat," he said as he smirked at her. "You're welcome to have that if you're hungry."

I walked up behind him, placed my hands on both shoulders, and then slid them down to his chest. "No, that's all right. I don't want to deprive her of the extra calories. She looks like she could use a little more meat on her bones." That remark was met with a bit of an unpleasant glare from Casey, but I didn't care. The little voice tried to tell me I wasn't being very nice, but this time I told it to shut up.

I gave Mitch a kiss on the top of his head and stood back up as I began to rub his shoulders. "Well, I should probably head back home and let you two get back to whatever it was you were discussing. I'm sure it was some important work thing."

Casey stood quickly and placed her napkin on her empty plate. "Oh, no, Dana, we were just chatting. It's time for me to get back to the dining room anyway." She smiled at Mitch. "These breaks go by far too fast, don't they?" She picked up her plate and glass as she headed toward the door. "Thanks for sharing with me, Mitch. It was really nice."

"No problem. Thank *you* for bringing it to me."

Now, she's his personal waitress? Hold your tongue, Dana; hold your tongue.

As Casey left the room, I started to follow.

"Not so fast," Mitch said, catching me by the arm. "I'd like to talk to you." He closed the door and turned around to face me. "Okay, go ahead. Chew me out."

I looked at him as if I had no clue what he was saying. "For what?"

He gave me that stunned look again. "Aren't you upset that I was having pizza with Casey?"

I swallowed my true feelings and smiled. "No. Is there a reason I should be?"

"Well, I did tell you that I wouldn't have any free time tonight, and I don't want you thinking that I only said that so I could eat with Casey. I wasn't planning to take a break; but when she brought me the pizza, I didn't want to be rude."

I placed a hand on his cheek and looked into his eyes. I only hoped he couldn't read mine. "Honey, it's fine. I understand."

He reciprocated the action. "I was thinking you might be feeling a little, uh, territorial, judging by the way you were coming on to me in front of her."

I gave him a small laugh. "Territorial? Mitchell, for heaven's sake, I'm not a wild animal!"

He gave me his impish little grin and a flash of that adorable dimple. "That's a matter of opinion, my dear. You do have a tendency toward acting that way whenever another woman is near me."

I folded my arms and puffed the air from my lungs in a huff. "I absolutely do *not* act that way, and I resent your saying that. Did you ever stop to think that perhaps I simply felt like being close to you? We have spent the last eleven hours apart, you know!"

He chuckled. "Sorry, love. My mistake." He pulled me into his arms and held me close. "How could I have ever possibly thought you'd be jealous of Casey?"

"I don't know," I muttered. "I'm not."

He pulled back to look into my eyes, and his own were glowing with a soft affection. "That's good to know because you have no reason to be. You are the only woman I care anything about."

"That's good to know, too. Judging by the way you two were carrying on last night and just now, I might have gotten the impression that you have a slight attraction to her."

We stared at each other for a moment, and he smiled. "I'm certainly glad we cleared all that up. I wouldn't want any misunderstandings."

I smiled back. "Neither would I."

As I downed a bowl of fettuccine—I couldn't stomach the thought of eating a pizza I knew had Casey's fingerprints on it—Mitch shared with me the details of his demo recording and what he'd gotten accomplished so far at work. In turn, I told him about my day spent on cleaning the house, washing baby clothes, and putting away items from my shower. He told me about the case of nerves he'd fought during his solo recording and the fear that he was going to suddenly squeak like a mouse. I relayed the five cases of Braxton Hicks, three cases of being kicked in the ribs, and two cases of 'fetal' hiccups I'd experienced during the day. When I had finished eating and all had been said, I gave him a kiss and left him to get back to his work.

Just before I reached the front door of the bistro, I felt a set of eyes upon me. Pausing for a moment to turn around, I caught Casey's stare; and she smiled nervously.

"Good night, Dana. Drive safely," she managed to squeak out.

"Thanks," I said and headed out the door.

Casey watched through the window as Dana climbed into her car and pulled away from her parking space. *This might turn out to be a bit more of a challenge than I thought*, she said to herself. Dana was the jealous type. That could only mean one thing: she would stick to her husband like glue. If she felt the least bit threatened, she'd make sure she eliminated the source. Although Mitch was technically the manager of Gartano's, she was sure that Dana had some influence over the staff. If she felt at all like Casey was trying to make a move on Mitch, she'd convince him to fire her for sure. She couldn't afford to let that happen. She'd have to figure out a way to befriend Dana and make her feel comfortable with her. Once that happened, the rest would be a piece of cake, but she'd have to take things slowly so no one would become suspicious.

When I was safely back at home, I retreated to the family room, sat down in the chair, and reopened the book of baby names. Earlier I had jotted down a few names that I liked and thought that now I could add them to the list. When Mitch got home later, I could share them with him.

"Let's see now," I said to myself aloud. "Aaron and Amanda, Brooke and Brandon...I need C's. But there weren't any C names I liked." I sighed and flipped through the pages again. There it was, staring up at me as if I were being haunted by it. "Casey."

"No way! I'd name these kids Bozo and Bimbo before I'd name either of them Casey!" I rubbed my stomach and spoke soothingly to my children. "Don't worry, guys. I promise you'll have good names." I moved my finger rapidly through the pages until I came to the names that began with D. But now, because I'd been reminded again by seeing her name, I started to think about her.

Just seeing Casey sitting across from Mitch, chit chatting away like she was as content as could be—oh, how that had sent a fire racing up my spine that made every nerve stand on end. And *she* brought *him* the pizza! Clever of her to think of it just before her own break as she had known full well that he'd invite her to join him. I had to wonder what it was they'd talked about. Undoubtedly, she brought up more memories of their happy, carefree courtship. I was sure their conversation didn't include me at all; and on the small chance that it did, I was certain my name was only mentioned in passing. The more I thought about how she'd been pouring on her charms to Mitch, the angrier I got. Casey had him hook, line, and sinker, and was trying her best to reel him in. However, she didn't know there were bigger fish in the sea who planned to bite the line right in half. She was definitely up to something, and I was now even more determined to find out what.

I rubbed my stomach again as I began to feel gentle kicks coming from within and a soft grumbling. "What's wrong? Didn't the fettuccine fill you up?" I placed the book on the coffee table and maneuvered myself into a standing position. "Okay, let's go find something we can snack on."

Making my way to the kitchen, I rummaged through cupboards and drawers, not exactly sure what I wanted but knowing I would know as soon as I found it. Finally, I decided on a PB & J and in less than two minutes had one whipped together. I started to take a bite, but hesitated. *It still needs something,* I said to myself. With a little more searching, I located a few *Cheeto's* Mitch hadn't managed to eat in the bottom of the bag. I stuffed the crunchy puffs in between the slices of bread and took a bite. *Perfect.* After pouring myself a tall glass of orange juice, I headed back to my haven on the couch.

Mitch turned the key in the lock and checked the door to make sure it was secure. He took the watch from his pocket and pressed the button on the top to open the case: ten forty-five. Since he'd started back with the band, his days at the bistro usually ended around five or five-thirty. He had forgotten what it was like to go through the closing routine of totaling out the cash drawers and making sure everything was clean and in order for opening the next morning. That had become the responsibility of Jimmy and Kayla, and they had handled it well.

But, due to his erratic schedule with everything else that day, he'd given the pair an evening off and taken on the duty himself. It wasn't that it was a particularly difficult one at all. He simply enjoyed having his evenings with Dana. *Oh, well,* he thought. *Tomorrow, things will be back to normal.* He yawned as he unlocked his car door and stepped inside.

Feeling very fatigued, Mitch turned the air conditioner on full power and pointed the air vent directly into his face. The last thing he needed was to fall asleep at the wheel. Thankfully, the drive from Gartano's to home was only ten minutes. It had been a long day; and at that moment, he wanted nothing more than a hot shower, a soft bed, and a little TLC.

He saw the porch light shining from a few houses away, and he smiled. Dana was anticipating his arrival home as much as he looked forward to being there. He pushed the button on the garage door opener. When he saw her sweet smile as she peeked out through the front curtains, he smiled himself and sped up the driveway.

I positioned myself by the door and greeted Mitch with a hug as he stepped inside.

He chuckled softly and hugged me tightly. "Hi, sweetheart! You're awfully nice to come home to!"

"I missed you so much," I said as I snuggled into him. "This house is big and lonely without you here."

He stepped back and looked into my eyes with a loving smile. "Don't you like the house?"

I nodded. "Yes, I do—very much, but I like it better when you're here."

He hung his keys on the hook by the door and draped an arm around my shoulder as we walked into the kitchen. "I like it better when I'm here with you, too—much better than being at work." He noticed the empty *Cheeto's* bag still lying on the counter where I'd left it. "I see you had some cheese puffs."

"Actually, I had a sandwich."

"A sandwich and some cheese puffs, huh? You must have been hungry."

"Not a sandwich *and* cheese puffs—a sandwich *with* cheese puffs."

He chuckled as he tossed the bag into the trash. "Honey, it really doesn't matter how you say it. It's still the same thing."

"No, it's not. I had a sandwich *with* cheese puffs, not a sandwich *and* cheese puffs. There is a definite difference."

He gave me a confused stare, and then his face contorted in such a way that I could clearly see the disgust. "Hold on—you mean you put the cheese puffs *in* the sandwich?"

I nodded, and his face contorted even more.

"I'm afraid to ask, but what kind of sandwich was it?"

"A PB & J. I had a glass of orange juice, too."

"Good grief, Dana! That makes my stomach hurt just to think about it!"

"Well, it tasted good."

He shook his head and gave me a lopsided grin. "And I thought the banana-grapefruit-lemonade smoothie you made last week was weird? I think this one tops it, love."

"Don't make fun. It isn't like I tried to make you eat it."

He began to loosen his tie and unbutton his shirt as he headed toward the stairs. "It's a good thing because I wouldn't have!"

I followed him up the stairs and into the bathroom, virtually picking up a trail of his clothing as I went along. He was stripped down to his boxers by the time he reached the middle of the room. After he'd turned on the shower, he shed those as well and stepped in: the only sound coming from him being a rather loud yawn. I tossed his clothes into the hamper and moseyed off to the bedroom to wait for him.

About five minutes later he emerged slightly damp with a towel wrapped around his waist. He moved rather slowly to his dresser as he yawned again. The towel dropped to the floor as he dressed in boxers, a t-shirt, and old track shorts. I simply pointed to the towel lying by his feet, and he looked down as if he expected it to jump back into his hands. He sighed loudly, picked it up, and trudged back into the bathroom to hang it to dry.

"You're really tired, aren't you, sweetie?" I asked as he appeared once more.

"Exhausted," he said as he ran a hand through his wet, mussed hair. "I can't remember a time when I felt this wiped out. In fact, I'm going down for a quick snack, and then I'm hitting the hay." He extended his hand, and I took it as I slid off the bed. "Come down with me and keep me company, okay?"

I followed him to the kitchen where he made himself a bowl of cereal and then headed down to the family room to stretch out in his chair. Noticing the book of baby names I'd left on the coffee table, he picked it up and placed his bowl where the book had been.

"Been picking out names?" he asked.

"A few. I actually found some I liked this time," I replied as I took a seat on the couch.

"Oh yeah? What are they?"

I ran through my list with him, and he smiled.

"You didn't mention anything that began with a C. Any reason for that?"

"I didn't like anything that started with C."

He shot me a sideways glance as he opened the book to that section. "Sweetheart, there are tons of names here. You can surely find two that you like."

I shook my head. "Nope. None."

He shot me another sideways glance—this time mixed with a hint of his dimple—and slid his finger down the page until he came to the most dreaded name of all. "Here we go. How about Casey?"

I knew he was only trying to ruffle my feathers, and I decided I wasn't going to let him. "I thought we agreed not to name the babies after anyone we know."

He tapped his finger against the page and looked up at me. "We did say that, didn't we?"

I smiled, gloating in the fact that I had apparently outsmarted him. Or, at least I thought I had.

He twisted his jaw in thought and then snapped his fingers. "I know what we can do! We can name the *boy* Casey. Then no one can say we named the baby after the Casey we know. What do you think?"

That I need to think of something else and fast! "I don't know. There's kind of a fine line there, don't you think? I believe I'd rather come up with something else. Besides, to be honest, I'm not crazy about the name anyway."

He gave me another flash of his dimple. "Really? I think it's a nice name."

I'm sure you do. Just like you think everything else about her is nice. "Let's just find something else, okay?"

At long last he sighed in defeat and decided to give the teasing a rest. "Well, I guess maybe we should if you're really that dead set against it." He laid the book on the arm of the chair and extended his hand to me. "Come on over here, love, and we'll take a look through this together."

I smiled and inwardly patted myself on the back for managing once again to curtail my true feelings about Casey. Mitch had put me to the test, and I'd passed with flying colors. I was sure he knew that I didn't like her, but I would never admit to it. I couldn't. I wanted to prove to him, first of all, that I trusted him. Second, I wanted to make sure he didn't find out about my plan to dissect her and possibly try to stop me.

I took his hand, and he pulled me onto his lap. I deduced that he couldn't be very comfortable with a 150-pound woman sitting on his legs, but he simply placed an arm around me and kissed my cheek as he opened the book. For the next few minutes I remained there with him, and we talked and planned for the children that we would soon be blessed with. Finally, the fatigue overtook him; and he gently placed me on my feet as he stood up.

"I really can't stay awake any longer, love. I'm sorry," he announced through a yawn. "Are you coming to bed with me?"

I picked up his cereal bowl and started off to the kitchen to place it in the sink. "Yeah, I'll be there in a minute. You go on up."

Less than three minutes later, I crawled beneath the covers next to my husband and positioned myself so that my head was resting on his shoulder. I could hear the faint sound of his heart beating, and I wondered if the twins had sensed it as well because at that moment they began to kick and move. After I kissed the palm of my hand, I tenderly placed it on my stomach and fell into a blissful sleep.

Over the weeks that followed, life seemed to move at a pace almost faster than we could keep up with. It was during this time that Mitch decided to move into family mode and sacrifice his sporty Mustang convertible for something he deemed more 'practical.' After spending two days arguing over the situation—I knew that he loved his car, and I would be the one driving the twins around the majority of the time anyway—he finally gave in and agreed to allow me to give up my Camaro instead. However, four hours at the dealership provided us with not one, but two new Jeep Cherokee's—his and hers. A second set of car seats would be purchased for his vehicle, thus allowing us more flexibility than having to switch one set between the two of us. As he secured the final strap on the second seat, we smiled at one another and realized that it was official—we were no longer just Mitch and Dana, but instead had become The Tarrington Family.

Four more sessions and a 'graduation' ceremony marked the end of our childbirth education classes. Although Mitch had the utmost confidence in my abilities, I still had concerns about being alone with two babies at once. To ease my anxieties, he surprised me with a copy of 'Baby's First Year' and a promise that he would set up a round-the-clock response team—better known as his family and himself —that I could call upon should I feel the need. Each person he spoke to readily agreed to the task, and I was once again thankful for the people in my life.

The pregnancy continued to progress normally—and I continued to grow abnormally—to the point where Dr. Bradley began to caution me on gaining much more weight. I was already close to forty pounds heavier than I had been pre-pregnancy; and with about four weeks left to go, he didn't want to risk any sorts of complications that might come with excessive weight. To help curtail my cravings for sweets, Mitch and I decided to eliminate those items from our home and replace them with healthy alternatives such as fruit and low-fat yogurt. To make sure I didn't sneak anything we might have left lying around, Mitch volunteered to make the ultimate sacrifice and eat those goodies that remained. He said it was the least he could do for his family; and although it was tough, he'd somehow get through it. I simply rolled my eyes at him and laughed.

As for Mitch, the day-to-day ritual of work and rehearsals kept him going as always. The business at Gartano's remained steady, and he was exceedingly grateful that he had a strong staff who could handle it. Claiming that she had "settled in nicely," Casey remained a subject of praise for him—and a thorn in the side for me. Rarely did I visit the bistro that she wasn't somewhere within his line of vision, either pouring out her sugary sweetness to him in conversation, or making eyes and smiling at him from across the room. But, no matter what she said or did, I remained steadfast in my quest to keep my feelings to myself. Every once in a while he would try to put me to the test as he had the night with the baby names, but I remained strong. Although I did my best to do nothing more than say hello to her at any given time, for some reason she seemed to have begun to go out of her way to make contact with me over the last few weeks. I wasn't sure what was behind her sudden interest in becoming my friend—I certainly had little interest in becoming hers—but decided for the sake of my investigation that I wouldn't snub her completely. After all, I still needed to find out what she was up to, and it would be easier to do that if I interacted with her at least a little.

That opportunity presented itself in full form when I least expected it, and more so, was least ready for it. One evening Mitch arrived home from work to find me as I awoke from a much-needed afternoon nap. I opened my eyes to see him perched on the coffee table next to the couch with his hands folded neatly in his lap and a soft smile on his face.

"Hey, sleepyhead," he said as he reached out to brush the hair off my face. "Did you have a nice nap?"

I pushed myself to a sitting position—not an easy task for a woman with my girth—and stretched. "Yeah, I did. I can't believe how tired I've been getting. I swear I'm starting to need naps to recover from my naps."

He laughed and held out a hand to help me to my feet. "I guess that's to be expected, love." Once I was standing, he placed an arm around my shoulders. "What's for dinner? Something smells wonderful."

"I made beef stroganoff. I turned off the flame just before I lay down, but it should still be hot if you want to eat right away."

He followed me up the stairs into the kitchen. "Did you make a lot?"

I giggled as I moved to the sink to wash my hands. "Why? Are you hungry?"

"Well, yes...but I'm really asking if there's enough for three."

I reached for the kitchen towel that was hanging on the handle of the oven door. "Three? You mean four, don't you?" I patted my stomach. "Twins. Remember?"

"Then I guess I should really ask if there's enough for five. Casey's going to sit in on rehearsal tonight—she's been wanting to hear us play—and I told her to come a little earlier for dinner." He must have noticed the steam starting to rise from around my collar because he grimaced. "You don't mind that I asked her, do you? I guess I should have called to let you know, but it was kind of a last-minute thing."

Just as I was about to answer, the doorbell rang. *Gee, what impeccable timing, Casey. You just saved your ex from the wrath of a hormonal pregnant woman. Lucky for him. It could have been ugly. Really ugly.*

Mitch opened the door to Casey who greeted him with a radiant smile. As she stepped inside, just one look at her made me instantly become self-conscious. I glanced down at my favorite maternity sweater—now faded from a multitude of washings—and the knit stretch pants which seemed to be stretched to the very limit. I was sure there had to be sleep lines which still shown on my face amidst the faded makeup, and my hair was pulled back in a loose ponytail. Casey's curvy little figure was enhanced by her tight jeans and sweater, and her hair fell in soft, perfect waves on her shoulders. Making a quick comparison, she looked like a million bucks—I came in somewhere around $12.50.

Before either of them had a chance to notice, I made a beeline for the stairs and disappeared into the bedroom.

Mitch ushered Casey into the living room and offered her a seat on the couch.

"Where's Dana?" she asked.

Mitch chuckled. "She's right...." He turned toward the doorway to the kitchen where she'd been standing just moments before, and a bewildered look came over him. "That's weird. She was right there a minute ago." He started in that direction as he called out for her. "Honey? Are you out there?"

Not finding her, he returned to the living room and pointed up the stairs. "Maybe she had to go upstairs for something. You make yourself comfortable while I go see."

Casey simply nodded as Mitch took the stairs two at a time.

I heard a soft knock on the door, and I turned to see Mitch enter the room with a concerned look on his face.

"Dana, are you okay? Why'd you run off like that?"

I was in the master bathroom rummaging through my makeup drawer in search of a blue eyeliner pencil. "I hadn't planned on company, Mitch. I looked like a mess! I came up here to clean up a little and change clothes."

He smiled and shook his head. "Baby, you look beautiful all the time. Why do you think otherwise?"

I turned slowly and gave him a sarcastic sneer. "Because I know better. *No one* looks beautiful all the time. Well, *almost* no one."

"You wouldn't be referring to Casey, would you?" he asked with a smirk.

I turned back to the mirror and gently drew a line along the lower lid of my left eye. "You look at her more than I do. What do you think?"

He suddenly seemed at a loss for words. "I think...well...."

I tossed the pencil back in the drawer and started my search for a lipstick. "Come on, Mitch. Just admit that you think she's pretty and get it over with."

"If I do, will I get in trouble?"

I found the shade I wanted, applied a coat to my lips, and blotted it with a tissue. "It's okay. I already know the answer. I've seen you checking her out more than once."

I could almost hear the walls of defense going up around him. "I didn't check her out, Dana. I'll admit—I may have looked her way a time or two, but I definitely didn't check her out—not by my definition anyway."

I turned around to face him and crossed my arms in front of me. "Well, by mine you did. What's *your* definition?"

He hesitated. "What's yours?"

"I asked you first."

He started to bite his lip until suddenly something seemed to click, and his eyes lit up.

"In order to check her out, I would have had to stare at her—*really* stare at her—for at least three minutes or more. Kinda like this." He fixed his gaze on me as the hint of a smile tugged at his lips. "I would have smiled a little to let her know I liked what I saw. The eyes would have moved slowly from top to bottom and back again. If she was *really* hot, they may have made a few stops in between." He demonstrated as he raised his eyebrows at me. "At some point I'm sure the hormones would have kicked in, and I may have thought about repeating the process for the shear pleasure of it all." He shrugged. "But, a simple look—such as what I *may* have given Casey—involves the eyes either looking straight at her or moving more rapidly from top to bottom. Then I turn away and get back to my business." He thrust his hands into his pockets and looked very matter-of-fact. "The look is definitely associated with a general lack of interest on an emotional level—kinda like looking at a tree. It's pretty—nice to look at—but it doesn't do a lot to get me fired up."

Surprisingly enough, I actually found myself somewhat convinced by his explanation. I had to hand it to him. He was a quick thinker and clever, too. However, I also knew he was trying to cover up his guilt and save my feelings at the same time. I thought for a moment about how to react and decided to give him what he wanted.

"So, you're telling me that you never 'checked out' Casey—you only looked at her."

"Uh-huh. That would be correct, my love."

"Like a tree."

"Yeah, like a tree."

"Okay, then. If Casey's a tree, what am I—an entire forest?"

He chuckled as he reached out to hold me. Pointing his eyes to the ceiling in thought, he smiled as he brought them back down to meet mine. "No, sweetheart, you are a car."

I twisted my jaw. "A car?"

He nodded. "Yes, but not just *any* car. You are a '66 Mustang GT Convertible: a rare find, breathtaking to behold, and hard to keep your hands off. Any man who has one is very lucky."

"Is that so?"

"I wouldn't say it otherwise." He looked down at me with bright blue eyes that reflected the feelings of his heart. "I love you, Dana Tarrington. Now, I think we should get back to our guest before she thinks we left her." He took my hand, and we made our way back downstairs together.

Casey stood at the sofa table with her back to the stairs. She was holding the small, heart-shaped frame containing the ultrasound photos of the twins, and she turned to face us as we approached.

"Sorry about that, Casey," Mitch said. "My lovely wife here was trying to make herself even lovelier, which just isn't possible."

I smiled up at him, but it seemed Casey chose to ignore the comment.

"Hi, Dana," she greeted with a smile as she placed the frame back down. "I hope you don't mind my coming for dinner. I know it was sudden. When Mitch extended the invitation and told me what a great cook you are, I couldn't resist."

Mitch glanced at me as if he expected a reaction, but I simply shrugged.

"No, I don't mind. I hope you like beef stroganoff."

"Sure, that sounds fine. Let me help you."

You can help me by telling me what you want with my husband. "Oh, no, that's okay. I just need to put everything on the table, and then we can eat."

She followed me into the kitchen like a lost puppy. "I insist. I came unexpectedly. The least I can do is offer some assistance."

I gathered three place settings and handed them to her. "You can take these into the dining room, and Mitch and I will bring everything else."

As she headed off, Mitch caught me around the waist and planted a kiss on my cheek. "Thanks for being so great about this. Casey said she was looking forward to the chance to talk to you again, and I thought it might give you another chance to get to know her better."

I gave him a basket of rolls and sent him to the dining room. *Maybe one of these days he'll get the hint that I don't want to get to know her any better.*

A few minutes later, the three of us were seated at the dining room table with Mitch in the head seat and Casey and I on opposite sides of him. She took a few bites of her meal and looked up at me with a smile of approval.

"Dana, this is delicious! The last time I had beef stroganoff was in Chicago at some little Mom and Pop joint. It certainly doesn't compare to this."

"Thanks," I said. "I do my best."

Just as I was about to say, "Speaking of Chicago…" she turned to Mitch with a sort of light in her eyes that told me I was about to be shoved out of the conversation—again.

"Do you think your friends will mind my watching your rehearsal, Mitch?" She shot a glance my way. "With dinner and all, I'm really starting to feel like the intruder here tonight."

I looked across the table at her. *Then why don't you go back to wherever it is you came from? That way you won't have to worry.*

"Nonsense," Mitch said as he set his glass back on the table. He chuckled. "If anything, they'll be doing everything they can to impress you. Just to forewarn you, three of them are single; and they can act kinda goofy when they get close to an attractive girl."

Casey giggled and touched his arm. "That's okay. I can handle 'goofy'—I dated you, didn't I?"

Mitch smirked and rolled his eyes at her as she laughed. I tried to keep down my last bite of food.

She continued on her quest to annoy me. "I'm only kidding, you know." She looked at me with a hint of contention in her voice. "Mitch was the perfect gentleman the entire time we dated. He made me feel like I was on a pedestal all the time." She touched his arm yet again. "Everyone used to remark about how well we got along. I don't think we ever had an argument, did we?"

Mitch seemed a bit uncomfortable with the question and didn't look up from his plate as he answered. "I don't think so," he said quietly.

Seeing another opportunity to chime in, I opened my mouth to speak only to have Casey seize the moment once more by completely changing the subject.

She looked out through the sliding glass doors and pointed. "That must be the outbuilding you told me about, Mitch. You say you got it soundproofed?"

He nodded. "Yeah. Tony Sheppard, the brother of my bass guitarist, did it for me. Now, we can pound around out there and not worry about bothering any of the neighbors. There's plenty of room for all the instruments and some sound equipment. I was thinking about installing a permanent system at some point so the guys don't have extra stuff."

"Sounds like the studio Jason's band had in Chicago. It was really nice—actually took up the entire basement of his home—all soundproofed, built in sound system, mixing boards, the whole nine yards. Of course, they were semi-professional." Then she smiled brightly. "But hey! You could say that about Ace now, too, couldn't you?"

Mitch laughed. "I wouldn't go that far just yet."

I couldn't sit there a minute longer without saying something. "Why not, honey? You guys did cut a demo; and when Remington signs you, you will be pros."

He smiled at me. "Well, that hasn't happened yet, and I don't want to jump the gun. We are what we are for now."

"When will you know something—about the demo, I mean?" Casey asked.

Mitch wiped the corner of his mouth with his napkin and placed it back on his lap. "I'm not really sure," he answered. "I got a call about a week ago from Steve Garrett—he's the guy that recorded us—and he said they want a few more of the 'big shots' over there to listen to the cuts before they decide. It could be another couple of weeks at least."

"Wow. It sounds like they're pretty thorough."

"Yeah, they are, and the guys are going crazy waiting to know what's going to happen. I guess if they're going to sign a band, they want to make sure they're getting someone worth having on the label."

"I for one can't wait to hear you," Casey said. "I'm sure you're wonderful." She turned toward me as if she needed to explain. "I can't believe I've been home more than a month, and I haven't met these guys yet. The few times they came into Gartano's I wasn't there, and it seems like every night and weekend I've been tied up with family or something." She took a drink of her iced tea and smiled. "But, everything's finally settling down, so now I have some extra time to do things."

"That's nice," I answered, not caring much. Mitch gave me a funny look, and I tried to ignore him.

The next few minutes were spent with Casey and Mitch engaged in idle chatter about all things musical and nothing I had any concept of. Once again, as I had the night at Charley's, I found myself on the outside looking in. Once again as well, I found myself no closer to solving my mystery of Casey Tomlin.

As the two continued to chat, I excused myself—not that either of them noticed—and made my way into the kitchen to retrieve the spice cake I'd made for dessert. As I pulled three small plates from the cupboard, I mumbled to myself.

"I can't believe he actually invited her here for dinner. What on earth was he thinking? It's not enough that I have to think about him spending all day with her at the bistro. Now, he's bringing her home, too. Next thing I know he'll have her moving in with us!" I found my serving tray and placed the cake on it along with the plates, a pot of coffee, and three cups. "What is up with his zealous attitude toward her anyway? It's been a month. I'd think the newness would have worn off by now. I'm beginning to wonder if he doesn't regret breaking up with her, and he's trying to make up for lost time by playing Mr. Nice. Well, I've just about had enough of all this. If he doesn't stop...."

"Honey, who are you talking to?"

I wheeled around to see my husband standing behind me.

"Oh, uh...." The twins began to kick and once again saved the day. "The babies. They're doing tricks in there again."

He smiled and reached out to place a hand on my stomach. "They sure are! Guess they must have liked your dinner, too, huh?"

"I guess so. And why are you out here, anyway? You have company."

"*We* have company, and I came to see if I could help with anything."

I pointed to the tray. "You can carry this for me, please. It's a little heavy."

"Sure, love. Anything for you." He paused to give me a kiss on the forehead before he walked away.

Anything? How about getting her out of your life?

After the post-dinner session of 'Talk and Ignore Dana,' I started to clear away the dishes as Mitch and Casey headed outside to greet the band who had just arrived. Hurrying through the motions, I stepped out the back door just in time to see Casey and Mitch disappear into the outbuilding. Unless my eyesight was failing me, it looked like his hand was in the middle of her back as he guided her through the doorway.

As I walked to the outbuilding, I placed a hand on my stomach and talked to my children. "Guys, don't you worry. I'm going to get to the bottom of all this. Guaranteed."

I slipped into the building just as the introductions started and found the guys around Casey with huge smiles and wide eyes that were focused on everything but her face. Mitch stood closest to her, and every once in a while she looked up at him with that sickening sweet smile. I had yet to be noticed by any of them—which didn't surprise me at all—so I quietly sat down to observe the mating rituals of the young North American Musician.

Zach was the last to step up to her, and he kissed her hand as he offered a chivalrous bow.

"Last but certainly not least," Mitch started, "this is Zach Daniels, my back-up lead."

Zach's eyes met Casey's, and I thought I actually saw a spark ignite between them—at least I hoped I had. Maybe an interest in Zach would take her mind off Mitch.

"Nice to meet you, Zach," Casey said in her syrupy tone.

"The pleasure's all mine," Zach answered. He stepped back and smiled at her. "I hope you'll enjoy listening to us tonight."

"I'm sure I will," she answered. "Mitch has been bragging about all of you, and I already know how wonderful he is." She shot him a flirtatious glance. "I used to love to hear him sing."

"Exactly how do you two know each other?" Shep asked.

Mitch and Casey looked at each other as if they had a secret they weren't sure they should reveal. Finally, Mitch spoke up.

"We dated about a year and a half ago...."

"Then I moved to Chicago for a while, and things didn't work out," she finished. She smiled up at him again. "I decided to come back; and as fate would have it, we found each other again. Now, I have the pleasure of working with him at Gartano's, and I'm loving it so far."

"That's cool," Ty chimed in. "Did you go to Chicago for school or something?"

Mitch decided to answer for her. "Actually, Casey sings and also plays piano. She went to audition for a band."

She shrugged and gave another flash of her sickening sweet smile. "Unfortunately, that didn't work out, either. I guess some things are meant to be," she looked at Mitch, "and others aren't."

I don't know who you think you fooled with that line, but it certainly wasn't me, I thought. *I know you wish Mitch was single, but he's not. The sooner you come to grips with that, the better off you'll be.*

After a few more minutes of letting the guys form puddles of drool around Casey's feet and fawn over her musical escapades, Mitch pointed to a chair which, unfortunately, was right next to mine.

He looked at Casey. "Why don't you have a seat back there, and we'll put on a little concert for you."

"Sounds great, but first I think I'd better go and use the ladies' room. Can you point me in the right direction?"

Mitch smiled. "Downstairs, just off the family room in the house. Take your time."

She thanked him and hurried off.

Casey made her way down the stairs into the family room. The wedding picture hanging above the fireplace caught her attention, and she stopped to look at it. *They're so happy together,* she thought to herself. *I remember when he used to kiss me that way.* She closed her eyes to savor the feelings that swept over her. *He was always so gentle, his lips were so soft, his hands so warm and strong....* She opened her eyes once more and gazed at the picture. *If only I had told him. I guess I'll have to get used to the fact that it can never be.* Then she smiled. *But, if I play my cards right, maybe other things can.*

By the time Casey returned to the outbuilding, the guys were in the middle of the first song; and she moved into the chair beside me. Her expression showed clearly that she was in awe, and she turned to me and leaned in close.

"Mitch was right, Dana. These guys are amazing!" she said.

"Yes, they are," I replied. "Let's just hope Remington Records thinks so."

Yes, let's hope they do, Casey thought.

After three more tunes, Mitch stopped the guys and took off his guitar.

"Take five guys," he said. "It's sounding pretty good so far."

He walked to the back of the room where the two of us sat, and he smiled. "Well, what do you ladies think so far?"

I opened my mouth to speak; but, of course, I wasn't quick enough.

"My gosh, Mitch! You guys are amazing! I always knew you were talented, but all six of you together? There's no way that record deal won't come through."

"Thanks! I'm glad you think so, but I guess we'll just have to wait and see."

Casey decided she hadn't flattered him enough. "As far as you go, I could listen to you sing all night! You are so talented."

Just then, Newbie shouted from the front. "Hey, Casey, we'd like to see how talented *you* are. Why don't you come up here and sing something for us?"

Casey blushed as the other four men attempted to encourage her. Finally, she turned to them with a smile.

"I'll only sing if Mitch sings with me."

He began to chuckle and shake his head. "Come on, Casey, they hear me all the time. They want to hear you."

"We could do that tune we used to do together. You know the one."

Mitch glanced toward the guys as he bit his lip, and then focused back on Casey. "Okay, but then you have to give us one on your own. Deal?" He extended his hand.

She sighed. "Okay, deal. But, just one." She shook his hand and started toward the front of the room.

Mitch sat down next to me for a moment and placed a hand on my stomach. "How are you doing back here? Haven't heard much from you tonight."

Not surprising since I can't get a word in edgewise.

"I'm fine," I replied softly. "Just taking things in."

He felt a strong kick beneath his palm, and he laughed. "Do these two ever settle down?"

"Sometimes, but not very often."

"I think we're going to have our hands full, but that's okay. It's gonna be great." He gave me a kiss and turned his eyes to the front of the room where the guys were once more surrounding Casey. "Can you believe them? They act like they've never seen a woman before."

I shrugged. "They're just young and hormonal, that's all. Typical men."

He turned back to me and cocked his head to one side with a grin. "Typical, huh? I'm not like that!"

I laughed as I patted my stomach. "Oh, no, not you. Not at all."

He joined in. "All right, maybe I am; but, only with you." He kissed me again before he rose to his feet. "You sit back, relax, and enjoy, okay? When you hear her, you won't believe how good Casey is. In fact, I might go as far as to say she'll blow you away."

And she did. The minute she sang her first note, my mouth dropped open; and I was sure I was listening to the female equivalent of my husband. Her voice was strong and pure. When she harmonized with Mitch, their voices blended perfectly into a tone that grabbed you, pulled you in, and held you captive. I hadn't wanted to believe she'd be that good, but she was. I admitted to myself that, while I wasn't particularly enjoying her company, I was enjoying her musical talents. She, like Mitch, was a natural. As I watched them wind up the song, I began to wonder again why they ever broke up.

After the last note was played, you could have heard a pin drop. The band stood in awe—none of them sure how to react or what to say. Suddenly, Ash began to clap followed by Newbie; and within a few seconds, all six men were gathered around Casey applauding wildly. She looked from one to another with a bright smile and a blush in her cheeks.

"Casey, that was awesome!" Ash said. He turned to Mitch and laid a hand on his friend's shoulder. "Buddy, I think you just met your match."

Mitch nodded in agreement. "I told you she was good, didn't I?"

"Good?" Ty chimed in. "She's fantastic!"

Mitch looked at Casey with a light in his eyes. "Okay, now it's time to fly solo," he said as he moved the stool he'd been sitting on and placed his guitar on the stand. "We have a deal, you know."

Casey sighed and nodded. "Yeah, I know, but I'm not sure what to sing."

Mitch picked up a set list and handed it to her. "I'm sure you know most of these. Pick one."

She studied the sheet for a moment as she ran her finger down the list of songs. Finally, a decisive smile came to her face as she pointed her selection out to Mitch. "This one's good if your guys can take it up one key for me."

"Consider it done," Mitch said. He lowered the main mike to accommodate Casey's height difference from his, and the guys moved back into position. "Okay, on four. One, two, three...."

Ace began to play again as Casey took control of the moment and belted out the tune like she'd been singing it all her life. Mitch backed off and let Shep and Ty take the harmony so as not to drown out Casey with the strength of his voice, and the three of them sounded like they'd done it all before. She finished singing, and once again the room was filled with applause and cheers. When everyone had settled down again, Casey looked at them with a smile.

"Thanks for letting me do that, guys," she said. "I'd forgotten how much fun it was to sing with a band—not to mention how much I missed it."

The six of them looked at each other as if they all had the same thought. I sat at the back of the room and held my breath because I was fairly certain of what that thought was.

Confirmation came when Ty stepped forward and spoke up. "What do you guys think about adding a song for Casey at the club Saturday night?"

Everyone nodded in agreement, and Mitch smiled at Casey. "Sure, why not? I can talk to Rob, and we can feature you as a special guest. What do you say?"

I say you're playing all the cards just right, Casey thought to herself. "Gee, Mitch, I don't know. I mean, I am flattered and all, but I don't want to intrude on your routine."

Mitch laughed. "I think the regulars will like a change in routine. They get to hear us all the time. It'll be a treat for them."

She glanced around at the men and then turned to Mitch and nodded. "Okay. Count me in!"

Excitement swept through the musicians' circle and the spectators—made up of my unborn children and myself—sank down in the chair with disbelief. *Just what is happening here?* I asked myself. *First, she weasels her way into a job at Gartano's; and now she's trying to.... Wait a minute. Is that what's going on? She wants to be a part of Ace?* I sat up and glared at her as she and the band chatted gleefully about their plans for the show at Studio 14. *Does she think that because she didn't make it in Chicago that she can come here and fulfill her dreams through my husband?* As I contemplated that thought, she looked toward the back of the room; and our eyes met. An uncomfortable expression crossed her face as if she knew what I was thinking, and she quickly turned away. *That's right, Casey. I'm on to your little game; and before long, Mitch will be, too.*

Later that night as I lay in bed, my thoughts were focused on Casey and the newfound knowledge of her potential plans. I had to let Mitch know what was happening, but it was a matter of finding the right words and the right time to tell him. I glanced over at him sitting next to me, engrossed in the book he was reading. I turned my eyes back toward the ceiling. It wasn't going to be easy. He liked Casey, and he was all for the idea of her singing with them on Saturday night. He and his five band mates were innocent to her scheme. They simply thought it would be one song, one time, and life would move on. In Casey's mind, this was only the beginning of an ongoing thing. She'd hook the crowd and leave them wanting more. Mitch, being the type of guy who put his audience first, would probably oblige and boom!—she'd be in. To think she'd pretended she only wanted to be in the background tonight. She'd most likely plotted all along to come here and show off for them. It had all fallen into place nicely. She'd stalked her prey, pinned them down, and was about to go in for the kill. But, if I had anything to say about it, I'd have them running from her in no time.

Chapter 18

For the next few days, Casey made a nightly appearance at our home to rehearse the song she would sing at the show that weekend. The guys always gave her a warm reception as well as a multitude of praise after she sang, and she ate it up like a child would devour a favorite treat. I would sit at the back of the room and simply observe, seemingly forgotten for the majority of the time they played. At the end of their sessions, Mitch would find me again and lead me to the house where he would say goodbye to his friends until the next evening. Then I would spend the rest of the night contemplating how I was going to tell him Casey's ploy and try to determine the right time to do it.

After rehearsal on Friday evening, Mitch invited Casey and his band mates to stay for pizza and a little pre-performance pep rally for Casey. Although she was excited about her chance to be on stage, it was obvious that her nerves were taking their toll on her as well. I didn't want to be cruel, but a part of me secretly hoped she'd get too uptight and decide to bail altogether. That would eliminate the possibility of anyone hearing her, anyone liking her, and anyone wanting to hear her again. Most importantly, it would eliminate the possibility of her becoming a part of Ace.

"Okay, everyone, dig in!" Mitch placed the four pizza boxes on the dining room table; and like vultures on a fresh kill, they all moved in. Casey wasn't shy with her appetite, and I secretly seethed at her ability to suck down 500 calories with the knowledge that she would not gain a single ounce. Looking down at the bulges that I once called my thighs, I resigned myself to the fact that for me those days were long gone. While the seven of them savored the strings of cheese bridging between their mouths and the pizza slices, I headed to the kitchen for a cup of low-fat yogurt.

Knowing the temptation in the dining room would be much too great, I peeled the lid off the container, took a spoon from the drawer, and leaned against the counter to enjoy my 'treat.' I tried my best to tune out the sounds of indulgent bliss coming from the others and told myself this was all for the best. I knew I would never have the willpower to stop at just one piece, and the last thing I needed was another ten pounds.

As I stood there focused on fishing the last blueberry from the bottom of the cup, my husband entered the room with a concerned expression. He placed a hand on my shoulder and bent down to look into my eyes.

"What's wrong, sweetie? Why aren't you having pizza?"

I slapped my hand against my thigh. "Need I say more?"

He gave me a sweet, soft smile and pulled me into his arms. "Dana, you're so beautiful. I know you've gained a little extra weight with the pregnancy, but you'll lose most of it when the babies come." He snuggled into me and placed his cheek against the top of my head. "Even if you don't, I don't care. I love you, and I always will."

His arms felt warm, strong, and secure around me; and I allowed myself to get lost in the feeling of love they were giving me. I could hear his heart beating, and it soothed me. He always knew what I needed to hear and just when I needed to hear it. Right then—and especially with Casey in the next room—I needed the reassurance that he still wanted me just as I was. He pulled away from me with a smile in his eyes and a soft glow on his face that radiated what was in his heart.

"You're my everything. You know that, don't you?"

"Am I?"

"Absolutely!" He pulled me to him again and placed a soft kiss on my cheek before he let me go. "Will you at least come and join us? I'd like you to."

"I will only if all the pizza's gone. Too tempting."

He glanced at the room filled with his friends and then looked at me once more. "I don't think you have to worry, love. They all acted as if they hadn't eaten in a month."

I tossed the empty yogurt cup in the trash and tucked my arm around his waist. "Again, typical men."

"What about Casey?"

"She was just trying to get some before they ate it all."

We started into the dining room, and I hadn't taken three steps before I stopped suddenly and turned to Mitch. "Wow—another one."

"Another one what?"

"Another Braxton Hick's contraction. I've had four of them since I came out for the yogurt."

His face began to grow pale. "Are you sure that's what they are?"

I placed a hand on his back and rubbed it gently as I smiled at him. "Yes, honey, that's what they are—nothing to be alarmed about. I just don't remember having that many this close together before."

"Maybe it has something to do with the fact that you went on a cleaning spree today. You may have strained some muscles or something."

"Could be," I answered. "Well, I'm not going to worry about it. Besides, the house really needed it; and now it looks good."

"Absolutely," he quipped again as he put his arm around my shoulders. "You did a great job."

Mitch kissed me as we stepped into the room, and Shep's face held an ornery grin.

"I swear that must be all you two ever do. Every time I see you lately you're slobbering all over each other." He turned to the others and pointed in our direction. "Don't you guys agree?"

Everyone nodded in agreement, and he addressed Casey. "It seems like every time we leave them alone for more than thirty seconds, they turn it into a make-out session. You'd think they're newlyweds or something."

"Yeah, it has gotten out of hand," Zach agreed teasingly.

Mitch grinned at both of them. "You're both just jealous." He turned to me with that light in his eyes again. "You wish you had someone even half as beautiful as my wife."

Out of the corner of my eye, I noticed Casey as he said that; and she looked a little more green-eyed than normal. I moved closer to Mitch and rested my head against him. She turned away, and I smiled inside.

As I settled into a chair, Mitch took a seat beside me and placed a hand on my shoulder as he began to rub it. "I have everything worked out with Rob for tomorrow night. We'll go on as usual, do the first four in the set, break, and then bring Casey out right after." He turned to her with a little smirk. "Will you get too nervous waiting that long? If so, we can try something else."

"No, that should be fine," she said. "Will you have me waiting backstage or in the audience?"

Mitch twisted his jaw in thought before he answered. "You can sit at the table with my family until the break. Then I'll come get you, and you can wait backstage until you go on. How's that?"

Lovely, I thought. *I get to spend more 'quality time' with her. I can hardly stand the excitement.*

"I like that idea," she answered. "That way I can scope out the crowd a little, too."

The seven of them visited for the next hour or so; and after the last goodbye was said to the group, Mitch closed the door and turned to me with a smile.

"She's really nervous," he said in reference to Casey. "I hope she doesn't pass out or anything."

I decided to try being sly. "Gosh, you don't think she will, do you? Maybe you should reconsider this whole thing. She does strike me as somewhat flighty anyway."

Mitch bit his lip for a moment and then shook his head. "No, I think she'll be all right. I gave her the day off tomorrow and told her to rest up. I know I get nervous sometimes, too—well, at least I did at first—but once I get out the first line or two of the song, I just start to relax. If the crowd's into it like they normally are, the excitement will overpower the nerves."

"What if the crowd makes her more nervous?"

He smiled. "That's what the six of us are for. We'll back her up, and no one will see it. It's the fine art of performing—never let them see you sweat."

I could see my tactics weren't working, so I decided the only thing to do was hope that her day spent in anticipation would jostle her nerves even more. It looked as if the show was going on no matter what.

A short while later as I got ready for bed, I caught Mitch out of the corner of my eye watching me with a bit of a smile tugging at his lips. As I crawled up next to him, I let out a heavy sigh.

"Do you really think I'll lose all this extra weight, Mitch? I've really gained a lot." I patted my thighs. "Look at me—I'm enormous!"

The smile spread into a wide grin, and he turned so that he was now on his side facing me, his head propped on his hand. "No, you aren't. Enormous would be...." He paused for a moment in thought.

"Enormous would be something like the Atlantic Ocean. You look nothing like the Atlantic Ocean."

I felt a tear trickle down my cheek. "Well, maybe I'm not water, but I am a large body!"

He reached out for me and prompted me to lie down next to him. "I thought we talked about all this earlier, love. Remember, when everyone was here and we were in the kitchen?" He brushed the hair off my face and tilted my chin to look into his eyes. "You are an incredible woman, and I'm very attracted to you."

I wiped a tear from my eye and glanced down again before I looked up at him. "You are really attracted to all this? I look nothing like I did even three months ago."

He smiled softly and pulled me closer to him as he lowered his voice to a seductive tone. "No, you don't. You look better to me. You get prettier each day. And yes, I'm attracted to you. Do I need to show you how much?"

I looked into his eyes filled with desire, and I kissed him softly. "Mitch, you know that Dr. Bradley said we need to be careful now that I'm getting closer to delivering. We probably shouldn't."

He gave me an ornery grin. "Ah, what does he know? He's only a doctor," he teased. "Besides, I have to prove my point, don't I?"

"I suppose you do."

And he did.

By the time Saturday afternoon rolled around, I had convinced myself that I had to find a way to tell Mitch about Casey before the show that evening. I couldn't stand back and allow her to take advantage of his kindness—let alone that of the other five men as well. I was certain that she had every inch of her plan worked out right down to the last detail and that she had plotted it since the day she and Mitch had met at the hospital. I deduced that she'd purposely put off meeting the guys and coming to rehearsal. She wanted to give Mitch plenty of time to get used to having her around again as well as get as much information from him about the band as she could. After all, ignorance is bliss; but knowledge is power. She would need all the knowledge she could get to have the power to carry out her plan. I wasn't sure yet how I would do it; but if I had any say in the matter, her plan would be foiled before the evening came in.

I heard the sound of the garage door going up and glanced out the window to see Mitch's deep blue Jeep Cherokee pulling into the driveway. Not wanting to be obvious, I grabbed the newspaper and quickly took a seat on the couch. A moment later, I heard the door open and the sound of Mitch whistling a happy tune.

Perfect, I thought. *He seems to be in a good mood. Maybe it won't be so hard to tell him what I need him to know.*

With a bright smile on his face he rounded the corner to the living room. "Hey, sweetheart! How are you?" He plopped down next to me as he tugged at the knot on his tie and planted a kiss on my cheek.

I placed the paper next to me and gave him a hug. Resting my head on his shoulder, I looked into his eyes. "Better now that you're here."

"Sounds like someone was lonely."

"I'm always lonely when you're away. I miss you, you know."

He pulled the tie completely off, tossed it onto the coffee table, and undid the first two buttons on his shirt. Kicking off his shoes, he propped up his feet and then pulled me closer to him. "I miss you when I'm away, too. I much prefer being here with you."

I ran my finger up and down his chest, and he began to follow the motion with his eyes. "Well, now that you are," I started, "there's something I need to talk to you about."

His face took on a look of concern. "Sure. What is it?"

Okay, Dana, you can do this. Just come right out with it. No sense beating around the bush. It's now or never.

I looked into his eyes as he waited for my answer; but when I tried to speak, the words just wouldn't come out. "I think...."

He smiled softly. "Honey, go ahead. Whatever it is, you can tell me."

I knew I needed to say it, yet I knew he'd never believe my theory about her wanting to join the band. I had to come up with another concept. *Maybe I should give him a little test to see if he's thought about letting her join Ace. That way, I'll have a better idea of how to approach the subject.*

"I was thinking about Casey. What if she misunderstood that you only planned to let her sing tonight, and she thinks it's going to be an ongoing thing? How will you tell her it's not without hurting her feelings?"

He kissed my forehead as he brushed the hair gently off my shoulder. "There's nothing to worry about, love. We're announcing her as a special guest—one song—and it's a done deal." He rubbed my arm with his hand. "I'm pretty sure she understands that. It's just for fun. After all, it was really the guys who talked her into this whole thing. She didn't ask to do it. She only agreed, but I think it's sweet of you to consider her feelings in all of it."

Gee, that idea sure flopped. Now what?

"Well, what if the crowd really likes her, and they think she's a regular ? Won't you run the risk of losing people when they find out she's not?"

"I think the special guest label will clear up that misconception." Then he chuckled. "Sweetheart, I'm beginning to think that there may be a reason why you don't want her to sing tonight." He pulled back and looked into my eyes with a smirk. "Do you feel like maybe she's getting a little too close to your man?"

I've felt that way for a month and a half—not that either of you have done anything to change it! "No, Mitchell, my jealousy has nothing to do with this."

I hadn't realized what I said; but, of course, my husband didn't miss a trick.

"Ah ha!" he exclaimed. "Now, you admit that you *are* jealous of Casey?"

"What?"

"You just said it. You said that your jealousy has nothing to do with the fact that you don't want her to sing tonight."

He was grinning from ear to ear, obviously enjoying himself. Why did he always decide to tease me when I was trying to be serious? He knew it would only make me angry, which right then was definitely the case.

I folded my arms stubbornly and moved away from him. "I'm not jealous of her—I trust you, remember?"

"Yes, I remember. Thank you."

"But, I *don't* appreciate your teasing me all the time. I was trying to help you...her...but if you won't take me seriously, then forget I said anything at all!"

As I started to stand, I felt a sharp pain race through my lower back. Instinctively, I placed a hand there and winced. Mitch noticed this, too, and placed a hand on my arm to help lower me back to the couch.

"What's the matter? What happened?"

I was far too upset just then to take his sympathy. "Nothing. I'm fine."

"That look on your face was not one that said "I'm fine." Tell me what's wrong. Is your back hurting?"

I nodded as I began to rub against the throbbing that had actually been plaguing me most of the day.

He stood up, repositioned a few pillows, and then slowly lowered me down on my back. "Lie still for a minute or two. It's probably nothing more than a muscle spasm." He took off my shoes and gently straightened my legs. "There you go. I'll go get the heating pad for you. That should help."

I heard him rummaging through the linen closet, and a moment later he returned with it. Placing a hand beneath me, he managed to lift me enough to slide the pad under my lower back and told me to lie flat against it. He plugged it in and turned it to the 'low' setting.

He took a seat on the coffee table and smiled sympathetically. "Better now?"

I nodded. I still didn't feel like answering him.

He reached out for my hand and brought it to his lips for a tender kiss. "I'm sorry I was teasing you. You really have been a good sport about all this, and I appreciate it. In fact, Casey really likes you."

She won't like me once I figure out how to call her bluff!

I nodded again as I tried to relax and let the heat penetrate my aching muscles.

He leaned forward to give me a kiss before he stood up. "I'm going to go take a shower. You try to take a little nap. I love you."

I heard the bathroom door closing and the sound of Mitch starting to sing. *What song is that? 'Endless Love'?* I sighed softly, and a gentle smile came to my face. *He's such a sweetheart. I'm sure he knows I can hear him, and he's doing that for me. How did I get so lucky?*

I closed my eyes and tried to go to sleep; but each time I got close to unconsciousness, my back would start to ache, I would have a Braxton Hick, or one of the babies would decide it was time to play 'Kick Mommy's Internal Organs.' Besides the physical aches, my mind wouldn't let go of what was to transpire in a few short hours. I couldn't stand the thought of sitting idly by and letting Casey weasel her way into Ace, but there didn't seem to be any way to stop that from happening. She was going to sing; and once the crowd—and Rob—heard her, they would surely insist on another performance regardless of how Mitch planned to announce her. Our conversation of a few moments ago proved that he thought there was nothing to fear. To make matters worse—because I had opened my big fat mouth—he would think that anything else I said against Casey was only out of jealousy. I was at an impasse with the situation—or wasn't I?

Perhaps I could handle this in an entirely different way. Instead of working on the prey, why not work on the predator? I could try to talk to Casey and propose the same issues I did with Mitch to see how she reacted. If she seemed distant or apprehensive, that might give her a clue that I'm on to her and perhaps be enough to make her back out. If she seemed calm, then she might be innocent after all—or simply a very good actress.

As I contemplated possible dialogues for the evening, I heard Mitch's footsteps on the stairs; and soon he appeared next to me.

He held his glasses in one hand, breathed onto both lenses, and proceeded to wipe them with the corner of his shirt. "How are you feeling? Did you get a nap?"

"No, I couldn't sleep." I glanced at the clock on the wall opposite me. "Anyway, I need to get up and fix some dinner so we can get to the club on time."

He held his glasses at arms length to inspect them, wiped another spot from the right lens, and then placed them on. "That's better. I don't know how I could even see out of those things before." He smiled. "About dinner—why don't I order in something tonight? What would you like?"

"Thank you, but I'm fine. My back only hurts a little. I can cook."

He let out a deep sigh; and although he was smiling, his face took on that stubborn look I knew all too well. "No arguing, young lady. It's a done deal. Now, tell me what you would like to eat."

"How about Chinese?"

"Sounds good."

He headed off to the kitchen; and a minute or two later, I heard him place the order. He hung up and returned to sit in the chair next to me. "Mr. Chang said they'd have it here in about half an hour." He sunk down a little and stretched out his legs. "So tell me about your day. What did you do?"

I tried to turn to my side to face him. When I did, another pain shot through my lower spine; and I grimaced. Mitch noticed and looked at me—his eyes filled with concern.

"Dana, how long has your back been hurting?"

"Pretty much all day. I'll be okay."

"Maybe you should stay home and rest tonight. I can fix you up on the couch down in the family room, and you can watch TV. That might be best."

I sat up as slowly as I could and gave him a look. "I want to go with you tonight. I'll be all right. Really. I probably just did too much yesterday."

He sat up, folded his hands in his lap, and leaned toward me with a flirtatious grin. "Have I ever told you that you're stubborn?"

"Yes, you have—many times."

"Have I ever told you that you're really cute when you're acting that way?"

"I don't remember that but thank you."

He moved to sit down next to me and placed an arm around my shoulders as he drew me to him. He glanced down at my stomach and placed his other hand there. "I don't feel anything. They must be sleeping, huh?"

"They sure weren't earlier," I said. "That's one of the reasons I didn't get a nap while you were showering. They kept trying to dislodge all my organs with their feet!"

Mitch laughed. "That doesn't sound very pleasant."

"Well, it's not so bad until they decide to wedge themselves under my ribcage. Then there's no way to turn to get comfortable until they decide to move."

He gave me a gentle kiss on the forehead and began to rub my arm. "Pretty soon you won't have to worry about that any longer. Just think—this time next year we'll probably be chasing them all over the place."

I nodded. "Probably." I let a soft sigh escape and snuggled close to him. "I can't even imagine what that's going to be like. Heck, some days I still can't believe I'm married and pregnant."

He chuckled. "And you have me to thank for both."

I poked his side playfully, and he laughed. "Yeah, I guess I do."

A little over an hour later, we arrived at Studio 14; and Mitch tucked an arm around my waist as we walked to the door. Because the back pain had not eased much, he wanted to offer me some extra support. As we stepped inside and approached the table, I noticed the form of someone sitting there and quickly identified the figure as Casey. Her eyes were fixed on the guys as they busily put things in place onstage, and she appeared to be wringing her hands nervously in her lap. Mitch smiled at me and leaned close to my ear.

"I didn't expect her to be here this early. Either she's really excited, really uptight, or both."

I was secretly hoping for the latter. It would make my plan go a lot smoother.

I decided to try one more sneaky plea. "I'd guess she's nervous. Maybe you should tell her to go home."

He gave me half a smile in response and shook his head.

"Hi, Mitch. Hi, Dana," she greeted as we got to the table. "I hope I'm not too early. I couldn't stand sitting at home a minute longer."

Mitch gave her a sweet smile. "No, you're fine. Are you all set to do this?"

She nodded and began to twist a strand of hair around her finger. "I think so. I've gotta admit though—I am a bit nervous."

He had let go of me and placed his hand on her shoulder. "Don't worry about it. You'll do fine. Like I told you in rehearsal, the guys and I will back you up. There's nothing to be concerned about. Just let the crowd see the talent."

She smiled up at him and batted her eyelashes. "Gosh, Mitch, you sure know how to make me feel better. Thanks."

I wanted to be sick.

"No problem." Finally remembering I was still standing next to him, he pulled out a chair with one hand and extended another to me. "Come on, love. Take a seat here and relax. How's your back?"

"It's okay," I replied. I didn't want to tell him that my stomach was starting to hurt, too.

"I'll be back to check on you in a few minutes." He pulled the watch from his pocket, opened the case, and looked at the time. "The others should be getting here shortly. Do you need anything before I go?"

I shot a look in Casey's direction before I looked up at him with big puppy dog eyes. "Nothing but a big kiss and maybe a hug from you."

"Sounds like a request I'll be happy to fill."

As he leaned down to kiss me, I opened my eyes for an instant and caught a glimpse of Casey's jealous stare. Just for show, I made the kiss last a little longer.

He stood back up and addressed her once more. "You relax, too. If you need anything, Dana or one of the others can point you in the right direction. I'll check back in before the show starts."

"Okay, Mitch, thanks."

He headed up the stairs that led to the stage, and soon he was caught up in the weekly pre-show ritual with his band mates. I watched them for a moment or two until I felt Casey's eyes fall upon me. I turned toward her, and we both smiled uncomfortably—an awkward silence between us. I decided that it was time to put my plan into motion, and I glanced back to the stage before I made eye contact with her again.

"You know," I started, "I've been around these guys practically every day for the past ten months or so; and it still amazes me how well they click together. They have everything down to a fine science. I don't think they'd ever let anything come between them."

She nodded. "Yeah, I noticed that they do seem to get along well. That's great that they have that camaraderie. I guess when you work together that closely, you need it."

"They definitely are close. I'd even go as far as to say they're almost like brothers to one another." I looked at them again for effect. "In fact, it's like they have a tight knit circle that they will do anything to protect. They don't want anyone to leave, and they don't want anyone to come in."

Casey's expression changed to one that I could easily have mistaken for defiance. "Well, they're letting me in," she said in a mocking tone.

I took a deep breath so I wouldn't hiss back at her. "Oh, yeah, you're right. They are letting you in for tonight. I meant *permanently*. They're a pretty tight group."

I could see the gears turning in her head; but before she had a chance to formulate an answer, Jim and Angelina approached with Paul and Julia following close behind.

"Good evening, ladies," Paul greeted with a smile. "I hear we're in for a treat tonight, huh?" He looked at Casey, and she blushed.

"I'm not sure if it will be a treat for anyone, but Mitch did agree to let me sing this evening. He's so sweet."

I must have been glaring daggers through her because Paul and Jim both looked at me and then exchanged smirks.

Jim smiled at me. "I'm sure Dana can vouch for that." I returned the expression.

"Vouch for what?" Chris asked as he and Trudy came up behind me.

"What a sweet guy Mitch is," Julia answered.

Chris laughed. "Mitchell? All I remember is an ornery little boy who grew up to be an ornery young man. I'd hardly call him sweet."

Trudy gave him a look and folded her arms. "Christopher Tarrington, that's your brother you're talking about; and yes, he is a sweet guy. Absolutely."

Chris began to chuckle, and he placed an arm around her waist. "Don't get all bent out of shape, dear. I was only joking." Then he winked at me. "Well, kind of."

"Oh, I'll agree he's ornery all right. But," and I made sure Casey was paying attention, "he's also a big sweetheart."

The guys ran through a few sound checks and retreated offstage while Mitch made his way to the table. He stopped behind me and began to rub both shoulders gently. I reached up and placed my hand atop his.

"You guys keep an eye on my girl here, okay? She isn't feeling well tonight."

Jim shot me a look. "What's the matter, Dana?"

I gave him a reassuring smile. "Nothing really. I did a lot of cleaning yesterday, and now my lower back is hurting some. I'll be all right." I smiled up at Mitch. "He's just being overprotective again."

He sighed but then smiled down at me. "Somebody has to keep you in line."

"You do a good job of it, sweetie. Thank you."

He turned his attention to Casey. "We'll be getting things underway in about twenty minutes. Looks like we're gonna have another huge crowd."

Casey's eyes scanned the room. "It's already packed, and it looks like more are coming in."

"This is only about half of what will be in here shortly," Trudy told her. "Once the word got out about how fantastic Ace is, they've been packing them in every week!"

Mitch grinned as he noticed the nervous look on Casey's face. "I used to get a little uptight at first, but now I kinda feed off the crowd. If they're riled up, then it gets me riled up, too. The object is to do your best and have a good time with it." He pointed toward the stage. "Why don't you come back with me for the preliminaries, and then you can head back to the table?"

She stood up with a shrug. "I don't know what the 'preliminaries' are, but okay. I'll come with you."

Mitch took a few steps away from the table, stopped suddenly, and turned around. "Gosh, I almost forgot." He walked up to me and gave me a long, warm kiss. "I'm sorry, sweetheart. I love you."

"I love you, too, Mitch. Good luck."

As the two of them walked toward the stage, Mitch was pointing out various things to Casey; and she was leaning close to him as if she was trying to hear above the crowd. As they ascended the stairs, I noticed once again his hand resting gently in the middle of her back as if to steady her. He turned to smile at me before they disappeared backstage, but I didn't smile back.

Fifteen minutes passed quickly, and Casey made her way back to the table just as Rob went onstage to announce Ace. The crowd was on its feet as the band took the stage, and Mitch cued them into the first song. Casey was sitting on the edge of her seat with her eyes glued to my husband and a grin as big as Texas plastered to her face. Mitch turned toward our table and smiled brightly, so I blew him a kiss and waved. I didn't want Casey to think his expression was for her, and I tried to believe it wasn't.

The third song wound down, and Mitch stepped breathlessly to the mike as the crowd roared.

"How's everyone doing tonight?" He wiped his forehead with a towel Zach handed to him and tossed it behind him next to an amp. He turned back to the cheering audience with a grin. "Sounds like you came here to have a good time, and we're going to make sure you have it. We're gonna do one more, take a break, and then we have a surprise for you all. Let's keep this thing rolling, shall we?"

As they started to play again, I looked around me. There was not one person I saw that wasn't standing and not one face that didn't hold a smile. Some were dancing, some were clapping their hands to the music, and others were singing along. I looked back at Mitch singing and playing his heart out, and a feeling of pride swept over me. That was my husband holding the crowd in his hands and having the time of his life. There wasn't a doubt in my mind that this was his passion, and there was no way I was letting Casey take that away from him. The song ended, and Mitch announced their break. I had exactly fifteen minutes to take one last shot at stopping her.

I stood up slowly and gained my footing with both hands on my lower back. Jim, who had been lost in conversation with Chris only a moment before, turned to me with true concern.

"Is your back still hurting, Dana?"

I didn't have time for a medical evaluation. I needed to get to my husband. "Oh, it's feeling better. I think I'll stretch it out a little. I'm going to go see Mitch."

"Isn't he going to come out here?" Angelina asked. "He usually does."

"Uh, well, I'll just meet him halfway. I really could use a short walk."

I hurried away from the table as quickly as I possibly could before anyone else could try to stop me. Mitch reached the top of the stairs at the same time I reached the bottom, and he hurried down to take my hand.

"Honey, what are you doing? Shouldn't you be sitting down?"

"I'm stretching out my back. I'll only get stiffer if I sit all night." I took hold of his other hand and stepped up close to him. "Besides, I wanted to come and see you."

He took me into his arms and planted a soft kiss on my lips. "I was coming to see you, baby. I want you to rest."

I looked into his eyes filled with love and knew I had to tell him then, or I never would. "Actually, Mitch, I have something to tell you about Casey."

He smirked. "Are you going to try to convince me again that you aren't jealous of her?"

Come on, Mitch, don't start teasing me again. Not now.

"Please be serious. This is important."

He chuckled. "I'm sorry. What do you want to tell me?"

I opened my mouth to speak, only to be interrupted by none other than Casey herself.

She'd crept up behind me without a sound—like a sneaky cat ready to pounce on her prey. I turned around, and she shot me a glimpse of her sickening sweet smile.

You know that I know your secret, you conniving little brat. That's why you hurried over here. You knew I was going to tell him, didn't you?

She turned to Mitch. "Sorry, but Rob was at the table looking for you, Mitch. He said it was kind of important."

He sighed and looked down at me remorsefully. "I'd better go see what's going on. Come on. I'll walk you back to the table."

I gave Casey a look that would have peeled paint off a wall, and she just smiled as she led the way. I tugged lightly on Mitch's arm, and he stopped momentarily.

He gave me a soft peck on the cheek. "Baby, we can talk later, all right? I promise."

I knew 'later' would be too late, and there wasn't a thing I could do about it. Not one thing.

"Yeah, I guess so."

We reached the table, and I sat back down. Rob and Mitch rapped up the last-minute details for Casey's big performance; and with a quick kiss on my forehead, he was off for the second half of the show. I sat back and said a silent prayer that my worst fears wouldn't come true. Somehow, I knew better.

About the time Mitch walked to the microphone again, I felt my stomach beginning to ache even more; and the pain in my back was starting to radiate into my legs. *You're just tense,* I told myself. *It'll be all right. You'll figure out what to do. Just relax.*

I took a slow, deep breath and let it escape silently. The last thing I needed was to bring attention to myself. Trudy looked my way, and I mustered up a smile. She smiled back and turned her attention back to Mitch.

"I told you all that after the break we had a surprise for you," Mitch said and everyone applauded. "It gives me great pleasure to introduce to you our special guest tonight, my good friend Casey Tomlin!"

Most of the crowd stood up as she came onstage with that smile and a wave. Mitch stepped away from the mike and smiled at her. She nodded to the band and started into her song. Evidently, nerves weren't an issue for her after all. She sang like she'd been born on the stage and within mere seconds had the crowd right where she wanted them—not to mention Rob. He stood on the floor next to the stage for a minute just grinning and shaking his head before he disappeared toward the back of the room. I tried to follow him with my eyes, but the pain in my back prevented me from being able to turn very far in my chair. Soon he was lost in the crowd, so I focused back in on the Queen of Deceit.

Mitch's family was as taken with her as everyone else seemed to be, and they chatted excitedly about how wonderful she was. Julia turned to me.

"Wow, she's really great, isn't she?"

"Yeah, she's pretty good," I replied as I thought to myself: *good at getting people to think she's good.*

Casey sang the last line, and the sound from the crowd was deafening. Even the guys in the band were applauding her, and Zach and Shep were both whistling as well. Mitch turned and said something to Shep. He quickly moved through the other four and said something to each before he raced off stage. He returned with two stools which he placed next to Casey and Mitch, who now stood at the mike. Mitch gave a signal to the crowd to settle; and when the noise was down to a low roar, he began to speak.

"You know, the six of us had a feeling you were going to love this girl," he hesitated as he waited for the cheers to subside once more, "so we planned a little something else; and we hope you'll enjoy it."

Mitch took a mike off the stand and handed it to Casey as she sat down. He did the same; and as soon as I heard the first few notes of the song, I realized what was about to ensue.

'Endless Love'? Is that why he was singing it earlier? He wasn't singing it for me at all—he was practicing for tonight!

I watched in amazement as my husband sat across from his ex. His face was full of emotion and his eyes were focused completely on her. *I don't like the way she's looking at him—and I <u>really</u> don't like the way he's looking at her. What's happening here?* Casey's expression was undeniable. Everyone in that room at that moment could clearly see that for her the words weren't just lyrics to a song. She truly meant every one of them. Maybe being a part of Ace wasn't the only thing she wanted after all. And now, even though I didn't want to believe it, I wondered if maybe there was a chance he knew that, too.

This isn't going to happen, I told myself as I stared at the stage. *We've been through too much...we have babies on the way....*

The song ended, and the crowd went wild as Mitch and Casey stood up and took a bow. Casey turned to him with a bright smile; and as he returned it, she extended her arms and he stepped into her embrace. Only this time what had been a friendly hug in the past seemed to hold a bit of true emotion as I saw them tighten their grip for a moment before they let go. They turned toward the crowd, joined hands, and bowed again.

"Ladies and gentlemen, Casey Tomlin!" he shouted into the mike, and he smiled at her again.

I rose to my feet and grabbed the jacket off the back of my chair. Chris placed a hand on my arm.

"Dana, are you okay?"

I fought to hold in my emotions, and I managed to squeak out a response that sounded at least halfway convincing. "I'm getting a little warm. I'm just going to step outside for some air."

"Would you like me to go with you? You shouldn't go out there alone."

"No, Chris, thanks. I'll be all right. I'll stay by the door."

As I made my way toward the door and got lost in the crowd, I turned to see Casey back at the table with Mitch's entire family gathered around her. Glancing up at Mitch again, his eyes were fixed on the scene; and his face glowed. *No, this won't happen. It won't!*

Composing myself as best I could, I turned away as I heard the band start again. Once I was out the door, I let go.

Chapter 19

Chris looked nervously at his watch and started to stand. "I'm going to check on Dana. She's been out there for fifteen minutes."

Trudy placed her hand on his back as she stood herself. "No, honey, let me go. I think I might be better equipped to handle this one."

He gave her a quizzical stare. "Handle what?"

Trudy shook her head; and with her hand still in place, she prompted him a few steps away from the table and lowered her voice. "Chris, didn't you see the way she looked when Casey and Mitch were singing together? It upset her. You know how jealous she is, and I'm sure that the extra hormones right now don't do much to calm her." She kissed his cheek lightly. "You stay here. This is a girl thing."

He sighed and moved his eyes toward the door. Looking at Trudy again, he reluctantly nodded. "Okay, but please don't go far from the door, and don't stay out there for long."

"I won't."

I stood outside the entrance to Studio 14. I was careful to keep my back to the door as I didn't want anyone to see the tears that streamed down both cheeks. I held my gloved hands over my mouth to muffle the sobs. I had known from the first time I saw Casey that she was trouble, and my instincts had been proven right tonight at every turn. Everything she had said and done pointed to her desire to be a part of Ace—to live out her dream even if it meant she'd have to intrude on, or even shatter, Mitch's dream. Now, after seeing them sing that duet, I had to wonder what else she was contemplating. Was it also a part of her plan to try to win Mitch back once she'd wedged her way into the band? Could it be that she was still in love with him? I pondered that thought. *Still in love with him.* Mitch had never told me how deep his feelings for Casey had gone—only that their breakup was of mutual consent. After tonight, it was no secret how deep her feelings were for him.

I was trying to put it all together in my mind, but there were still too many pieces of the puzzle that didn't fit. For one thing, he never mentioned her to me until the night he hired her. Could it truly be that she hadn't meant that much to him; or was it that she had, and he didn't want me to worry about it? Was being around her stirring up old feelings, or was it creating new ones? Is he starting to realize that perhaps there was more to their relationship that he never knew, and he gave up on it too soon? Were his attempts at getting me to become friends with her really nothing more than his way of ensuring that he didn't allow himself to get too close? After all, if I was her friend as well, he would be too uncomfortable to cross any lines with her, or, at least I *hoped* he would be. As my mind raced, the thoughts became even more tangled. I wasn't sure if I'd ever get them sorted out.

I heard the door open behind me, and Trudy stepped out into night. She wrapped her jacket around her and zipped it up all the way as she stood the collar on end to keep out the chill. She placed a gentle hand on my shoulder.

"We were getting worried about you. Is everything all right?"

I wiped my eyes as best I could and turned to face her. "I don't know, Trudy. I can't believe she's doing this to Mitch—to us. It's so mean and rotten. How can one person be that cunning?"

"Dana, I'm sorry, but I'm not following you. Are you talking about Casey or someone else?"

I decided to try out the family policy of 'no secrets' and began to pour out my entire theory on Casey Tomlin for Trudy. The more I told, the angrier I became; and soon my emotions were in control of me completely. The tears strangled me, and my lungs began to gasp as

I gulped in the cold night air. The pain from my back had taken over my legs as well, and the tension was causing Braxton Hicks so close together that it had become hard to distinguish when one ended and the next began. As I finished speaking, throwing in one last derogatory remark against Casey, Chris appeared at the door and stepped outside. Seeing my less-than-stable emotional state, he quickly came to my side and placed a hand on my back.

"What's going on?" His eyes searched mine, then Trudy's, for some kind of answer. When neither of us gave him one, he placed an arm around my shoulders. "I think the two of you need to come back in. It's awfully cold out here." He saw the look on my face and read it with precision. "You don't have to go back to the table. I'll keep Mitch and Casey at bay for a little while, if you want, until you feel better. Please come back in where it's warm, okay?"

Trudy held open the door, and I had only taken one step when a strange sensation came over me. With wide eyes, my hands instinctively went to my abdomen; and I looked at the two of them in complete panic.

"I think my water just broke!"

The pair glared at me as if they had seen a ghost. Trudy let the door slam shut and rushed to me. "Are you sure?"

I could only nod as I felt another Braxton Hick. Only then, I realized these were no longer practice contractions. These were the real McCoy.

"Christopher, go get Mitch!"

Chris nodded obediently to his wife and disappeared into the club. In what seemed like record time, Mitch and Chris appeared at the door with Jim close behind. Mitch's face was pale, and he hurried to place an arm around me as Trudy helped me through the door.

"Is it true, Dana? Are you...are you...."

I nodded, and he shook his head.

"But you can't be! You still have over three weeks left. It's too soon!"

Chris smirked. "Yes, little brother, she's in labor."

Mitch gave him a deer-in-the-headlights sort of stare, and Jim stepped in between them as he looked Mitch directly in the eyes to take control of the situation.

"Mitch, listen to me. I'll drive the two of you to the hospital in my car. That way if we get pulled over for speeding, I can tell them it's a medical emergency; and they'll let me through. Give Chris your keys, and he can bring your car. Trudy, you go back to the table and tell the others what's happening. Then please call Jake, Olivia, and Kayla so

Mitch doesn't have to worry about that." He smiled as Mitch nodded nervously and fumbled for the keys in his pocket. "Just relax, buddy. It's going to be fine. Yes, she's early, but that's not unusual with twin births."

As Chris and Trudy disappeared into the club, I had another contraction—only this time, it hurt. I started to double over, and both men placed their arms around me.

I could almost feel Mitch's body trembling as he held me close to him; but he took a deep breath, gained his composure, and spoke to me soothingly.

"It's okay, honey; just relax. Take a deep breath and let it out slowly. Remember how Kathy taught us?"

I didn't know whether or not it would help, but I figured it couldn't hurt either; so I followed his instructions. I was still upset over the whole Casey thing but decided the impending birth of our children was more important at that particular moment. Jim ran across the parking lot to his car; and a moment later he pulled up next to the door, jumped out, and opened the back for us.

"Mitch, you sit back there with her and let her lean against you, okay? Dana, when was your last contraction, sweetheart?"

"She just had one before you pulled up," Mitch answered.

Jim took a look at his watch. "Okay. I want you to tell me when you have the next one and about how long it lasts." After he had us both situated in the back seat, he got back in and headed out of the parking lot. "Don't worry," he chuckled. "I'm an expert at this sort of thing—once with Angie and a couple of times with Chris and Trudy. We were lucky to make it to the hospital on all those accounts; but if your babies decide to make an early appearance, I know what to do."

I knew he was only trying to get me to relax, but his attempt at humor didn't help. I looked at Mitch through misty eyes and said in a trembling voice, "Oh, no, please. I don't want to have these babies here. I'm scared."

He wrapped his arms around me as tightly as he could and kissed me softly. "I know you are, but I'm here, baby. I'm right here. We'll be all right."

We arrived at the emergency entrance to Mercy Hospital twelve minutes later—a drive that would normally take about twenty—and I said a silent prayer of thanks that Jim was an excellent driver. During the ride I had one more contraction, and Jim announced that they were coming around ten minutes apart according to his best calculations. Instructing us to stay put, he ran inside for a wheelchair. An orderly helped me into it and wheeled me inside. Just like Mr. Lane in our

Lamaze class movie, Mitch kept right by my side and held my hand tightly as we boarded the elevator to the maternity ward; and every few minutes he would tell me to breathe.

We stepped off the elevator, and the orderly handed the wheelchair over to a nurse who smiled brightly at both of us. Somehow, Jim had managed to make it to the floor ahead of us, and he had everyone on standby. The nurse turned to Mitch and put up a hand.

"Mr. Tarrington, we'll be taking your wife into Room 3. You can wait right over there in the fathers' lounge while we start her IV and get her prepped. Someone will come back and get you in a few minutes."

He started to protest, but Jim quickly moved up behind him with a smirk. "Don't argue this time, Mitch. She's okay."

I glanced back at him standing there helplessly biting his lip and looking very lost.

Jim led Mitch toward the fathers' lounge as Chris and Trudy stepped off the elevator. Chris quickened his pace to catch up and put his arm around his younger brother.

"How are you doing, little brother?"

Mitch smiled. "I'm okay—nervous, excited, scared—but okay." His eyes moved in the direction the nurse had taken Dana. "I just hope she is." He turned to Jim. "How much longer before I can be with her again?"

"It'll take about ten minutes or so. I paged Mark—Dr. Bradley—so he should be here shortly." He walked over to a rather old and stained coffee pot surrounded by stacks of Styrofoam cups. "Anyone want a cup of coffee? It probably tastes like motor oil by now, but it's warm."

"Sure, I'll try some," Mitch answered.

Jim poured a cup and handed it to him and then took one for himself. He took a sip and nodded. "Yeah, I was right."

Mitch walked to the doorway and stared into the hall. He let out a soft chuckle and then turned to his family. "You know, I can't believe this is happening. For the last eight months or so, we've been getting ready for it. I knew the day would come, but it still seems surreal to me. I just wish she was closer to her due date. Those kids shouldn't be coming out for another three or four weeks." Then he remembered Dana's comment the night before and sighed heavily as he allowed the hint of a smile to emerge. "Guess that's my fault though. I'm the reason she's in labor three weeks early."

The three of them laughed softly, and Chris stepped up to his brother. "Well, Mitchell, you *are* the one that fathered those children, but that doesn't mean that's why she's delivering today."

Mitch shook his head—a serious look on his face. "That's not what I meant. She wouldn't admit it, but I know Dana was upset with me tonight over Casey." He started to bite his lip. "And, well, last night we...even though she said the doctor advised against it...I kinda insisted...."

Chris and Jim smiled at each other. "Those things probably have nothing to do with any of this," Jim said. "The only common factor between this and you is that the babies are impatient."

Mitch laughed. "That's great! I hope that's the only trait they take from me!"

Jake, Olivia, and the rest of the family arrived just as the nurse came to summon Mitch back to Dana's side. He paused briefly to exchange hugs with all of them.

He took a deep breath before his expression turned to a radiant smile. "I guess it's time to go become a dad, huh?"

"Keep us posted, Mitchell, and give Dana our love," Jake said, and he watched with pride as his youngest hurried off to his wife.

The nurse ushered Mitch into a room much like the one they had seen in the Lane family film. Two clear bassinettes stood waiting on the opposite side of the room next to a small table that had a bright light shining down upon it. A stool was positioned at the foot of the bed along with a cart holding a sterile tray of instruments that could be used to assist with the delivery. The sight of Dana in bed with an IV and monitors strapped to her brought back painful memories Mitch would have rather forgotten. However, when she smiled that beautiful smile and looked into his eyes, he was reminded that tonight—unlike months earlier—the reasons for those things were joyous. Tonight, they would welcome their children into the world. Tonight, they would become a family.

Mitch bent down and softly kissed me—his expression one of tenderness and love.

"Hey, sweetheart," he said as he reached out to stroke my hair. "How are you feeling?"

"I'm not sure," I replied. "I'm feeling all sorts of things, but right now I guess I'm mostly nervous."

He took my hand and gently caressed it with his thumb. "Well, I'm here now, and I'm not moving from this spot until those kids are born. You hold on to me, love, and I promise you'll be just fine."

Dr. Bradley stepped into the room and shook Mitch's hand. "Hi, Mitch, nice to see you again. Ready to become a dad tonight?"

Mitch smiled at me and then nodded to the doctor. "Absolutely!"

"Good, because it's official. Dana and I chatted a little before you came in; and based on my exam as well as her information, I'd say she's been in a mild state of labor most of the day. The back pain and what she thought were Braxton Hicks were actually the beginning stages. Most women don't experience the painful contractions until the membranes rupture."

"How long will she be in labor?" Mitch asked.

"Unfortunately, we can't predict that; but right now she's almost fully effaced and somewhere around five centimeters dilated. We gave her something to make her comfortable; and when she's ready to go, we'll back it off a little so she can help us out. Right now she can't feel the pain of the contractions, but the monitor here will tell us when she's having one."

Mitch glanced to where the doctor was pointing and noticed something that looked like the markings on a seismograph. He smiled.

"I'm guessing that peak was one that she just had?"

"Yes, it was. About four minutes ago. Right now, we've timed them about eight to ten minutes apart."

"I don't care if they are ten seconds apart as long as I don't feel them," I chimed in. Both the men chuckled.

"I'm going to go check on a few other mothers since I'm here, and then I'll be back to check on you, okay? Mitch, I'll have one of the nurses bring you something to put on over your clothes. If you need anything at all, let them know. For now, just try to relax." He laid a gentle hand on my shoulder and smiled down at me. "We're going to take good care of you, Dana. Nothing to worry about."

"Thank you, doctor," Mitch said as he shook his hand again.

As Dr. Bradley exited the room, Mitch let out one big puff of air and looked at me with a smirk. "Well, here we are. Anything you want to do before we officially become parents?"

"I suppose right now a ski trip to Switzerland might be out of the question, huh?"

"As would hunting lions in Africa," he smiled. "But, we could talk. If we did, I'd probably tell you how much I love you and how you make each day of my life worth living. And I might even tell you how much I've enjoyed being your husband for the past nine months and how I'm looking forward to spending every day of the rest of my life with you."

I felt a sentimental tear fall down my cheek, and I looked up into his bright blue eyes. "I'd probably tell you how much I love you, too, and how I don't ever want to spend a moment without you next to me." I began to think of Casey again and all that had transpired that night.

My voice began to tremble. "I'd also tell you how much—how very much—I needed to hear you say all those things to me. I really hope you never stop meaning any of them."

He bent down close to me and kissed me with true compassion—his arms holding me as closely as he could at that moment. He moved back enough to search my face, and he wiped away the tears that had begun to fall softly on the blanket. He sighed softly and placed his cheek next to mine.

"I won't, love; I promise. I really do promise."

A young nurse holding a set of surgical scrubs interrupted our moment. "Excuse me, Mr. Tarrington," she said timidly, "but Dr. Bradley asked me to bring these to you. You'll need to put them on over your clothing. I wasn't sure what size you needed; so if they don't fit, let me know."

Mitch took the outfit from her and smiled as he held up the shirt. "Thank you. I think these will be fine."

"Are you doing all right, Mrs. Tarrington? Is there anything you need?"

"Just two babies. Other than that, I'm good for now."

She smiled. "Those should be here before long." She checked the monitor. "Looks like you just had another contraction." She held out the tape, and an odd look came to her face. "How do you feel?"

"Like nothing's even happening," I replied. "I'm not having any pain at all."

Mitch took my hand as he noticed the nurse's expression. "Is something wrong, miss?"

She gave a smile which I'm sure was meant to reassure us, but it really didn't work. "I don't think so, but I'm going to have Dr. Bradley come back in to check your progress. Unless I read this incorrectly, your contractions are down to about two to three minutes apart."

She quickly left the room, and I squeezed Mitch's hand. He simply held on tight and kept his eyes fixed on the door.

Dr. Bradley entered the room not two minutes later with two new nurses plus the one who had left to find him. He checked the monitor and nodded in their direction. All three moved into various positions around the room as the doctor pulled on a pair of latex gloves and took a place on the stool at the foot of my bed.

"Let's take a look here and see where things are," he said as he gently placed my feet in the stirrups. I glanced down at him and then at Mitch. The doctor smiled and extended a hand toward one of the nurses. "Valerie, could you hand me a sheet, please? Let's give her a little privacy."

Mitch looked down at me with a half smile. "Do you want me to step out, sweetheart?"

I shook my head. "No, but this *is* a little embarrassing." I was sure my face was turning red. He bent down and kissed my forehead.

The doctor stood up and proceeded to change his gloves as he addressed one of the nurses. "She's at ten. Let's call Dr. Rayburn in to crank down the drip, and we'll get the show underway." He looked at Mitch and me with a smile. "As soon as Dr. Rayburn gets here, we're going to start coaxing these little ones out into the world, okay? You're fully dilated, Dana, and everything looks good. You're progressing fairly rapidly for a first birthing, but that's all right."

Dr. Rayburn stepped into the room and extended a hand to Mitch as Dr. Bradley introduced them. "Dr. Rayburn is our anesthesiologist. He's going to stay with us and monitor the epidural drip while we do this." He turned to me with a determined look on his face. "Dana, within a minute or so you should feel a contraction starting. When I tell you, I want you to bear down as hard as you can. Mitch, you can hold her hand; and as she pushes, try to steady her head and shoulders, too. Any questions?"

"Do you have to shut off the medicine? I really don't like pain. I don't tolerate it...oh my GOSH!" I concluded that my question came about two minutes too late, and I squeezed Mitch's hand as hard as I could. I thought I saw him wince in pain, but he didn't let go.

"Dana, push for me and breathe through the contraction," Dr. Bradley instructed.

Mitch must have suddenly decided it was time to coach me because he jumped in with a well-timed, "Breathe, honey. Come on, you can do it. Hee hee hee ha. Hee hee hee ha."

The contraction subsided, and I fell back against the pillow as I panted for air. Mitch smiled down at me and began to brush the hair back from my face. Another nurse had slipped in without my knowledge and stood next to me on the side of the bed opposite Mitch. She glanced at the monitor and then to the doctor.

"Another contraction starting," she announced.

"You didn't have to tell me that," I muttered. I didn't think I'd said it loud enough to be heard, but apparently I had because everyone snickered.

"Push a little harder, Dana; that's it. You're doing just fine...."

"Come on, baby, focus. Remember your breathing—hee hee hee ha." I glanced at Mitch and tried to pay attention, but it felt as if not only the babies but everything else inside me was being forced toward my groin.

"Contraction is subsiding, doctor."

I looked at the nurse in disbelief. *I'm sure we all would have figured that out ourselves*, I thought. *To think you get paid for that. Wow.*

For what seemed like an eternity—but in reality was only about thirty-five minutes—I pushed, breathed, grunted, groaned, strained, and panted—only to have Dr. Bradley proudly announce to Mitch, "Dad, would you like to see the top of your baby's head?"

Only the top of a head? Heck, with all that effort, I feel like I should have birthed an elephant by now!

Two of the nurses and an intern who had decided to join in the fun gathered around the foot of the bed to stare at my private parts. Mitch broke into a wide grin and headed in that direction as well. *So much for modesty*, I thought to myself.

Suddenly, I felt that gripping pain that was becoming all too familiar. "Mitchell! Get over here—NOW!"

He flew to my side, took my hand, and began to try to coach me again. By now, I'd concluded that no amount of breathing was going to ease my pain. When he looked at me and said, "Dana, come on, love—you need to focus, and you need to breathe," I glared back and said, "*You* breathe—*I'm* trying to push out babies here!" He bit his lip to hold back his smile.

Another forty-five minutes passed, and it seemed that the only thing progressing was my fatigue. I looked up at Mitch as a tear of frustration fell down my cheek. "I'm so tired, Mitch. I can't do this anymore."

He dabbed the perspiration off my forehead with a cool cloth one of the nurses had given him. "Yes, you can. You're strong. You are doing so well. Just a little while longer."

I felt the next contraction; and this time as I pushed, I heard Mitch say, "You can do it, sweetheart. Just push—it's not that hard."

Not that hard? What planet is he from? "Then you get up here and do it!" I managed to squeak out between breaths.

He chuckled. "I don't think that's physically possible," he said as the contraction subsided; and he gently placed an oxygen mask over my nose and mouth. I inhaled deeply and felt myself start to relax.

As Mitch took the mask away, he looked down at me with a soft smile. "I'll bet you really hate me right about now, don't you?"

I shook my head. "No, not you," I replied as I shifted my eyes downward, "just certain parts of you. In fact, if the doctor would hand me a scalpel...."

"Yikes!" Mitch exclaimed, and the staff all started to laugh. He joined in, too, as he added, "Guess I'll be sleeping with one eye open for a while!"

As I felt the pain beginning again, the nurse next to me turned toward the doctor quickly. "Dr. Bradley, the monitor is picking up signs of distress."

He motioned to Dr. Rayburn, and suddenly I felt the tingling numbness return to my lower half. Taking a quick look at the strip of paper the nurse handed him, he began to bark orders to his team; and they moved at lightning speed. I felt an overwhelming panic sweep over me, and I clutched Mitch's hand as tightly as I possibly could.

"What's the matter? What's happening, doctor?" Mitch asked—his face and voice filled with fear.

Before an answer could form on his lips, I found myself being wheeled from the room and down the hallway in record time.

"Fetal distress—we need to get them out of there right away."

My hand flew to my mouth, and I felt tears begin to flood down my cheeks as my entire body trembled. "Oh, my...no...." I reached for Mitch's hand, and he tried his best to grab hold of it while he kept pace with the others as they raced toward the delivery room. My heart pounded wildly from the anxiety, and I felt as if I couldn't breathe. "Please, save our baby. Please...." I heard myself say.

From somewhere that seemed light years away, I heard Mitch's voice. "It's okay, baby; it's going to be okay."

The walls of the delivery room were a putrid grey, and everything smelled of industrial-strength disinfectant. Dr. Bradley disappeared behind a set of swinging doors as four more staff members suddenly appeared: two male and two female. The men positioned themselves—one at my head and one at my feet—and on a count of three hoisted me carefully onto a cold, hard table. While one nurse placed my head on a pillow, another placed a drape over my midsection to block my lower half from view. Although I couldn't see anything, I could smell the scent of iodine as they swabbed it over my abdominal region. Dr. Bradley reappeared with fresh white gloves and took his place next to the table.

"Mitch, you stay right there next to her. Dana, we're going to do this as quickly as possible. You may feel a little pressure, but no pain. Just relax."

Relax? How can I possibly relax? I just spent the last two hours trying to give birth, and now you're telling me that you have to cut me open to take out my distressed infants!

Mitch held my hand tightly and gently stroked my hair as he fixed his eyes on the doctor. I knew he was nervous, too. When I looked up at him, he was biting his lip; and his expression was very solemn. No more than a minute passed when I heard the doctor announce, "Baby number one—a boy," and our son's first cries.

Mitch let out a long deep breath, and his face filled with emotion as the nurse laid our child on my chest. His eyes were filled with tears that he fought to hold back. I stared in awe at the most beautiful sight I had ever seen in my life.

"Welcome to the world, little one," I whispered. Mitch kissed his hand and gently touched the baby's head before the nurse whisked him away.

"One down, one to go," Dr. Bradley said, "and here we have...another boy!"

But, he wasn't crying.

I looked up at Mitch, and his eyes were filled with such fear that I felt my heart drop to my knees. I wanted to ask what was wrong, but I couldn't speak. I squeezed his hand and he glanced down at me for only a moment before turning his attention back to the doctor.

"More suction, please," I heard the doctor say. "Hold the mask on for a moment—there we go—he's turning pink now. That's what we want."

Suddenly, the room was filled with the echo of our second son's cries, and it was then that the tears raced down Mitch's cheeks. He looked up to the ceiling and whispered, "Thank you, God. Thank you so much." Then he leaned down and took me into his arms as best he could and held me close.

"I love you, sweetheart. I love you so much. You did such a good job. I'm so proud of you."

"Would you like to see your other son?" the nurse asked.

Mitch brushed the tears from his cheeks with the back of his hand. "Absolutely!" he quipped with a smile.

She placed the child on my chest. I shook my head as I gazed into piercing blue eyes and gently touched the crown of dark hair with my fingertips.

"It figures that you should look like your father," I said softly to him. "You're starting out stubborn, not wanting to cry. What's that all about?"

Mitch looked down at me with a smirk and then addressed his son. "Don't pay attention to her. She just likes to give people a hard time. You're wonderful."

A short time later I was taken back to my former room with instructions that I would stay there for about an hour to recover and then transfer to a regular room. The babies had been taken to the nursery to be examined more thoroughly by Dr. Renaldi, the staff pediatrician, who like Dr. Bradley, came highly recommended by the Tarrington family. Mitch was sitting in a chair close to the side of my bed, still holding my hand and stroking my hair as the nurse finished settling me in. Both of us were drained and yet neither of us could rest as we continued to bask in the excitement of the evening. As she smiled and left the room, he stood up with a smile of his own.

"Well, Mommy, I think I should go and let our family know about the new additions. They're probably all frantic with concern by now."

I nodded as he bent down to kiss me. As he stood back up, a thought came to me; and I grabbed his hand gently to pull him back.

"What is it?"

"We never named them, Mitch! We have two sons who don't have names! You know everyone's going to ask. What should we do?"

He chuckled. "We name them."

"Name them what?" He got an ornery grin that spread all over his face, and I shook my head. "Don't you dare say Casey!"

He laughed. "I wasn't going to. What I was going to say is that since we're kinda down to the wire here, let's do the one thing we weren't going to do."

"What? Name them after someone?"

"No, name them something that begins with C."

"I didn't like any C names, remember?"

He grinned. "Yes, you did. But, after Casey came into the picture, so to speak, you were too stubborn to go back to that section of the book and see that the first time we went through it we had circled two names."

"We had?"

"Yes—Cameron and Cody."

I looked across the room, momentarily lost in thought. "Cameron and Cody," I repeated slowly. Then I looked up at him and smiled as I nodded. "Yes, I like them. I like those choices a lot." Then another thought popped into my head. "What about middle names?"

He sighed and twisted his jaw for a moment before I saw something click. "Well, they are *my* boys...."

Everyone rushed upon Mitch as he stepped into the fathers' lounge. Angelina, Julia, and Paul had arrived as well as Kayla, Mitch's band mates, and Casey.

"What's the news, Mitchell?" Julia asked.

His smile was as bright as the morning sun, and he held up two fingers. "We have two sons—two wonderful, beautiful sons!"

Mitch suddenly found himself the recipient of hugs, kisses, and a lot of love. As they all stepped away from him, Chris smiled and patted him on the back.

"Well, little brother, your wish for boys came true after all! But, I'll bet it had more to do with your 'superior masculinity, didn't it?" Everyone laughed, including Mitch.

"Give us all the details—but first, how's Dana?"

"She's fine. They have her in a room for about another fifty minutes or so to recover, and then she'll go to a regular room. She ended up having an emergency C-section though; one of the boys was in distress. But, he's okay now. Everyone is fine." His face began to beam again, and his eyes sparkled. "They are so beautiful. I can't believe it—I really still can't believe it!"

"Okay, Mitch, you haven't told us anything about the babies, not really," Angelina stated. "Names, weights...."

"Sorry," he said. "Their names are Cameron Mitchell and Cody Jacob. We actually figured that out about five minutes ago." Everyone chuckled. "One weighed six pounds three ounces, eighteen and three-quarter inches long; and the other one was six pounds five ounces, nineteen inches long. One of them has a lot of dark hair; and the other, a little fuzz. They're just little guys, but both of them are amazing."

"When can we see them?" Olivia asked.

"Dr. Renaldi is checking them out right now, but the nurse promised she'd bring them to us as soon as he's through."

Jim decided to speak up. "Actually, everyone, it might be best—considering all Dana's been through tonight—if we allow her to get some rest and visit tomorrow. But, what I can do is go down and ask one of the nurses to bring them to the nursery window so you can all take a look."

A few minutes later the Tarrington family and their friends gathered around the nursery window as two nurses held the twin infants up for them to see. Mitch stood proudly front and center gazing at the miracles that love had created—the love between him and the woman of his dreams. He noticed, out of the corner of his eye, his parents step closer together and his father as he drew his mother to his side. Olivia looked to her new grandchildren and then to her husband as she placed a finger on the glass.

"He looks like Mitchell when he was a baby. Do you remember?"

Jake nodded with a smile. "Yes, dear, I remember." Then he glanced at his son. "Just like it was yesterday."

"Mitch, which one is Cameron and which is Cody?" Kayla asked.

Mitch got a dumbfounded look on his face. "Gosh—I don't know!"

Everyone laughed again. "Well, I think you and Dana better figure that out," she said.

Mitch bid goodbye to everyone except his parents and Kayla, who remained behind to have a brief moment with Dana. Mitch went ahead to make sure she was open to visitors. He stepped into the doorway of the room, and the scene before him filled his heart with love.

Dana was sitting up in bed with a pillow propped haphazardly against the side rail to support her arm. She gently cradled one of the twins while the other lay sleeping in a bassinette next to her bed. He could see a tiny oxygen tank suspended by a pole and tubes into the infant's nose. He was evidently the one who had suffered the distress earlier. She was speaking in a soft, tender voice as her finger lightly caressed the tiny face of the one she held. Mitch stood silently for a moment to listen.

"Cameron, there's something I need to tell you," she started. "I don't know much about babies. I've never fed one, diapered one, or even held one until right now. But, I promise I'll do the very best I can to be a good mommy because I really love you and Cody." She carefully touched the edge of the blanket and moved it away from the baby's face. "I'm not the only one, you know. There are a lot of people who love you: Daddy, Grandma and Grandpa, and all your aunts and uncles and cousins. Oh, yeah, Aunt Kayla, too." She smiled softly. "Well, Kayla really *isn't* your aunt. She's my best friend. Actually, she and her husband Joseph kinda look out for me since your Grandma and Grandpa Walker and Great Grandma Branson are in Heaven now." Mitch could see the expression on her face change, and his own heart ached for her as she continued. "I really wish they were here, Cameron. I miss them so. They would love you and Cody so much." She took a deep breath, and a sweet smile came to her face. "Anyway, you'll really like Kayla and Joseph. I know you will. You'll like everyone else, too. Being a Tarrington is a pretty neat thing to be. You just wait and see."

Mitch decided to make his presence known, so he cleared his throat loudly as he stepped into the room.

"Hi, beautiful," he said as he bent down to give me a kiss. He smiled as he moved the edge of the blanket back to look at Cameron's face. "Being born must be a tough job. He's sleeping pretty soundly."

"So is Cody. In fact, I haven't even held him yet. I was afraid I might wake him." I looked at the tiny form lying next to me and smiled. "Dr. Renaldi said that he swallowed some of the amniotic fluid, so they want him on oxygen for a day or two to make sure his lungs stay clear." I looked back at Mitch. "He also said that, even though they came a little early, it appears they're both healthy."

Mitch smiled brightly and nodded. "That's great news, love," he replied. He pointed to the hallway. "You have a few people out there waiting to see you. Are you up for visitors?"

As long as Casey isn't one of them, I thought. "Sure, I guess so."

"Okay, I'll be right back."

He disappeared; and a minute later I greeted Jake, Olivia, and Kayla who all sported huge smiles. Mitch took the baby from my arms and handed him to Olivia.

"Grandma, meet Cameron Mitchell Tarrington, our firstborn and...." He gently wheeled the bassinette toward them, lifted Cody from it, and handed him to Jake. "Grandpa, meet Cody Jacob Tarrington, his twin brother."

Mitch took a step back, and we both watched as Jake and Olivia welcomed their newest grandchildren into the family. After applying gentle kisses to each infant's forehead, they exchanged babies and did the same. Then they gave Kayla a turn.

"Kayla, meet Cody," Olivia said softly.

Kayla's face beamed as she cuddled the infant close to her. "Why, hello there, little Cody," she said. "You are just the sweetest little boy I ever did see!" She looked up at Mitch. "You can't deny this one at all. Look at those big, blue eyes of his. Those came straight from you, and all this dark hair—what a ladies' man he's gonna be some day!"

Mitch chuckled. "If his mother lets him out of her sight, that is!"

She kissed him softly and handed him to Mitch, who wheeled the crib closer to my bed and gave him to me. "Here you go. Now, you can hold him."

As I cuddled with my younger son, Kayla took Cameron from Jake.

"Well, now you're just as handsome as your brother, aren't you? Your mommy better lock you up and throw away the key because those girls are gonna be knocking down doors to get to you!" She grinned at Mitch and me. "Of course, with pretty parents like you have, you couldn't help but be pretty yourself, could you?"

Mitch looked at me and rolled his eyes as he smirked playfully. "There's that term again. Pretty. It's *handsome*, not pretty."

Kayla handed the baby to Mitch and giggled. "What if I say 'pretty handsome'? Will that work?"

He nodded. "Much better."

For the next few minutes, we shared the details of our birthing experience with our guests. Just as we finished, a nurse appeared in the doorway.

"Excuse me, but I'm going to have to break up the party. We have a room ready for you now, Mrs. Tarrington." She turned to the group and smiled. "These little ones are going to the nursery for a diaper change and a bottle; and after a good night's sleep, they'll be ready for visitors around nine in the morning."

I looked at Mitch with sad eyes. "Do they have to go to the nursery? Can't they stay with me?"

He gave the nurse a questioning look, and she she shook her head. "I'm afraid not tonight, Mrs. Tarrington. Dr. Bradley gave orders that he wants you to get as much rest as possible. Don't worry. We'll take good care of them. When you wake up, just call the nurses' desk; and someone will bring them to you."

"May I kiss them goodnight?"

"Of course," she said, and she held them up one at a time for a soft kiss and a whisper of 'I love you' from both Mitch and me.

Settled safely in my room, I reached out to push Mitch's hair back from his forehead. He sighed softly as I ran the back of my hand down his cheek.

"Sweetie, you're so tired. Go home now and get some sleep, okay?"

He shook his head. "No. I'm okay. I want to stay with you."

I let out an exasperated breath and gave him a soft, yet stern, look. "Mitch, we agreed that if the babies and I were all well that you would go home and sleep. We are, so go and rest. You've had a long day." I smiled and tried to make light of the situation. "Besides, that pain medicine the nurse just gave me will kick in shortly, and I won't know that you're here anyway."

He stared into my eyes and said softly, "I won't sleep much. I already know that. Not without you there." Reluctantly, he stood and looked down at me—his eyes full of love.

"You did a great job tonight, love. I really am proud of you. A beautiful wife and two beautiful sons. I'm so blessed."

He leaned down to kiss me, and he let his lips linger near mine as he whispered, "I love you so very much. Good night, sweetheart."

I stretched my arm as far as I could before I let go of his hand, and he turned to walk out the door.

"I love you, too, Mitch—so very much."

Making his way toward the elevator, Mitch paused briefly by the nursery window. A sea of pink and blue spread throughout the room before him, all wrapped around tiny, sleeping figures. In the very first row, just to his right, rested his children; and he smiled warmly as he looked at them. "Sleep well, guys," he whispered as he placed a hand against the glass. "I'll see you in the morning. Daddy loves you."

As he stepped away from the window and turned to board the elevator, he suddenly felt as if the reality of it all finally kicked in. *'Daddy'—wow! From this night on, for the rest of my life, nothing will ever be the same.* As the elevator doors began to close, he glanced back toward the nursery window one more time. *That's fine with me.*

Chapter 20

The ringing of the telephone pierced the air and caused Mitch to sit bolt upright. It took a moment for his senses to become oriented. He'd temporarily forgotten where he was. Filled with adrenaline and unable to sleep, he'd stretched out on the couch the night before and tried to get the TV to help him relax. Apparently, it had worked because he was still there this morning: fully clothed and well rested. He reached for the remote, shut off the TV, and jogged as quickly as he could to answer the call.

"Hi, Mitch. I was beginning to think I might have missed you. This is Steve from Remington Records. First, let me say congratulations on your new family. I hope everyone is well."

"They're all fine, thanks," Mitch replied with a lilt to his voice. "My wife had to have an emergency Caesarian, but everything went well. Two boys; both wonderful."

"That's great," Steve replied. "How's the new dad this morning?"

Mitch smiled at the use of the term. He was still reeling from all that, and it never occurred to him to wonder how Steve even knew. He'd had no contact with him since the demo; and to his knowledge, neither had anyone else. "Not bad. I actually managed to get some sleep last night." He chuckled. "Guess I'd better do that while I can, huh?" He stretched the phone cord as far as he could, pulled the coffee pot off the base, and moved to the sink to fill it with water. "So what can I do for you?"

"I know you want to spend the day with your family, but would you be able to spare about an hour at some point? There's something I need to talk to you about."

Mitch poured the ground coffee into the filter and placed it back on the base as he flipped the 'on' switch. His curiosity was piqued. "Uh, yeah, sure, Steve. I'm sure Dana will be getting plenty of visitors today, so I should be able to sneak out this afternoon sometime."

"Great! How about two-thirty at the studio?"

"That sounds fine." Mitch paused as a thought occurred to him. "Should I bring the rest of the guys?"

"No, not this time," Steve replied. "I'd like for us to talk first."

Now Mitch's curiosity level was as high as it could go. "Oh, well, all right. I'll see you around two-thirty then."

Mitch hung up the phone and stared at it for a moment before he shook his head and went to pour a cup of coffee. As he took a long drink, he inhaled deeply and allowed the aroma to stir him into full consciousness. Walking to the front door, he opened it up; and a heavy draft of cold air hit him as he reached out onto the porch to retrieve the morning newspaper. Shivering against the chill, he closed it quickly, turned the lock, and went to take a seat in the chair.

He took another sip of coffee before he placed the cup down and opened the newspaper. He tried to read an article or two that caught his interest, but his mind was too occupied with other things: Dana, the twins, and Steve's phone call. He missed Dana. He missed waking up next to her. Her smile was the first thing he saw when he opened his eyes. He was surprised he'd even been able to fall asleep last night without her there and knew for certain, that had he gone up to bed, he probably would have tossed and turned all night. Next were those two precious lives that had captured his heart at first glance. He was looking forward to being a father, to watching them grow, helping them learn, and simply loving them.

He breathed a heavy sigh as he lay the paper down, picked up his cup, and savored the warmth between his hands. What could be so important that Steve would give up a Sunday afternoon to meet with him? More so, what could be so important that he thought it worthy of taking him away from time with his new family? Perhaps his colleagues had made a decision about signing the band. Then why wouldn't he want the others there today as well? Could the reason for their meeting be something else entirely; and if so, what? He tried to rack his brain as to what other news it might be, but nothing came to him. Although patience wasn't one of his stronger points—which he had proved many times recently—he resigned himself to the fact that he would simply have to live in suspense until two-thirty that afternoon. No longer interested in the daily news, he retreated to the kitchen for another cup of coffee.

In order to save time, Mitch opted for an overly ripened banana and a granola bar instead of typical breakfast fare. Visiting hours in the maternity ward for fathers began at 8:00 a.m. That gave him just fifteen minutes to shower, shave, and dress before he would need to be out the door. Thinking that he should probably make a stop at the gift shop before he headed up to see Dana, that reduced his time to ten minutes. He gulped down the last of his coffee and rushed off toward the bathroom.

In eight minutes flat he was ready; and after he filled a travel mug with coffee, he switched off the pot and was on his way. Turning the radio on low, he tried to focus his thoughts on the days ahead. He began to make a mental to-do list of the things he would need to accomplish: arrange for Jimmy to cover until he returned to work, change his rehearsal schedule with the band, and just make sure he was doing all he could to make the transition from couple to family a smooth one. He knew Jimmy and the guys wouldn't be a problem. It was the third matter that filled him with the most trepidation. All the months of planning they had done were finally going to be put into play. Would everything fall into place like they both hoped it would? He couldn't answer that question. All he could do was pray for the best and deal with each day as it came. Deciding to dismiss his cares for now, he turned up the radio and began to sing along.

"It's okay, Cameron. Mommy will get to you in just a minute." I looked down at the tiny face wrinkled in an unhappy expression. "Don't cry, sweetie. Please don't cry!"

As I tried to soothe him, I glanced briefly at the one I held in my arms. A dribble of formula flowed down his cheek, so I pulled a tissue from the box on my bedside table and gently dabbed it away as I pulled the bottle from his mouth. "Why aren't you swallowing that? You were a minute ago," I said in a soft tone. "Are you getting full already?" Cameron started to wail. "Oh, no, baby. Please don't cry. I promise I'll feed you in a minute. It's okay." Cody must have sensed my frustration as he, too, started to whimper. I sighed heavily. "I certainly hope your daddy gets here soon. I could use another set of hands. Please don't cry. I'm doing the best I can."

Placing the bottle on the table, I carefully maneuvered the baby to my shoulder. "Maybe you need to burp," I said as I began to pat his back gently. Suddenly feeling moisture against my chest, I realized that wasn't the issue. "Well, now I know what the problem is," I said as I pulled him away from me. "Guess I need to get the diaper tighter next time, huh?"

By now, both boys were exercising their lungs to the fullest, and I had to wonder how two people so tiny could emit so much noise. Limited in my mobility due to the discomfort from the surgery, I did my best to reach for a clean diaper on the shelf below the bassinette. Barely reaching it with my fingertips, I tried to pull it toward me while being careful not to roll my leg onto the infant now lying between them on my bed. Just as I thought I had it in my grasp, my fingers slipped off; and the diaper fell to the floor.

"Drat!" I exclaimed as I looked down at Cody once again. I let out a long, exasperated breath. "Maybe I should call the nurse."

"Hey, what's all the commotion in here?"

I looked up to see Mitch standing in the doorway with a vase full of beautiful red roses. He walked to the bed, bent down to kiss me, and placed the vase on the bedside table.

I was sure Mitch could hear the frustration and panic in my voice. "I was feeding Cody, and Cameron was sleeping. Then he woke up and decided he was hungry, too, and he started to cry. Then Cody started to cry, and I thought he needed burped; but he actually needed his diaper changed. When I tried to reach the fresh diaper, it fell on the floor—and I can't get up to get it. Now, they're both crying, and I don't know what to do first!"

He placed a hand against my cheek and smiled sweetly. "Just relax. I'm here to help." He reached down on the bed and picked up Cody. "Boy, you're soaked all the way through, aren't you? No wonder you're crying so hard." He laid the baby in his bassinette and then lifted Cameron from his and handed him to me. "Here, love. You take care of this little guy. I'll handle the diaper issue."

I kissed Cameron's tiny cheek and placed the tip of the bottle in his mouth. Instantly, he began to settle down. "There, now. Everything's okay."

I turned my eyes toward Mitch for a moment and watched as he expertly removed the baby's wet t-shirt, wiped him off, replaced it with another shirt, and moved to his diaper. Within another minute, the infant was calm, clean, and dry. After he washed his hands, Mitch smiled down at him, wrapped him in a fresh blanket, and lifted him to his shoulder. Sitting down in the chair next to the bed, he rocked him gently. Suddenly, the baby burped, and Mitch chuckled.

"Gosh, that was a pretty mighty sound from one so small," he said. "Guess that was part of the trouble, too, huh?"

Soon Cody was sleeping soundly, and Mitch gently placed him back in his bassinette. He stood up and reached out to tenderly stroke my hair as I glanced from Cameron to him.

"Maybe you should take over here," I said softly. "I don't seem to be doing a very good job."

He smiled. "You're doing fine, sweetheart. It's only the first day. It'll get easier."

He kissed the top of my head. "How do you feel?"

"I'm very sore, but I'm kinda used to pain," I replied with half a smile. "Been there, done that."

"Yeah, I know. You're quite the little trooper." He pointed to the baby lying contentedly in my arms. "And you *are* a good mother, too."

A short while later with Cameron now settled into his bed, Mitch pulled the two cribs together and gazed lovingly at his sons. I sat for a moment just watching him watching them, and the expression of love and pride on his face warmed my heart. I knew without a doubt that he would be a strong role model for them and that there would never be a day that he wasn't there for them physically and emotionally. He would raise them to be independent and yet allow them the opportunity to lean on him for strength. He would scold them for wrongs, praise them for rights, and love them no matter what.

"I'm glad you showed up when you did," I said to Mitch. "I was getting ready to hit my button here and call in some reinforcements. You don't plan on going back to work anytime within the next three years, do you?" I said teasingly. "I'm going to need some help when these two go home."

Mitch laughed. "Actually, love, I think you'll need more help *in* three years! By then we'll probably have another one...."

My eyes grew as wide as saucers, and my jaw dropped to my knees. "*Another one*? I'm not even used to the two I have yet!"

His eyes twinkled mischievously, and he came to sit on the side of my bed as he put his arm around me. "What are you telling me? I thought we could start trying right away."

I pushed him away as he laughed. "Don't even think about it, buddy!"

"Now, come on—you have to at *least* let me think about it."

"Mitchell Tarrington, you're terrible."

"Maybe, but I know you love it!"

I pointed toward the vase full of roses and smiled. "Those are so beautiful, honey. Thank you."

"Not as beautiful as you," he replied. He took my hand and looked into my eyes. "If you'll notice, there are actually fourteen roses in there. Twelve for you and two for the boys."

I smiled up at him. "You're really happy that both of them are boys, aren't you?"

The prideful expression returned to his face. "Absolutely!" he said. Then he quickly added, "Of course, girls would have been fine, too," he smirked, "but at least this way I don't have to pay for weddings or deal with all those extra hormones. "

I smirked right back. "Gee, sweetie, you should be an expert on that latter one by now!" He simply laughed.

The hours passed quickly as Mitch and I enjoyed each other's company. Around noon, Cameron began to stir, and Mitch smiled at him as he opened his eyes.

"Hey there, sport," Mitch quipped. "You knew it was lunchtime, didn't you?" He lifted the baby from his bed and cradled him lovingly in his arms. "Well, you're in luck. I think we have a bottle right over here for you."

I watched while Mitch in one motion picked up the bottle, replaced the cap with a nipple, and shook it up—all as he held the baby. He sat down in the chair as Cameron began to fuss, pushed the blanket away from his face, and began to feed him. He made it look so easy. Had I tried it, I would have dropped the baby or spilled formula everywhere.

"Now, you're a happy guy, aren't you?" He pushed the blanket back even more and studied the baby's face. "You know," he said as he addressed me, "I can't figure out which one of us he resembles the most. It looks like he has my nose, maybe your eyes, but that mouth...."

I giggled. "That can't be from you. It's too small."

He rolled his eyes at me and smirked. "Very funny."

Just then, I heard the beginnings of a soft cry from beside my bed, and I turned to see Cody's blue eyes turn my way as he followed the sound of my voice.

"It's lunchtime for you, too, isn't it?" I pulled his bassinette closer and carefully lifted him from it. "I'll take care of you. Don't get upset." Once I had everything in place, I began to study the baby's tiny face the way Mitch had studied Cameron's.

"There's no denying who this one looks like," I told Mitch. "He's the spitting image of you."

Mitch smiled. "Such a handsome boy," he teased.

I laughed and shook my head. "They both are," I replied, and Mitch agreed.

Absorbed in the wonder of the new lives we held, the sound of a soft knock on the door startled us.

"Hey, parents!" Chris said as he and Trudy entered the room. "Looks like we're just in time for lunch." He walked up behind his brother and lightly patted him on the shoulder. "So, little brother, has it all sunk in yet?"

Mitch withdrew the bottle from Cameron's mouth, dabbed away the dribble of formula, and placed him against his shoulder to be burped. "It still seems a little like a dream sometimes; but if it is, I hope I don't wake up."

Chris smiled. "It is a pretty awesome feeling. I'll give you that." He bent down slightly to look at the baby's face. "Who have we here?"

"This is Cameron," Mitch replied. "Dana's handling Cody this shift."

I noticed Trudy give Chris a desperate look, and she cleared her throat as if she wanted to gain his attention. He held up a hand and then touched Mitch's shoulder again.

"Why don't you let Uncle Chris have a shot at it? It's not like I haven't done it a few times."

Mitch looked up at him. "Well, okay, if you want to." He stood up and handed the baby to Chris who expertly placed him in burping position.

Trudy moved a little closer. "I was really hoping to get a cup of coffee, Mitch. Could you show me where I could do that?" She gave him the same desperate look she'd given Chris a moment earlier, and she moved her eyes toward the door.

Mitch looked at her strangely but tried to play along. "Sure. It's right down the hall in the lounge. I'll take you."

Wonder what that was all about, I thought. *I'll just have to pick Mitch's brain a little later.*

As they stepped outside the door, Trudy took Mitch by the arm and quickly led him away from Dana's room. She looked around as if she needed to make sure no one heard her and leaned close to him.

"Listen, Mitch. I saw Casey in the gift shop downstairs as Chris and I got on the elevator. I think it might be a good idea if you intercepted her before she gets to Dana."

Mitch seemed perplexed. "Why? I don't understand."

"After last night at the club, I have the distinct feeling that Casey is the last person Dana would want to have a visit with."

Mitch shook his head. "Trudy, I'm not following you. I know Dana's a bit jealous of her, but I really don't think she'd be all that upset about her visiting."

Trudy sighed. "Didn't you wonder why Dana was outside when Chris came to tell you she was in labor?"

"I guess I never thought about it. I was too caught up in what was going on."

"Well, I'll tell you why. She went out there because she was upset. She told me some things in confidence, so I'll let her decide how much she wants to share with you. However, I will tell you that Dana really doesn't like Casey. She told me that there's just something about her that rubs her the wrong way, but she's been trying to tolerate her for your sake. She knows you like Casey, and she wants to show you that she trusts you. Up until last night, she thought she was doing all right; but the duet was really what did it for her, Mitch. She honestly thought the two of you were singing more *to* each other than *with* each other. Understand?"

Mitch dropped his head, shook it, and let out a long, deep sigh. He lifted his eyes to meet Trudy's once more. "Man! I knew that she was a little uncomfortable with the whole situation, but I had no idea...." He sighed again and motioned toward the elevator. "What am I supposed to tell Casey? 'Hey, Dana hates your guts so you probably shouldn't visit her?'"

Trudy smiled. "I think 'hate' is a little strong, but I don't think now's the time to try to buddy them up." She twisted her jaw in thought. "I know—tell her that Dana's not up for visitors today. Tell her...tell her that she's on heavy pain medication, and it kinda loops her up or something."

Mitch looked surprised. "What do I tell her when she comes back tomorrow? Come on, Trudy. I can't lie to her. I *shouldn't* lie to her."

"No, you shouldn't, but you can't very well tell her the truth, either—now can you?"

Mitch was starting to get nervous. He knew Casey could step off the elevator at any moment. "I don't like this, Trudy. Not one bit."

He sent Trudy back to Dana's room and put his brain on overtime. *What am I going to say to her? Will she be able to see through my fabrication?* He began to bite his lip. *What reason can I give her for hovering around the elevator? I can't let her know I'm actually waiting for her.*

He hurried back toward the door of Dana's room and waited just out of her sight. When Casey stepped off the elevator, he could pretend to be exiting the room at that precise moment. Within mere seconds the doors opened and off stepped Casey, a large gift bag in one hand and a small vase with two blue carnations in the other. She spotted Mitch and smiled brightly as he walked toward her.

"Hey, Mitch," she greeted. "How's the new daddy doing?"

"I'm good," he answered. He began to bite his lip unconsciously.

Casey noticed. "Is everything okay? Is Dana all right?"

I can't do this. I can't lie to her. I have to tell her the truth.

"She's okay, but I don't think it would be a good idea if you visited today."

Casey gazed at him—her eyes filled with questions. "Is there some sort of problem?"

Okay, Mitch. You have to be honest. Casey would want you to be honest. He hesitated. "Well, I'm not exactly sure I'd call it a problem myself, but maybe more of a misunderstanding."

Casey smiled softly. "I have a feeling I already know where you're going with this. Does it have anything to do with the show last night?"

He nodded. "Actually, it does. I found out inadvertently that Dana was a little upset about the duet. She wasn't aware that we were planning to do that, and I believe she may have read something into the song we chose." He decided to coin Trudy's phrase. "I believe she thought we were singing *to* each other, not just *with* each other."

Casey's expression changed to one that could easily have been mistaken for panic. "Oh, my gosh, Mitch—does she think we're having an affair?"

He shrugged. "I don't think so, but I can say that I definitely believe she wonders if we have feelings for each other. I mean, I've told her we're only friends; but Dana has what I would define as 'trust issues.'" He briefed Casey on Dana's background and the incident with Eddie. He finished by saying, "Given the fact that you and I used to go out, I'm sure you can understand why she might feel the way she does."

Casey took a brief moment to collect her thoughts before answering. This was the very thing she had hoped wouldn't occur. If Dana was truly that uncomfortable with her—and especially if she suspected that she and Mitch were being adulterous—she would definitely want her out of the picture—and soon. She couldn't let that happen. Not after last night. Things had gone so well. The crowd loved her. She knew that if she could just get Mitch to let her sing there again, it might give her the edge she needed. She would have to think of a way to get around this and most of all, gain Dana's approval.

"I had no idea, Mitch. I'm so sorry," she finally said as she tried to sound sympathetic. "Maybe it would help if I talked to her and told her there's nothing going on." *Not that I don't wish it were otherwise!*

Mitch shook his head. "Thanks, but I think I'd better field this one. She might get more upset knowing that I shared all this with you." He smiled. "I'm sure once I explain everything to her, it'll be just fine."

Casey shrugged and blew out a puff of air. "Okay then." She glanced down at the gifts she held in her hands. "Here. I picked these up for Dana and the twins. Could you give them to her for me? Just tell her that...." She paused as she searched for an excuse. "Tell her that I stopped by your house this morning and asked you to bring them for me because I wasn't sure if she wanted visitors today." She gave him a desperate look. "Will you do that for me? I really would like her to have them."

He smiled. "Okay. She's gonna wonder why I was gone so long anyway. I told her I was going for a cup of coffee. I can always say I forgot them in the car and went down to get them." He knew he would eventually tell Dana the truth, but for now, this story would make Casey feel better.

Casey handed the gifts to Mitch and then touched his arm. She smiled softly into his eyes. "Thanks, Mitch. Look, I'm sorry if I did anything to upset Dana. I really do like her."

"No need to apologize. Like I told you, she's been through a lot. I'm sure everything will turn out fine."

Casey shifted her purse to the opposite shoulder and smiled at him again. "Well, I guess I'll be going. Maybe I'll give you a call tomorrow or something to see how everyone is—if that's okay."

"Sure," he replied, and she gave him a little wave as she walked away.

Mitch watched Casey until she was out of sight and then turned to go back into Dana's room. As much as he hated to have that conversation again, he'd have to talk to her about her jealousy of Casey. He'd have to reassure her that the song was simply a song and that Casey was simply a friend. He wondered how long it would be or how many more reassurances he would have to deliver before Dana would finally believe him and relax. He also wondered how long it would be before she allowed herself to like Casey. He chuckled. That would probably never happen, not completely anyway. He knew she'd never allow herself to get close to anyone he had ever been close to. But, he understood, and he didn't fault her for it. In fact, if anything, he loved her for it. Her jealousy—even though it drove him mad at times—actually proved to him that she valued what they shared. As long as he had that, it was all he needed.

"Hey, little brother, where did you go for that coffee? Columbia?" Chris asked as Mitch reentered the room.

"No, just down the hall," he answered. "I had to go out to my car and get these." He walked to the side of the bed and handed the gift bag to me as he placed the vase next to the one he'd gotten me. "Casey dropped these off this morning and asked me to give them to you. She...." He hesitated as he shot a quick look at Trudy. "She said that she knew you'd have a lot of family visiting and didn't want to get in the way."

I glanced at Mitch and could immediately tell that he was lying, but I didn't know why. I decided that since Chris and Trudy were there, I would put on my game face and play along. I could always interrogate my husband later.

"Oh, how nice," I said as I hoped I sounded at least halfway convincing. "She didn't have to do that."

Mitch took a seat on the end of my bed as I removed the tissue paper from the gift bag and reached inside to pull out two matching sleepers, two bibs, and two tiny blue rattles. While I wasn't crazy about Casey, I had to admit that it was a thoughtful gesture.

"These are nice," I said as I carefully placed the items back in the bag. "Tell her I said thank you."

Mitch slid off the bed and walked over to the bassinettes where the boys were both sleeping peacefully. He reached down and gently caressed Cody's cheek with the back of his finger. Smiling as the baby crinkled his face against the sensation, he removed his hand and did the same to Cameron.

"Don't wake him, Mitch," I scolded. "I had a terrible time getting him to go to sleep. He was really fussy while you were gone."

He glanced up at me momentarily but kept his hand in place. "I won't wake him. Stop worrying," he replied. He looked at Chris. "Only one day and I'm already catching static from her," he teased through an ornery grin.

"Don't expect that to stop," Chris replied. Trudy rolled her eyes at him, and he grinned.

A short while later, a young lady from the kitchen showed up with my lunch tray. Chris and Trudy took this as their cue to leave, so they said their goodbyes and left Mitch and me alone once more. Mitch took the lid off the entrée and raised his eyebrows.

"Wow, check this out—baked chicken, corn, mashed potatoes. I want to be in the hospital if this is the kind of food you get!"

I picked up my fork and patted the bed next to me. "I'll share with you," I said.

"No, love, you go ahead. You need to keep up your strength. I was planning to go and grab something when Kayla gets here, if you don't care." Mitch hadn't told her he'd gotten the call from Steve that morning or about their impending meeting that afternoon. He'd decided to keep it a secret and share with her what he hoped would be good news once he returned to the hospital.

"That's fine, sweetie," I replied.

The next hour was inundated with visits from friends and relatives, each one with a gift and well wishes for our new family. I ate quickly in between bits of conversation; and not wanting to appear rude, I was thankful that most of the people were more interested in the babies than in talking to me anyway. Promptly at two o'clock, as promised, Kayla arrived with a bright smile and a warm hug.

"There's that new mommy," she said as she embraced me gently. "How's my baby girl today?"

"I'm sore, but other than that, I'm great," I answered.

"That's good," she said as she turned to Mitch. "How are you, Daddy? Still grinning over those boys, I see."

"I don't think he'll ever wipe that smile from his face, Kayla," I said.

"Definitely the proud papa," she replied.

"Absolutely!" Mitch said. "Just look at them. What is there not to be proud of?"

"Not a thing, honey, not a thing."

As Kayla stood by admiring the twins, Mitch gently pushed the hair off my face and bent to kiss me. "I'm going to run out for a little while now. Is there anything I can bring you?"

I thought for a moment and nodded. "Yes, actually there is. Since we didn't get the chance to go home after the show last night, I need my suitcase—you know, that little one I packed last week to bring with me."

"Yes, I know the one. I'll bring it." He started to kiss me again; but I began to speak once more, and he pulled away.

"I also need you to find my makeup bag—you know where I keep it—and bring that along with my hair dryer and the round styling brush. Oh, yeah, I'll need my mousse, and don't forget to throw my robe into the suitcase, maybe a nail file and my crossword puzzle book...."

"Whoa! Hold on there, sweetheart," he said as he raised his hands. "You're only going to be here another day or so. Why do you need all those things?"

I sighed in such a way that implied he just wasn't thinking. "Because I have visitors, and I don't want to scare anyone off. Besides," I added, "Dr. Bradley said he keeps C-section patients at least three days. Therefore, I have two more to go."

He gave me that look that husbands give when they know they won't win the argument, and he handed me a pad of paper and a pen. "Here. Write it all down so I don't forget anything."

I made out the list, checked it over, and handed it back to him along with the pen. He shook his head in disbelief as he looked at it and then bent to kiss me again. "Have a nice visit with Kayla. I'll see you in a little while. I love you."

He gave each of the boys a soft kiss and then turned to Kayla. "Keep her out of trouble for me, okay?"

"I'll try my best," she replied, and he smiled as he walked away.

Mitch swung his car into a spot near the side entrance of the Remington Records studio. He turned it off and sat for a minute to calm his nerves. He had no reason to feel that way; if anything, he should be excited. Everything had gone well during the demo. In fact, one could even say it was nearly flawless. He and the guys had never sounded better, and the reactions from Steve and Jerry that day hinted of success and promise. Still, he couldn't help the thought that Steve had been vague at best as to the reason for today's meeting. He'd never said the news he had was good, or even that he had any news at all. Mitch took a deep breath and let it out slowly as he pulled the keys from the ignition and reached for the door handle. Whatever would be would be, and he would take it in stride.

A buzzer sounded as Mitch opened the door and stepped inside the studio. He unzipped his jacket and waited only a moment before Steve appeared with a friendly smile and extended a hand.

"Hi, Mitch," he said. "First, let me say congratulations again on those twins. I'm glad to hear everyone's doing well." Steve couldn't help noticing the prideful grin his words brought to Mitch's face. Even though Mitch was young, Steve knew he was a man with his priorities in the right places.

"Thanks, I appreciate that," Mitch answered. "I'm still walking on Cloud 9!"

Steve chuckled and patted Mitch on the shoulder. "I can tell, but that's how it's supposed to be." He started walking down the corridor with Mitch beside him. "I remember when my own children were born. It's an incredible feeling."

He led Mitch into a large office where two other men waited. They stood up as he and Steve entered the room and welcomed him with warm smiles.

"Gentlemen, I'd like you to meet the front man for Ace, Mitch Tarrington; Mitch, this is Alex Kincaid and Shawn Powers." The three men shook hands and exchanged greetings. Steve turned back to Mitch. "These two are the ones that have the final say about new talent."

Alex gestured toward the chair next to Mitch and prompted him to sit. He undid the button on his jacket before he took his own seat and crossed one leg over the other. Mitch studied him for a moment. He was a stocky man with graying hair and a kind face that drew Mitch in and made him feel at ease. His soft brown eyes seemed to study Mitch as well, and his smile broadened.

"Well, Mitch," he started in a jovial tone, "Steve has given us a bit of background on you, but the most important thing as I understand it happened last night?"

Mitch's face lit up, and all three men exchanged a look as they smiled themselves. "Yes, sir, it did. My wife and I became parents—twin boys."

"Congratulations!" Shawn chimed in. "How long have you been married?"

Mitch blushed and shot a quick glance at Steve. "We got married in February." Even though she wasn't there, he knew Dana would want him to clear up any possible misconceptions. He grinned. "Honeymoon babies."

They all chuckled, and then Alex's face grew serious. "We want you to know how much we appreciate your taking the time to meet with us this afternoon. I promise we'll try to keep things as brief as possible so you can get back to your family."

"First of all, we want to tell you that we've reviewed your demo," Shawn said. "While we were very impressed, we were having difficulty with the idea of signing another band such as Ace. It isn't that you don't have the talent—we're sure you could easily make it in the industry over time. Right now, however, that industry is saturated with bands such as yours. They're a dime a dozen. We want something different—something that stands out from what everyone else is doing."

Mitch tried to keep the disappointment out of his voice. "I see," he said quietly.

"Now, before you get discouraged, let me finish," Shawn continued. "We listened to the demo again, and again, and again. We conferred with one another, we struggled, we conferred some more, until finally a decision was made. Before we wrote the idea of Ace off all together, we decided to sit in on one of your live shows and hear what you could do. Last night, that's exactly what we did."

Mitch perked up. "You were there last night? No one told us...."

Alex jumped back into the conversation. "That was the idea. We didn't want you to be 'rehearsed' for us. We wanted you just as you are each week. What we got was beyond our expectations." He smiled brightly as he leaned toward Mitch. "Mitch, you are an extraordinary talent. I still can't believe you have no vocal training and yet can produce a sound that pure. You have an unbelievable energy, and your crowd absorbs that from you. That's the mark of a true showman."

Mitch was beginning to fill with nervous energy—his curiosity at an all-time high. What were these two working up to?

Alex leaned back in his chair again and brought his hands up in front of him as he placed the tips of his fingers together. "During your break, we went around the table again. We bounced back and forth on the idea of signing you as a solo act, but we could easily see the connection you have with your band. There's a loyalty there, isn't there?"

"Yes, sir, there is. I'm not a solo act. I'm their front man."

"I can certainly understand your feelings on that. In fact, I admire them. So, we were back to square one."

"Then you brought your friend Casey on stage, and you sang that duet," Shawn interjected. "Suddenly, it was as if the light came on, and it all made sense. We knew what we needed to do that would be a win-win for everyone." He opened a steno notebook lying on the desk in front of him, flipped through a few pages, and placed his finger on the page as he read his notes. "She's magnificent, and your range is just so that you were able to take it up a key—yes, I noticed that—and handled it without faltering. Your voices blend in such a way that you sound as if you're meant to sing together. I haven't heard harmonizing that astounding since *The Carpenter's*."

Steve, who had sat idly by until that point, finally spoke. "Let's cut to the chase here, Mitch. As Alex and Shawn have expressed, we feel Ace possesses phenomenal talent. However, we're in search of something that the average studio isn't producing at this time. Our goal here at Remington is to produce acts that are a cut above the rest. We feel that you and Casey are just that. This is our proposal: we'd like to sign you and Casey as a duo. There are plenty of bands, plenty of male soloists, and plenty of female soloists; but as we know it, there are no male-female duos. You'd be unique to this area, unique to our label, and most of all unique to the industry. There's no doubt in my mind—in any of our minds—that you will be a top producing act. While you're very talented individually, I think in time you'd get lost in the shuffle. But, together you could become legends."

Mitch simply stared at them as his eyes moved from one man to the next. He couldn't speak.

Alex noticed the displaced look on the young man's face. "Mitch, is there something you'd like to say?"

He nodded slowly. "I don't quite understand how we went from being considered as a band to being accepted as a duo. I'm even more confused because part of that duo is someone who isn't a regular part of our act. Casey was only a one-show deal. We just agreed to let her sing last night for fun."

"You happened to pick the right show," Shawn answered. "Not only are you getting a break, but so is your friend. If it hadn't been for you, she may have never gotten this chance."

"If I may add something," Alex said as he leaned toward Mitch again, "I know you have that loyalty to your band, son. As I said, I admire that. But, *you're* the true star here. I don't mean to diminish your friends' talents in any way, but they're simply the background."

Mitch shook his head emphatically. "With all due respect, sir, that's where you're wrong. Those five guys possess more talent than I could ever hope to have and hearts of gold to go with it. A few months ago, I was ready to quit the band. I was afraid my job along with the demands of a new family would be more than I could handle. I just wasn't sure that being part of a club band would fit into my life anymore. Then the chance for the demo came along. It was like a dream come true for them. But, you know what?" Mitch had to swallow against the lump of emotion coming up in his throat. "They kept it a secret from me. They didn't want me to feel obligated to stay with the band if my heart wasn't in it. They were willing to give up the one thing that meant the most to them for me." He sat up a little taller in his chair and fixed his eyes directly on Alex and Shawn. "Those men are *not* just background. Not to me. They're part of me, and I'm part of them. Thank you for your offer; but if you aren't interested in Ace, then that means you really aren't interested in me either. As I said earlier, I'm not a solo act. We're a package deal."

While Alex and Shawn exchanged expressions full of disbelief, Steve glanced at Mitch with eyes full of understanding. Even before today's meeting, when Alex and Shawn had proposed their idea to him, he somehow knew in his heart that Mitch would decline. While he hated to see Mitch let the chance to showcase his talents slip away, he also admired him for holding true to his convictions. He knew this was a young man who, regardless of what he seemed to be walking away from right then, would be rewarded richly at some point for doing so.

Shawn looked at Mitch with determination. "Mitch, let me reiterate what we're offering here. We're giving you and Casey an exclusive recording contract with Remington Records. This will not only include the production of albums and singles for full release and airplay, but also the assignment of a publicity agent and business manager to take care of the background work for you. A national tour will start shortly after the release of your first single, and you'll appear on highly prominent radio and television shows. You'll have only the best of everything as our artists. Along with all of this, we'll place you with our top studio and touring band. These men are professionals with a history of working with some of the best in the business. Here at Remington, we're looking for what the others can't offer, and we know we would have that in the two of you. If you sign with us, we can promise you, it will be more than a dream come true."

Mitch smiled. "Thank you, but I'm not interested. Being a star was never my dream. It was theirs. Now it's gone, and I have to give them that news. But, they'll be all right. All of us will." He rose to his feet and extended a hand. "I appreciate your time. It was a pleasure meeting you both."

The men stood as well and shook his hand. "The pleasure was ours, Mitch," Alex said. "If you have a change of heart, you know where to find us."

Mitch nodded and turned toward the door.

"I'll see you out," Steve said, and the two exited the room.

They walked in silence to the door and paused briefly. Steve turned to Mitch with an expression that reflected pride and understanding. He extended his hand and placed the other on Mitch's shoulder as he looked squarely into his eyes.

"Mitch, it's been a true pleasure working with you. I'm sorry things turned out the way they did, but I understand your reasoning." The two shook hands; and Steve added, "To be quite honest, when they talked to me last night about their proposal, I was fairly confident as to what your response would be."

Mitch shrugged. "How could I possibly walk away from my band and live out the very dream they've worked so hard for? It would be like slapping them right in the face, Steve." He smiled. "Besides, this year has been full of dreams come true for me already. This is one I can leave for someone else."

"Well, if it were solely up to me...."

"I know," Mitch answered. "Thanks."

"Good luck to you," Steve said. As he watched the door close behind Mitch, he added, "You'll make it big someday. All of you will. Just wait and see."

After a stop at home to retrieve the items Dana had requested, Mitch made his way back to Mercy Hospital. His mind was filled to capacity with all that had been discussed at Remington Records. He wasn't sure if he should be honored or offended by the offer he received. Alex and Shawn had almost acted as if he should simply blow off his friends, steal their dream, and make it his own. How could anyone think that would be a noble thing to do? However, he needed to remember one thing and that was Remington Records, when it came right down to it, didn't care much about anything except making a buck or two. They were out to sign the act that would return the most revenue for them. Sure, they hadn't worded it that way, but that was the bottom line. It was just the way corporate America worked. But, he didn't have to play into it, and he didn't intend to.

Aside from all that came the bigger issue—how was he going to break the news to the guys? Although he'd prepared them for a possible letdown, it wasn't going to make it any easier to actually deliver. He knew they'd be disappointed and that a few of them—Shep in particular—would be almost devastated. He, more than anyone else, seemed to want this more than anything. Mitch thought back to their college days and the very first time they stepped onto a stage to perform. He remembered the look in Shep's eyes as he turned to him and told him that he knew they'd make it big someday. He could just feel it. Mitch had dismissed it as a schoolboy's dream at the time; but since he'd gotten back with the band and especially after the demo, Mitch realized that it was truly the man's heart's desire. However, life was full of disappointments, and this was simply another they would have to face. The one good thing they had to go on, though, was that they would be facing it together.

Then came the matter of Casey. From the overtones of the conversation at Remington, he gathered that she knew nothing about the proposal. To back up that assumption, he knew that if she had, she would have mentioned something to him at the hospital that morning or even the night before. Like Shep, to make it big in the music industry would be like the completion of a lifelong mission for her. She had sung since she was a child, had taken up piano at the age of eight, and had skillfully mastered both. Now her chance had come; and unless he told her, she'd never know it. When he agreed to let her perform last night, he never gave a moment's thought to the possibility that one song would lead to this sort of opportunity for her. But, if he thought about it, there really *wasn't* any opportunity for her—not without him anyway. Alex and Shawn had made that point clear: both of them or no one at all. He sighed. Should he even mention it to her? She'd already suffered one disappointment in Chicago. Did he really want to be the bearer of more bad news for her? There was that saying that some things are better left unsaid; but as he thought back on the past several months with Dana, he'd learned that it was actually better not to keep secrets. He'd have to give the entire situation some careful thought.

As he pulled into the visitors' lot of the hospital, he felt his stomach grumble and suddenly realized he hadn't taken the time to have lunch. He could have eaten a sandwich or a bowl of soup at home; but his thoughts were consumed with too many things, and food wasn't one of them. Although he'd already been away much longer than he'd planned, he decided to stop in the hospital coffee shop for a quick bite before he returned to Dana's room. He knew she'd be upset if he didn't eat; and with everything else going on, it was better to avoid that confrontation all together.

I glanced up at the clock on the wall and then shifted my eyes nervously toward the door.

"He's been gone over two hours, Kayla. I'm starting to get worried. How long does it take to get something to eat and pick up a suitcase?"

She smiled sympathetically. "Maybe he had other things to tend to while he was out. Don't go getting yourself all worked up. You don't need to be doing that right now. You'll make those babies nervous."

I shook my head. "If he had other things to do, he would have told me. He said he'd only be gone for a 'little while.'"

"I'm sure he's just fine," she stated with confidence. "These little ones are all settled down now. Why don't you do the same and try to catch a cat nap? I'll sit right here and wait until Mitch gets back." I gave her a look, and she returned it with her disciplinary stare. "Go on now, girly. Close your eyes."

I puffed out a breath of air and settled into my pillow. I'd humor her although I knew sleep would never come. I had too many things on my mind. First, I wondered where Mitch had gone. He told me he was going out to get something to eat. Unless he went to The Mark or Chandlers, that wouldn't take more than forty-five minutes at most. Then my mind—even though I tried not to allow the thought in—brought up the possibility that he was with Casey. I knew she hadn't dropped off the gifts at home that morning. Most likely she came to the hospital; he'd met with her, and she gave them to him. But, why didn't she come in to see me? Did she really think I would have too many visitors, or was she afraid to face me because she knew I was onto her scheme? I decided it was probably the latter. That caused a fear to creep over me. Perhaps when she'd shown up to deliver the gifts, she'd made arrangements to meet with him this afternoon so she could plead her case to join the band. She'd know that with me in the hospital there would be no way I could intervene. What a conniving little....

"Hey, sorry I was gone so long." I opened my eyes to Mitch's warm smile. He held up my suitcase. "I have your things here, sweetheart. I'll put them over...."

"Where have you been, Mitchell? I've been worried sick!"

Kayla shot a look at Mitch and slowly rose to her feet. I guessed she sensed the impending confrontation.

"Well, now that he's back all safe and sound, I'd better get home. There's a dinner at the church tonight, and I need to make my casserole." She offered a hug to each of us; and as she got to Mitch, she whispered, "It's just hormones, honey. Don't let it get to you."

Once Kayla was out of sight, he cautiously approached the bed. "I'm sorry, Dana. I had some business to take care of."

I sat up and secretly prayed that it wasn't what I had thought about earlier. "Business? With whom?"

"Remington Records. I met with Steve and a couple of other guys—Alex and Shawn. They're the big shots over there who make all the decisions about new talent."

My entire attitude took a complete turn. "Oh, Mitch! What did they say? Did they like the demo? Are they signing the band?"

He lowered his eyes and shook his head slowly. "No, they aren't. They weren't interested in the band."

My heart sank as I saw the hint of sadness on his face. "Honey, I'm sorry. What happened? How could they possibly say no to you?"

He lifted his eyes to meet mine, and he shrugged. "Actually, they didn't say no to me. Just to the band."

"Mitchell, you're confusing me. What exactly happened?"

He briefly filled me in on the meeting he had with the team at Remington. Then he elaborated on a few points.

"They don't want to sign any more bands or soloists—they think the industry already has enough of them. In fact, they were going to blow us off all together until Alex and Shawn sat in on the show last night and heard Casey and me sing the duet. They loved the way we sounded together—not to mention the concept of a male-female duo—and they wanted to sign us to the label."

I couldn't believe what I was hearing. "Let me get this straight. These guys came to hear the band. They liked them; but when they heard you and Casey, they decided that's what they wanted? A duo?"

He nodded. "Yep. That pretty much sums it up. We either sign as a duo, or we're out completely."

My heart dropped to my knees. "What does Casey think about all this?"

He shrugged. "As far as I can tell, she doesn't know anything about it. The guys at Remington appeared as if they wanted to talk to me first. I guess the final decision is all mine."

I closed my eyes and said a silent prayer that he hadn't agreed to this proposal. To think of him becoming a duo or anything else with Casey Tomlin made my stomach turn and my blood boil. I held my breath as I asked the million-dollar question. "What was your answer to them?"

"I told them I'm not a solo act or a duo or anything other than the front man for Ace; and if they don't want the band as a whole, they don't get anything. End of story."

I breathed a silent sigh of relief; and if I could have jumped from the bed to hug him, I would have.

Mitch continued. "How could I possibly even consider signing a contract with them and embarking on a career of my own knowing I was fulfilling the very dream that my friends had been denied? I couldn't live with myself." He smiled softly as he glanced at the twins and then at me. Taking my hand he said, "My dreams are right here in this room, Dana. Everything I want in life. I don't need a record contract or celebrity status. I'm perfectly happy with things the way they are."

"So am I," I replied.

He kissed my hand tenderly and gave me a hint of his dimple. "Do you still love me even though I'm not going to be a famous musician?"

I pretended to think about it, and he laughed.

I traced circles on the back of his hand with my index finger. "When are you going to tell the guys? Better yet, *what* are you going to tell the guys?" I hesitated. "Are you going to say anything to Casey?"

"I don't know," he said. "I know how disappointed they're going to be, and I can hardly stand the thought of doing that to them. Casey's already had one dream destroyed, and the guys have dreamed of making it big for what seems like forever—especially Shep. He's wanted this for as long as I've known him."

I gripped his hand, and he looked down at my fingers wrapped around his. "He'll be okay, honey. Todd's a strong guy. They all are." I tried to offer a bit of comfort. "Sure, it'll be a disappointment, but you'll still be able to play together like you have been. And who knows? Maybe once the word gets out that you didn't sign with Remington, some other company will seize the opportunity to sign you."

He chuckled. "It's okay by me if that doesn't happen. As long as the six of us can stay together, I'm fine with it." Then his voice softened. "I just hope they are."

I noticed the way he worded his response, and I decided to confirm what he said. "You mean you and the guys?"

He gave me a strange look. "Yeah—who else would I mean?"

"No one, I guess. I wasn't thinking."

Cody began to stir. Mitch kissed my hand, let go, and then stood up to look lovingly at his baby son.

"Hey there, champ. Want Daddy to cuddle with you a little bit?" He smiled and picked the baby up in his arms. Cody's blue eyes meshed with those of his father, and he seemed to settle. "You probably get tired of lying in that nasty old crib all the time, don't you?"

He held him close and gently rocked him as he placed his finger inside the infant's hand. "Man, I can't believe how something so small can be so perfect." He looked up at me and smiled. "God sure knows what He's doing, doesn't He?"

"Yes, He does," I answered, "in all things."

Mitch smiled. There was no explanation needed. He knew what I meant, and I knew he agreed.

The hours passed quickly, and soon the afternoon sun began to sink in the sky. Mitch stood at the window and gazed out at the city skyline. Streetlamps and buildings began to light up the world below and mocked the darkness that settled in around them. Dr. Renaldi had taken the twins back to the nursery for their one-day checkup, and Dana was lost in a much-needed nap. He'd walked to the lounge at the end of the hallway for a cup of coffee. He brought it to his lips and blew away the steam before he took a sip of the bitter, hot fluid. Jim had been right. It did taste like motor oil, but it somehow seemed to soothe him just the same. Tonight he'd make calls to the band and arrange to meet with them tomorrow to break the news. He'd tell them everything that had transpired in the meeting that day—with one exception. He wouldn't tell them Remington Records had wanted him. The very last thing he would ever want to do is appear as if he felt his talent was superior to theirs. He'd meant what he said to Alex and Shawn. He was a part of them, and they were a part of him. Yes, he could sing, and yes, he was a good musician; but the band made him better than what he was. In his mind, there was no Mitch Tarrington. There was only Ace.

As for sharing any news with Casey, he now leaned toward keeping quiet. He'd decided that what she didn't know wouldn't hurt her. If he didn't plan to share any of that information with the guys, he simply wouldn't share it with her either. If she happened to find out on her own somehow, well, he would deal with that when he needed to. Until then, life could go on as usual, and there would be no hurt feelings. Yes, that was the way he would handle it.

He poured the remainder of his coffee down the drain in the water fountain nearby, tossed the cup in the trash, and wandered back to Dana's room. There was one more order of business on the agenda, and he would take care of that right now.

As he entered the room, he saw that she was still asleep and quietly sat down in the chair next to her bed. *She is so beautiful*, he thought to himself as he gazed at her. *How could she ever believe I could fall for anyone else? I'd have to be totally insane.* He reached out to touch her hair tenderly, and he smiled. "I'll always be yours, Dana. Always," he whispered.

I slowly opened my eyes and reached up to wipe the sleep from them. I smiled as I noticed Mitch in the chair next to me with a soft smile on his own face.

"Hi, handsome. Have you been sitting there the whole time?"

"No," he said as he shook his head. "I went for a cup of coffee a little while ago, and I just got back. Did you have a nice nap?"

Noticing that the twins weren't in the room, I avoided his question. "Where are the boys?"

"Dr. Renaldi took them back to the nursery for their one-day checkup. They'll be back soon."

"How long have they been gone?"

He shrugged. "I don't know—half an hour maybe." He patted my hand and smiled. "Don't worry about it, love. He'll give them back." He reached out and rubbed my cheek with his thumb. "Sounds like you're a little attached to them already, huh?"

I nodded. "They're wonderful, Mitch—so small and beautiful and wonderful. I loved them when they were inside me, but I never imagined how much more I'd love them once they were here."

He smiled sweetly—his eyes full of love. "Yeah, me, too. They are pretty great."

I watched as the smile slowly faded into an expression I couldn't quite read, and he seemed to study my face as he continued to look into my eyes. He reached down and wrapped his fingers around mine, and my eyes followed his motion before I looked into his once more.

"Mitch, is something wrong?"

He shook his head. "No, not really. But, there is something I want to talk to you about. Well, actually, I'd say first that I need to ask you a question."

I was feeling a little uneasy, but I nodded. "Okay. What would you like to ask me?"

He gave me a bit of a crooked grin. "How on earth could you ever believe—even a little bit—that I was singing that song to Casey last night?"

He'd caught me off guard with his question, and I immediately found myself to be embarrassed. I thought that perhaps I would try to play dumb. "Who told you that?"

He continued to grin. "Sorry, I can't reveal my source, but let's just say it's a reliable one." He folded his arms in front of him and sat up straight. "Now, do you plan to answer my question?"

He didn't have to reveal his source because it only took me a moment to figure it out. "Is *that* why Trudy called you into the hallway earlier? I wondered why she didn't bring any coffee back with her," I said with a slight annoyance to my voice. *So much for things told in confidence*, I thought.

"Before you get upset, you should know that my source had to disclose some pertinent information in order for me to understand the reasoning behind another action she wanted me to take. I might add that action saved you from what could have been a rather uncomfortable visit." He moved to sit on the side of my bed. "So, actually, my source was only trying to help you."

I concluded that my pain med had to have some sort of magical brain boosting power as I was quickly putting everything into perspective. I had been right. Casey *had* been at the hospital that morning, and Trudy took Mitch out into the hallway to stop her from coming in to see me. While Trudy was back in the room visiting with me, Mitch was handling matters with Casey. It must have been then that she gave him the gifts for the boys.

"Casey was here, wasn't she, Mitch?"

He nodded. "Yeah, love, she was here. I headed her off at the pass."

He made his confession about everything that had taken place while I listened and grew increasingly upset—not so much at the fact that Trudy had broken my confidence—but because Casey now knew my true feelings. Since she was armed with the knowledge that I really didn't like her, Casey could do one of two things. Just to spite me, she could make herself appear like the innocent victim to everyone and ultimately make me look bad. Secondly, she might work that much harder to try to drive a wedge between Mitch and me. When Mitch finished speaking, I simply gazed into his eyes—my face clearly filled with annoyance. He noticed it right away.

"You look angry."

"Why shouldn't I be? First, Trudy tells you things that I specifically asked her not to, and then you go and tell Casey that I don't like her."

He chuckled. "I never told her that you didn't like her, Dana. What I told her was that there was a misunderstanding and that I believed you might think she and I had feelings for one another. That's it." He folded his arms somewhat defensively. "Besides, you *don't* like her; and if anyone here should be angry, it's me."

"You? Why you?"

"Because once again, you don't trust me. Frankly, it's getting a bit old."

"No one ever said I didn't trust you."

"It was implied."

"No, it wasn't. The only thing implied was that I don't like Casey. And you know what? You're right, I don't, so that's not even an implication any longer. It's a fact, and it's out in the open. Now, are you happy?"

Mitch slid off the bed and stood next to it. "Gee, Kayla wasn't kidding."

I gave him an odd look. "Kayla? What are you talking about?"

He wasn't about to say he thought I was being hormonal, but I suspected he felt that way anyway. "Nothing, dear. Nothing at all. It's not important." He took a seat in the chair and leaned forward. "Anyway, we've gotten off the main subject here." He softened the tone of his voice and took my hand once more. "I guess I've known all along that you weren't comfortable with the whole Casey thing. But, I also wanted to give you a chance to get to know her. I hoped that once you did you'd see that you had nothing to worry about. I guess things didn't work out quite that way, did they?" He smiled at me again. "Now, tell me—why did you think I was singing *to* Casey as opposed to *with* Casey?"

"Because of the way you were looking at each other, Mitchell. Especially the way Casey was looking at you. I really think she's...." I hesitated, almost afraid to let the words escape from my mouth. "I really think she's in love with you!"

A look of surprise, shock, and total disbelief covered his face. Mixed with the hint of a smile, it was the kind of expression that said he thought I'd gone completely insane.

"What?! In *love* with me?" He began to laugh. "You're kidding me, right?"

I didn't think he would believe me, but I hadn't expected him to find the situation humorous. "Mitch, I've suspected it all along. I've wondered about it from the very first time I saw her with you. The way she looks at you, the way she touches you all the time, the way she laughs at everything you say." I swallowed against the emotions I felt rising in my throat. "Then last night when you sang the duet, I knew it for sure. It was much more than just a song to her. She meant every word she was saying." I swallowed again and lowered my tone to just above a whisper. "I had to wonder if you didn't know it, too."

Mitch sat down, took off his glasses, and rubbed his eyes. He exhaled loudly, replaced his glasses, and stared at me for a moment as his laughter subsided. He fell back hard into the chair and tilted his head slightly.

"You're completely serious about this, aren't you? You actually think she's in love with me?" He ran a hand through his hair and shook his head. "Come on, Dana. That's crazy." He leaned forward as he lowered the tone of his voice. "Casey definitely doesn't have those kinds of feelings for me. Even if she did, she knows I'm married." He sighed. "Honey, she knows how much I love you. And she likes you. She told me she thinks you're sweet. She would never do anything to come between us. She's just too nice a person."

There was that term again—nice. I was becoming so frustrated I could have easily screamed and been heard in New Jersey. I decided right then it was time to let Mr. Tarrington know exactly how I felt about Miss Casey Tomlin.

"No, she *isn't* nice. She's anything *but* nice. All that is just an act so she can manipulate you into thinking she's nice and she can get what she wants. You *do* know what she wants, don't you, Mitch?"

The hint of a grin tugged at the right side of his mouth which allowed his dimple to show just slightly. "Let me take a stab in the dark here—me?"

I nodded emphatically. "Among other things. She also wants to...."

"Good evening, Mitch, Dana. How are the proud parents?" Dr. Bradley's entrance abruptly ended my train of thought as well as our conversation.

Mitch stood and exchanged a handshake with the doctor although his eyes were still fixed on me. "Just fine, thanks."

Dr. Bradley moved to the foot of my bed and removed the chart that hung there. He shuffled through the pages, laid it on the bed, and came to stand next to me.

"How are you feeling, Dana?" He placed the ends of his stethoscope into his ears and touched the device to my chest. "Are you doing all right?"

"I guess so," I answered as he stood up again and hung the stethoscope around his neck. "I just feel kind of sore. I also had a few pains earlier that felt like contractions, but the nurse told me that's normal."

He smiled. "It is. Your body's simply working its way back to a pre-pregnancy state. You may have those for a few days, but don't worry. The pain medication should keep you comfortable. I'll write an order for something slightly stronger in case you feel what you're on now isn't helping, okay?" He pulled down the blanket and started to lift my gown—which attracted my husband's immediate interest. "Let's take a look at your incision and make sure there are no issues."

Mitch watched intently until the doctor removed the bandage to reveal an ugly line across my lower abdomen. He winced and sat back in his chair as he turned his attention to something outside the window.

"It seems to be healing nicely. No sign of infection. We'll keep it bandaged for a few more days." He replaced the dressing and put my gown and blanket back into place. Noticing the look on my face, he smiled reassuringly. "Don't worry. Once that's healed, you'll barely notice a scar." He picked up the chart, made a few notes, and hung it back on the end of the bed. Then he turned to me with a smile. "Now comes the fun part. We need to get you up and around before I can release you to go home."

Mitch turned back to the doctor. "When do you think that will be?" he asked.

"I like to keep my C-sections at least two full days; so I'm going to say early Wednesday, unless anything changes, which I don't foresee. She's doing very well." He turned so that he faced us both. "Do either of you have any questions for me?"

Mitch and I exchanged a look and both shook our heads. "No, I don't think so," he answered.

"That's fine." Dr. Bradley turned back to me. "I'll leave some orders with the nurse for that pain med as well as ambulatory instructions. You'll need to take things slowly at first because you will be weak, but it is important to get you moving, okay?"

"Okay," I answered.

The doctor caught the twinge of uncertainty in my voice. "Don't worry. This won't be as bad as when you had your accident. You'll be fine." After shaking Mitch's hand again, he bid us farewell and exited the room.

Mitch sat down again and rested his elbows on his knees as he leaned toward me. "Where were we? I believe you were saying something about Casey wanting something from me," he smirked, "or wanting *me*?"

Just as I was about to open my mouth with a response, Dr. Renaldi and a nurse stepped in with our children. Mitch shrugged, and with a smile stood to greet his sons and the doctor.

"Well, Mr. and Mrs. Tarrington," the doctor began, "both boys seem to be doing well. Cody's lungs still sound clear; however, I'd like to continue the oxygen through tonight. I'll stop back in the morning; and if he's still in the green, I'll discontinue it at that time." He smiled as he noticed Cody beginning to fuss. "Well, it sounds as if someone is waking up. I'll leave you to attend to him, and I'll see you in the morning."

"Thank you, doctor," I said as he walked away.

As Cody's cries became more urgent, his brother began to stir as well. I realized then that the window of opportunity to discuss Casey's intentions had slipped away. I allowed the subject to die a natural death and mentioned nothing more about it as I helped Mitch care for our sons.

Before I realized it, three more hours slipped away and visiting hours were almost over. Mitch leaned down to kiss each of his sons tenderly and then turned to me with an affectionate glow on his face. He took my hand; and after he kissed it, he placed it between his hands and looked deep into my eyes.

"Promise that you won't be upset anymore over Casey. I can assure you that she doesn't want me, and you have nothing to worry about."

I decided to go in for a bit of insurance. "Only if you promise me that you'll stop being so friendly with her." I dropped my eyes from his for a moment and lowered my voice. "It really bothers me a lot, Mitch."

He looked down at me and squeezed my hand tightly. "Dana Patrice Tarrington, you are the love of my life. There is no one else, and there never will be ever again. I hope with all my heart that you'll believe me because it's true. You mean the world to me."

He pulled me to him in a loving embrace, and in his arms I felt all my anxieties slowly melt away. At that moment, I experienced a bond so strong that I knew nothing—not even Casey—could break it. As Mitch kissed me tenderly and stood up again, I smiled into his eyes; and he smiled into mine.

"Good night, handsome. I love you."

He touched my cheek with the back of his hand. "I love you, too. Sweet dreams."

Chapter 21

Mitch hung his keys on the hook by the back door and yawned as he turned on the kitchen light. He unzipped his jacket but didn't bother to take it off as he moved to the cabinet, withdrew a cup, and filled it with the remainder of the coffee he'd made that morning. He placed the cup into the microwave to warm it and turned to pick up the phone. He would call his band mates and tell them he needed to see them tomorrow morning at nine sharp. Although it would be early, he knew that work schedules would take a back seat once he told them he had news from Remington. They'd be eager to hear it—and he was eager to tell them, for no other reason than to get it over with. He only wished that what he was going to tell them was what they wanted to hear.

Within ten minutes he'd completed his task and consumed two cups of stale coffee along with a day-old chocolate donut he'd confiscated from the fathers' lounge at the hospital the night before. Trudging up the stairs toward the bathroom, he felt a strong need for a hot shower and a good night's sleep despite the caffeine that now coursed through his veins. Shedding his clothing just inside the doorway, he pulled back the shower curtain and turned on the faucet. Stepping in, he turned his face toward the water, craned his neck back, and let the steaming-hot flood wash over his shoulders and chest. He stood there for what seemed like an eternity until he began to relax, and the tensions of the day flowed along with the water down the drain. When he felt sufficiently calm, he lathered up from head to toe in an effort to wash away the rest of the stress that had crept in with the thoughts of what was ahead. Rinsing off, he ran a hand through his hair to slough off the water, opened the curtain, and reached for the towel on the rack to his right. Once dried, he stepped out, wrapped the towel around his waist, and moved to the sink to comb his hair.

He stood for a moment and gazed at his reflection in the mirror. He was an average looking guy, he thought. He just couldn't see why Dana thought he was so handsome—as she put it—the kind of man that women were naturally drawn to. But, he was glad she felt that way—not because he desired the affection of other women—because he wanted her to be attracted to him. He smiled. Now, what was it she found so adoring about that dent in the side of his face? His dimple. She'd always told him it was cute. *Okay, whatever,* he thought. Then he thought about her smile. She had dimples, too, and on her they *were* cute. They brightened her face somehow, not that her face needed any help with that. She was the most beautiful sight in the world to him. He ran the comb through his hair and then sighed as he replaced his glasses and looked into the mirror once more. Suddenly, everything became clear and focused. How he wished he didn't need those glasses. He thought they added at least ten years to his appearance. There again, Dana told him they made him look intelligent and distinguished. Once more, she found the good in something where he just couldn't see it. She had that way about her. She had a way of making everything in his world better, including himself.

Making his way into the bedroom, he placed his glasses on the nightstand, pulled back the covers, and fell into bed. With a heavy sigh he closed his eyes and soon drifted off to sleep.

Mitch reached into the box of doughnuts Zach had brought along with him, pulled out a cream-filled pastry, and took a large bite. He sat at his dining room table surrounded by the men who had become like brothers to him. Before their arrival minutes earlier, he had mentally prepared himself for the words he was about to deliver. Although his head was telling him to move forward, his heart was aching just knowing that he was about to break theirs.

"Guys, I called you all here this morning because yesterday I met with Steve from Remington and a couple of other guys, Shawn and Alex. They're the big shots who make all the decisions about signing new talent." He paused long enough to take a drink of coffee with the hope that it would wash the lump back down his throat. "First, let me say that they were totally impressed with the demo. In fact, they were so impressed that they decided to come to the club last Saturday night to listen to us."

He glanced at each one of them and noted the expressions of eager anticipation on each face and the prideful smiles that told him they expected good news. He allowed the hint of a smile to come to his own lips before he dropped his eyes from theirs. The hesitancy to continue caught him; and as always, Ash's perception picked it up.

He gave Mitch's shoulder a gentle push to prompt him. "Hey, buddy, go on and tell us what they said. It's all cool."

Mitch lifted his eyes and moved them over each man. "They like what we have to offer, but, well, it's just not what they're looking for."

In the blink of an eye each smile disappeared, and the disappointment set in. "What do you mean, we 'aren't what they're looking for'?" Ty asked.

"Yeah, why'd they come to the club to listen to us if they weren't interested?" Zach added.

Mitch sighed and shrugged. "When they came to the club, they were still undecided; but I guess what it comes down to is that they think the industry already has too many bands like Ace. They're looking more at signing unique acts—you know, things that other companies haven't already done."

"Like what?" Newbie asked.

His eyes met Ash's for a moment; and when he noticed his were being read, he quickly turned away. "I don't know. They really didn't say."

Shep stood up and exhaled loudly. "So, that's it?" He placed his hands on the back of his chair, dropped his head, and then looked at Mitch again. The pain on his face and in his voice was almost too much for Mitch to bear. "I thought Steve told us he had good feelings about us. I thought he said we really had a shot."

Mitch took a deep breath. "If it makes any difference, he told me that if it were solely up to him, we would have been signed weeks ago. But, it isn't. There's nothing he can do about it. Alex and Shawn run the show over there. He's just the scout."

Shep began to chew on his bottom lip and fought to hold his emotions in. "This really stinks. The whole thing just really stinks."

"It does," Mitch agreed, "and I know it hurts. We just have to accept it and move on. We have to try to look at the positives...."

"What positives?" Shep shot back. "That was a once in a lifetime chance, dude. We'll never get a break like that again. You know it, and I know it. We'll always be the band that didn't make the cut. We'll always be the rejects." He took his coat off the back of the chair and slipped it on. "Thanks for the news. I gotta go. I told my boss I'd be in late today."

As he made his way to the door, Mitch looked at the others and then quickly rose to his feet to follow his friend. Mitch's hand covered Shep's as he placed it on the doorknob.

"Todd, come on, man. I know how much this is hurting you, but do you know how it hurt me to tell you? Do you know how much I hated saying those words to you, knowing that I was shattering your lifelong dream? I knew everyone else would be disappointed, but I knew you'd be devastated." He placed a hand on his friend's shoulder and positioned himself so that Shep was forced to look into his face. "We aren't rejects. We've done more than most other amateur bands out there. We were given a shot, and it just didn't work out. Everything happens for a reason. We still have everything we had before. We have a packed gig every weekend. We get a good pay, and," he chuckled, "we even have groupies. Most importantly, we have each other. What's wrong with that?" Shep stood up straight, and Mitch knew his words were starting to penetrate the clouds of doubt. "I know things didn't turn out the way you wanted, but it doesn't mean we still can't make music. We'll always have that, and who knows? Just because Alex and Shawn said "no" doesn't mean at some point they won't change their minds. It's their loss, dude. That's the way you have to see it."

Shep turned his head to look at the others still seated in the dining room. He noticed a few smiles; and although they still seemed sad, he knew they had already begun to move forward. He kept his eyes focused on them as he spoke.

"I've wanted to be a famous musician ever since I can remember," he started. "My dad bought me my first guitar when I was only nine. I never put it down. I'd listen to old albums—anything I could get my hands on—that had a good guitar part in them. Didn't matter who the artist was—B.B. King, Jimi Hendrix—heck, I even listened to classical guitar. I learned to play, and I ate it up." He let the hint of a smile come to his lips as he recalled the memory. "Then I got my hands on my older brother's bass, and I fell in love with the sound. I fell in love with the heartbeat it gave to the music thrown out by the other instruments. I loved the way it seemed to pull everything else together. That's when it all started, and I never let it go." He turned back to Mitch. "Now, I have to."

Mitch smiled and shook his head. "No, you don't. All you have to do is put it on hold. Maybe Remington doesn't want us, but that doesn't mean no one else will sometime down the road. Anyway," he said as he, too, glanced at his friends, "you are famous. Just for a smaller group."

A slow smile came to Shep's face, and he nodded. "Yeah, I guess you're right."

"Hey, do either of you want the last jelly doughnut?" Newbie called out.

"Keep your mitts off. It's mine," Shep called back, and Mitch patted him on the back as the two returned to their band mates.

A short while later Mitch bid goodbye to the band as Ty shook his hand and headed out the door after the others. Ash had lingered behind pretending that he'd misplaced his car keys—which unbeknown to the others had been in the pocket of his coat the entire time. Mitch closed the door and walked back to where he stood.

"You find them?"

Ash reached into his pocket and withdrew the keys. "They were never lost. I just wanted an excuse to stay behind and talk to you without the others around."

Mitch looked at him inquisitively. "About what?"

"There's something you didn't tell us," Ash stated. "I want to know what it was."

Mitch sighed heavily and took a seat as Ash followed his lead. "You figured that out, huh?"

Ash nodded. "I saw it in your eyes, man. We've known each other a long time. I think I know how to tell when you aren't being straight with me." He sat back and placed his hands behind his head so that his arms jutted out on the sides like wings. "Remington wanted you, didn't they?"

"Casey and me," Mitch replied softly. "They were blown away by the duet, and they wanted to sign us as a duo. But, I told them no—that I'm part of the group, and it's all or none."

Ash let out a long breath, placed his hands on the table, and leaned toward Mitch. "That was a noble thing to do, but do you realize what you're giving up?"

Mitch shook his head. "Doesn't matter. I don't want to sing with Casey. I want to front Ace. And, that's what I'm going to do. Case closed."

"What does Casey say about that?"

Mitch sighed and leaned forward himself. "She doesn't know."

Ash had to laugh. "Very smart, my friend, very smart! The last thing you need is an irate woman on your case."

Mitch laughed as well. "No kidding! Especially when I'll already be dealing with Dana. One hormonal female is more than enough for me." He let his smile fade to a more serious expression. "Actually, I just can't bring myself to tell her. She's already had her dream squelched once. I can't do that to her again." He took the last sip of his now cold coffee. "I figure what she doesn't know won't hurt her."

"You better hope she doesn't find out some other way."

Mitch shrugged. "I don't see how she could. I purposely didn't say anything to the others about it for that reason. I didn't want the word getting out to her." He gave Ash a nod as he spoke. "I know I can trust you not to say anything either."

Ash nodded in response. "You have my word, Trip. What we've discussed won't go beyond this room." Then he grinned. "Now, one thing you haven't told me yet. What does Dana think about your giving up the chance at stardom?"

"I think she's a little disappointed that Remington didn't want Ace—well, actually a little shocked. She's told me from the get-go that she thinks we should go professional." He chuckled. "As far as the duo thing, well, I'd say she's probably ecstatic. She really isn't very fond of Casey."

"I kinda picked up on that, too," Ash answered. "A bit of jealousy aimed at the ex-girlfriend, huh? For some reason, wives can't fathom that we ever had a life before them. I remember running into one of my ex's when Cindy and I went to dinner about a year ago; and just because I stopped and said hello to her, Cindy wouldn't speak to me for two days!"

Mitch laughed. "Well, at least she didn't say that she thought your ex was in love with you."

Ash's jaw dropped, and he started to laugh. "No way! Dana thinks Casey... or you and Casey...whoa, dude, that's pretty wild. How'd you handle that one?"

Mitch shrugged off the question as if it was nothing unusual. "The same way I always do. I simply told her that she was wrong and that she had nothing to worry about."

"And she bought that?"

"I doubt it. But, what else can I do? I can't very well fire Casey from Gartano's. She's done nothing wrong. The duet was a one-time thing, and I'm not signing with her at Remington. Other than at work, I won't have any contact with her. I'll give Dana a little more attention than usual, and she'll be okay." He chuckled. "I think some of her issue is hormonal anyway."

"Just pray she doesn't get post-partum depression," Ash countered. "You don't want to have to deal with that, trust me."

"I'll take your word for it."

An hour later, Mitch arrived at the hospital just in time to witness my first attempt at standing since giving birth. With orders given by Dr. Bradley only moments before, a nurse stood close to my side with a hand gently placed on my left elbow as I eased myself from bed to floor. I stood still for a moment to calm shaky muscles still weak from attempts to push out two children a few days earlier. I could feel gravity pulling at the bandage covering my incision and causing it to tug at my skin in an unpleasant way. Instinctively, I placed my hand on my midsection which alerted the nurse to the situation.

"You'll be sore for a while, Mrs. Tarrington," she stated. "That's quite normal with a C-section." She moved her hand to my back to offer more support. "Do you think you can stand on your own?"

I nodded, although I wasn't quite convinced that my wobbly legs would support me. "I think so," I replied.

Mitch, who had been standing just inside the doorway until then, decided to get involved. "I can take over from here if you'd like," he told her.

She smiled as she stepped away from me, and Mitch placed an arm around my shoulders. "That's fine. The doctor would like you to stay in the room until you feel steady. Whenever you're comfortable, you can feel free to walk in the hall or down to the lounge." She smiled again and headed toward the door. "If there's anything you need, ring for us; and someone will come."

"Thank you," I said as she exited the room.

Mitch offered a gentle kiss on the top of my head. "Where to, beautiful?"

I pointed. "How about back to bed?"

He snickered softly. "I don't think that's going to help you get any stronger, love. Why don't I put the chair by the window, and you can sit over there and look out?"

"Okay, but only because you won't let me go back to bed!"

With everything in place, he took my hand and slowly led me toward the chair. Once I was seated, he positioned himself in front of me and leaned against the wall next to the window.

"Well, I broke the news to the guys," he started. "Just as I had suspected, they were all pretty bummed, especially Shep. He really took it hard, but I think he'll be okay in a day or two."

I gave him a sympathetic smile. "I know it was hard, but you did what you had to do, sweetheart. Don't worry about the guys. They'll bounce back."

He let the hint of a smile emerge. "I know they will. They're good guys, Dana. I couldn't ask for better friends."

"What did they say about Remington wanting to sign you and Casey?"

He turned to look out the window for a moment before he turned back to me. "I decided not to say anything about that," he replied. "I don't want them thinking that I have some sort of awesome talent that they don't possess. Besides, I figured if they didn't know that there would be no worry about anyone slipping up and telling Casey."

"You decided not to tell her anything about the meeting either?"

He shrugged. "I thought that would be best, considering the whole Chicago ordeal. What she doesn't know won't hurt her. The only one out of the group that knows is Ash. That's only because he sensed there was something I wasn't saying, and he stayed behind to ask what it was. I know I can trust him not to say anything to the others."

"I'm sure he won't, not on purpose anyway. I just hope it never slips out in conversation."

"Yeah, me, too. That would be tragic."

Mitch had no way of knowing how true that statement would prove to be.

Wednesday brought the promise of our release from Mercy Hospital, and Mitch arrived at eight sharp in eager anticipation of taking his family home. I had to laugh when he bounded into my hospital room with an infant's snowsuit in each hand and two blankets stuffed into a large diaper bag.

"I hate to disappoint you, but the doctor hasn't been in yet," I told him as I watched the smile slowly leave his face. "I have to wait for Dr. Renaldi to release the twins, too. So, it's going to be a while, sweetie."

He placed the things on the chair and moved to take Cody from my arms. "I just want to get you all home and settled in, that's all," he said. "I suppose I can wait a little longer if I must." He snuggled into the warmth of the baby's neck and kissed him softly. "Hey, Cody, how's my boy today? I'll bet you'll be glad to get out of this place, won't you? Well, Daddy's going to be glad to have you home. It's been pretty lonely around there these past few nights." He pushed the blanket away from the child's face and smiled at him. "You really are a handsome guy, aren't you? And so is your brother. Daddy loves you very much, do you know that?"

He laid the baby down and gently lifted his brother from his bassinette. Cameron stretched and made a soft grunting sound but didn't wake. Mitch repeated the snuggle and kiss that he'd delivered to Cody and held Cameron close.

"Hi, sport," he whispered softly. "You're sleeping it up pretty good right now. I'll bet you won't be doing that tonight when Mommy and I want to sleep, will you?" He kissed the infant on the forehead. "Well, that's okay. You'll learn soon enough, and I won't mind getting up with you at all. In fact, I'm looking forward to spending time with you. I'm gonna do that as much as I can and teach you and your little brother all sorts of things, okay? Daddy loves you, little guy."

He placed the baby back in his bed and turned to deliver a wide smile to me. "Then there's the pretty little Mommy over here." He walked to the side of the bed, bent down, and delivered a long, lingering kiss. "How's my girl today?"

"I'm fine," I replied as I slid my hand into his. "I'll be even better once I get out of here. I'm getting a little burnt out on hospitals."

He nodded. "I know what you mean. We've seen a bit too much of this place in the past several months, haven't we?" He took a seat on the side of my bed and reached out to tuck a strand of hair behind my ear. "I, for one, have no desire or plans to come back here until the next baby comes along!"

I gave him a horrified look. "Don't you start that again, Mitchell Tarrington. I'm definitely not in the market for another child anytime soon."

"Gee, I'd hoped you changed your mind about trying right away," he teased with a smirk.

I had to smile at the mischief in his eyes. "I think I may have to send you to your parents' house for a few years by the sounds of things."

Mitch laughed. "A few *years*?"

I giggled. "Yep. I'm not taking any chances."

He moved toward me a little and leaned down very close to me as he whispered, "It's not *my* fault you're so irresistible." He began to place quick, playful kisses all over my face. "See, I can't even resist you right now."

I giggled as I pushed him away. "Mitchell, behave yourself, would you?"

He moved away long enough to look at me with a playful grin. "No."

I was still busy fighting off my husband—both of us now laughing—when I heard a voice.

"Hey, buddy, better learn to control yourself. You have at least eight more weeks to go."

Mitch stood up to see Jim and Dr. Bradley standing behind him, both sporting wide grins. His face turned instantly red, and I blushed as well.

"Don't you know how to knock?" Mitch shot back as a grin of his own began to emerge.

Jim patted him on the back teasingly. "Next time hang a tie on the doorknob, okay?"

"I wouldn't have to if you'd learn to knock," Mitch said.

"Well, Dana," Dr. Bradley began as he moved to the side of the bed, "while these two argue, why don't I see how things look and then discuss your discharge instructions with you? I'm sure you're eager to get these little ones home."

After a quick check of my vitals and a peek at the ugly incision, Dr. Bradley ran through my list of do's and don't's which included a reiteration of the 'eight-weeks' waiting period' for Mitch. When asked if we had any questions, Mitch's only response was, "Why eight weeks? I thought it was only six."

Dr. Bradley smiled. "I generally say eight weeks for Caesarian births. However, we'll see how things look at the six-week checkup, okay?"

"That sounds fine," he replied with a smile of his own.

The doctor signed all the necessary paperwork with instructions to call his office for an appointment. He shook our hands and was on his way.

"Well, love, one down, one to go," Mitch said. "Now, all we need is Dr. Renaldi to release the boys, and we're good to go."

"Why don't I see if I can round him up for you? No sense having you sit here all day when you could be at home settling in," Jim volunteered.

No more than five minutes passed before Jim returned with Dr. Renaldi close behind. Another exam—this time of both boys—and what seemed to be an almost endless list of instructions later, we were finally ready to leave the confines of Mercy Hospital far behind. When Mitch and I were alone again, he closed the door and curtains as I slipped out of bed to get dressed. In eager anticipation, I placed my small suitcase on the bed and opened it to reveal a sweater and pair of jeans I hadn't worn in several months. Accepting the reality that I would be nowhere near pre-pregnancy weight only days after the delivery, I had chosen this particular outfit as it was one of the bigger ones I owned. Most importantly, it wasn't maternity wear. I'd had my fill of loose tops and pants with expandable waistbands. Those things were definitely something I wouldn't miss.

As Mitch dressed the twins, I proceeded to pull the jeans over my hips—only to have them stop halfway. *Oh, no, this isn't happening*, I said to myself. I glanced down. *Maybe they aren't unzipped all the way.* I tugged on the zipper and then tried to pull them up again; but still there was no way they were going any further than they had the first time. In frustration, I climbed back into bed and lay down as I attempted to suck in my stomach as much as I could and at least get the jeans to my waist. If I could do that much, I figured the sweater was long enough to cover up the fact that I wouldn't be able to button them. With my coat on as well, no one would ever notice.

Mitch finished with the boys and turned to stare at me as he did his best to contain his laughter.

"Sweetheart, what on earth are you trying to do?"

"Trying to get dressed. What does it look like?"

"Well, it looks like...." He stopped himself from completing the sentence. "Why don't you just wear what you came here in? I put it in the suitcase for you so you wouldn't forget it."

I gave him the death stare. "Are you insinuating that I still look like I'm pregnant?"

He looked genuinely frightened. "No, no, not at all. All I meant was that, well, it doesn't look like those jeans are going to work out. At least not yet."

I lifted my backside off the bed and tugged a little harder. "Yes, they will. They're a size larger than what I normally wear—wore—before I got pregnant. They were always baggy, and they should...*ugh*...fit me... if I can just get them...*ugh*...."

Mitch sighed and shook his head. He walked over to the bed, grabbed a pant leg with each hand, and in one tug had the jeans off me. He then handed me the maternity pants I'd worn to the hospital and looked down at me as he shook his head again.

I folded my arms stubbornly. "I am not leaving this hospital in maternity clothes, Mitchell. No way."

He snickered. "I wouldn't mind if you went home in your underwear, but I think you might get cold—not to mention a few unappreciative stares from passersby who might find the attire indecent." He reached out to stroke my hair lovingly. "Dana, I know you're eager to get back to normal, but you can't expect it to happen overnight. Now, get yourself dressed so we can go home, okay? I'll check around to make sure we haven't forgotten anything."

I glanced down at myself again and sighed heavily. He was right. It *wasn't* going to happen overnight—as much as I wanted it to. In fact, it might not even happen for several weeks, maybe even months. I didn't have a huge protrusion in my abdominal area any longer, but I still had what I defined as blubber; and my hips were wider than two football fields. I may not have looked like I was nine-months pregnant, but I still looked at least three or four. I slid back to stand on the floor and pulled on the maternity pants—which much to my dismay, were now only slightly big. Deciding to give up the fight, I put on my maternity top, knee-high nylons, and shoes and then sat down in the chair. Mitch turned to me and smiled.

"I'll go get the nurse while you bundle these little guys up, all right? It looks like we have everything in order."

While I attempted to stuff two tiny bodies into snowsuits almost double their sizes, Mitch went off to find a nurse who could escort us to the exit. He returned a moment later with a nurse and an orderly who took my suitcase as well as the diaper bag and two vases of flowers. After chuckling at his sons and the way they looked lost in their clothing, Mitch handed Cameron to me and took up Cody in his arms; and we started toward our new life as the Tarrington Family.

With babies strapped safely into car seats and belongings tucked away, we set out for home. While Cody seemed to sleep comfortably along the way, Cameron fussed continuously. About five minutes into the ride, I became frustrated that I could do nothing to change the situation. Mitch took my hand and smiled sympathetically as I glanced into the back seat for the twentieth time.

"He's fine, love—probably a little uptight. You have to remember he's never been in a car before."

"I know. I just don't want him to cry, that's all."

Mitch shook my hand playfully. "Toughen up, Mommy. He's going to cry a lot before it's all said and done. You have to get used to it."

I shook my head. "I'll never get used to it. How can I? He's sad, and that makes me sad."

Mitch chuckled. "I'd say he's probably more ticked off than sad right now. There he was, all warm and cozy in that little bassinette; and then we took him, dressed him up, stuffed him into a snowsuit, strapped him into a car seat, and put him in motion. If I were him, I'd be mad, too."

I smiled at the picture his analogy created in my mind. "I suppose you're right," I glanced backward again, "but I still don't like to hear him cry."

Much to our surprise, it didn't take long to establish a routine with the twins. By the end of the week, most of the day-to-day tasks associated with their care had become second nature. Unless both boys were awake at the same time, Mitch and I took turns getting up in the night to feed and change them. Whoever stayed up the longest was given the luxury of an afternoon nap the following day. Since I was somewhat restricted as far as bending and lifting, Mitch took on the majority of the household chores as well which left me with little more to do than care for the twins. As they had after my accident, Mitch's family brought in meals which helped us settle in that much easier. Over the weekend, we found ourselves entertaining various members of the family and friends between feedings and diaper changings.

By the beginning of the week, I honestly had to wonder if Mitch wouldn't be glad for the chance to return to work simply as a means to get some rest. Jimmy had insisted that Mitch take Monday off as he knew that the bistro's annual inventory was scheduled to begin on Tuesday. Since this would be Mitch's first year as manager, Jimmy agreed to start the preparation for the event. Mitch could simply oversee the crew to complete the task from there. I knew that Mitch was grateful for Jimmy's assistance, and I was grateful for another day with him at home.

Early on Tuesday morning, Mitch sauntered down the stairs as he yawned, a baby monitor in one hand and a half-empty bottle in the other. Taking both from him, I offered a kiss before I placed them on the counter and returned to the stove to finish breakfast.

"Sounds like he finally settled down," I said in reference to Cody, who had been exercising his lungs only moments before.

"He didn't want to go to sleep," Mitch answered through another yawn. "But, I'll tell you what—I sure could fall asleep myself right now."

I delivered a plate filled with pancakes and sausage to him and kissed the top of his head. "I know, sweetie. You look pretty wiped out. Are you sure you're okay to go to work?"

Although I tried not to show it, I was sure he knew I was still nervous about being alone with the boys; and he smiled. "I'll be fine and so will you. If you get too overwhelmed, just use our backup list, okay?" He pointed to the sheet filled with names and numbers that hung on the refrigerator door. "Don't be too embarrassed to call someone if you need to."

I feigned an air of confidence as I sat next to him with my own plate. "I won't need to call anyone. I think I can handle my own two children, don't you?"

He nodded as he took a drink of coffee. "Absolutely! You're a good mother. I don't think you'll have any issues."

Famous last words.

Mitch left home at exactly two minutes past nine and arrived at work no more than fifteen minutes later. He started a pot of coffee in the kitchen, went to the men's room, and sat down at his desk within eight minutes. He glanced up at the clock on the wall—nine twenty-five. *No, Mitch, it's too soon. You can't call her yet—she'll think you don't have any confidence in her at all. Wait a little while longer.* Maybe getting absorbed in some work would take his mind off Dana and the twins. He opened the drawer on his desk, withdrew the daily ledger, and opened it to peruse through the figures from the past week. Jimmy had done well to keep the books up to date; and as always, the numbers pleased Mitch. He closed the ledger and sighed. Now what? Remembering the photo he'd brought along for his desk, he stood up and retrieved it from the inside pocket of his coat. He glanced at it and smiled.

One of the nurses had taken a picture of him holding both boys shortly after their birth. For reasons which he knew were mostly due to vanity, Dana had declined being included in the shot. He remembered, however, her comment about the prideful smile that graced his face and the love that radiated from his eyes as he glanced down at his children, not bothering to look straight at the camera. As he studied the picture, now he saw it himself; but what's more, he felt it. Smiling again, he tucked the photo into the corner of the frame that held the one of Dana and him and set back to work.

At home, the fun had just begun. With Cody fed, burped, changed, cuddled, and put back to sleep, Cameron was still in need of all of the same. However, he'd decided that instead of being fully cooperative he'd rather give his mother a challenge. First, I watched as most of his bottle dribbled down his cheek, and I had to wonder whether or not he'd gotten enough inside to fill him up. As I put him to my shoulder to be burped, that question was quickly answered when the contents of his stomach emptied onto my sweater. After I had cleaned off what I could with a baby wipe, I retrieved a fresh sleeper and t-shirt from his dresser and laid him on the changing table. Sometime in his nine days of life, he'd decided that he preferred to be clothed. The moment I set out to unsnap his garment, he began to fuss. The cry began to escalate as I wiped him down and gently slipped his clean t-shirt over his head. Moving to his diaper, I tried my best to talk to him in a tone meant to soothe, but he only cried louder. I removed his diaper, wiped him down, and turned just for an instant to throw everything into the diaper pail. Remembering Mitch's advice to "always cover him first," I turned back a moment too late.

"Cameron Mitchell, why'd you do that? Now, I have to scrub down that wall." I sighed as I looked at his tiny face. "You have no clue what I'm even saying, do you?" I glanced at the wall again. "I suppose it won't be the last time I'll have to do that, but let's get you dressed first and back in bed."

Cameron wasn't interested in going back to sleep. He was now wide-awake and fully intended on making sure I knew it. Each time I thought he'd drifted off, the moment he touched the crib he immediately awoke and began to fuss. Finally, a full hour later, he surrendered the fight; and I lay him back in his crib. Just as I began to scrub down the wall, I heard the phone ring. Dropping the sponge into the bucket, I raced off to answer it.

"Hello?" I panted, quite out of breath from running down the stairs to the kitchen. Somehow I'd forgotten that we had a phone on the nightstand in our bedroom which was right next to the nursery. I'd also forgotten about the fourteen stitches in my stomach that were now aching like mad as a result of taking a flight of stairs in less than ten seconds.

"Hello, hello, is this Charlotte?

I almost killed myself for a wrong number? "No, I'm sorry, you have the wrong number."

"Well, is this 555-7824?"

I sighed heavily. "Yes, but I'm sorry, there's no one here named Charlotte."

"Are you sure?"

I held the receiver out for a moment and stared at it before I put it back to my ear. "Yes, I'm certain. Have a nice day." I hung up quickly, shook my head, and started back toward the stairs. I'd only taken about five steps when the phone rang again.

"Not again!" I picked up the phone. "Hello?"

"Is this Charlotte?"

I dropped my head. "No, sir, this isn't Charlotte. You're dialing the wrong number."

"Sorry."

I hung up the phone and counted to ten. I picked it up on the second ring.

"This isn't Charlotte, is it?" the voice asked.

"No, still not Charlotte."

"Sorry. I think I'll just go to her house."

"Good idea."

This time I laughed as I started to walk away.

I made it as far as the second step when the phone rang yet a third time. Now, I was downright annoyed and snapped as I lifted the receiver, "Sir, this isn't Charlotte, and I thought you were just going to her house!"

Silence filled the air for about thirty seconds. Then I heard, "Baby girl, I don't know what on earth you're even talking about. Are you all right?"

I sighed. "Sorry, Kayla. I thought you were someone else."

"Okay," she responded with a bit of skepticism to her voice. "I thought I'd check in before I went to work. How are things going?"

I wanted to go into detail about all that had taken place in the last two hours, but I knew that she would tell Mitch and that would only cause him to worry. I put a smile in my voice and said as cheerfully as I could, "Nothing much to report, really. I fed Cameron and did a little cleaning. That's about it."

Just then, I spotted something lying on the floor next to one of the kitchen chairs. Stretching the phone cord to reach it, I neglected to keep an eye on the vase of flowers sitting in the middle of the table. As I picked up what turned out to be a speck of dirt off someone's shoe, the cord hit the vase and sent it to the floor with a loud 'crash!' I stood and stared down at the remains of my best vase surrounded by rose petals in a puddle of water.

"Oh, for crying out loud!" I exclaimed.

Kayla must have heard the noise as well. "Dana, what was that? What happened?"

"Oh, I just knocked something over. No big deal." I heard Cameron starting to whimper once more. "Kayla, I'm sorry, but Cameron's waking up again. I need to hang up now. I'll call you later, okay?"

"Are you sure you're all right?"

I glanced down again at the mess by my feet and then up the stairs toward the sound of my son. "Yes, I'm fine. Thanks for calling. I'll catch up with you later."

As Cameron's cries grew louder, I let out a long breath. The mess would have to wait. I headed toward the nursery to start Round 2.

Chapter 22

Mitch glanced at the clock again. Ten-fifteen. In just forty-five minutes the bistro would be open for business. Most of the crew had arrived with the exception of Kayla and Casey, and he knew they should be there at any moment. There were things he needed to do before he opened the doors, but he couldn't concentrate. Every time he looked up, he saw the pictures of his family; and he thought of Dana at home and wondered how she was. *This is insane, Mitch. Just give her a call and get it over with. She knows you trust her. Besides, you always call her before you open. Why should today be any different?* He picked up the phone and dialed the number. Two rings, then three, then four. *What's going on? Why isn't she answering?* On the sixth ring he hung up and redialed. Maybe he'd inadvertently called the wrong number. Once more, it rang without answer. With an uneasy feeling, he placed the receiver down and began to bite his lip. What if something had happened? Should he go home? Just then, he heard the sound of Kayla's voice, and he went to meet her as she stepped inside the front door.

"Good morning, Mitch," she greeted cheerfully. "All ready to dive back into the grind?"

Mitch ignored her question. "Kayla, I'm thinking I may have to run home for a little while. I tried to call a few times, and Dana didn't answer. I'm afraid something may be wrong."

Kayla didn't seem to be phased by his concern. "Don't go getting your feathers in an uproar, honey," she said. "I called her right before I walked out the door, and she said everything was fine. Maybe she was caught up with the babies and couldn't get to the phone. Why don't you wait and try her again in a little while?"

Mitch began to bite his lip again, and he noticed Kayla smile at the gesture. "Yeah, okay. I'll wait. You're probably right."

Kayla decided to try to take his mind off things. "What's on the agenda for today? Anything special we need to do?"

Mitch knew she was referring to the inventory. With his thoughts burdened with Dana and the twins, taking count of stock was the furthest thing from his mind. He looked out the window at the cars streaming by and expelled a heavy sigh.

"Today, let's just concentrate on using up what's already out. If you need to get anything from the back room stock, let me know before you take it, okay? It's a lot easier to count full cases than bits and pieces. In fact, I'll try to get back there and empty any partial boxes. I may go home for dinner to check on the family and then come back to do some work this evening. We can plan on closing early tomorrow to get in the final counts—you know, like we did last year." He smiled as he remembered that day—the day he'd finally met Dana face to face. He remembered the way she'd looked at him, the shy smile that had graced her beautiful face, the warmth of their first kiss. Now, here he was, a full year later, her husband and the father of her children. He'd never understand why God had chosen to bless him so richly, but he knew for certain he was happy for it.

Kayla brought him back from his daydream. "That sounds like a plan, boss," she said. "You know I'll do whatever I can to help."

"Yeah, I know you will. Thanks." He started to walk toward the office once more but paused instead and turned around. "Hey, did Jimmy leave a copy of the report from the fire inspection? I didn't see anything on my desk this morning."

Kayla looked puzzled. "He told me he was planning to call and talk to you about it when you got in today. I guess there were a few issues you needed to know about."

Mitch seemed shocked. "Really? Do you know what they were?"

She shrugged. "I'm not sure exactly, but I think I overheard something about some faulty wiring and an outlet or two that weren't up to code."

"What about everything else? Any issues with the sprinkler system or alarms?"

Kayla shook her head. "I don't know. You should probably talk to Jimmy about that. I wasn't paying much attention to be honest with you."

He nodded. "Thanks. I think I'll go and give him a call before we open. Then I'll make a few calls to see if I can get someone in here to take care of those things today or tomorrow. I'm sure we have a deadline to have the issues resolved anyway."

Mitch returned to the office, closed the door, and took a seat at his desk. As he reached for the phone to dial Jimmy's number, he noticed the light blinking on the answering machine. *Why didn't I notice that sooner,* he thought to himself. *Guess I really was distracted.* He pressed the button and sat back to listen.

"Hey, Mitch, it's Jimmy. I wanted to let you know that a copy of the fire inspection is in the front of the filing cabinet, top drawer. There are a few things there you'll need to check out, so take a look; and if you have any questions, give me a call. Have a good day. I'll see you tomorrow."

Mitch stood up to retrieve the paper while the second message played:

"Hi, honey, it's me." Forgetting about the paper, Mitch closed the drawer and slid back into his chair. He leaned toward the machine as if that would help him hear the message better. "I know you just left, and you aren't even at work yet." She giggled, and it made him smile. "Gee, that was a brilliant deduction, wasn't it? If you were there, I wouldn't be talking to your machine. Anyway, I just wanted to say that I hope you have a good day and…and that I miss you." He heard the faint sound of a baby whimpering in the background. "Well, that's Cody, so I'd better go. I love you, Mitch. Bye."

Mitch sat back. He played the message again and smiled as the sound of her voice washed over him. His sweet Dana. Even though he really hadn't said a word, she'd known somehow that he was faced with a long, hectic day and that just that simple message—the knowledge that she had thought of him—would make it easier. As he basked in thoughts of her, he didn't hear the footsteps behind him and jumped when Casey placed her hand on his shoulder.

"Oh, gosh, Mitch, I didn't mean to scare you!" she said with a bit of a giggle in her voice. "You must have been really concentrating on…." She looked at his desk but saw no evidence of what he may have been doing. "Well, something."

Mitch snickered, seemingly amused at himself. "Yeah, I was totally zoned out there for a minute." He turned his chair around and stood up as Casey placed her coat on the rack. "How'd it go for you here last week? Anything to report?"

She shook her head as she turned to face him. "Nope. Not a thing. How was your week? Did everyone get settled in?"

Mitch folded his arms and sat down on the corner of the desk. "Everyone's fine—we all adjusted a lot better than I expected. We even have a bit of a routine worked out already."

Casey smiled a little. "That's great, Mitch." She felt a bit apprehensive but decided to say what was on her mind. "I was going to call; but, well, I wasn't sure if it was such a good idea—you know, after what you told me at the hospital and all."

He stood up again and leaned against the desk. He crossed one foot behind the other and stuffed his hands into his pockets. "Hey, look, I'm really sorry about all that. As I told you, Dana has a real jealous streak. I can assure you she probably would have felt the same way had it been anyone else, so try not to take it personally. Besides, I talked to her, and she understands there's nothing going on between us."

Casey hoped her disappointment in that fact wasn't apparent. She cleared her throat and tried to put a bit of a lilt in her voice. "Well, that's okay—that she got upset, I mean. I can understand how she might have misunderstood. I just hope she doesn't resent me working here with you. I really do enjoy it, and I wouldn't...." She was going to say that she wouldn't want Dana to tell him to fire her, but decided to keep quiet. Confident that he would most likely share this conversation with Dana, she didn't want to risk that idea getting planted in her head.

Mitch took her pause as a cue to finish her sentence. "You wouldn't want her thinking we're having a fling?" He snickered. "Don't worry about that. She knows we're only friends. As far as the song, well, to be perfectly honest I wouldn't doubt that she didn't actually enjoy it." He stopped long enough to give her a full flash of his dimple. "Not that she'd ever admit it, mind you."

Casey looked at Mitch, and she felt her heart skip a beat. Closing her eyes for a moment, she allowed herself a chance to secretly savor his smile. She opened them again and gave him one of her own. "Well, I'm glad to hear that because I was really hoping that we could do it again sometime—maybe even this weekend."

"*This weekend?*"

Casey nodded as she took a step closer to him. "Actually, I was going to propose that we do it every weekend." She placed a gentle hand on his arm and looked so deeply into his eyes that he felt as if she were trying to hypnotize him. "When the deal fell through in Chicago, I pretty much gave up the idea of ever performing again. I knew there wasn't much chance of anything materializing in Philly. After all, I'd already been down all those roads—or so I thought. Then when I heard the response of the crowd that night at the club, it was like my dream came alive again, Mitch. I knew I was being given another chance. They loved me, and I loved being there." She looked away for a brief moment; and when she turned back, her face held a pleading expression. "I don't want to lose that feeling; and if you'll only agree to let me be a part of your show, I won't have to. What do you say?"

Mitch stared at her, taken completely off-guard by her proposal. He hadn't expected her to ask if she could sing again. He'd allowed himself to believe that she'd be satisfied with just one performance. Obviously, what had been meant as a simple night of fun had now become the night that Casey viewed as the beginning of her newfound career. As his mind grasped at straws trying to formulate an answer, he turned away from Casey long enough to catch a glimpse of Dana's picture on the corner of his desk. Immediately, his mind filled with her presence, and he began to think about how she would react to the subject at hand. Actually, he didn't have to give that issue much thought at all. She wouldn't be happy about it. If he let Casey become a regular, he was sure that it would spell disaster for his marriage. There was no way he would ever let that happen, and it was for that reason above all else that he would have to tell Casey no.

He turned back to her now and saw the same expression on her face—her emerald eyes filled with hope. It was then he knew that using his wife as a reason for his refusal would never work. It may have been the truth, but it would be far too easy for Casey to argue, especially since he'd already told her that Dana was fine with their friendship. He needed to tell her something that would end the discussion there— perhaps blame it on a situation that was out of his control. He smiled to himself as it came to him.

"I'm sorry, Casey, but I have to say no. The guys and I hold contracts with the club, and I don't think they can let you perform again since you don't."

She appeared baffled by the comment. "I didn't have a contract before, and they let me perform. What's the difference?"

He sat back down on the desk. "Well, Rob agreed to the guest appearance because I told him it would only be a one-time deal. There is a difference between allowing you to go on and do two songs versus an entire show, let alone doing it on a weekly basis. Since we hold contracts, the fact that you don't could get him into a legal mess. I'm sure you can see my point." Confident that he'd squelched the topic with his explanation, he crossed his arms smugly. He wasn't prepared for Casey's response.

"Why couldn't I have him draw up a contract for me, too? If compensation is the issue, he doesn't have to worry about that. I have the job here. Between my salary and tips, I don't really need anything extra from the club. I only want the chance to perform. That's it. Nothing more. He can't say no to that, and the contract can serve as his way around any legal issues."

Great. I sure wasn't ready for that! Now what? Mitch's brain scrambled for a counterattack. "Unfortunately, I don't think it's quite that simple. The guys and I are signed as the house band at Studio 14. As far as I know, that makes it kind of an exclusive thing. I'm not sure he could just add you on like that. Like I said, two songs in one night are a lot different than ten songs every week."

Although her expression held a bit of skepticism, Mitch thought she was buying it. "So, you're saying you don't think there's any way to make this happen?" Then she smirked. "Or, is this your way of saying that *you* don't *want* to make this happen? You're not making excuses just so I won't join your show, are you?"

Yes, but I can't tell you the truth and have you thinking my wife is a shrew either. "No, Casey, of course not! Why would I do that?"

At that moment Kayla walked into the room, and Mitch was glad for the distraction.

"Should we go ahead and open the door? That line is getting pretty long out there."

Mitch shot a glance in Casey's direction and then nodded to Kayla. "I guess that wouldn't be a bad idea. Wouldn't be good for publicity if we let our customers starve to death on the sidewalk."

"I think they'd freeze before they'd starve, but I get the picture," she answered with a laugh and followed Mitch toward the door.

As Mitch concentrated on pulling orders from the kitchen, Casey offered a smile to the two men in suits at table twelve. She fought to hide her discomfort when the oldest of the pair seemed to stare at her incessantly. When his eyes followed her back to the counter for their drinks, she tried not to glance back.

"Mitch, tell me if that man at table twelve is still looking at me," she whispered as she discreetly pointed a thumb over her shoulder.

Mitch turned slightly toward the table where the two men now seemed to be engaged in conversation. He shrugged. "Not that I can see. Why?"

"I just took their drink orders, and the one's eyes were glued to me the whole time. It's kinda creeping me out."

Mitch turned back toward the window full of plates and continued his task. He allowed a playful smirk to grace his face. "Maybe he's trying to flirt with you or something. Don't let it get to you." He handed a tray full of food to Katie and began to fill another. "But, do let me know if he does anything inappropriate, okay?"

"Yeah, sure."

Pausing for a moment before she reached the table, she placed another smile on her face and set the drinks in front of the men. "Are you all set to order, or did you need a few minutes?"

"You're Casey Tomlin, aren't you?"

"Yes...."

"We knew this was Mitch Tarrington's place, but we had no idea you worked here with him. It's very nice to see you again, Casey." The older gentleman stood up and extended a hand. Casey looked at him apprehensively.

"I'm sorry, but should I know you?"

Both of them laughed softly as the other stood as well. "I'm sorry. I'm Alex Kincaid; and this is my partner, Shawn Powers. We heard you sing at Studio 14 a few weeks ago, and I must say we were quite impressed."

She felt a bit relieved now that she knew the reason behind the man's stares. Obviously, they had been at the club that night and had simply recognized her. "Thank you," she said shyly. "I'm glad you enjoyed it."

"To say the least," Shawn replied. "You and Mitch have remarkable talent: talent that we were really hoping to share with the world."

"That's right," Alex continued. "We were really quite surprised—shocked, in fact—that Mitch turned down that opportunity. We were hoping he'd change his mind," he gave her a bit of a grin, "or that you'd change it for him once he talked to you. However, I'm guessing that didn't happen."

Casey took a step back and stared at them with pure bewilderment. "Forgive me for sounding dumb, but just what opportunity are you referring to?"

The two men exchanged a baffled look of their own before Alex spoke again. "The opportunity to join our label. We're from Remington Records."

Casey turned her eyes toward Mitch who was now engaged in conversation with Joe at the counter. She looked at the men again. "You mean you offered to sign him, and he turned you down? I don't get it. Why would he do that?"

"He's very loyal to his band. When we explained to him that we only wanted the two of you, the conversation ended right there. It didn't seem to matter at all that we were willing to set you up with one of the best studio and touring bands around. Mitch didn't want any part of it." He gave her a bit of a smile. "Well, no sense beating a dead horse. If you weren't able to change his mind, then I guess the matter is as good as closed."

She only heard one phrase out of everything Alex had said. "You wanted to sign the *two* of us?"

"Yes, you and Mitch." His face held a bit of a guilty expression as he realized that until right then Casey had not known anything about their meeting with Mitch. "I'm getting the impression that he never shared any of this with you, Casey."

She turned back to the men and shook her head as she tried to keep her anger in check. "No, I didn't have any idea until just now. Mitch never mentioned anything to me," she replied as she tried to keep the tremor out of her voice.

"I'm sorry, Casey. I assumed that you knew. I hope I haven't caused any problems."

She shook her head and turned to glance at Mitch again. This time he caught her stare with a smile; but when he noticed her expression, his own changed as well.

"No, you haven't caused any problems." She forced a smile as she looked at Alex and Shawn once more. "It was nice meeting you both. If you'll excuse me, I'll see if your orders are ready."

As Casey approached the counter, Mitch ended his conversation with Joe and walked up next to her. Doing her best to ignore him and keep her cool, she placed the plates on a tray and turned to walk away from him.

"Casey, is something wrong?" Mitch asked as he placed his hand on her shoulder.

"I have to deliver these orders," she replied shortly without giving him so much as a glance.

Mitch watched as she moved to the table. Suddenly, he realized the source of her problem. His heart dropped to his feet as he recognized the two patrons she was serving.

"She knows," he whispered to himself. "Good Lord, she knows."

Mitch was pacing the floor of the office when Casey walked in. He stopped to look at her as she closed the door and wheeled around with fire in her eyes and a rage in her voice that caused him to keep a safe distance.

"How could you do this to me, Mitch Tarrington? How could you keep this from me especially knowing how long I've worked for it? I finally had a chance to live my dream, and you went behind my back and stripped it away from me. What made you think you had the right to do that? Who gave you the authority to make decisions that affect *my* future without even consulting me?"

He took a cautious step toward her. "Just let me explain...."

"Explain what? How clever you think you are for coming up with that cockamamie story about contracts to keep me from singing with the band again? Did you think that keeping me away from the club would keep your secret safe?" She laughed disgustedly. "I never pegged you as being the scheming type, but I guess everyone has a dark side." She hastily pulled her coat and purse from the rack near the door. "I have to wonder if your wife knows what a low-down creep you really are—unless she was in on this, too." She put a finger to her chin and tapped it as if she was deep in thought. "You know, that does make some sense. Maybe this was her doing. After all, you did say she was jealous of me; and if we signed with Remington, that would mean we'd spend a lot of time together. That wouldn't make her happy now, would it, Mitch? You had to tell them "no" to keep wifey happy, didn't you? Is that what happened?" She nodded. "Most likely. Wouldn't want that fire at home to grow cold for you." She gave him a look of mock pity. "That's so sad. You're the puppet, and Dana holds the strings."

Mitch's face filled with anger at the accusation. "Dana doesn't control me. The reason I refused Remington's offer was because they wouldn't take us and the band, too. I won't walk away from my band." He took a deep breath and lowered his voice. "The decision was all mine, Casey. My wife had nothing to do with it."

The tone of her voice told him she wasn't convinced. "What kind of fool do you think I am? The woman hates me. She's been scared to death from the first time she saw me that I'd try to steal you away from her, and I'm sure she's been trying her best all along to get me out of here." She threw on her coat and placed her purse on her shoulder as she fought to hold in the tears that now filled her eyes. "Well, she doesn't have to worry anymore. She got her wish. And besides, now that I know how you really are, I wouldn't want you."

"Casey, wait!" Mitch called as she rushed down the hallway. "Casey, please come back. I can explain."

Suddenly noticing the curious stares of several patrons, Mitch stopped at the counter and watched as she let the front door close behind her. Slightly embarrassed that he was now the center of attention, he turned and headed back to the office.

I strapped Cody into his infant seat and placed it in the center of the table next to his brother's. It was rare form for both of them to be this wide-awake at six o'clock in the evening and more so for them to be awake at the same time. I was glad for the change, however, as I knew Mitch would be home soon for dinner and would welcome the chance to see them.

Hearing the garage door lift, I smiled and gave both boys a kiss as I admired their sleepwear: Cody's in a baseball motif and Cameron's in football. Each had a matching bib and a pacifier imprinted with the respective game ball that hung from a cord attached to the bib.

"That's Daddy," I said. "He's going to love these little sleepers I put you in. One thing you'll learn fast is that Daddy really likes sports, especially baseball and football. He'll be happy that Mommy's not dressing you in those pink and yellow outfits your Great Aunt Katherine bought. He said they were too 'girly.'"

As the door opened, I turned to greet Mitch. Although he offered me a smile, a certain aura about him told me something wasn't quite right. My first inclination was to pry it out of him, but I decided to wait a few minutes and give him the opportunity to divulge the information on his own.

He welcomed me into his arms and softly kissed the top of my head. "Hey, beautiful. How was your day?"

Ah, the beauty of a random opportunity. "Why don't you tell me about yours first?"

"I'm sure yours was much more positive, trust me."

I followed him to the table where the twins were waiting. "Is it safe to say your first day back was a little rough?"

He bent down to kiss his sons and took Cameron's tiny hand within his fingers. "To say the least. Casey quit."

I put a bit of sympathy in my tone and suppressed the urge to do cartwheels around the kitchen. "Wow, Mitch! What happened?"

He kissed Cameron again and then began to caress Cody's cheek with his thumb. "The guys I met with at Remington—Alex and Shawn—stopped by for lunch today; and Casey just happened to wait on them. They told her about the offer." He sighed heavily. "Had I noticed they were there, I would have made sure to keep her away from them. But, I was busy with other things when they came in." He kissed his son and pulled out the chair to sit down. "She came back to the office and totally went off on me about everything. I wanted to explain why I did what I did, but she wouldn't even let me talk. Then she walked out."

As I looked at the troubled expression covering his face, I almost felt ashamed that I couldn't bring myself to share the pain this event had obviously caused him. The only thought I had was that it hadn't happened soon enough for me. I was glad that Casey Tomlin was finally out of Mitch's life—and mine—for good.

I had to think of something to say that would make him think I really cared. "Honey, if you tried to talk to her and she wouldn't listen, it seems there really isn't anything more you can do. After all, you didn't keep the news from her to be mean. You were trying to save her feelings. She should appreciate that."

He put a little smirk on his face. "You didn't. In fact, when I tried to spare your feelings with that whole strip club thing, we both know how that turned out."

I didn't feel much like debating the topic with him and decided to nip it in the bud. "Well, that was a different set of circumstances entirely. Anyway, we're past that, so why are you even bringing it up?"

He stood and gave me a peck on the cheek as he moved to the sink to wash his hands. "Just trying to make a point, dear."

"What point would that be?"

"That she has every right to be angry with me. Regardless of whether I was trying to spare her feelings or not, I should have told her about the meeting. I definitely should have told her about Remington's offer. She had a right to know."

I carried our plates to the table while Mitch poured two glasses of water. "But think about it, Mitch. Even if you *had* told her everything, what would it have changed? You still would have declined their offer, wouldn't you?"

He nodded as he sat down and spread his napkin across his lap. "Absolutely. There's no way I would have signed without my band, regardless of Casey's feelings on the matter. I *did* tell her that."

I shrugged as I reached for the basket of rolls he handed me. "Then I'm sorry, but I don't see what else there is you can do. Remington doesn't want you without Casey, and they don't want Casey without you. Since they don't want Ace at all, that means no Mitch, either." I took a bite of chicken and held my fork in the air as I spoke. "Look at it this way. You didn't tell her, and she got mad: but if you *had* told her and still declined the offer, she would have gotten mad about that, too. Either way, you can't win. So as far as I can tell, the issue seems to be closed."

"I suppose you're right," he conceded.

We spent the next half hour sharing the rest of the events of the day until Mitch announced that he needed to return to work. He helped me clear the dishes from the table, kissed the twins, and then wrapped his arms around me as tightly as he could while he buried his face in my hair.

"I really wish I could stay right here with you," he said. "But, I've got to get the inventory started, or it'll take me a week to finish everything."

He moved so that we were now touching foreheads. "I'll be thinking about you, and I'll try to give you a call later, okay?" I nodded as he took me into a tight hug and then delivered a long, sweet kiss. "I really do love you, baby. I won't be too late."

Reluctantly, I let go of him and followed him to the door where we kissed again before he left me with a smile.

Mitch sighed loudly and wiped his dusty hands on the legs of his trousers. For two straight hours he'd been a prisoner of the stockroom. He was beginning to feel claustrophobic. He had closed the door to keep his employees from coming in and taking supplies without his knowledge. The last thing he needed was for the counts to be inaccurate and his efforts to be in vain. Now, he silently wished they would come and take everything so that he could forget the rest of his tedious task.

After marking down the number of items in the box he'd just gone through, he tossed the clipboard on a nearby shelf and sat down on a crate. He shivered against the cold and decided that a bare concrete floor and thinly plastered walls did little to hold in any heat. It was then that he remembered, and he smiled to himself as he moved to the far back corner of the room. Inside a broom closet, a small space heater beckoned him like a long lost friend. He searched through a few dusty crates until he located an extension cord and then happily carried the heater to the area where he had been working. Once he had it in place, he ran the cord to the outlet in the hallway right outside the room. Upon inserting the plug, he heard a 'pop,' and a small spark shot from the outlet, causing him to jerk his hand back. *That was strange*, he told himself, but thought nothing more about it. He welcomed the fact that he could now continue his work and be at least a little more comfortable. He reentered the stockroom and closed the door behind him once more.

Before he realized it, another hour had passed; and Kayla knocked lightly before she entered the room.

"I see you found that old heater," she said as she approached him. "At least you'll be all warm and toasty." She pointed to the racks full of boxes and open merchandise filling the room. "Are you sure you don't want any help tonight?"

He shook his head. "No, thanks. I can handle it. I'm not planning to stay much longer anyway. I'm thinking we can tackle the remainder tomorrow evening after we close. Jimmy will be here, too, so it shouldn't take long."

"Well, if you're sure you don't need me, then I'm going to head home. Everything's spiffed up out there, and the others are leaving now, too."

"Sounds good. You can just use your key to lock up out front, all right?"

She smiled. "Sure enough. I'll see you tomorrow." She started to walk away and then turned around once more. "Would you like me to check in with Dana and tell her you'll be heading home soon?"

He managed to smile as he tried to stifle a yawn. "Sure. That'd be great."

Now alone, Mitch found himself struggling to stay focused on the task at hand. The faint noises from the bistro had served as a bit of a distraction and trying to tune them out had forced him to concentrate on his work. But, now in the silence, he found that his mind was wandering everywhere but where he needed it to be. At that moment, it had decided to settle on Casey and the events of earlier that day. Once again, his attempt to spare feelings had backfired. *Maybe I shouldn't try to be nice anymore*, he thought as he chuckled to himself. *Seems like all it does is cause me trouble.* On the drive back after dinner, he'd rehearsed an entire explanation to Casey, along with an apology; and he promised himself that he'd call her the minute he was back in the office. But, all he'd managed to do was pick up the phone a half dozen times only to quickly place it back down and convince himself that it would be a waste of time. Dana had been right. If she had already refused to listen to his reasoning, there was nothing more he could do. However, for some reason, he wished he could. He didn't quite understand why making things right with Casey meant so much to him. It wasn't as if he really cared what she thought about him—he didn't. But, he did care what she thought about Dana. Maybe that was the reason it mattered. Even if the two never saw each other again, he didn't want Casey to think Dana had put him up to anything. True, he loved Dana and would do anything to make her happy; but she didn't control him. He had a mind of his own, and it was solely his decision to decline Remington's offer. He sighed. *Why are you even wasting your time thinking about this, Mitch? Just forget it and move on with your life. Casey will never give you a chance to tell her any of this anyway.*

As he turned to place a box on a nearby shelf, he heard a loud clamoring coming from just outside the delivery entrance. *It's probably just those stray cats Kayla's been feeding*, he told himself. *The scraps she put out tonight must not have been enough, and now they're rummaging through the trash cans.* He laughed. *Cats that like Italian food. Oh, well, at least they won't starve.*

He dismissed the sound and turned back to his work until he heard it again; but this time, it seemed as if it was coming from the front of the building and sounded more like someone tapping on the window.

Cautiously, he moved toward the dining room, taking care to peek out as discreetly as possible. Suddenly, he breathed a heavy sigh of relief and moved quickly to unlock the door.

"I certainly didn't expect to see you tonight," Mitch said.

Casey stepped inside, and Mitch closed the door behind her. "To be quite honest, I almost didn't come." She held out a small container covered in aluminum foil. "Here. I brought you something. Consider it a peace offering."

Mitch looked at her curiously through a crooked smirk and lifted the edge of the foil. "What is it?"

"Brownies."

"Laced with arsenic, no doubt?" He raised only his eyes.

"No, just walnuts."

Now, he allowed a full grin to emerge, and she once again found herself lost in his bright blue eyes. "Gee, thanks." He placed the container on the table next to him and turned back to her as he folded his arms. "Why the sudden change of heart? You called me everything short of despicable when you stormed out of here earlier. I figured I'd seen the last of you."

She hung her head and spoke softly. "I know, but I've had most of the day to think things over, and I decided that I wasn't very fair to you. I should have at least given you the chance to explain." She sighed heavily and looked up at him. "All I saw was a missed opportunity, Mitch—an opportunity that I may never get back again. I only had you to blame for it."

"I can understand why you feel that way," he answered. "And you're right—at least partially anyway." He pulled out a chair and prompted her to sit. He took the seat across from her and took a deep breath before he began to explain his meeting with Alex, Shawn, and Steve. Casey listened intently and silently, not breathing a word even when Mitch paused to find his own. He completed his story with one final clarification. "If you look at the whole situation from another angle, they never really offered *you* a contract. They were only interested in us as a package deal. If either of us wasn't willing, then there was no chance for the other one. Understand?"

Casey began to giggle as she watched a slow smile come to Mitch's face. "Now, you're just trying to sweet talk your way out of trouble, Mitchell Tarrington." She smiled back at him and reached across the table to touch his hand. "But, that's all right. I'm not angry with you anymore. In fact, I think I actually understand everything now."

He glanced down at her hand on his. "I'm glad because I really didn't mean to hurt you, and I'm sorry that I did. In fact, when I chose not to tell you, it was actually so I *wouldn't* hurt you."

She pushed out the chair and stood up. Mitch followed her lead. "I know, and I accept your apology. I hope you'll forgive me for flying off the handle at you earlier. I was upset, and I really didn't mean any of those things that I said." She giggled again. "You should know what a terrible temper I have."

"Apology accepted." He pushed in his chair and started to walk with Casey toward the door. "Well, does this mean I'll see you at work tomorrow morning?"

She glanced down the hallway at the light shining out of the stockroom. "One better. Why don't I help you work on the inventory for a little while? I'll even make a pot of coffee, and we can have a brownie or two."

Mitch glanced at the clock just above his right shoulder. "I was only going to stay until about eleven or so...."

"Then we have another forty-five minutes. If we team up, we can get a lot done. What do you say?"

That Dana will kill me when she finds out I was here alone with you. I could use the help, though, and that would mean that much less to do tomorrow.... "Okay, you start the coffee, and I'll pull down a few more boxes."

"Consider it done, boss."

Only a few minutes had passed before Casey entered the stockroom with a small radio in hand. Mitch gave her an inquisitive look.

"What are you doing with that?" he asked as he pointed to it.

"I thought we could listen to some music. Is that okay with you?"

He shrugged. "Sure, why not?"

"Cool! You set that up while I go get the coffee."

A short while later the two were working side by side, and Mitch was relieved that the burden of Casey's animosity toward him was no longer on his shoulders. He was grateful that she had now seemed to have accepted the situation; and more than anything, that he would not only keep a friend, but a waitress as well. As selfish as it may have seemed, he really hadn't relished the thought of undergoing that search again.

"Oh, wow! Hey, Mitch—do you remember this song?" Casey called to him from a few feet away. "I haven't heard it in ages."

He paused a moment to listen to the tune, and he nodded in her direction. "Yeah, I do."

She started to walk toward him with a reminiscent expression on her face. "Do you remember the first time we heard it?"

He remembered exactly the time; but he wasn't interested in dredging up memories of their romance, so he shook his head. "That part I'm not sure about."

She rolled her eyes as if she couldn't believe his memory had failed him. "It was the night we drove up to Fantasy Ridge. It was on the radio. After it played, we had our first kiss. I can't believe you don't remember that."

He smiled. "Hey, I'm a guy. You shouldn't expect me to remember stuff like that. Heck, Dana has to remind me what my name is half the time!"

Casey dismissed the fact that he had brought his wife into the conversation, and she moved closer to him. "You know what would really be nice? If you would dance with me...."

Mitch took a step back and gazed at her. "Thanks for asking, but I don't think that's a good idea." He quickly fumbled for something else to say. He didn't want her to know he was beginning to feel awkward. "We really should keep working. There's a lot to do."

Casey ignored him as she turned the music up and then placed her hands on his shoulders. "Come on, just one dance. All work and no play makes for a dull boy, you know."

Before his reply had the chance to escape his lips, Casey had wrapped her arms around him and placed her head against his chest. She began to sway gently to the music as she prompted him to do the same. "Relax, Mitch; I don't bite," she said.

What seemed like forever to Mitch was only a moment, and the song ended. As Casey lifted her head and looked into his eyes, his heart took notice; and he stepped away just as her lips grazed his.

"No, Casey. I can't do this. I'm married." He put up his hands and took yet another step away from her.

"I thought you wanted to," she replied softly.

He furrowed his brow in bewilderment. "What on earth would make you think that? You know I love Dana. She's my life and so are my boys. *Our* boys." He let out a heavy sigh. "Look, Casey, I'm sorry if I did anything to make you think I was still interested in you—romantically, that is. I'm not. I really am happy with Dana, and I would never do anything to jeopardize what I have with her."

Casey backed away now and shamefully lowered her eyes from his. "Oh, Mitch, I feel so foolish," she said. "I guess I mistook your attempts at friendship as something more." She looked at him once more. "I suppose I need to extend another apology."

He smiled as he thought of how Dana always accused him of flirting unconsciously with other women. *Maybe she wasn't so far off the mark after all*, he thought. "It's okay, just a misunderstanding," he replied.

She sighed. "I suppose this means I'm out of a job now, huh? You won't be comfortable around me anymore."

He laughed. "Heck no! I'm not that cruel. Now that you know where I stand on things, I don't think I have to worry about anything else happening."

She smiled. "You are a sweet man. Thank you." She extended a hand. "Still friends?"

He nodded with a smile of his own. "Still friends."

Casey glanced at her watch. "Well, I think I'd better go and let you finish up on your own, okay?" She pulled on her coat and placed her purse on her shoulder. "Goodnight, Mitch. I'll see myself out."

Mitch began to follow her. "Let me walk you out. It's late."

She quickly turned around and shook her head. "It's only ten thirty-five, and I'm parked right around from the delivery entrance. Thank you, but you stay here, turn up the music, and finish your work. I'll switch off the coffee pot; and then I'll slip out that way so you don't have to come up front and lock the door. Everything will be nice and secure." She pushed open the stockroom door and turned to him with another smile. "See you tomorrow." She closed the door behind her. "Now, don't you dare follow me, or I'll be mad," she called out. "You get back to work."

"Yes, ma'am," he laughed as he took another box off the shelf.

Mitch reached down to turn off the heater and ran the back of his hand across his forehead. He snickered. *Gosh, two hours ago I was freezing, and now I'm burning up! Guess this old dog of a heater works better than I thought.* And then, he heard it.

At first he wasn't sure what the sound was: a steady, rhythmic buzz, first appearing somewhat distant, then suddenly growing louder until it screamed in the hallway outside the door. He turned off the radio and listened as his heart filled with fear. The smoke alarms were sounding—his bistro was on fire.

How could this happen? What could have started.... Then it hit him, and he looked at the heater. *That spark—I should have unplugged it. How could I have been so stupid? I did this. I did this....*

He shook his head to chase away the guilt as he rushed to the door and reached for the knob. Pulling his hand back quickly, he shook it against the throbbing heat that had penetrated his skin. In slow motion, he placed his other hand against the door to confirm his theory. He couldn't open it because he knew what waited on the other side if he did. He was trapped.

Like a shroud, his fear engulfed him and took control of all his senses. Rational thought no longer had an existence in his being. Now he acted purely on instinct—he had to escape. His pulse raced and caused his heart to pound so hard he was sure it was going to break right out of his chest. The adrenaline rush through his veins pushed him toward the door. He reached for the knob again, took a deep breath, grabbed on and twisted. *No, it can't be! There's no way it could be locked! No way!* The intensity of the heat sent bolts of pain up his arm, but he gritted his teeth against them and tried again. *Maybe it's just stuck for some reason.* This time he placed both hands around the knob and pushed against the door with all of his upper body strength. Still, it wouldn't budge. Slowly he backed away—his left hand gripping his right wrist as he stared at the blood-red palm of that hand. He watched in horror as small white blisters began to emerge in dots on the seared flesh. He felt his breath start to come in short, quick spurts as the panic filled him to the very core. *I can't get out of here. I'm going to die. I'm going to die right here, tonight....*

Unconsciously taking a few steps backward, he stood in the middle of the room and stared at the door, completely dazed. For some reason his eyes dropped to the floor; and he removed his shirt, wedging it as best he could into the space under the door. He wasn't sure how long it would be for the flames to take notice and set it ablaze; but for now, it would act as a shield against the smoke that had begun to drift into the room and cause a light haze to hang in the air. As if it would help somehow, he waved his hand in front of him to cut through it and then rubbed his eyes beneath his glasses as they began to sting. He returned to the door, getting as close to it as he could without actually touching it. "Hello!," he shouted as loudly as he could. "Is anyone there? Can you hear me?" He picked up an empty metal bucket sitting nearby and threw it against the door with all his force. "Please somebody—anybody—help me!" Realizing that there was no one around to hear his cries, he dropped to the floor and hung his head as his voice faded into a soft, half-hearted plea. "Please, please help me. Anyone. I don't want to die."

He closed his eyes and let his mind drift outside the four walls surrounding him. Perhaps by now someone had noticed the blaze and summoned help; perhaps the fire crews who would come to douse the flames would find him there and lead him to safety. It was his only hope, and he wanted to cling to it. But yet, his heart knew that the chances of that were slim at best. Even if help were on the way, even if someone from his crew happened to show up on the scene, he or she would assume he'd already gone home. He took the watch from his pocket and opened his eyes to look at it. Eleven-fifteen. Not even Dana would be missing him yet, especially if she was busy with the twins. Even if she wasn't, if Kayla had told her he was staying until eleven, she would simply think he was enroute or had possibly gotten caught up in a task and lost track of time. By the time she started to worry, it would probably be too late.

His heart began to ache as she came to mind—his beautiful bride of only nine months. His mind filled with her laughter, her smile, her touch; and his arms longed to hold her just one more time. But, he knew that time would never come. How he loved her and wished that he didn't have to break the vow he'd made to her. He'd promised her a lifetime, and now he was leaving her all too soon. His tears began falling like raindrops as he realized that once again he was letting her down. He knew that she'd be angry, hurt, confused. She'd had so much pain in her life, and the last thing he had ever wanted to do was give her more. He closed his eyes and whispered her name; it fell from his lips like the soft kiss of an angel. That's what she had been to him—an angel sent from God for him to love. He'd loved her from the moment he first saw her, and he would love her throughout eternity. "Keep me in your heart, my sweet Dana," he said softly. "That way, I'll always be with you."

For just a moment he smiled as he thought of Cameron and Cody. What pride had filled his heart the night they came into the world. Two sons: two wonderful, beautiful sons, perfect in every way. Two blessings entrusted into his care to love, teach, and nurture—to act as their father, role model, playmate, and friend. Now, it would be up to Dana to do those things—to take on both roles and raise them alone as best she could. He knew his family would be there for her. He would just have to know that somehow, even without him, the three of them would be all right. Although the twins would be too young to remember him, he was confident that Dana would make sure they never forgot.

Feeling a sudden, intense heat, he opened his eyes to see his shirt blazing up in front of him, the blue-tipped flames reaching toward him and threatening to take him in. Frantically, his eyes searched for something to put out the fire—the closest extinguisher was, unfortunately, outside the door. On a nearby shelf rested a stack of tablecloths, and he rushed to grab one. Awkwardly, he gripped it as best he could with his stinging hands and beat the fire until nothing remained but his smoldering shirt, lying in charred, black pieces on the ground. He coughed out the smoke that had filled his lungs and moved closer to the back of the room, shrinking down to the floor once again. The fire outside was making its way to claim its one and only victim. He knew he was in his final moments. For some reason, this was his fate.

It was at that very second in time that something caused him to turn his eyes upward to what he'd forgotten was even there. On the back wall of the room, two small windows sat high above his head, placed there only to bring some natural light into the room during the day. If he could get to one of them, perhaps he could break it and crawl through—or, at the very least, call for help. Moving as quickly as he could, he returned to the broom closet and located a large crescent wrench in the box of tools he had stored there. It might hurt to grip with his injured hand, but it would do the job when it came time to shatter glass. He then hurried off for the stepladder, carried it to the back wall, and opened it up. He hung his head with a heavy sigh. The ladder was only four feet tall. Even if he stood on the very top, he wouldn't be able to reach the window. Unless....

Without another moment's hesitation, he secured the wrench from his belt and scaled the ladder. When he reached the top, he grabbed onto the shelving unit that rested between the two windows. He was a bit uncertain as to the safety of doing so. He knew that the units, though sturdy enough to hold supplies, were not designed to be climbed by a 190-pound man. But, he couldn't think about the risks involved with a wobbly shelving unit at this point. His life was at stake now. He glanced toward the door one more time and then turned to focus his eyes on the window. He had to make it. It was his only hope.

Please, God, be with me, he silently prayed as he carefully placed one foot and then the other on the shelf of the unit. He could feel it start to sway; but he took a deep breath, waited for it to steady itself, and pressed onward. One shelf at a time, he moved slowly toward his destination. Blood began to drip from the cuts the metal was making in his already-wounded palms. Spying a bottle of wine near his right hand, he chuckled for a moment as he remembered the occurrence last year when he'd pulled Dana off this same unit. She'd needed a bottle of wine for a customer; and unable to reach it on her own, she had decided to scale the shelf instead of using the step ladder. When he found her on the unsteady apparatus, he had scolded her for doing the very thing he now found himself attempting. With his thoughts focused once again on the woman he loved, he set forth with determination.

Just two shelves from the top, he glanced down at the floor below. He could barely see it now through the smoke that had started to fill the room from beneath the door. He knew that soon it, too, would become a victim of the fury just beyond it. Turning back to the window, he had to wonder why Jimmy had ever purchased units that stood so tall. Because they had no means to reach anything stacked higher than four or five shelves from the ground, the tops of the units were always nothing more than barren, ugly pieces of metal filling the room. When Mitch had first taken ownership of Gartano's, one of his goals had been to replace those units with smaller, more efficient ones. Like many other things, that project had gotten placed on a back burner, and eventually, forgotten. Right then, he was thankful for that. Had he followed through with his plan, he truly wouldn't have any chance for escape.

Two more steps found him at his destination, and he coughed against the smoke that hung in a thick, dark cloud around his head. His lungs wheezed, but he knew that soon this would all be behind him. Carefully, he positioned himself as close to the window as he could get and slowly took out the wrench. The unit began to sway again, and he placed both hands back on it as he stood perfectly still and waited for it to steady. His eyes burned, and he felt as though he could hardly take a breath; but he squinted through the smoke and brought the window back into focus. *You can do this, Mitch,* he told himself. *One hard swing should do it. Make it count.*

His hand shook again as he eased his grip on the unit and lifted the wrench once more. Just as he prepared to swing, a loud, deafening crash outside the door drew his attention away. Instinctively, he turned toward the noise. His motion shifted his weight and position on the unit. It began to rock; and though he quickly scrambled to recover his security, it was too late. He felt himself and the unit begin to fall. In no more than a heartbeat, it was over. His body lay, broken and defeated, on the cold concrete floor.

The pain that had filled him only seconds earlier was gone. He felt nothing until suddenly it seemed as if a set of arms surrounded him, and he opened his eyes to see who was holding him ever so tenderly. She stood before him, all dressed in white, glowing with love. He smiled.

"Dana, is that you? I knew you'd come. I knew you'd find me."

He felt a peace come over him as he reached out for her, and he closed his eyes.

"I love you, Dana," he whispered. "Forever."

CPSIA information can be obtained at www.ICGtesting.com
Printed in the USA
BVOW04s1923180314

348048BV00001B/4/P